The Final Battle

Maria Albert

DESCENT of KINGS Book 4

Dreamspinner Press

Published by
Dreamspinner Press
5032 Capital Circle SW
Suite 2, PMB# 279
Tallahassee, FL 32305-7886
USA
http://www.dreamspinnerpress.com/

The Final Battle
© 2014 Maria Albert.

Cover Art
© 2014 Paul Richmond.
http://www.paulrichmondstudio.com
Cover content is for illustrative purposes only and any person depicted on the cover is a model.

ISBN: 978-1-62798-244-3
Digital ISBN: 978-1-62798-243-6

Printed in the United States of America
First Edition
February 2014

Acknowledgments

Special thanks to Rachel, Ariella, and Joylyn, my beta readers, first fans, and staunch supporters. Particular thanks to all the folks at Dreamspinner, for enabling me to fulfill my dream. Elizabeth, Lynn, Paul, Andi, and Ian, you are the greatest! And a special shout-out to the often unknown and unnamed proofreaders, production assistants, and others who have contributed so greatly, and shared their thoughts and feelings with the editors and along the margins. I am truly grateful for your extraordinary work and support.

A warm welcome to all my new readers and welcome back to those of you who have been on this journey from the start. Heartfelt thanks to the wonderful folks on Goodreads, especially Pixie, Catherine, and Mel, for your well-considered and thoughtful reviews. Yes, authors read them, and they can either be a balm to the soul or a knife to the heart. Thank you for providing the former! And don't worry, this is not truly the end, merely a well-deserved rest at a way station after a long journey. Next stop, the sequel series Legacies!

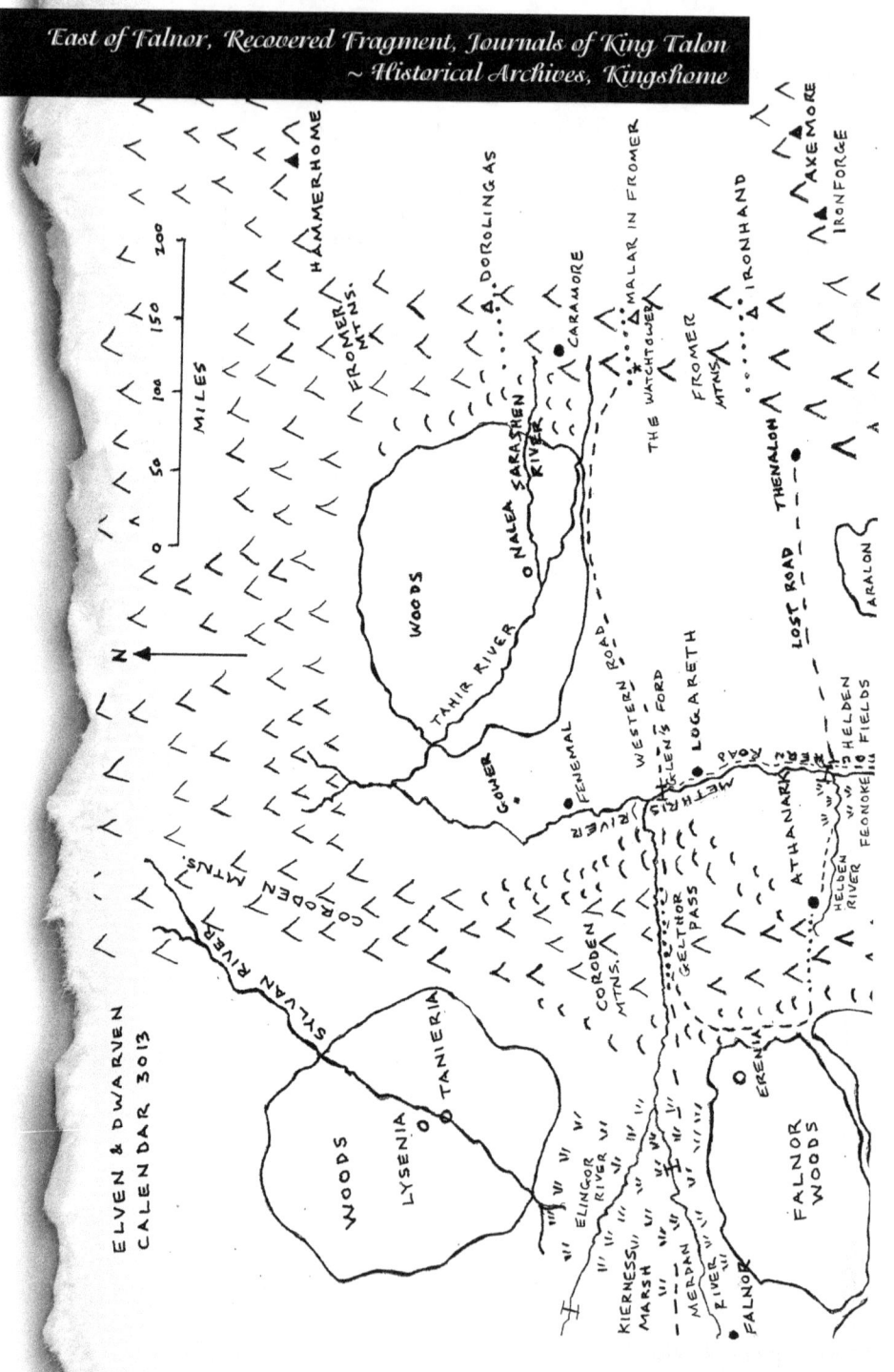

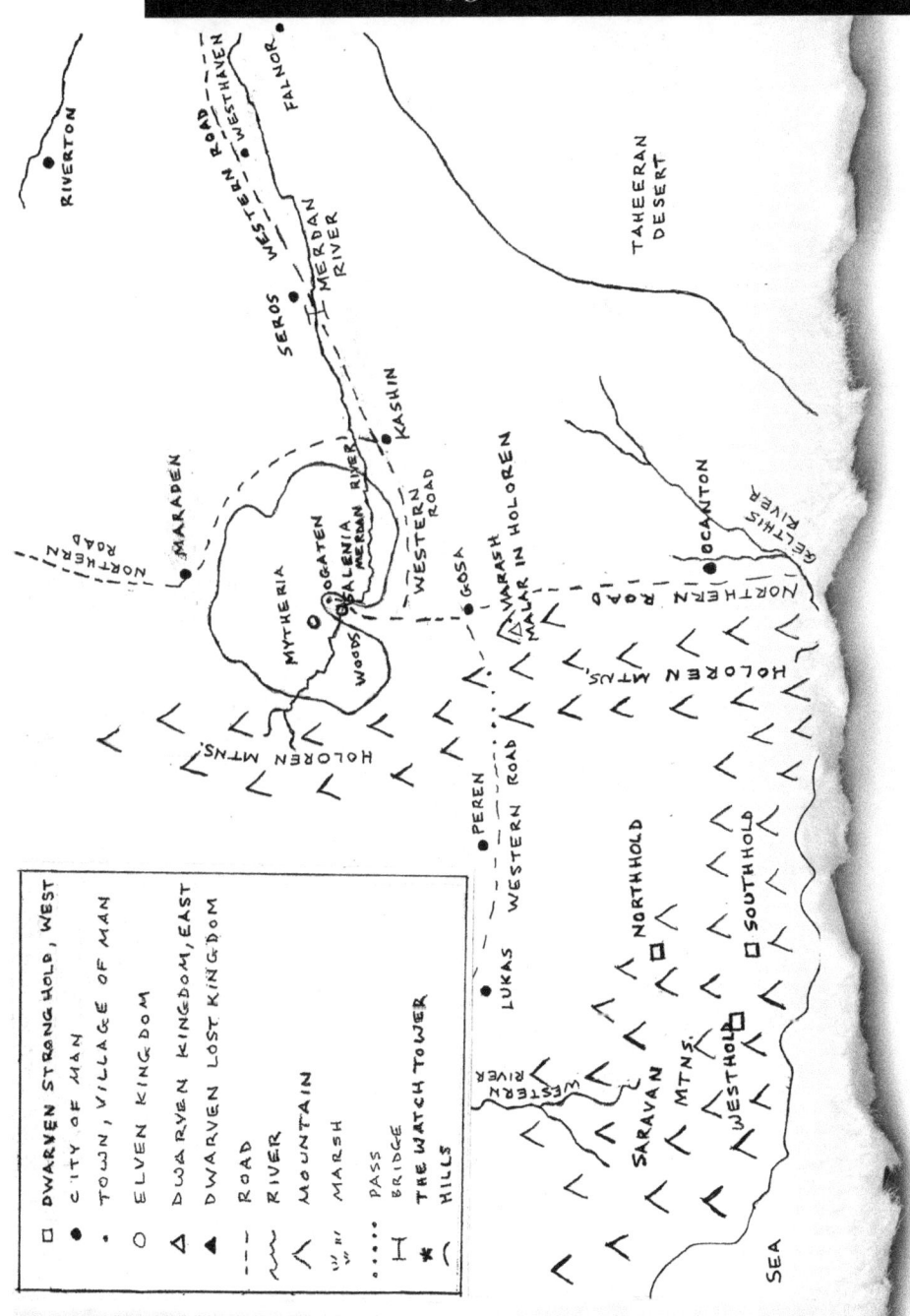

Chapter 1
Retaliation and Retribution

RION walked through the Market with two of his guards, Jathran and Lerdon, admiring the cloudless blue sky. It was a beautiful sunny day and would have been perfect for traveling had they not only just finished their long journey from Athanark here to Gosa, their new home. Rion turned, smiling, as he heard a familiar voice call his name and spotted three of the Ogaten brothers.

"Ron, Ara, Gar! We haven't seen you for weeks! How have the three of you been?" Although all three of their former guards still wore their swords, Ron and Ara were dressed in richer clothes than he had ever seen them in, while Gar was still in his old guard's livery, though he was now guarding his older brothers instead of Rion and his guardian, Tarrell.

Ron smiled fondly at him. "We're doing well. Business has been good. And you've got your cast off! Your arm's healed well? It doesn't pain you?"

"Not at all! It's as good as new, see," Rion assured him, flexing and twisting his arm. "I've even been sparring with Tarrell, to keep in practice, though there's little need with Jathran and Lerdon and Rarnak to guard us."

"You still haven't found a fourth guard?" Gar asked, surprised and concerned.

"Not yet, but we will. Few good men are interested in guarding a pair of merchants in the City. It's too boring! They want adventure and bonuses, the kind guarding a caravan brings. None of the men who were interested were good enough. Or maybe we're too picky! You four are hard to measure up to, you know. But we're doing fine. Enough about us! How are Van and Liana?" Rion asked, eager for news of their youngest brother and his new wife.

Ara grinned. "They couldn't be happier. The inn's open for business, and Liana's expecting."

"Already? That's wonderful!" Rion said, beaming.

"How about we come by the shop later and talk? We'd love to catch up on everything, but we've got someone we need to see," Ron said apologetically.

"Of course! Stop by any time. You know the door's always open for all of you."

They parted company, and the brothers were quickly lost in the swirl of shoppers. The Market was bustling this morning. Rion would have to visit Ogaten with a gift for Van and Liana, but he had no idea what they might need. He'd have to ask Van's brothers later today when he saw them again.

Rion walked past a stall selling ceramic dishes with only a quick glance and headed toward another, this one offering wood carvings that appeared to be of exceptional quality. Just as he reached it, he heard an odd sound, like the flapping of a bird's wings, only far too loud to be. A large shadow fell across the ground before him. He was surprised; there hadn't been any clouds a moment ago. He looked up as he heard a horse scream in terror, the screams of two women joining it.

Frozen in shock, he stared at the nightmare descending from the sky directly above him. It was an impossible creature, with the sleekly furred head and forepaws of a long-fanged cat, a pumar, but scaly reptilian hindquarters and belly, and a tail like a snake. The hind feet were like the taloned claws of a giant eagle, and the wings were an eagle's as well, only of enormous proportion, to scale with the rest of the beast. It was the monster Uncle Farion had told him of in Ardock six years ago—it seemed a lifetime ago—somehow come to life again. A chimaera, Hardred had called it.

But even more horrible was the thing riding astride it. It had the body of a man, but the head of a wolven. It was naked, and it was staring at something held in its left hand. Rion could not tear his eyes away as the wolven-man's gaze left its hand and its yellow eyes fixed upon Rion. It bared its fangs in a hideous rictus of triumph.

Before Rion could move, Jathran and Lerdon had drawn their swords and leapt protectively in front of him. Rion belatedly drew his own blade, barely able to clear the scabbard for the shaking of his hand.

The Market around them had erupted into chaos. People were screaming and running everywhere. Rion could hear them, but he couldn't take his eyes off the creatures as they dove to attack them.

As the chimaera swooped down toward them, it lashed out at Jathran and Lerdon with its forepaws. It was so fast! The claws of its right paw sliced downward, raking Jathran's face and chest before he could even bring his blade up, and he fell. Lerdon was faster. He parried the paw that slashed toward him with his sword. Rion saw blood well from the thing's foreleg as the blade scored it. But then its left rear leg jerked out and down, exactly like a hunting bird striking its prey, and Lerdon fell too. Rion saw that the monster's talons dripped red.

Rion ran, expecting at any moment to feel agony in his back as the thing tore it to ribbons, astonished that he yet remained whole. There was a laden wagon! If he could just get under it!

As he dove for cover, he heard the terrible flapping sound overhead, accompanied by the screaming roar of a hunting cat. The cry raised the hairs along the back of his neck, even as the heavy wagon was lifted off of him, as if it weighed nothing. The creature had it in its rear talons, leaving its forepaws free to attack. How could it be so strong?

It tossed the wagon into a panicked mob of people, and there were screams, some of them abruptly cut off as people were crushed by the shattering wagon and crates of goods. The horrible thing with the yellow eyes leered at him, ignoring the dozens of other fleeing men, women, and children. It was hunting him!

Unexpectedly, a flight of arrows hit the chimaera. One imbedded in its left shoulder, but the other three glanced harmlessly off its scaled back and belly. The chimaera roared in fury and pivoted midair, turning to head for the four City Guard, standing less than fifty feet from him with bows in their hands, who had so bravely attacked it.

They desperately nocked more arrows, but only two of the four were fast enough to let them fly. Both those arrows flew wild, and then the monsters were upon them, the chimaera clawing and rending with forepaws and rear talons, the rider engaging them as well, with fangs and a dagger. Knowing he was powerless to save them, Rion turned and ran, sobbing as he heard their screams abruptly end.

He dodged over and around boxes and bags and bodies. The ground was littered with things people had dropped or knocked over in escaping the creatures, as well as people who had either been injured or trampled in the ensuing chaos. Rion tripped and fell, landing hard, and stared in horror at what had once been a face. He could tell from the livery and hair alone that the body was Jathran's. A shadow and a rush of air passed overhead, and Rion realized the creature had dived over him, missing him only because he had fallen.

Rion looked around frantically from where he lay. He saw people everywhere, cowering under wagons, in stalls, in doorways; there was nowhere left to hide, no cover near enough. He stood then, shaking, and raised his sword as the creature came for him. Its paws lashed out and he vainly slashed at them, knowing it was his turn to die. But though the chimaera knocked the keen-edged blade from his hand, as easily as a kitten bats away a ball of yarn, it did not hurt him. Instead, to his horror, he felt hands grasping for him, and he looked up directly into those nightmarish yellow wolven eyes. He could smell the fetid breath of the panting wolven-man, and he almost vomited in terror when drool splattered down upon his face as he felt himself lifted from the ground.

This could not be happening to him! He was supposed to have been safe here! How could this thing be here when the Elven Kingdoms yet stood?

He kicked fruitlessly as he was dragged onto the back of the beast, in front of the wolven-man. But then the cat-creature screamed in rage and pain and wheeled around, a trio of arrows miraculously sprouting from its right shoulder. The chimaera had pivoted so violently that Rion almost slid from the wolven-man's grasp, even as hope flared.

Hope turned quickly to horror as Rion saw it was Ron, Ara, and Gar standing over the fallen City Guard, bows raised, and he realized they had retrieved the Guardsmen's bows to try to save him. They had wounded the creature, and now it was going to kill them for it! It would tear them apart as easily as it had the men at their feet, as effortlessly as the wolven and their riders had massacred all but one of his guards outside Athanark.

No, not them! No more would die for him! Rion twisted and kicked and pulled, and suddenly he and the wolven-man were falling from the sky.

Hitting the ground hard, on his back, Rion huffed as the breath was knocked from him. Fortunately they had still been close to the ground. The wolven-man landed lightly on its feet and came for Rion, grinning, rows of glistening fangs showing.

Rion kicked upward with all his might, between the thing's legs as it reached him, and it howled in agony and rage as it fell to its knees on top of him. He saw its eyes burn with hate as whatever reason it once had fled from it. It had not hurt him before, but now those terrible teeth were coming for his throat.

As he desperately raised his arm to block the savage attack, a vision of Tarrell flashed into Rion's mind, of his ripped arm, the muscle and bone showing through the blood. He felt the razor points of the thing's teeth and pain, but not agony, as the monster shuddered. Its jaws did not close upon his arm as he expected. Instead, the creature fell forward, twitching, pinning him with its weight. Rion pushed frantically against it, and it toppled off of him and fell to the ground. He saw the quick flash of a blade and then booted feet by his head.

Rion realized someone was speaking to him, but the words made no sense, as he lay there shaking violently and gasping. He tried to speak, but he couldn't utter a sound. The words wouldn't come. He heard a whining sound, and thinking it was the wolven-man, turned toward it in terror.

There were three arrows protruding in a neat cluster from the back of its skull, and it had been beheaded as well. He realized then that he was the one whining, whimpering, and fought to stop.

"RION, are you all right? Elmoth, look at him, he can't even hear me," Ron said in despair.

"Ron, his arm," Gar said, horrified.

"Quiet, Gar!" Ron snapped as he set his bloody sword onto the body of the werewolven he'd just beheaded, knelt down beside Rion, and grasped him by the shoulders.

SOMEONE was shaking him. Rion felt strong hands around his shoulders and he struggled. Abruptly, water cascaded over his hair and face, drenching him. He stopped resisting as the world snapped back into focus. He knew the arms, the voices, the words. "R-R-Ron," he forced out, his teeth chattering badly.

"Thank Elmoth! It's all right, Rion. You're safe now. It's dead. They're both dead. Can you stand?" Ron asked, releasing Rion's shoulders and reaching out a hand to aid him.

Rion nodded, accepting the hand, and stood shakily. Ron put his arm about Rion to steady him.

Rion examined his arm fearfully. He hadn't thought he was gravely wounded, until he'd heard the fear in Gar's voice. He was relieved to see he was barely bleeding. He wasn't hurt even as badly as Talon had been, and Talon had healed quickly and fully.

Rion studied the body of the chimaera. There was an arrow protruding from each eye and another from its mouth. He marveled anew at the brothers' bow work.

People began shakily coming out of hiding, to the jingle of chainmail and the sound of running feet. Rion's gaze fell upon Jathran and Lerdon, lying where they had fallen, and he cried out in dismay.

The four of them went to their two fallen friends and knelt beside them.

Gar stared in horror at Jathran's face. "Elmoth, was I as bad as that?" Gar asked, looking up at Ara, who nodded grimly.

Rion knew this time not even the Elves could save Jathran, as they had saved Gar after the obearn had mauled both him and Ara.

Ron confirmed what Rion already knew. "I'm sorry, Rion. Jathran is dead."

Ara said sadly, "Lerdon's gone too."

"N-N-Not a-a...." Rion's brow creased with the effort, but he couldn't speak further. He'd meant to say, "Not again. I hadn't wanted anyone to ever die for me again," but he couldn't. What was wrong with him? He'd been afraid before. He'd been terrified by the ogres in the mountains, when he had thought they wanted to take him to their village and eat him. He'd been so afraid he'd passed out. And when he had seen Jargas's eyes burning and feared Circe had yet ensorcelled his friend and had tricked him, when he'd been certain he was going to die, he'd stuttered a little. But he'd not lost his voice even then.

"You there! You're coming with us," a hard voice said, and they all looked up.

There were three of the City Guard standing a few feet behind them, their swords drawn and pointed at them.

"What's the meaning of this?" Ron asked, incensed.

"You're all under arrest. We've two dozen witnesses who say that thing came for the boy specifically, that it chased him. We've got at least a dozen dead, four of them Guard. We're going to find out what the boy knows. And the three of you are carrying our fallen Guards' bows. Now drop your weapons, all of you!"

Ron removed and dropped the quiver in disgust. He'd already set the bow down. "We took the bows to slay the beasts! We've no intention of keeping them. Would you rather we'd let them kill more people?"

The Guard's eyes narrowed. "The boy's a wizard, and you're too friendly with him by far. No one could make shots like that without magic helping him," he said, pointing to the fallen winged cat-creature with the tip of his sword.

Ron rolled his eyes. "The thing's head wasn't ten feet from us! We couldn't miss!" he said scornfully, as he picked up his sword.

"Your swords, too, and silence your tongue or I'll silence it for you!" the Guard said, fuming, likely both at Ron's disrespectful attitude and the implication of incompetence against the fallen Guard. Rion reluctantly dropped his sword and Gar followed suit, as did Ara.

Ara put a restraining hand on Ron's shoulder. "Ron, you're not helping us any."

Ron cursed and dropped his sword as well.

"G-G-Guardian T-T-T-T...," Rion forced out, but try as he might, he couldn't say Tarrell's name.

Another of the Guard said, "Captain, the boy's scared out of his wits. Look at him! I know we have to arrest him, but can't we at least...."

The Captain glared at him and he fell silent.

"B-B-Bury," Rion said explosively, stomping his foot as if to force the word from his mouth as he pointed at Jathran and Lerdon. Why wouldn't his tongue do what his mind told it to?

Gar spoke in his stead to the Guard. "He's trying to tell you he wants his guardian, and to be sure his guards get a decent burial." Gar turned to Rion. "Rion, I'm sure they'll take care of them. You need to calm down. We'll be with you. You'll be safe until Tarrell comes for you." He turned back to the Guard. "The trader Tarrell's his guardian. They've a shop on Amster Way."

Another squad of City Guard approached. Bolstered by the added numbers, the Captain said sharply. "All right, move it! You can tell it to the interrogators."

Rion paled, and Ron put his arm about him again and urged him forward.

TALIA burst into the shop. "Tarrell! Rarnak! Are you here?"

Tarrell came out from behind a display. "Talia! What's wrong, what's happened?" he asked, as she rushed into his arms.

"Oh, Tarrell! I was afraid you were in the Market. I thought you might have been killed! Is Rarnak here, too? Is he safe?"

Apparently hearing his sister's voice, Rarnak came out from the back room as Tarrell paled. "Talia, what happened at the Market?"

"The monsters! They came out of the sky and started killing people. Jenny was there. She told me she ran for her life as it threw a wagon at her. It nearly crushed her. She…."

"Rion! He's there!" Tarrell cried, cutting her off, terrified for him. "Rarnak, come on!" He headed for the door with Rarnak, and Talia followed, wide-eyed with horror at the thought Rion had been there too.

TARRELL stared in frustration when they arrived. They couldn't even get close to the Market. There was a huge crowd of people rimming it.

Rarnak said confidently, "I'll get us through." He started shouldering people roughly aside, shouting "Make way! Step aside!" and glaring at any who protested, hand on his sword hilt. Most people moved aside when they saw the uniform, even though it wasn't the uniform of the City Guard, perhaps figuring he must have business there.

Tarrell gaped in shock and dismay when they broke clear of the crowd. The Market was a shambles. Things were overturned and spilled everywhere, and there was a row of what appeared to be bodies, under blankets, in the middle of it. Off to the side was another covered body, and something huge lay near it, under a tarp.

"Hey! You there! The Market's closed! We don't want any gawkers here," a City Guard said, coming toward them, appearing annoyed.

"Please! I'm looking for someone: my ward, Rion. He has light-brown hair and blue eyes. He's dressed in fine clothes. He'd be with two guards, with uniforms like this," Tarrell said, pointing toward Rarnak.

The Guard looked about to protest further as he glanced at Rarnak, but then stopped walking and scrutinized his livery carefully. His expression became grim. "They're here. The Lady should stay here, though. She shouldn't see them. It's not pretty."

Tarrell started breathing fast and shallowly as the Guard began leading him and Rarnak to the row of covered bodies. Oh, Elmoth! Rion!

The Guard pulled aside a blanket. Tarrell recognized Lerdon. Something had sliced him open from throat to groin. His entrails were hanging out in a ragged, bloody clump. "That's Lerdon, one of our guards," Tarrell said hoarsely.

The Guard scratched his name with a stylus on a piece of slate and then pulled aside the blanket beside Lerdon's body.

Jathran. Tarrell could only tell from the uniform and the hair. There was a bloody ruin where his face had been. "That's Jathran," he choked out, fighting not to vomit.

The Guard wrote that as well and reached for the next blanket.

Shaking, Tarrell turned to see. He could tell the body beneath was shorter than the other two, and more narrow at the shoulders. He forced himself to look as the blanket was pulled away.

He almost fainted in relief. It wasn't Rion. It was a boy with brown hair. His eyes were closed, so Tarrell couldn't see the color. He was younger than Rion and had been crushed or trampled. He shook his head, "That's not him. It's not Rion," he said, feeling a wild rush of relief, even as his heart went out to the boy's family.

Rarnak said, "Can we check the others?"

"There's no other boys that I saw, but we can make sure," the Guard agreed.

They checked the rest of the bodies, but none of them were Rion.

"Where were the injured taken?" Tarrell asked. Rion would have either come back to the shop or stayed with the bodies of his friends. He'd only have done otherwise if he were badly injured or unconscious and couldn't.

"Everywhere. They—" the Guard started to say, but was interrupted.

"What's going on here, Regus?" a sharp voice asked.

"Captain! This man is searching for his ward. Those two guards are his, but the boy isn't the right one."

The Captain's eyes narrowed. "Light-brown hair, blue eyes, rich clothes, dressed in blue?" he asked, eyeing Tarrell's own fancy attire and Rarnak's uniform.

Tarrell felt suddenly weak with fear again. "That's him. Please, tell me where he is! Tell me what's happened to him!"

"He's been arrested for wizardry, and multiple counts of murder, assault, and destruction of property. If you're his guardian, since he's under age, then you're legally responsible for his crimes as well. You're under arrest," the Captain said coldly.

"What? But Rion's no wizard, and neither am I! And he'd never hurt anyone! Why would you even think such a thing?" Tarrell exclaimed, shocked.

"We'll ask the questions!" the man snapped at Tarrell. He turned to Rarnak. "You, if you work for him, you're under arrest, too. Both of you surrender your swords."

TALIA stared wide-eyed from the edge of the Market. She'd seen the naked despair on Tarrell's face when he had looked at the first two bodies and then the relief. From his reaction, Rion must be the one he hadn't seen. He'd viewed the rest of the bodies and talked animatedly with the Guard. But then another Guard came and suddenly Tarrell and Rarnak were surrendering their swords. The Guard called out to the others and more came, surrounding them. She realized they were being arrested, though she had no idea why. She knew better than to confront them about it herself. Instead, she turned and began forcing her way back through the crowd. She had to tell Madame Genevieve, the seamstress she worked for. She had connections at the Palace. She'd know what to do.

RION couldn't stop shaking. He'd felt cold, even before they had entered the stone building and descended the stairs. It was dark and damp here, and the air smelled stale. It was so cold, his teeth were chattering again. His hair and shirt were still wet from the water Gar had dumped on him in the Market.

This couldn't be happening! How could this be happening to him? That thing had tried to capture him, and now he was being blamed, as if he'd loosed it upon his own guards. He stifled a sob. They were dead! Lerdon and Jathran were dead!

He was pushed into a cell. There was a wooden cot, though only the frame, no padding. A thin, worn gray blanket lay in a heap upon it. The rest of the room was of featureless rough stone, except for a pair of rusted iron manacles on the wall and an empty sconce by the door for a torch. The Ogaten brothers were still in the hall. Apparently, he was going to be locked in here alone.

The City Guard began leading him to the wall, to the rusty shackles.

"Chain him," the Captain commanded.

Rion felt suddenly weak and fell to his knees.

The Captain grabbed him roughly by the collar at the back of his neck. "On your feet!" he demanded, but Rion couldn't stand. He would have fallen in a heap but for the hand on his collar. "Suit yourself," the Captain said coldly. "Drag him!" he ordered the Guard, as he pushed Rion forward. His men caught Rion, grabbed him by his armpits, and began dragging him to the chains.

RON had tried to keep quiet, but he couldn't, seeing how terrified Rion was and how cruelly they were treating him. Rion was like a baby brother to all of them, even Van. At sixteen, Rion was only a year younger than Van, but he was over a head shorter and still had a boy's build, though he'd officially come-of-age on their journey. "You can't! He's just a boy! He hasn't done anything! At least let us in there with him! Can't you see he's terrified? He can't even speak!" Ron begged, outraged on Rion's behalf.

"If he truly couldn't speak then he wouldn't be able to summon anything to free him. But he can't fool us. We'll bind him in cold iron. Then he can speak all he wants, but his magic won't work," the Captain said smugly. "Put them in the next cell. Chain the one with the loose tongue. Maybe then he'll learn to keep quiet."

RION heard the footsteps recede and Ron's curses, and then the sounds of a scuffle and a grunt and a thud. There was the creaking of a rusty door opening. The Guard beside Rion tested the manacles he'd fastened about Rion's wrists and turned to go. Rion stared after the Guard, watching as the light headed for the door, terrified they were going to leave him in the dark. But mercifully, the Guard put the torch into the empty sconce by the door before he left. The door closed with the screeching whine of aged metal. It clanged shut, the bang echoing loudly across the stone all around him.

Suspended by the chains, Rion's arms, which were held up and out over his head, hurt already. They were shaking from the strain of his weight and the cold. Rion's feet barely reached the floor of the cell. He'd not yet attained the height of a full-grown man.

They'd taken his purse. He was relieved he'd carried so little coin, only a hundred gold. He knew he'd never see it again. He'd taken to leaving the bulk of his coin in the shop, now that they had a home. There was a loose board in the floor they hid their coin under. But the City Guard had taken the Elfstone too. He always carried it with him. It was the one token he had from Elanara, though it hadn't been meant for him, and they'd taken it! And Tarrell wouldn't know what happened to him. He'd be frantic searching for him. The thought that Tarrell would be looking for him warmed him a little.

Rion could hear a string of expletives coming through the bars of the little window on the door, and he recognized Ron's voice, though he'd never heard half of the words he used.

"Rion, if you can hear me, we're all right," he heard Ara call out. "I know you're frightened, but don't be. Tarrell will come for you. He'll get you out."

Rion tried to respond, but he couldn't. His teeth were still chattering violently and his tongue wouldn't obey him at all.

He knew it was real, now. He'd known it was before, but the cold, rusted manacles about his wrists drove away any delusions that this might be some sort of fantastic nightmare, that he'd wake in his own bed, warm and safe. He had to get mastery over his tongue again. Was it fear or wizardry that had robbed him of his voice? Had Arcanus somehow found out about the message he'd given Elavar for Talon, warning Talon against him? Or was it even worse? Was it because he'd betrayed all three of the wizards, after swearing to keep silent, when he'd told Elavar too much: about Arcanus losing his powers, Magus being tainted by Incuban, and Circe changing into some terrible, dark creature of the night?

That thing hadn't tried to kill him, as it had killed everyone else. It had tried to capture him. What horrific things would the wizards do to him, if they caught him?

He tried to calm himself, but his heart was hammering. He tried to speak, but he couldn't utter a sound—not even the awkward stutters from before. His tongue was completely frozen.

RON was twisting and struggling in the metal cuffs that held him fast to the wall when Ara scolded him for it. "Ron, stop it! All you're doing is tearing your skin! Look at those manacles! Do you want the rust to get into your blood and kill you?"

Ron cursed and tried to force himself still. He inhaled deeply and exhaled just as strongly, over and over, breathing in the sweet, cool scent of the rock all around him. It was quarried stone, but they were underground, and there was enough of it that he felt the same calm fill him that he used to find only in the secret cave he would visit late at night when he was a boy.

Long after his chores were done and he and his brothers and sister had gone to bed, he'd lay awake and then sneak off to explore the riverbank of Salenia and the surrounding Elven Wood, though both were forbidden ground. The Elves had come upon him more than once, but they had seemed more amused by his trespass than threatened by it.

He hadn't even known what he'd been searching for, until he'd found it, a narrow crevice between two large slabs of rock peeking out from the forest loam. He'd wormed his way inside, into the darkness beyond. His eyes had grown accustomed to the dim lighting that filtered in from the entrance, and he'd started exploring his find. It was small, a single chamber with a low ceiling, but it was enough. To this day, he didn't think his brothers had ever learned of his secret refuge from the ills of the world, from the unending pain of his childhood.

He'd lived through all of it. He'd learned to fight and survive. He'd protected his three brothers for the two years of their journey and brought them safely home. He'd even reconciled with his father and discovered he was not the monster Ron had thought him to be. And now here he was, chained like an animal in a cell, with two of his brothers beside him, and he was helpless to aid them. And worse, he was unable to protect Rion, who was smaller and weaker than Van, in body if not in spirit, and who was alone and injured.

His hard-won calm shattered. "They arrested us! Just because their own Guard was too incompetent or terrified to make a decent shot, they think no one should be able to!"

Ara sighed. "Be fair, Ron. We would've been just as bad off if we'd not had Swiftsong to teach us how to focus when we shoot. All I saw was its eye as it came for us. I almost fainted when I saw clearly what I'd been shooting at, even with it dead. When we heard about chimaera in Thenalon and saw those etchings, I hadn't believed they could be real. I thought it was some of the survivors' madness."

"That werewolven is the thing that worries me," Gar said. "We were lucky we knew to aim for its head to destroy it, that it wouldn't be affected by anything else. The chimaera even I could believe, easier than that thing. It can't be true, can it, that when one of the werewolven bites you, you turn into one? But I didn't think any of it was true." His eyes were wide with fear. "You saw Rion's arm. He was bitten and it drew blood and he's losing his power of speech and…."

Ara grasped him by the shoulders and shook him. "Gar, stop it! I can't believe that part of it. I won't. What frightens me most is why it was after Rion at all. Those people were right. We saw it, too. It was hunting him, specifically. It killed anyone that got in its way. And the werewolven wasn't interested in killing Rion, until he angered it. It was trying to fly off with him. Who wants Rion, and why, and how are we supposed to protect him when we're prisoners ourselves? What if they come for him again, in his cell?"

As if Ara's words had summoned the evil to Rion, they heard a scream of pure terror echoing down the stone corridor.

Gar and Ara ran to their door and began banging against it and pulling at if futilely, as Ron strained against his chains. "Rion! What's happening? Rion!" Ron yelled, but more screams were his only answer.

Rion was staring at the torch. He remembered it had comforted Hunter to stare at a flame, that he'd used it somehow to focus his thoughts; he'd chanted over it. Hunter had told Rion he'd been chained in a cell once too. If Rion concentrated on the flame, and pretended he was on the road again, sitting by the campfire with his guards all around him, and Tarrell, maybe he might feel warmer. Maybe then he could stop shaking. Perhaps even speak. He knew the brothers were worried about him, and he ached to reassure them. But he also knew the Guard would eventually come back, that they'd want to question him about the attack in the Market. They'd never believe he couldn't talk. They'd think he was keeping silent deliberately. They'd torture him to make him speak, and he wouldn't be able to, and they wouldn't stop hurting him.

This was madness! All of it! This morning he'd had breakfast and laughed and joked with Jathran and Lerdon, and now they were dead, he was going to be tortured, and Tarrell didn't even know anything was wrong. Half the day would pass before he even started to worry, and then more time would go by before he had any hope of finding out what had happened, of figuring out where Rion was. What if even then they wouldn't let Tarrell see him?

He was giving in to panic and despair. Neither would help. The flame would, though, he was sure of it. He focused on the torch.

But then he felt something on his leg. He glanced down and saw, to his horror, a big brown rat with beady black eyes and chiseled teeth. It started to run up his leg, toward his face. He screamed and kicked, flinging it off him, but even after it was gone, he couldn't stop screaming and writhing in the chains.

"RION!" Tarrell cried. The City Guard was leading him down another dark corridor when he heard the screams and knew it was Rion. He broke into a run, but the Guardsmen to either side tackled him. "Let me go! You're hurting him!" One of the Guards cracked him hard across the face and the world vanished.

RARNAK silently cursed as Tarrell fell limply to the stone floor of the corridor. Rarnak had forced himself not to resist, knowing it was hopeless. There was nothing they could do to help Rion, not like this.

The Guards were looking at each other uneasily as the screams continued echoing down the hall. The Captain said, "It's just him trying to trick us into opening his cell. We'll look in as we go past. Now move!"

One of the Guards grabbed Tarrell under the arms and dragged him along the corridor as they proceeded warily, some muttering prayers to Elmoth.

The Captain peered into the barred window of a door on the left ahead of Rarnak. The man exhaled in relief and then glared at his men. "I told you! There's nothing there, and he's still chained. He can scream all he wants, but he won't be able to summon his monsters bound by cold iron as he is. We'll toss these two in with him. Maybe they can get him to shut up."

They opened the door and dumped Tarrell onto the floor, then pushed Rarnak in after him. Rarnak barely managed not to trip over Tarrell as the door was slammed shut behind him. He left Tarrell lying on the floor and ran to Rion. "Rion, it's all right! It's me, Rarnak. Can you hear me?"

Rion was kicking and flailing about wildly and screaming, his voice hoarse, as if he'd been screaming for a long time. He didn't react to Rarnak's presence or his words at all, as if he didn't even know Rarnak was there. Then, without warning, he collapsed, hanging limply from the chains.

"Rion? Rion! For the love of Elmoth, please answer us! What's happening?" a terrified voice called, echoing from the darkness into the sudden silence.

Rarnak looked around, baffled, recognizing the distinctive but mild Thenalonese accent of one of the Ogaten brothers. "Gar? Is that really you? Where are you?"

"Who are you?" Gar's voice called back, uncertainly.

"It's Rarnak. Where are you?"

"Rarnak! We're in a cell, about twenty feet past the one Rion's in. He's been screaming and screaming. You must have heard him. We've been going mad not being able to help him, and now he's stopped."

Rarnak went to the cell door to hear Gar better. "I'm in here with Rion and Tarrell. They're both unconscious. They brought me and Tarrell here and hit Tarrell, knocking him out. I don't know why Rion was screaming. There's no one else in here. But he's passed out, now."

"We thought something had come for him again," Gar called out. "He was attacked in the Market by a chimaera and a werewolven, two beasts we heard of in Thenalon. They were hunting him specifically for some reason. We managed to kill them, but Jathran and Lerdon are dead, and lots of others who were there. They're blaming Rion for all of it. They arrested him for wizardry and murder and other things, and us too. They think he's an evil wizard and that we're in league with him, because we saved him. How does he look to you?"

Rarnak went back to Rion. He looked terrible. His hair and shirt were wet and he was shivering violently. His skin felt very cold. His wrists were torn and bloody from the manacles, and there were teeth marks and congealed blood on his right arm. Something had bitten him. But although the wound hadn't been treated, it wasn't deep and it wasn't bleeding any longer. Rarnak went to the cot and lifted the blanket, then dropped it quickly in disgust, brushing off the things that crawled on his hand. He took off his own shirt instead and wrapped it around Rion, and began chafing his hands up and down Rion's arms, hoping to warm him.

"He's in a bad way. I've done what little I can for him," Rarnak said, shivering from the chill of the cell as he checked on Tarrell. Rarnak tried to rouse him, but Tarrell didn't waken. "Tarrell's still out. They hit him pretty hard." He walked back to the door. "You said 'we' before. Are Ron or Ara or Van with you?"

"Ron and I are here too," Ara called out. "Van's in Ogaten, thankfully. We're all right, though Ron got himself chained. We were hoping Tarrell might be able to get us all out. Why'd they arrest the two of you?"

"Talia came by the shop to see if Tarrell and I were safe. A friend of hers had been in the Market and told her about the attack. We went there to find Rion. We saw Jathran's and Lerdon's bodies, and then a Captain of the Guard came over and described Rion to us. When Tarrell said that's who else we were looking for and told him that he was Rion's guardian, the Captain said Rion had been arrested and since he wasn't an adult, the killings were Tarrell's fault, too. Tarrell didn't tell them Rion's a man now. He'd hoped to see him. They blamed me just for working for him, apparently. I'm only glad they didn't get Talia, too. One of the other Guard was decent enough. He hadn't wanted her to see the bodies, so she wasn't with us when we looked."

Rarnak imagined Talia captive, being forced into one of the cells, screaming and crying as the Guard took turns on her. He forced the images from his head. She was safe and she was smart. She'd know not to come here asking after them. He made a silent prayer to Areth, thanking her for keeping Talia safe again and entreating the Goddess to keep watching over his sister.

Tarrell stirred, and Rarnak went to him, glad for something to distract him. Tarrell moaned, and his hand went to his head as his eyes opened. "Easy, Tarrell. They hit you pretty hard."

Tarrell stared up at Rarnak's concerned face. "Where's your shirt?" he asked, sounding befuddled.

"Rion needed it worse than I did," Rarnak said grimly.

"Rion!" Tarrell cried, sitting up suddenly, and then falling back, clutching his head, gasping in pain.

"Easy, Tarrell! He's not going anywhere. Take it slow," Rarnak advised. He told Tarrell about the brothers being arrested as well.

Gar called out. "Rarnak, there's two things you'd better know about Rion, before he wakes up again. He can't speak, at least he almost can't. He's able to choke out a word here and there when he tries really hard. And he was bitten. That werewolven bit his arm. I know it doesn't look bad, but it might be. We're not sure if it's true or not, but from the stories we heard in Thenalon... he might change into one of them. And they're vicious, and cunning, and preternaturally strong. He'd be dangerous. The manacles might not even hold him."

Tarrell sat up. He saw Rion dangling from chains on the wall. He tried to stand, but was a bit unsteady on his feet, so Rarnak helped him over to Rion. "Rion? Rion, can you hear me?" Tarrell's hand was shaking as he brushed the hair from Rion's eyes and ran his fingers through Rion's hair. Tarrell lifted him to his feet and hugged him, then began chafing his arms, obviously hoping to warm him. Rion was shivering violently. "We have to get him out of here!" Tarrell said desperately.

Rarnak said, "I can't see as how any of us will be getting out. They'll come for us soon enough, but I doubt it will be to let us go."

Rion moaned and stirred and then started struggling before he was fully conscious.

"Rion, hush. It's me. It's Tarrell. It's all right. I'm here now," Tarrell soothed as he held him.

Rion opened his eyes and at first stared wild-eyed, as if he didn't recognize or even see Tarrell, but then his eyes focused on Tarrell's face and tears began to fall. "T-T-T...." Rion stuttered, and then he stamped his foot backward against the wall in frustration and began sobbing.

"Hush, Rion. It's all right. You don't have to say anything. Don't worry about that now," Tarrell soothed.

Rarnak went to the door and called out. "Rion's awake again, but he's not doing too well."

Gar called out in concern. "Is he acting odd? Does his arm look different?"

Rarnak really didn't know what to look for. He'd never heard either of the names Gar had given the monsters, and they hadn't seen what lay under that separate blanket, or the tarp. "Nothing I can tell," Rarnak called back.

Rion took great shuddering breaths, apparently trying to calm himself. Then he twisted in Tarrell's embrace, trying to see his arm. Tarrell let go, and Rion examined the wound. "Wh-wh...." He stamped his foot again. "What?" he yelled explosively and then stood breathing heavily, as if he'd fought a great battle.

Rarnak came over to him. He wished Gar hadn't said anything while Rion was awake to hear. "Nothing, Rion," he lied. "Gar's just worried your arm might fester, since it hasn't been treated, but it's not a bad wound. You'll be fine."

Rion stared at him intently, and Rarnak grimaced as he realized Rion didn't believe him. "T-T-T-Tell... m-m-m...." He stamped his foot again and struggled further to speak, but he couldn't say more.

Rarnak said, "Please, Rion. I'm not even sure what he's talking about. I've never heard of either of the names they gave those creatures. Please trust that we'll try to keep you safe, all right?"

Rion's expression remained fearful, but he nodded.

TARRELL looked at Rion in agony. Rion not being able to speak was terrible. If only they could get him out of here! Once he was home, and warm and safe again, maybe then he'd find his voice.

Footfalls sounded in the corridor, and Tarrell put his arms protectively about Rion. A face peered through the barred window of the cell door. "Stay there, by the wall. We're coming in."

A Guard Captain came in, a different one than before, with eight men, all with drawn swords.

Tarrell stiffened, afraid they'd come to kill them.

"You two, stand back by that far wall. We're taking this one for questioning," the Captain said, pointing to Rion.

Tarrell let go of Rion and fell to his knees. "Please, I beg you! Take me with you. I'm his guardian. He can't even speak after what's happened."

The Captain stared at Tarrell, begging on his knees, and then at Rion, chained to the wall, trembling, his face tear-streaked, and muttered disgustedly, "'Dangerous wizard,' he says." Tarrell continued to gaze at him beseechingly, and the Captain said, "All right, but watch what you do, if you don't want the boy to suffer for it."

"Thank you, Captain!" Tarrell said in relief. He stood aside while they unchained Rion and tossed Rarnak his shirt. They fastened shackles they'd brought with them to Rion's wrists and ankles and led him shuffling from the cell, with Tarrell following. They relocked the door, leaving Rarnak in the cell.

The Guard took Tarrell and Rion up a long flight of stairs. They didn't object when Tarrell helped Rion negotiate them, after he'd tripped on the heavy chains a few times.

They were led to a brightly lit room, with a sturdy wood table and four chairs. Tarrell sagged in relief. He had thought they were going to torture Rion.

The Guard Captain told them both to sit, and they did so. The cuffs of Rion's shackles made rattling noises as his hands shivered on the table. The Captain turned to one of the Guard. "Geffen, get the boy some kakla. Make sure it's hot. And bring a blanket, one of ours, not one of the ones from the cells."

Apparently noting Tarrell's surprised expression, the Captain said, "You're lucky you had someone speak on your behalf, or you'd not be in this room."

Tarrell was eager to know who might have spoken for them, but kept silent, lest he antagonize the Guard.

"I need to hear everything that happened in the Market this morning," the Captain said to Rion, his voice surprisingly kind.

Rion appeared panicked. "Wr-wr-wr...." He looked at Tarrell desperately, and licked his lips, then held his right hand as if holding a pen and pulled it across the table as if writing, while nodding his head.

Tarrell said, "Captain, excuse me for speaking. He's trying to tell you he can write it for you, he'll be happy to tell you anything you want to know, if you'll give him pen and ink and paper. He writes fast and well, but he honestly can't speak."

The Captain studied Rion appraisingly. "Not even if it means I lock your guardian back in the cell, and take you downstairs to the room we usually question prisoners in?"

Rion paled and started shaking more violently. "P-p-p.... D-d-d...," he begged, unable to say even a single word, as tears started to stream down his face again.

"Captain, please don't hurt him!" Tarrell begged. "He hasn't done anything to deserve this, I swear!"

The Captain raised his hands. "Calm yourselves, both of you. I needed to be sure you weren't trying to deceive me. I've no wish to harm the boy, but I've a job to do. It's the Guard's responsibility to keep the City safe, and I'll do everything in my power to see to it."

Geffen returned, but he wasn't alone, and he'd done more than the Captain had asked. Instead of carrying a single mug and the blanket, he was bearing a tray, which he set down. There were three empty mugs, a large steaming pitcher of kakla, two smaller ones of sweet cream and honey, a plate of six slices of honey cake, three cloth napkins, and three spoons. There was another Guard behind him, holding a folded, thick wool blanket. Tarrell recognized him in surprise as the Guard they'd first spoken to in the Market: Regus, the compassionate one.

It was Regus who spoke. "I figured you could use a mug too, Captain, so I offered to carry the blanket for Geffen so he could bring extra. And I knew it was likely the prisoners weren't the only ones who'd not had any lunch. I thought you might be a bit peckish and that a few slices of my sister's honey cake would tide you over," he said, appearing embarrassed, his eyes darting to Rion's shivering form and back to the Captain's face again.

"Well, then, as you seem so eager to help, after you give the boy's guardian the blanket for him, we'll be needing pen and ink and paper as well. The boy can't speak," the Captain said.

"Yes sir!" Regus said, handing Tarrell the blanket and leaving the room quickly.

Tarrell put the blanket about Rion's shoulders, as he was hampered by the thick, heavy length of chain that bound his wrists.

The Captain said to Tarrell, "You may pour the boy some kakla, and yourself some as well. Also, Regus must have forgotten I don't have much of a sweet tooth. I wouldn't want to insult his sister, though, or for good food to go to waste. Help yourselves to the honey cake," he offered, as he poured a mug of kakla for himself and, true to his words, didn't add either sweet cream or honey, drinking the bitter black brew appreciatively instead.

After Tarrell poured and sweetened a cup for each of them, Rion held the mug of kakla in both hands, the chain dangling between them, and drank carefully. His trembling eased a little. "Th-th-th...." Rion said, looking frustrated and on the verge of tears again.

"You're welcome," the Captain said kindly. "Take another drink or two to warm yourself, and eat at least one of the pieces of cake, so Regus will think I had some," the Captain ordered.

Rion nodded, picked up a piece of the cake, and obediently and gratefully began eating it.

"Thank you, Captain," Tarrell said sincerely. "His father and uncle were City Guards in Ardock, before they fell. Elmoth bless you and your men for being the kind of Guard they were." His thanks were heartfelt, but also, he thought it wouldn't hurt to establish that bond between them. The City Guard, at its finest, was a brotherhood of sorts, at times respected even in a city not their own.

The Captain nodded slightly in acknowledgement, and then sipped again from his mug of kakla.

When Regus returned with the writing supplies, Tarrell noticed he glanced surreptitiously down at the table in front of Rion, and suspected it was to ensure he'd been given some of the cake.

"Now then, I need you to write down all that happened: what you saw, what you did, what you know," the Captain commanded Rion.

RION nodded and complied. It was hard to write with his hands chained without smudging the ink, but he was careful.

The Captain read his statement aloud, after he was done. It was very thorough, including descriptions of the two beasts, and it detailed everything he'd seen. Rion saw that Tarrell listened intently and was horrified to hear what they had faced.

Then the Captain began asking questions, the first being why Ron, Ara, and Gar would have risked their lives to save him if they no longer worked for him.

Because they love me, as I love them, and we would die to save each other, Rion wrote sincerely.

The Captain appeared surprised and impressed by such loyalty. Then he asked Rion if he was a wizard, or knew any magic.

Rion wrote honestly, *I am not a wizard nor do I know any magic. If I did, I would have used it to protect myself from the monsters and to keep the Guard from arresting me.*

The Captain eyed him shrewdly. "Do you know why a wizard might want to harm you?"

Rion had been expecting that question, he had been bracing himself for it, and was careful to appear puzzled, and write with a steady hand. *No, I don't know why a wizard would take interest in me. I'm hoping he might have mistaken me for someone else and realized his mistake. If I'd known a wizard hunted me, I'd not be walking around openly with only two guards. I'd be in hiding, with armed men all around me.*

The Captain studied him intently, and Rion met his gaze levelly. He'd been able to lie to Hunter without him suspecting, when he feared Hunter was marching against Talon. He could do so now, to a stranger.

The Captain appeared satisfied and asked a few more questions. Then he stood. "All right. We're going to take you back to your cell. We need to question your friends, next. You can keep the blanket, and you'll stay in the shackles you're in. You need not be chained to the wall again."

Rion nodded his thanks.

RARNAK was relieved to see the two of them come back as quickly as they did and appearing unhurt. He'd been imagining what they might do to poor Rion. He'd hoped Tarrell might have been able to convince the Guard that Rion couldn't talk. But still, Rarnak was sure they would have tortured him. How else would they know he spoke the truth? Of course, a man in pain will say anything to make the pain stop, even damn himself to death, but such truths mattered little in a place like this. He'd been afraid Rion and Tarrell might have confessed to all kinds of crimes, in an effort to protect one another.

Rion actually looked a little better than he had when he'd left. He had a thick wool blanket about him, and he'd stopped shivering. And they didn't chain him back to the wall as he had expected them to. Rion sat down on the wooden cot frame, as far from the other blanket as he could get.

Then Rarnak heard the brothers being taken for questioning.

Tarrell eyed the cell door with a concerned expression. "I hope that our mysterious benefactor put in a word for them, too. I hope they are as civil to them as they were to us." He turned to Rarnak before he could voice the question. "The Captain said someone spoke on our behalf. I wish I knew who."

A while later they heard footfalls and the sound of a cell door being opened and then closed again. After the Guard left the corridor, Tarrell called out to make sure the brothers were together and all right.

Ara called back, "We're fine. They were remarkably restrained, and Ron had the sense to hold his tongue this time. Rion seems to have impressed the Captain by what he told him of us, whatever it was."

Tarrell told them that someone had spoken on their behalf, but none of them could figure out who it might have been, or why they'd have taken the risk of being branded an accomplice of a wizard in order to help them.

A LONG while later, there were footsteps once more. Rion glanced nervously at Tarrell as Tarrell and Rarnak moved to stand beside him. Rion knew it was both to protect and reassure him. He was somewhat relieved to see it was the same Captain, the kind one, with the same eight Guard as before. All of them had been the type of Guard his father and uncle and their friends had been: decent people.

"You've an audience with the Magistrate," the Captain said. "The three of you are to come with us." To Rion's surprise, he unlocked the fetters from Rion's hands and feet. He hoped that their removing the shackles was a good sign. Did it mean they believed he wasn't a wizard, that they realized they had no need of cold iron to protect themselves from him? Rion rubbed his wrists, careful of the torn skin.

They left with the Guard, down the hall to the left, and stopped at another cell. The Captain opened it, and Rion saw the brothers peering tensely out. Ron was no longer chained to the wall. The Captain said, "The three of you have an audience with the Magistrate. Come." When they came out, Rion studied them anxiously, but they truly appeared unharmed, except for a ring of dried blood around each of Ron's wrists that matched his own.

RON examined Rion critically. He looked terrible, but he still seemed himself. But he was quiet. Rion was seldom quiet, and he was far from smiling.

They walked together, surrounded by the Guard. They were escorted upstairs to the Judgment Hall. There was an imposing man there, older, with graying hair and a stern but honest-looking face, and more Guard.

The Guard led them in front of the man and then stepped to the side, joining the others. "You will step forward when I call your name, for verdict and sentencing. Rion, ward of Trader Tarrell of Ardock?"

Rion stepped forward. Ron could see he was nervous. He offered up a silent prayer to Elmoth on his behalf. Ara, who was by far the most devout amongst them, had softly spoken a number of them in their cell.

"You have been charged with foul wizardry and the resultant murder of seventeen citizens, including four Guard, the injury of twenty-nine other individuals, and the destruction and damage of an as yet unassessed amount of goods."

RION tensed for the verdict, holding his breath.

"You have been found not guilty of these charges. However, it is clear that, for an as yet unfathomed reason, you are a target of such foul wizardry and as such are a danger to the City. For the safety of the citizenry, you are hereby banished from Gosa. You will have twenty-four hours to leave the City. You will be escorted to your home by the Guard, and from there to the City gate. Should you ever choose to return, you will be subject to immediate arrest and potential execution, as deemed necessary at that time."

Rion sagged, both in relief and dismay. They had lived through so much to come and then spend only a few scant weeks here. He didn't think he would ever have felt safe here again, after being attacked twice now in such a brief time. But where were they to go now?

"Trader Tarrell of Ardock, guardian of Rion of Ardock?" Tarrell stepped forward, and all Rion's concerns for himself vanished. He was terrified that his own punishment might have been lenient because they thought him still a child, that Tarrell might face something worse. "As guardian of Rion, you are likewise found not guilty of all charges and likewise banished, under the same conditions as your ward," the Magistrate said. Tarrell clenched his jaw but kept silent, and Rion almost collapsed in relief.

"Guardsman Rarnak of Gosa?"

Rarnak stepped forward.

"You are found not guilty of the charge of guilt by association, and if you agree to terminate your employment under Trader Tarrell and his ward Rion, you will be free to remain in the City."

Rarnak nodded wordlessly.

"Trader Ronamark, Trader Aramark, and Guardsman Garamark of Ogaten?" the Magistrate called, and the three brothers stepped forward. "You are found guilty of the charge of theft of weaponry of the City Guard."

The brothers stiffened, but all of them, even Ron, kept their jaws clenched tight as the Magistrate continued. "You are found not guilty of the murder of said Guard. Due to the circumstances surrounding the theft, the use to which the weapons were put in service to the City, at risk to your own lives, and the cooperation rendered during your imprisonment, there will be no punishment meted out for the first charge. You are free to remain at liberty in the City. Further, you are each hereby rewarded fifty gold pieces for your heroism in the face of grave danger and foul wizardry and are offered positions in the City Guard, should you choose to accept them." He gazed expectantly at the three men.

"Thank you, your Honor, but I will decline that honor," Ron said, without rancor or sarcasm. His brothers echoed his words.

"Your purses and weapons, which were confiscated, are hereby returned to you all," the Magistrate said, and the Guard came forward with their belongings.

Rion's heart quickened when he saw the little bag he kept the Elfstone in. It, or something of similar size and shape, was inside, he could feel it, but he dared not insult the Magistrate or Guard by checking.

The Magistrate then called each of the brothers forward to accept his reward and gave each five ten-gold pieces. They each thanked him, politely.

"The Guard will accompany you to your homes and will remain at watch outside the home of Tarrell and Rion to see that they leave the City as ordered. You are all dismissed."

They turned and followed the Guard from the chamber, through a number of corridors, up a flight of stairs, and outside.

By unspoken agreement, the brothers came home with Tarrell, Rion, and Rarnak. Once they were all safely inside, with the City Guard on watch about the house, Ron broke his silence, letting loose a tirade against the whole affair.

"No apologies, just a single night and day to pack and leave! He gives us a reward for what we did, after calling us thieves! That was nothing compared to Rion! He stood and faced them with nothing but a bared blade, after he saw what they did to Jathran and Lerdon! He knocked the werewolven and himself off the chimaera in midflight, trying to keep them away from us! Those gutless, pompous, self-serving—in chains! Rion and me, in chains!"

The others stood back and let him rant. He needed to vent his frustrations, and he was speaking their hearts as well.

Tarrell said, "Rion, you were wise to rent the shop and not buy one. I should have listened to you before, when you told me you didn't like it here and wanted to leave. This City is no place for us. I won't be sorry to leave. But where will we go now?"

He turned to Rarnak. "I know it's asking a lot of you, as it appears Rion has somehow made a powerful enemy, but could you come with us? We've not the time to find other reliable guards. As it is, it will be treacherous for us on the road with only one."

"Of course I'll come," Rarnak said, appearing surprised that Tarrell even thought to ask. "I've no desire to stay here after today, welcome by them or not."

Ron spoke up, sounding calmer. "You're talking as if it'll only be the three of you. You don't think we'd let you go by yourselves? The three of us will guard you as well, as we have before."

Tarrell argued against it. "But Ron, you can't. You and Ara are traders now. There's no need for you to risk yourselves for us like that again. We'll manage."

Ron said firmly, "It's not open for discussion. We're coming with you, and don't you dare try to pay us for it, either. We're doing so as your friends."

Rion was moved beyond words, even had he been able to speak. He hoped he conveyed his thanks sufficiently with his eyes.

Tarrell sighed. "I've no idea where to go. I'll certainly not endanger Ogaten or the mill, and we need a large City to settle in, in any case, if we're to be traders."

RON shook his head. "First you're going to Salenia. The Elves might be able to help Rion." He didn't say they needed to see him. Only they might be powerful enough to save Rion, if he was indeed turning into one of those wolven-headed monsters. But he could not tell Tarrell that in front of Rion. Poor Rion had been terrified enough for one day.

Ron addressed everyone. "We'd better treat Rion's injuries and all have baths and some dinner, and get to bed early, if we're going to be packing up Rion's and Tarrell's things as well as our own tomorrow. Fortunately we only have a single wagon's worth of goods and it looks like you're down to about the same," Ron said, looking around the sparsely stocked shop. "It's lucky you've sold so much of what you brought and not had the opportunity to buy more."

Rarnak spoke up. "I'll cook this time, Ron. You need to get cleaned up and bandaged too."

Ron nodded and then turned to his brothers. "Ara, Gar, you go to our rooms and get our clothes for tomorrow. We'll pack the rest tomorrow morning or afternoon, dependent upon when we finish up here."

Ara and Gar left without comment.

"Tarrell, I'd recommend you sell the wagons you don't need for the journey. You can always buy more wherever you end up," Ron suggested.

"We'd actually already planned to sell them," Tarrell agreed. "We knew it would be more economical to buy new ones later if we needed them than to store and maintain the ones we have. We'll sell them tomorrow."

They continued to talk over their plans while they heated water for their baths.

There was a knock on the door, just after Rion and Tarrell had finished bathing and dressing, and both Rion's and Ron's wrists had been tended to.

"It can't be Ara and Gar. They'd not be back yet," Ron said. "Get into the back, you two. Rarnak, get the door." Ron drew his sword and moved to stand behind the door so he could spring out, if needed.

Rarnak approached the door and warily asked, "Who is it?"

"Nicky? Thank Areth! It's Talia. Please let us in," his sister said, using her childhood name for her older brother.

Talia entered, with Madame Genevieve and a large, armed man in the livery of a private guardsman who stepped between the two women and the door, hand on his sword hilt. Rarnak released his grip on his hilt, and Ron sheathed his blade and came out into the open.

"I was so afraid they would hurt you!" Talia said, studying him critically. "Are Tarrell and Rion here too? Are they all right?" she asked, looking around anxiously.

They came out from the back, and she ran up to Tarrell and hugged him.

Madame Genevieve smiled at Tarrell and looked in concern at Rion. "I'm happy to see I was able to gain you your freedom. I am sorry my influence was not sufficient enough that you might stay. I fear I will be losing a brilliant seamstress on the morrow."

Talia blushed.

"You are the one who helped us?" Tarrell asked, and the older woman nodded. "I owe you a debt I can never repay," Tarrell said fervently.

"You can repay me easily enough. Tell me you will wed Talia and be good to her always. That is all I need to hear," Madame Genevieve said sincerely.

Talia's blush darkened and Tarrell blushed as well. "This is not how I had planned to ask you, Talia," he said, holding her hand.

She turned to Rarnak for his approval. Rarnak's expression of surprise transformed into a grin of joy. When she saw her brother approved, Talia squealed in delight and kissed Tarrell, and he returned the kiss enthusiastically.

Madame Genevieve left after dinner, with Talia and her guard. Ron stood guard in the shop with Rarnak, while Rion and Tarrell went to bed.

Chapter 2
Lost to Darkness

IT WAS bright out tonight, but the moon's light did not bring comfort. Instead it was disturbing. The moon was large and full, but it was red, the color of blood. Shadala shivered. A deathmoon, her people called it. Such a moon in the past had presaged the death of a Chieftess or a War Leader. But what danger could she be in here, surrounded by the might of half the Elven Army and Navy? She swallowed, hard. Her brother was also protected by half the Elven Army and Navy, but by the other half, the ones who had left with King Talon and most of the rest of her kin. He was far from here and most certainly in greater danger than she.

An equally chilling possibility occurred to her. This time, might it foreshadow the death of a King? She no longer hated King Talon for what he had done to Akarhad, the Elven High-Prince others called Aras. She could not hate the King after he had humbled himself to her and admitted he had wronged the son-of-her-heart. She did not wish to see him fall.

Shadala was crossing the huge field surrounding the Lords' Grove far more slowly than her usual ground-eating stride. It was getting harder to come each day, but she needed to see her Tree as much as Taradala needed to see her. Shadala could not bear her loneliness without her Tree. Akarhad was gone. Three hundred of their people had marched to war with King Talon, her beloved niece and nephew Falara and Veran amongst them. Taratur had left as well. She had named the one the others called Beryl "tree-talker" in her native Urwani tongue, for he both spoke with and for the special sentient Trees of the Lords' Grove. Only Leonas, of all those she cared for, remained.

From here, she could make out the individual Trees, as well as the faces of each of the Grove Guard. She spotted Leonas, who was watching her approach. Leonas was usually here. He lived and ate and often even slept under the Trees. She almost smiled. It lightened the burden of her heart to see him. He was like a brother to her, far more than Haran had ever been, in spite of the bond of their blood.

Even as she studied them as she approached, the Grove Guard in turn watched her. They always watched. They treated everyone as the Enemy, until the Trees assured them they were not. Not even the High-King was trusted, by his own order. He would not risk Arandrin's life, not when his Tree had only just been returned to him, when he could hear Arandrin's voice again after one thousand years of silence, and even feel his leafy embrace.

She wondered anew at what Akarhad had told her of that. When she had parlayed with Akarhad those many nights ago, when she had first learned the name given to him by his own people, Aras, and that he was the son of the High-King, he had told her that Elves live to be a thousand years old. From Akarhad's own words about Arandrin then, High-King Laedrin should already be at least ancient and withered, and probably dead. Yet he was instead strong and hale, with no look of advanced age upon him.

She was not nearly so old, yet she had begun to feel old since the sons-of-her-heart had left her. She was forty-nine. She *should* feel old. She should look far older than she did. It was her Amontir blood that kept her so young. Only the few remaining pureblood Urwani of her tribe died at sixty as Men should. Others of their mixed tribe, those of pure Amontir blood, had lived to be over two hundred, some even reaching two hundred fifty years.

She would not live so long. She might live to be one hundred fifty or so years. She was not of pure Amontir blood, but one of the many who shared the mixed blood of both tribes. Her mother, a pureblood Amontir, had married one of the few pureblood Urwani left. There had almost been civil war because her mother had done so. Her brother Haran had nearly died for it. His coming-of-age ceremony had almost become his funeral, when he was challenged for Lordship of House of Gryphon by their cousin. The King's Knife had almost been lost before it could ever be gifted to King Talon. She was the only one who had known its hiding place, and she would not have survived if her brother had fallen.

Shadala forced her thoughts back to the present. She was pleased to see Leonas still looked so well. She knew he missed both Akarhad and Taratur as fiercely as she. The three men had become as brothers. She had thought nothing could ever part Leonas from Taratur, especially once Akarhad had gone. But Taratur had spoken to the High-King. He had told him he must follow King Talon to Caramore. Taratur had asked that Leonas be named the new Lord of the Grove, Protector of the Trees, in his stead. He said that he had already consulted with the Trees, and they had approved him for the appointment, though Taratur alone heard the voice of all the Trees, not just his own.

Before Akarhad had gone, he and Taratur both had convinced the High-King to form and appoint a special new Guard, the Grove Guard, to see to the protection of the Trees. Members of both the Elven Army and Navy had been carefully selected for the task. One hundred forty-seven had been chosen in all, three Captains, each with forty-eight men, to guard in three shifts so the thirty-seven Trees of the Grove would be protected day and night. All knew that at any moment, the Enemy might seek to burn them, as he had tried to burn the Wood around them, or attack them with poison or other vile magicks, as he had used upon her people's fields when he had started their war against the Elves, the war Akarhad had ended.

Leonas's friend Gaius was one of the Captains, his former Commander, Daras, another, and Thanadrin of the Army, the third. She saw Gaius was here as well today. Gaius too often stayed well past his shift. She had begun to suspect his interest might be more in Leonas than dedication to the Trees, though Leonas appeared oblivious to it.

She had been surprised to learn that it was not uncommon for the Elves, or even her newly discovered pureblood Amontir kin, to form such pairings: man to man, or woman to woman. The Urwani certainly did not share the practice, and her people had forgotten they once did. But she could not view it as unnatural and be appalled by it, as some of her people were. Leonas had told her that Taratur had wistfully spoken to him of a secret love he yet held in his heart for a man he would not name. And she had seen firsthand the love Akarhad held for King Talon. Once, she would have been jealous of the King, but now she was content to love Akarhad as a mother might.

Gaius and Daras both had helped Leonas bear the loss of Akarhad and Taratur. She wished she in turn had others to whom she might have turned, to ease the burden of her own heart. But save for Leonas, there was no one. They were gone, all of them, and her heart gone with them.

GAIUS was watching Leonas, as he always did, surreptitiously, discreetly, from afar. Until only recently he had been subordinate to Leonas, only a lieutenant, and worse, assigned to a different squad. Then he had been promoted to Captain. His heart had sung with joy when he had been assigned as a Captain of the Grove Guard, where Leonas also was a Captain. Now that they were both the same rank and in the same unit, he had hoped that someday soon he might finally express the love he had kept hidden for so long.

They had trained beside each other for five years. From the moment he had first set his eyes upon Leonas across the training ground, he had known they were destined to be together. They became close friends, and every moment since had only reaffirmed his conviction. But as cadets they were yet children, unable to express love verbally or physically, even had Leonas felt the same.

Gaius had hoped to celebrate his graduation with Leonas. As Leonas had not chosen the path of the Reservist, Gaius had assumed Leonas would not be returning to Tanieria. He was devastated when he first learned that Leonas was going home for the four weeks allotted to him before his active duty began, thinking Leonas was keeping a promise to one he had left behind there. Gaius had been relieved beyond naming to learn that he had gone only to visit his parents.

Leonas had told him that his mother was expecting another child, and that he ached to see his baby brother or sister. Noble Leonas had thoughts only for his family. He had proudly confided in Gaius that he loved his parents dearly, for their strength of character, and their love for one another, and for him, their son. Leonas's mother was an Oceana, a River Elf of Tanieria, but his father was an Aerta, a Wood Elf of Lysenia. They had not let racial prejudices interfere with their happiness, though their path had not been an easy one. Nor was Leonas's.

Gaius knew Leonas's heart's desire had been to be one of the King's Guard, so that he might someday guard and perhaps even enter the Lords' Grove. Leonas had been crushed when he had been forced into training for the Guard instead of the King's Guard, for his mixed blood, thinking he would never know the grace of the Trees. Leonas had never dreamt that he might one day be appointed Lord of the Grove, their Protector.

Gaius bit back a moan of despair. Though officially still a Captain in rank, Leonas had been elevated to the title of Lord when Lord Beryl left them. Just when Gaius had thought to press his suit, Leonas had once more become unattainable, promoted out of his reach.

Gaius turned and gazed upward as he heard the soft rustle of branches overhead. He stood beneath Aranonas, Leonas's Tree, his favorite position within the Grove. He could almost swear the Tree was whispering to him, though he could not hear him. Unlike Leonas, no Wood Elf blood ran in his veins. Yet still, at times like this, he fancied that Aranonas somehow knew of his affection for Leonas, that he even approved of it.

He was a heartsick fool. What could these magnificent, ancient Trees know or understand about love, particularly the love of one Elf for another?

LEONAS watched the Chieftess approach, worried for her. Almost her entire tribe had left to fight King Talon's war. The Urwani-Amontir City was deserted now. The fields surrounding it were still poisoned from the treachery of former Lord of the Guard Ahrnad. All the warriors that once guarded it had left. Only the farmers and the children remained. The farmers needed to be near their new fields, on the Elves' land, by the River, where the fire had leveled the forest. Even the Hall of History in their City was empty. Six of the precious ancient tapestries that had once hung there and even some of the books had gone with the combined Urwani-Amontir Army and Elven Army and Navy, as symbols of their endurance as a people.

It was too dangerous for those people remaining to be so isolated, so poorly defended. It had been hard for Shadala to abandon the City she had fought so hard to protect. But she had seen the danger; she had moved with her people. She lived in Field House now, though she spent little time there. She was lost without her people, but especially without Aras, and Lunahr, the Man most knew only as Beryl. Leonas was lost without them as well. He could not have borne it were it not for Gaius and Daras, and the Trees.

When Lunahr had told him he must stay here as Lord of the Grove, to protect the Trees in his stead, he had refused. He had sworn himself to Lunahr's service, at first because his High-Prince, Aras, had commanded it of him, but since then he had done so because his own heart commanded him to. Lunahr had become as a brother to him. Leonas had told Lunahr that nothing he said might make him leave his side.

It was then that Lunahr entrusted him with the true secret of the Grove and of the Elf Lords and Ladies. Leonas had known that each of the Elf Lords and Ladies was bound to one of the Trees, that they loved them and spoke with them, although until recently the voices of the Trees had been silenced. But he had never guessed that the Elf Lords' and Ladies' very lives depended upon that bond.

They were not as the rest of them, the Wood Elves of the Army, who relied upon their Wood for their survival, or the River Elves of their Navy, who needed their River. They were Wood Elves also, but actual survivors from the lost Homeland, refugees from the Annihilation three thousand years before. They would not live for one thousand years, but for ten thousand. It was the Trees of the Lords' Grove that gave them their strength, their health, their longevity, that fueled their Power. If ever a Tree was felled, the Lord or Lady it sheltered would die as well. High-King Laedrin and High-Prince Aras, as well as Jarnath, Meloneth, Areth, Laneth, and all the others whom Men, in their ignorance, worshiped as their Gods and Goddesses, would perish if the Grove did. Leonas wondered again if he might live to be so old, now that Aranonas had bonded to him, or if Shadala might, for one of the remaining two formerly unnamed Trees had bonded to her as well.

When he heard of the importance of the bond, Leonas had known true fear, not for his own life, nor even for the life of Lunahr, whom he loved so dearly. Of all of them, it was Aras who must not fall. Leonas had been told some, overheard more, and surmised much. Aras must survive, even if his father and the very Gods and Goddesses of Man were to perish. Aras was one of the four great wizards battling for the fate of the world. He fought Incuban, seldom spoken of by name, often called only the Enemy. He fought Arcanus, whom the Amontir, especially their King, Talon, had followed blindly as a savior until a few short months ago. And he fought one other, whom Aras would not name, even to him.

Leonas thought Lunahr might know who the other one was, but he had not asked. Lunahr was still not strong, not whole. He had not yet fully recovered from his capture by

Incuban, from all the terrible things He had done to him when Lunahr had been turned into His servant. Lunahr never should have left his protection, or that of the Grove, for the Trees shielded him as much as he guarded them.

Leonas's musings abruptly ended, as without warning the calm of the Grove erupted into chaos. It was as if a hurricane had suddenly seized the Trees. The branches of the Trees at the edge of the Grove nearest to the High-Prince's Tree began swaying wildly, as if lashed by strong winds. "Be vigilant! I must speak to Aranonas!" Leonas called out to the Grove Guard as he ran into the Grove, toward his Tree. He feared some attack by the Enemy, that the wind was some terrible magic of dark purpose.

For the moment ignoring Gaius, Leonas reached out and touched his Tree, completely unprepared for the result. He was deafened by the scream, he was driven to his knees by the pain, as he fought to stay conscious, to understand what was happening.

It was not Aranonas who was in pain, who was screaming. This was only what he felt along the bond he shared with his brothers and sisters in the Grove. He begged for Aranonas to tell him what was wrong, even as an invisible crushing weight pressed against his chest. He fought to breathe, but he was overwhelmed by pain and the darkness that claimed him.

GAIUS stood frozen as Leonas was first driven to his knees, screaming, and then stiffened and toppled over soundlessly onto the ground. Gaius broke free of his paralyzing shock and ran to Leonas's side. Leonas's face was twisted in agony, his eyes wide but unseeing. Gaius felt desperately for the beat of Leonas's heart and knew terror when he could not find it.

No! He could not be gone! He could not be dead! He stared in horror at Leonas's Tree, that he might have killed one he was bonded to, that he had killed the one named Lord of the Grove, Protector of the Trees.

SHADALA was running now. Something terrible was happening. There had been a scream, abruptly silenced, and then her Tree, Taradala, was calling to her, pleading for her aid. One of the Trees was dying.

She saw one of the Grove Guard run from the Grove with the speed of a deer, heading toward the Palace. Taradala was frantic. None of them could reach the dying Tree to help him. She begged Shadala to go to him.

Shadala's face paled when she realized the horrible significance of Taradala's thoughts. It was Akarhad's Tree that was dying, the young birch. That was why none of them could reach him. Akarhad's Tree was the smallest, set apart from the rest, outside the circle of the Grove, the only one that had sprouted upon this land. She saw the branches of the others straining toward him, thrashing wildly, trying vainly to reach him.

"Chieftess, stay back!" one of the Grove Guard ordered, and she saw to her horror they had nocked arrows against her, to a man.

"I am not here as an enemy, but as a friend!" she said, desperately looking toward Aranas, Akarhad's Tree.

"You may not enter, for your safety as well as that of the Grove. The Enemy controls the Trees. Lord Leonas has been slain. We have sent a runner. The High-King has been summoned. No other may approach," the Elf said.

Shadala paled. "Leonas? He cannot be!" She could not lose Leonas as well. "Please, I am Healer as well as Chieftess. I beg you, let me see Leonas. I will not enter the Grove. Bring him here to me, so I might tend to him."

The Elf appeared agonized. "We cannot. The Trees will not let us enter the Grove. They have expelled us. Only Gaius is within, held captive with Leonas's body. The Trees will not let him leave."

"Then let me try to go to him! The Trees must let me. I am bonded to one of them, as none of you are," Shadala begged.

"We cannot," the Guard said, tortured but unyielding.

Shadala fought her hammering heart and remembered all Taratur had told her. She did not want to harm the Grove Guard and she feared she might do worse, that she might kill them in her ignorance and inexperience, but Leonas was too precious to her and to the Grove for her not to fight to save him.

She touched her Power, shaped it, and then spoke, weaving it carefully into her words. "**You will let me enter,**" she commanded, using the King's Voice for the first time, as if she were King instead of Chieftess.

The eyes of the Elf before her lost their focus, and he obediently lowered his bow, as did all of his men within sight of her, within the sound of her Voice. She ran inside the Grove, toward Leonas's Tree, and the Trees did not impede her.

Gaius was there. Leonas lay near him, just beyond his reach. One of the roots of Leonas's Tree had torn up from the ground and was pinning Gaius, who was slashing desperately at the grasping branches above them with his sword, keeping the Tree from touching Leonas, though a second root was wrapped around Leonas.

She fought the urge to go to them and instead ran to Taradala and touched her. Shadala spoke wordlessly to her Tree and to her intense relief was answered with a cascade of images, of knowledge, part whispered, part sung, part shown, nearly overwhelming her in Taradala's frantic haste to be understood.

Shadala called out to Gaius, even as she ran toward him. "Gaius, lower your sword! You must allow Leonas's Tree to touch him! Quickly! It may already be too late!"

"Chieftess, I will not! He has killed him!" Gaius sobbed.

"His Tree did not mean to harm Leonas. He wishes now only to save him. Gaius, please, as his friend, you must give him the chance to live." Shadala could not use her Power, not here, within the Grove; the Trees would never allow it. Aranonas must save Leonas, if he might still be saved. She reached for Leonas, ducking the sword that swung wildly toward her, realizing Gaius was mad with grief, that what she had suspected must be true: Gaius truly loved Leonas.

One of Aranonas's branches knocked the sword from Gaius's hands, and others entangled him, pinning him.

Shadala picked up Leonas's limp body and held it up to where the branches of the tree could reach him. Her arms shook with the effort, even with her Amontir blood. He was far heavier than he appeared. Elven bones were very strong, very dense. But the branches reached down and lifted her burden from her, the trailing root releasing him as soon as the branches touched him. Leonas was engulfed completely by the branches.

Gaius cried out in loss, sobbing wildly.

Shadala ran back to Taradala. She could not attempt to comfort poor Gaius, not yet. She must learn more about what had happened, now that Leonas might live, so that she might aid Akarhad's Tree, if she could.

A short while later her thoughts were drawn back, away from her Tree. She wiped her tear-streaked face with her hand and fought to stand as she heard voices outside the Grove. She heard her name being called in anger by the High-King, Laedrin, and to her horror, the sound of breaking branches. "Do not harm the Trees! I will come to you!" She left Gaius, still struggling in the confines of the roots and branches of Leonas's Tree.

"I lay my knife down in the Grove. I am unarmed!" she called out and did so, knowing better than to appear before the Elven High-King armed. Just before she emerged from the safety of the Trees she called out, "**You are released**," removing the hold of her Voice upon the Grove Guard. As she left the sanctuary of the Grove, as soon as she was clear of their branches, she was seized roughly by the King's Guard and forced to her knees. She clenched her jaw as they searched her for weapons. They were very thorough and not at all gentle.

"It is safe to approach, Majesty," one of the King's Guard said.

Laedrin strode before her and glared down at her. "What evil have you done to the Grove, Chieftess, that the Trees will not let me enter, that they kill my men and rob them of their will?" he demanded harshly.

"There has been evil done this day, High-King, but not by me, and not by the Trees. Leonas's Tree did not mean to stop his heart. He is trying even now to save Leonas, with the aid of the others. The Trees are all linked to one another. When one suffers, they all suffer. It was the dying Tree that Leonas felt through his link to his own that felled him, the scream, the fire." Her voice caught on the last word, and it ended in a sob.

Laedrin's eyes narrowed. "I see no fire, I smell no smoke. You are lying to me, Chieftess, but I will have the truth from you," he said coldly.

"I wish I were not speaking the truth, but I am. It is the birch that is dying. You can see them yet trying to reach for him, to save him. It is your son's tree that is dying… because Aras…." Her voice caught on the Elven name she seldom used. "Aras was dying…. Aras was the one screaming…. Aras is the one… who was on fire…." She sagged as she began sobbing, supported only by the strong hands of the soldiers who held her.

Laedrin's face paled. "No. No, he cannot be," he said in denial. He grabbed her by the shoulders and shook her. "Why do you say that to me?"

Lost in her grief, Shadala did not answer, nor even hear him.

THE King's Guard tensed as the High-King released the Chieftess and strode into the Grove, but did not try to impede him, in spite of the danger, nor follow him. They watched as the Trees let their High-King pass, when only moments before they would not. They waited breathlessly as he disappeared within the Grove. Then they heard a howl of anguish and ran inside, cursing themselves and fearing him dying. The Grove

Guard raced to their High-King's aid at their side, and the Trees did not move to stop them.

They thought they would find the High-King dead as well, but what they saw chilled them even more so. Laedrin was crumpled upon the carpet of dead leaves at the base of his tree, lying in the dirt, sobbing. They had never seen their King grieve before, nor cry, for anyone or anything, not even when he watched his son bleeding to death in the arena at the age of fourteen, or when the wizard Magus showed him a false scry of his son's death in the jaws of a wolven only a few short months ago.

The Grove Guard found Captain Gaius, pinned helplessly by Lord Leonas's tree. The Guard ran to their Captain's aid, though they knew they could do nothing. They could not harm the Tree even to aid one of their own. But the confining root moved, stiffly, not like a snake, but like a stick dragged upon the ground by a tired child, and the branches drew back as well. The Tree freed Gaius of its own accord.

Then as the Guard watched cautiously, many of the branches lowered, and then rose again. To their shock, they saw that Leonas stood before them, living and breathing, the expression of puzzlement on his face instantly replaced by one of grief and compassion.

As his startled men clustered about him, while Gaius only stared, dazed, Leonas pushed past them. "The High-Prince's Tree, I must go to him. He needs me."

LEONAS left the Grove, his men trailing behind him, and approached the slender birch that stood apart from the rest. He embraced the Tree as if it were a child who had lost his father, or a father who had lost his child, and began whispering words of comfort to him.

He turned to his men, still holding Aranas. "Someone, please comfort Gaius for me. I have frightened him terribly, but I must go to him later, if I am to save this Tree. And fetch Healer Jarnath, for High-King Laedrin." Then he turned back to Aranas and spoke once more.

"My Lord, what about the Chieftess? She is in our custody. The High-King accused her of harming the Grove," one of the King's Guard boldly asked.

"Release her, on my authority. I do not think the High-King should be disturbed with such matters now, while he is grieving for his son. High-Prince Aras is dead. He died horribly, in agony. By fire," Leonas added in a whisper. "His Tree felt him die. I am trying now to save his Tree. Please, I will explain more later."

Leonas fought the pain in his heart even as he tried to comfort Aranas, though he hoped that Aranas might feel it, that Aranas might realize he shared the depth of his loss. He hoped he might convince Aranas that Aras would never have wanted the Tree he had loved to suffer or die for him.

He still could not believe the horror of what he had felt. He could not believe Aras had died so terribly. Even for a Man such a death was terrible, but for a Wood Elf, there was no more horrible death imaginable. He fought the sudden urge to immerse himself in the River, although he was not surprised that his mother's blood might call to him now. Instead he let the cool image of the River, the sound of its waters, wash over Aranas, hoping that it might calm him, that it might soothe him, that it might wash away the feeling of flame consuming one he loved.

Jarnath came and Leonas saw that both Laedrin and Shadala were borne away on litters, the King's Guard following closely behind them. Leonas hoped they might find some comfort in their mutual grief, that they might somehow ease their loss by sharing their thoughts in the days to come, as he did now with Aranas.

Many hours later, Leonas finally fell asleep holding Aranas. Even in sleep, his thoughts were of Aras. He dreamt of him.

When he awoke, he could not be sure if the dreams were his own or ones sent to him by Aranas. He wondered that he could hear Aranas at all. He should not be able to. Only Lunahr had been able to hear all the Trees.

His fear for Lunahr was now far stronger. They never should have let him leave, to face such danger. Leonas fought the dread in his heart that Lunahr, too, might be lost, without him knowing. He could not bear to lose them both.

Aranonas and Aranas had told him that Aranahr was greatly troubled. He could no longer hear Lunahr. The further Lunahr had ridden from them, the fainter his voice had become. And only a few days ago, when Aranahr could hear Lunahr's voice only as a whisper, he thought he heard another whisper in his mind as well. Aranahr feared that Incuban was trying to take Lunahr from them again, that without Aras or the Grove to protect him, He might succeed.

LEONAS spent the entire next day with Aranas. Gaius came to him more than once, with food, with a blanket, with words of comfort. Leonas suspected Gaius came mostly to reassure himself that Leonas was not dead. He knew that Gaius still could not believe he had recovered.

Leonas had not realized the depth of Gaius's love for him. He had been blind to it all through training and beyond. He had thought of him only as a friend. Even friendships were dangerous in the High-King's Navy. But they were both of the Grove Guard now. Though even the Guard was different at present, no longer in such peril from the High-King as it once had been, thanks to Aras.

Leonas fought the despair in his heart, hugging Aranas tighter. His bark was smooth and cool. Leonas pressed his face against him and closed his eyes, afraid he would see images of Aras again, not just the terrible ones of him burning and screaming, but also the wonderful ones of him smiling and laughing. He could not bear to see more.

Instead, an image of Gaius flashed before his mind's eye. He was strong and warm and alive. He wished for a moment it was Gaius whom he held.

Go to him, Aranas whispered to him.

He looked at the Tree in surprise. "I cannot leave you, when you yet need me."

I will need you for a long time, Leonas. If I am to live, I will need you forever. That does not mean I cannot share you with another who loves you.

"I cannot betray Aras like that," Leonas argued. "You were never meant for me to love. You were meant for him."

He felt pain so sharp he gasped. "Forgive me my words. I had not meant them to harm you," Leonas apologized.

I was meant for Aras, that is true. But he is gone. I am yet young; I am not so ancient as the others. But still, I waited a long time for one to hear me. I spent many decades without anyone who could. Then, when Aras first came, I spoke to him, and he heard me, though he was not allowed to approach me, nor touch me. Aras chose me when he was yet a child, as I chose him. Then finally, we were allowed to embrace.

I have known his touch for such a short time, but he was so bright that I cannot help but be lost without him. But you have loved him too, Leonas, from afar, for a long time, and you have also walked with him, if only for a short time. I can share my love of him with you, and it will be enough. Aranonas will allow it. But you are an Elf, and Elves must love other Elves. You must find peace. You must find happiness with your own kind, as well as mine.

"I will come back to you when the sun is high above you," Leonas promised.

I will be here to greet you when you do. I have already told the others they need not fear for me any longer.

Leonas caressed Aranas and then let go of him. He walked, stiffly at first, toward Gaius; he had stood and lain in one place for many hours. Gaius appeared startled to see him approach and came to him.

"You are not supposed to be here, Gaius. Daras is here. Your shift is done. You have not left the entire time I have been here. You should lie down," Leonas gently scolded.

"I am not tired, Leonas. I do not want to sleep. Are you all right?" Gaius asked, reaching for him in concern, but then dropping his hand awkwardly without touching him. "I am sorry. I forget your station," he said softly, his voice touched with sadness.

"I did not tell you to sleep, Gaius, I suggested you lie down. I am glad you are not tired. While it is true that I have the title of Lord, now, my rank is still Captain, as it was before my title was granted. I do not outrank you in that regard, Gaius. It is not improper for you to touch me. In fact, I would welcome your touch far more than I would welcome sleep. I would have company tonight, if you might wish to join me. The Guest House is too quiet a place for only one," Leonas said carefully. He did not want Gaius to mistake his offer for an order.

Gaius eyed him in surprise and dawning excitement. "But... but the High-Prince's Tree...," he said, dutifully.

Leonas smiled at him, shocked that he could still smile after what had happened, his smile turning to a grimace of pain at the thought that he betrayed his High-Prince's memory by smiling, when he should instead weep.

He heard a soft whisper and looked in surprise at the birch and then nodded. "The High-Prince's Tree has told me to go to you. How can I deny such a request, when it follows the desire of my own heart?"

Gaius's eyes widened in hope. "You have never voiced such thoughts to me before, Leonas, though I have longed to hear them."

"Sometimes one must lose someone dear to him to find someone who might become even more precious to him. The High-Prince would wish such happiness for me, were he here. He ever only wanted to see all of us happy. He ever only hoped that he, too, might someday be so loved. It was my honor that I was able to love him as I did, even if it was for such a short time. Even if it was not the same love I hope to now share with you. I loved him as a brother, for his heart no longer dwelt in our Wood,

Gaius, but in the world of Man. I only hope that the one he loved might someday find joy of his own, without him."

The two of them began walking side by side to the Guest House.

DEWALAREN laid about desperately with the King's Sword. He had made a costly strategic error. He should never have sent all five thousand Elves, his three hundred newly discovered Urwani-Amontir kin, and ten thousand of the Dwarves on the march back to Nalea. When he had feared from Lunahr's words that the Enemy would target the Lords' Grove, to destroy Aras by destroying his Tree, he had thought that Incuban meant to divide His forces evenly. Dewalaren had thought that now that Incuban knew of Aras, once He heard of his Power, Power that rivaled His own, He would perceive Aras as a great threat. But Incuban desired the King's Ring also, and must have realized it was here. How else could they have freed Lunahr from His control for a second time?

Dewalaren had kept ten thousand Dwarves here, fully half their number, and all two hundred of the Varash. He had thought it would be enough. But it was belatedly obvious that the Enemy had turned the full force of His attentions here. Dewalaren had realized in dawning dread that the Enemy must be planning to seize the Sword and the Ring, to use them to slay the three wizards He battled against. There was no other explanation. Dewalaren would not let Aras die by the Sword he wielded!

They had lost Caramore, the remnants of their forces barely retreating steps ahead of the Enemy's army. Lunahr had told them that He had at least fifty thousand Revenants at His command, as well as wolven-riders and other foul creatures, and Dewalaren was certain they had faced the Enemy's full force. The airborne attacks of the chimaera and hippogryphs in particular had decimated their ranks. They had already lost five thousand of the ten thousand Dwarves who had remained. He feared at least another thousand had already fallen during today's battle and that those remaining would join them in oblivion by the end of it.

Dewalaren cut a bloody swath to the Dwarven King Rongas, through the last of a horde of wolven-riders, realizing in dismay Rongas was desperately protecting his fallen son, Jargas. There was no sign of Sarnon, King Rongas's Steward and self-appointed bodyguard. Just before Dewalaren reached Rongas, he saw him stumble and falter. Rongas's axe was wrenched from his hands by one foe, and a blade wielded by another was coming for his unprotected throat. Dewalaren knew he would not be in time to save him.

But then a giantess appeared, swinging her axe viciously, and the arm bearing the sword threatening Rongas fell to the ground, its former owner joining it there, headless, a moment later. The bulk of the Enemy's army were Revenants, the walking dead, twisted corpses of animals, Dwarves, Men, and Elves, fused whole and brought to a semblance of life. Beheading them or destroying their heads was the only way to stop them. They could not be killed, for they did not truly live.

Dewalaren yelled over the roar of battle. "Shanti! What are you doing here? Where's Archer?" Dewalaren feared that if her father, the Dwarven High-King, was lost, their army would shatter. There was a momentary lull in the fighting around them, and Rongas took advantage of it to reclaim his axe and climb to his feet.

"King Talon! We feared for you! Father's got fifty Dwarves around him. I couldn't get near him if I tried. I sensed Jargas fall. Father told me to go to him," Desenia replied.

Dewalaren nodded. Desenia would not have abandoned her father to danger to save her husband, nor would Jargas have wished her to. He knelt beside Jargas, checking him for injury. He could find none, but Jargas was scarcely breathing. "Did anyone see what happened to him?" Dewalaren asked, fearing poison or some other foul treachery. Then he sprang to his feet, as a new wave of Revenants attacked.

The three of them worked intently to remove the enemy from their section of the field. When she had breath to talk, Desenia answered. "No, but I felt it, across our link. Jarina's fallen."

"Jarina is dead?" Dewalaren asked. Rongas's face showed his anguish. He had not known his daughter had fallen.

But Desenia shook her head. "Worse, much worse. She's been taken prisoner," she said, her eyes taking on a haunted look as she shivered involuntarily.

Horror filled Dewalaren, followed quickly by fear. "Hunter! Has anyone seen Hunter?" If Jarina's twin brother Jargas had fallen, then her husband Farad might have as well. Dewalaren began scanning the field desperately for signs of his cousin, cursing Aras's shield around his core that kept him from being bonded to Farad as he should be. Farad might be anywhere in this madness.

A shadow passed over Dewalaren, and he ducked instinctively, but it was not a chimaera, only a bird. So, the battle was not yet over and already the carrion birds were circling overhead. But wait! That was no vulture; it was an eagle. It dove upon a cluster of the enemy with complete disregard for its own safety. One of the enemy fell back, and then Dewalaren saw why Lunahr's bond-eagle Quickwing flew so eagerly to danger. There was a flash of blond hair, quickly covered by the creatures surging forward. Lunahr! What was he doing on the field? Dewalaren had ordered him to stay in camp!

Dewalaren ran for him. Lunahr was terrified of Revenants, of all the Enemy's dark servants that had tortured him while he was Incuban's captive. Only one thing could have brought him into their midst: Farad. Lunahr would brave any danger for Farad. Dewalaren desperately hoped that Lunahr had found him, that they both yet lived.

Finally, Dewalaren reached Lunahr. Lunahr was sobbing and shaking in terror, standing over Farad's still form, desperately slashing at the undead things that surrounded him. His frantic gaze found Dewalaren's. "Laren! Don't let them take me again! Don't let them take me!" Lunahr's swordwork faltered as his panic began to consume him.

"Lunahr, you must be strong in order to save Farad," Dewalaren commanded in Amontirin, with the voice of a King, as he could not use the King's Voice, crippled as he was by Aras's shield. But it worked. Loruthanar steadied in Lunahr's hand.

As the two of them fought back the horde that had threatened to overwhelm them, Dewalaren spared a glance at Farad. He appeared lifeless, limp, motionless, and pale, pale as death. What tortures was his wife, Jarina, already enduring, that he had fallen?

THE battle had been a disaster from the start, the most recent in a series of many. Before today, they'd already lost nearly a full half of their remaining fighting force: five thousand of the Dwarves who had accompanied them on their long march from the west and at least fifty of her own tribe, the Varash, of the two hundred who had come. Jarina did not want to think about how many must have died in the valley, today, to add to that toll, how many were dying even now. Those left would not find victory, but perhaps their shattered forces could withdraw and they might save some of the men, to battle another day.

Jarina shuddered, even as her skin crawled at the touch of the undead monsters that held her fast, as if the shackles about her hands and feet were not enough to imprison her. She would not be saved. She was beyond saving. If only the blow that had struck her had robbed her of her life instead of her consciousness! Farad might eventually have recovered from losing her, had her death been quick. But what was to come would drive him to madness, or death. And Jargas. If only Desenia might be strong enough to save him! Her fear for her husband and twin kept all thoughts of fear for herself at bay, until Incuban entered the tent.

She knew instantly who He was, from Farad's memories of Him, the ones he'd tried to shield her from. The second she saw Him, terror rose within her. Strength of will alone kept her knees from buckling under her, kept the fear from showing upon her face.

She clutched desperately at the two coppery strands in her mind that bound her to her husband, Farad, and to her twin brother, Jargas, carefully keeping the shield in place, ready to sever the bonds as soon as it became necessary. She should do so now, but her fear ruled her for the moment. She felt them desperately pounding upon the shield as they had since she first awoke and realized she had been captured, that she was a prisoner of the Enemy, that she had scant days to live and those days would be filled with such torture and horror she would already have taken her own life, had she been able to do so.

Incuban walked toward her slowly, His eyes upon hers. She met His gaze coolly, but she could not slow the hammering of her heart. If she had the power to slow the pounding of her heart, she would have stopped it altogether.

Incuban's eyes left hers, traveling slowly downward. He was undressing her with His eyes, fondling her with them. Such eyes! They were not brown, nor blue nor green as eyes should be, but red, the red of blood. His face was ageless, exquisite, His lips full and red and moist. They would be so soft upon her. His hair was the red-orange of flame, hanging past His shoulders. Broad shoulders, beautiful shoulders. His shirt was unlaced, barely gathered at the waist. His smooth, hairless chest was perfection, each muscle chiseled as if by a master sculptor.

Jarina looked downward. He wore silk pants. She could see the bulge of His thigh and calf muscles through them easily. And another bulge as well. Her heart started hammering harder as she gazed with desire at His manhood straining against the confines of those thin pants. All she need do was pull upon the lace. A single leather thong stood between her and her desire.

She tore her eyes away angrily, feeling a wave of bile rising in her throat, which she forced back down.

Incuban laughed at her and then spoke. His voice was as sensual and pleasing to her ears as His body had been to her eyes. "Why fight it, Jarina? You already desire me. I can feel the heat of your need for me. Although I do so enjoy a good fight. Perhaps you should resist me. Victory is always the sweetest after a long, hard struggle, when you know you've overcome an opponent worthy of you. And you are worthy of me, Jarina.

"I have been so patient, waiting for you to come to me. Food always tastes its best when you are at your hungriest, don't you agree? I am not alone in my desire. Imagine how I might taste, to one such as you, who has waited so many long, lonely decades for me." He reached His hand toward her face.

Jarina pulled angrily at the shackles binding her hands and feet, futilely struggling against the cold hands of the undead creatures that held her arms. She turned her head, straining away from His hand, forcing herself not to cringe as she felt His fingertips against her cheek. But even then, a shiver of desire raced through her at His simple, gentle touch, and her stomach churned. She twisted quickly, trying to bite Him, but His hand pulled back just out of reach.

He laughed. "So very hungry. My servants have not fed you yet. But don't worry. They are as eager to ease your hunger as I am."

As if silently commanded, one of the undead monsters shifted his grip upon her arm, and his cold, clammy, dead fingers thrust under the bodice of her dress and fondled her breast. Her skin crawled at the touch. Incuban was at least warm, He was alive. His heart beat strongly, so strongly. Everything about Him was strong, powerful. How could any man or woman born not want Him?

Jarina bit back a whimper of desire. He was trying to manipulate her, to make her come to Him as if of her own free will. His face, His body, might be beautiful, but He was a monster, worse than the undead creatures that held her.

Incuban chuckled good-naturedly. "Good, Jarina, good. That's it. You can resist me. Hour after hour, day after day, you can fight my will. Food is for the weak, sleep as well. You have your cold honor to keep you warm, your love to replace food and sleep.

"You are married, now, are you not? In a manner of speaking. Many, of course, don't consider a marriage valid until it is consummated. Tell me, Jarina, has Farad consummated his marriage to you? Has that old, worn-out, scarred body of his been up to the task of quenching your youthful fire, of releasing you from the burden of your innocence? Or have you found your new husband to be sadly lacking in certain manly attributes?"

Incuban laughed, already knowing the answer. His words tore at her heart. Farad had tried so desperately to love her. He had thought himself healed, but the King's Ring and King's Knife had proven powerless against the century of torment he had endured. Incuban's violation of his parents and his brothers while Farad was linked to them, and then what He had done to Farad's mind, had left him impotent. Jarina had loved Farad anyway, but it had formed a breach between them. "He is my husband, my friend, my lover. You are nothing to me. You will never claim me as he has," she said, proudly, defiantly.

"The others may believe you, Jarina. You may even have deceived Jargas. But you cannot keep your dirty little secret from me. I see the truth in your mind. But, if you insist I find other proof...." He reached for her again, but not for her face. She struggled vainly as His hand touched the inside of her right thigh. He stroked her gently, lovingly, down, then up again, His hand disappearing under her gray Dwarven dress. She stiffened at his touch and her eyes burned with rage.

"Your heart is so cold, for one so lovely, but your body is warm. You are in need of my services." He shifted His hand upon her and she gasped and began trembling with terror and revulsion. He laughed in delight. "You have felt fingers there before. But you have yet to feel what a woman truly desires. You have yet to feel the true strength of a man inside you. I will be the one to release you from the burden of your innocence, as Farad cannot." He pulled His hand away, bringing it to His mouth, and sensually sucked upon His fingers one at a time.

"My brother will kill you," Jarina spat. Fury served her better than horror, which would only paralyze her.

Incuban laughed. "You do not say Farad will. You know he is not man enough, even for that. But neither is your brother, it seems. He has fallen on the field of battle."

"You are lying. Jargas is stronger than you are," Jarina said proudly. "He will defeat you."

"I had actually hoped to face Jargas in single combat. It would have made taking him in my bedchamber so much more satisfying. Although Desenia took him first." He laughed. "But of course, I took Desenia first."

Jarina raged at the memory of His cruelties to her sister-in-law.

Incuban continued. "It seems Jargas was unable to bear the strain of your imprisonment. He has fallen. Touch your link to him. You will see."

He was trying to trick her, to make her call to her brother. She would not lift the shield. She would not touch the link.

"You are so brave, Jarina. No begging, no whimpering for you, is there? You are not one of the lesser women I have been forced to feed upon. I might as well try to take pleasure from the beasts in the fields, those the one you know as Arcanus feeds upon, cattle or horses, as from them. They feel only terror for me. But you... you burn with hate. I feel the flame of your rage. Few of the women of the Amontir have true Power, but you do, bastard daughter of a Dwarf and a wildwoman of the hills. I hunger for your fire, Jarina. I will feast upon your core, your essence, as my body feasts upon yours. Remove her chains. Tie her and leave us," He ordered the Revenants surrounding her abruptly.

As the manacles fell away from her hands and the shackles from her ankles, she grabbed for one of the chains, vainly hoping to strangle herself with it, or dash out her own brains, but dozens of grasping hands yet imprisoned her. All her struggles proved futile as they tied her wrists tightly to the post in the center of the tent, over her head, and then moved to bind her feet. "No, leave them free. I will feel her twist and writhe against me. Now go."

The Revenants obediently left.

Incuban stood beside her and slid a hand between her breasts. She tried to bite Him, but could not reach.

"Such an eager mouth, Jarina. I will have use for such an eager mouth, but first I will teach you not to bite."

He reached with both His hands and unlaced her dress, pulling the lace free and tossing it aside, baring her breasts. Then He encompassed one breast in each hand and began massaging them. He ran His fingertips along her areolas. "Your body betrays you, Jarina. Your nipples stiffen at my touch. You have hungered for the true touch of a real man for too long. Poor Farad. Poor Jarina. I will teach you all you have been missing."

He bent downward and His tongue traced the path His fingers had taken. "I will nurse upon you, as if I were your own," He said, and started to suckle her.

Jarina roared in rage and pain for a lost joy she would never know, twisting desperately, trying to wrap a leg around Him, to pull Him from her.

"So, your loins ache for me, as well as your mouth," He said, laughing. He placed a hand on her taut stomach. "You are eager to grow new life inside you, despite the danger to you. You would take that risk for the tall stranger you have lusted after all your life." He smiled. "Ah, yes, I know of that. I know you well, Jarina. I have made you hunger for me. Did you truly think it was Farad?" He laughed again. "No, sweet one. I have turned your thoughts often to me."

"You lie!" she cried in fury, fighting the terror and despair that threatened to overcome her, to weaken her. He was trying to break her, but she would not be broken, no matter how He defiled her body, how He hurt her. He would not sully her core. She would remain pure and inviolate.

Incuban spoke as if He heard her thoughts, as He well might have. "Oh yes, Jarina. I will hurt you, over and over again. At first, you will beg for me to stop. But I will not stop. Then soon, so very soon, you will beg for more. That is when I will stop. When you ache for me, when you burn for me, when your need consumes you."

Jarina could not shield Jargas and Farad any longer. She was not strong enough to shield them from what was to come. She needed her strength for herself. Quickly, so He could not stop her, so they could not, she severed her links to her brother and husband. She fought down a whimper as their light left her, cold and alone with this depraved monster.

"No, Jarina. You cannot shield them from what I will do to you. You see? I restore the links you have severed. I bond them both to you again, so the brother you love and the man you love may both feel all that I do to you, this night and every night, until I tire of you."

Jarina felt them again, inside her mind, and fought against them, as if they were the ones violating her, as if they were the ones who were going to rape her. But she could not sever the bonds Incuban had forged. Her pure love was no match for His dark magicks.

"Farad, especially, must feel my touch upon you, inside you, to know I go where he could not. And not only my touch. I am a good master. I reward my servants well for their loyalty." Incuban whistled piercingly and a huge shaggy wolven trotted into the tent and came to Him. He patted the vicious beast upon the head. "Slash was in the valley. He fought well for me. His entire pack died for me there. He is lonely now, Jarina. He has no brothers, nor mate. He is in need, like Farad. Although he has something Farad does not. You can help him, Jarina, as you meant to help Farad. You will be his new mate, once I have taken all the pleasures I can from you. You will beg for him. You will be glad for his attentions, when I no longer want you."

He turned to the wolven. "Taste her, Slash. Know what it is I gift to you."

The vile beast walked over to her as if an obedient dog. She tried to kick it, but suddenly she could not move her legs. They were held rigid and apart by Incuban's gaze. The wolven looked at her, scented her, then tucked his muzzle up under her dress and began licking her.

She cried out in outrage at the feel of the animal's hot tongue upon her womanhood. Jarina cursed Incuban and began telling Him all she would do to Him and His servants.

Incuban laughed. "You are so hot, Jarina, so delicious. You burn so brightly. That's enough, Slash. I'll not have you spoil her with your tongue. I will be the first to pleasure her."

The wolven backed obediently and stood, licking his muzzle, watching her intently, his eyes burning now with red-gold fire.

"Farad and I have shared a woman before, after a fashion. Did he never tell you, Jarina? I made myself known to Farad's mother. I made sure her links with her sons stayed sound while I took my pleasures from her, while I fed upon her. They tried so desperately to save her. I held her for only one week, seven days. I saw to it that the line would end. Neither he nor his brothers could ever lie with a woman again, after feeling all I and my servants did to her. That is why he can never want you as you want him." He laughed. "Why he cannot rise to the occasion.

"I took his brothers, as well. The most fun I had was with Alarad, the youngest, the innocent one. Much like you, he had never known sweet caresses upon his flesh. I made sure my servants and I showed him all that he had missed. Do you know that he put out his own eyes, so he would not have to watch what they did to him? But he felt it still, all the more keenly, for having no eyes to distract him. Yes, I have strong ties to Farad. That is why I chose you for him. He has not suffered enough, I think.

"Everything that I have ever done to those he loves will pale beside what I will do to you now, Jarina." The laughter was gone. Incuban's eyes were burning with hunger, with lust, with Power, with madness. "But you mean nothing to me. You will begin to hate Farad, knowing your torment is all to punish him. He will see your hatred of him. You are the one who will reduce him to a whimpering, sobbing madman. Then I will heal him, and he will be grateful to me for it. He will fawn upon me as Slash does. He will have forgotten all about you. Then I will take him. But I will not be the gentle lover he will crave. Oh no. His screams will be heard all the way to the sea. I will keep him alive, year after year, in endless torment."

Jarina watched, horrified, as Incuban drove Himself into a frenzy with His fantasy of Farad. He had already forgotten her. Then He looked her in the eye, and a glimmer of reason showed through His madness. "But first I must break you, to break him."

He disrobed in front of her and stood naked before her. She felt a wave of desire flame across her body as she beheld Him in all His magnificence, followed by a wave of terror. Wordlessly, He went to her, His strong hands gripping the insides of her thighs as he forced her legs apart.

Suddenly, with a snarl of fury, the forgotten wolven lunged at Incuban, knocking Him to the ground, his teeth tearing at His throat. The savage beast ripped a great hole, bloody bone and cartilage hanging from his mouth. Incuban lay gasping for breath as air whistled through His ruined throat, gurgling through the welling blood as the light left His eyes. The same terrible teeth bit hard upon Incuban's groin, tearing a bloody mouthful off and flinging it away, as if in revulsion. Then the huge, shaggy animal turned his blood-soaked muzzle toward Jarina.

Jarina yanked desperately at the ropes that bound her to the pole as the monstrous creature approached her. The wolven whined and crouched down onto his forepaws and crawled toward her. She screamed and thrashed. With Incuban dead, there would be no one to stop him from taking his pleasure from her, or from merely eating her alive.

He touched her leg with his bloody muzzle and she began kicking furiously. The wolven jumped back from the fury of her attack. Her screams became incoherent, her efforts frantic until her fear overwhelmed her. Her body, strained beyond its limits, finally betrayed her and she fainted.

THERE was the sound of growling and screaming from outside the tent as the camp erupted into a chaos of carnage. Not all of Incuban's servants were the walking dead, nor did most of the wolven love their riders, those who had sent them to die by the dozens in the valley, and the Master who had held them in his thrall had fallen.

The wolven in the tent whimpered and nuzzled Jarina's leg gently. He saw the blood from his muzzle on her leg and rubbed his shaggy shoulder against her until the blood was gone. Then he leapt at the binding ropes over her head, severing them with his teeth, and twisted to catch Jarina upon his back as she fell. He took one bloody wrist, torn from the manacles and abrading ropes, carefully into his mouth to keep her from falling off his back and walked from the tent with his precious burden.

The other wolven were leaping and tearing at the living and undead around them. He walked fearlessly through their midst, and none challenged him for his prize. He left them to their revenge and trotted into the woods, Jarina limp and helpless upon his back, as the roaring, circling chimaera and hippogryphs entered the fray, driven into a hunting frenzy by the scent of blood.

LUNAHR knelt by Farad's side and felt his wrist, then cried out in despair and laid his ear to his chest, to his heart. Lunahr reached frantically for Farad's core with his own. It was dark and dull, motionless, lifeless. It did not pulse with energy or thought, or even pain.

Farad was gone! He was dead, truly dead! He had survived over a century of torment and haunting loneliness, only to be killed by his love for Jarina.

Lunahr knelt by his side and sobbed, hugging him tightly. "He is dead! Oh Laren, Farad is dead! I am too late to save him!" Lunahr lamented and wept.

Dewalaren fell to his knees and began to sob with him.

There was the sound of shocked voices and then cheering from the left flank. "The enemy is in chaos! They retreat!" The scattered force rallied and renewed their attack and began driving the fleeing enemy from the field. But Dewalaren, who should have led them, was lost in his grief and would not leave Farad's side.

JARINA moaned and stirred. Something hot and wet and gentle washed her face. She recoiled from the gentleness of the touch and heard a soft whining. She sat up suddenly, eyes wide. The wolven was there, the one from the tent. She saw the dried blood upon its face. It had been licking her own. It had licked her before, but not there.

Jarina whimpered and curled herself into a ball. Then resolutely, she forced her head up and looked around desperately for help, but she was alone in the woods with the beast.

She reached out tentatively with her mind for her brother, for Farad, afraid of what she might find, knowing the Enemy had tormented them through their links to her.

Her brother's core was alarmingly dim. She saw the same image of the obearn cub she had seen once before, biting at the trap that held its foot, its mouth torn and bleeding. But this time, though she tried touching and animating the pumar cub that lay beside their dead mother, it remained as still and lifeless as their mother.

She fled back up the strand. The image had chilled her. She followed her bond to Farad, desperate for his warmth, his light. She stared in horror at what she found. His core was completely dark, black, lifeless, all trace of his enduring strength, his selfhood, gone. She laid her hand upon his core and sent a wave of Power into it, but there was not so much as a flicker.

She fled back down the link to her own core, her own body, and began sobbing, not caring if the wolven killed her for it. "Oh my love! He cannot have killed you!"

THE wolven was whining. He began pawing at the dirt with his forepaw, but Jarina's head was in her hands and she did not see him. The wolven grabbed her hand in his teeth gently and pulled. Jarina shrank from him. She yanked her hand away, across his sharp teeth. He tasted blood and howled in such agony that she was startled from her terror. He lay at her feet and batted his forepaws upon the ground.

JARINA looked up and her eyes widened. Scratched into the dirt by the wolven's paw, barely legible, was a word: FARAD. Jarina looked into the wolven's eyes and remembered the red-gold fire of them, but this time understood it for what it was.

"Oh, Farad! What have you done for me? You cannot come back! There were no bonds leading to your core other than mine and its core cannot be strong enough for me to bond to. You should not have been able to go to it." Still she tried, extending a strand to the wolven. "Leap to me, my love, as you leapt before." But there was nothing. As she had feared, she could not touch the small, dark core of the animal with her link. Belatedly, she realized how Farad must have been able to: he was Lord of House Wolven, somehow in fact as well as name. The beast was of his House. But Farad was last of his House! No one else would be able to do what he had done, to go to his aid.

She began to succumb once more to despair, but then a sudden desperate hope flared. "The King's Ring! We must use the Ring. I can use my bonds to you and to Jargas to find your body. But we must hurry, for if I thought you dead, so must they. We cannot let them bury you. Your core is already so cold. Without your spirit and the sun to warm it, your body will surely die."

Jarina leapt onto his back. "This way, my love! I will find your body, when you cannot. I am still linked to you. Even now, I know where to go."

THE wolven whined in fear. They would not bury him. They would burn him. They would build a pyre around him and turn him to ash, as soon as they thought him dead. It might already be too late.

FARAD'S body lay upon the pyre. All but the last of his kin had said their good-byes. They had been brief. Farad was loved by only four of them, and two of those were notably absent.

"Try once more. He's the one who should light it," Rolin said.

Aramis nodded wearily and returned to the tent. Dewalaren and Lunahr were still there, watching over Jargas. Their victory this day had been a costly one: they had lost Jarina, Lady of House of Pumar; her brother, Jargas, Heir to House of Obearn, lay near death; King Rongas looked like he might soon join his only two children in death; and Farad, Lord of House of Wolven, was dead.

Aramis had never thought Farad might fall, after all the decades he had survived. He was one of the four who truly mourned him. The others had always shunned Farad, feared him, hated him. Not long ago he had been amongst them. Aramis cursed himself for the many lonely, lost decades Farad had suffered, when Farad might instead have been his friend. He spoke into the terrible stillness of the tent. "Majesty? Please, Majesty, you must come. Please let Farad go to his rest in honor," Aramis implored.

Dewalaren rose and approached, as if one of the walking dead they had been fighting. Lunahr stumbled along beside him. Their youngest cousin was trembling, and tears were streaming down his face so heavily that Aramis did not think he could even see to walk. "I will come, but I won't say good-bye to him. I cannot," Lunahr sobbed.

They exited the King's tent and slowly approached the pyre. Dewalaren stood beside it and cleared his throat twice before he was able to speak, his voice hoarse with grief, barely intelligible. His words were simple and brief. No words could convey the depth of his loss. "Good-bye, cousin. Know that I will always hold you in my heart." His voice broke on the last word, as he lifted the torch and then stopped, a look of horror on his face. "I cannot."

"Majesty, please! He is dead, he is gone!" Aramis's voice was agonized.

"No. The fire. I cannot. How could I have forgotten my pledge to him? It was at Father's funeral. Farad was overcome by memory of Thenalon, the smell of the fire. He made me swear to him that I would not burn him. When his time came, he wanted a cairn of cold stone. It was so long ago, I had almost forgotten."

"But he hates stone, after the dungeon and the Dwarves," Lunahr argued. "I know. I saw it! But... but fire terrifies him, you are right. I remember now. In the Mountain, Incuban made him try to burn himself alive. Even stone is better. I will build the cairn for him."

"I will help you," Dewalaren said. He turned to Aramis. "Wash the oil from him and lay him in his tent, in a new shroud. Lunahr and I will ready the cairn."

Aramis nodded wearily. At least they no longer argued that Farad was not dead. They might yet bury their fallen kinsman before he began to rot.

IT TOOK many hours to return to their camp from the Enemy's. Incuban had flown Jarina far from the field of battle on the back of a chimaera. It was well into the night by the time they reached camp, but the eyes of Farad's new body saw well in the dark, and the moon was bright.

Farad could not believe his true body yet survived, when it should have burned. When Jarina led him to the cairn of stone, he was baffled. His people did not bury their dead, they burned them. The thought had repulsed him, ever since Thenalon, that screaming, burning city. Thenalon! Memory suddenly flooded him. At Evanaren's funeral, he'd fallen to his knees, gagging and retching. The smell had brought back the stomach-churning, decades-old memories. Afterward he'd begged Dewalaren when his time came not to burn him. Dewalaren had sworn he would not. It was so long ago, but his cousin had remembered. Dewalaren had saved him.

He began pawing at the rock. At his side, Jarina began removing stone after stone from the mound that covered him.

LUNAHR sat shivering, alone in his tent. Almost alone. Quickwing was there. He stroked his bond-eagle's proud head gently, fighting the urge to hug him tightly. He had found Quickwing when they had retreated from Caramore. One thousand Dwarven troops had sacrificed themselves, following the four thousand who had already fallen into oblivion, so the rest of them could escape Incuban's army. The eagle was in the valley, its left wing torn. Lunahr had heard its cry, he'd understood it somehow; it had sounded so much like a Man in need of rescue calling for help.

One of the Dwarves had raised his axe to put the injured eagle out of its misery, when Lunahr had stopped him. Lunahr had taken the wounded bird into his arms, even as Elanara had tried to protect him. But the eagle didn't claw him with its talons or tear at him with its razor sharp beak. Instead, he'd seen pictures in his mind of the eagle soaring, of a chimaera attacking it, hunting it, of its fight to escape from it. It had pecked out one of the chimaera's eyes even as the chimaera slashed its wing. They had both plummeted from the sky. The eagle had lost sight of the monster as it desperately tried to land, to live.

The eagle had survived the fall, only to slowly starve, unable to fly, to hunt. But still it fought to survive. Lunahr had touched it somehow with his mind, bonded to it, as if it were a kinsman. Even Laren had been shocked: in all their long history, no one had done such a thing. But Lunahr's core, his Power, had always been strong, and he'd been stronger still since Farad had used the Ring and the Knife to heal him.

Farad! Farad was dead! Farad had saved him, rescued him from Incuban, healed him as well as he could, bonded to him and been named his guardian. He'd needed Farad so desperately, but now he was dead.

Lunahr began sobbing. It did not matter if anyone heard him. The others still thought him a child. He did not even have to make the pretense of holding back the grief that consumed his heart.

The others would have sought to console him once. They had all loved him. Once they would have flocked to him in his grief. But now they shied away from him. Many of them feared and loathed him, even worse than they had feared, mistrusted, and despised Farad. Lunahr had been tainted by the Enemy, defiled by Him. They all knew what the Enemy had done to him. He had lost the love of his kin when the Enemy had loved his body, when Lunahr had turned Eladar and Elanara against them, when they had almost lost their King because of him. They could not forgive him for Caramore.

Farad had forgiven him, and Laren. The two of them at least had. But now Farad was dead. Elanara had tried to forgive him, but still, he saw fear and revulsion in her eyes sometimes when she looked at him, where there had once been love and compassion. Eladar was the worst. He had been like a brother to Lunahr once. He had been far more. They were to have been *lythenia*, once they both came-of-age; they had secretly promised themselves to one another. They were to have spent the fullness of their lives together. But now Eladar hated him. Lunahr saw it in his eyes. Worse, Eladar hated all of them.

The Dwarves had almost brought Eladar back to himself. Lunahr had heard about how he had been, as their prisoner. Lunahr had so desperately hoped that Eladar might be healed. But it had all been turned to ash by what Lunahr had done to him. Now only anger was left, and bitterness, and a terrible, burning lust for revenge. There was nothing left of the Elf he had loved. He had begged Farad to help Eladar with the Ring, but Eladar would not be helped.

Quickwing screeched loudly in protest. "Forgive me," Lunahr said, releasing him from his tight embrace. He fell upon his bed and wept.

He had hoped building the cairn might help him sleep. He had carried most of the rock himself, and he was not used to such physical labor. His hands had been scraped raw from it. He refused to wear Laren's gloves. Laren no longer wore them to conceal the true nature of the King's Sword. Lunahr shuddered at the mere thought of those gloves. The Enemy had made him wear gloves, once, and Arcanus's magic coated these. He would not touch them.

Even though he was grief-stricken and exhausted, sleep was a long time coming. Lunahr was terrified he might have more nightmares of his time spent as Incuban's prisoner. He'd been tormented by dark dreams nightly since the fighting began. Worse, he was afraid he would dream of Jarina now. He kept imagining he could hear her screams as the Enemy savaged her. He had such horrific visions of what the Enemy and His minions would be doing to her, even in the light of day. They had already held her for many hours.

Lunahr had wanted so desperately to save her for Farad, and to save Farad, as Farad had saved him. But Jarina was as good as dead; she would be better off dead. And Farad was already dead, buried under that small mountain of stone Lunahr had so painstakingly gathered.

Finally, Lunahr drifted off to an exhausted sleep. But sleep was not the mercy he had so desperately needed it to be.

It was night. The moon shone brightly, but such a terrible color: it was neither yellow nor white tonight, but red, the color of blood: a bloodmoon, an ill omen. He looked away from it. Lunahr realized he was not in camp, but in the hills outside camp. He saw the cairn, but it was not as he and Laren had left it. It was not deserted, as it should be. Someone was there!

It was a woman, dark-haired, wild, and beautiful. She wore a gray dress, but not as it was meant to be worn. It was a Dwarven dress, she had once been a Dwarven Lady, but the lace that had previously secured it was gone, and though her breasts were exposed to the chill night air, she did nothing to try to conceal them. Nor was she wearing a veil. Her eyes burned with fervor, with passion.

Those eyes! He knew those eyes. Jarina, it was Jarina, or had once been her. She was working, intently, removing rock after rock from the cairn at her feet. A huge, shaggy wolven stood beside her, pawing at the rocks. "Soon, my love. Soon you will be returned to me. Soon you will be free."

Lunahr woke up, heart pounding. A nightmare, it had only been a nightmare. Idare, please don't let it be real!

He fought the urge to run to Laren. He could not tell him such an awful dream when he was already living the nightmare of Farad's death. Lunahr looked to his tent doorway, fighting his fear of the night, longing for the sun. But the crisp air might calm him and perhaps clear his head.

Lunahr slipped on his boots. He was already dressed. He strapped on his sword as well; he'd not leave his tent without it. He opened the flap and exited quickly. Lunahr closed his eyes and breathed the cool air deeply, until he felt the pounding of his heart begin to slow. He opened his eyes.

It was so bright out tonight. He looked up into the sky. The moon hung low and large. And red, the hue of blood, exactly as it had appeared in his dream!

Lunahr ran then, for Laren's tent, heart once again slamming in terror, past the startled guards surrounding it. He dove though the doorway and leapt to Laren. He was shaking him awake even as strong hands seized him, as hard bodies tackled him, forcing him to the ground. He felt their hands upon him, so many of them, clutching at him, their bodies pressing against him and he began thrashing and screaming wildly, as the memory of other hands upon him, nightmarish hands, overwhelmed his fragile control.

Even in his hysteria, he could hear the guards trying to get Laren to leave the tent, and the knowledge brought a measure of control back to him. "Let me go!" Lunahr cried desperately. "Laren, please! You have to stop her! She's turning Farad into a Revenant!"

Laren fought to his side. "Don't hurt him! Hold him, but don't hurt him," Laren commanded.

Laren knelt beside him. "Lunahr, please, you must calm yourself. They think you've gone mad again. What's wrong?" he begged.

Lunahr could see Laren feared for his sanity also. He could see the guilt naked upon Laren's face and knew he blamed himself for leaving Lunahr alone in his grief.

"It's Jarina," Lunahr said, forcing himself still, trying to keep the panic from his voice. "I had a nightmare. No, more than that: a vision. The bloodmoon, I saw it. She's at his cairn. She's opening it. She was talking to him, telling him she was freeing him so they could be together again." The horror overwhelmed him again. "Please don't let her do it, Laren! I can't bear it! Not Farad!" He began sobbing.

A CHILL of pure dread threatened to paralyze Dewalaren. Oh Idare! Either Lunahr was falling to madness, or madness had come to claim them all.

"Hold him here. Watch him carefully. Don't hurt him, but don't release him," Dewalaren commanded as he buckled on the Sword. "It might just be night terrors. It might be worse. Or, Idare help us, it might be true. Call ten guards, but none of them Amontir. I'll not have them witness this," he commanded the Dwarven guards inside the tent.

"No! Laren, you can't go alone! Please, Laren! Let me help you!" Lunahr begged. His voice....

"Forgive me, Lunahr," Dewalaren said, agonized. "Bind him and gag him, lest he use his Voice upon you. Quickly." He stood there as they did so. They stuffed a cloth in Lunahr's mouth and tied it, then bound him tightly with rope.

Dewalaren took one last look at Lunahr, at his pleading eyes, at him shaking in terror, either for him or the confining ropes that bound him, or both. Then, resolutely, he strode out into the night.

It was bright out. He looked up. It was as Lunahr had described: a bloodmoon. Ten Dwarven guards took up position around him. Ten would be enough against a single Revenant or a Resemblant, whichever Jarina might now be, and a corpse, even one that had been awakened. The thought of Farad being turned into one of the monsters he had fought against his entire life would have paralyzed him, did it not fill him with a spirit-consuming rage.

It was hard to retrace the steps to the cairn. He had not wanted to see it again, ever. He was angry at these hills for holding the body of one he loved. He knew Farad was not truly there, not his spirit. His spirit was forever lost to him. He pictured the lonely gray mass of stone under the bright moonlight. But when they came upon the cairn, it was neither deserted nor intact. Idare, it was exactly as Lunahr had described!

Dewalaren's stomach turned. She was there. She'd done it. She'd dug Farad out of his grave. Farad's body was lying slumped next to the violated cairn. His face had been unwrapped from the burial shroud. It was pale, lifeless. A huge, shaggy wolven stood beside Jarina, fawning upon her, ignoring the body by its feet.

Eyes burning with hate, Dewalaren drew the Sword, silently cursing Aras once more for binding his core in the thrice-damned tree when he desperately needed to unleash the dormant Power of the Sword. He had sworn to Farad he would not use the Ring to break the shield that protected him until he came face-to-face with Incuban himself, until he could use the Sword and the Ring against Him. But the Enemy yet remained hidden.

Incuban had tormented Farad for over a century in life, but by Idare, his cousin would finally find peace in death! He should have beheaded the body. He'd been a fool not to! He'd not been thinking clearly. His grief had overridden rational thought. There was a reason they burned their dead! How could he have been so stupid? How could he not have seen the danger? He'd let sentiment stand in the way of ritual.

Jarina saw him coming for her, but she did not shrink from his attack, nor try to defend herself with a weapon. Instead, her eyes flashed with golden fire. **"You cannot move to harm me."**

Her Power! He had not thought what was left of her might still be able to wield it. The ten Dwarven guards around him froze, helpless against the King's Voice she wielded. He suddenly found himself facing her and the wolven alone, blessing the protective shield of Aras's tree that he had only moments ago cursed. Without it, he too might have fallen under the thrall of her Voice, were his own Power not strong enough to resist her.

He dove for her, so focused upon her that he forgot the wolven entirely. The previously docile-looking beast lunged at him with incredible speed, sinking its teeth deep into his right wrist, trying to force him to drop the Sword.

He pounded upon its muzzle with his left hand in a tight fist, as he had seen Lunahr do in his vision of his capture, just as ineffectually. His fingers weakened and the Sword fell from his grasp. But the wolven did not release him. Instead it was dragging him to Jarina by the wrist, oblivious to his punches and kicks.

Jarina's hand clawed at his, and he belatedly realized she was trying to seize the Ring. Desperately, he tried to reach for the Power of the Ring to shatter Aras's shield. All was lost if the Enemy obtained their one true weapon against him! But he was heartsick and exhausted, his thoughts in chaos, and he could not focus. He turned his kicks toward her then, and she cried out when one of them connected. But the wolven growled and bit down harder and Dewalaren felt the bones of his wrist splintering in its powerful jaws. He fell to his knees, gasping in agony, his attack upon her crippled.

The wolven was whining now, around his wrist, which was still firmly held in its mouth. Blood was gurgling from between its fangs. Jarina wrested the Ring from him with a triumphant cry. Then she turned to comfort the distressed wolven.

"Hush, my love! You had to injure him, but he will be all right. We'll have the Ring and the Knife to heal him. Hold him tightly. He cannot interfere." Dewalaren felt her hands at his side as she pulled the Knife from its sheath.

She turned from him. He could not see what she was doing. Then the Ring suddenly flared to such brightness he was blinded by it. He was appalled that they were somehow using the Ring against him, defiling it as the Enemy had sullied the Knife, when He'd had Lunahr poison the blade and had Eladar thrust it into Dewalaren's back. He expected to feel the Knife rip into his throat, to feel something even more horrible while he was so injured and blinded and helpless, the army too far away to hear his screams. But no attack came.

Instead, his vision gradually cleared and he stared in astonishment. Farad was kneeling before him, the shroud wrapped only about his waist, now, and the Sword lying flat against his outstretched hands. Jarina was kneeling beside him, the Ring and the Knife in her hands.

Farad spoke then, with the voice of one Dewalaren knew and loved still, a voice his ears had ached to hear. "Forgive me, my King! But you'd never have believed her. Lunahr is still bonded to me. He can test me for you, as you cannot, for the tree that blinds you to me.

"I was never dead. I'd only left my body to save Jarina. It worked, but I was trapped in the wolven: I could enter him, as he is of my House, but his core was not strong enough to release me. My body appeared dead to your eyes, when it merely slept, in that strange breathless sleep you have also felt. Have mercy, Dewalaren. Do not slay us now, as my father, Jarad, did not slay you and Evanaren when you terrified the Lords with a similar trick, when you were but a child of ten.

"Incuban did not take Jarina. She is well. I'll have Slash release you now. Please do not slay us." He turned to face the wolven. "Come here, boy! That's a good boy! I'm sorry he hurt you. You did well."

Dewalaren stared at the wolven, stunned, as it began wagging its tail with a happy thud as if a great mastiff, as it released his wrist and limped obediently over to Farad, or the thing that had taken his form.

Dewalaren snatched the Sword from Farad's hands with his left hand and clumsily fumbled the Knife and the Ring from Jarina's hands with his injured right hand, unable to believe they surrendered all three willingly, instead of bringing them to their master. Why would they do such a thing? What might possibly be gained by it? Why trick him into trusting them when there was no need, when they had already held the tools the Enemy needed for instant and absolute victory over them within their grasp? Instead, they now left themselves completely at the whim of his mercy, when he should have none. Could they truly be who they claimed to be? "Release the guards," he ordered, both stalling for time and testing them.

"**You are released**," Jarina said, her words once again resonating with Power.

The Dwarven guards sprang to motion again, in anger and terror. They raised their axes and surged toward the kneeling figures. Jarina flinched as they came, but neither she nor Farad moved to defend themselves.

"Hold!" Dewalaren commanded, leaping between the Dwarves and Farad and Jarina, to protect them, exposing his back to the two who should be his enemy. "Do not harm them! Bring Lunahr to me at once. And bring King Rongas as well. He may yet regain his daughter, his son-in-law, and his son this night," Dewalaren said as hope flared.

The guards eyed the two figures warily as two of them ran to do the King's bidding.

"Majesty, your arm. Please, let me bandage you," Helvan said.

Dewalaren nodded, his eyes never leaving the two who still knelt at his feet.

Lunahr and Rongas came quickly and they did not come alone. All the remaining Amontir were with them, save for Desmond, Desenia, and Jargas.

Dewalaren said in Amontirin, "Lunahr, they have told you? You must test this Man for me, who claims to be Farad."

"LAREN! I... I am afraid," Lunahr said, trembling. He did not want to touch his mind to one of Incuban's creatures.

"I won't hurt you, cousin. I could never hurt you," Farad said softly in Amontirin. "Forgive me for frightening you, Lunahr. It must be terrible for you to have thought me dead, to have buried me, and to see me now risen from the grave. But I was trapped in the wolven. His core was not strong enough to send me back. We needed the Ring. We had no idea Dewalaren would be so obliging as to bring it to us," he said, and he actually smiled and then held Jarina's hand.

Lunahr approached him slowly, fearfully. He lowered his shield, forcing it down. Then he closed his eyes and reached out carefully, along the link that still bound them one to another. The bond! Shouldn't death have broken it, if Farad were truly dead?

Lunahr followed the link, a glimmer of hope warring with a wall of fear. When he reached Farad's core, he found it shone brilliantly, aglow with light and life again. It was not possible! It had to be a trick! Farad had been dead! Lunahr had seen it, felt it. This must be a Resemblant, but how could one shine so brightly?

He placed a trembling hand on Farad's core, bracing himself for something horrible, for an attack, for a monster. But instead, a wolven appeared, which melted quickly into a Man, into Farad's form. Farad slowly extended his hand, and Lunahr took it, still terrified of treachery, but also in sudden desperate hope. He felt the familiar rush of strength and love he'd thought he'd never know again.

Lunahr embraced his beloved cousin. "It is you! It truly is! You are not dead!" he cried. He looked outward and fell to his knees and hugged Farad with his flesh and blood arms, as he had hugged him within his core, crying tears of joy.

FARAD smiled warmly and hugged him in return. "Lunahr, my cousin! I thought I might never come home to you, that I might never hold you again," he whispered in Amontirin. He looked up at Dewalaren and spoke louder. "I can assure you Jarina is herself as well, but you may test her also, and quickly, for she is eager to help Jargas. And for Idare's sake, Dewalaren, please use the Knife upon your wrist. I am truly sorry for what I had to do. I have only had to injure you so terribly once before. I was only able to do so now because I knew the Knife might heal you."

He looked at Slash. "I ask that you forgive Slash for it as well, and use the Knife upon him also, for you have harmed him and he has become dear to me. I never truly understood before tonight what it means to be House of Wolven. Now I understand Lunahr's bond to Quickwing even more keenly. I have bonded to Slash in the same manner, as if he were one of us." The wolven was whining at Farad's feet, in obvious pain, and Farad comforted him.

Dewalaren eyed the wolven distrustfully. "You mean to keep that beast in camp?"

"He obeys me. I'll keep him from the horses. His teeth are the ones I used to rip out Incuban's throat and more besides. Incuban is dead, at least for a while. I know only the Ring and Sword can truly destroy Him. He is powerful beyond anything you or I have ever imagined. I could feel it, taste it. He has fed upon hundreds of thousands. We must act quickly. Once He recovers, Incuban will be enraged by what I have done to Him. His vengeance will be terrible. With Jarina safe from Him, at least for now, I fear for Rion. Rion alone of those I care for is vulnerable to attack. Lunahr has told us Incuban spoke of him. We must see Rion safely beside us."

Dewalaren shook his head. "Rion is safer where he is, Farad. War is no place for a boy. We know the Enemy is not truly dead, which means He will renew His attacks upon us as soon as He heals from the damage you inflicted upon Him. We must flee to what safety we can, while we can, before He recovers. We must go to the Watchtower. It is our last, safest stronghold. Lunahr knows nothing of it, so Incuban could not have stolen the knowledge from him. We must behead the dead and AIEEEE!"

Dewalaren's sentence ended in a scream. He clutched the sides of his head and collapsed, writhing upon the ground.

To THEIR horror the Dwarves and Amontir saw blood begin to flow from King Talon's nose, ears, and eyes. Many hands reached for him as he began convulsing. But then the Ring on his hand flared brightly and his entire body was enveloped in a blaze of red light. There was heat as well, this time coming from the sheathed Knife at his side. Then the glare softened and flickered out, though none beside him could see to know that it did.

There was the sound of many Dwarven voices as armed warriors ran from the camp to the cairn, High-King Archer leading them. They had seen the blazing light. When they saw King Talon fallen and everyone blinded and helpless, and saw Jarina and Farad, they would have torn them to pieces, did the blinded Amontir, Dwarves, and King Rongas not defend them, sheltering them with their bodies until they could convince Archer that they were not to blame and the High-King was able to ensure his men would not act against them.

They begged for those who could yet see to tell them of King Talon. They were told that he lived, but he was not conscious. Donovar had been summoned and came quickly. Sight began to slowly return to those who had been blinded.

FARAD saw that Dewalaren's face was still bloodied. He feared that, though Dewalaren's body might live, his mind might not have survived.

Donovar examined him and told them he seemed perfectly healthy now. Too perfect. The minor wounds, which he had been bandaged for, from the battle, had fully healed, vanished as if they had never been. And his wrist bore a bloody bandage, yet it appeared fine.

"We bit him, Slash and I. We broke bone. We broke several. If he was healed of even that, it must have been the Knife, but none of us used it upon him. It worked its magic upon him of its own accord. We had not known it could do so. Please, let me view his core. His body might be whole, now, but the blood upon his face. I fear…." He could not put voice to his fears.

Rolin said, "Hunter's Power alone has ever been strong enough. Beryl has told us he is free of the Enemy's influence. Please, Hunter, do what you can for him. We must not lose him, not now."

Aramis said, "Do it, Hunter. None will try to stop you. We support you."

Farad reached with a shaking hand and touched Dewalaren's bloody face. As he did so, he realized how hopeless it was. The tree! He had forgotten Aras's tree! It encased Dewalaren's core completely. He would not be able to touch him.

But there was no tree. It was gone, vanished as if it had never been. There was only the gleaming sheen of pallenteum, Dewalaren's naked core. Carefully, fearfully, Farad touched it. There was no pain, but there was sound. Farad heard sobbing. He followed the sound, though it was not easy.

His cousin's core hummed with Power, but it was so complex, the feelings and images so strong, yet there was little pattern to it, or perhaps too much pattern. He had known before how unstable Dewalaren's core was, for his Power, but he had only once before risked touching him so deeply, and that other time, he had been intent upon forming the bond and containing his Madness. He had thought the convolutions all part of the Madness. He had not realized they were part of his core as it always stood.

Dewalaren had been screaming for help the last time Farad had come. He had aided Farad in finding him within his core, helping him, soothing him. This time it was all Farad could do to find him. Finally, he saw him. Dewalaren was on his hands and knees, sobbing, surrounded by bright images of Aras, memories of Aras smiling and laughing, of his warmth.

"Dewalaren," Farad said softly, approaching him slowly. But Dewalaren seemed to neither see nor hear him.

"Dewalaren, please! Let me help you." Farad walked over to him and knelt beside him and reached for him, yet still Dewalaren did not react to him. He embraced Dewalaren and instantly tore himself away, gasping and trembling, horrified.

When he had touched Dewalaren, the core around him had changed. There was fire all around him and a terrible endless scream of agony. It was Thenalon all over again, except without the horrid smell of burning flesh Farad remembered so vividly. He could not help Dewalaren, not against fire! Anything but fire! But he could not leave him here like this.

Farad steeled himself and hugged him again. He remembered Desenia's burning core and the wave of cool Power Jargas had sent him, which he had used to extinguish it. He wished he had Jargas's aid now, his Power to help him. Then the Power was suddenly there and he realized it came from the Ring upon Dewalaren's hand; Farad was holding Dewalaren and the Ring responded to his need.

He heard the roar of a wave break against Dewalaren's core, and he drew it in toward him. It penetrated the pallenteum shell around his core and enveloped them both in soothing, cool waters, the thundering flow drowning out the unbearable scream, until the flame and the scream were washed away.

"Dewalaren, can you hear me? Can you feel me now? I am here, cousin. You are not so alone as you have feared, as you have felt. I love you. I am with you and I will not leave you."

"Farad?" Dewalaren asked, turning to face him. Then he crumpled fully upon the ground and began sobbing anew. "I've killed him! I made him go before he was ready. It's all my fault! I never told him how much I love him, and now he is dead! He is forever lost to me! And I could not see anything but the fire, nor hear anything but him screaming. Oh, Farad! How am I to live without him?"

The tree was gone and images of Aras surrounded Dewalaren. Now Farad thought he understood what must have happened. Aras was dead, and his death had almost caused Dewalaren's.

"Hush, cousin. I am here. And Lunahr and Rolin and Aramis. All your kin. We have all lost someone. We have all lost many. Let us help you." He hesitated. "Dewalaren, forgive me, but I must be sure. It is Aras who is dead, who is gone?"

Dewalaren nodded. "There was fire, shooting up from the roots of the tree, and a horrible scream and terrible pain, so much pain! Then the tree shattered and the splintering metal of it lashed my core until I could see only fire, hear only screaming, though I tried so hard to see, to hear him as he had been. Then you came, and there was coolness and the fire left me."

He looked up in wonder, in reverence at the shining images all around him. "I can see him now, I can hear him, feel him," he said, reaching for one of the bright memories, caressing an image of Aras's smiling face. "I will stay here with him, and we will be together, always," Dewalaren said reverently.

Farad felt fear. "Dewalaren, you cannot. He is dead, he is gone, but your kin still live. They need you. We all yet need you."

"No! I have given enough! What more can you ask of me? I have given too much! I have nothing left to give!" Dewalaren cried angrily.

"Please, Dewalaren! You must return to us. You are our King. You must lead us to the Watchtower. Your hand is the hand that must hold the Ring. You are swordmaster. Your hand is the one that must wield Kathalanar to slay our Enemy. Jargas uses a staff, I use a bow. The Enemy would disarm us quickly. And Lunahr! Though Lunahr has the skill to wield the Sword to such purpose, he loves Incuban still. Lunahr would sooner hand the Sword to Incuban than try to slay Him with it. Dewalaren, please! Lunahr needs you. We all do. Don't make it all have been for naught," Farad pleaded.

"ALL for naught," Dewalaren mouthed silent. He remembered those same words being uttered to him in Nalea by Lunahr, when Lunahr had told him his suffering was needless. Lunahr's heart had ached for him. Lunahr loved him, trusted him, needed him so desperately, lest he fall to the Enemy a third time. Aras had loved Lunahr as a brother. It was his fault Aras was not here for Lunahr, to see him safe. It was his fault Lunahr had been taken a second time. The Chieftess had told him he must help Lunahr in Aras's stead, as his King. And he had knelt to her and he had sworn to Lunahr that he would keep him safe. But he had failed him. He could not fail him again. He could not stay here and let Lunahr fall to darkness again.

He looked at Farad. "It is so dark with Aras gone. I do not want to awaken."

FARAD'S desperation turned to despair. But then Dewalaren put his hand on Farad's shoulder. "But I will, if you and Lunahr will stay by my side."

"We will stay with you always," Farad swore, grasping his other shoulder in relief. "Come, my friend, my cousin, my King. Your people await you."

Farad's eyes opened and with them Dewalaren's.

The anxious expressions on their people's faces melted into relief and joy.

"The King is awake!" Rolin cried.

"Long live the King!" Aramis called, and the cry was taken up by them all, and then by hundreds of other throats around them, as the Dwarven warriors added their voices to the roar.

King Rongas approached. Farad could see how terrible his grief for his daughter and for his fallen son was. He looked like he could barely stand.

"Do not despair, Majesty. Jargas will soon be well again," Farad assured him. "Jarina needs only to touch him. I will help her. Jargas will hear us. We will wake him for you."

Dewalaren also looked like he could scarcely stand, though his core now hummed with the Power of the Ring. "King Talon must rest, but the rest of us must work quickly, as he has described. We must behead the fallen, pack up camp, and be ready to move at first light. Beryl, you must walk with King Talon to his tent. He must speak with you, and he must not be alone."

Lunahr nodded, looking at Laren in concern.

"Come, Jarina. Jargas has need of us," Farad said and headed for King Rongas's tent with her and her father in tow and Slash at his side.

DESENIA stared in wide-eyed disbelief and fear as Farad and Jarina entered the tent. Farad was in his shroud, Jarina's dress was scarcely covering her, and a huge wolven limped at their side as if an obedient dog. She stood protectively before Jargas, braced for battle, until she saw Rongas was with them. He raised his hands in a gesture of peace and spoke reassuringly to her. "Do not worry, Shanti. Neither of them was lost as we had feared. They can explain it to you later. Please, as you love Jargas, let Jarina aid him."

Desenia looked at Jarina with pleading eyes, all haughtiness gone. "Please, Sister-of-my-husband! He does not even hear me. I beg you, bring him back to me."

"You need not beg, Sister. I will go to him and all will be well," Jarina promised. She moved to stand beside her fallen brother. "Jargas, it is all right. I am here. You have not lost me as you feared," Jarina soothed as she touched her brother's face lovingly.

A few moments later Jargas sat up and Desenia and Rongas both hugged him in relief. Jargas returned their embraces and then swung his feet over the bed and made as if to stand.

"Jargas, you must rest," Jarina scolded.

"I have rested more than enough, Sister. From what you have told me, it is Talon who must rest. I have much work to do. It sounds as if we've a long march ahead of us. But you both need to get dressed first. It is unsettling to see you in your shroud, Hunter."

FARAD nodded tiredly. "Come, Jarina," he said and headed for their tent. They passed Dewalaren's on the way, and Farad heard the sound of sobbing and hushed voices and stiffened, until he realized who it was. He sent a wave of warmth and strength across his bond to his young cousin. "Courage, Lunahr. I am here," he whispered aloud.

He turned to Jarina. "Aras is dead. It is what felled Dewalaren. He has just told Lunahr. I need a bath and some clothes and to sleep for a week." He sighed wearily. "I will have to settle for the first two."

There was a soft whine from behind them, and Farad felt Slash's pain along his bond. "Hush, Slash. It is all right. I will have Donovar tend to you. We should not disturb Dewalaren and Lunahr. They must grieve in order to heal."

"I WILL take him," Jarina volunteered. "He will allow it. Won't you? That's a good boy," Jarina said, scratching Slash behind the ears. She had forgiven him for what he had done in the tent. He had been under Incuban's control as much as she had been, he had suffered great loss at that monster's hand as well, and he had helped save her. "You go bathe, Husband, and dress, and rest, at least for a little while. I will join you shortly."

Jarina hugged Farad spontaneously and kissed him full upon the mouth, so passionately she stole his breath away.

FARAD'S eyes widened in surprise as he felt his body respond with sudden stirrings in a way he had not thought it ever could again. He hugged her tightly and kissed her just as passionately, and then joyfully. He could no longer doubt what he felt. "Do not be long, Wife. I have great need of you this night," Farad said hungrily.

Her eyes widened as well and then lit with corresponding joy as his desire resonated across their bond. Farad knew she felt the unmistakable swell of his manhood against her, and understood the full extent of his meaning. "Your victory against Him has healed you, when the Ring and Knife alone could not!" she said joyfully. "I will hurry," she promised. Then she left, heading for Donovar's tent.

Farad entered their own. He bathed quickly and dressed only in a tunic when he was done. Jarina returned a short time later, with Slash by her side. His leg was bandaged and Farad could tell from their bond that he was no longer in pain. Slash started to follow Jarina inside, but Farad instead asked that he lay before the door, guarding it, to ensure no one might enter and disturb them, petting him as he requested his aid. Slash licked his hand and eagerly assumed his position outside the tent.

THAT night Jarina and Farad finally experienced the true ecstasy of their union, which had been so long denied to them. Their cores merged as their bodies intertwined, as they lost themselves to the passion of their love. Neither of them got any sleep that night, but neither cared.

When morning came, they dressed and packed up their tent and began the long perilous march to the Watchtower. The army marched with grim purpose and great speed. They had left behind one thousand brave Dwarves to cover their escape, to distract the Enemy, to obscure their tracks and set false trails and ensure they were not followed. Men they knew none of them would likely ever see again.

RION lay in bed unable to sleep for a long while, though his body was weary. He fingered his Elfstone, thinking of Salenia and Elavar. He wondered again if Arcanus had sent those creatures after him, or whether it might have been all three of the wizards.

He hadn't told the others yet. He was too ashamed and too afraid. He'd betrayed a trust, and now he and all his friends might die for it. He debated sneaking away, so that the danger would pursue him alone, but he knew he couldn't, and not just because of the City Guard outside. He wasn't strong enough. He was too frightened. It tore his heart to know that the brothers had saved him, yet he was bringing them all to danger. And Jathran and Lerdon were dead, gone forever. They'd died for him. It was his fault they'd died. He would never be able to forgive himself for it.

He tried to clear his mind, staring at the soothing green stone in his hand. He'd been dreaming of Elanara every night since he'd seen her elder brother Elavar. He couldn't help his dreams, but he was ashamed of them anyway. He betrayed Talon with his dreams of Elanara. They were betrothed to one another. Even were they not, he was a fool to think she might ever choose him over Talon. What would someone like him have to offer an Elven Princess? Though his head knew the folly of his heart's desire, he still ached to see her face again tonight, to hear her sweet voice, if only in his dreams. Finally he fell asleep, thinking of her.

RION was standing naked in a room rimmed with burning red candles, hot wax dripping like blood from them. The scent of incense was heavy in the air, and there were crimson and orange silks everywhere, hanging on the walls and strewn about the floor, covering both completely, giving no hint as to where he might be. There was a single red wooden chair in the center of the room, oddly out of place. It looked strong, sturdy, but it had no seat, only a frame where the seat should have been, arms, legs, and a solid back.

"Ah, Rion, we meet at last," a voice said, silky, sensual, yet very masculine as well. "I have heard so very much about you. And I think you have heard of me, as well. I am known by many names, but there is only one you will have heard: I am Incuban. Your friends might have told you about me: Farad, Jargas, and Jarina. They all think so highly of you. You are right, Farad, he is exquisite."

Rion looked around, but the room was empty. He could not see who spoke. Then someone came out from behind one of the silks. It was Hunter!

The voice said, "Yes, Rion. You miss Farad, don't you? He is your friend. He is my friend as well. That is why he led me to you, so that I might meet you. So I might get to know you." The way he said it made Rion shudder.

The voice had called him Farad, but it was Hunter. His eyes were horrible, far worse than they had been when he'd seen him on the road, and his face.... Hunter was leering at him. There was a look of such lechery and hunger on his face that it sickened Rion.

"Farad wanted to watch, Rion. How could I deny him the pleasure, after he has gifted you to me?" the voice said. "Your friends are all so loving, so loyal: to me. You have many friends, both alive and dead: your new guards and your old. You miss Jathran and Lerdon already, do you not, Rion? Lerdon's gentle touch, his healing hands. You are hurt now, aren't you, Rion? Lerdon would help you still. I have the Power to see him aid you. Go to the chair, Rion, that's a good boy."

To his horror Rion began walking to the chair, as if he did not have control over his own body. He fought to stop, but he could not. When he reached the chair, he tipped it over at Incuban's command, so that the back faced the floor, and the chair was supported by the ends of the arms and the forward side of the two front legs. He knelt on the floor between the chair legs, as instructed, and then lay face down, so that his chest and stomach lay across the back, and his groin was pressed against where the seat would have been, framed by the wood. His legs were braced along the chair legs that rested upon the floor, and to his humiliation and confusion, his bare buttocks was blatantly exposed.

"Tie him for me, Selene," Incuban said.

Rion's eyes widened in fear, and he struggled vainly to move. Then Circe appeared from behind one of the silks, naked, as he had seen her in the woods. She was eyeing him hungrily, yet sadly. "I warned you that you might not like what you found when you saw me again. But I still like you, Rion. I still ache for you."

She headed to him as he fought with all his will to move, but he still could not.

One by one she ran the silken red cords along his arms, his hips, his back, his legs, as she skillfully bound him to the chair. Then her hands were upon him, touching him, lightly, gently, everywhere. He trembled as she caressed him, in terror and, to his mortification, desire. His manhood had stiffened at the first brush of the soft ropes against his bare skin. His body thrilled to her touch, even as his mind recoiled from it, as she caressed him all over, except his groin. He felt a terrible, wonderful, unbearable pressure building within him, until he thought he might die if she did not offer her touch to the one place she had denied him.

His mind fought against the sensations even as his body fought to embrace them. Oberas had always told him he was too young for such things. Oberas had been so strict. Tarrell had been as well. Tarrell had warned him about losing his innocence, and his heart, to someone who might trick him, use him, to someone who sought only his full purse and cared nothing for his heart. But this was far worse than that could ever have been. He heard an amused chuckle, and burned in shame, knowing Incuban was watching him. "You can make her stop, Rion. All you need do is tell her so," Incuban urged.

"St-st-st...," Rion stammered. He could not speak! Such a simple word and he was powerless to say it.

Then Circe knelt before him. "I hunger for you," she said. As she retraced the path her fingers had taken with her tongue, all rational thought fled.

Rion ached, he burned, he was in an agony of ecstasy, an ecstasy of agony. He should have succumbed long ago. At her first touch he should have.

He gasped as her mouth finally settled fully upon his manhood, and she began sucking, slowly and sinuously. Incuban must be controlling his body still, keeping him from reaching release.

Finally, when it felt as if his desperate need must be fulfilled, that even Incuban could not possibly hold the torrent that raged inside him at bay any longer, she stopped without warning. She pulled away, licking her lips languidly, and he let out a cry of loss as he strained wildly toward her, pulling with all his will against the ropes, against the invisible restraints of Incuban's wizardry.

"He is ready for them, Master," Circe said, licking her finger and then sucking it slowly, sensuously.

"We've missed you, Rion," Lerdon said, appearing from behind one of the silks. Rion's eyes widened in disbelief and denial: Lerdon was naked, his intestines hanging out from his slashed gut—he was undeniably dead, but he was walking toward him. Rion stared in horror at his dead friend, his gaze traveling down from his spiritless eyes to the horrible wound that had killed him, and then further down. Rion paled in shock and revulsion as he saw his groin, his engorged manhood; he began straining frantically against the ropes in terror. No, oh no! This couldn't be happening!

"We're here to help you," Jathran's voice said from behind him. Rion's head snapped around easily, apparently not confined at all, as the rest of him was. He looked over his shoulder to see Jathran, also naked. He was even more horrible to look upon: his chest was torn open and his face was a bloody ruin. Rion felt his head dip against his *will, forcing his gaze to Jathran's groin, to his hideous, dripping erection. Rion bucked and kicked wildly, straining against the ropes, the chair, Incuban's wizardry, desperate to escape, but unable to move at all.*

"You can make them stop, Rion. All you need do is tell them so," Incuban taunted, laughing.

"St-st-st...," Rion stammered desperately, as little pricks of light appeared before his eyes, and dizziness flooded him.

"No, Rion. You will not escape that way," Incuban scolded, and the torments in the room snapped back into crystal clear focus.

Rion realized in terror that Lerdon was standing before him now, less than two feet from his face. Lerdon's cold, dead fingers reached down and grasped Rion's chin. He was so strong! Lerdon dug his fingers into his jaw, forcing Rion's mouth open. At the same moment, Rion felt Jathran's clammy caress on his back, and then something cold and wet dripped onto his calf.

To his horror, at their terrible, lifeless touch his body began jerking and spasming in the release Circe had denied him.

"That's it, Rion. Show us how much you love us," Lerdon said, his voice laced with seductive promise. "We miss you, Rion. We love you, as you love us. Now it's our turn. Let us show you how much we love you."

Even as Lerdon took the final step to his face, Rion felt something thick and cold and wet slide against his inner thigh, toward his buttocks. Incuban laughed gleefully as Rion screamed.

RION awoke screaming, kicking and thrashing against the blanket that covered him. Tarrell was at his side, groping for him in the dark to calm him, and put strong hands on his shoulders. Rion shrank from his touch, lashing out hard with his fist, knocking Tarrell from him.

Rarnak and Gar flung open the door and ran into the room, swords drawn. In the light spilling in from the hallway, they saw Tarrell on the ground by Rion's bed, clutching his stomach, and Rion striking out wildly with his hands and feet, screaming, eyes wide open but unseeing, as if fighting invisible demons.

They sheathed their swords and ran to his side. Gar said, "Rion, it's us," and put his hands on his shoulders to shake him.

Rion flailed wildly, cracking Gar across the face. Rarnak slapped him hard, and suddenly Rion's eyes focused and he stopped screaming. He cowered back from Rarnak and curled into a ball, tucking his legs under his chin, arms around them, whimpering and trembling.

Tarrell staggered to his feet and went to him. "Rion, it was only a nightmare. It wasn't real. Whatever you saw wasn't real," he assured him.

RION shook his head violently. It was real! It had been horrifyingly real. He'd released his seed upon the blanket, he felt the horrible sticky wetness of the wool, but worse, he could still smell the incense from that terrible room, still feel the bite of the ropes as he'd struggled against them, still feel Jathran's and Lerdon's cold, dead hands on his naked skin. They'd almost…. He whimpered louder, whining, sounding almost doglike.

GAR looked at him sharply, and Ron and Ara, who had come in as well, were staring at Rion in concern.

Tarrell gazed at Rion helplessly. He reached for him, but Rion shrank back from Tarrell again.

Tarrell pulled back, hurt and worried for him. "All right. I won't touch you. You might feel better if you drank some water," he said. Tarrell got up and got him some, and held the cup out to him.

A DRIP fell from the cup onto Rion's bare leg, unnoticed by Tarrell, and suddenly Rion turned over and started vomiting violently. His body was wracked by dry heaves long after his stomach was empty.

Tarrell said, anguished, "This isn't just night terrors. I've never seen him like this. Rion, I'm going to get you pen and paper. Write what you saw."

Rion shook his head violently. He was shivering and wrapped the blanket around himself. Hunter had betrayed him to Incuban. He remembered what he'd said to Hunter, about him being a trader, and that losing his tongue, his voice, would be the worst thing that could happen to him, and Hunter had Incuban do it! And Incuban had spoken of Jargas and Jarina too. They must all be His as well now.

Talon! They had been marching against him, he was sure of it. What if Talon had fallen to Incuban too? Lerdon and Jathran were dead, but somehow they were His pawns as well. All his friends were becoming his enemies, one by one. Incuban would control and corrupt them all. He looked fearfully at his friends in the room. Who would be next? Would he lose them all to Incuban?

Ron pulled Tarrell aside and spoke softly, so Rion wouldn't overhear.

Gar shook his head, not taking as much care with how loud he spoke, and Rion heard every word. "A healer can't help him. I doubt the Elves can. He needs a wizard's aid."

Rion began shaking his head violently again. Incuban haunted him, Arcanus wanted him dead, Magus was Incuban's servant, and now Circe was His as well. If only they could help him, then he was beyond help.

No, he couldn't believe that. The Elves could aid him. If they had the power to banish Aramark the Elder's nightmares, maybe they might keep him safe as well. Even from his friends. Incuban couldn't truly turn them all against him, turn them all to darkness, could He? He indicated he wanted pen and paper and Tarrell seemed relieved.

Rion snatched the paper from Tarrell's hands and wrote quickly, underlining the first two words so vehemently that he nearly tore the paper. _No wizards!_ Take me to the Elves. They will help me.

Ron read what he had written and said, "Then we go to the Elves. Maybe they can help him, if he believes they can. Rion, why don't you go into the main room? We'll clean up in here so you can sleep."

Rion shook his head. He would not sleep, not until they were out of the City. He got dressed and walked into the shop and silently started packing their wares into the wooden crates and sacks the brothers had brought for them.

TARRELL said, "I'm going to try to get some more sleep. Someone needs to be awake tomorrow," and headed back for his room.

The others were almost done cleaning the room, but the smell was still foul.

"Tarrell, we have to talk," Ron said softly. "Those creatures that attacked Rion, they're legend in Thenalon, myth, from the War. Most people never heard about them, and many of those that did don't believe they were real. We didn't believe it, either. How could we? How could things such as that be real? But we've seen them now, we've fought them. We can't pretend they're nightmares. They came with the ogres and the pumar. They savaged the City with them.

"Part of the legend is that when one of those wolven-men, the werewolven, bites you, you begin to change. You turn into one. I know you can't believe it, but Gar believes it and I'm starting to. Rion can't speak, Tarrell. He's acting wild, violent. He attacked you and Gar. He's losing his reason. You have to be prepared. We all have to be. If he changes, truly changes, into one of them, you need to be ready to do what's necessary," Ron said grimly.

Tarrell did not have to ask him what he meant. "Keep an eye on him, Ron," Tarrell said despondently.

FARAD stared in horror and revulsion at the beautiful creature beside him. Incuban was standing next to him, in the dark, His pale face glowing as with an inner light, His red eyes burning.

Farad knew he was asleep, knew he was dreaming, but Incuban should not be able to enter his dreams, not now. "You cannot be here. You no longer have Power over me. I banish you."

Incuban had not invaded his dreams since the Ring had healed him. He did not think Incuban was strong enough to, especially not after what Farad had done to Him, the physical damage to His body. Incuban must be using much of His Power to be here now. The dream was so vivid! Farad knew he would remember every sight, every sound, every smell, every taste, every touch as if it were real, upon awakening. He tried to force himself awake, but he did not waken.

Incuban laughed, the same terrible laugh Farad had heard in the past. "You did not truly think you'd destroyed me?" Incuban asked, appearing astonished. "No, I can see you knew. Did you like the taste of me, Farad, as you held me by the throat? And not only the throat. I have always enjoyed the taste of you, Farad, and my grip upon you has always been further down as well." He said it with a laugh and eyed Farad's groin appreciatively, as if what Farad had done to Him had been trivial, even amusing.

"But I am not the only one who holds such a grip upon you now, am I, Farad?" He continued. "It was foolish of you to give yourself to Jarina. You have weakened yourself

when you most need strength. And it was selfish of you not to share Jarina with me, Farad. But just to show you there are no hard feelings, I will share Rion with you."

Suddenly there was light. Farad saw Rion then, naked, tied to a tipped over chair, struggling. There was a woman fondling him. Her features were Dwarven, but she was naked, and she was kneeling before Rion.

"Rion? Rion!" Farad screamed and tried to run to him. But he was frozen in place, powerless to aid him.

"He cannot hear you, Farad. He hears only me and my servants. But he can see you. He sees you watching him. I have made you look monstrous to him, amused by his suffering, reveling in it."

Farad listened and watched helplessly as Incuban taunted Rion. Then Incuban turned to him, "Did you see his face, Farad? Did you see how he recoils from you? He thinks you repay him for his betrayal of you to Talon. He burns with shame for his betrayals. Now I make him burn with something else.

"Do you like what you see, Farad? He is so easy to manipulate, so young, so naïve, so innocent, so desperate to be a man, so like Lunahr when first I took him. His spirit is so strong, so pure. He is exquisite. I will take special delight in breaking him. I did not know I would be able to sustain him long enough to enjoy him fully, but he is proving very amusing to me.

"I sent a Revenant, one of my special ones, and a chimaera for him this morning. They almost brought him to me. I am glad now that they failed. The thrill is in the chase, is it not?"

Farad saw to his horror that two Revenants were approaching Rion, both men, naked and fully aroused.

Incuban continued, "But I did not depart empty-handed. I took the lives of two of his friends, as you see. I've taken their bodies as well, so they may serve me. These, of course, are mere shadows. Then I took Rion's voice from him. The City took his liberty. They bound him in chains for me. He thought himself free when they released him. Poor boy! He will never be free. Tonight, I take his innocence."

Farad strained, trying to overcome Incuban's hold on him. He had to save Rion from the horror Incuban was planning for him. Rion would go mad; even one of Farad's people would go mad, when faced with such terror. Rion was barely a man, and he had no Power to aid him. His core was so small and dark; it could shatter at any moment.

The scene before him vanished, and Farad cried out in denial. More awful than seeing what was happening to Rion was not seeing, not knowing, but imagining.

"Perhaps I should allow him to awaken? Should I savor such a delicacy, Farad? I savored Alarad, remember? We both did. I shared almost all I did to him with you, until you spoiled it. He died too quickly.

"You remember how Alarad died, don't you, Farad? You have blamed me for his death, yet I was not the one who killed him. You did. You fed from him, through your link to him. You stole all his essence from him and left him an empty husk.

"You've tried so hard to resist the hunger that brought, haven't you? But you have grown so weak, so weary. You fed upon Jargas so greedily before, in Malar. That is why you do not renew your bond to Dewalaren. He is too tasty. It would be regicide. Although you have developed a taste for that as well," Incuban said, laughing.

"I lied before, Farad. I did share Jarina with you. I was there, when you took her for the first time. I felt her tremble, I felt you thrust, I felt the pain as you breached her maidenhead, and the passion afterward. I felt every caress, every kiss, every touch. I let you take her. I wanted to reward you for trying so hard to kill me. I had become so bored with you. I am glad you are amusing to me again.

"What will we do to your wife tonight, Farad? Will she be as willing, knowing I am with you, inside her? Perhaps she will be more willing. You felt how much she wanted me in the tent. She was so eager to feel a real man, after having suffered your poor attentions.

"But we were speaking of Rion. Alas, Rion's core is not nearly bright enough to bond to, is it? You cannot feed from Rion. You cannot take him from my pleasures. Rion will pay for all your crimes against me, Farad, and there have been so very many. Thenalon was merely the first.

"After I take Rion's innocence, I will teach him all the pleasures of the flesh. He has so very much to learn, and as in all things, I am sure he will prove an apt, even eager, pupil. Then, once I tire of him, I'll take his hands, so he can neither speak nor write. He will go mad rather quickly, I think.

"No, too quickly. I will instead take one finger at a time. Yes, that is it. Oh, the things he will do for me to keep them! The betrayals, the pain he will cause, the treachery he will bring to you!

"Sleep well, Farad. You will see Rion often in your dreams, now, although you will not like what you will see. I won't reveal the rest to you tonight. You must use your imagination to determine what I have done to him."

Incuban laughed. "I release you from your sleep, now."

FARAD awoke, screaming Rion's name and Jarina awoke instantly. She tried to put an arm around him, but he shrank from her touch. He lay gasping and trembling.

"Farad, Husband, what is it? What is wrong?" she asked, hurt by his rejection.

Farad roared in frustration and helpless rage. "I'm going to kill Him! I have to kill Him!" He turned to Jarina, his face creased in agony. "He's found Rion."

Jarina paled. "Rion is His prisoner?"

Farad shook his head. "Not yet, but He is torturing Rion all the same. He is sending dreams to him, the same kind He almost drove Shanti to madness with. And He's made Rion think I'm his enemy. How can I help Rion when he'll flee from me now, if ever he sees me?"

"Will you not let me hold you, Farad, to comfort you? You have not shrunk from my touch for many nights now," Jarina said. Far from it. Her touch had finally awakened him, now that his defeat of the Enemy had released him from his decades-old curse. The night he had returned to his body, they had made love, first cautiously, then joyously, passionately. They had spent many hours pleasuring each other. And that had been only the first of many such nights.

"I cannot! He knows, Jarina. He has been watching us. I am sorry, Jarina, but I cannot, knowing He is watching, that He might even be feeling what I do," Farad said, anguished.

"Faradan, he is lying to you. He would not have watched. He would have stopped you, if He could. He wanted me for Himself, but more, He has wanted you. Do not give Him such a victory over you, Husband. You have fought Him for so long. Do not give in to Him now."

"BUT it doesn't end! He doesn't stop, ever! He never lets me rest. One hundred years, Jarina! Not in one hundred years have I found peace, until I met you, and He almost took you from me, like He took Mother, and Alarad, and everyone I have ever loved. And now Rion. Rion was the one person I was able to save, but not from Him."

Alarad. Incuban had said Farad had killed him. Did He say so just to goad Farad, while knowing the truth, or did He truly believe it? Alarad had killed himself. He had sent all his energy down their bond, leaving none for himself, like Dewalaren's mother had, when she sacrificed herself to save her husband, Evanaren. But Alarad had done so to end his own agony, as well as to save Farad from the torment of enduring it along with him. Yet Farad still blamed himself for it, for living when Alarad died, for his youngest brother suffering in his place, when Farad should have been the one tortured to death. He was the older brother. He should have been able to protect Alarad, save him.

JARINA eyed Farad in concern. He was quiet now, his mind lost in old agonies. It was dangerous for him to dwell amongst those memories, those thoughts. She must pull him from them. "Farad, you must hear me. Listen to me. You tore out Incuban's throat; you tore off much more. You tasted His blood upon your tongue. He torments you because you fight Him, you weaken Him. Of all of them, you alone He has not been able to defeat.

"You must endure, Farad. The Elves would say so to you, were they the ones beside you. You must stay strong. We cannot defeat Incuban without you. You heard what happened when the others thought you dead. Dewalaren would crumble to dust without you, especially now, with Aras lost. Lunahr would fall without you. You saved Lunahr as well, and me and Eladar and Elanara. How can you have forgotten? Now I will hug you, and you will not only allow it, you will take comfort from it." She wrapped her strong arms around him. She felt him shudder, and then he relaxed against her, clinging to her tightly.

"I cannot ever lose you," Farad said into her hair. "You are my strength now."

"I will be so always, Husband. In life or in death, I will never leave you. You are never alone now, Faradan, my love. Now, tell me what you can of your dream. We must try to discover how He found Rion, when He should not have been able to. Rion's core is not strong enough."

Farad appeared surprised and then thoughtful. "You are right! He should not have been able to—Circe! She was in the dream. She was Incuban's puppet. Perhaps she was the one who found Rion for Him, somehow."

Jarina breathed a sigh of relief. Farad was thinking clearly again. The pain, the despair, no longer clouded his mind. Rion might have a chance now.

Chapter 3
The Road to Ogaten

TARRELL rose early the next morning. He'd barely slept, but he'd forced his body to at least rest. He was surprised by how much work Rion had done during the night. He looked better, too. Keeping himself busy had apparently helped. Ron's words of last night still haunted Tarrell, but with the light of day, the danger seemed somehow farther away.

The brothers and Tarrell recovered their respective hidden purses from beneath the floorboards. Tarrell, Rion, Rarnak, and Ron started loading the wagon. When Ara and Gar returned with their own loaded wagon, Rarnak left to get Talia.

A short while later, Tarrell left with Ara and Gar. He needed to make sure the burials had been taken care of, that Lerdon and Jathran had been properly laid to rest.

RON was concerned to see his brothers and Tarrell return grim-faced. Ara and Gar spoke quietly to him, telling him troublesome news: Lerdon's and Jathran's bodies were gone. The City Guard told them they'd found only the empty blankets the corpses had lain under.

At the sound of a whimper behind them, they all turned. Ron cursed. Ara and Gar should have told him in Thenalonese, but they weren't used to keeping secrets from Rion, and he had apparently gotten close enough to hear without their realizing.

Rion was staring at them in horror, trembling. "N-n-n...," he said, shaking his head in terrified disbelief.

Rion stumbled to the table. He grabbed for his pen and paper, knocking over the inkwell as he did so, sending ink pouring everywhere. He ignored it, dipping his pen into the puddle. *Walking dead! Not a dream! Hurt me. Revenants*, he wrote, underlining the odd final word three times.

Tarrell's eyes widened as he read what Rion wrote.

"Are you trying to tell us they were in your dream? Lerdon and Jathran were dead but hurting you?" Ron asked carefully.

Rion nodded his head frantically.

"Rion, they're dead. They can't hurt you," Ron reasoned. "And they wouldn't. They'd never hurt you. They loved you."

Rion looked at Ron as if he'd said something unspeakably vile, something terrifying. He stumbled from Ron and tripped backward over a chair. He fell, tangled in the chair legs. He pushed the chair away as if it were burning him, then sprang to his feet, grabbed it by the back, and began slamming it against the floor, over and over, smashing it to kindling.

Ron leapt at him and seized him, pinning Rion's arms to his sides. "Gar, Ara, help me! He's going to hurt himself."

Rion struggled violently in his grip, lashing out with his feet, trying frantically to free himself, apparently not even realizing he was hurting them.

Tarrell stared at Rion, obviously appalled.

Ron cursed as Rion's foot connected hard with his shin. "Tarrell, get a rope! We have to tie him!" Ron yelled, galvanizing Tarrell. But Rion stiffened at his words and stopped thrashing. Ron heard that horrible whimpering, whining sound again. Mention of the rope had terrified Rion. Elmoth, what was wrong with him? It was as if he'd lost control not only of his tongue, but of his mind as well, that friends and ropes and even chairs horrified or enraged him.

"Rion, you have to calm yourself. You can't keep losing control like this, or we're going to have to tie you, for your own safety. Do you understand?" Ron asked.

Rion nodded, and Ron saw tears begin to fall. "Rion, I wish you'd tell us what's wrong. Why won't you trust us to help you? We've always helped each other before. What's changed that?"

Rion started to sob and hugged Ron tightly. Ron was surprised. He looked at Tarrell helplessly and then awkwardly started to comfort Rion. The others gave them some privacy. "We kept you safe from the chimaera, and we'll keep you safe from whatever demons are haunting you now, if you'll only let us," Ron swore.

Ara and Gar helped Tarrell finish loading the wagon, and then, after Rarnak returned with Talia, they headed out to sell the ones they wouldn't be needing. After Ara and Gar came back, as the others made a last check of the house, Rion fell asleep in Ron's arms, his head against Ron's chest.

Ron carried Rion in his arms effortlessly, as if he were a child. He feared Rion might waken, but he was sound asleep, exhausted from all he had suffered. Ron sat in the bed of the wagon with Rion on his lap; the others had left space for him. With Jathran's horse, Blaze, tied to the back of the wagon beside Ron's horse, and Lerdon's horse, Bramble, tethered to the back of the second wagon, where Ara and Gar had loaded their goods, they began the journey to Ogaten.

Rion slept deeply. All the fear and heartache left his face, and he looked at peace again.

They'd been traveling for half the day, until well past noon, when the wagon hit a ditch in the road and lurched. Rion's eyes opened. Ron braced himself for Rion to be violent again, but instead, he looked up at Ron in wonder.

RION looked up at Ron worshipfully as he saw the trees all around and realized they were well on the way to Ogaten. He must have slept for hours, yet he hadn't dreamt. Incuban hadn't come to him again. Ron had kept Him away somehow. Rion smiled at Ron in joy and love.

RON smiled back at him in relief. "Do you think you might like some lunch?"

Rion looked thoughtful, then nodded. He'd thrown up his dinner and not had breakfast. Ron hoped if Rion could sleep and maybe eat again, he might get well. He might even get his voice back.

Ron called to Tarrell casually, "Rion's hungry, Tarrell. What say we stop for lunch?"

TARRELL looked back in surprise. Rion was still in Ron's arms, but awake. He appeared sane and calm and normal again, gazing at Ron with worshipful eyes. "Lunchtime, everyone," Tarrell called out simply, as if a miracle hadn't just occurred.

There was a field on their left. Tarrell pulled the wagon off the road, and Gar did likewise with the one he was driving.

They'd packed bread, meat, fruit, and cheese for the trip. Tarrell was encouraged to see that Rion ate some of everything. Lunch passed without event. Afterward, to Tarrell's further relief, Rion sat on the bench next to him, as eager and alert as he'd always been.

After finishing his own lunch, Ron untied his horse from the wagon, and mounted him, free to guard them, now that Rion had apparently recovered.

"LUNAHR, I need you to help me," Farad said. "Incuban has found Rion. He knows what Rion means to me. You told Him I love Rion, and He's seen it to be true, so now He's trying to hurt me by torturing Rion. He hasn't caught him yet, but He's harmed him, through his dreams. I need to find Rion and bring him to safety."

"I'm sorry, Farad, I didn't mean to betray you to Him. How can I help?" Lunahr asked, sounding upset, but not despondent.

Farad was relieved. "Rion should still be in Gosa. I need you to send Quickwing with a message for him, telling him to head for the Elves in Salenia, so they might bring him to us. Can you see through Quickwing's eyes from so far away?"

"Of course! I truly wield the Power of House of Eagles now," Lunahr said proudly. "My Power was brought to fruition by the Ring, as was your own."

"I will tell you where Rion was staying when I was there, though he'll probably be elsewhere in the City by now. I will have Eladar write a note to put in a band on Quickwing's leg." Farad's face crumpled in despair. Rion would not trust him now. He'd seen the look of terror and revulsion Rion had given him. And that would have only been the first dream. By the time Quickwing reached Rion, he would have had more, any one of which might bring him to madness. He was such a bright light, yet his core was small and dark. None of them could touch it to help him. Only the Ring and the Knife might save him now, and even so, Farad did not know how much they might be able to do.

Lunahr put his hand onto Farad's shoulder. "Courage, Farad. You will not help Rion by surrendering to despair. Quickwing has carried such messages before. He will do well, you will see."

Farad nodded. But he could not hurt one friend to help another. He must warn Lunahr. "First, I must be sure you know the danger. Incuban sent a chimaera and a Revenant to Gosa. Quickwing may well face chimaera or hippogryphs. He may be killed."

Lunahr looked fearful, but he swallowed and said bravely, "Still, he will go."

"Thank you, Lunahr. I know what Quickwing means to you. I would not have before I bonded with Slash. We gained much when the Ring was found."

Farad sought out Eladar. Eladar's look of annoyance changed to one of surprise and concern as he listened to Farad. "Eladar, I need you to write a message to Rion for me. I will tell you what to say. The part for him should be in Common, with an additional note in Elvish for the Elves in Salenia."

Eladar looked at Farad in surprise. "Would it not be easier to write the note to Rion yourself and for me to write the second part?"

"No, it cannot be in two different hands. Rion would become suspicious. He is terrified of me now. He cannot know this is from me, or he'll not trust what it says," Farad said, agitated.

Eladar's eyes narrowed in suspicion. "You must tell me why Rion fears you, if you desire my aid."

"I won't speak of it. All I can say is that Incuban snared Rion in a nightmare to torture him, and me, by forcing me to watch his torment. He is hurting Rion, solely to punish me by it." Farad grimaced. "And He has tricked Rion. He has convinced him I am his enemy. Rion might even think Talon is, now. But he trusts you, Eladar. He'll listen to you. If we can get him here, we might help him. Incuban's stolen Rion's voice from him. Rion can't speak, and… and I'm afraid He's hurt him terribly. He didn't show me all He did to Rion, but I saw enough. I saw too much."

Eladar's jaw set in cold fury. "Rion should not be harmed, ever, in any way. Tell me what to say."

Farad was surprised. He had not realized how strongly Rion had touched Eladar as well.

Farad dictated the message to Eladar, and Eladar wrote it as he spoke, and then wrote it a second time, changing the wording and adding to it so that it sounded like it truly came from him. Farad read it and looked at him in surprise.

"You are not the only one whose life Rion has touched," Eladar said simply, confirming Farad's earlier thoughts.

Farad nodded and took the note, inserting it in the metal message tube to be strapped to Quickwing's leg.

TARRELL called their small caravan to a stop when it was time for them to make camp for the night. He was relieved to see Rion eat dinner with the rest of them. He seemed much more himself again, although he still could not speak. He even wrote in his travel journal, as he used to on their trip to Gosa. Then he stretched and settled down for bed.

RION reached into his little side purse for his Elfstone and found to his shock it was empty. He tried to remember when he'd last seen the precious stone, held it. He brought it with him everywhere and often touched it within its pouch to feel its reassuring presence.

He remembered his relief when it was returned to him after the Magistrate passed judgment. He'd been holding it while lying in bed, thinking of Elanara, before he finally fell asleep. But he'd woken from the nightmare thrashing. It must have fallen to the floor. It was still back in Gosa, in his room! He got up and wrote a quick, panicked message and then showed the page to Tarrell. *Elfstone on bedroom floor! Must go back!*

"Rion, are you sure?" Tarrell asked.

Rion nodded. He picked up a pebble, feigned sleeping and waking, and then dropped the stone.

Tarrell sighed. "Well, we can't do anything about it tonight. And you and I can't go back in any case. Our day of grace is over. Tomorrow we'll send Gar to look for it, with a note for our landlord to let him in, since we no longer have the key. We paid our rent through the end of the month, so he shouldn't take issue with it. Gar's horse is the fastest of any of ours. We'll keep traveling. He should catch back up to us in a day or so. He'll be able to travel much faster by horseback than we are by wagon."

Rion sighed and nodded reluctantly in agreement.

"Why don't you lie back down? It's been a long, hard couple of days. You need to get some sleep."

Rion nodded again and headed back to his bedroll. He lay down, but he was afraid to close his eyes. Every time the fire cracked, he jumped. And there were noises from within the trees of a kind that had never bothered him before in their travels. But now he imagined them twigs snapping under heavy feet.

Ron was on guard duty. Tarrell had finished speaking to Gar and had settled down to sleep by the fire. Talia was asleep in the wagon. Rion rose and headed for Tarrell, who appeared to already be sound asleep. He laid his blanket down close to Tarrell and, after a moment's hesitation, laid his head gently on Tarrell's chest. Rion heard Tarrell's strong heart beating rhythmically, reassuringly, like Ron's had been earlier. The dead didn't have beating hearts. They were cold. Tarrell was warm. Rion laid an arm across Tarrell's chest carefully, hoping not to wake him, and Tarrell didn't stir. Gradually, Rion relaxed, his own breathing slowing as he finally drifted off to sleep.

AS SOON as Rion was safely asleep, Tarrell gently put his arm around him. Tarrell had been careful not to move before, once he realized what Rion was doing. He had been so afraid when Rion had risen and appeared so agitated that he'd go wild again. He was glad they were away from the City. It seemed to be helping Rion. He smiled tenderly at Rion and then truly fell asleep.

THE next morning, Rion awoke and blushed, embarrassed. He was acting like a child. But he didn't pull away from Tarrell's strong arms. Instead, he listened to Tarrell's steady heartbeat. It was just as soothing in the morning light as it had been by firelight. Rion smiled at Tarrell when he woke up in turn.

"Good morning," Tarrell said.

"G-g-g...." The smile fled Rion's face, as he struggled to speak. Why couldn't he utter even a single word? It was so frustrating!

"It's all right, Rion," Tarrell said firmly, and Rion nodded.

TARRELL was relieved to see that although Rion still didn't have control over his voice, he seemed in far better control of himself now. They ate breakfast together, and then Gar began the ride to the City, after Rion made sure he knew to check against the walls, in the corners, and between the cracks in the floorboards, so that he wouldn't leave without finding it.

The day passed uneventfully, other than for a brief, unexpected thunderstorm that drenched them all, except for Talia and Rion, who huddled under the tarp covering the wagon. Tarrell had made Rion get under the tarp with Talia, to stay dry. He didn't want Rion getting sick.

RION felt awkward under the tarp with Talia. Her hair smelled like jasmine. His heart started to beat faster. She was so beautiful and so near. He blushed when he realized the effect her scent and nearness was having on him, but then he felt terror at his growing arousal, as memory of the horrible dream flooded him.

He clawed his way out from under the tarp, almost falling out of the wagon into the mud in his haste to get away from her. He tilted his face up into the chilly rain, almost sobbing in relief as the deluge washed away the feeling of cold, dead hands on his skin and Circe's terrible touch. He could see the brothers and Rarnak and Tarrell were all worried. He tried to reassure them, but resolutely refused to get back under the tarp, instead sitting beside Tarrell on the bench again, against his protests. Ara was driving the other wagon in Gar's stead.

THAT night when they made camp, Tarrell had trouble starting the fire. All the wood they'd gathered was wet, and it was very dark and hard to see. Clouds were obscuring the moon and even most of the stars. Tarrell had finally gotten a small flame going and was carefully fanning it to make it grow when Rion kicked dirt over it, putting it out.

"Rion! What... mpfh," Tarrell said, his exasperated complaint cut off as Rion clapped his hand over Tarrell's mouth. Just then, one of the clouds drifted away from the face of the moon, providing a dim bit of light, and he could see that Rion was looking up in terror.

"Shh...." Rion hissed, almost inaudibly, in his ear. Tarrell listened intently, straining to hear what might have Rion so upset. He was about to try to speak anyway when he heard it, a distant, roaring sound, coming almost imperceptibly closer as he listened.

Rion let go of Tarrell and drew his sword, and Tarrell could hear the brothers and Rarnak drawing theirs as he drew his own. He could feel Rion trembling against him.

There was another roar, much closer, accompanied by the sound of loud flapping, like birds' wings, only far too loud to be a bird. Something big passed overhead, shadowing the sliver of moonlight, and the horses stamped nervously. Fortunately, they'd not caught the creature's scent, or they might have screamed and attracted it. It continued flying, following the road in the direction they were traveling, heading away from Gosa, toward Ogaten.

"Chimaera," Ron said, his voice grim and sure. "It was too high up. I couldn't see if it had a rider."

Tarrell couldn't believe he'd been able to tell that much in such poor light. But then again, what else could it have been?

Rion sheathed his sword.

Tarrell went to him and hugged him. "You were very brave. I'm very proud of you." He was incredibly relieved. Rion was acting himself, even with such a creature so near. He'd been only as afraid as he should be, ready to fight for his life if need be, though he'd had every right to panic, after surviving the attack in the Market and seeing their friends killed before his eyes.

"G-G...," Rion said, then took Tarrell's hand and stroked Tarrell's palm with his finger. Tarrell was confused, until he realized Rion was making the same strokes over and over. Rion was spelling upon his hand.

"Gar? You're worried about Gar?' Tarrell asked.

Rion nodded.

"He should reach us by tomorrow afternoon. The rain kept him from getting all the way back, that's all," Tarrell said reassuringly. "We'd better post extra watch and eat a cold supper tonight."

Tarrell was relieved the monster had flown past them, but puzzled as well. If the thing had been hunting Rion, as the one in the Market apparently had, it appeared it couldn't find him in the dark. Yet another of the creatures had found him easily in the City, in a crowded market. No one had seen it until it had attacked Rion. It hadn't circled low over the City looking for him, it had just dropped out of the sky, directly over him.

He made sure Rion was out of earshot later when he talked to Ron about it, but Ron had no insight as to why the creature couldn't find him. They both agreed that perhaps Rion wasn't the target of this one.

THE night passed slowly. Rion did not sleep, he could not. He kept listening for the sound of wings and of hoofbeats, but neither came.

That morning they proceeded cautiously, constantly looking overhead. By afternoon Rion was looking back along the road as frequently as he was looking up, but no hoofbeats came to join them.

By evening Ron and Ara were visibly upset as well, no longer trying to hide their concern. Ron told Tarrell, "Gar should have joined us yesterday, or at the very least, this morning or this afternoon. Something's happened. We're already halfway to Ogaten, and you two can't go back in any case. We'll not leave you underguarded with one or no bowmen, not with those creatures flying about. But as soon as we get you safely to the Elves, we're going to look for Gar."

"Maybe something delayed him in the City," Tarrell said. "Perhaps the landlord was away and he couldn't get the key. Or maybe he had to tear the floor apart to look for the stone. He still might join us." But Tarrell didn't sound as if he believed it.

NIGHT came, but Gar did not. Rion appeared distraught. He wrote on Ron's hand, "My fault. Sorry." The moon was out tonight, and Ron could see tears of despair on Rion's face. Ron had almost sent Gar to his death, once, for a horse. Now it appeared Rion had done the same, for an Elfstone.

Ron hugged Rion. "You couldn't have known about the chimaera. You mustn't blame yourself."

Rion didn't eat dinner that night, nor did he sleep.

The next day he ate neither breakfast nor lunch nor dinner.

THAT night Rion lay awake again, remembering Gar laughing and joking, all the times they had shared on the long journey to Gosa and since.

He refused breakfast in the morning and then lunch, when they stopped for it. Ron finally spoke to him. "Rion, Gar wouldn't want you to get sick on account of him. Please, you must eat something."

Rion shook his head. He couldn't eat, knowing Gar might have been killed because of him. He had missed the brothers terribly when they had left, but he had been relieved they had all survived the crossing, that no one else had died for him as Elkrum and all their other guards had, outside Athanark. And now Lerdon and Jathran were dead and Gar was dead, too. He knew he was.

He kept picturing how it must have happened. Gar had been alone on the road, and the chimaera had swooped down out of the sky at him. He'd have tried to shoot at it with his bow, but it was so fast, so vicious. It would have torn him to shreds. It would have ripped his face off as it had done to Jathran, just like the obearn in the hills had done to Gar before. Only this time Gar had been on his own. Ara hadn't been there to save him, to bring him back to be healed enough that he might survive a journey to the Elves. This time he would have died alone and terrified. Rion curled up in the wagon and began to cry, muffling the sound against his arm.

ARA said stubbornly to Ron, "Gar might still be in the City. Something truly might have kept him. We can't know that he's gone. I won't mourn him until I see a body."

Ron said in a low tone and in Thenalonese, to be sure Rion couldn't overhear, "There might not be a body. It could well have been eaten." He forced himself to say it. "Or taken. But we'll look. We have to look. What will we tell Van? What will we tell Father? Why did I let him go?"

RION refused dinner. No amount of cajoling could get him to eat. That night he lay awake, imagining Gar's corpse following their trail now, coming after them for revenge for being slain. No, Gar wouldn't do such a thing. But Incuban could make him do worse. He'd twist him the way he'd twisted Lerdon and Jathran. All three of them might come after him, in the middle of the night, out of the woods. They'd drag him into the woods where the others couldn't find him, and they'd torture him and violate him. Or worse, they'd take him to Incuban, and He'd tell them what to do. They might kill him too quickly on their own. Incuban would make sure he suffered as long as possible. And they'd take his friends, too, and torture them. All the usual soft night sounds were terrifying. He kept expecting them to pounce upon him at any moment.

The next morning, Tarrell sounded desperate and upset, knowing Rion hadn't slept in over three days and hadn't eaten in four. "Rion, the Elves won't be able to help you if you do this to yourself. Please, you must sleep and eat, if not for yourself, then for me? Please, Rion! I can't bear to see you like this."

Rion shook his head. He couldn't, not even for Tarrell. Ron and Ara tried to get him to eat also, but he wouldn't. Finally, Talia came up to him. "Rion, I know how you must feel. I felt the same when Father died. I felt it was my fault that he'd gone back for the chest, as much as he did it for himself, too. I wished so many times to wake up and find it all a nightmare. But I survived it. The hardest part of death isn't dying: it's living on after someone you love has died. But I was alone. You're still surrounded by people who love you."

Rion stared at her, agonized. Her words had hurt rather than helped. They would all die for him, all his friends. They hadn't seen the chimaera again, but Rion knew Incuban still hunted him. He would never give up. He would never stop tormenting Rion, or killing his friends to get at him, or even just to hurt him by it. He had thought it was Arcanus or Magus or Circe who was angered against him. He didn't know why Incuban was hunting him, unless it was because Incuban was aiding Circe? Or was it because of Rion's knowledge of the three wizards, or of Talon, or maybe even of the Elves?

No, it wouldn't be because of Talon. Talon was His now, as was Hunter—Farad, Incuban had called him. And Jargas and Jarina. Incuban had told him as much. Were they still alive or were they all dead? Hunter had looked alive: horrible, but alive. Now Gar was lost as well. And he would come for Rion. It was only a matter of time.

TALIA looked at Rion in dismay and went to Tarrell. "Oh Tarrell, I wanted to help. I thought maybe I could, but he looks worse for my having spoken to him."

"It's not your fault, Talia," he assured her. "It's wizardry. It has to be, for him to be like this. The Elves will help him. They must. We went too slowly, to help Gar catch up to us. Now we've another night until we reach Ogaten, but we'll be there by midafternoon tomorrow. We've just one more night."

They got into the wagons and continued their journey. They didn't stop for lunch, instead pressing on. How could they eat, knowing Rion wouldn't?

RION turned, startled. He thought someone had been behind him. His eyes closed and he jerked them open instantly.

Rion sat shivering. They'd come for him in the dark. Incuban would have realized by now that he could not visit Rion's dreams, not when he refused to sleep. Incuban's minions would have to come for him in the flesh. When they did, all his friends would be hurt, he knew it. He should sleep instead. Then he'd be the only one hurt. And it wasn't really real. Except it felt real and sounded real and smelled real. He would go mad if he had a dream like that again. He remembered every detail of the terrible room. He could still smell the incense, feel them touching him. Dreams weren't ever so detailed, so vivid, days afterward.

If he slept, his friends would be safe. But he'd be helpless. Incuban would control his body, as he had before. At least awake he could fight. He could die quickly. His friends were all ready to fight for him, to die for him. He was so selfish that he could not sacrifice himself to save them.

The afternoon passed with agonizing slowness, but the sun was finally setting. They'd be stopping soon for the night. Rion fought to stay awake.

What was that? Rion turned. Hoofbeats. No, he must have imagined them. He'd wanted to hear them for too long. He listened intently. No, there truly were hoofbeats. They were real, he was sure of it. Rion strained to see.

The others heard them too, now. Ara, who had the advantage over Rion of being on horseback and having slept said, "It's a single horse. A man, it's.... Elmoth, it's Gar! I can't believe.... Wait, he's not alone, and something looks odd about him...." He took off down the road toward Gar.

Rion's eyes widened in terror. They'd come for him! They were here for him, Jathran and Lerdon and Gar! Rion bolted up and over the side of the wagon in a blind panic and headed for the trees.

"RION! Stop! Come back!" Tarrell yelled after Rion, who inexplicably stumbled wildly toward the trees, a look of sheer terror on his face.

Tarrell thrust the reins at Talia as she scrambled onto the bench and then jumped down from the wagon and ran after Rion. He was dimly aware that Rarnak had leapt from his horse and was following him. Ron, however, after a moment's hesitation, rode off after Ara, leaving Talia alone with the wagons. She would be safe for a short while, surely? Tarrell couldn't worry about her or the brothers. Rion was the one who needed him most.

Ahead of Tarrell, Rion was running blindly. He tripped over a tree root, but kept on his feet. He apparently misjudged the distance to dodge around a tree and slammed his arm into it, but he went on as if he barely felt it.

Tarrell tried to follow Rion, but he was small and fast, and not at all cautious. Tarrell soon lost sight of him. He could still hear Rion, banging and crashing through the woods, but it was impossible to tell where the sound was coming from.

ARA rode up to Gar cautiously, and then his eyes widened and he headed for Gar in relief. "Gar, Elmoth, it really is you! You're alive. When I saw you I thought.... What happened? Who are they?"

Gar was on Thenagar. His guard uniform was completely black with soot, though his hands and face were clean. In front of him was a young girl, maybe twelve years of age, with big brown eyes, and long brown hair, surprisingly neatly combed, considering the rest of her appearance. She wore what appeared to be a filthy, blackened nightdress, covered by one of Gar's shirts, and her feet were wrapped in bandages. Behind him was a second girl, about the same age, dressed and groomed similarly, except she wore Gar's pants over her nightdress, tied tightly with a piece of rope. Her feet were also bandaged.

The girl behind Gar was peering shyly out at Ara and blushing, and the girl in front of him had tried to bury her head in Gar's chest.

"It's all right, Gisela. This is my brother, Ara. We finally caught up to them, though I hadn't expected to. I thought they'd be at the mill already," Gar told the girl in front of him. "Ara, this is Gisela." Gar nodded to the girl in front. "And behind us is Anabelle."

Ron came thundering up and Gisela squealed and clutched Gar in fear.

"Ron, you're scaring her," Gar scolded his elder brother.

"Scaring her? We thought you were dead! We thought the chimaera took you! I won't even ask who they are. We've not the time. Rion's run off into the woods. We have to find him," Ron snapped and then he wheeled his horse and took off back for the wagon.

Ara followed right behind Ron, but Gar came at a much slower pace, clearly mindful of the girls.

RION heard Tarrell and Rarnak calling for him, searching. He'd completely lost track of the road and wasn't sure which direction he was headed in now, but he was still running. His right shin slammed into a low branch, and he almost fell. Even the trees wanted him. They were trying to catch him for Gar.

He felt a sob welling up as he staggered and began running again. No, not now! He could not cry! It would be like in that storage room back in Gosa, when those men had taken him for ransom. Gar would hear him and come for him and hurt him.

Rion skidded to a halt and froze. He still heard Tarrell and Rarnak calling to him, but now he heard Ara and Ron. But worse, horrifyingly worse, he heard Gar. Gar was coming for him!

Rion ran again, renewed terror giving his feet wings. He bashed his right knee and then his left arm. It truly was as if the trees were leaping into his way.

He tried to duck under a branch but didn't bend low enough. He cracked his forehead on it and flipped onto his back, lying half-stunned. He heard someone coming and then a shadow fell over him.

"Rion, it's me! It's Gar."

Rion whimpered as Gar loomed over him. He looked terrible. Gar's face was in shadow in the fading light of the setting sun, but his uniform was black, filthy, and he was reaching for him. Rion screamed and started scrabbling along on his back, kicking out with his feet at the monster that was trying to seize him.

"Rion, it's all right! Calm down," Gar said, as he reached forward and grasped Rion under his arms.

Rion kicked him hard in both shins, and Gar fell over onto him. At the weight of Gar on top of him, Rion began screaming and thrashing hysterically, punching and clawing and struggling as Gar tried to pin him to the ground, his mind awash with the horrible memories from the dream.

"Ron, Ara, Rarnak, Tarrell, help me! I've found him!" Gar called out. "Rion, stop it! You're hurting yourself as well as me. What's wrong with you?"

Ara ran up. "Rion, calm down! It's all right. Gar's not dead. It's really him. He's safe. He's come back to us," Ara soothed.

"Dead? He thinks I'm dead?" Gar asked, completely flummoxed. "But if I was dead, how could I…. Oh, Elmoth, his dream! No wonder he's terrified! So that's what you and Ron meant."

RON found them and grabbed Rion by both sides of the head, holding him immobile, forcing him to look at him. "Rion, it's Ron. Stop. You have to stop. Listen to me." He was looking into Rion's wild eyes, and he saw a spark of something, recognition maybe, or perhaps rational thought. "Rion, come on. You can do it. That's it. It's all right. Everything's all right. Gar's not dead. He's not coming after you. He's alive, he's safe. You're safe too. No one's going to hurt you, I swear to you."

Rion shuddered and finally stopped struggling. Then he started crying wildly, clutching Ron tightly. Ron hugged him, patting his back, and talking to him as if he were a small child, as Rion sobbed his terror out into his arms.

"It's all right Rion. Let it all out: all the fear. That's it. That's better. You're safe. I know you're frightened, but everything's all right." Rion was sobbing so hard Ron doubted he could even hear him, but the words weren't important.

"Ara, try to find Tarrell and Rarnak. Let them know we found him," Ron commanded, and Ara left.

Gar looked on helplessly, and when he spoke, his voice was thick with despair. "But when I left he was better! What's been happening?"

"He thought you were dead. We all did. A chimaera flew over us the night you left, coming from Gosa. When you didn't come back, we thought it had killed you. Rion has neither eaten nor slept since. He blamed himself. Come on. Let's get him back to the wagon. Can you walk, Rion?"

Rion nodded, bravely choking back the last of his sobs, though he kept his head against Ron's chest. He winced as he lurched forward, his leg buckled, and he would have fallen when he tried to walk, had he not been leaning against Ron.

"You've hurt yourself," Ron chastised gently. He picked Rion up in his arms and began carrying him as if he were a child, as he had before.

Tarrell and Rarnak were at the wagons with Ara and Talia and the girls when they approached. Tarrell paled when he saw Ron carrying Rion.

"It's all right, Tarrell. Rion's just hurt his leg a little, but he'll be fine," Ron assured him. "Why don't we pull off the road and make camp here, while there's still enough light to see by? I think a fire might even be safe tonight. We're far enough off the Western Road now, and we haven't seen anything flying for the past few nights. Once we're settled, we can hear Gar's story and find out what happened."

They made camp and Talia fussed over the two girls. She unpacked some of her clothes and had them change while she held up a blanket to screen them from the sight of the men. Then she expertly pinned up their skirts, which were too long, carefully arranging the pins so they wouldn't prick them. She frowned at the bandages she saw upon Gisela's arm and Anabelle's leg and both girls' feet as they helped each other dress.

Ron had sat down on the ground near where Ara was stirring a pot over the fire. Ron was holding Rion on his lap as he had in Gosa. Gar said, "That smells good. The girls and I have been getting pretty tired of roast rabbit, haven't we, girls?"

"Oh no, Gar! They were wonderful," Anabelle assured him.

"You're such a good hunter," Gisela said simultaneously.

They both gazed at Gar worshipfully, and he looked embarrassed. "Thank you for the clothes, Talia." He nodded at the girls. "You both look beautiful," he told them, and they smiled at him shyly.

"So, Gar, when do we hear what happened?" Ara asked.

"Not now, Ara. I'm too hungry," Gar said. Ara started to object, but Ron caught his eye and tipped his head toward Rion. Ron realized Gar didn't want to chance upsetting Rion.

"You're right. Dinner first," Ara said, nodding in understanding.

Rion was almost asleep in Ron's arms again. Ron figured Rion needed the sleep more than he needed to eat, though he was in desperate need of both.

Rion seemed to just have drifted off to sleep when he suddenly jolted awake again in a panic. Ron soothed him and calmed him.

Five more times, Rion jerked awake, until finally his breathing slowed and steadied. After Rion seemed sound asleep for a good long while, Ron risked laying him down and joined the others for dinner.

"Here, we saved you a plate," Rarnak said, handing it to Ron.

"Thank you, Ron," Tarrell said sincerely. "Though I wish he'd still be able to seek comfort from me. He keeps going to you instead."

"I'm older, Tarrell. He needs a father now, not a brother, and I'm almost old enough to be one for him. I'm hoping that now that he can't blame himself for Gar, he might start to get better again. We need to make sure he eats well at breakfast. We'll need to make sure it's something he can keep down, too, as he's not eaten for so long. I'm hoping he sleeps through the night tonight. He sorely needs to."

"He's not the only one who needs to," Gar said. "Now that you've finished your dinner, it's bedtime, girls. You want to be well rested for tomorrow. Remember, you'll be seeing Liana in the afternoon. You don't want her to worry. I'm glad Talia had clothes for you. You look much more presentable now. Let me change your dressings, and then it's off to bed with you, after you've washed your faces and cleaned your teeth."

"Yes, Gar," they said in tandem.

Gar took a kit out of his pack, unrolled some bandages, and took out some ointment. "You first, Gisela," he said. She pulled up her loose sleeve to reveal a bandage from mid forearm to shoulder. Gar unwound the bandage, revealing a horrible burn, which appeared to be partly healed. "That's looking better, Gisela." Gar carefully applied the ointment to it and rewrapped it in fresh bandages. Then he did the same to her feet, which were also burnt and blistered. "Now drink your medicine," he urged. She made a face but drank it, quickly.

"Now you, Anabelle," Gar said. Anabelle pulled her skirt up to her knee and then hesitated, blushing darkly. He smiled reassuringly. "It's all right. Ron, Ara, Rarnak, why don't you help Talia clean up dinner?" he suggested, and the three of them left to do so.

Ron peeked over and saw Anabelle had lifted her skirt to her waist. Gar was treating a burn that went from knee to midthigh, while she watched calmly. Then he treated her feet and gave her something to drink.

After he finished tending to them, Gar brought them some water and tooth powder. They washed their faces and scrubbed their teeth with the dentifrice, using their index fingers.

Finally, Gar tucked the two of them in, and Ron meandered back over.

"… were we?" Gar was saying.

"The Elf!" Gisela said eagerly.

"Prince Thorn," Anabelle corrected.

"I knew that! I remembered too!" Gisela pouted. Then she gazed at Gar worshipfully. "Tell us what he looked like again!"

Gar smiled at her. "He had long silver hair, straight, like yours, not curly like Liana's, and bright blue eyes, and he was tall and thin. He was as pretty as Liana, too, except he was all dusty and scraped and bruised, and his broken arm and leg were bandaged. But he still smiled and laughed all the time."

"Ooh, the poor man," Anabelle said.

Gisela corrected her. "He's not a Man, he's an Elf! And he was brave and strong!"

"I know! Shh…," Anabelle scolded.

Gar smiled at them again. "So, after the second ogre attacked us, Thorn could barely talk. But he told Rion the secret words to get into the Elves' Wood. He knew otherwise we would never find the Elves, that we'd just walk about in circles looking for them. And Rion learned the words, all of them, in Elvish, though it's not a language he speaks. Then Thorn fell unconscious, and he wouldn't wake up.

"Rion and the others brought Thorn and Ara and me in the wagons to the Elves' Wood. Rion spoke the secret words aloud and the Elves came, appearing all of a sudden from amongst the trees. Only these weren't the friendly Elves we'd hoped to find. These were soldiers, with shiny metal armor and scowling faces. And they took Thorn from us and left the rest of us behind, in the woods."

"But what about you and Ara? How could they leave you? You said the Elves healed you!" Gisela said indignantly.

"Shh! Don't interrupt. It's rude. Go ahead, Gar," Anabelle encouraged.

"So they left, but Rion called out after them. He ran after them too, and called out that they couldn't leave, that Ara and I needed their help, and that he had a message from Thorn. And the Elves came back. Only they weren't helpful-looking at all, but angry. They tried to get Rion to tell them the whole message, but he said he wouldn't unless they helped us."

"He was so brave! He didn't look brave tonight. Why was he so scared of you, Gar? I thought you are friends," Anabelle said, appearing troubled.

"We are, Anabelle. But Rion's been hurt a lot. Not just once, like you and Gisela, or me, but over and over. And he's been very brave, but he's not as strong now because of it. It's not his fault. He's under an evil spell the bad wizard put on him. The wizard stole his voice and he's been trying to steal his courage, but Rion's been fighting him."

"Fighting a wizard? The one that burned the City and killed everyone?" Gisela asked wide-eyed, and Gar nodded.

Ron's eyes fastened onto his brother, riveted, but he didn't interrupt.

"That's right. But that's way too far ahead in the story, Gisela. So, let me see.... So the soldiers scowled at Rion but agreed to take us to the Elven City. They blindfolded us so we wouldn't see where their City is. It's a secret. And then they led us there. That's when we met Princess Brook, Thorn's sister. She was even more beautiful than Thorn, with long silver hair to her feet and flowers in her hair. She wore a dress the blue of the evening sky and had blue eyes, like Thorn's. But she was sad, because Thorn was hurt.

"Rion said he'd tell her the message even without her helping us, but he begged her to help us anyway. And she did. She sent all of us to the Elven healer. And soon the terrible claw marks were gone from my face and body, without even a single scar, and I could talk and breathe and move and eat again. And they healed Ara's back, and even Ron's head and Van's leg, though they weren't too badly hurt. They healed Thorn too, and his sister was happy again. Now, that's enough for one night. I'll tell you the rest later," Gar said.

"But we'll be at the mill tomorrow!" Anabelle complained in distress.

"I'll still tuck you in and tell you the rest. I promise. Now, get some sleep, both of you. It's getting late. Sweet dreams," he said and kissed each of them on the forehead. Then he headed for the fire. His face flushed in embarrassment when he saw Ron.

"I didn't realize you were listening," Gar said sheepishly. "I started it the first night, when they were in so much pain and afraid no one would want to marry them, for their scars, and because they might not be able to walk well enough, and they were still afraid they might die from the chimaera, too. I wanted them to know they could still have a happy future, if they were brave and careful. I told them the Elves could heal them, that they'd healed me, and they wanted to hear all about it, so I've been telling them of our travels a little each night before bed."

"What happened to them?" Rarnak asked.

Ron said, "Gisela said a bad wizard burned the City and killed everyone."

Talia gasped and paled, and the others looked at him sharply, and then at Gar.

"That's why I didn't want Rion to hear. He blames himself for enough, already, and I didn't want them maybe even blaming him too. They loved Algor and Verna like a father and mother, and they died with the rest," Gar said somberly.

"After I left you, I rode to the City. I knew something horrible had happened long before I got there. I could see the smoke from miles away, even smell it. The sky was black with it. Once I was there, it was like a nightmare, all smoke and ash and charcoal where the buildings used to be, and it was still burning. Two thirds of Gosa is gone. I couldn't even get near where we used to live, or your house, Tarrell, it was all still so hot, but there was no point in trying. The Elfstone would be gone. Your street was completely destroyed, and ours, and Tailor Street, everything between Westgate and Eastgate, everything south of Aylebourne Way. From what I heard, the fire started on your street, Tarrell, on Amster Way. And that's not all. While the City burned, the chimaera came.

"There were three of them. Most everyone who survived the fire was huddled in Elinor Cemetery and the Downs. The chimaera circled low and started picking people up out of the refugees, holding them up and then dashing them to the ground: all teenage boys, all about Rion's age. I figure the wizard that sent those things came to your house looking for Rion, or his servants did, and when they didn't find him and saw that he had left for good, they got angry and started burning the City to flush him out, and then searched the crowd for him," Gar said grimly.

The others were listening, spellbound and horrified.

"I was trying to help where I could, learn what I could, when one of the chimaera came back. I felled it, arrows in both eyes. I made it tumble from the sky and then finished it off with my sword." He shuddered. "And that horrid thing riding it, just like the one we'd destroyed in the Market.

"Elmoth, you should have seen those poor people! They thought I was a wizard, for having slain those monsters. They were terrified of me, too. I was trying to go then. I had to tell you all what had happened, and I was afraid the crowd might turn on me, when I heard this girl scream, 'Van! Wait, Van! Help me!'

"I didn't realize she was talking to me, but her voice was so desperate. I could hear whoever she was needed help, so I turned and trotted Thenagar back. I saw Gisela, only I didn't know who she was. I'd never met her before. She was covered in soot, in that nightgown, on her knees, and her feet were all burnt and blistered. She got a good look at me then, and said, 'You're not Van!' and seemed frightened, and I realized it was the uniform she'd seen and recognized. It wasn't quite so black then, and from a distance I knew I looked enough like Van. I told her my name was Gar and that I was Van's older brother. I asked how she knew Van. She said she was Gisela, Liana's sister. I was such a fool! I'd worried whether Madame Genevieve survived—I'd been keeping an eye out for her—but I never even thought about Liana's sisters."

Gar turned to Talia. "I didn't see Madame Genevieve anywhere, but she might have gone to the Palace. It was still standing, and they'd maybe have let her in."

Talia nodded, her face pale, and he continued his story. "Gisela told me Anabelle was hurt saving her. She'd pushed her out of the window first and burnt her leg on the way out. She said the bakery burnt so fast. I realized it was because of the flour. You know how flour burns, Ron. They'd been asleep, and Algor and Verna's screams woke them. They both burned to death in their bed in their room downstairs.

"The girls barely made it out the window. They fell onto a pile of garbage in the alley. They had to walk from there, barefoot, with all the smoldering rubble everywhere, until they couldn't even stand: their feet were all burnt and blistered. Then someone with a cart found them and carried them to the Cemetery, where everyone else was gathering. And then Gisela crawled away from Anabelle, to look for help.

"I picked her up and put her on Thenagar. We found Anabelle, and I put her on him too. And I searched until I found someone helping the injured. When they saw it was me, they gave me the bandages and the ointment. They'd seen me kill the chimaera and were grateful for it. I tended to the girls as well as I could. I wanted to get clothes and food, but there was nothing available at any price. And I knew with all the dead, the plagues would start, like grandfather told us had happened in Thenalon. I knew I had to leave quickly. So we left.

"They've been so strong and brave. Liana will be so proud of them. I was afraid you might worry about me, but I had to go slowly. Thenagar could have gone faster, even carrying the three of us, but they're hurt and hadn't ever ridden a horse before and we also had to stop here and there so I could hunt, so we could eat.

"I'm sorry, Tarrell, I didn't think it might upset Rion so much. I didn't know one of the chimaera had come this way and that you'd think it had gotten me. There's at least two more of those things out there, from what I heard, but at least I killed one of the three."

"Don't fret, Gar," Ron said. "I'm proud of you. You rescued the girls and got them here safely. You tended to their injuries and kept their spirits up. You'll make a fine father someday."

Gar seemed surprised.

"I've told you before: I can give praise too, when it's warranted. You're right, Gar, to have kept Rion from hearing. Rion shouldn't learn any of this. He has enough on his conscience—though he shouldn't blame himself—and enough troubles and fears of his own. We'll have to warn the girls not to say anything. He'll figure out some of it, but the less he knows the better."

They agreed. Ara said, "I'll stand watch with Rarnak. The rest of you should get some sleep. Ron, why don't you go back to Rion? We don't want him running off if he wakens in the middle of the night. He'd likely panic if he found you were gone."

Ron nodded and went to Rion, who was still sleeping soundly.

WHEN Lunahr came to Farad, his features were creased in despair.

"Lunahr, what's wrong? Is it Quickwing? Has he been hurt?" Farad asked.

Lunahr shook his head. "He's flying over Gosa. I know what Rion looks like from your thoughts when we touched, but, Farad, how am I to find him for you? Gosa is gone, burnt, most of the City. And there are so many people, all covered in soot. They all look the same! I will try to share my link to Quickwing with you. Your mother was House of Eagles as well as my own. It might work. Try to see from his eyes."

Farad cleared his mind with a quick, practiced exercise and followed his link to Lunahr. Then, very carefully, he crept down the fragile strand binding Lunahr to Quickwing.

It was unsettling at first, flying. He felt dizzy and nauseous as Quickwing swooped and turned. It was horrible. The eagle flew low over a sea of faces, banking and diving over and over again, effortlessly dodging the rocks people threw at him. When Farad realized he was the one guiding Quickwing, his heart soared with the bird. He rose into the air, then banked and dove, tucking his wings for the sheer joy of the speed of the plunge. He saw people cowering, and he turned away, ashamed. Why should they be so terrified of an eagle? Then he saw the body. A chimaera! Of course! No wonder the eagle frightened them. He continued his search more cautiously, soaring over the crowd again and again, and then searching the City street by street.

QUICKWING was not tiring yet, though they'd spent many hours in their search. Would Rion have left the City? The City was certainly no longer the safe haven they'd told him it would be. Jargas had lived near there, but Rion knew he was gone.

The brothers! They had also been from near there, from Ogaten. It was a little town, a few days ride, perhaps five by wagon. Rion might need a wagon, depending upon how hurt he'd been, what Incuban had done. Rion might be dead, either from the nightmares or the fire.

Farad forced the thought away. If Rion was dead, then he was at least free of pain. Incuban wouldn't be torturing him.

He could still torture you with Rion's body, a soft voice whispered in his mind. Farad recognized it in relief as a dark thought of his own. He would not listen. Rion yet lived, he must. Farad set off along the Western Road, heading north toward Ogaten, to find him.

THE enticing aroma of roasting meat greeted Rion as he awoke to the sound of bubbly, cheerful girlish chatter and the feel of warm arms around him. Where was he? Who was holding him? Flummoxed, Rion opened his eyes warily and realized to his mortification he was in Ron's arms. "Are you feeling better, Rion?" Ron asked cautiously, and Rion realized Ron had been careful to phrase it as something he could nod to.

Rion's face flushed in embarrassment and he nodded, sitting up. He winced. He was sore; he hurt everywhere, especially his right leg and left arm and head. He vaguely remembered banging into trees when he fled. It all seemed so surreal, in the bright light of day.

"Are you hungry?" Ron asked.

Rion nodded eagerly.

Ron smiled in obvious relief. "Well, all right, then. Let's see what smells so good."

Rion walked over to the fire with Ron. He was limping, but at least his leg supported him. The girls looked up and smiled at him. "Rion's awake! Hello, Rion. I'm Gisela and this is Anabelle. We're Liana's sisters. We're twins."

"We are not twins, Gisela. We don't have to pretend anymore. I'm thirteen, I'm older. She's only eleven," Anabelle said proudly.

"You're older, but I'm prettier," Gisela said with a flounce.

"You're louder, you mean," Anabelle sniped back.

Rion was overwhelmed by the two of them. He smiled timidly at them.

"He smiled at me!" Gisela said. "I told you he'd like me better!"

"He smiled at both of us," Anabelle said. "We're glad you're feeling better, Rion. Gar's told us so much about you."

Rion looked at Gar quizzically.

Gar said sheepishly, "I've been telling them of our trip, for bedtime stories. Last night was the part with the Elves. They were very impressed by you."

"And we're going to get to meet real Elves too! They're going to heal us!" Gisela said rapturously.

Rion's brow creased and he studied them carefully. He belatedly realized their feet were bandaged. He hadn't noticed at first: their skirts were so long little showed.

"There was a fire at the bakery, and we got hurt," Anabelle explained.

Gisela nodded. "See," she said. She pulled up her sleeve and showed him her arm and then lifted her skirt and showed him her feet.

At Rion's obvious concern, Anabelle said, "It's all right. Gar's been taking care of us." She looked over at Gar lovingly.

"He's so wonderful! I'm going to marry him!" Gisela said.

Gar's face flushed in embarrassment at her declaration, and Rion grinned. He couldn't help himself.

Gisela squealed in delight at his smile and beamed back at him.

"Are you married, Rion?" Anabelle asked shyly, and Rion blushed and shook his head. Anabelle gazed at him with worshipful eyes.

Gar came to his rescue. "Girls, let Rion eat his breakfast, all right?"

Rion sat and eagerly filled a plate. He was about to start eating when he heard the sound of flapping wings. He jumped, startled, knocking his food to the ground, scanning the sky in alarm.

"Rion, relax. It's just an eagle," Ron assured him.

Rion spotted it. Ron was right: it was only an eagle, not a chimaera, but it was a large one, with an impressive wingspan. It circled once overhead and then dived down toward them.

Rion drew his sword in alarm at the bird's unusual behavior, and Gar snatched up his bow and nocked an arrow and let fly. The eagle unexpectedly banked and the arrow missed.

"Did you see that? It dodged my arrow! Rion's right, there's something odd about it. It was headed for him," Gar said, nocking another arrow, tracking it.

The eagle let out a cry and circled again and made to land down the road from them, but Gar shot again, and it veered away. It began circling over them, at a distance.

"I think it's spying on us. It might be signaling someone as to where we are," Ron said. "We need to get to the Elves."

They packed up breakfast and headed for Salenia.

Rion had been ravenous when he awoke, but now he was far too anxious to eat. The eagle wasn't flying off to alert anyone to their presence, but merely by watching and following them at a distance, it was betraying their position. Tarrell tried to distract him by talking, urging him to look at the road and the trees as they traveled, anything instead of scanning the sky. Tarrell encouraged him over and over again to eat, too. Rion knew Tarrell was upset that he hadn't eaten for so long, but he couldn't. His stomach was tied up in knots again.

They had traveled for about two hours when Rion heard the eagle start crying out as if in distress. It dove toward them, skimming just over their heads and then banked and dove again, so fast even Gar could not track it. Then they heard a terrifyingly loud flap of wings.

Rion paled, searching the sky, belatedly realizing the eagle had been trying to warn them with its seemingly aggressive behavior. A chimaera was coming!

"Gisela, Anabelle, Rion, get down!" Gar yelled.

Rion hunkered down in the wagon as ordered and felt a blanket being tossed over him.

"Look out!" Gar cried, and Rion heard the distinctive noise of bowstrings releasing arrows and the screams of horses. There was a loud crash and the sound of splintering wood.

Rion threw off the blanket and stood, drawing his sword. They wouldn't die for him! No one would. He saw in dismay that the wagon with the brothers' goods had been shattered.

"Rion, get down!" he heard Tarrell holler. Then a shadow passed over Rion. He thrust upward with his sword, but a huge taloned foot grabbed him by the waist, and Rion was lifted from the wagon. He stabbed up desperately, but his sword hit scaly hide.

His eyes widened in horror. There was a rider. It was too terrible to be real. It was Lerdon! He leered at Rion, the way he had in the nightmare. Rion slashed at him in revulsion. He was still afraid, terrified, but his fear no longer ruled him. He was not bound and weaponless and helpless, nor trapped in a dream, not this time. Righteous anger filled him. Incuban had killed gentle, kind Lerdon, and turned him into a hideous creature, a cruel monster to be used against his friends. He would see Lerdon find peace, even if he died for it.

Rion started hacking with his sword at the enormous bird leg that held him. The creature's grip tightened instead of loosening, and Rion felt the talons pierce him like daggers. He slashed at the base of the right wing, where it met the creature's back, and tore a great rent along it. Rion looked down and realized to his horror that they were at least a hundred feet in the air. He saw the brothers firing their bows, but the arrows couldn't reach him at such a sharp angle. They were falling back to the ground. Rion heard the girls screaming his name.

It was taking him! He was going to be a prisoner of that sadistic madman from his nightmare. He renewed his attack, this time focusing on Lerdon, stabbing him in the leg. His sword hit with a dull thud, but Lerdon didn't flinch and there was no blood. It was as if he was piercing clay, or a piece of mutton. Lerdon reached for the sword. Rion reversed the blade, turning it toward himself, grasping it with both hands. He wouldn't let this monster take him. He couldn't. He'd kill himself if it was the only way to prevent it.

Suddenly there was a dual scream, the hunting cry of an eagle and the yowl of a cat in pain, and without further warning, the chimaera began falling. It recovered, after plummeting for a short distance, and the eagle cried out once more. The cat-creature screamed again in pain and rage, bucking wildly. Rion was tossed about, and the sword flew from his hands and fell toward the woods below. The cat-creature was twisting and turning, spinning and tumbling from the sky. Lerdon slid from the monster's back, grabbing out as he fell, catching Rion's leg, the way that man had clutched at him and dragged him down into the shark tank so long ago, in Ardock.

Rion kicked Lerdon hard, in the face, over and over, but he wouldn't let go. Finally, Rion felt the sickening crunch of shattering bone beneath his booted foot, and Lerdon fell into the trees. Without Lerdon's weight, the chimaera's frantic flapping was more effective. It slowed its fall somewhat before hitting the trees, at the last moment spinning to take the impact on its back as its wings encircled Rion. Rion heard the cracking of dozens of branches as the monster tore through the forest canopy, plunging toward the ground, taking the brunt of the fall, cushioning Rion from the worst of it, until it finally hit the ground with a resounding thud.

TARRELL had watched Rion's abduction helplessly. He saw the eagle battling the chimaera, gouging its eyes, and then stared in helpless terror as Rion fell from the sky.

He ran to where Rion had fallen. He saw someone moving and thought it was Rion, but then realized to his horror it wasn't. No, it couldn't be! Lerdon was dead! He couldn't be here, he couldn't be alive! Then Tarrell realized in shock that he wasn't. Lerdon's head was tilted at an unnatural angle, his neck broken. His nose was smashed and his jaw hung open, half ripped from his face. And the chimaera in Gosa had gutted him: Tarrell could see the swollen mass of entrails bulging from the wound. He was dead, he must be dead! But he was moving, coming toward him. Tarrell stood paralyzed in revulsion and denial as Lerdon reached for him.

There was a roar from behind Lerdon, and Rion, wielding a thick tree branch like a club, cracked Lerdon across the back of the head with a horrible, dull thwacking sound. Lerdon fell to his knees and Rion brought the branch down upon his head again. With the sound of an overripe melon bursting when dropped upon stone, Lerdon's skull was crushed, and he pitched forward and lay still.

Rion was breathing fast and deeply. He cautiously poked at Lerdon with the branch, but the corpse no longer moved. Rion dropped the branch and limped over to Tarrell, dragging his right leg behind him. He looked at Tarrell in concern, touching his face, patting him on the back, as if he was trying to comfort him, despite what he had just gone through. Then Rion hugged him, but Tarrell was too overcome by all he'd witnessed to embrace him back.

Ron and Gar ran up to them.

"Rion! Thank Elmoth! We thought you'd been killed," Ron cried in relief.

Rion let go of Tarrell and pointed to him, obviously worried for him.

"Tarrell? Are you all right?" Ron asked.

Tarrell didn't answer, he couldn't. He just stood there, shaking.

RION pointed at the rider, and Ron bent to take a closer look at the face, what was left of it. "Lerdon?" he asked sharply, and Rion nodded. Then Rion swayed and almost fell.

"Rion, for Elmoth's sake! You're bleeding! You've fallen out of the sky! Let me help you," Ron scolded.

Rion smiled weakly at them. He was bruised and bashed and bloodied, he could scarcely stand, but he felt better than he had in weeks, since before he'd been captured by those terrible men when they first arrived in Gosa. He would never be made a helpless victim again. He had found himself.

Ara came out from the trees. "Blessed Elmoth be praised. The chimaera's dead and it's truly a miracle that you survived such a fall."

Ron helped Rion to the wagon and Gar helped Tarrell.

The girls were staring wide-eyed at Rion. Gar stripped off Rion's shirt. The talons had pierced his back and his side. The wounds were relatively small, but deep. Ron started tending to them. "We have to make sure these are thoroughly cleaned. Puncture wounds from a creature such as that are bound to fester if not treated properly."

GAR heard an eagle cry and looked up. The eagle had come out from under the trees, more staggering than hopping, dragging its right wing limply behind it. Gar drew his bow to put it out of its misery.

Gisela cried, "Gar, no!"

"It's cruel to leave it so hurt, Gisela," Gar reasoned.

"Please, Gar? Can't we bring it to the Elves? It saved Rion from that horrible thing. It made it fall!" Gisela pleaded.

"Gisela," Gar began, but he saw her face and sighed. Gar put aside his bow and drew his sword instead, holding it at his side. He approached the eagle cautiously.

It cried out to him, fell over, and then shook its leg. Gar saw a little metal tube on the leg it was shaking. Then it stood again, lurching toward him.

Gar stared at it, astonished. It looked as if it had been showing him it was bringing him something! "I won't hurt you. Can I see what's on your leg?" Gar asked, feeling foolish.

The eagle obediently lay down and held out its leg to him.

Gar stared at it in disbelief. He reached for it carefully, well knowing the damage its talons or beak might do to his hand. But it was docile, as if it were a tame songbird, rather than a hunting bird that had just felled a chimaera.

Gar took the little metal tube off its leg. It was lightweight, as if it was hollow, and there was a seam down the center. He twisted and it opened, revealing a tightly rolled piece of paper. He pulled it out, unrolled it, and read the name at the top. "It's for Rion," he called to the others in astonishment. "It's a message for him and for the Elves." His eyes flew to the bottom. "Elmoth! It's from Thorn!"

Gar started to head for the wagon, but the eagle called out, and Gisela did as well. "Gar, you can't leave him!"

Gar turned back to the eagle and swallowed. "I'm going to cover its eyes, to keep it calm," Gar said, snatching up his blanket and heading for it.

The eagle cried out and started to hop away from him, as if it had heard and understood him. Gar covered it anyway, but it didn't calm: it clawed and fought. It yanked the blanket off, then called out and lay still.

"Can't you just carry it?" Gisela asked. "It promises it will be good. Don't you see? It doesn't want to be blinded."

Gar glared at it. "Do you promise you'll not try to claw my face off, if I carry you to the wagon?" Gar asked skeptically. He must be mad to even think of risking it, after what the obearn had done to him!

To his astonishment, the eagle bobbed its head up and down, as if answering him. Then it lay very still.

Gar gritted his teeth and lifted it, fearfully. It was huge, but lighter than he'd thought it would be. His misgivings evaporated as it remained perfectly docile while he carried it to the wagon. "Be careful, girls. It seems tame enough, but it's hurt, and it's a wild bird, not a pet," Ron cautioned.

The eagle called out, cocking its head, peering at Rion.

"Look, it's worried about Rion," Gisela said.

RION stared at the eagle, wishing he could speak. Ara cut through Rion's right pants leg from ankle to waist. His leg looked terrible. His kneecap was twisted to one side, and his knee was swollen to at least twice the size it should be. Ara bandaged his knee. Talia tried to pin the pieces of his pants back together after he was done, but she gave up apologetically. Between the swelling and the bandages, there wasn't enough fabric to cover it.

Gar handed Rion the note once they were done tending to him, and his eyes widened as he read it.

> *Rion, my dear friend,*
>
> *I know this note will not find you well. You will have been hurt, I fear more than once, by the time this finds you. But you are strong and brave, and you must endure.*
>
> *I beg you not to listen to anything Incuban, King of Lies, tells you or shows you. We would have warned you of Him, had we ever thought there was the need. It hurts us almost beyond bearing that He injures you to harm us.*
>
> *Your friends have not turned against you as you fear. They would not. Incuban feeds upon fear. He delights in terror and torment. He seeks to weaken you. You cannot withstand Him alone. Your friends are your greatest strength. Talon holds the Power to heal you, to restore your voice, your health, your spirit, even your smile.*
>
> *You must leave Gosa and go to the Elves in Salenia. Show this message to them. They will bring you safely to us. Your friends, any who you might choose to bring, are welcome amongst us as well, but there is danger here. We are at war, and they would be safer and happier where they are.*
>
> *Please believe that Hunter, Farad, for his given name was not a lie, would pay almost any price to see you safe. When next you see him, remember the Man you knew and trusted in Gosa, not the dark shadow from your dreams.*
>
> *There are so many secrets of this world you have yet to unlock, Rion, so many friends yet to meet, so many good memories yet to be forged. Do not surrender to despair. Stay strong and know that you are truly loved by many. We await you.*
>
> *—Thorn*
>
> *P.S. Please see the eagle who bears this message returned safely, or if so fated, buried in death, for he is more than he appears and is very dear to a friend. If he yet lives, he will accompany you on your journey, and aid in guiding you to us. You could ask for no finer or more loyal guardian.*

There was more, a second, shorter portion, but it was written in Elvish.

Rion showed the note to the others. Tarrell read it aloud. When he finished, he said, "Thorn would have been proud of you, Rion. I'm so proud of you. You fought them and kept fighting them, even when you were falling. Then, on the ground, I had a sword, and I just stood there when that… thing… came for me. And you stopped it with a branch! You did what Hunter told you to do, it seems so long ago. You didn't let the dead make you feel less than you are. Not even the walking dead." He shuddered. "I've been so worried about you, but it sounds like you might even get your voice back now."

RON said, "We'll need to have the Elves take you to them as soon as we can. I told you not to worry about being a danger to Ogaten and the mill, but after this attack, and what we heard of Gosa, you'd best leave as quickly as we can manage."

Rion looked at him oddly, and Ron realized he'd broken his own edict about Gosa. "I'll not tell you more. All you need to know is that it will be safer for the town once you're gone. It's time we got moving again."

Rion shook his head. He laid one hand down and mimed scooping with the other, then covered his other hand over and over, and pointed to the woods.

Ron thought he understood. "You want to bury Lerdon?" he asked.

Rion nodded a firm "yes."

Ron said, "It's only right we do so. He deserves to be at peace. It's not his fault his body was used to evil purpose. He was a good friend and a fine man."

The girls were watching, wide-eyed. "Who are you talking about burying?" Gisela asked.

Gar said, "Never mind. We won't be long at it." He and Ron went to lay Lerdon to rest, while Ara and Rarnak stayed by the wagon to guard Rion, Tarrell, and the girls.

RION tapped Tarrell and his sword, indicated falling with his hands, and then pointed toward the trees and mimed searching.

"Your sword? I saw it fall. It was my coming-of-age gift to you. You want me to try to find it for you?" Tarrell asked.

Rion nodded eagerly.

"I'll do my best," Tarrell said, and went with Ara to look near where Rion had landed, leaving Rarnak to guard Rion and the girls.

Rion watched the eagle, intrigued. The eagle looked right back at him and let out a call. Rion tentatively reached out a hand, and when it seemed safe enough, stroked its feathers gently.

It was not long before Ara came back to join Rarnak guarding Rion and the others. The rest soon returned with Rion's sword, explaining that Ron and Gar had finished the burial as quickly as they could, and then helped Tarrell search for the blade. It was Gar's keen eyes that had spotted it.

Rion smiled his thanks to all of them and then carefully cleaned the blade and sheathed it.

BEFORE they set out, Ron said, "Rion, please, as I told Tarrell before with the bandits, next time let your guards do your fighting for you and stay down when we tell you to."

Rion shook his head, pointing at his purse.

Ron said, "Paid or not, Rion, we are here to protect you. It's our decision."

Rion pointed to himself and his sword.

Ron turned to Tarrell. "I warned you this would happen, when you bought it for him."

Tarrell said, "But you still helped me pick the blade."

"Of course. At least I knew he'd have a good one, then. If he bought his own, and he would have, he might not have selected as well. Many a young man as slender as he is has picked a sword too heavy or too long, and it's led to tragedy." Ron was careful to say "slender" rather than "small." Rion was sensitive about his boyish build, and Ron didn't want to say anything to upset him. He sighed. "Come, we'd best go now."

"But your wagon! Everything you own is here. We can't just leave it," Tarrell argued.

"We'll have to and hope we are able to come back for it before someone else comes down this road. Few enough people usually come to Ogaten, though I suspect we'll soon have many." He did not say a flood of refugees. He'd already said too much before Rion.

LUNAHR watched Farad, worried. He had been guiding Quickwing for many hours now. He was afraid Farad might lose himself, as he had when he first controlled Slash, though he realized the circumstances were far different.

Suddenly Farad started breathing quickly and heavily. Something was wrong! Quickwing was in danger. Lunahr felt it instantly. He tried to extend into the link to Quickwing's core, but he could not: Farad was already there, and neither the core nor the link was strong enough for more than one person to communicate with him at a time.

Farad gasped and tensed. Lunahr could tell he was in pain. He realized Quickwing might die and feared for him. But if Farad was in Quickwing's core, so far down the link, might he not die as well? Farad might not be able to leave quickly enough to return to his own core in time.

Lunahr tried calling to Farad, with his voice and his mind, but was thrust away by both Farad and Quickwing so violently Lunahr feared the link might shatter.

WHEN Farad found Rion and his guards and friends already on their way to the Elves, or perhaps to the mill or the town of Ogaten, he was so overjoyed, so relieved to see Rion sitting and eating, instead of lying lifelessly on the wagon, or worse, writhing and howling in madness, that he made a mistake. He came diving out of the sky toward him, calling to him. Rion heard and saw him and leapt up, but Farad saw fear on his face, rather than joy.

Rion was drawing his sword and Farad saw Gar unsling his bow and nock an arrow against him. He thought he need not worry, that Gar's arrow would surely fly wild. How could it near him when he dove so fast? But he dodged from it instinctively and it was fortunate he did so: it was all that saved Quickwing. Aramark the Elder must not have been the only one to train Gar! Even a Horseman of Aralon would not have made such a shot, and Aramark was from Thenalon. He would have thought only an Elf could have shot so well. Farad knew even he could not have matched that shot. He admitted that Gar was a better bowman. It had been decades since he'd met anyone who could outshoot him. His respect for the brothers grew.

Farad tried a different approach, a less threatening one. Incuban had said in the nightmare He had sent a chimaera after Rion. Again he had forgotten that, as an eagle, he would be feared. Farad tried to land down the road and hop to them, but Gar was ready for him.

Frustrated, he climbed to a safe distance and circled them. Perhaps he would wait down the road for them? Or just accompany them, until they reached the Elves. The Elves could read the note first and give it to their group. He watched them break camp and start their journey anew.

When he had gotten closer to Rion, he was concerned again. Rion appeared gaunt and wearied, as if he had neither been sleeping nor eating well. Farad well knew the look: frazzled, haunted, and so afraid. Farad wondered at all that might have happened to him and his friends in Gosa and upon the road.

He flew overhead, shadowing them, but not trying to approach again for a while, not until Farad saw the chimaera following the road, heading toward them. He threw caution to the winds, calling and diving, trying to warn them, fearing an eagle's cry was not enough. They must have understood it, though, for Rion and the two young girls that traveled with them hid.

The chimaera was so fast! It swooped out of the sky and dove for them. Farad saw the horses go wild in terror and he saw the riders fight them. Only Gar had mastery of his mount. The chimaera picked up one of the wagons and threw it at Gar, just as he was trying to fire. Still, he shot it and wounded it, barely dodging the splintering wreck that shattered on the ground.

At the sound, Rion rose, sword drawn, revealing himself, and Farad cried out in dismay. Rion looked afraid and desperate, but he attacked the chimaera as it came for him. It snatched Rion from the wagon and rose with him. Instead of cowering in fear, Rion renewed his attack, striking at both beast and rider, although to little avail. Then Farad looked on in helpless horror as in desperation, Rion turned the sword upon himself.

Farad dove for the chimaera, clawing at its face, and pecking at its eye with his chisel-like beak. He felt the eye burst like a grape in his mouth. He could not risk looking at Rion as he dodged the chimaera's claws and headed for the other eye. If he blinded it, it would have to land. He hoped it could do so safely enough, but Rion was right: even death was better than capture by the Enemy.

Farad scored a hit to its other eye, but at a terrible price. Quickwing was hit by a slashing paw; it batted him and tore his wing. The pain was agonizing. His right wing all but useless, he started tumbling from the sky, desperately flapping with his left, trying to control or at least slow his fall, so Quickwing might survive it. He would abandon neither him nor Rion.

Just before they hit the trees, Quickwing tucked his left wing in, trying to protect it, but he could not shield his right. Farad did the best he could to control his fall as Quickwing plunged through the branches of a fir, the cushioning needles tearing at him even as they slowed his fall further. By the time he finally reached the ground, he hit hard and lay stunned.

He heard a louder crash, and a second one, louder still. The Revenant and the chimaera, or Rion and the chimaera? As he hopped and staggered toward the sound, he heard the sounds of battle, quickly ended. He heard people talking but the voices were becoming softer. They were heading for the road! They were moving too fast! He struggled toward them, afraid they would leave him here, the note undelivered and Quickwing unable to fly.

He emerged from the trees and approached them. He saw Gar draw his bow against him again, though this time his face showed only sadness. Farad had not thought they might attack him again. He was as good as dead. He knew Gar would not miss, and he could not dodge this arrow. Farad knew he must leave Quickwing to die alone. He would flee along the link in time to save himself, and hope they might find the note on Quickwing's body.

But one of the girls called out, and pleaded for mercy for him, and instead of attacking him, Gar came for him. He spoke to him, and Farad did all he asked and more, to Gar's astonishment.

Farad saw Rion then, further wounded. He could scarcely walk. But incredibly, to Farad's overwhelming relief and joy, although Rion did not appear strong, he looked enduring and proud. He'd battled his demons, true demons, and won.

Gar took the note from him and gave it to Rion, who read it silently. Then Tarrell read it aloud. Afterward, Rion gestured to the others that they must bury someone, and they named him: Lerdon, his murdered friend, one of the two Revenants that Incuban had tortured Rion with in the nightmare. He marveled at Rion anew, that he might still find compassion in his heart for the Man, when all that remained was the monster that had attacked him.

Farad wished either he or Rion could speak, but for now it was enough to see him alive and relatively well and whole, when he might have found a shattered husk instead of the bright light before him. Rion called out to him, then reached out his hand and gently stroked his feathers.

THEY urged their horses forward. Rion was sitting in the back of the wagon. He unpacked Talon's book and opened it to the Elvish dictionary, peering intently at the Elvish postscript to the letter. He took out a paper and a thin piece of artist's lead. The eagle was riding in the wagon next to Rion, since it could no longer fly. It cocked its head, looking from Rion to the letter to the book. At first it appeared puzzled, and then agitated. Rion smiled at it, and stroked its head lightly with his finger, and the eagle quieted.

Rion smiled triumphantly as he wrote a word in Common. His many long hours with the book were paying off. By early afternoon, he had translated the Elvish message. He'd already known many of those words by sound, though not by sight, having concentrated on the Common phonetic equivalent when learning the language. He was far better at spoken than written Elvish. Their elegant script was still a struggle for him.

Rion showed the translation to Tarrell and gestured, speaking with his hand, and pointed to the others. Tarrell read it aloud.

> *Cousins,*
>
> *I hope this letter finds you well. Forgive me my brevity, but there is great need for it.*
>
> *Aid the bearer of this letter, Rion, as you would aid me. He is precious to me, and to my sister, as well as those of the Watch.*
>
> *He is in terrible danger and in dire need of aid. Incuban has been tormenting him. Already he cannot speak and by the time he finds you, or his friends find you for him, he may well have been driven mad or been terribly injured, or both.*
>
> *Do all you can for him. Deliver Rion and his friends, if they choose to accompany him, safely to the Watchtower. Our forces are massing there. Lithunia of your people knows of it. He can guide Rion there. Once there, Talon will heal him.*
>
> *May we meet in brighter days.*
>
> *Eladar, Prince of Riviera-that-was*

Ron asked, puzzled, "Who is Lithunia?"

Ara said somberly. "That's Swiftsong's given name. Grandfather spoke it to me. Please, none of you should repeat it. Elves are very protective of their names."

Gar said. "What do you think he meant by Riviera-that-was? You don't think—I mean, nothing could have happened to Riviera, could it?"

Ron said, "It might mean it's been changed somehow. Perhaps Eladar's family no longer rules there? Something might have happened to his father, King Laranela. I suppose we'll find out when we see him."

LATE in the afternoon, the wagon pulled up to the mill. Ron was relieved to see it still stood. He'd not said anything to the others, but he had been afraid the chimaera they'd seen that second night might have come this far and destroyed it and Ogaten as well.

Van came out of the mill doorway with a sack of flour on his shoulder just as they pulled up. He glanced up in surprise then cried out in joy, dropped the bag, and ran to them. When Van saw that Rion was bloodied and bandaged and his wife's sisters were with them, his joy turned to concern. "What's happened? What are you all doing here?"

Ron was about to answer when Gisela piped up. "Van! We've missed you! Gar saved us from the fire and from the chimaera, and we're going to see the Elves so they can heal us, just like Gar told us about!"

"What fire? What do you mean a chimaera? Why heal you?" their youngest brother asked in concern.

"We were burnt in the fire," Gisela said matter-of-factly. "Van, where's Liana? She's here, isn't she?"

"Of course. I'm sorry, I'll go get her." Van went back inside and a few moments later Andra, Liana, and Markara came out.

Liana squealed and ran to her sisters, hugging them joyfully. But when they didn't leap from the wagon to follow her, she realized something was wrong and belatedly saw their bandaged feet. "What's wrong with your feet?"

Gisela said, "It's all right, Liana. We burnt them in the fire, but the Elves are going to heal us, just like they healed Gar and Ara and Ron and Van in Erenia, when Gar and Ara almost died."

Markara looked at them sharply and Ron winced. They'd not told their father anything about that when they'd recounted the story of their travels.

"What happened to you, Rion?" Van asked.

Anabelle piped up. "Oh, he can't speak, Van. You mustn't ask him questions he can't nod to. It makes him feel bad. An evil wizard put a curse on him and then, on the way here, a chimaera grabbed him and flew off with him, but the eagle saved him. Only he fell and the eagle's hurt now, too."

Gar said, "Anabelle, I think you've said enough. You're going to upset your sister, Father, Lisandra, and Van. They'll want to hear all about it, but we have to bring you three to the Elves first, or four, I suppose. There's the eagle, too. Ara, can you and Van and Rarnak go with a wagon to get our things, while Ron and Tarrell and I take the girls and Rion and the eagle to see the Elves?"

"Of course, Gar. Pay my respects to Swiftsong when you see him," Ara said.

Markara turned to Ron and eyed him sternly. "And then I'll hear all that's happened, both what you neglected to tell me before of your journey, and what's happened since we last saw you."

Ron nodded reluctantly.

THE one group left for the Elves and the other for the shattered wagon, leaving Andra with her father, Liana, and the beautiful woman who'd traveled with her brothers. Andra eyed her fancy dress, which had obviously been handmade just for her. "Ara or Gar?"

"Excuse me?" the woman asked politely.

"Are you here with Ara or Gar? It'd not be Ron. You're much too young for him and not at all his type, and he'd not waste his coin on such fancy clothes," Andra said bluntly.

"Lisa," her father scolded. "That's enough." He turned to the young woman. "I'm Markara. This is Liana, my son Van's wife. And this," he said with a disapproving glare, "is my daughter, Lisandra."

"I'm not here with Ara or Gar. I'm Talia. I'm Rarnak's...."

"Excuse me. I've work to do," Andra interrupted, turning and leaving quickly. She'd heard enough. She let her bluster hide her pain as it always did. Rarnak! Talia was Rarnak's, either his sweetheart, his betrothed, or his wife. What did it matter which?

Andra hadn't been able to stop thinking about Rarnak since his visit, when Van had returned, and later when he'd come again with her brothers. He'd even brought her a gift.

No one ever thought to give her things, other than Van or Ron. He'd put thought into it too. And he'd helped her work, and he'd talked to her. He'd been so sad, but she'd even gotten him to smile the way she sometimes got Ron to. She'd thought maybe Rarnak had liked her, just a little bit, too. She'd hoped she might see him again, the next time the others came to the mill. But now he had found Talia.

She was beautiful. They were always beautiful, all the other women. She'd hoped for too much. She'd been painfully reminded again how foolish she was. What use were hopes and dreams to one such as her, who'd live and die here, alone and unloved, unwed and childless?

It had been bad enough with Liana here and Van and Father fawning all over her. But then Liana had gone and got herself pregnant, and of course mustn't do any of the heavy lifting or the real work. She dabbled at cooking, but many days claimed to be too ill to do it. It seemed she could do nothing but sit and look pretty. And now her two frilly little sisters had come. Father didn't only have one pretty little new daughter to replace the big, bony, ugly one he'd never loved: now he had three. And Talia, too.

Andra was sobbing, now. She ran around to the back of the mill, to her mother's grave, and fell over it, crushing the delicate flowers that grew there, watering them with her tears.

MARKARA studied the fine Lady before him, his face flushing. "That's just Lisa's way. Pay her no mind. You were saying?"

Talia blushed. "I'm Talia, Rarnak's sister. And I'm betrothed to Tarrell."

Liana beamed at her. "Talia? Rarnak found you? That's wonderful! Welcome! But what's been happening? You can tell us. We've no need to wait for the rest of the men."

"Of course," Talia said, and she went into the mill with them and began telling the story of all that had happened.

Chapter 4
Sanctuary

TARRELL, Ron, and Gar walked along the riverbank with Rion and the girls. Ron was carrying Anabelle and Gar was carrying Gisela, to her delight. Tarrell had his arm about Rion, to aid him. Rion's teeth were clenched against the pain from his leg, and he walked slowly, holding the eagle in the crook of his arm as if it were a baby. It was docile, but alert.

A beautiful female Elf stepped out from amongst the trees toward them. Her silver hair flowed well past her waist, nearly to her knees, and her dress was filmy, almost transparent, of the palest green, made of many layers, each adding a depth of color. Her eyes were the same peridot shade as her clothes.

Rion was surprised by the hue of her eyes. From all he had seen and read, if she was a Wood Elf, she should have had blond hair, or if a River Elf, blue eyes. Perhaps she was of mixed parentage? As far as he knew, that was not a common occurrence.

The girls stared at her wide-eyed and smiled timidly.

Ron bowed to her. "*Sehla*, Meander. *Alethia hapo un*," he said in Elvish.

Rion translated automatically in his head. Ron had said "Hello" and then the formal phrase "Please help us," which always preceded any request for assistance when speaking to the Elves.

Ron switched to Common. "Our friend Rion is injured. He is a friend of Prince Eladar of Riviera and bears a note to your people from him, requesting your aid. Rion has lost his voice to foul wizardry and cannot speak to ask for your aid on his own behalf. But also, these are the sisters of my brother Van's wife. They were injured in a fire and are in need of healing as well. Might you grant the favor of your aid to our family?"

Meander's eyes widened. "Fire? They have been burnt?" A shudder passed through her body as she uttered the last word. Her voice was soft and low, and she spoke Common musically.

Ron said, "Yes."

Her eyes filled with tears. "Yet still they can smile?" She gently touched Anabelle's face but then snatched her hand away. "She is in pain!"

Anabelle said, "My burn's a lot bigger than Gisela's. It hurts a lot, sometimes, but it's not so bad with the medicine Gar's been giving us. And he tries to keep me from thinking about it. It's much worse when I do."

"She is so brave!" Meander said. She turned to Rion. "It is our honor to aid both them and the Prince's friend. Please, come with me," Meander said and headed for the water.

Rion watched her curiously. So she must be a River Elf, then. That made sense, as from what the brothers said, they were in Salenia. But the Elves couldn't actually live in the River, could they? Rion hadn't seen a path, but where her feet touched the ground, one became plainly visible.

As they approached the bank, Rion saw it was high here, sloping steeply downward, almost ten feet above the level of the water. It was made of mud and clay, with some bushes rooted here and there.

Meander touched a large clump of bushes, and they moved aside from her hand to form an opening. Rion saw in surprise that there was a crevice or cave, but it was lit, instead of dark.

They entered a cool, moist tunnel of earth and river rock. As they walked deeper within the bank, it branched several times, and Rion soon lost his way. Then the branch on the left unexpectedly opened into a large room.

It was well lit and surprisingly warm and dry. The floor of the room was made of smooth river stones. There were soft-looking cushions upon large slabs of rock that appeared to be beds, with short stone pillars on either side of them. There was also a large stone slab along the opposite wall, with flattened boulders around it that might have been a table with chairs. Everything was very simple and primitive, nothing like what they had seen in Erenia. Did all River Elves live like this? Was Elanara's home Kingdom of Riviera the same, or different?

"I will help the children first," Meander offered. She opened a drawer in one of the stone pillars Rion had thought were solid and produced a jar of glass with a wax-sealed top and a bundle of fresh bandages. She had the girls sit on one of the beds and asked to see their injuries.

Anabelle lifted her skirt. She was no longer so shy, now that she knew Rion, Tarrell, and Ron better. Rion saw she had a bandage from her knee nearly to her waist. Gar gently unwound the bandage, exposing a large, horrible burn.

Meander cried out at the sight of it and collapsed. Ron dove toward her and somehow managed to catch her before she struck the stone floor. She appeared to be unconscious. The jar, fortunately, fell onto the bed instead of the floor, where it would have undoubtedly shattered.

"I've never seen Meander or any of the Elves look ill before. We need to get her to one of the others, to help her," Gar said, his voice fully of worry.

Anabelle's eyes had filled with tears. It was obvious she was frightened.

"I'll carry Meander to them," Ron volunteered. "You and Tarrell take care of the girls." He swept Meander's legs out from under her with his free arm, cradling her like a child, the way he had carried Rion earlier in the woods, and headed for the door.

"She'll be all right," Gar reassured the others, but he didn't sound certain of it.

RON took Meander from the room and looked about. He knew the way back outside, in spite of the many twists and turns of the route they had taken, though he realized there was no guarantee the tunnels still led in the direction they had before. He suspected individual Elven dwellings might be as protected by their magic as their Kingdoms were. He headed to the left, intending to head farther into the riverbank, but then he saw a male Elf whom he did not recognize coming quickly down the corridor toward him. Ron had never seen an Elf move in haste before. He opened his mouth to speak, but the Elf spoke first.

"Give her to me," the Elf demanded abruptly and abrasively in Common as he approached, his face twisted in rage. He snatched Meander from Ron's arms. "What have you done to her?"

Ron had never seen an angry Elf and hoped to never see one again. The soldiers in Erenia had been cold and harsh, even cruel, but this Elf was truly enraged. Ron had to fight the urge to fall prone at his feet in obsequiousness. Though oddly, instead of the Elf glaring at him as he would have expected, now that he was before him, or even looking at Meander, the Elf kept his face down and turned to the side and the floor.

Ron remained upright, refusing to grovel, but he did bow his head in deference to the Elf. "Forgive us. We meant no harm. I am Ronamark, son of Markara. I came with three friends in need of healing, as well as my brother and another friend. Meander started to tend to the injured but suddenly fell ill."

"Go and do not return!" the Elf commanded imperiously. He turned to go, but then Meander stirred in his arms and he stopped, speaking to her tenderly and gently in Elvish, his voice now warm and compassionate.

Meander's eyes opened and she spoke weakly to him. He seemed to argue with her. Then he glared at Ron. "She asks if the jar broke," the Elf said reluctantly.

"No, it fell upon the bed," Ron assured them both.

"Inside is an ointment. It is very special and very rare. It will heal them when Meander cannot. Spread it on the… burns," the Elf hesitated on the word as if speaking it was difficult for him. "Use it sparingly. Only a thin coat is needed, but be sure their wounds are covered fully. Then bandage the girls and remove them from our tunnels. When the sun has set tomorrow, you may unwrap their bandages, but not before. The sun's fire must not touch their wounds too soon. Meander will return when the girls are safely out of the tunnels, to help the Man you brought," he said, scowling, obviously not approving of the idea.

"If Meander is ill, perhaps someone else could help us? We never meant to cause Meander harm and would not want to risk worsening whatever affliction she might be suffering from," Ron said solicitously. He would never knowingly cause harm to one of the Elves, nor would he want them to harbor ill will against his family, as they dwelt within their Kingdom only by their grace.

The Elf stared at him intently, and some of the tension and much of the anger left his face and his posture and bearing became far less rigid. "Your compassion is unexpected and appreciated, but do not concern yourself. From her words and your own, I understand now that you did not harm her intentionally. She will recover, once she is away from the girls. But she is our only true healer. No one else here can aid your friend as she can, and now that she has seen his pain, she will not rest until she has healed him. It is not something a Man might understand."

"Then I will do as you ask. But please, know that we did not mean to cause distress to Meander or to you. We would not have come had we known we might harm her by it," Ron said sincerely.

The Elf nodded in acceptance of his words without speaking further and then carried Meander down the hall.

Ron returned to the room. Rion was sitting upon one of the beds, stroking the eagle's head lovingly.

"Don't get too attached to it, Rion," Tarrell cautioned. "Remember, it belongs to a friend of Eladar's."

Rion nodded.

Both girls still looked sad and frightened, in spite of Gar's efforts to soothe them. "Gar, I want to go back to the mill," Anabelle said, tears dripping down her cheeks.

Ron spoke up. "Anabelle, it's all right. Meander just isn't feeling well. She told me how to help you and Gisela. She'll be better soon, and then she'll come back to help Rion."

Ron told Gar in Thenalonese what had happened and suggested Gar be the one to tend to the girls.

GAR opened the jar. There was a viscous paste inside that smelled of honeysuckle and somehow of rain as well. He dabbed his finger into it and started covering Anabelle's burn.

A look of surprise came over Anabelle's face. "The pain is gone! It feels strange: sort of warm and tingly."

Gar finished her leg and then treated her feet. Then he bandaged her, in the Elven bandages. They were incredibly soft and elastic, and the material stuck to itself, making it amazingly easy to use.

Then he turned his attentions to Gisela and tended to her as well. Gisela laughed. "It tickles!"

They were all relieved as the girls started chattering about the Elves, their pain and despair forgotten.

Ron said, "The other Elf said to take the girls back outside."

"How are we supposed to do that? I have no idea which way to go," Gar said, vexed.

"THEN I guess you're lucky I was here. Next time, pay better attention, idiot!" Ron scolded. Then a subtle shift in the air behind him made him turn toward the door.

"Now that they are no longer in pain, it is safe for me to return," Meander said from the doorway. She was not smiling, nor did she look well, but she was walking unaided.

She entered the room and handed each of the girls something. "These are for you, for being so brave. They are a gift from my husband, Whitewater. They are shells from the sea. If you place them to your ears, you can hear the crash of the waves upon the shore."

The girls took them timidly, thanking her, and then pressed them to their ears and squealed in surprise and delight.

Meander's face was lit by a smile, and some color returned to her face, as if merely seeing their joy physically renewed her. "Much better. But now I would have the rest of you return to the mill, so I may tend to your friend. He will be here for some time. Whitewater will show you the way out," Meander assured them.

The stern-looking Elf from before appeared in the doorway, only now he did not appear nearly as forbidding. Ron was surprised. He had not known Meander was married. No wonder he had been so angered, so protective!

Whitewater gestured for them to follow him.

Tarrell glanced uncertainly at Rion, but Rion smiled and waved him away. Tarrell turned to Ron for reassurance that it was all right to leave him.

"He'll be fine, Tarrell. Meander will tend to him," Ron said confidently.

Tarrell turned to her and bowed to her. "Thank you for your aid."

She smiled at him. "You are quite welcome."

Ron picked up Anabelle and Gar carried Gisela. Their feet might not pain them any longer, but they did not want to risk damaging them further. Pain often prevented one from worsening an injury, to help ensure it might properly heal.

They exited the room, Tarrell gazing behind at Rion as he departed.

RION made a shooing motion with his hand and smiled, trying to reassure Tarrell that it was all right to leave.

Tarrell did so, with obvious reluctance.

Once Tarrell was gone, Rion pointed to Meander and then the eagle.

"Of course, I will heal him as well. But you first," Meander said.

Rion shook his head.

She seemed surprised. "You wish me to heal the eagle before you?"

Rion nodded.

"Why?" she asked, curious.

Rion was frustrated for a moment, but then saw a glass pitcher of water by the bed he had not noticed before. Had it only now magically appeared? Had it been masked, hidden somehow, like the trail, so he'd not notice it? Or had he just been so overwhelmed he'd failed to see it? He realized it did not matter, though he yearned to know the answer. He poured some of the water into his hand even as he marveled at the look and feel of the glass, as he had admired the jar. Glass vessels were a prized rarity in the Lands of Men. Only those of Thenalon had mastered the art of glass blowing.

Meander watched, appearing intrigued, as Rion dipped his finger into the water on his palm and wrote with it upon the stone stand by the bed, "HURT SAVING ME."

To his astonishment, Meander looked a little flustered then, almost sheepish. "Forgive me. I forgot about your voice. I'm still not thinking clearly, although the pain and nausea is gone. You wish me to help the eagle first because he was injured aiding you? Then so I shall."

Meander ran her hands lightly along the bird, taking special interest in his damaged wing. From the expression upon her face, and the way she grew rigid, she seemed to somehow share the bird's pain when she touched him. She got out a small flask from another concealed drawer, poured the contents into a bowl and held it out to the eagle. "You must drink this, Proud One. I will mend your wing while you sleep," she said in Common.

The eagle obediently drank. Rion wasn't sure whether it had truly understood her or had just been thirsty, but he thought it might be the former. Only moments later, the eagle fell limp.

Meander turned to Rion. "We must allow time for the elixir to take full effect upon him. I can see your leg is injured, but I must examine it, as well as the rest of your body, while you are awake, so you can tell me of your injuries, if I require it. I will need for you to get undressed."

Rion blushed at the thought of undressing before someone so beautiful.

Meander smiled at him, and her smile was like Aras's and Elanara's, full of warmth, but with a hint of mischief, rather than like Eladar's, which was much more full of mischief. "You may keep on your undergarment. I don't have to examine you that fully," she added, eyes twinkling.

Rion blushed more darkly and began undressing self-consciously.

"Please lie down on your back," she said, once he was done, and he did so.

She examined him carefully, as she had with the eagle, not merely with her eyes. She ran her fingers lightly over him everywhere. He shivered at her touch, thankful his manhood somehow did not stiffen with it. He had only felt something so wonderful once before, in his dream, and the horror surrounding it had made it into torture rather than pleasure. He marveled that the memory did not bring the terror it should. He suspected Meander might be keeping it at bay somehow.

Meander noted the puncture wounds and cuts and bruises and scrapes, and of course, the terrible injury to his leg. "You have done much damage to your knee. It is a wonder you can walk at all. You have all but crippled yourself. Were a Man to treat you, you would never be able to run again, nor kneel, nor even bend your leg, and you would live in constant pain until the end of your days," she said in sympathy.

Rion swallowed hard, at the thought of being permanently crippled, when he was already mute.

"Forgive me! I perhaps should not have told you so. I am still not quite myself. I was merely anticipating the length of time it will take to heal you, and the amount of pain it will cause me to do so. But I can assure you, you will heal fully. It will be as if you were never injured."

Rion looked at her wide-eyed. Healing him would harm her? He could never allow such a terrible thing! He began sitting up, shaking his head adamantly, reaching for his clothes, but a gentle hand upon his arm stopped him.

"I have done it again," Meander said with a sigh. "I should not have told you healing you will harm me. I forget sometimes how little Men understand of such things, when few enough of even my own people understand.

"All of us used to wield such Power, once, long, long ago, for healing, for art, for music, for growing plants, for so many things. But the soil of this land is weak, compared to our own, and so the water that flows over it and the trees that grow upon it do not have the Power they should. Of all of us in Salenia, only Whitewater and I and one other possess such Power."

Her face lit with love and joy. "And my husband is yet young. I am almost five hundred whereas he came of age only a handful of years ago. He would be lost without me, I fear. He is so protective of me, one might think he is the older one. But he angers so easily, and his rage is quite dangerous to all but me and one other. It saddens me that the rest keep their distance from him because of it. I worry, sometimes, what he will do, once I am gone, for we were born for one another, and no other can complete him as I do."

Her voice held such sadness, now, that Rion wanted to weep at the thought of Whitewater living in loneliness for four and a half centuries, until he might join her in death.

She shook her head and smiled again. "Forgive me again! I do not know why I have said such things to you. I have told you too much! Yet I felt that you would somehow understand. I see you have. You understand much, Rion. You are very special. No wonder Prince Eladar has asked for our aid to see you safe. Your friend spoke of a note from him. Might I read it?"

Rion nodded, relieved to see her smile again, the heaviness shrouding his heart lifted with it. Elves had such an amazing affect upon him! He wondered if they affected everyone as much. He suspected they did, from what he had seen of people reacting to Aras as he interacted with them in Athanark.

She read the note he handed to her, eyes widening, and then she looked at him in sympathy and compassion. "You poor Man! I had no idea. How is it you appear so well? It is a wonder you have even survived. Please, you must turn over onto your stomach, so I may finish examining you."

Rion did so, wishing the admiring expression from before might return. It hurt him to know she might hold only pity in her heart for him now. But when she had him turn back onto his back, he saw she was gazing at him only in fondness.

"You must sleep now, Rion, so I might begin healing you." She handed him the bowl Quickwing had drunk from.

Rion was suddenly afraid. He had not slept without Ron or Tarrell since the terrifying nightmare.

She saw the fear upon his face and understood. "You will not dream here, unless they are dreams we give you. You cannot be harmed in your sleep while you are here. The River will not allow it. I will not allow it."

There was such a fierce note of protectiveness in her voice, he could not even think to doubt her. Rion nodded and drank, his heart overflowing with trust and faith in her.

Meander stroked his face gently as he drifted off to sleep.

"YOU do not usually caress those you aid, Misteria," a jealous, beloved voice said in Elvish, from the doorway.

Misteria looked up at Evanadar levelly as her hand stilled. Her husband's eyes were sparking with Power. Only she and Lithunia could survive such a gaze with their minds intact. "No, I do not. This Man has touched my heart in a way I allow few to. You will perhaps understand once you read this," she said, handing Evanadar the note. "It is from Prince Eladar. We had suspected when Crown Prince Elavar came seeking his mother, who was not here, that ill might have befallen his family or his Kingdom or both. I fear now, from reading Prince Eladar's closing, that Riviera has been destroyed and perhaps Loatia with it. We will find out soon enough.

"I sense that the King will summon me soon. That he will ask something terrible of me. I see a whirlwind of pain and coldness and darkness, and perhaps even madness, coming for me. So do not blame me for seeking what calm and warmth I can. I will feel pain enough when I tend Rion. Please do not add to my anguish."

Evanadar went to her and embraced her. "Forgive me, my love! Though your blood called to mine, you never should have joined yourself to me. I still cannot understand why you would, how you might love me, when there is nothing lovable about me. Please, let me help you aid him! We have tried it before and it has worked. I can share in the pain, so you feel it less keenly. I only wish I shared that aspect of the gift of your touch, so that I might treat him and you need not suffer at all," he said, his voice thick with sorrow.

Misteria smiled at him. "You are so wonderful that you would say and do such things, yet still you can think so ill of yourself? Come, my love. We will live only in the pain of the moment and not worry about what the future might bring. But first, before we heal Rion, we must heal the eagle, for I promised Rion I would do so."

FARAD left Quickwing as soon as he drank Meander's elixir, rising quickly up the strand of the bond toward his own body. He was free of pain now. He opened his eyes and saw Lunahr's concerned face hovering over his. He smiled reassuringly at him and sat up, feeling large and heavy, clumsy and awkward. Possessing Slash had been far different from flying with Quickwing.

"Farad! Please don't ever do that again! I thought I had lost you!" Lunahr said, hugging him tightly, trembling.

Farad hugged him back and comforted him. "It's all right, Lunahr. I'm all right and Quickwing will be as well. Forgive me. I hurt him when we fought the chimaera, but Rion is taking good care of him and the Elves are healing him."

"A chimaera? You forced Quickwing to fight a chimaera?" Lunahr was appalled.

"Of course not! Surely you realize he would not allow me to do something against his nature, especially having barely survived such a battle once before? But he was as eager as I was to attack. I am sorry, Lunahr, but we had no choice. The chimaera had seized Rion and was taking him to Incuban, or trying to. By the time we attacked it, Rion had already turned his sword upon himself and was about to kill himself. It was the only way we could save him.

"We went for the eyes. We blinded the chimaera and it fell from the sky. But it broke Quickwing's right wing and we fell too. As did Rion. Fortunately, Quickwing and Rion survived the fall and the chimaera did not. Rion even destroyed the Revenant who had been riding it, afterward.

"Rion and Quickwing are being healed by the River Elves of Salenia. From what I know of Elven healing and the extent of their injuries, they'll both sleep for a couple of days at least. Rion will be surprised upon waking that Quickwing will act differently, although Quickwing is already quite fond of him. Rion, of course, did not realize I was inside Quickwing."

Joy lit Farad's face. "I flew, Lunahr! I dove, I banked, I soared! Thank you, cousin! I owe you much. I never knew my mother's blood flowed so strongly in my veins. I never thought I could be Eagle as well as Wolven. I feel close to her again. I can remember her grace, her courage, her strength. And I will fly again, I must." Farad was intent, now. "I will bond to an eagle as well, if I am able. You must summon one for me, or we will have Quickwing bring one to me, one that might not mind binding to me."

"I will put out the call, cousin. But you must promise me you'll not lose yourself to him. I know how it feels to be so wild and free. I have been tempted to stay within Quickwing always, but the temptation has not been so great that I might ever do so. Yet I fear for you, cousin," Lunahr cautioned.

Farad smiled at Lunahr tenderly. "You need not. I will be careful, Lunahr. I'd not risk hurting you and Jarina and Dewalaren. I promise you I will always come back. How could I roam so far, when those who love me are here?"

Lunahr hugged him fiercely. "My heart sings to hear you say so, cousin! I never want to lose you again."

Farad saw the anguish of burying him was yet far too keen. "You won't, Lunahr," Farad swore.

RON, Tarrell, and Gar returned with the girls to the outside of the riverbank. Whitewater turned to go.

Ron said, "*Lashay ya fa hapola un.* Again, I am sorry Meander was somehow hurt by doing so, but we are, as ever, very grateful to you."

Whitewater looked at Ron, nodded curtly, and then disappeared back inside the riverbank, and the opening vanished with him.

"Come, let us go back to the mill. We still have to give Father an accounting of what's happened," Gar said.

"I'd rather face the chimaera again," Ron grumbled.

Gar smiled fondly at his older brother. "Don't worry, Ron. We'll all take responsibility for it. We'll not let Father blame you alone for it."

When they returned, Liana was obviously dismayed to see the girls were still being carried and were still bandaged. "You said the Elves would heal them!" she accused.

"Meander had me treat the girls. She fell ill and she's tending to Rion," Gar said, and explained what had happened.

"It doesn't hurt anymore, Liana," Anabelle assured her older sister.

"It doesn't even tickle anymore," Gisela said.

"Perhaps we're healed already! Gar, can you take off the bandages so we can see?" Anabelle urged.

Gar shook his head. "Not until tomorrow after the sun sets, as we were told. I'll not risk undoing the healing."

"All right," Anabelle said, with a pout.

Markara spoke then. "Now, Ron, I'll hear all you neglected to tell me before, and the new tale as well. And I mean all of it. I've heard some from Talia."

Gar said, "Liana, why don't you and Talia come with me and Ron? We'll carry the girls to your room, so you can all talk with one another. You've got a lot of catching up to do too. While you're going about it, we'll speak with Father."

They were all enthusiastic about that, to Gar's obvious relief. It was clear he hadn't wanted the girls to hear much of what would be said.

When Gar returned to the grinding room with Ron, Ron took a deep breath and told his father and Lisandra everything he'd omitted earlier, even about Circe. Gar told his story about what had happened in Gosa. Then they both told them about the encounter with the chimaera.

Markara eyed them sternly after they were done. "Promise or not, I'd not have sent you—Father would not have asked me to—had he realized the danger. I almost lost the four of you. I'll not soon let any of you leave the safety of the mill again. Ogaten needs traders as well. I've a feeling the town will soon be bursting with refugees from Gosa, from what you've said."

Ron shook his head. "I'm sorry, Father, but I won't be staying. I'll be accompanying Rion on his journey. I'll not leave his protection solely to the Elves."

Gar said, "I'm going as well. I'll not let Ron go with no one to watch his back. I'm the best archer of all of us, and there's no telling what might come after Rion on the road. I'm sure Ara will want to come with us, also, but Van's place is here."

Ron agreed. "Van definitely won't be coming with us, not with the baby coming and the girls to take care of. A man's place is guarding his family first and his friends second."

A WHILE later, Ron heard Ara, Van, and Rarnak return with the wagonload of goods. When they entered the grinding room and saw him and the others all looking grave, Ara asked in concern, "What's wrong? Couldn't the Elves help the girls?"

"No, they've helped them. So, how much did we lose? Half? Or worse?" Ron asked, expecting the worst.

"Less than a fifth," Ara said happily. "It's amazing how much survived the fall. We'll be able to sell most of it after all."

"Ara, I won't be doing any trading for a while, now," Ron said. "Gar and I are going to accompany the Elves to guard Rion on his journey. We thought you might want to come as well, but neither of us would think less of you if you'd rather stay in Ogaten."

"No wonder Father is looking so grim. Don't be ridiculous! Of course I'm coming. But what about Van? You didn't mention him," Ara asked.

Van appeared torn and opened his mouth to speak.

"He's doing the responsible thing and staying here with Liana and the girls. Now that the baby is coming, it wouldn't be right to leave her," Ron said firmly, bracing himself for an argument.

"That's what I was going to say. With the baby on the way and the girls, my place is here," Van agreed. "But please, be careful, all of you."

"Of course we'll be," Ron assured him, surprised and relieved he wouldn't need to argue with Van into doing what was right.

"So, it will be the three of us. We're used to fighting as two teams of two. We'll have to adapt," Ara said.

"I'll be the fourth," Tarrell volunteered. "I've seen you fight. I'll soon learn your pattern."

Ron looked at Tarrell levelly. "Tarrell, you can't come. What of Talia? You promised Madame Genevieve you'd wed her and take care of her. You can't abandon her and go off into danger."

ANDRA looked at Ron sharply. Tarrell marry her? But she'd thought Talia was with Rarnak. Hadn't Talia said she was his?

"Why do you think Van is staying? Rion can make this journey without you. He's a man now. You saw how well he fared on the road here, even hurt as he is. It's time you let him go, Tarrell. If you came with us, you'd be a danger to him. You know he's as protective of you as you are of him. The Enemy could use you against him," Ron reasoned.

"But he can't even speak," Tarrell argued.

"He's been getting by well enough," Ron reminded him. "He thought to use the artist's lead you'd brought from Athanark, so he could write easier than with pen and ink on the road. Ara, Gar, and I can all read, so we'll have no trouble understanding him. We don't plan on leaving him unguarded for a moment, but if for any reason one of us isn't with him, if others he needs to converse with can't read, he can still use gestures to communicate, as he's been doing. Besides, the note said Talon can heal his voice, once he reaches their sanctuary, that Watchtower of theirs. Then he'll not need paper and lead any longer."

"But if I let him go, I might never see him again! Talon's at war, Thorn said so. Rion wasn't born to be a swordsman, despite his father and uncle being City Guards. I was. I can still protect him," Tarrell argued.

Ron shook his head. "You can't, Tarrell. Not from the foes he now faces. Don't make it harder on him than it needs to be. He is being so brave. Don't weaken him."

"But he could die!" Tarrell said, agonized.

Rarnak spoke up then. "So could Talia, while you're away. Would you want to come back to find Ogaten and the mill gone and no sign of her, as I found our farm? Knowing that if you'd stayed, you might have saved her? Knowing she was lost to you forever? Could you live with yourself? Could you still love Rion after losing her because of him?" Rarnak clasped Tarrell's shoulder. "I'll be protecting Rion for you. Please protect my sister for me."

Tarrell crumpled and nodded.

Andra felt incredibly foolish. His sister! Talia was Rarnak's sister! That's what Talia had been saying when she'd run off so she'd not hear. She'd thought—but Rarnak said he'd be protecting Rion. He was leaving. He was going with them. She'd be all alone again. Van would have no time for her. He'd be thinking only of his wife. And she'd be surrounded by the four of them, frilly, giggling, useless creatures, in their lacey dresses and—no. No, she'd not. Andra had to get Van alone. She had to talk with him, and she needed some things.

Ron said, "Tarrell, after we're gone, can you inventory our salvageable goods against the list we have? And perhaps sell what you can of them? You can take whatever commission from the sale you deem fair. Some of those things are perishable."

"Of course. I'll do whatever I can to help you," Tarrell swore. "And you wouldn't accept our coin. Why would you think I'd take yours? I won't take a commission. You'll see every copper from the sale."

Ron nodded his thanks.

"It's a good thing the inn's almost finished," Van said. "The mill has been getting pretty crowded, and now we have the girls and Tarrell and Talia as well. They can all stay at the inn once it's done. The girls will be a big help. They're both trained as bakers. The inn will be able to bake all its own goods, now. Liana's learned a lot about cooking, and I have as well, but we're not quite up to baking yet!" Van said, grinning. Then he grew more serious. "And if there are truly so many refugees on the way, I can see they'll be needing an inn. It's a good thing we built it as big as we did, though I'd feared it a folly, when so many told me I'd made it too grand. I wish now it was bigger."

Everyone went to work. There was still grain to grind, and beds to be set up for everyone. Andra finally found her chance to speak with Van before dinner. Ron was cooking, as Van and the others would be doing plenty of cooking in the days ahead.

"Van, I need your help," Andra said.

Van looked at her curiously. Andra knew it wasn't often she admitted needing anyone's help. "Of course."

"I plan to go with Ron, Ara, and Gar, but I'll need a few things for the journey," Andra said firmly.

"But Andra, you can't! It sounds like they're heading into a war!" Van protested, horrified.

"That's right. And I'm better with a bow than you and even Gar, much better than Ron and Ara. I had Swiftsong teach me while you were all away. I was going mad. Learning is all that kept me sane. And I didn't only learn the bow. I had Uncle Donara teach me how to use a sword as well. He felt bad for me, that neither of his sons had helped doing the work at the mill as he'd promised they would. And I've practiced both the bow and the sword, day and night, after all the work was done. I never did so while I still had a job to do, but I wanted to be sure that if you came back and ever decided to leave again, there would be no reason you might not take me with you. I just slept less. What need has someone like me for sleep? There's no beauty my rest might give me. And what use for time to have dreams, when they've always ever only gone unfulfilled," Andra said bitterly.

"But Andra, you don't understand! It will be so dangerous! Worse than our last trip: they'll be facing chimaera and maybe even wizards and Incuban, the Enemy the Watch has been on guard against all these years. You could die!" Van said, tears in his eyes.

She hugged him tightly. "You're one of the three who would even think to mourn my passing," she said softly into his ear. Van, Ron, and Swiftsong were the only ones who would care. "I can't stay, Van. Can't you see? I can't stay because I love you, as much as you love me. You're more than a brother to me. I raised you. You're like a brother and a son to me, both. Your love keeps me going, keeps me strong. But if I stay, that would change. I wouldn't mean it to, but I can't help how I feel."

"I hate Liana, Van. I hate her as much as you love her. I'd soon grow to hate her sisters too. They're all of them everything I'm not. It was bad enough with only Liana. The three of them, four with Talia, the girlish giggles, the hair, the dresses, while I work like a dog. I know you love Liana and you should: she's your wife. You deserve her. I know she's sweet. I choke on my dinner at how sweet she is. Van, if I stay, you'd start to hate me, for hating her, and then I'd just give myself to the River. I've thought about it often enough since she's come."

Van shook his head in denial. "How can you say that? How can you feel it?" he asked, stricken.

Andra pulled back and peered intently at him. "You know, Van. You alone have ever known what's in my heart. Please, Van, I need you to support me, against Father and the rest. If I don't go with them, I'll follow them. I'll catch up when we're far from here, if I live to. But I can help them, Van. The partner system works best with four. With three one's back is left unguarded. And it would be Ron, and I'll not see him die when I might save him. I'm strong, I'm tough. I've never had the chance to do anything I've wanted to, Van. You all left me behind, all alone, for two years. But you won't be alone. You've a second family, now, when I've never really had even the one."

Van hugged her and started to cry, as if he were still the little boy she'd cared for all those years.

"You're a man now, Van, not the boy you were when you left. You'll do fine without me here," she soothed.

"You'll come back, won't you, Andra? Please, promise me you'll come back!" Van begged.

"I'll do my best, Van. I love you. I always will. Now, much as I do need it, I came to you because I need more than your support. I've the sword Uncle Donara gave me and the bow Swiftsong gave me," she began.

Van stared at her in wide-eyed awe. "Swiftsong gave you one of theirs? An Elven bow?"

Andra's lips creased in the slightest of smiles, softening the harsh planes of her face. "I told you I was better than you and Gar. I so impressed Swiftsong, he gifted me with a bow and two dozen arrows. But wait, I was telling you what I need. I've the sword and bow, but I need your guardsman's livery. Also, I'll need traveling coin. None of you thought to give me any of the coin from the sale of the pearls, but at least one hundred fifty of those pearls were mine, from my labor, half of what Father earned these two years past as well as a portion from the years before, when all of us worked. Minus the fifteen percent commission, that's one hundred twenty-seven gold and change. Father's given you all the coin from the sale for the inn and told you to hold what you don't need of it for Gar, for his stables, but I need my share."

"Of course! It's only fair. Andra, please take more. Take two hundred or...."

She shook her head. "I've no need for more. I plan to give you the twenty-seven, in exchange for your horse. He's been in battles before, though it's a shame he's not the one Gar trained. That will leave me with one hundred gold, for whatever I might need. I can't imagine spending all of it, unless I kill three horses, and I don't plan to."

Van looked at her in surprise. "You've really thought this through. You've planned all of it."

She nodded. "I almost followed you all two years ago, but I wouldn't leave Father alone, when he's getting so old. But now, with his three new daughters, he'll not even notice me gone. No, he will, for the three of them together can't do the work I did alone."

Van winced.

"I'm sorry, Van," Andra said sadly. "You see why I have to go? I've so little softness left in my heart now, I'd turn all to rock and ice if I stayed." She hugged him, gently. "Who knows? Maybe I'll even earn someone other than a brother to hug, on this trip." She turned quickly away. She'd not meant to say so aloud. She'd not meant to tempt the Gods into taking Rarnak from her, before she'd even had a chance to win his heart.

"I've always wished I wasn't your brother, Andra," Van said softly.

Andra almost fell, she was so wounded to hear him say so.

Van saw her stiffen and was in front of her with his strong arms around her instantly. She still wasn't used to him being taller and broader than she was. "Andra, you heard my words, but not my tone. I meant—I love you, Andra. I've always loved you, more than as a brother, more than as a son to you, more than I should have. I never thought I'd be able to find someone I could love as a wife, for loving you," he admitted, blushing darkly, as he let her go.

Andra stared at him, astonished.

"I never told you. How could I? But you had to hear, Andra. You had to know others might love you the same, too," Van said sincerely.

She hugged him tightly. "Oh, Van! I'm so glad you found Liana! I'm so glad you're happy and you've a baby coming. I thought I was a fool to be so jealous of her, and now I understand why I've felt as I have."

Van took a deep breath. "Let me get the coin for you now, and I'll help you pack for the trip. You'd be surprised what we wished we'd had along, that we had to buy along the way. And I've a few tricks I picked up along the way too, that are useful in a fight, things Father and Uncle Donara never taught us."

"Poor Ron! He's no idea what's coming," Andra said, with that slight smile again.

THE next morning, Ron cooked again, and they all helped finish unloading and sorting the wagons. By late afternoon the girls were clamoring to have their bandages taken off. Gar insisted they wait until after sundown.

Van and Liana herded everyone off to Ogaten to show them the inn. Ron looked in surprise at the wooden sign over the door. They had named the inn The Silver Swan, and there was both a picture of one and the words saying so below it. "How did you pick the name?" he asked. He'd always marveled at the odd names inns had, often those of animals, and had wondered how people named them.

Van grinned. "I named it after Princess Brook. She uses the swan as her seal, with silver wax, and her hair is silver, and we're so near the River and the Elves, I thought it was appropriate. It's in honor of the help she gave us in Erenia, for saving Gar's life and healing all of us."

"It's a fitting name, Van," Ron said approvingly. "Now let's take a look inside."

After the tour, Ron said, "You've done an impressive job, Van! I think many a night over the next few months we'll wish we had a place so fine to sleep in." His other brothers echoed his words and Van beamed in pride.

AFTER they were done at the inn, Gar checked on Thenagar. He'd corralled him with one of his father's three mares. He was hoping to stud Thenagar to all of them before he left, to get a start on the stables he was planning. He was pleased to see Thenagar seemed as excited by the prospect as he was, and the mare was more than willing.

Finally it was time for the girls' bandages to come off. Everyone watched breathlessly as soon as Gar told them it was time.

"Me first, me first!" Gisela insisted and Anabelle agreed. Gar unwound the bandages. He was nervous they might be disappointed with what they saw, from Meander's reaction, that there might be horribly disfiguring scars after he'd promised them there wouldn't be any. But when the bandage came off her arm, it was as if she'd never been hurt. Gisela hugged Gar. He unwrapped her feet then and they were healed as well.

Anabelle was pulling at her own bandages. She beamed when Gar helped her remove them, and she saw her leg whole again, and her feet fully healed as well. "Oh Gar, it's just like you said!" she squealed in delight and hugged him.

Gar was surprised to see Andra smiling with the rest of them. He was amazed when she cooked dinner for everyone without complaint and then brought out a surprise. She'd made a cake to celebrate the sisters' reunion. He'd thought he'd smelled one baking, but had convinced himself he must be imagining things.

Tarrell was the only one who appeared glum, though Talia tried her best to cheer him. "Rion will be fine, Tarrell," she assured him. "If the Elves could heal such terrible burns, they can heal him as well."

That night it took a lot of coaxing for Gar to get Thenagar into his stall, but Gar promised his stallion he'd have another fine mare for him in the morning.

OVER the next two days Gar was able to stud Thenagar to the other two mares as well. That third day, Tarrell asked him and his brothers if they could check on Rion for him. Tarrell was concerned that Rion had not returned to them yet. Ron spoke to the Elves and came back with the message that Meander hoped Rion would be fully healed by the following morning.

Later Ron spoke to Andra in private. "I didn't want to say anything in front of Tarrell, Andra. You've been living here these two years past. Is something going on we don't know about? Meander didn't speak with me herself, it was her husband Whitewater who did. He looked awful, as if he's been ill. When I asked whether Meander was well, he gave me an odd look. And it's not only him. I saw others as well, Elves I know at least in passing. I've never seen such despair. It was all I could do to keep from throwing myself in the River, after seeing them."

Andra looked at him in concern. "There's nothing I know of. Perhaps the word has spread about Gosa burning? You told us how Meander reacted to the burns the girls have. Maybe they're afraid the refugees who will come will be burnt as well? Even thinking about it seems to harm them."

"I hope that's all it might be. I'm afraid it's something worse, that something even more terrible has happened," Ron said grimly.

That night at dinner, everyone was on edge. Those who would be going were eager to be on their way, and those who were staying were already anxious about them.

RION awoke from a dreamless sleep, his brows crinkling in puzzlement. What an odd ceiling. It couldn't truly be made of dried clay as it appeared to be, could it? Where was he? Not his room in Gosa, certainly. An inn?

"Good morning, Rion," a lilting voice said in Common.

Rion sat up and looked about. Memory and awareness returned as he saw Meander, but neither brought fear or pain. Meander looked terrible, though, far worse than before. She looked as if she were dying.

He reached out to her. She drew back from his touch, but smiled reassuringly. "Please, Rion, it is not your fault I am unwell. Nor am I alone in my affliction, as you will see, though I feel it more keenly than the others. You are well? There is no more pain?"

He nodded, still eyeing her in concern.

"Please walk for me," Meander requested.

Rion slid carefully from the bed, stood cautiously, and began to walk. His face burst into a grin. The pain was gone. He walked effortlessly, as he always had.

Meander smiled in return. She looked better for a moment, as if his smile had strengthened her somehow. Rion looked about for the eagle and the smile fled his face. It was still lying limply upon the bed it had occupied before. He went to it in concern.

"It's all right, Rion. I was about to waken him as well. It is fortunate he is a bird, that his bones are so small and hollow. Broken bones normally take a much longer time for me to heal." Meander glided to the bed and lightly stroked the eagle's head. He sprang to his feet and let out a shrill call and stretched his wings, then tucked them. He cocked his head, stretched his wings again more slowly and stared intently at his right one, then tucked them again and bobbed his head to Meander. Then he looked with just as much concentration and apparent concern at Rion.

"This is the fourth day since you came to us. Rion is well also, except of course for his voice, which is beyond my Power to heal," she said, speaking to the eagle. Then she turned to Rion. "Come. I will bring you to your friends, Rion. They are eager to see you. Your friend Tarrell in particular has been quite anxious. He has asked about you."

Rion swallowed. She was so wonderful and she had suffered for him, and he couldn't even thank her.

"Please, Rion. I told you, much as healing you caused me pain, such pain passes quickly. I have already recovered from it. What I now suffer from, I cannot say. But perhaps it will brighten your heart to hear that I will be traveling with you, for a time. Whitewater and I and many others will share a portion of the journey you will undertake. We will accompany you as far as Westhaven. Then you and your guards must continue along the Western Road, while we undertake a far different journey." Her voice sank to a whisper. She was terrified, he could see she was. What could terrify an Elf, other than flame?

Rion realized he wouldn't be traveling through Falnor this time, on his way to the Coroden Mountains, though he and his friends had traveled through that City on their journey east, to Gosa, having taken a shortcut through the Wood Elf Kingdom of Erenia and the Falnor Woods. Falnor was the last City of Man before the Coroden Mountains, but it was on the wrong side of the Merdan River, and over thirty-seven miles from the Road. To the southeast of it were the Falnor Woods and Erenia. Elanara was in Erenia, or had been. Rion wondered if she might yet be, or if Elavar had succeeded in freeing her and Eladar from the soldiers there.

Meander was eyeing him thoughtfully. He could not read the expression on her face. Without realizing he did so, until she commented upon it, he cocked his head and looked at her curiously.

To his surprise and relief Meander laughed. "Be careful, Rion! You are adopting the eagle's mannerisms," she teased. "Come, it is time you both saw the sun again."

Rion nodded and put the padded cloth she offered to him over his arm and held it out for the eagle to perch upon. The eagle watched him with what seemed to be wariness. Rion tapped his arm, indicating he wished to carry him. After another moment's hesitation, the eagle hopped onto his arm. Rion grinned and gently stroked the bird's head.

The three of them navigated the complex maze of tunnels and exited into the bright light of day. Meander stumbled and Rion instantly reached out to steady her, but another hand beat him to it. "You will not touch her!" a harsh voice snapped in Common.

Rion pulled back as the eagle screeched shrilly.

It was Whitewater. He had his arms around Meander. He paled as he held her, but she seemed to draw strength from his presence.

"You should not speak harshly to Rion, Evanadar. It is not his fault I nearly fell," Meander scolded her husband in Elvish.

"I know. I did not mean to. Please, Misteria, you must not go! I fear you will not survive it," he pleaded.

"I will. I am stronger than you know, Evanadar. And you will be there to aid me," she reminded him.

Rion felt guilty for eavesdropping. They obviously had no idea he spoke Elvish. He felt especially bad about hearing their given names. He knew how carefully Elves kept them from strangers.

Whitewater, she'd called him Evanadar, turned to him and spoke in Common. "Forgive me my rudeness. I know you sought to aid my wife. But Elves do not welcome Man's touch."

Rion nodded, remembering the brothers had warned him similarly, when they'd first come across Eladar in the Gelthor Pass.

They walked silently onward. Rion was surprised. They did not seem to be heading for the mill. They emerged instead in a field. Rion's eyes widened as he gazed worshipfully at the small herd of horses grazing there. They were the most magnificent horses he had ever seen. A male Elf was standing amongst them, stroking them lovingly and speaking to them. Rion recognized him. He was one of the few Elves he had met here before: Swiftsong, or Lithunia, he realized, chagrined that he knew his given name also, when he should not have.

Swiftsong approached them. Rion was disturbed to see that he appeared ill as well, although not nearly as unwell as Meander and Whitewater.

"Are the horses ready, Swiftsong?" Meander asked in Common. "And the others? We hope to be off as soon as Rion has had a chance to say good-bye to his friends."

"Yes. We are all eager to be away," Swiftsong replied in Common. But then he continued on in Elvish. "The busier we are kept, the less time we will have to dwell upon what has happened. Have you ascertained whether the boy can ride?"

Rion fought his usual resentment at being called a boy. They did not realize he could understand them, and all Men were children to the Elves. Amongst themselves, they considered forty-nine to be adult. He realized he shouldn't be insulted. Besides, he admitted ruefully to himself, he still looked like a boy, and he'd been acting child enough on the trip to the mill. He wondered what might have happened that had the Elves so upset, what Swiftsong was referring to.

"Rion, have you ever ridden a horse before?" Meander asked, in Common.

Rion blushed, embarrassed, and shook his head, *No*. He'd only ever traveled by wagon before.

"Then we must be especially sure your mount suits you and will respond to you, particularly as you cannot speak and do not know Elvish, even if you could," Meander said. "*Famsala*, you would call her Seafoam, has been trained to respond to whistles. Can you whistle?"

Rion nodded and began whistling "A Summer's Faire," his favorite song from Ardock.

Meander smiled warmly. "Excellent! I had thought to only try to teach you the four most basic commands, go, stop, right and left, but I can teach you all twenty-five signals if you wish. You may learn them as we ride."

Rion nodded eagerly and pointed to the herd and shrugged.

"Ah. She is the mottled white mare there," she said, pointing. "This is 'Come,'" Meander said, whistling a distinctive note.

The mare lifted her head and came trotting toward Meander. Quickwing flew from his perch upon Rion's arm and settled upon a tree branch to watch. When Seafoam reached them, Meander spoke to her in Elvish. "Seafoam, this is Rion. He will be your rider, for a time. You must take special care of him. You must guard him with your life."

The mare nodded, as if she understood.

Rion petted her gently. She was so soft! It felt more like he was stroking rabbit fur than horsehair. Then he backed up ten paces and whistled, *Come*. Seafoam walked to him and Rion grinned in delight.

Meander smiled also, the illness leaving her face for a moment with the warmth of it. "That was perfect, both tone and pitch. I did not even need to repeat it. Can you learn more without confusing them? Should I teach you four a day? Or less?"

Rion shook his head, *Yes*, then *No*, twice, and he held up both hands as fists and spread his fingers, flashing them twice, and then only his right hand once, signaling the number twenty-five.

Meander laughed. "Are you trying to tell me you would learn all of them now?" she asked, amused.

Rion grinned and nodded eagerly.

Meander smiled and began teaching him the other twenty-four commands: go, stop, left, right, faster, slower, prance, jump, push, pull, play dead, stay still, find, bow, lie down, roll, swim, backward, follow, hide, conceal trail, attack, protect, and do not.

Rion was astonished by some of the commands. He knew horses would normally not lie down nor walk backward. And when Meander commanded Seafoam to hide, she disappeared completely into the trees. Meander told him Seafoam would do far more than seek out rock or firm ground, when told to conceal her trail. She would actually swish her tail to erase her tracks when walking along sand or leaves, and blur them with her hooves when walking in mud. But it was *Attack* that was the most startling. The gentle, obedient mare lashed out with her hooves, trampled the ground, and bit the air as if she were a King's war stallion. Then, as if sensing she had frightened Rion with her display, she trotted over to him, nickered softly and thrust her nose under his hand to be petted. Rion stroked her and then hugged her tightly. He loved her already. He couldn't bear the thought he would eventually have to part from her.

"Why don't you get a feel for riding her?" Meander suggested.

Rion nodded. He looked at Seafoam. She wore neither saddle nor bridle. Rion remembered Aras complaining bitterly about having to use them on Janahar, when they both would have preferred he do otherwise. Aras! He was eager to see him again. He knew he would still be with Talon. Rion couldn't imagine him ever leaving Talon. They'd been like brothers, for all the brevity of their time together. Rion wondered how to mount Seafoam without stirrups. He'd asked Aras how he did so once, and Aras had leapt onto Janahar effortlessly. Aras was taller than Rion, with the agility of an Elf. Rion knew he could not mount as Aras had. Then Rion grinned and whistled, *Bow.*

Seafoam did so, and it was easy to mount her then.

Then he whistled, *Do not bow*, and she rose. He wound his fingers in her mane and whistled, *Go*, and she began to walk. He was relieved to see that he had no trouble staying on her. He took a deep breath and whistled, *Faster*, and she broke into a trot. After only a few moments, he whistled, *Slower*. Ah, that was better. Then he tried, *Backward*, and *Hide*. Then, because he knew it might well become necessary, he whistled, *Attack*, to see if he could stay seated. He was relieved to see he could. He thought he should try, *Jump*, and did so, but regretted it. He half fell from her. He realized he must be pulling her mane painfully. He reseated himself, and rubbed along the roots of her mane and patted her shoulder. Then he rejoined the Elves, looking sheepish, feeling clumsy and awkward.

"I cannot believe you have never ridden before today, or that you have mastered all of the commands so quickly!" Meander said approvingly, to Rion's surprise.

Rion grinned at her. He would miss Meander terribly. He hoped wherever she and the others were going that they'd be safe.

"You make my obligation far easier than I had any right to expect, Rion," Swiftsong said. Rion realized that from Eladar's letter, Swiftsong might have had to try to deliver a howling madman, or worse, to the Watchtower.

Rion pointed to Swiftsong, then held up his fingers and counted one, two, three, four, five and then shrugged and pointed to himself.

"You wish to know how many are to guard you?" Swiftsong asked. "I am one, then there is Quicksilver, Meadow, and Rain. The four of us will stay with you until you reach Thorn. But Meander, Whitewater and eighteen others will accompany us for part of the journey."

Rion pointed to Meander and Whitewater and shrugged.

"I am sorry, Rion. I cannot tell you where we are going," Meander said softly, and all the life and joy that had so animated her while she watched him with Seafoam died.

"Please, Lithunia! You have the King's ear," Whitewater said in Elvish. "Tell him she cannot go! You see that she cannot. He gives her and the others a hopeless task. How will her death help others?"

Rion fought not to reveal his shock at Whitewater's words.

"We are under Martial Law, Evanadar. The High-King now dictates all our actions. Our King has no say in the matter," Swiftsong stated grimly.

"I am going, Evanadar. I will not let our people suffer when I might help them. I will aid those I can," Meander said.

Rion was greatly troubled by what he overheard. Had the Enemy unleashed some terrible new weapon, a plague, perhaps? Is that why all the Elves appeared ill, and why their healer was being ordered to go into danger? And there was Eladar's cryptic closing: he'd written Riviera-that-was. Had his Kingdom fallen to illness?

"Bring Rion to his friends. We must ready ourselves for the journey," Swiftsong said.

"I know I must go, but I still do not understand how you can risk such a journey, Lithunia!" Meander protested in Elvish. "We have heard that the High-King has gifted King Talon five thousand soldiers. What if he comes to review them, or join them with his own forces? You cannot risk that he might see you! You wear no masking spell. Even after three millennia, there is no question Laedrin would recognize you were he to see you. Surely your life would be forfeit, the moment you were revealed to him!"

"Fear not. You of all people know that, even in such an eventuality, I would be far from helpless. Now come. There is yet much to do to prepare and little time."

Meander nodded, as if speaking had become too great an effort.

Rion was shocked and horrified by all he had heard. Why should the High-King wish to kill Swiftsong? He had never heard of Elves slaying other Elves! What possible transgression might inspire such an act? What unforgivable crime might Swiftsong have committed? Treason? The brothers spoke highly of Swiftsong. Could their faith in him be misplaced? And what had Meander meant by three millennia? Had he misremembered the meaning of the Elvish word? Surely she must have said centuries? Aras had told him that Elves live to be one thousand.

Seafoam butted his head with her own, as if sensing his distress, and he gave her a lingering caress as he followed Meander and Whitewater. At the edge of the field, he bid Seafoam good-bye distractedly, with a brief pat, and he and the Elves reentered the woods.

A short while later, they heard a snort of frustration. Rion turned in surprise. It was Seafoam. He'd not realized she'd been following them, she'd been so silent, but now she was unable to proceed further. The woods here were too dense for her to pass between the trees.

Rion approached her and whistled, *Do not follow. Go,* and pointed back toward the field.

Seafoam shook her head stubbornly.

"Seafoam! You have never disobeyed before," Meander said, exasperated, in Elvish. "Why would you do so now?"

Seafoam nickered and nuzzled Rion.

"Ah, I see. You see he is sad and upset and you are trying to aid him already? You like him, too, don't you? He is easy to like, is he not? And he makes you want to protect him? It is the same for me. But you must let us take care of him for a little while longer. He will ride you soon enough," Meander assured her in Elvish. Then she whistled, *Go*, and Seafoam whickered, apparently reassured, and turned back for the field.

Rion was incredibly moved, both by Seafoam's loyalty and protectiveness of him, after so short an acquaintance, and by Meander's. He again felt guilty for eavesdropping. Meander had no idea he knew Elvish. He wished for the hundredth time he could speak. He was relieved to see Seafoam's affection seemed to have helped Meander. In turn, his own heart was less heavy as they headed for the mill.

Van spotted them as they approached, and he ran to the mill door and called excitedly "Rion's back!" before rushing over to greet him. Van was soon joined by his siblings, Rarnak and Tarrell, just as the eagle came out of the sky and perched upon Rion's arm. Rion greeted him and held him with all the familiarity of a Lord and his favorite hunting bird.

"Rion, you look wonderful!" Tarrell cried happily. "Do you feel as well as you look?"

Rion nodded, smiling, his concern for the Elves momentarily forgotten in his joy at seeing his friends.

"He is as healed as he can be here. We must go now, but Rion needs to say good-bye to you all before we leave," Meander said.

"We're going with you," Ron said. "Gar, Ara, Rarnak, and I, to help protect you."

The smile fled Rion's face and he shook his head, *No*.

"It's not open for debate," Ron said. "We already decided, days ago. We're all ready to go. We just need to saddle our horses and pack some food for the journey. The rest is ready. It won't take us long to prepare."

Rion was still shaking his head, pointing to Meander and Whitewater.

Ron said, "I know the Elves are guarding you, but we can still be of use to you. The Elves can fight when they have to, we've seen it, but it's hard for them, Rion. They're not like the soldier Elves. And the Enemy knows their weaknesses, too. If He finds you again, He'll likely use fire against them."

Meander paled and swayed. Whitewater held her tightly. "I must take her to the River. Rion, we will be back for you shortly. We will bring Seafoam to you," he said and then he led Meander quickly away.

"What's wrong with her? With him as well? They look ill," Gar said in concern.

Rion pointed to the mill and they went in. He got out his journal and writing lead and told them his conjecture regarding a plague and about the twenty other Elves that would be accompanying the four guards. He tried to convince them he wouldn't need any of them to come because of it, that they should stay to guard Ogaten and the mill instead. He assured them he'd be fine. But the brothers wouldn't hear of it.

"Have you warned them yet that you can't ride?" Tarrell asked.

Rion wrote, *I can ride. I've ridden Seafoam this morning already, and I know all twenty-five whistle commands. Meander taught them to me. All I do is hang on. Seafoam does the rest. I've trotted and even jumped and ridden her going backward. She is amazing. Gar will be jealous when he sees what she can do.*

Gar grinned. "I've already seen what the Elves' horses can do. It's not me you need to worry about: it's Thenagar! He's been mounting mares for three days now. I hope he shows some restraint on this journey."

Rion hoped so too. He'd seen what Seafoam could do to Thenagar if she weren't in a receptive mood.

Rion wrote to Tarrell that he would be leaving all his coin with him, except for one hundred gold. He doubted he'd need anywhere near that much, but wanted to err on the side of caution. And he asked Tarrell to take care of the book Talon's father had written.

"Shouldn't you bring it to Talon?" Tarrell asked.

Rion shook his head. *Talon gave it to Brook, and Brook wants it here,* he wrote. He did not say it would be safer here with him. He knew it was hard enough already for Tarrell to let him go into such potential danger.

Ron, Gar, and Ara changed into their guardsman's livery and went to the stable for their horses.

Van came from the kitchen with an armload of packs. Rion realized there was one too many and looked curiously at Van, who evaded his gaze and swept past him as if he weren't there, but then hesitated at the door and took a deep breath before heading outside, as if girding for battle.

Intrigued, Rion followed Van outside, and saw that Gar was having a tough time leading Thenagar away from the stable. The stallion trumpeted shrilly and snorted and pawed the ground in complaint, displaying none of the behavior Gar's normally obedient mount was known for. He apparently liked his new role as stud, and was reluctant to leave his stable of mares. Gar was frowning as he led Thenagar up to the mill. Rion assumed he was upset with Thenagar, until Gar voiced his true concern. "What's the idea, Van? Why is your horse saddled? I thought we'd been through this already. You're not coming."

Van said innocently, "Of course not, Gar. I've already told you I'm not. I don't have a horse. I sold him three days ago. The new owner is departing today as well." Then his eyes widened. Rion saw twenty-four Elves had emerged from the trees, without a sound, even though they were on horseback. They were soldiers; every one of them wore gleaming armor.

Rion shivered until he recognized some of the approaching Elves: Meander, Whitewater, and Swiftsong were with them. Seafoam was there also. She whinnied in greeting and trotted over to him, whickering as she rubbed her velvety nose against his cheek.

Rion petted her enthusiastically and then whistled, and she knelt. He mounted and then with a second whistle, she rose.

Rion saw that Tarrell, Ara, and Ron, who had stopped halfway from the stable to the mill, finished their approach, apparently recognizing them as well. Ara and Ron were leading their horses, and Tarrell was looking lost. Tarrell walked over to Rion. "Promise me you'll be careful. Promise me you'll come back."

Rion nodded and tried to smile, but he was fighting tears.

Ara approached Swiftsong, his eyes widening in surprise. "I didn't know you were a soldier, Swiftsong. I'd never even known of the soldiers amongst you, until Erenia."

Swiftsong winced as if his words had caused him pain, somehow. "We are, all of us, Reservists: every Elf in every Kingdom. But we have all been called to active duty now. We are officially at war. Meadow, Rain, Quicksilver, and I will accompany you four and Rion on his journey. The other twenty will travel with us for much of the way, but then we will part company. If you are ready, we must begin. We cannot delay the others. Their mission is vital."

"What do you think you're doing?" Rion heard Ron say indignantly, and he turned to see who he was speaking to and what was happening. To his surprise he saw Andra walking up to them, leading Van's horse. She was dressed in the livery of his guards, and her hair was tied back as usual, but without the veil of flour that habitually covered it. She had a bow and quiver upon her back and a sword at her side.

"Accompanying you," she said bluntly.

"No, you are not," Ron said hotly.

Ron glared at Van, as Van handed her a pack. So that was who the extra pack was for! Van had apparently known his sister planned to join them. "Are you mad, Van?" Ron fumed. "I thought you loved her. How could you encourage her like this? Do you want to see her get killed? She's no guard!"

Van visibly winced and swallowed under Ron's assault, but then faced him bravely. "I know she might die. Any of you might. But she's taking no greater risk than the rest of you. She's just as well trained, if less experienced. Andra's a better shot than I am with a bow now, Ron. She's better than Gar. And her swordwork is fine as well. I tested her. I wasn't about to give her my uniform, until I saw she was as good as she said she was. She's an adult, Ron. She's every right to do as she pleases. You can't stop her. If you try to leave without her, she'll simply follow you."

"She's not coming. That's final," Ron snapped.

"You can't stop me, Ron." Andra looked over her older brother's shoulder. "Good-bye, Father, Liana." Rion realized belatedly they'd emerged from the mill. Andra smiled tenderly at Van. "I love you, Van. Take care of yourself." She hugged her youngest brother good-bye.

Markara turned to his eldest son. "Ron, as much as you love her and want to see her safe, you must let her go with you. There's no place for her here, now, not because others have made it so, but because she has. She can take care of herself well enough to survive. She's strong: she has her mother's strength of spirit and my strength of body. It's a comfort to know she at least received one good thing from me. You watch her back and she'll watch yours, and Elmoth willing, you may all yet return safely to me, if you have the luck."

He turned to Andra. "Take care of yourself, Daughter. I love you and I'll miss you. May you find the happiness on the road that has always eluded you here."

Andra looked stunned. She hugged him quickly, awkwardly. "Good-bye, Father. I love you, too, but I won't miss you. I'm glad I'm going." Then she turned abruptly and went back to her horse and mounted him.

"Welcome, Andra," Swiftsong said.

Ron sighed in defeat and mounted as well. Then the thirty of them began their long journey.

Rion glanced over his shoulder one last time at the friends he was leaving behind. Van was hugging Liana tightly and Tarrell was embracing Talia as he and the others headed down the road. With a final wave, the four of them went inside the mill. But Markara was still watching them when the narrow road curved and the mill disappeared behind the trees.

Chapter 5
The Harbinger

"YOU must sit up, Chieftess. You have a visitor," Jarnath said, his voice kind, but firm.

Shadala did not open her eyes. The one she wanted to see was only in memory, now. She had not known of the special magicks of the Elves, so long ago. She had not even known of the Elves. Neither of her two peoples had stories, nor legends, nor warnings about them. She was so very tired. There had been a single bright spot of light in her life, thirty-four long years ago, so bright it had burnt her heart as the sun burns the eyes and left her numb, instead of blind. She had lived in longing until she finally saw hope flare again, and then accepted that Akarhad, the one true love of her heart, must instead be as a son to her, and it had been enough. But now he was gone forever.

"Chieftess, you will sit. I suffer your people to farm my land. I will be shown the respect of my station. You will either sit or kneel, the choice is yours, but you will not lie there and ignore me, unless you wish the children of your City to starve," a hard voice threatened.

Anger flashed brightly, singeing away indifference. Shadala opened her eyes to glare at High-King Laedrin, but the light of the room was too bright after having lain for so long in darkness. She closed her eyes against the glare.

"Who are you to lie here in such grief for him? You are neither father nor mother to him! You have no claim to a parent's grief!" Laedrin roared at her.

Pain cut her like hot knives and she opened her eyes again and lashed back at him. "No, I am neither father nor mother. I am only one who loves him, when neither of you ever did!" She had meant to scream it at Laedrin, but her voice was only a hoarse croak. She fought to sit, to glare at him, eye to eye, but fell back weakly. It was too much effort to sit. Her eyes closed again. Too much effort even to feel hate, or bitterness.

"Do not tell me I do not love my son!" Laedrin challenged.

"You have never loved him. He has begged you for five decades to love him, with every thought, every word, every deed. You know nothing of what he has done to earn your love. Your heart is made of ice."

"I cannot hear your insults, Chieftess. Drink. I would not strain to hear," Laedrin commanded, holding a cup to her face.

She turned her head away from him. "You cannot trick me so easily. I wish only for death. Water will only prolong what must come to pass."

"I am not here to trick you. I am here…." Laedrin's voice caught and Shadala turned back to him in surprise at the unexpected hesitation. "I am here to regain what I can of the son I have lost. He is gone," Laedrin said, and his voice broke again, and to her astonishment, his eyes were bright with unshed tears. "And I find I knew nothing of him. All I thought I knew is false. I had only just begun to see him and now he is forever dark to me. You were his friend. You were more. You truly were as a mother to him, despite what I said, if only for a few months. I have learned all I can from Leonas and from Jarnath, and even Meloneth, though his music drives me to madness, and Etheria, though her serenity makes me want to choke the life from her, if only to see if she would try to stop me. You now must tell me what you know of Aras."

"Why?" Shadala demanded, raising herself briefly in challenge, her voice acid. "To kowtow to the will of the mighty High-King?"

"No," Laedrin said, his voice surprisingly soft and forlorn. "Out of pity. Pity for a man who sought to coax immortality from a Tree, when he had a son to gift it to him unasked. It is a terrible thing to be childless, Chieftess, for those who have never borne children, but even more so, for those of us who have borne them and then lost them."

"You are not who I thought you to be," Shadala said, eyeing Laedrin carefully.

"My heart was lost for a very long while, until Arcanus found it again, and Arandrin and Aras. I did not even know Aras was a wizard, until he showed me, when he broke Arcanus's spell upon me. He has told me you are one as well, after a fashion, that many of your people have magic to them. There is much I will never know. Much he was afraid to tell me. Will you share your memories of him with me? Though I wish I could see him, rather than only hear of him. I have some few memories of him I would share with you, as well, but I do not have the words for it."

"I would see what it is you might wish to share, High-King. My people have a way, though we have never thought of it as wizardry, only Power." She sank back onto the bed. "But I am too tired. I am so very tired. I would rather sleep," she said, closing her eyes once more.

"No!" Laedrin cried loudly, startling her with the force of his denial. "Chieftess, please! Jarnath has told me, when next you sleep, you will not waken. Do not keep your memories from me. Do not make me beg to see them. I would not know how," Laedrin pleaded.

Shadala opened her eyes again. "Yet you are begging, even now. Perhaps as you beg without knowing you do so, you love, and are also blind to it. I must touch your face. And you must not fight against me. I would not survive it."

Laedrin nodded and braced himself for something hard and cruel, or cold, like Ithelia's touch. But Shadala's touch upon his core was soft and gentle. Everywhere their minds touched, Akarhad, Aras was there: as Shadala had first met him, at fifteen, when she had fallen in love with him; in her longings over thirty-four lonely years; months ago, as her bound prisoner, when she would have tortured him to death; as savior of his people, the night of the Great Fire; as diplomat and healer, teacher and student, farmer and builder, wizard and child.

In turn, Laedrin shared his disgust and disappointment, his resentment, and finally his pride, all his memories, but he saw them anew, through her eyes. He saw the treasure he had held so long yet always overlooked. Laedrin felt his heart, so long asleep, waken again. He felt it flood with love for his dead son. When Aras had removed the change Arcanus had made to him, he had grown cold again. Arandrin had brought some warmth back to him. He had been able to feel gratitude toward Aras; he had some small inkling of the terrible, noble sacrifice his son had made by removing the change Arcanus had wrought in him. But through Shadala, he saw the depth of his son's love for him, in spite of all he had ever said and done to him.

Laedrin had wept for Aras in the Grove because the Trees had made him weep. Arandrin's grief had washed over him, and he could not control himself. He had been so distraught his men had needed to carry him from the Grove. Once away from the influence of the Trees, he had been ashamed and humiliated that he had appeared so weak before the Grove and the King's Guard, and especially before Jarnath. He had angered, he had raged. But now, he wept for Aras of his own accord, not only for the future time they would never spend together, but for all the lost years that had already passed.

SHADALA'S heart went out to Laedrin, and she wrapped her arms around him in her thoughts, well knowing he might lash out at her for it, in the pain of his loss. Instead, he leaned against her and embraced her. The depth of his grief overwhelmed her, and she wept with him, when she had thought all her tears spent. And somehow the coldness and the darkness around her lifted and she felt warmth and light again, and knew wonder that it came from Laedrin.

"Please do not leave us, Chieftess," Laedrin entreated. "We—I... need your strength, your guidance. I am hated by many. I am hated by everyone. Only Aras has ever loved me, and Arandrin. Even my wife, Aras's mother, Ithelia, always despised me. It pains Arandrin still that I could not hear his warnings about her. He was able to forgive himself for her harm of me only because it brought Aras to me and to the Trees. They love Aras. They all but worship him. They have always protected him and he has protected them. They are in terrible danger now, without him."

"My people have all gone to war," Shadala said. "I fear few of them will return. I also am not well loved. My heart has been cold for so long, though mine never turned fully to ice. My brother's children have always been close to me. Their mother died in childbirth, and I was the one who nurtured them. Having Akarhad, Aras, go so suddenly, then having Veran and Falara leave, with Taratur, Beryl, was almost too much for me to bear. I thought losing Aras forever was. But perhaps life is the better choice. I will stay, High-King, because you are the one who has asked it of me. But I fear I have lain here, neither eating nor drinking, for too long. I can no longer even sit."

"My body is strong, though my heart is weak," Laedrin said. "I will gift my strength to you, Chieftess. Aras once showed me how."

The warmth Shadala felt as a soft blanket before flowed over her, into her, from all around her. She embraced Laedrin again in her thoughts. "Thank you, High-King," she said, as he let go of her.

Shadala turned her eyes outward again and saw Laedrin standing over her, his familiar scowl slowly being replaced by a smile. It looked awkward upon his face. She smiled back and sat up slowly, with the strength he had gifted to her. He reached out and helped her. "Might I have some water?" Shadala asked hoarsely. "I find I am suddenly thirsty."

Laedrin held the cup up to her lips again, but this time she drank from it. She would have drained it dry, had Laedrin not forcefully encouraged her to drink it more slowly.

She was grateful to him instead of angry. As a healer, she knew better. She was not used to being a patient. "Jarnath will be pleased," she commented.

Laedrin's stiff smile was replaced by a true grin of delight. "Jarnath will be astonished. It will be one of the few times I have ever surprised him. He had despaired you would be lost to us. Leonas will be overjoyed also. He has visited you here often."

"I knew I was causing Leonas pain. I did not wish to further burden his heart. He is fully recovered? He is well?" Shadala asked.

Laedrin nodded. "One of the Grove Guard has been comforting him: Captain Gaius. When I learned of it, I thought to reassign Gaius to patrolling the mountains. I thought it inappropriate to Leonas's station. But Arandrin would not allow it. He said I would harm not only Leonas and Gaius by it, but Aranas and Aranonas as well. I did not understand before, though I bowed to Arandrin's wishes. I do now. I am glad Arandrin stayed my hand."

Shadala smiled. "I am happy Leonas has found someone to ease the burden of his grief."

"I should go now, Chieftess," Laedrin said. "I am sure Jarnath is waiting outside anxiously. I was loud before, and it is quiet now. He might be worried for your safety." He grimaced and then looked Shadala in the eye. "I did not kill my wife, Shadala, despite what you may have heard. I hated Ithelia, I wished her dead, but I did not act against her. I could not kill her. Nor did I exile her. She left, without word to anyone, of her own accord." He had never before called the Chieftess by her name, instead of her title.

"I know, Laedrin. Aras knows the truth. He told it to me," she assured him.

LAEDRIN nodded and left. Jarnath was indeed in the corridor outside, appearing anxious. Leonas was with him. They both turned toward him.

"Jarnath, the Chieftess is in need of you," Laedrin directed.

Jarnath studied him intently.

"I have helped her, as much as I am able. She is stronger now. She can sit and she has drunk some water, but there are medicines you might give her, and you will know what it might be safe for her to eat, with her having not eaten for so long."

Jarnath nodded wearily, apparently too worn, too numbed, for astonishment.

Laedrin continued, his eyes bright with tears. "And, Jarnath, you must share the pain in your heart with her, and with Aranath, as much as you are able. Aras would never have wanted to cause you harm, by his life or by his death. You were like a father to him, more than I ever was. You must fight to live, in memory of him, as must we all."

Now Jarnath stared at him in astonishment.

"As much as I have helped the Chieftess, she has helped me far more," Laedrin admitted. "Go to her, Jarnath. She is not yet well."

Jarnath nodded and entered her room.

LEONAS had watched the exchange in surprise. He had not wanted to intrude, but he could not leave the High-King's presence without his permission. He hoped Laedrin might pass by him without noticing him, but he did not. He turned his focus upon Leonas, his eyes boring into his own. "Leonas, I would have words with you."

Leonas stiffened. "Yes, Majesty?" he asked, carefully keeping all emotion from his voice.

Laedrin was direct. "Though you have tried to be discreet, it has come to my attention that Captain Gaius has become a frequent visitor to Guest House."

Leonas paled and his heart began hammering, his worst fears suddenly realized.

"I think you would find it more convenient were he to instead live at Guest House with you. Captains Daras and Thanadrin would, of course, be assigned to comparable quarters elsewhere, if they choose to be. Would that be acceptable to you?" Laedrin asked.

Leonas began to breathe again and found his voice. "Yes, Majesty," he said, afraid to say more, suspicious this might all be a trap of some sort.

"Then it is settled. I will have my son's things moved from the House to the Palace." He hesitated a moment. "I also wish to thank you, Leonas, for sharing your memories of Aras with me, when I commanded you to. I know it was very difficult for you. And I want to thank you for being such a good friend to Aras as well, when he was so desperately in need of one." Laedrin looked as if he suddenly felt awkward. "That is all. Dismissed," he added, with familiar abruptness.

"Yes, Majesty. And thank you!" Leonas said, much more enthusiastically than before. Then he left. He did not know what had come over Laedrin. He only wished Aras might have been here to share it. But he must tell Gaius. The two of them had been living in fear of discovery. They had dreaded that one or both of them might be reprimanded and forced to cease their relationship, or more likely, be reassigned or incarcerated for it. And Shadala was suddenly recovering when even Jarnath had feared today would be her last day amongst them. He hurried to the Grove, eager to share his joyous news with Gaius.

Leonas only hoped Lunahr might yet be safe, wherever he was. Lunahr should not have marched to war with King Talon. It eased Leonas's fears to know that five thousand Elven soldiers had marched with them, in addition to three hundred of Lunahr's newly discovered kinsmen. Lunahr might yet return safely to them.

GAIUS stroked Leonas's face tenderly. "Leonas, my love. What is wrong?"

Leonas nuzzled his cheek against the gentle caress, and Gaius ran his fingertips across Leonas's lips. Leonas reached for him wordlessly and drew him into an embrace, kissing him tenderly. Then he sighed and said with obvious reluctance. "I have to go back. The Trees are restless as well. There is danger coming."

It was Gaius's turn to sigh. They were in the beautiful garden of the Guest House where they had lived these weeks past, away from prying eyes. Gaius had hoped they might be away from duty, from responsibility as well, for a single afternoon. "Leonas, I am worried about you. Ever since the High-Prince's death, you have not spent more than a handful of hours away from the Grove. You will get ill if you do not take care. Even the Trees know it. Remember, it was Aranas that sent you here to me today."

Leonas looked at Gaius, anguish naked upon his face. "Gaius, I cannot rest. We still do not know how Aras died." Gaius knew it still felt wrong for him to say it, both to call Aras by name, as he teasingly would not in life, but also, to say that he was dead. The truth of it was too painful.

"You fear for the Grove," Gaius said.

"I fear for all of Nalea, but especially the Grove. Ahrnad is the Enemy's pawn. He is still out there, somewhere, filled with hatred and treachery. He will target me, Gaius. I am the only one left of the three he most hated. Aras is gone and Beryl is safe from him. I fear Ahrnad will seek his revenge. Alwen can no longer aid him, now that he has been replaced by Laedrin with Phaedrus, as Lord of the Guard, but still, I fear for the Trees. I fear...." He hugged Gaius tightly.

"You are afraid for me, as well, that Ahrnad will seek to gain his revenge upon you by harming one you love," Gaius surmised.

Leonas nodded. "I fear for you, as well as for Aranonas and Aranas and the others," he said, naming the two Trees of the Grove he was bonded to, although he was now able to speak to all of them, as Lunahr had been.

"The High-King must share your fears," Gaius said. "He has not marched southwards with the Army and Navy as he had told King Talon he would. At first he was lost in his grief for his son, and now, I realize, worried for the Chieftess. But even now that she is recovered, he does not go, although, were the Enemy to attack us in numbers, we are too few to resist. We have a mere five thousand soldiers, against the might of the Enemy. It was a mistake, I think, for the High-king to go to King Talon's aid, to so split his forces. I fear he waited too long to activate the Reservists."

Leonas smiled wearily at him. "If you are still trying to put me at ease, my love, you are doing a poor job of it."

"I am unsettled as well, and my uneasiness grows. Come, Leonas, we will return to the Grove," Gaius said. "Unfortunately, vigilance is still our strongest weapon against the Enemy. Would that we were better armed."

C APTAIN Antonius and his eleven fellow King's Guard on door duty watched warily, hands on their sword hilts, as twenty-four Guard, only a handful of whom he recognized and knew by name, approached the doors of the Palace.

Captain Taras of the Guard spoke. "We are escorting a messenger, an Aerta whom we waylaid in the woods. He is in the livery of Erenia. He did not resist us and surrendered his arms to us willingly. He says he has a message for the High-King's ears only. We found none upon him, but he claims it is an oral one." The Guard parted, revealing the blond-haired, green-eyed Elf in their midst, who was indeed dressed in the livery of a King's Messenger of Erenia.

"Well done. Hold him here," Antonius commanded. He knocked in the correct pattern for the afternoon shift and the doors were opened just enough for him to slip inside, and then were closed behind him. Once inside, he sent a handful of men to alert Lord of the Guard Phaedrus and also summoned twenty-five additional King's Guard to his aid, two dozen to replace the Guard in escorting the alleged messenger within the building, and a Captain to replace him at his door post. Lord of the Guard Phaedrus might not have objected to such a large force of Guard within the Palace, but he was not of sufficient rank to be comfortable allowing it without direct orders.

Scant moments later he reappeared outside with his new men and the Captain replacing him took up position by the door. "We will escort the messenger to the Audience Chamber. You and your men will return to your patrol duty in the Wood, Captain Taras."

"Understood," the Guard Captain replied with a curt nod, without the challenge or bite of bitterness another might have betrayed in his place. Taras was a good man, a good warrior, even if he was an Oceana.

Antonius and his men formed up around the foreign Aerta and escorted him to the Audience Chamber.

The messenger balked, stopping short only a handful of steps inside the room. "That is not the High-King. My message is for his ears alone."

The male Aerta standing before the empty throne said, "I am Lord of the Guard Phaedrus. No one speaks to the High-King. All messages are relayed to him, through me." His voice was firm.

"This message cannot be," the messenger insisted.

"Then there will be a slightly delay in delivery. Take him to the dungeon," Phaedrus commanded. "I am confident he will tell us his message with the proper persuasion."

The messenger's eyes widened. "No! Wait, you can't," he said, his voice tinged with fear. "I... I was told if I could not speak to the High-King, I might speak with Lord of the Grove Beryl. Those are the only two he trusts."

Phaedrus eyed him coolly. "Who trusts?"

"I cannot say. I am sworn to silence," the messenger said. "Your men have searched me. They see I carry no weapons. I am not a danger to the Lord of the Grove."

"You wish to speak to the Lord of the Grove? Very well. Captain Antonius, bring the Lord here. Tell him of this messenger," Phaedrus commanded.

"At once, Lord." Antonius noted that Phaedrus had not mentioned to this supposed messenger that Lord Beryl was no longer Lord of the Grove, that he was no longer here. He was curious to see how this man might react to the appearance of the new Lord of the Grove in his place.

PHAEDRUS watched as the messenger shifted uneasily from foot to foot after Captain Antonius departed on his mission. He and the remaining King's Guard stayed perfectly still as they waited.

Phaedrus silently calculated the time it would take for Antonius to complete his mission and was not at all surprised when the doors reopened, precisely when he expected them to. Leonas entered, escorted by Antonius. "I come as commanded, Lord of the Guard Phaedrus." He turned to the messenger. "I am Lord of the Grove. Speak your message to me."

The messenger eyed him in dismay. "But... but you cannot be! Beryl is a Man, not an Elf."

Leonas said warily, "Lord Beryl is no longer here. I am Leonas, Lord of the Grove, Protector of the Trees."

"Can… can you speak to the Trees, as Beryl could? Part of the message is for one of the Trees," the messenger said nervously.

Leonas turned to Phaedrus. "This man is no messenger. He has neither the nerve nor the bearing of one. I will compromise my own safety by coming here willingly, to keep the High-King safe. But I will not compromise the safety of the Trees I am sworn to protect."

Phaedrus nodded calmly, in full agreement with Leonas's assessment. "Take him to the dungeon. Tell the Healer Jarnath we will have need of his elixirs and perhaps his services as a healer, if we are forced to use other means as well, and decide that the prisoner should then live."

The messenger's hand plunged into his shirt, but before he could pull it free again, dozens of hands pinned him to the floor. "No! Let me show you the letter! Keep Jarnath away from me!" the messenger cried in panic.

"Bind him and carry him to the dungeon!" Phaedrus ordered.

"Lord! There is a letter in his hand! I do not understand. The Guard said they searched him for both weapons and messages and found neither," Antonius said, confounded.

"Then the Guard was obviously less than thorough. See that you do better. Search him, now!" Phaedrus barked.

There was the tearing of cloth and then the man on the floor started screaming hysterically and thrashing wildly. There was the sound of fists on flesh, then silence, then more tearing. "Sir, the prisoner is unarmed," Antonius reported.

"Bring the letter to me," Phaedrus said, "But do not touch it. I suspect the paper is poisoned."

Antonius's hand trembled slightly, as he held the letter aloft. "Forgive me, my Lord. I have already touched it."

Phaedrus sighed. Of course he would have, when he found it. "Then open it, and hold it up for me to read. If we are fortunate, we both will live."

LEONAS stepped back as Antonius approached, eyeing the letter warily. Antonius held it up for Phaedrus. Phaedrus began reading it, and his face paled. He motioned to Leonas and when he came, whispered softly into his ear, so no other could hear. "I do not know the High-Prince's hand, but you must. Tell me, is this genuine? Is it truly from him?"

Leonas's eyes widened, and he looked at the letter and began to read. He nodded wordlessly. He could not speak.

Phaedrus took the letter from Antonius. "Antonius, you and your men are to bring the messenger to Jarnath at once. Tell Jarnath he is to be kept unconscious until I call for him, but he is not to be harmed. He is to be healed of any injury you and your men dealt to him and dressed in new clothes before he awakens. You are to tell Jarnath to watch you closely for signs of poisoning or other dark magicks. Your men are to stay with this man as his personal Guard. You are to guard him as if he were the High-King. Do you understand?"

"Yes, Lord," Antonius said, his voice betraying his confusion at the change in treatment of the Elf from prisoner back to messenger, and perhaps also that Phaedrus had taken the letter from Antonius, when he yet suspected it might be dangerous. Leonas knew that Antonius was not in a position to ask questions and he did not. The naked Elf and the shredded remains of his clothes were borne swiftly away.

Phaedrus inspected his fingertips. "We must wait and be sure there is no ill effect from handling this letter. I do not believe the Guard would have missed finding it. How could they have? I am not so prejudiced to believe they might be so incompetent. I sense wizardry here, either fair or foul, I know not which."

"Please, Lord Phaedrus, let me finish reading the letter," Leonas pleaded. "The messenger said either the High-King or Lord of the Grove might read it. I am Lord of the Grove, now, and Aras trusted me, with his life. He and Beryl and I were like brothers. Even though I was not named, I must read it."

Phaedrus studied his face intently and nodded. "I will allow it. I cannot read it, as I was not named, but I have seen enough that I am desperate to know what it might say. Please, tell me only after you are done, whether the High-Prince might have survived what the Trees felt, whether they were somehow led astray. I must know whether or not he is truly dead."

He sighed. "I will hold it for you, in case it is a trick or trap of some sort, perhaps a poison which works slowly, to give an intermediary time to hand the letter to the High-King. The Enemy would know how suspicious we would be of messengers, after the High-King was almost assassinated by Lord Beryl. I might at least die honorably, if such is the case. I suspect I might instead be executed for my actions this day. Although the High-King's temperament has been more forgiving of late, he is still unpredictable in matters concerning his son."

"I will speak on your behalf, if I am needed," Leonas assured him sincerely. "The Navy has fared much better since you assumed command of our combined forces. I appreciate the fairness you have shown to my friends. You truly do not seem to share Ahrnad's or Alwen's prejudices against us."

"I in turn appreciate that you did not exclude the Army from your Grove Guard, when you selected them, though you well might have. You even elevated Thanadrin to Captain, an honor which he deserved. And the King's Guardsmen have been treated well, as equals, under your command."

Phaedrus lifted the letter and Leonas read it from the beginning, his heart pounding.

Dearest Father,

It pains me that I did not say good-bye to you before I left. My departure was so abrupt that I did not say good-bye to anyone.

I know you do not understand why I left, but you now must. I have kept far too many secrets for far too long. Yet even now, facing death, I cannot fully bare myself to you, as I wish I could. I can tell you only this: there are four wizards who battle for the fate of the world. The first is Incuban, most cruel; he would see every Elf, Man, and Dwarf consumed by his rapacious desires and the very world itself consumed by flame. The second is Arcanus, whom the Watch once worshipped as a God and whom I thought at first to be no less a villain than Incuban, for I am not as perfect as I need to be. I have now allied myself with Arcanus, to battle the other two. The third is Ithelia, who was once your Queen and is my mother still, but in body only. She bore me solely as a source of Power to feed upon. She is made of ice that burns as cruelly as Incuban's fire. She cares not for the fate of the world or its peoples. She would destroy all to obtain her twisted revenge. I have suffered terribly under her vile hand for decades, without your knowledge. Would that she had truly abandoned me, as she had appeared to you to have done! She must see me dead when she is done, even should I survive the coming battle, and the deaths of the other two. For you see, beloved Father, I am the fourth wizard. I could never reveal myself to you before. I tell you now only out of necessity, yet there are still secrets I must keep, so many secrets!

All I seek, all I ever sought, is that every man, woman, and child, be he or she Elf, Man, or Dwarf, be given the chance to live in happiness. I once thought, in order for the world to survive, the other three wizards must all perish. But, I have seen now that instead Arcanus will aid me, without treachery. I have shown him a different path.

Father, you must forgive Arcanus for what he did to you, that which I put to rights again, as you have forgiven Beryl. And you must aid Arcanus, his pupil Magus, and his other allies, in order to aid me, to aid us all. The bearer of this message, Willow, is of vital importance. If we are to see victory, he must be kept safe at all costs. If he falls, we may all be lost.

I have given him a verbal message for my Tree, Aranas. You must bring him to the Grove and allow him to touch Aranas so that he may deliver it. The Grove itself must be protected, not only for my love of it, but because it is also crucial to victory, as I fear the Enemy has now discovered. It is the Grove that must shelter Willow as it once sheltered Beryl.

Willow must dwell in the Guest House with Beryl and Leonas, and perhaps Gaius, to help Leonas watch over him, for Leonas guards Beryl still and Willow needs his own protector and friend. Willow is as desperately in need of friends as Beryl was, when first he came to us. The three of them will protect him and I hope love him, for Willow has endured much, and I fear his trials may have only just begun.

Forgive me, Father, for speaking of love to you. I should perhaps instead have said, "Willow is of strategic significance," so that you might understand me, and that "every Guardsman and King's Guardsman under your command is expendable, to see Willow and the Grove safe." Would that I were expendable in their place! I am a fool for writing this. You will send hundreds, even thousands, to their deaths easily enough, without my encouragement.

I wish I could rewrite this letter, for I have said too little, I have said too much, but there is no time. We are out of time. I am out of time. I fear I will die too soon. I fear death, but more, I fear failure, that I will die with the task at hand yet unfinished, and that all the innocents of the world might soon follow me to oblivion.

Forgive me again, Father, for showing you such weakness. I know you are ashamed of me, that you have ever only been ashamed of me. As always, I will try to make you proud of me. As always, I will fail. Even if I save the world, it will not be enough. Nothing is ever enough.

With all I have endured, I have never experienced despair until today, nor terror. There are so many things I have yet to experience, so many things that now I fear I never shall; it is a pity despair and terror are two that I have. They are not two I would have picked, had I a choice. But I have never had a choice, Father. So very few days of my life were ever lived as I chose to live them. I cherish those few days; I weep for them.

Yes, I know, tears are weakness, so you tried to teach me. Yet you wept once, Father. I—no, I cannot say more, not now. I fear not ever. I have so much else I wish I could say, but for now, this must suffice. I will try to hold hope in my heart instead of despair. I will try to hope that you might somehow understand, this one time, that you might see what is in my heart. For now, know that I love you, more than you have ever been able to comprehend. I will love you always.

But I love you no less for loving others. Please tell Jarnath, Shadala, Beryl, and Leonas that I love them, that they are in my thoughts often, and that I will do my best to return to them, to all of you. Aiee, you will not, I know you will not!

If only you would show them this letter, folding it so only the last paragraph shows. Do not show them the entire letter. It would wound them terribly to read it. I speak of wounds, yet still you will not understand. I will pretend I am the Commander and you my subordinate this one time.

"High-King Laedrin, I command you to fold this letter and show Jarnath, Shadala, Beryl, and Leonas this passage, and Talon, should you by some miracle ever see him again. It is for your eyes also, though you will be as blind to my written words as you have always been deaf to my voice:

"Though I do not like to think I might not see any of you again, should I fall, hold me in your hearts always. But do not let my memory prevent your hearts from healing, from someday finding the happiness you all deserve, that I have ever only wished for all of you. Forgive me for any pain I have ever caused you or might yet cause you. Remember, it is always darkest before the dawn, and the days to come, though they look bleak now, will be filled with more light than you can imagine. Be safe, be well, be strong."

All my love, always,
Aras

Leonas was shaking with silent sobs as he finished the letter, his eyes streaming with tears. He wrapped his arms about his own shoulders as if embracing Aras's spirit. He fought for control. "You must… you must give this letter to the High-King. But first, let me summon the Chieftess. He should not be alone when he reads this. He is no longer the man Aras knew when he wrote this. Aras would not ever have wanted his words to harm his father."

Phaedrus clasped him on the shoulder. "I wish there was something I could say to comfort you. Go, Leonas. You serve the High-King well. I will do as you ask."

Leonas left the Palace, inhaling the comforting scent of the Wood desperately, wishing again for the River as well, his mind playing Aras's last desperate words of hope against all that he had written before, against the pain and terror of the flame that had consumed him. He headed for the Grove first. He could not face the Chieftess alone. He knew he could not embrace Aranonas for strength, lest the Trees learn of the message before the High-King. But there was one other here he could turn to.

The Grove Guard eyed Leonas suspiciously as he approached, hands gripping their weapons. He realized he must not appear himself. He tried to master control of his expression. "Do not worry. I have not been taken. Yet I need come no closer. Captain Gaius, you are commanded to accompany me. We are to summon the Chieftess for the High-King."

GAIUS came when called, keeping his face as emotionless as he could. "At once, Lord." He walked three paces behind Leonas, all the way to the stand of trees surrounding the Guest House, wordlessly, lest Leonas's fragile control shatter. Gaius could see something was terribly wrong.

Leonas looked about half-dazed, as if to ensure they were safely out of sight of the Grove Guard. Then he embraced Gaius. "Hold me, Gaius. Let me hear your steady, strong heart, for my own is breaking anew."

"Leonas, please tell me what is wrong! The King's Guard summoned you to the Palace. Have you lost your position? Is the High-King angered? Are you in danger?" Gaius could not keep the fear from his voice.

"No, Gaius. I am sorry I have frightened you with such thoughts. It is something else entirely. There was a letter, from Aras." Leonas sobbed as he spoke his name. "It is like a knife in my heart, knowing he is gone! But I must heed his words to me, the only ones he thought I would see. I must stay strong for him. We must go now to bring the Chieftess. The High-King will have need of her, now that his heart is no longer made of stone, as it once was. I will explain on the way."

SHADALA knew at once something terrible had happened, seeing Leonas. She was relieved to hear it was an old grief, reawakened. She was outwardly solemn as they returned to the Palace. Inwardly, she was in renewed anguish over Aras, but more, for his father, knowing how terribly this letter could wound him.

Shadala and Phaedrus appeared before the High-King in the Audience Chamber, while Leonas and Gaius waited in the hall. Phaedrus told Laedrin of the messenger and the letter, and suggested that the High-King might wish to clear the room and the observation areas of King's Guard before reading it.

Shadala was deeply moved when Laedrin looked from Phaedrus to her, silently seeking her counsel. Laedrin had been betrayed by the Lord of the Guard he had appointed once before, by Ahrnad, thanks to wizardry brought by a false messenger. He would not be deceived again. He could not trust Phaedrus fully. But he trusted her. Warmth for the father flooded her heart, not drowning out the anguish over his son, but muting it, making it more bearable.

"Phaedrus will guard you with his life, as will I, should there be need," she assured Laedrin. "But it would indeed be best if we two were the only ones present, High-King. There are passages within the letter of a personal nature, which you might wish to discuss with us, which should not be for other ears." Her voice spoke one message, but her eyes told another, as she urged him to listen to what she would not convey with words. She knew he could not bear to break down in front of his men once again, this time of his own volition. From what she had heard, this letter would crush him, but succumbing to grief before his men could destroy him.

WHEN Leonas and Gaius were finally summoned to appear before the High-King, Leonas saw that Laedrin was pale, and appeared shaken. Shadala stood beside him, and his hand was clutching her shoulder, as if he might fall without such support.

"You have read the letter, Lord Leonas. I do not think, considering all that has happened here in my son's absence, he would now wish it were otherwise. You will escort Willow to the Grove, to Aranas. Willow is to be allowed to touch him. The Grove Guard is charged with protecting Willow, as if he were a Tree of the Grove. He will live with you and Gaius in Guest House. I am quartering Captains Daras and Thanadrin there as well, as Beryl is no longer with us, to ensure that Willow is never alone.

"But, in fulfilling a portion of my son's wishes, I do not ignore his other concerns. This is not meant to prevent you and Captain Gaius from finding happiness, as long as Willow's safety comes first and you use the utmost discretion, as you have been doing already. Is my meaning clear?"

"Yes, Majesty, thank you," Leonas and Gaius said in unison, the sincerity of their thanks evident.

"You must try to find out from Willow if Arcanus yet lives. If he truly supported my son, he may also have been slain. If he lives, he is now our one hope. From what I have learned I suspect... Ithelia... was the one who killed Aras, may she burn for it," he swore, shaking in rage and grief.

"Go. And have the Healer Jarnath report to me, when you collect Willow. Do not speak of the letter to him. Say only...." Laedrin hesitated, his eyes seeking Shadala's, for the first time in Leonas's memory appearing lost, speechless. Leonas felt an unexpected surge of compassion for the man who had once shown Aras only coldness and cruelty. He suspected Laedrin's mind was in turmoil, in agony, that Aras's words had burnt him like the fire that had claimed him, as they had tormented Leonas.

Shadala interjected, "Say that I suffer a relapse, that he must bring medicine to ease my grief. We fear for Jarnath. He will have need of such medicine. He will undoubtedly insist upon reading the entire letter. The three of us will drink together, grieve together."

Laedrin looked at her in gratitude. "Do as the Chieftess suggests. Dismissed."

"Yes, Majesty," Leonas said. Then he and Gaius left the High-King and headed for the Healers' Hall.

"It is far more than I hoped," Gaius said, sounding nearly breathless with relief.

"I had been so upset over Aras, I had not realized what it might have meant for us," Leonas admitted. "Aras has again saved us, by naming you, and his concerns for my happiness, in his letter." Leonas fought the tears that threatened to come. "I thought I knew how much I loved him. I see now that my love for him will grow, rather than fade, with time."

They entered the Healers' Hall. The King's Guard let them pass. Jarnath turned from the bed where Willow lay as they approached. "Leonas, what is wrong? What ill has befallen you?" the healer asked, his voice warm with concern.

"None more than any of the rest of us, Jarnath. I am as well as I can be, for now. How is Willow, the messenger?" To Leonas's eye he appeared to be sleeping peacefully.

"He was not harmed overly much by the King's Guard. I gave him something so he might sleep, as the High-King commanded. Am I now to waken him?" Jarnath asked.

"He must wake, but it would be best if you not be here when he does. He is terrified of you, for some reason. He spoke as if you did him some great ill in the past," Leonas admitted.

Jarnath seemed surprised. "Truly? To my knowledge, I have never seen him before."

Leonas shrugged. "In any case, there is also somewhere you need to be. The Chieftess is in need of your services. She is at the Palace with the High-King. She has been overcome by memory again, for the High-Prince. The High-King has instructed you to bring medicine to ease her grief."

Jarnath looked pained, then nodded. "I will bring her sharesh. It does not take the pain away, but it softens it so the memories are not so raw."

Leonas nodded. He did not like lying to Jarnath. The healer had not been well since Aras's death. Jarnath appeared far older than he had even a few short months ago, when he had thought Aras, whom he loved as a son, dead in the jaws of a wolven. Leonas feared that to have had Aras miraculously return, hale and strong, only to lose him again, even more terribly, to fire, was too much for the elder Elf to bear.

"Courage, Jarnath," Leonas said, placing a comforting hand upon his shoulder. "Of all of us, Aras would have wanted you to suffer least of all. You must value your own life as much as he treasured it."

"I know, Leonas, and I try, for his sake, I truly do. I eat, I sleep. I try to pretend life still has purpose, still has meaning, with him gone. I am still needed. Yet it is cold comfort at best. But Shadala must not suffer further, not with all her people gone." He removed a vial from a drawer. "When I have gone, tilt Willow's head back and have him drink this, all of it. He will still be able to swallow it, even while unconscious. And try to learn if it is truly me he fears, or all healers. I fear he might have need of us, again, if he is truly in such danger."

Leonas waited until after Jarnath left, then he did as Jarnath had instructed. Leonas studied Willow, curious. None of the tension and fear of before were reflected in his face now, in his sleep. His long blond hair hung nearly to his waist. He was fine-boned, even for one of their kind: delicate seeming, yet he had fought against the King's Guard strongly enough.

Willows eyes snapped open, the vivid green showing terror as he saw Leonas before him. He scrabbled away from him on the bed, eyes riveted to the pallenteum container in his hand. "Stay away from me!" he yelled in fear.

"Hush. It's all right," Leonas said, as if calming a frightened animal. "It's empty, see?" he assured him, holding the vial upside down to prove it, before putting it down. "You must calm yourself. No one here will harm you. The High-King has read the letter. We are taking you to the Grove, to Aranas, as Aras asked us to. You will be safe there. You will stay in the Guest House, with me and Gaius, as well as Daras and Thanadrin of the Grove Guard, for Beryl no longer dwells in our Wood. The King's Guard will accompany us to the Grove for protection only. You need not fear that they might harm you. They will guard you now as if you were the High-King. Come. It is time you met Aranas. I can see you are in need of the tranquility of the Grove," Leonas soothed, extending his hand.

Hesitantly Willow placed his own hand in his. It was cold and it trembled.

"Gaius, he is cold. Fetch him a cloak," Leonas commanded.

"No! No cloaks!" Willow said, panic rising, snatching his hand away.

"All right, Willow. No cloak. Come, you have need of the Grove. I can see that plainly enough," Leonas urged.

Willow nodded and stood. He looked down at himself and wrapped his arms about his middle, fingering the strange clothes, his gaze darting nervously to the King's Guard. He shivered visibly.

"My apologies. Your own clothes were torn beyond repair," Leonas explained. "Please, you need not fear the King's Guard. I have told you, the High-King has instructed them to guard you as if you were him. The fervor they showed protecting the High-King's representative, Phaedrus, against you, when they thought you sought to harm him, is no less than that they will show to any who now dares try to harm you."

Willow nodded, and appeared to force his arms down to his sides. He walked away from the bed, allowing himself to be encircled once again, but Leonas could see the tension in him. He could almost smell his fear, it was so strong.

They exited the Palace. Willow did not relax at all once outside.

They continued onward, toward the Grove, but stopped well before it. Every member of the Grove Guard had their bows at the ready and arrows nocked against them. Captain Daras stepped forward and ordered them to drop their weapons.

Leonas kept silent, deferring to Captain Antonius, as he tried to puzzle out what could possibly have the Grove Guard so on edge they would draw against two of their own, as well as a contingent of the King's Guard, even if they did have a stranger in their midst.

"We cannot," Captain Antonius argued. "We are guarding a messenger, at our High-King's command. We are escorting him to the Grove. He is to be allowed to touch the High-Prince's Tree, and to be given shelter in the Grove, and to be guarded by you and your men as if he were himself a Tree, as per the High-King's order. Lord of the Grove Leonas and Captain Gaius accompany him."

"Then I would speak with them. Lord Leonas, Captain Gaius, disarm and show yourselves, that we may determine whether it is safe for the King's Guard to approach," Daras commanded. Leonas could hear the tension in him.

"We will approach," Leonas said, wondering what was wrong. He and Gaius were allowed to exit the circle of King's Guardsmen. They divested themselves of their swords and bows, handing them to one of the soldiers to hold and then walked forward.

Daras met them halfway. His sword was drawn, in his hand, but held at his side. He studied them both intently.

"Leonas? It is truly you. What is going on?" Daras asked.

"Antonius has told you. We are bringing a messenger to the Grove. His name is Willow. He was sent by High-Prince Aras, before he was killed. He carries a letter from Aras, commanding that he be allowed to touch his tree, Aranas, and that he be given shelter in the Grove, as Beryl was once sheltered here, and at Guest House," Leonas said, perplexed by Daras's actions and those of the Grove Guard.

"The men reported you were acting strangely before, and that you summoned Gaius away from his post, without providing a replacement. You look yourself, you sound yourself, yet still, the Enemy is treacherous. I will search you for concealed weapons and bind your hands. You will come with me and you will touch Aranonas. You might be able to fool me, but you will not be able to fool your Tree, and you will not be able to live long enough to cause harm amongst those of the Grove if you are other than you appear," Daras challenged. Daras tensed, clutching his sword, as if he expected Leonas to lunge for him, or run into the Grove.

"Of course," Leonas said, belatedly realizing how odd his actions had seemed. He held his arms away from his body, so he might be searched.

Daras was thorough. He searched them both and then bound their hands before them. Then they were escorted to the Grove. He had six men encircle Gaius at the edge of the Grove and then led Leonas inside.

The Trees permitted them both to enter unimpeded. Daras did not guide him to his tree, but instead hung back, as if testing to be sure he knew which one to approach. Leonas walked to Aranonas and caressed his Tree with the fingertips of both bound hands. The tension and pain he had felt since reading the letter vanished as if they had never been. He breathed deeply, again at peace. Aranonas reached down a branch and stroked Leonas's face with it and then gently brushed the same branch against Daras's sword hand.

Daras exhaled in relief. "I might not be able to speak to him as you do, Leonas, but I can see that he seeks to tell me you are yourself, and that I may sheathe my sword." He embraced Leonas, briefly. "I had feared you were lost to us. You have no idea how close we have come to slaying you, for what you have done."

Leonas smiled ruefully. "Forgive me, my friend. I was not thinking clearly. It did not even occur to me I left the Grove Guard without a Captain when I summoned Gaius. I will report myself to the High-King for doing so. If I am fortunate, I will have cost myself my station, if I am not, perhaps my life. You must not say anything to Gaius of this. I will leave Gaius here as guard for Willow, and you here in charge of the Grove. When word comes of my fate, you must comfort Gaius as well as you can."

Daras looked at him in pain. "Surely the High-King would not execute you! Any other man under his command, certainly. He has done so with far less cause many times, or at least, has sent many to their deaths. But you are bonded to a Tree. He would not injure the Grove." Daras hugged him fiercely again. "We must go. The rest of the Grove Guard will begin to suspect treachery, if we are too long gone, and it is no easy thing to hold a drawn bow so long without releasing your arrow."

"I almost forgot to inform you. You and Thanadrin are to move into the Guest House, to help us guard Willow there, as well," Leonas said, as they exited the Grove.

"Lower your bows. Leonas and Gaius are well. The King's Guard may approach with the one they escort armed," Daras called out loudly.

Leonas could see the tension leave his men. He gazed longingly at the Grove, at the men, and then steeled himself. He must not betray his thoughts to Gaius. The King's Guard parted and, to Leonas's surprise, Willow made a beeline for Aranas.

Of course. Aras must have described his Tree to him. Yet when Willow reached the slender birch, he stopped. He appeared afraid. He spoke softly to the Tree and then reached out a cautious hand, as if it were a wolven and he feared being bitten. He grimaced as if with pain, or fear, but then his face broke into a beatific smile, and he embraced the Tree as if it were a long lost lover. Indeed, Aranas embraced him as well, wrapping leafy branches around him, so he was nearly concealed from their sight.

Leonas felt pain then, knowing he might never again feel his own Tree's touch. He turned to Gaius. "Gaius, you are to guard Willow. I must go tell Thanadrin he will be moving into the Guest House with us. Daras already knows."

Gaius nodded and Leonas fought the urge to embrace him. Leonas studied Gaius's face, memorizing every line of it, and then left quickly, before he could betray the terror and despair in his heart to his lover.

TIME passed with painful slowness for Daras, who waited anxiously for word of Leonas. But finally, as the sun began to sink into the sky, and dusk approached, Daras was startled to see Leonas himself approach, even more so when he saw his apologetic smile. Leonas went straight to Daras. "I must speak with you amongst the Trees, Captain," he commanded formally, and Daras joined him in the solitude of the Grove.

"FORGIVE me for keeping you in such suspense, my friend! All is well. High-King Laedrin is so changed these past weeks, I can scarcely believe it. He acknowledged that I was derelict in my duty in calling Gaius from the Grove and not assigning a replacement. He relieved me greatly when he told me that Gaius was not to blame, for following my order to leave it. But then he astonished me.

"He said that I was under extreme duress, for having read the letter, when Aras had warned him I should not. He told me that losing Aras was akin to losing a brother."

Leonas did not tell Daras the rest. Laedrin had also told him that he'd had a brother, once, long ago, and that he had made many terrible mistakes following his death. Laedrin said that at least no one had died because of Leonas's mistake. There was such a wealth of guilt, regret, and self-condemnation in his voice when he told him, it was a wonder Laedrin could yet stand. But he could not dwell on that now. Leonas continued his report to Daras.

"The High-King said that no one is as perfect as he needs to be, but he told me that I am an excellent soldier, valued by both him and the Trees and… he has forgiven me." He could not hide the shock and wonder at the memory of his words. "He said he was impressed that I came to him, knowing that it might mean loss of my position or of my life. He freely admitted that not long ago it well might have. But he trusted that it would never happen again. I swore to him on my life and by my sword and my bow that I would never again fail him." Leonas hugged Daras, grinning in relief and joy.

He heard a gasp, as if someone was in pain. He released Daras and turned. Gaius was standing there, at too great a distance to have heard his softly spoken confession, but obviously not far enough to have failed to see their embrace.

Gaius's face was completely expressionless, and when he spoke, his voice was wooden. "Forgive me my trespass, Lord. I came to inform you that Willow has released Aranas. He says he is ready to go to the Guest House and has inquired about dinner. I will bring him there and see that he has whatever he requires. I can see you are otherwise occupied." Gaius turned stiffly to leave.

"Return to your post, Captain Daras. Captain Gaius, I have not dismissed you. Approach," Leonas commanded imperiously.

Daras left the Grove as Gaius approached with blatant reluctance. "Talk to me, Gaius," Leonas said, softly, in the voice of a friend and lover, rather than a Commander.

GAIUS'S heart ached to hear the sweet tones of his voice. "As my Lord commands it, I must," Gaius said, unable to staunch the flow of bitterness in his voice. "I saw you, Leonas. Not only now, but before as well, when you were whispering secrets to him, hugging him. I have been so afraid, living as we have. I knew I might die for it or that you might. But I thought it worth the risk I thought—I was a fool, I see it now. I thought you loved me, Leonas, that you truly loved me, as… as lythenia… not merely as some pleasure love, to be cast aside, without thought for how my heart would break…." He could not continue. He was trembling already and he would not cry. He had humiliated himself enough.

"Ah, Gaius, you are a fool. A proud fool. A jealous one," Leonas said, embracing him, kissing him softly upon the cheek.

"Please, do not," Gaius begged, his control shattering. He sobbed and clung to Leonas.

"Hush, it is all right, my love, my lythenia. You were right in that, at least. You are lythenia to me, Gaius. I would never betray that. Do you not trust me better than that? Daras is my friend, only. He was my Commander, have you forgotten? Though I command him, now, instead, still I value him as a friend, as a confidant, as a comrade. Gaius, you must know why such relationships as ours are usually forbidden. Such passions, such jealousies can be ruinous to a command. We have been given a rare gift, that we are allowed to express our love for each other," Leonas said.

Gaius's trembling stilled at his words and his embrace tightened. Then he released Leonas. "Forgive me, Leonas! I—so much has happened. I have lived with such fear and—you must think me so weak. I can see from your face you forgive me, that you love me still. I...." He kissed Leonas passionately. Words were not enough to express what he needed to say. Then he pulled gently away. "I will be stable. I will be discreet. I will be whatever you need me to be, I swear. We should go. Willow is hungry. I would not shirk my duty to him."

Leonas smiled at him and they left the Grove together.

LEONAS was surprised to see Willow smile as they approached. "Aranas has gifted me with strength enough that I think I might safely leave him, for a time. I find that I am surprisingly hungry, though I have not been eating well, of late," Willow admitted.

Leonas shook his head. "It is uncanny. You sounded so like Beryl before, in need of his Tree, and now as well, having held him. I only hope that Beryl is yet well. It has been so long and he is far from us. Aranahr tells me he can no longer hear him."

Willow looked at him oddly. "You spoke to Aranahr?"

Leonas nodded. "Yes. I both hear and speak to all the Trees now, as Beryl once did. I have been able to ever since I touched Aranas, after Aras was killed. I began to hear all the Trees, through him. Now I can hear them all directly." He grew solemn. "Would that I could hear only my own. Would that Aras yet lived!"

Willow appeared uncomfortable.

Leonas eyed him in dawning surprise. "I had not thought when I mentioned it, that you would think Aras still lived. Yet you do not react strongly to my words. You knew of his death already, though you bore his letter as if he were still alive."

Willow swallowed. "His words were no less true. Please, I cannot speak of him to you. I am forbidden. I will not. You have been commanded to aid me. You must."

"I will do as I am commanded. But if you will not speak to me, you might speak to the High-King. He will be far less easy to refuse than I, and once he learns you know of his son's death, he will not rest until he hears all you know," Leonas said.

Willow looked at him in fear. "Please, you cannot tell him! Not for my sake, though I'd be a fool not to fear him. But because there is no choice: what must be must be, if the world is to survive."

Leonas sighed. "I will not keep secrets from the High-King." He did not say that at one time he well might have, that he had. "But neither will I disturb him now. The morning will bring what it will bring. Come, you need to rest and eat. You must keep up your strength. We all must. There are yet dark times ahead that we must face."

Hesitantly Willow accompanied them, and the three of them walked to the Guest House. Thanadrin was already there. Leonas introduced him, and the four of them engaged in rather strained conversation, until dinner arrived. Willow commented that the food was excellent, but Leonas noted he did not eat much of it, despite his earlier words.

After dinner, Leonas stared into the fire, a crystal goblet of wine in his hands. It was so silent. The Guest House should not be like this. Lunahr should be here, and Aras. They should be laughing and talking and singing. An image of Aras writhing and screaming as flame consumed him tore across Leonas's mind. He threw the glass into the fire and it shattered against the stone fire pit, sending tiny glass shards everywhere.

Leonas fled outside, into the garden, but Aras was there also: he saw his smiling face by every bush and flower, and heard his laughter. Leonas ran for the solace of the stream. He stripped off his clothes and sank into it, gasping as the cold, clear water flowed over him.

GAIUS had followed his lythenia in concern. He had told Thanadrin to stay with Willow. Gaius stood on the stream bank, watching critically as Leonas's beautiful hair flowed with the current across his leanly muscled chest and arms. He was more lean than he should be. Leonas had neither been eating nor sleeping well.

"Why is he in the stream? I thought him Aerta," a voice said from the darkness. Gaius jumped, startled, hand on his sword hilt, until he recognized Willow.

"Why are you alone? Where is Thanadrin?" Gaius asked, concerned.

"I told him I was only going into the garden and that you were already there. But I did not see you, and I remembered the stream and felt compelled to come. I love these waters. This stream saved my life once. I thought I might find calm here. Is Leonas Oceana?"

"His Mother is Oceana, of Tanieria. His Father is Aerta, of Lysenia. And you?" Gaius asked.

"My mother is also Oceana, of Riviera," Willow said.

Gaius said sympathetically. "Forgive me for asking. My condolences, then. No wonder you are so in need of the Trees."

Willow paled. "What... what are you saying? Why do you speak to me in such a tone?"

"Surely you must know? Loatia and Riviera... no, forgive me. Never mind," Gaius said, realizing to his horror that Willow did not know his mother's Kingdom, and likely his father's, that of Loatia, though he had not mentioned him, had been destroyed.

"What has happened? Tell me!" Willow commanded, though it sounded more like a plea.

"I will tell you, but first you must go back to Aranas. You have left too soon. You should sleep with Aranas to shelter you, to keep your dreams from becoming too dark," Gaius said.

"I will walk with you," Leonas said, rising from the stream, reaching for his clothes. He had apparently heard and determined Willow needed him more than he needed the stream.

"No! I want no more questions from Aranas! My core is strong enough. I need the River, or at least this stream, that is all. What has happened?" Willow demanded.

Leonas looked grim. "Loatia and Riviera have both fallen to Incuban. He has dried up the River and burnt the Wood... and our people. There are some few thousands of refugees, survivors of the many thousands who once dwelt in both Kingdoms. They are in Erenia. The Army has quarantined the City to all but the healers who have been called to come from every Kingdom. The City is all but lost to chaos, to madness. There were so many with such terrible burns, and all the rest, even those whose bodies are whole, their spirits—they are dying, all of them, for want of their River and Wood, their friends and families. If your mother still dwelt in Riviera, there is scant hope she yet lives."

Willow's expression changed from shock to bleak despair to rage. "He knew! He knew and he did not tell me! May Incuban take him, he knew!" He looked up and screamed into the night. "You want the Power of the Trees of Nalea, Father? Then come take it, if you dare! I am through being your pawn and Aras's, and Incuban's plaything!" His figure and his face glowed and shifted and a different Elf stood before them, his silver hair blowing with a wind of its own and his blue eyes crackling lightning. Then he cried out in sudden terror.

"No! He sees me! He is here, His army, He is already here! The Grove, the Trees! Hurry! He comes for them, He comes for me!" the Elf who had been Willow screamed, clawing at invisible demons in the air.

Gaius slung Willow over his shoulders and began running for the Grove. Leonas, unburdened, outdistanced him and ran ahead to warn the Grove of a pending attack, and of Willow's true form, lest they attempt to repel him and Gaius as they approached.

"Father, forgive me! Help me! Don't let Him take me!" Willow cried.

Gaius heard the sound of the alarm being raised in the City over his own labored breathing, as he ran to the Grove with his burden. That the alarm was already being sounded heartened him, until he saw the gray haze in the distance over the woods before him and understood why. Terror clutched his heart. It was smoke, so much smoke! He stopped running and spun about, scanning his surroundings. There was smoke everywhere, in every direction he turned, even from the River. Fire, they were surrounded by fire!

Gaius fought down his panic and continued toward the Grove. The Grove was in the center of a field; it would be harder for those Trees to catch. It was difficult to run with Willow writhing in his grasp, but he finally reached Aranas. Gaius saw more than the usual complement of Grove Guard was there, but perhaps only double the forty-nine, not triple, as there should be. He hoped more were on the way. He laid Willow beside Aranas and forced Willow's arms about the trunk of the Tree. Willow calmed instantly and clung to Aranas desperately. There was a strong breeze in the Grove. It worried Gaius: wind would make the fire spread more quickly.

Gaius unslung his bow, glad he had brought it outside with him when he had gone to the stream. He took up position in defense of Aranas and Willow, though there was no enemy in sight yet. It gave him time to worry. He could not fear for Leonas. He must not let his affections weaken him. Instead, he feared for the High-King and the City, but also for the Urwani-Amontir. So many of their people had gone with King Talon and those remaining were mostly women and children. Though the women could all fight, they would be poorly defended against a large force, and the woods by the River were already burning. Gaius pictured Field House and the fields around it already in flames, the women and children already horribly slain.

Willow had said Incuban was here with his army, though he did not understand how he might have known before them. He feared tens of thousands of the walking dead might already be slashing their way through their forces, heading toward the Grove. But the attack, when it came, came from above.

There was a terrifying, ear-piercing screech and out of the night, lit only by the moon, came a living nightmare, a winged creature, part eagle and part horse. It swooped down and snatched up one of the Grove Guard, not twenty feet from him. It was too dark to see who had been taken. A flight of arrows hit the beast and it fell to the ground, thrashing, but its prey lay motionless. Six of the Grove Guard ran up to it and dispatched it.

Then there was a roar from the sky almost directly above him and something part pumar, reptile, and eagle dove toward him. Gaius nocked an arrow and fired, aiming for the right eye, which glowed eerily green in the darkness. He saw the light go out and realized his arrow was not the only one to strike. The creature fell, not ten feet from Aranas, pierced by at least a dozen arrows. Its remaining eye burning with hate, it began dragging itself toward him and Willow.

Gaius dropped his bow, drew his sword, and set upon the critically wounded creature, thinking to dispatch it easily. His blade sliced cleanly into its neck, but he hissed in pain as the creature's leg spasmed, and its talons raked his right calf, a moment before it shuddered and collapsed lifelessly to the ground. Gaius staggered back to the Tree and sat, bracing his back against it; he could feel one of Willow's arms pressed into his lower back.

Gaius sliced off his other pants leg, and improvised bandages from it, which he bound about the wound. He could not tell how badly he was injured, in the poor light. He knew pain was no indication. Light wounds often hurt terribly and severe ones sometimes not at all, from shock. This one hurt fiercely.

The sky was alive with the heavy beating of wings. The wind from them was lashing Gaius's hair about his face, making it yet harder to see. Then he realized another creature was diving toward him and he braced his sword to impale it. The wind rose in crescendo to a roar and Gaius saw that the creature that had been heading toward them veered clear, not of its own accord. The wind had become so strong now that it threatened to pull Gaius away from the Tree, into the air. He twisted about and clutched as desperately at the trunk as Willow.

He would have thought he would not be able to hear anything over the roar of the wind, until he heard the things that broke into the clearing from the woods around the Grove. The Enemy's army was attacking in force. He hoped they would find the strong gusts as daunting as the airborne creatures had.

The branches of the Trees of the Grove were lashing wildly in the gale and Gaius was afraid he would see them torn lose and that the Trees might even be uprooted and crash to the ground, but the Trees remained surprisingly unharmed. To his shock he heard a strong whisper from Aranas and belatedly understood. The Trees were not being lashed by the wind: it was their furiously waving branches that were somehow causing the wind.

Gaius's arms tingled where his skin touched Aranas, as if hundreds of ants were crawling upon him. He had known the Trees were ancient and powerful, that they spoke and even moved, they soothed the mind and heart, and in Beryl's case, had even healed him of injury, but he had not dreamt that their Power was true magic, or that they might be able to focus it and wield it as a weapon.

Gaius saw that the Enemy's army could not approach, at least, not yet. But the fire was approaching. The dark smoke now blotted out the stars and was accompanied by a horrific orange glow. Gaius wondered how many of the Army and Navy were already dead.

A wave of dizziness hit him and he fought against it. He forced his right hand to his bandaged leg, still clinging to the trunk with his left hand against the force of the wind. He discovered to his dismay that the bandage was soaked through, that it was dripping. So, the injury had been serious, after all.

He remembered the story of the High-Prince, decades before, in the Arena, where he had been besting Marlaenus of the Navy. Aras had been mortally wounded in the leg, saving Marlaenus from harm. The High-Prince had applied a special type of healer's bandage to his own leg, a tourniquet, and Aras had lived. But Gaius knew nothing of such arts.

His heart fluttered in fear as he realized he would not live. He thought of Leonas, already mourning the brother-of-the-heart, Aras, and his fear for Beryl. He must not die! He must live, for Leonas! It was his last thought as he succumbed to the darkness, his life's blood pooling beneath him on the carpet of dead leaves upon which he lay.

SHADALA stood in front of the fallen High-King, slashing at another of the horrific creatures who attacked them, but though her strike sliced through the monster's neck, in what would have been a fatal blow to either Man or Elf, the cut was too shallow to sever the head. The bloodless creature felt no pain. Instead, it grinned triumphantly at her as its own blade came for her.

Despair seized her. It had been an Elf once, a Wood Elf, like Aras, like Laedrin. Despair flared to pain, then rage. She would not let Laedrin and his brave warriors be turned into monsters such as these. She twisted away from the weapon and slashed again. The headless thing staggered and fell.

She felt a brief moment's triumph, until she looked about. She was the only truly living person still standing in the courtyard. All around her were the High-King's fallen Guardsmen, Army and Navy both, and dozens of the Enemy's fallen soldiers. But hundreds more yet stood and were closing in upon her. She had time for only a single act before they reached her. She dove for Laedrin with the hunting knife she now wore in place of the King's Knife. They would not use Laedrin's body. She would see that his head joined the heads of the undead monsters that lay around her.

But suddenly her body froze. She and the High-King were lifted into the air, as if by a great wind. "**No, Chieftess,**" a voice boomed, awash with Power, though not directed upon her. A Man floated in the air before her, his red robe lashed by the winds, his long white hair whipping about his face. One hand was outstretched before him, palm upward, fingers rigid, as if grasping something, and she realized it was her and the High-King that he held.

"Incuban!" she spat in hatred. This was the creature of fire that had injured Taratur, Lunahr, who was yet a child, so terribly. He had ripped away his songs and laughter and replaced them with terror and tears.

"Not exactly," the voice said. Then his eyes blazed red flame and the creatures on the ground below them began howling as they caught fire by the dozens and stumbled about, burning, slashing mindlessly at everything around them, devastating their fellow undead.

"I am Arcanus. The City is lost, but the Grove yet stands. I will take you there," he said, and flew her and Laedrin toward it.

Arcanus! He had tried to kill Aras, to burn him. Aras had told her of his treacherous attack. But Aras's letter said Arcanus had become his ally. She now owed Arcanus her life, certainly, as did the High-King. But magicks or not, if he betrayed them, she would kill him.

"I have rescued some few other Lords and Ladies also, all those I could find amongst the carnage. I was delayed elsewhere."

They flew over thousands upon thousands of the Enemy's undead. All of them were heading for the Grove, apparently unconcerned that fire closed in all around them. Shadala could see by the bright light of the moon, as yet undimmed by smoke, that where Field House had once stood and the buildings that had housed the hundreds of Urwani-Amontir women and children who remained at home, while their husbands and sons, brothers and nephews and fathers had gone to war, there were now only the blackened, skeletal remains of a few wooden frames of the houses. The Urwani and the Amontir were dead as a people, with an entire generation of children gone, and no one left alive to bear and raise another.

"You should have let me die!" Shadala screamed in agony at Arcanus, but lacking his Power, now that they were in flight, and not merely hovering, her words were whipped away by the wind, seemingly unheard. Shadala saw the Grove below, as Arcanus effortlessly lowered himself down amidst the Trees.

"Chieftess!" Leonas ran to her. His eyes widened in horror as he saw who had been laid at the ground at her feet. "High-King!" He knelt to him. "He's still alive! Chieftess, you must help him!"

Shadala shook her head. "It is better he die thus, unaware of the fate of his people. The City is lost, his people dead, the Enemy's forces all around us. We are dead, Leonas, we are already dead," she said, her voice disturbingly emotionless.

He grabbed her arms and shook her. "Shadala, he lives! But he will die if you do not help him! You are a healer! He is your friend! How can you let him die?"

"We are all dead, all turned to ash, all burnt, like Aras." Then her voice broke and agony ripped through her mask of calm. "Like the children! Leonas, they are dead! The children are dead!" she sobbed and collapsed against him, lost in her grief.

Arcanus spoke then, his voice an island of serenity in a sea of chaos. "No, they live. They are safe, for the moment. They are on the other side of the River. It is why I was delayed, why the City fell so quickly, why I could save so few of the Lords and Ladies. I saved my children first, the small ones, the women, the warriors, all of them. But if Incuban's forces overrun the Grove, they will fall to Him. You must save those injured Lords and Ladies you can, Chieftess. The Trees cannot. They use all their Power for the wind, save that which they channel through my son Magus to me."

His calm words broke through Shadala's despair. "They live!" she said, in shock and sudden hope. "They must not be taken. We must hold the Grove!"

Apparently confident she would do her part, Arcanus left for the edge of the Grove.

"What of Jarnath?" Shadala asked, daring to hope he might have made it to the safety of the Grove.

"He lies beside his Tree," Leonas informed her. "Aranath cannot aid him. Jarnath needs you. But first, you must save the High-King."

She nodded looking about. "So few! So few Lords and Ladies, so few of the Grove Guard!" Of those she did not see, she named only one. "Gaius! Leonas, I do not see Gaius! Is he hidden by the Trees?"

"He is not here," Leonas said, his voice wooden. "None of those outside the Grove live."

She stared at Leonas helplessly then knelt beside Laedrin, concentrating only on saving those she yet could.

Overhead a booming voice laughed, ripping through the wind. "**COME, PYRFIER! Why do you not face me? Why send servants to do the job of the master? But then, you were always nothing more than a mad servant, weren't you?**"

LEONAS looked up as a tremendous blast of flame blazed from the east, enveloping Arcanus. He feared the Trees would surely catch, but their wind yet kept them safe. When the flame finally died, Leonas thought there would be nothing left of the wizard who aided them, not even a blackened, charred ruin to fall to the ground. But miraculously, Arcanus still hovered there, glowing red and laughing. Somehow even his clothes had not been incinerated, as they should have been.

"Ah, delicious! Quite refreshing. And I thought the burning woods were tasty," Arcanus said gleefully. Then his voice turned deadly. "**See if my gentle caress is to your liking, monster! You dared take my sons and daughters? This is from Magus! And this is from Circe!**" he roared, and arcs of red lightning crackled from Arcanus's eyes toward the east. The boom that followed was nearly deafening.

"**YOU CANNOT FLEE, COWARD! I am not done killing you! This is from Lunahr! Alarad! Haranad! Sarad! Alaria! Jarad!**" he roared, an arc of lightning following each name, as he disappeared from sight, heading east, his voice lost upon the wind.

Leonas peered through the Trees. Past the wind-whipped swirl of leaves he could see the woods ringing the field around the Grove swarmed with the undead, though they did not advance further, apparently either awaiting their master's return, or for the wind to abate. He reached for Aranonas. "How long can you endure?"

Until help arrives. But I cannot talk, Leonas, I must concentrate. Already there are only thirteen of us healthy, nine dying, fourteen already dead, and one helps us not.

"Forgive me for failing you," Leonas whispered in horror, wondering which Trees yet lived as he took his hand away, thereby losing Aranonas's strength. He did not deserve the aid of his Tree. Fourteen dead! Nine dying!

He was startled when a branch reached down and touched him. *You have not failed us. What will be, will be. Courage, Leonas. I love you still,* Aranonas said and then released him.

Aranonas yet loved him! But Aras was dead and Lunahr might be also. Gaius... he fought the thought away, lest it cripple him. He looked toward Shadala. He saw that Jarnath was able to stand again, though shakily, after Shadala tended him.

"L-e-o-n-a-s," a voice called from outside the Grove, rising above the howling wind. It was a terrible voice, a taunting voice. For a terrifying moment Leonas thought it might be Gaius, risen from the dead and turned against him. "Come out, false Lord. You style yourself Protector of the Trees. Yet I know the secret of the Trees. The Trees will die without their Lords and Ladies. I have two of them here. Do you want them, Leonas? Come get them, come save them." He should not be able to hear the voice above the roar of the wind, but it cut through it like a knife.

Leonas peered through the branches. There was a monstrous winged beast, part pumar, reptile, and eagle, with a figure astride it. Leonas strained to see clearly, and a gust of leaves whipped out of his way. The nightmare creature's rider was a male Elf, naked, save for a collar about his neck. The blood froze in his veins. Ahrnad! It was Ahrnad!

There were two Elves beside him, held captive by the monstrous undead things that once had been Aerta, Oceana, Men, and Dwarves. The prisoners did not struggle, as if realizing the hopelessness of their situation. He recognized them and knew terror and despair: Meloneth and Etheria! No, not those two! Of all the Lords and Ladies, they were the most loved, the gentlest and the most treasured. Together they were the living embodiment of the culture of their lost Homeland.

"Perhaps if you see them suffer, you might wish to save them," Ahrnad taunted.

Leonas knew dread. Ahrnad would torture and rape them as they watched helplessly. He could not stand by and allow such horror! He ran for the edge of the Grove, even knowing he could never make it past the howling wind. But he did not make it even a few feet. One of the Trees grabbed him and held him fast. "Araneth! Araneth, please! It's the Lord you are bonded to, Meloneth! You must let me save him! You must let me at least try! He will die! You will die!" But Meloneth's Tree did not release him.

Then there was a bone-chilling scream and pain shot through him from the Tree that touched him. It let go of him and began thrashing. Leonas ran again for the edge of the Grove.

"No, Meloneth. You are too eager. It is not your turn. Ladies first," Ahrnad chastised. "Ah, Etheria, the artist amongst us. She has such talented hands. We Aerta have strong bones, yet it is amazing the damage a hammer can do to such delicate fingers."

Leonas's eyes widened in horror as he broke from the cover of the Trees just in time to see Ahrnad swing a sledge hammer viciously at her pinned arm. There was a piercing scream. Leonas fought to break through the wind surrounding and protecting the Grove, but three of the Trees further restrained him, their branches and roots holding him fast, even as the Tree Aratheria began thrashing in agony.

"Come to me, Leonas. Her left hand is yet intact, but I lose my patience," Ahrnad taunted.

"Lord, please! They cannot let you go to her! Even were they willing to see you slain, they cannot stop the wind. We would be immediately overwhelmed," Grove Guardsman Thavrin desperately reasoned.

There was another scream, and Leonas's head snapped back to the sadistic madman who held Etheria. "Too bad. Perhaps her art or maybe her voice was not to your liking. I will have Meloneth call to you. His voice has always been so pleasing to all of us." Ahrnad stepped in front of his other captive. Leonas fought to see. There was a scream, high and horrible, which ended abruptly. All the Trees were thrashing about as Araneth and Aratheria were, now. The howling wind was faltering. Leonas could hear it weakening.

"No! Please, I beg you, you must sustain the wind!" Leonas implored. "Thavrin was right! We cannot help them, but you still shelter other Lords and Ladies! And the Enemy will come, he will burn you or even twist you somehow, he will use you against us. You must not falter!"

To his relief, the wind strengthened again at his words, but then he knew a new horror when he saw Jarnath's face contort in agony and his hand clutch at his chest, even as he stiffened, gasping, and collapsed.

Shadala ran to him. "Help me, Leonas! His heart has failed him! Only Aranath might save him now, as Aranonas once saved you!"

Leonas helped her lift Jarnath, and they carried him to Aranath. Leonas wrapped Jarnath's limp arm about his Tree's trunk. "I will stay with him. Shadala. Please continue to help the others who are injured." He had purpose again, if only for a short while. Jarnath's Tree might repair the physical damage to the healer's heart, but Leonas knew it could not heal his broken heart. He doubted the healer might wish to live, having witnessed so much pain and suffering and death.

Leonas saw that Willow, who had fled to the comparative safety of the center of the Grove during the first of the airborne attacks, now headed toward Aranath. Leonas barred his way. "No! He is already dying. I will not have you harm him, while he lies helpless."

Willow drew back in surprise. "I will not. I wish only to save him, if I can, as he once saved me, though he knew it not, and though much ill later came from his aid. Please, I don't wish to harm you, but he has scant moments in which he might be revived."

Leonas hesitated, perplexed, and Willow pushed past him and knelt beside Jarnath. He shut his eyes and laid both hands upon his chest. Blue lightning crackled in a nimbus around his hands, and Jarnath's body jerked. Leonas would have expected Aranath to attack Willow for it, but instead, Aranath reached a branch down and caressed them both. Willow touched the healer's face for a few moments. Leonas realized the sound of the wind flickered and faltered, as Willow let go of Jarnath and stood. "He will live. I have given him reason to again. But Aranath's aid is lost to the others and they cannot maintain the wind for long with so few."

"I tire of this game. I can see your Trees want the Lord and Lady returned to them. Very well. As a show of mercy, I will release them," Ahrnad said. Leonas ran to the edge of the Grove and watched suspiciously as the unconscious Lord and Lady were carelessly tossed upon the back of the winged creature and Ahrnad mounted it. He began flying with his precious burden toward the Grove.

Leonas feared Ahrnad meant to try to break through, but instead he flew upward, until he was high overhead. Then, without warning, he pushed his helpless captives from the back of the unnatural creature. The two limp forms fell like rag dolls toward the treetops of the Grove.

The wind faltered and stopped altogether as straining branches reached for them. There was a triumphant, unnatural cry as the Enemy's army surged forward, and Ahrnad and the creature, as well as other airborne monsters, dove downward toward the Trees. The upper branches of two of the Trees cracked and broke under the weight of the plummeting Elves, as their fall was arrested, and they were caught.

Willow's eyes crackled with blue lightning as he rose into the air above the Grove, wind whipping his silver hair, as the cyclone protecting the Trees resumed its previous fury. "**BACK, FOUL CREATURES! It is not yet time for us to die!**" he thundered, as arcs of blue lightning crackled down around him, everywhere he gazed, and a number of the flying monsters fell from the sky, blackened and smoking. Leonas cupped his hands over his ears against the booming thunder that accompanied each blast.

THE Tree that had caught Meloneth lowered him to the ground and Shadala ran to his aid. He was alive, but she saw to her horror that his throat had been viciously slashed. One glance and she could tell that Meloneth's sweet voice had been forever lost to them. He might yet live, but his voice would never again rise above a whisper; he would never again raise it in song. She tended him, as her tears fell upon his unconscious form, and then went to Etheria. Her hands were completely crushed, the bones shattered, powdered. She would never again hold a brush, or breathe life from stone or clay. Shadala wept silently over Etheria as she bandaged her hands, knowing they would likely need to be amputated for Etheria to live, yet knowing that doing so would ensure she could not.

Jarnath stirred and Leonas went to him. "Easy, Healer. Lie still. Shadala tends to the injured. You must now heal only yourself."

To his astonishment, Jarnath smiled at him. "It is all right, Leonas. I will live. I had not realized Meloneth and Etheria might be healed by their Trees, after the battle is done. I had thought his music and her art lost to us. I had thought—I should have known better. Where is Magus, who helped heal me?"

"Magus?" Leonas asked, puzzled. Arcanus's pupil, the one who had done the scry that presaged Aras's death? The one Aras's letter said to aid? "Willow is Magus?" Leonas asked, in astonished revelation. Now Arcanus's words of Magus channeling the Power of the Trees made sense. He looked upward. "He is above us. He protects us, as the Trees no longer can."

Jarnath looked up as well. "He falters," he said, and his voice was tinged with fear.

Leonas shared his fear as he saw Magus was flailing in the air. He appeared to be desperately trying to stay aloft. He began to sink slowly toward them, in a series of jerky drops, but then the wind abruptly ceased, and he plunged toward the ground.

Leonas cried out, arms outstretched, knowing he could not break Magus's fall enough, that they might both die from it, but still, he stood prepared to try. But his sight was blocked by dozens of branches reaching out to catch him as they had caught the others before. Leonas could hear them breaking as Magus tore through the upper ones, but the lower ones held, and the Elven wizard was lowered gently down to the ground.

"Army... coming," Magus whispered, and then he lost consciousness.

"This is it," Leonas said. "Guards, man your bows. Aim for the eyes! We fight to the last arrow, the last sword, the last man!" Leonas cried.

Within his field of vision, seventeen bowmen stepped out from the Trees, facing thousands of undead creatures that had once been Dwarves, Men, Aerta, and Oceana. They had begun the battle with less than a hundred men, and there was no telling how many survivors remained, surrounding the Grove on the other sides, where he could not see. To Leonas's right, to his surprise, Laedrin stepped out from the Trees, a bow of one of the fallen in his hands. To his left, Jarnath stepped out, also armed with a bow. And to Laedrin's right was Shadala, armed only with her knife.

The undead army ran toward them. Leonas heard a loud cry of Elven voices come from the sides of the Grove that faced the Guest House and the River. He could not believe his men would cry out in fear after having confronted such terror so bravely, and he wondered if perhaps they saw some nightmarish new horror that was still hidden from the rest of them. But then their cry was answered by what sounded to be the battle cry of hundreds upon hundreds of men, as a volley of at least two hundred arrows shot along both sides of the Grove, toward the onrushing enemy.

The enemies directly in front of Leonas were sheltered by the Trees and sprang eagerly forward, unwilling to surrender their prize. But then, astonishingly, from around both sides of the Grove came first dozens and then hundreds of Dwarves, war axes gleaming in the moonlight. Some were bearing torches as well. They smashed into the undead army like logs in a raging flood shattering a dam, overwhelming and drowning the enemy with their might. Impossibly, a tremendous wave of Aerta and Oceana followed in their wake, their bows singing as they felled scores of the airborne creatures that threatened both the Grove and their unlikely allies.

Leonas belatedly realized Magus's words had been ones of hope. It was their own Elven Army, and apparently a Dwarven one as well, that had miraculously come to save them.

A force of Dwarves at least six deep ringed the Grove in front of Leonas, while hundreds of others sprang eagerly into battle. Leonas attempted to push his way forward to join them, but the Dwarves before him refused to make way for him.

"Nay, lad. You've done your part," one of them said. "Now let me and my lads do ours. It's a good thing King Talon thought to send us along with your brothers-in-arms. They needed our aid to break through the fire. It looks like Incuban himself has been at your woods."

"He has," Leonas said, stunned by the rescue and all that had gone before, and the Dwarf looked at him sharply.

"You must tell me all you know, then, after you have had a chance to rest. You look about done in, lad," the Dwarf said.

"My people," Shadala piped up, approaching the warrior Leonas spoke with. "The women, the children: Arcanus said they were safe, on the other side of the River, that he saved them. Have you seen them?"

"Arcanus! That traitorous conniver! King of Lies!" The Dwarf spat upon the ground for emphasis, and then his face darkened as if in shame. "Forgive me Lady!" he said, turning his face from her, and his eyes downward.

Shadala paled. "Then... then they are not?" she whispered in a voice filled with horror.

"Forgive me again, Lady, for my careless words, as well as my brutish manners, but we've had quite a journey and nearly arrived too late to be of aid," the Dwarf apologized, his eyes rising to her face for a moment, and then quickly flicking back down. He kept his gaze averted as he continued to speak. "Arcanus is enemy enough to King Talon, but friend to you, it would seem. He spoke the truth, for once, the miserable blackguard. The Urwani-Amontir women and children live. They are safely guarded by your kin, who have all returned with us, to a man." Then his eyes widened and darted up toward her face. He stared at her intently for a moment, and then forced his eyes down again. "Tell me, Lady. Might it be that you are their Chieftess?" he asked, his voice filled with dawning wonder.

"I am Chieftess and Healer Shadala," she confirmed.

"Ragnar be praised!" the Dwarf yelled, suddenly grinning, his head sapping back up, and then turning to the side to face Leonas, though from his words, he was still speaking to Shadala. "They thought they'd lost you, when they lost scant few of the others, only a few of the guards, but none of the women, or the children. I'd never have thought a Man like Haran might weep, but he is mourning you so loudly I thought I'd be able to hear him from here."

Shadala stared at him in astonishment. "Haran? My brother? He is crying? He is crying for me?" she asked, amazed. "He did not cry when his own son lay dying." She looked stunned.

The Dwarf's face flushed. "Earlier, when some of us spoke poorly of the Amontir women.... Not of the Urwani-Amontir, and not my men, but Dwarves nonetheless," he added hastily. "They spoke of those others, the Amontir of Caramore, for their loose ways, and Haran said his people did not do such things. He said that an Urwani-Amontir stays chaste until she is wed. He told us proudly that his own sister, the Chieftess, was forty-nine, that though she came of age at sixteen, she was still as virtuous as the day she was born, as any Dwarven Lady would be. He knows the Enemy's ways, Lady. I think he mourns you not only for your death, but that you would have been so dishonored before you died."

"Thank you for telling me. He should not suffer so for me," Shadala said. "I will go to him, as soon as it is safe to do so."

"That will be soon enough, I think. Though there may yet be stragglers from their forces, I will see you are well guarded. My name is Havron, son of Gavron of Cavernas, Westhold. The enemy is retreating. Once the field of battle is cleared, we will yet need to gather our fallen and theirs, and behead and bury the lot of them. Elves would not want to be burnt, though I fear most of the fallen will already have been. If you'll excuse me, I must see to my men," he said, and began calling out orders in Dwarvish.

WHEN the Dwarves told them it was safe to leave the shelter of the Trees, Leonas began searching for fallen Grove Guard. He could tell them from their uniforms only. Most were trampled and unidentifiable, by moonlight and torchlight.

He found one in a captain's uniform with silver hair and trembled. He pulled back the left sleeve, looking carefully for the crescent moon shaped birthmark he had traced lovingly many times, dreading he might find it, dreading also that he would not, that even Gaius's body might be lost to him. It was not there. This, then, was Daras. "Rest well, my Commander, my friend. You fought bravely and died well, and you have been avenged," he said softly. He wondered if Thanadrin had ever made it out of the Guest House. They should have gone to him, warned him, but they'd been so desperate to get Willow... Magus... to the Grove.

An uneasy muttering grew from the Guest House side of the Grove. From near Aranas! Of course! He was a fool! Gaius would have fallen there, defending Magus while he held Aranas, before he recovered and found shelter within the Grove. "Let me through, step aside," Leonas said, feeling as if he were wading through an army of children: none of the Dwarves stood scant inches higher than some four feet.

"Commander Havron! The Tree attacks us!" one Dwarf called out nervously, and the others warily drew back from the rest of the Trees of the Grove.

Peering over their heads, Leonas could see that Aranas was lashing out his branches. He swallowed. An Oceana in a Grove Guard uniform lay at the base of Aranas's trunk. He could not tell his rank from where he stood. Only a few feet from the Tree were two fantastic fallen creatures, one part eagle and horse, and the other part pumar, reptile and eagle.

"Shadala, Jarnath, aid me!" Leonas called, in frantic hope. "Please, step back. Let me calm the Tree," Leonas commanded in Common, and the Dwarves eagerly complied.

Leonas approached. "Aranas, it's all right. It is me, Leonas. Let me see whom you shelter," he said, speaking Elvish. The branches stilled at the sound of his voice and drew back. Leonas ran forward. His heart leapt to his throat. It was Gaius. But Leonas could tell from a single look it was hopeless. Gaius's face was so pale it made the moon appear dark by comparison. One leg was bare and appeared uninjured, but the other was thickly swaddled in cloth dark with blood, and Gaius lay in a pool of it, on top of a bed of fallen leaves.

Leonas cried out in loss and knelt beside Gaius, reaching for him, to embrace him. One of Aranas's branches slashed him across the face and he drew back, startled and in pain from the unexpected attack.

"Aranas, please! He is dead," Leonas begged, his voice ragged with grief.

Jarnath and Shadala knelt beside Gaius as well. "He cannot have lost so much blood and survived," Jarnath confirmed. The leaves rustled and the Dwarves watched the tableau uneasily and sympathetically. Jarnath touched Gaius's throat, then drew back his hand, astonished. "But it cannot be possible! How can he have a pulse when there is so little blood left for his heart to pump?" He rummaged through the vials in the bag at his side and then said in despair, "No! I have none left. I have already used what little I brought. I doubt the Healers' Hall still stands. There is no more."

"He lives?" Shadala asked, shocked. "What is it? What do you seek?"

"Anosar," Jarnath said hopelessly. "You will not have it, Shadala. You refused to use it again, after your kinsman injured himself by taking too much. But Gaius should already be dead. He has little of his life's blood left inside him. Only anosar might be strong enough to aid him."

Magus walked over to them and held out a trembling hand to Jarnath, containing a vial. "Here, Healer. It is all I have left of the vial you gave me. It is worse than poison, but you told me it is rare and valued, so I brought it with me to return it to you. I would not drink it before even to keep from falling from the sky. I would rather have broken my neck than to have tasted it again."

Jarnath thanked Magus for it and then reached for Gaius to minister it to him, but Aranas slashed his branches at Jarnath and he withdrew, appearing alarmed and perplexed by the Tree's renewed hostility. "Surely he cannot want Gaius to die!" He turned to Leonas. "Can it be because of you? Perhaps he is jealous of Gaius?"

"No. Aranas is the one who told me to go to Gaius," Leonas said, just as bewildered. "I had never before realized Gaius loved me as more than a friend. I will touch Aranas, if he will allow it, and ask him what is wrong."

Leonas reached out a cautious hand and was relieved when he immediately heard Aranas speak to him. After discovering what was wrong and reassuring Aranas, he pulled back. "I have learned what has been upsetting Aranas. We must not move Gaius's arm from about the Tree. He cannot let go, even for an instant. Without Aranas, Gaius will die.

"You were right, Jarnath. Aranas said that although Gaius's leg has been healed of the injury, there is not enough blood left in his body to sustain him. Until his body makes more, he must be tended to here, so Aranas can keep him alive. The anosar will aid him. I will hold Gaius's arm still so you might safely move his head enough for him to drink."

Leonas carefully held Gaius as Jarnath gave him the elixir. Leonas called out to the Dwarven warriors around him in Common. "It is all right. The Tree was only protecting him. The others will not attack you. And only this small stand of special Trees moves. You need not be concerned about the rest of our Wood." He was careful to say, "need not be concerned," rather than "need not fear." He did not wish to insult the Dwarves who had helped save them.

The others went back to the grisly task of collecting the dead. Leonas stayed with Gaius, speaking softly to him, though he knew he could not yet hear.

Shadala asked Havron, "Has King Talon sent his entire Army to our aid? Is he here also, across the River?"

"No. He sent all five thousand Elves back, and all three hundred of your people, and ten thousand of us Dwarves. There are ten thousand more of us beside him, along with two hundred Varash, and all his immediate kin are yet at his side."

"Havron, can one of your people bring word to my brother that I am alive and unharmed? He should not grieve for me, but I realize I must remain here for a time, to tend to the Elves who yet need me."

"Aye, Chieftess. Vernon! Go with eleven men, in case there's stragglers about, and cross the River to War Leader Haran and tell him his sister, the Chieftess and Healer Lady Shadala is alive and unharmed," Havron commanded.

"Aye, Commander! Come," Vernon said, selecting his men.

ARCANUS returned to the Grove, fuming, and reported to High-King Laedrin. "Majesty, I regret to inform you that Incuban has eluded me. Magus, come! We've work to do," Arcanus said, scowling at his son. He leapt into the air and flew toward the east, in a cascade of red lightning.

Magus looked sheepishly at High-King Laedrin. "With your permission, Majesty? I will return when I can."

"We thank you for your aid. We will not forget all you have done this day. And I must burden you with my gratitude for your father, as well, as he was in such a hurry to leave our presence," Laedrin said.

"May we continue to be of aid to one another, Majesty," Magus said carefully, his voice betraying his uncertainty regarding Laedrin's temperament. Magus bowed then leapt into the air after Arcanus, blue lightning arcing from his hands.

OVER the course of that day, the Dwarven army worked to extinguish the portions of the Wood that yet burned. The dead were collected and tallied, as best as they could be, considering a number of them had burnt so thoroughly it was impossible to tell whether they had been live or undead, friend or enemy, or even Man or Elf. The Dwarven Revenants alone were distinguishable, for their height.

Of the five thousand Army and Navy who had remained in Nalea, a scant eighty-two lived. Of the one-hundred-forty-seven Grove Guard, only forty-eight lived, and of the three Captains other than Leonas, only Gaius lived, and he still hovered at the brink of death next to Aranas. Leonas did not leave his side.

Of the thirty-three Aerta Lords and Ladies, including the High-King, only twenty-one lived. Of the thirty-seven Trees, only twenty-three lived, twenty-two named and one unnamed. Twelve of the fourteen dead had died with their Lords and Ladies. Shadala and Jarnath were able to save the nine injured Lords and Ladies, and their Trees recovered and were, in turn, able to fully heal the Aerta they were bonded to. Meloneth would sing again and Etheria would paint and sculpt, though his music and her art would likely be dark, at least for a time.

Five hundred sixty-one of the five thousand Elves who had returned from Caramore had perished and six hundred ninety-three of the ten thousand Dwarves. But over fifteen thousand Revenants had been destroyed, beheaded and buried or burnt in the Wood.

The Elven City of Nalea had been leveled by the fire, as well as the Urwani-Amontir City, and all their fields lay in ashes. The Lords' Grove and Guest House alone were spared. The surviving Lords and Ladies moved into the Guest House, while the Dwarven army set up tents to house the Urwani-Amontir. Both peoples were too numb to even think about rebuilding. They might have fled to the intact portion of their Wood along the Tahir River, but the waters of the Sarashen, fed by the Fromer Mountains, were richer in Power, nor could they relocate and abandon the Grove. The Dwarves, ever practical, offered a solution.

Havron was the one who spoke to High-King Laedrin, the surviving Lords and Ladies, and Chieftess Shadala and War Leader Haran about it. "We'll build each of you a new City," Havron offered. "We'll quarry the stone from the Fromer Mountains that border your Kingdom. You've shown us the abandoned Urwani City in the valley. We can move the Hall of History stone by stone and build in the same style for the rest of the new Urwani-Amontir City. And we can build a fortress around the Grove, should you wish it, large enough so the Trees won't mind it, but they'll be better protected. With all the burnt trees, there's plenty of land that can be cleared for both Cities, and for the new fields for your farms. We'll enlarge the stream by the Guest House, so the River Elves like it well enough, too. Once we're done with all the rest, we'll dig up and then relocate and plant a number of saplings from the intact portions of your Wood as well, to help restore the forest around the Cities."

"We do not have any treasure to offer you, for what you propose. All we owned was burnt in the fire," High-King Laedrin said, his voice skeptical.

His words clearly angered Havron. "We're not doing it for treasure. We're doing it for our brothers-in-arms. We know what it's like, to lose your home, your City, your Kingdom. The Kingdoms of the West have full treasure vaults. We saved much material wealth from our lost Kingdoms but, for the most part, value it little now. Our hearts are as full of pain as our vaults are of treasure, from all we've lost. We will not see others go unaided, when we might help them."

"Forgive me, Commander Havron! My words were ill chosen and unworthy of both my people and yours, particularly in light of the aid you have already granted us. I hope you might understand and excuse them. To have lost so many, when already we were so diminished as a people, and for most of those who fell to have been lost to fire, as... as my own son was only recently lost. I most humbly thank you for your offered aid, on behalf of my people. In turn, I would aid any of you that I could. Once the War is done, my people will aid you in reclaiming and restoring your Mountain strongholds, should you wish to. We will build gardens and fountains for them, the likes of which you have never imagined, and offer whatever other comforts we may."

"You are forgiven, High-King. Each of us has stood where you now stand. And we would be honored to in turn accept the aid you offer, when it might be available to us."

Plans were laid, as a semblance of order resumed in Nalea.

LEONAS was still terribly worried about Gaius, though Aranonas, Jarnath, and Shadala all assured him he would fully recover. He was also frustrated and concerned that Ahrnad's body had not been positively identified amongst the fallen, though there were thousands of unrecognizable corpses. He tried to assure himself that his must have been one of them, yet still, he feared Ahrnad might have somehow eluded his fate, as Incuban had.

Finally, five days after the attack, Gaius's eyes fluttered open.

FOR a moment, Gaius did not realize where he was or what had happened. He knew only that he felt both well-rested and tired, healthy and weak, hungry and oddly not. Leonas lay beside him, appearing drawn and gaunt. They were lying under Aranas for some reason. Gaius saw his arm was wrapped about Aranas. It should not be, he realized, to his mortification. He should not be touching Aranas. But when he tried to let go, Aranas's branches stopped him. To his astonishment, he realized he also heard the Tree's voice, when he should not be able to, though somehow it seemed as if he had heard that same voice many times before.

Do not let go, Gaius. Waken Leonas first, so he might be sure you are well enough. Elven physiology is still puzzling to us, even after all these millennia by your side. You are so fragile and oddly formed.

Gaius did not want to waken Leonas. He looked like he was in need of the sleep. He wished he could remember why he was here, in the Grove. Willow! His heart hammered. He had been protecting Willow. Where was he?

The memories came crashing back, like waves pounding upon the rock of the shore. They threatened to overwhelm him. The Enemy, the walking dead, the flying monsters, the smoke, the pain, the blood! He was dying!

He heard a song in his head, calm and soothing. It fell like a blanket of fog against the crashing waves of memory, replacing them with waters gently lapping the shore. At peace, Gaius snuggled against both Aranas and Leonas and drifted off to sleep again.

LATER, when Leonas awoke, Aranas told him that Gaius had awakened, but had been too upset to remain conscious. Aranas had cast him into sleep again, so he might waken once he was better able to cope with all that had happened. Leonas was overjoyed Gaius had wakened, but terribly disappointed that he had missed it.

THE following day, Aranas ceased his song, and Gaius awakened, when Leonas was awake also.

"Gaius," Leonas said softly.

"Leonas," Gaius said, contentedly. Memory stirred again and his eyes snapped open and he reached for his leg. His pants were intact. There was no trace of blood. "It was not a dream," Gaius said, unsure whether it might have been. His arm was about Aranas, when it should not be, but he remembered the gentle scolding, whether real or imagined, and did not let go.

"No, it was not. Nalea was attacked, and you were gravely injured. But the battle was won and Aranas both saved and healed you. We changed your clothes, so you might be more comfortable."

Gaius sat up and looked about. Warriors ringed the Trees shoulder to shoulder. Most of them were not in Grove Guard uniforms. Many of them were not even Aerta or Oceana. There were a number of both Men and Dwarves in the circle that surrounded the Grove, interspersed amongst their people.

"The battle was six days ago," Leonas explained. "The dead have been buried, and the signs of battle removed from the Grove and the field surrounding it, those that could be. The blood has all been washed into the soil."

"How is it we won when we should have lost? And the Men I see appear to be the Urwani-Amontir, but there cannot be so many. All but a handful of their warriors left to fight with King Talon. And why do Dwarves stand upon our land as if it were their own?"

Leonas explained. "It turns out that Willow was the wizard Magus in disguise. He and Arcanus aided us. But also, King Talon sent our own five thousand soldiers back to us, as well as his people, the Urwani-Amontir, and an army of ten thousand Dwarves, to aid us."

Gaius was eager to hear the details of all he had missed and Leonas answered every question he posed. The Grove was now guarded by one-hundred-forty-seven warriors at all times, including two Captains and one Commander. There were still three shifts, though each was three times the size it had formerly been.

Gaius was distraught to hear of their staggering losses. "So many comrades dead and the City itself destroyed! There is much to be done," he said and stood, then sagged as dizziness hit him. Leonas steadied him.

"Easy, Gaius," Leonas cautioned. "You can survive without Aranas now, but you are still weak. You must not strain yourself."

"The Trees have guarded me long enough. I must guard them, now. I am still Captain," Gaius said.

Leonas shook his head. "You are Captain no longer."

Gaius gasped in pain at the betrayal, that he might have been so easily cast aside.

Leonas hugged him. "You are Commander, now," he explained, and the words of protest that had been forming died stillborn upon Gaius's lips. Leonas continued. "But you will not guard the Grove itself. You are now Magus's personal guard and Aranas's, while Magus is yet within our Wood. He returned to us, after aiding Arcanus with whatever mission he had set for them. Both Magus and Aranas insisted upon you and no other, for your service to them in the battle. There is still much to tell you. But first, you must eat real food again, rather than what Jarnath has been sustaining you with. At Guest House you will meet the other two new Commanders. The High-King and the Lords and Ladies live there now. The Dwarves are almost finished building a barracks to house the entire Grove Guard. It is remarkable what an army of Dwarven stone masons can accomplish in a scant few days!"

They began walking slowly to the Guest House. Gaius eyed Leonas critically. "You must eat as well. I can tell you have been spending little time taking care of yourself this past week gone by. You have been worried about me and the Grove to your own detriment," Gaius scolded gently.

"I had thought you dead, forever lost to me, when I saw you lying so pale and still. Now I know how you felt the day Aranas stopped my heart by mistake. I would rather have it stopped again, than to ever lose you, my lythenia, my love," Leonas said, openly caressing his face, where any might see.

"Then I shall have to be more careful in the future," Gaius said and smiled at him.

Leonas returned the smile and they embraced and kissed, in full sight of the Grove Guard, and then continued on to the Guest House.

Chapter 6
Return to Athanark

SCANT hours after Rion and the Elves began their journey, Farad realized that Quickwing might become a danger to them, more than a help. He feared Incuban might somehow use Quickwing to find Rion and the others, that perhaps the chimaera had seen him circling Rion before and used the eagle to find him. He could not take the chance. Rion would be safe with twenty-four Elves around him and his five other guards. Besides, Dewalaren had need of Quickwing. He had proved invaluable as a messenger bird, and he fought as fiercely as any of Farad's kin. Reluctantly, Farad turned Quickwing toward home and departed.

RION watched the eagle fly away, thinking he meant to hunt or scout ahead. But when he rose into the sky, flying higher and higher, until he became a black speck, and then even the speck was lost, Rion's stomach fluttered uneasily.

The rest of the day Rion scanned the sky hopefully, vainly. That night he brushed Seafoam until she stamped her foot impatiently. He patted her in apology and impulsively hugged her, and she whickered at him, as if to assure him she was not upset with him.

Rion lay down and closed his eyes and tried to force himself to relax, to sleep. The Elves around him all seemed so cold, so hard, in their armor. Whitewater was also being very protective of Meander. She was nowhere near him. Rion was worried for her. She looked so ill.

It was his first night away from the safety of Salenia, the first night Meander was not watching over him. They were camped beside the River; he could still hear it, but he was afraid it might not have the same Power it had before, now that they had left the Elven Kingdom, to keep the terrible dreams from him.

He resisted the urge to go to Ron, to sleep beside him, as he'd done before, though he felt so vulnerable without the eagle watching over him. And he missed Tarrell desperately already. He fought the tears that threatened to overwhelm him.

He felt a warm fog on his cheek and opened his eyes in surprise. Seafoam was standing over him, her face over his own. It was her breath he had felt. He reached up and petted her and she nuzzled his face and nipped gently at his hair. He realized to his relief that Seafoam would not let him be harmed. Comforted by both that thought and her presence, as she stood protectively beside him, he drifted off to sleep.

EIGHT days later, Meander, Whitewater, and their eighteen companions left the rest of them, just outside of Westhaven, the last City of Man beside the Western Road on this side of the Coroden. Meander spoke for them all, and her words were brief. "We must leave you now, Rion, everyone. Our journey takes us elsewhere. I shall miss you. I hope we might meet again. Please take care."

Rion nodded, his eyes saying what his voice could not, as he watched her go. He could not believe he would be without her gentle presence, little contact though he had had with her on the journey. It was almost like losing his mother a second time. Having the light of twenty Elves leave him, even ones as grim as they had been, would have been unbearable, were it not for the four who remained.

He leaned over and wrapped his arms around Seafoam's neck desperately. She was a great comfort to him, especially as the eagle seemed to have left them for good. Even the Elves had seemed surprised by Seafoam's loyalty to him.

RON could see Rion was fighting tears. "Why don't we spend the night in Westhaven, now that the others aren't with us?" he suggested, hoping to take Rion's mind off the Elves' departure. "We bypassed both Kashin and Seros, but we need to replenish our supplies and I, for one, wouldn't mind sleeping in a real bed or taking a warm bath, instead of bathing in the River."

Ron was grateful when Swiftsong unexpectedly spoke in support of the idea. "I agree. You should restock now, while you can. We have not seen any danger these many nights past. It should be safe enough. We will sleep by the River. We would draw too much attention within the City, especially armored as we are."

RION fought a sense of dread. How could he sleep without the reassuring sound of the River or Seafoam standing over him? Then he remembered how he had slept before, listening to Ron's heartbeat. He was sure they would all rent a single room and share a bed. He could sleep, as long as he could lie against Ron and hear his strong heart.

It was comforting entering another city he was familiar with. They'd stopped at Westhaven on their way to Gosa. Rion remembered the meals at the Blue Boar had been exceptionally good and the rooms clean and was glad to see the others apparently remembered it as fondly, as that was the inn they were heading toward. Rion went in with Ron and Andra, while the others waited outside with the horses.

Rion inhaled deeply once inside. He loved the way inns smelled, of food and woodsmoke and people. He started to feel more relaxed, until he heard Ron speaking to the innkeeper. "We'll need two rooms, next to each other, one of them with two beds." He'd not thought Ron would get him a room of his own, though previously, he and Tarrell had shared one while the guards who weren't on duty had slept in the common room below. It was only once they'd reached Gosa and had fewer men that they'd gotten a room for their guards as well. There were so few of them now, he'd assumed they'd all want to sleep in the safety of a single locked room, rather than work shifts guarding him. He'd never be able to sleep all alone. He fought panic.

"Why two rooms and three beds?" Andra asked.

"You don't expect to sleep in a room with five unmarried men, do you, Andra?" Ron asked dryly. "Even if three of us are your brothers. You'll have the room next to ours.

And five is too many for a single bed. We'll sleep three and two. Rion usually shared a bed with Tarrell on our journey, so I figured he wouldn't mind. Unless you'd prefer a bed to yourself, Rion? We could sleep four and one. Sleeping with Rarnak as the fourth instead of Van wouldn't matter to us."

Rion shook his head, incredibly relieved. He counted three fingers, holding them up, then putting them down on the palm of his other hand and then did so with two, indicating three and two was fine with him. It wouldn't matter who he slept with. Any of them would make him feel safe enough.

ANDRA sighed quietly. She'd not particularly want to share a room or a bed with her brothers, but she certainly wouldn't mind sharing one with Rarnak. She fought the thought down. He'd not given her any indication so far on the trip that he'd be interested in doing so, although he had at least spoken with her, more than once. It seemed to her he tended to ride beside her more than beside any of the others, too. And in camp, he seemed to sit next to her for his meals, when given the chance. She hoped it might mean something.

RON ordered tubs be brought to both rooms as well. Then they went out to see to the horses, while their rooms and baths were readied.

The stable master looked at Seafoam in surprise. "How'd you lose your saddle and bridle, son?" he asked Rion.

Gar pulled the man aside. "Careful what you say around him. He's been in a state about it all day. The cinch broke on his saddle, when we were fording the Merdan, and two of the straps broke on the bridle. We had half a mind to let the River take him, instead of fishing him out. He's been no joy to work for. We'd told him he had to keep better care of his tack than that, but you know how rich boys are. It serves him right, for not tending to it nightly as he said he had. I feel sorrier for his horse than I do for him, having him bouncing around bareback on her for half the day," Gar said.

Rion grimaced, overhearing every word. It was humiliating, but they could hardly let the man suspect the truth, when it would draw attention to them. He hadn't thought how his riding Elven style might do so.

The stable master laughed. "Don't I know it! We get our share of wealthy folk in here, always thinking they know best about how to tend to their horses. If you're looking for good tack that'll be fancy enough to suit him, Cedron's on Chestnut Street has the best selection in the City. Tell him Temris sent you."

"Thanks, I'll do that. No offense, but I'm surprised Barton's not here. He was the stable master only a few weeks back, when my brothers and I came through heading toward Kashin," Gar said, careful not to mention Gosa. "I hope his health hasn't failed him," Gar added, in genuine concern.

Temris laughed. "That old goat will be around long after I'm dead and buried! He left here for the Gilded Lily. They hired away a few of our folk. It was a break for me. I went from head groom to stable master. They tried to get our cook, too, but luckily for us, Meribeth's sweet on the owner. It would take more than coin to get her to leave here."

"I'm glad to hear it," Gar said. "My mouth's been watering for one of her meat pies and a bottle of wine from Thenalon to go with it. You're the only ones west of the Coroden to have any."

"Ah. Well, the meat pie you can have, but I'm afraid we'll disappoint you about the wine, though we had a shipment of wine in from Gosa three weeks ago. What they had can't quite compare to Thenalon, of course, nothing can, but it's not too poor a second. We haven't had a supply caravan make it through from Thenalon in almost two months. This last one's over three weeks overdue. In fact, none of the ones from the east have come. We've started sending to Gosa for what we need. They're enough of a crossroads to have the more exotic goods. Though I'm surprised we haven't seen another caravan from Gosa by now. The one we were expecting is nearly a week overdue.

"I hope Falnor's your destination and not further east. From the few other travelers who've made it through, we hear the Kierness Marsh is twice the size now that it was: it's swallowed up the Merdan River as well as the Elingor. They say the Gelthor Pass is even worse, now, too. The stream that used to run through there is completely dried up, and the ogres twice as fierce because of it. You need to bring weeks of water with you just to make it from Logareth, now. From what we've heard, only the biggest caravans can make it through, but like I said, even so, it's been a while since we've seen one."

Gar forced a smile. "Lucky for us we're only headed to Falnor, but thanks for the warning." He went back over to Rion. "Come, honored sir, it's time for our dinner, if you've a mind," Gar said, not speaking Rion's name, so it couldn't be remembered later, if someone asked.

Rion gave Seafoam a quick pat and whistled for her to stay where she was. He heard her calling after him, as he left the stables, but fortunately she obeyed his command and didn't try to follow him. She hadn't before, but he was certain she might realize she and the other horses were being settled in for the night, now. She was the most intelligent animal he'd ever seen.

"Did you hear that?" Gar said to Ron, as soon as they were out of earshot of the stable master. "Weeks of swamp and then the entire Pass or more without running water altogether? The Elves will never survive it. Now what do we do?"

"We bathe, eat dinner, and sleep, and talk it over with them in the morning," Ron said firmly. "Rion, I don't want you worrying. We'll see you through this. No matter what the obstacles in our way are, we'll see you safely to Eladar, I swear."

Gar looked sheepish. "I hope you forgive me for what I said, Rion. I couldn't let him suspect the truth."

Rion nodded, his own embarrassment forgotten in his concern for the Elves.

The six of them went upstairs to their rooms and bathed. Afterward, the brothers and Rarnak put on the drinking clothes they'd brought, leaving their uniforms to be laundered, as they'd arranged with the innkeeper. Rion changed too, into his other shirt and pants. But where the brothers' clothes and Rarnak's were plain and comfortable-looking, his were just as fancy and rich-looking as what he'd been wearing, only clean. Rion felt conspicuously out of place amongst the others. Perhaps he should buy some less rich-looking clothes? He might be drawing attention with what he was wearing, he belatedly realized. At least the others treated him like one of them, even if he didn't look the part.

The six of them went downstairs and sat at a table. A serving wench came up to them promptly. "What can I get you and your guards, honored sir?" she asked, looking expectantly at Rion, after a brief, puzzled frown in Andra's direction, which she quickly hid.

"Don't mind him. He doesn't speak a word of Common, lucky for us," Ara lied smoothly. "We'll have meat pies and wine, bring the bottle. We hear you don't have any from Thenalon this time around, but we'll take the best you've got." Ara smiled and winked at her.

"Of course! I'm sure we have something that will please you," the girl said, smiling coyly at Ara, more than a hint of suggestion in her response.

"Oh, that you do indeed, lass," Ara agreed, grinning back at her.

She left the table and Andra scowled at Ara. "No wonder you were gone two years, instead of one. Sitting about in fancy inns spending your employer's coin, drinking fine wine, and flirting with serving girls," she said bitingly. "It certainly beat coming home and helping me carry flour."

"That's not how it was at all, Andra," Ron said, defending them. "Besides, we're paying for the wine, not Rion. He drinks even less than I do. And we always paid for our own meals. Rion would be the first to tell you, we always bought the cheapest meal, if that, and seldom drank a drop. Most of the time we still ate trail fare, when the rest of the guards indulged."

Rion nodded in mute agreement, wishing he had the tongue to speak in the brothers' defense.

"It's true," Rarnak confirmed. "The rest of us were always buying the fanciest meals and oushka, sometimes by the bottle, but your brothers seldom splurged. I was always impressed by their frugality. And they worked hard the whole time they were with us, more than their share. Going through the Pass, Gar drove one of the wagons part of the way, and still pulled guard duty with the rest of us, and that's just one example."

Andra appeared contrite. "Oh. Well that's different, then. I'm sorry, Ron. I still can't get over how you looked when I first saw you. I suppose I'll get over how jealous I was of you all eventually. Until I do, don't pay me any mind. You all never much cared before what I thought of you. I'm surprised you do now."

"I've always cared what you think of me, Andra," Ron said softly.

Rion was relieved when the food came. He paid for everyone's meal, in spite of Ron's objections. He pointed to his purse and them. Ron said, "Just because you're not paying our wages this time around doesn't mean you should have to pay for our meals. You already paid for both rooms."

Rion shook his head firmly.

"Let him, Ron, if it makes him feel better about it. He wanted you all on this trip as little as the rest of you wanted me," Andra said.

Rion patted her hand and peered intently at her.

"Oh. Well, thank you, Rion. It's good to know someone wants me here," she said.

Rion hadn't realized how hungry he was until he started eating. And the wine was good. He began to relax. He listened to the flow of conversation around him, wishing he could take part in it.

A minstrel began playing near the fire. Once Rion was done eating, and he saw Gar was too, he tapped Gar's shoulder, indicating he wanted to get closer to listen. Gar accompanied him.

THE serving girl came back to their table. "Since you're new in town, I thought you might like some company. I can show you the City, if you'd like," she said to Ara. "I'm done for the night. I've been working since before breakfast."

Ara looked at Ron for his approval.

"As long as you're back by dawn and ready to ride, whether you've gotten any sleep or not," Ron said in Thenalonese.

Ara grinned and stood. "I'd love the company," he said eagerly, and the girl smiled prettily. They left.

"I thought you told me you never went anywhere on your own in a strange City," Andra said, surprised.

"There are some necessary exceptions to that rule," Ron justified. "But I don't want you getting any ideas. You're to stay with Rarnak. I'm going to go over and join Gar and Rion."

Andra watched Ron's receding back, wondering at what he'd said. Had he realized that she'd hoped she might be left alone with Rarnak? She turned to Rarnak. "I'm sorry. I hope you don't mind being stuck with me."

"Not at all. You're good company, Andra. Would you like some kakla, or would you prefer oushka?" Rarnak asked.

"Kakla's fine," she said, though his words had warmed her enough.

"Then I'll get us some. They won't be so solicitous of us, now that Rion's no longer at the table. Or Ara," Rarnak added, smiling and Andra found herself smiling back at him.

A LONG while later, the minstrel played his last song of the night. The other patrons of the inn started settling down in the floor space of the common room they'd reserved for the night. "Come on, Rion, Gar. It's past time for bed," Ron said. "We should still try to keep to the same pace we've been making, if we can."

Rion nodded, yawning as he did so. He put a final silver in the minstrel's cap and smiled at him. The minstrel thanked him warmly. That had been a total of five he'd given him over the course of the evening.

When Rion turned toward the stairs, he saw in surprise that Andra and Rarnak were still at their table, talking animatedly, a pot of kakla and two mugs between them.

"Time for bed, Rarnak, Andra," Ron said, as they came up to them.

"What, already?" Andra asked.

"The rest of the patrons want to sleep. They're not all lucky enough to have private rooms to do it in. It's not like you can't pick up where you left off in the morning," Ron urged.

ANDRA sighed. She hadn't wanted the night to end. She'd never felt so at ease with someone as she had tonight with Rarnak.

"Ron's right," Rarnak said. It cheered her to hear the reluctance in his voice when he said it.

She nodded and stood and they climbed the stairs.

"Sweet dreams, Andra," Rarnak said.

"You too, Rarnak," she said. *I hope they'll be sweet, maybe even be of me. All my dreams will be of you, Rarnak,* she thought. She turned to the others. "Good night, Ron, Gar, Rion. Sleep well. See you in the morning."

RION looked at the others, then signaled to Ron for his hand and wrote, "ARA."

Gar had looked on curiously and then grinned. "Don't worry about him, Rion. If all goes well for him, we won't see him until morning. It looks like you get your own bed after all."

Rion's eyes widened in sudden fear, though he appeared to be trying to hide it.

Ron remembered how Rion had been on the road to the mill and thought he understood Rion's concern. "I don't know, Gar. After a day in the saddle, it would work better if we slept two and two, so we can stretch out more. Do you mind if I share your bed, Rion?"

Rion shook his head, *No,* enthusiastically, in obvious relief.

"Well, it looks like it's me and you, then, Rarnak. No offense, but I think Ara got the better end of the deal when it comes to bed partners tonight," Gar said laughing. "Next City, it's my turn."

ONCE they were in their room, Rion changed into his nightshirt. The others went to bed in their clothes. His wouldn't have been comfortable enough to sleep in, and they would have wrinkled badly if he had.

They all settled down. The others fell quickly asleep but Rion lay there stiffly, until he was sure Ron was asleep. Then hesitantly, blushing darkly and feeling like a child, he put his arm around Ron and lay his head against Ron's chest as he had on the Road. He heard his strong, steady heartbeat and finally felt safe enough to drift off into a deep and dreamless sleep.

THE next morning Ara joined them for breakfast, a contented grin on his face, broken by a wide yawn.

"You're in for a long, hard ride today, Ara. I hope she was worth it," Ron said.

Ara grinned. "She gave me a long, hard ride last night. Believe me, it was worth every missed wink."

Rion realized Andra looked as embarrassed as he felt at what Ara had said.

After breakfast, they headed for the stable. Seafoam whinnied happily upon seeing Rion, nuzzling him with her lips, as if checking to see he was in one piece, having spent the night without her. He grinned and showered her with attention.

They left the City and headed back to the River, to where they'd left the Elves.

"It's good to see one night away from us hasn't done you any ill," Swiftsong said, glancing over them, his gaze lingering upon Ara, and the ghost of a smile curled his lips. Rion wondered if Swiftsong could somehow tell what Ara had been doing.

"We're not the ones who are in danger now, Swiftsong," Ron said seriously. "We've heard some disturbing news about the Merdan. It seems the Kierness Marsh has doubled in size. We'll be in marshland for weeks, and afterward, the clear stream that used to run through the Gelthor Pass has gone dry. The four of you won't last through weeks of fetid water and another week without any. We need to find an alternate route."

Swiftsong shook his head. "There is no other way we can take that would not be more dangerous."

"What about the Falnor Wood and Erenia? They let us through once before. Perhaps we can go that way again," Gar said.

"No. You cannot use that route. The only other option would be to skirt the south edge of the Falnor Wood and then take the Thinabar Pass to Athanark," Swiftsong said.

"But we can't. It would mean weeks of extra journey, and besides, the Taheeran Desert lies immediately south of the Wood," Ron argued.

"It is true that in many places the Desert attempts to encroach upon our Wood, that because of it, you must travel within the Desert itself, for a time. But there is a small oasis, a water hole along the path you must take, where the outermost curve of the network of underground streams that nourishes our Wood breaches the surface. Later, in the foothills at the mouth of the Pass, there is a spring," Swiftsong said.

"But if you'd not survive the Marsh, surely you'd not survive the Desert?" Andra argued. "Why not go though Erenia?"

"We cannot. Erenia has been quarantined. We are forbidden to enter. All are forbidden," Meadow said adamantly.

Rion looked at her sharply. Quarantined? Had his fears of a plague been well founded? Elanara was in Erenia! Was it quarantined to keep disease from reaching her and the others, or because it already had?

Rion grabbed Ron's hand and began writing her name. "It's all right, Rion, calm down. I understand. Prince Eladar's sister is in Erenia. Is she safe? Is there illness there?"

"She is a Princess. She will be kept safe from the ill that has befallen those there. But Rion must be kept safe as well. We will escort him, as a Prince of our people has commanded us to," Swiftsong said.

"Even if it means you die doing so? You know you'll not survive the Marsh or the Desert!" Ara accused, appalled. "I won't allow you to try. You're our friend, our teacher. But even if you weren't, I'll never let an Elf die for lack of his water. You have to go back to Salenia."

"Our lives are not important," Quicksilver said, his voice and face unnervingly placid.

"Of course they're important!" Andra snapped.

Rion reached into his pack and got out his journal and lead and began writing.

"We're not going a step further, until you head back," Gar argued.

"Nothing you can say nor do will sway us," Rain said, with the irritating haughty smugness her kind was known for.

RION tapped Ron on the shoulder and handed him a piece of paper, folded more than once, then drew back as Ron took it and began opening it. Ron wished for the hundredth time that Rion could talk. He might be able to influence the Elves. They could waste hours arguing with them. He scanned the note quickly, then his breath hissed and he looked up sharply at Rion and confirmed what the note said.

Gar, Ara, and Andra were all arguing with Swiftsong and Quicksilver as Rarnak, Meadow and Rain looked on.

"Quiet, all of you! You can see what a fine job we're all doing protecting Rion," Ron said, his voice full of self-recrimination.

The others looked up and turned to where Ron was gesturing. Rion sat there on Seafoam, calmly, his hand steady, with the point of his knife pressed so tightly to his throat that a drop of blood was slowly dripping down his neck.

Ron held up the note and said, "He wrote this:

"No one else dies for me, ever. Swiftsong, you and Quicksilver, Rain, and Meadow must swear on the Merdan that you'll return to Salenia immediately, or I'll cut my own throat and even you won't be fast enough to stop me."

"He would not," Swiftsong said, in appalled disbelief.

"Elmoth, he would!" Gar swore. "Swiftsong, you've no idea! Please do what he says! He knows you'd not break an oath to your River. He'd rather die himself than see anyone else die for him ever again. He'd never let an Elf die for him, let alone four. Please, Swiftsong," Gar pleaded.

Swiftsong eyed Rion intently. "You would truly die for us?"

Rion returned his gaze steadily and gave a slight nod.

Swiftsong sighed. "Then at least if we leave you, there is a chance you might survive without our aid. You give us little choice. I swear by the Merdan that I will leave you now and return to Salenia," he said and nodded to the three others. One by one they swore.

Rion pulled the knife away, sheathed it, and then bowed slightly to them, rubbing his throat.

Swiftsong looked at Ron in sympathy. "He will not be easy to safeguard. We felt the Enemy searching for you earlier in our journey, but He was not able to find you for our presence. We suspect that He might well be responsible for fouling the River by expanding the Marsh and for drying the stream in the Gelthor Pass, to prevent our aiding you. He will yet be expecting you to head for the Gelthor Pass, by one route or another. That will be where most of His traps will likely lie. If you instead cross the River here and skirt the edge of the Taheeran Desert, as long as you swear you will not attempt to enter the Falnor Woods, you may yet make it safely to the Watchtower.

"We will tell you where to find the oasis and the spring. The Thinabar Pass is impassable to wagons. It was never as well traveled as the Gelthor Pass because of it. Few even know about it. But single file on horseback it should still be useable. From there you will proceed to Athanark, and then east and north and east again, to the Watchtower. We will tell you where to find it and how to approach it safely.

"Meanwhile, we will continue along the Merdan for a while, and attempt to trick the Enemy into believing we yet travel with you. We will try to hold His attention for a time and then we will conceal ourselves fully and double back for Salenia. We will give you our water pouches. You must fill them along with your own. We will be by the River always and have no need of them. You should acquire more waterskins in Falnor. Even so, there is a limit to the water your horses can carry. You must ration your water carefully, in order to survive. Your horses are larger and stronger than you are; they will live. Have them drink their fill deeply before you turn for the Desert. They will take whatever moisture they can from their feed and whatever small drinks you might spare them until you reach the oasis."

RION listened intently to all Swiftsong said. He'd been perfectly calm before, when he'd held the knife to his throat, but he was trembling now. He'd come terribly close to killing himself. He'd been afraid Swiftsong wouldn't believe him. He was glad Gar had pled his case so convincingly. He had no intention of dying so young, if he could help it. But he'd truly rather die than see another die for him. It frightened him that he would have carried through with his threat, if he'd had to.

"And I thought I harbored dark thoughts," Andra said. "I never would have suspected it of you, Rion. You're as born to smile as I was to scowl. I'll have to keep a more careful eye on you. Seafoam never would have forgiven herself. You know that, don't you? Nor Ron. Would you see them so hurt?"

Rion nodded his head, *Yes,* sadly. At least they would be alive.

"There is much more to you than meets the eye. I can see I seriously misjudged you, when first I saw you. You care more about others than you do about yourself. I never would have guessed it, from the way you looked." Andra smiled at him fondly.

Swiftsong told them everything they needed to know to get to the Watchtower. Then he focused his full attention on Rion. "As we will no longer be riding at your side, before we leave you, there is something I must gift to you, if you are to have any hope of succeeding in your journey. I am loath to part with it, for it has saved my life more than once, but I would not think to keep it. Still, for the memories it holds, I would ask that you return it to me, if you are someday able."

Rion nodded in acquiescence, wondering what Swiftsong could possibly be thinking to give him. Swiftsong reached into his pack and pulled out a slender coil of what could only be rope, though it gleamed as if made of spun silver. No, it shone like the dagger Aras had once shown him, which had looked like a beam of moonlight had been caught and rolled into the metal of the blade. The rope had the distinctive sheen of pallenteum.

"We are no longer capable of making cable such as this, for reasons which I cannot convey. For that, alone, it would be priceless. But the service to which it has already been put, and for which you will someday put it, is what makes it truly beyond price. I cannot tell you plainly why I gift it to you, for my visions are no longer as clear as they once were, and I will admit to you that at times, to my consternation, they baffle even me.

"I know that we are far inland and that you have no intention of heading to the coast anytime soon. I cannot imagine when you might next set your eyes upon the ocean. I can say only that, if ever you need an ocean to move a mountain, you now hold the key. Would that I were better able to prepare you for whatever trials might lie ahead."

Swiftsong turned so his gaze encompassed all of them. "Safe journey, my friends. May we meet again, in brighter days." Then, without further word, he and the others rode away, as Rion's friends called out their thanks and good-byes.

Rion watched them leave, feeling as if he were going to cry, but he forced the tears down.

"I feel it too, Rion, we all do—the emptiness with them gone," Ron said gently. "But they'll survive now. You've seen them safe. You must remember that. Come, we've still a long journey ahead of us, longer now that we must detour through Athanark, after all we went through to leave that City far behind us. The world never does what you expect it to, does it?"

Rion carefully added the coil of Elven rope to his pack, and then he and the others turned toward Falnor.

TWO days later they arrived at Falnor, in the early evening. Fortunately, the Market was still open, so they would yet be able to purchase what they needed. They acquired the additional waterskins and feed for the horses, and supplemented their own provisions as well. They debated buying a packhorse to help them carry the extra water and feed, but he would also require supplies and would likely travel more slowly than their own superior mounts. Also, they did not want to rely upon an animal of uncertain temperament on such a potentially dangerous journey. A cart or wagon would only impede them in a desert crossing.

They spent the night at an inn and left early the next morning after a bracing breakfast. They filled their waterskins in one of the wells on the way out of the City.

They traveled a day and a half along grassland and were still half a day's ride from the edge of the Desert when they unexpectedly came upon an ancient, weathered shrine to Areth.

"I need to make an offering," Rarnak said and dismounted, taking a waterskin and a loaf of *raeta* the Elves had given him.

Ron hated having to speak up. He tried to avoid ever commenting on another's beliefs, but he had to. "Rarnak, I know it's customary to offer food and drink to Areth, but you must at least save your water. We'll need all we have for the trip. You might die if you give Areth some now."

Rarnak looked levelly at him. "Elmoth has let me live, though I've never worshipped Him once in the seven years I've been a swordsman. Areth won't let me die for lack of water now, when I've always been faithful to Her. I need to pray to Her about the stream in the Gelthor Pass and the River, and I'll need water for the offering for both. There are those who depend upon them for their very lives, as well as their livelihoods."

Ron was surprised by the strength of Rarnak's faith. He and his brothers swore by Elmoth often enough, and Gar and Van worshipped Him, but only Ara followed Him devoutly, as their grandfather had. Ron had always wondered at his grandfather's continued devotion, in spite of the burning and rape of Thenalon, the horrible death of so many women and children, and of his friends and all his kin.

Ron had never forgiven Elmoth for allowing his mother and baby sister to die, and for not intervening when he was beaten nearly to death by the man he'd called Father his whole life. But Ron had since forgiven his mother, for him being the bastard child of a whore, and for her pretty lies to him and his brothers of how she and Father met. He'd even forgiven his father for the attack upon him, for the ills of his childhood, now that it had all been explained to him and he was man enough to understand it, as he never could have then. Perhaps it was time he forgave Elmoth as well?

Had Elmoth had a hand in him surviving as a child, and in him and his brothers surviving their two-year journey? Looking back upon it, mightn't Elmoth have been the one to see them all live through the ogre attack, even the obearn attack? Instead of being angered at the God for their injuries, should he perhaps have fallen to his knees and thanked Him for the aid of the Elves? Gar's healing had certainly been miracle enough, though he'd credited the Elves for it, rather than the God. How was one to know what was blind luck and what was divine intervention? Or were they one and the same?

Ron fought the ingrained urge to scoff at the thought that the God might care what happened to any of them. His brothers were all good men. If anyone deserved Elmoth's attention and compassion, they did. It was something to think about.

While he'd been pondering his own beliefs, Rarnak had been kneeling in prayer to Areth at the shrine. Now Rarnak put the full loaf of *raeta* on the small altar and ran a river of water from his skin across the stone. Ron held his tongue with effort. Rarnak must have used at least half that skin, perhaps more. He had others, but every drop was precious.

NEARLY three days later, Ron glared from the taunting, unattainable, lush Elven Wood at his left to the stand of dead trees on his right, which encircled the cracked, bone-dry former mud of what had once been a sizeable water hole. He swore graphically in Thenalonese as he again viewed the withered oasis in disgust, hoping for signs of water he'd somehow missed the first time.

"Now what do we do?" Gar asked in dismay.

"We move on. It's three more days to the spring at the mouth of the Thinabar Pass," Ron said determinedly.

"We'll be hard pressed to last long enough to reach it. But what if when we get there, the water's not there, either?" Gar asked, voicing all their fears.

"What choice do we have?" Ron asked. "You saw what happened when we tried to enter the Falnor Woods. The horses are terrified of them. Even Seafoam won't go near them. You felt it too, when you and I dismounted and tried to enter on foot, to look for water. I thought my heart would stop. I don't know if it's part of the quarantine, or just their usual magicks, but the Elves won't help us this time. They can't."

RION shifted nervously. His own waterskins were all painfully empty. He'd been sure there would be water here, and Seafoam had looked at him so forlornly, that he'd given her his last few drinks earlier in the day. He couldn't bear having her watch him drink and he'd thought they'd have plenty tonight. He patted her and hugged her neck. He didn't regret it. He'd do anything for her.

"We'll share evenly what we have left. We know Rarnak's already run out, though he's been denying it," Ara said.

"Hand me your skins, the ones with water remaining," Ron said, and Ara and Gar surrendered one each of theirs. He hefted them and nodded. "Andra?" he said. She handed two to him and he took them and looked at her in surprise. "How can they both be so full?"

She smiled ruefully at him. "I've been drinking only every other time the rest of you did. I'm more cynical than the rest of you. I was afraid we might run into ill luck."

"You're a marvel, Andra. Rion, hand me yours," Ron said.

Rion shook his head, *No.*

"I'll give it back as soon as we split what we have fairly," Ron said.

Rion again shook his head.

Andra eyed him appraisingly. "He'd not be selfish. I've seen enough of him now to know that's the last thing he'd be. It must be his are all empty, and he doesn't want to take any of ours. He's younger and he needs less. It's my guess he gave what he had to Seafoam."

RON was dismayed by Andra's words, though pleasantly surprised by his sister's tact. She'd not said Rion was smaller than the rest of them, only younger. She'd obviously noticed he was sensitive about his build. The surprise came from the fact that she cared whether or not she hurt him. Her tongue was easily as scathing as their father's, or his own.

Rion gave a guilty nod.

"Oh, Rion," Ron said. "Come, give me your skin."

Rion shook his head.

"Rion, I'll not see you weaken when you're the one we're here to see safely to Eladar," Ron said.

Finally, with obvious reluctance, Rion complied.

Ron carefully weighed what he, Gar, Ara, and Andra had. He was impressed by how sparingly even Gar and Ara had drunk. The skins they'd given him were both three-quarters full. He carefully poured all his own water into Rion's skin. He would have just swapped them, but he didn't want the others to know he wasn't saving any for himself. He gave Andra's second skin to Rarnak, and left Gar's and Ara's as they were. He'd pretend to drink when the others did. He was confident he'd survive until they reached the spring. He only hoped it truly still had water.

TWO and a half days later, the horses were all stumbling, except Thenagar and Seafoam. Rion fought the urge to really drink this time, when he pretended to. He hadn't drunk a drop of the water Ron had given him. He wouldn't deprive the rest of them what was rightfully theirs. They were only half a day from the spring. If only it truly held water!

Blaze stumbled badly, almost pitching Ron off. Ron dismounted and soothed him and then began leading him by the reins. The others, except for Rion and Gar, soon followed suit. Rion pulled out his journal and wrote with his lead, grateful again for Seafoam's smooth gait. *Gar and I are going on ahead to the spring to get water. Give us your empty skins and we'll give you ours with what water we have left.* Rion planned to keep riding down the Pass, if there was no water at the entry, but he had no intention of telling the others that. He showed Ron his note.

"No, Rion. It's too dangerous for the two of you to enter the foothills alone," Ron argued.

Rion shook his head and pointed to himself and Gar and then toward the Coroden.

Andra took the note from Ron and read it aloud to the others. She handed Rion her empty waterskins and took Rarnak's off his horse and handed them to Rion as well. Rarnak was looking dazed. "We've little choice, Ron. Gar will be with him, at least."

"I'll go on Seafoam," Ron said stubbornly.

Rion shook his head. He tucked the skins into his pack, since he didn't have saddlebags, and then held out his hand to Ara. Ara eyed Ron, then Rion, and handed his skins up to him, and Rion packed those away as well.

"I said no. I'll not risk you like that," Ron said vehemently. "If the Enemy's minions came upon only the two of you, or an obearn, or an ogre, or thieves, you'd be too weak to fight or even run."

Rion tossed his full skin to Andra, who caught it reflexively, and then he whistled "Go, faster, faster," to Seafoam, and Seafoam suddenly broke from a standstill into a gallop as Rion held on tightly.

"Rion, wait!" Gar cried and urged Thenagar after him.

ANDRA cursed as the two of them bolted away. There was no way she could catch them on foot. Then she realized the weight of what she held and cursed again. "Ron, how much water did you give Rion?"

"Why?" Ron asked, glaring after Rion's rapidly retreating form.

"Because I doubt he'd drunk a drop of what you'd given him, from the feel of this," she said, handing it to him.

Ron took it from her, hefted it, and swore.

"There's nothing we can do about it now," Ara said. "There's no way to catch him. I only hope he has the sense to slow Seafoam, now that he's gotten away, before she drops dead from thirst."

AS SOON as Rion was safely away, he slowed Seafoam to a walk, looking critically at her. He wanted to conserve what strength she had, as well as give Thenagar a chance to catch up to them.

Gar caught up with him soon enough and scolded him. "Don't do that again, Rion! But at least you had the sense to slow down to let me catch up to you. I know you hate seeing us suffer for you, but it's our choice. We're strong, we'll make it, but not if you take foolish chances."

Rion nodded seriously.

"Well, come on, then," Gar said.

It was early evening, yet a good while before dusk, when they reached the spring and water hole, or what had been them only a short time ago. A rockslide appeared to have choked off the spring. The tops of still-living trees barely protruded from the pile of rock, indicating that there must have been water there only recently.

Gar swore at length. "Either an ogre did this, or the Enemy. It matters little. After seeing the oasis and then this, I've no doubt whatever water might ever once have been in the Pass is gone as well. You'll have to risk going it alone, Rion. Seafoam can still carry you to Athanark. From what Meander told us, she can protect you, too. It's only another fifty miles to Athanark, though I've no idea what the terrain of the Pass might be like. Here. Take my water. Once you make it there, hire some guards and bring back water for the rest of us," Gar urged.

Rion shook his head adamantly. Gar and the others would die with such a delay. He was certain Gar knew that. They were all already dying. He dismounted and studied the rockslide before him, frustrated by the knowledge that the water they needed lay so close, but was unattainable, buried by a veritable mountain of rock. There must be some way to get at the water! If only he had the key!

Memory stirred: water, mountain, key. The Elven rope? He snorted in disgust at himself. He must already be sun mad. No matter how desirable the spring, it could not possibly be mistaken for an ocean, though it was also made of water. Besides, the ocean was supposed to move the mountain, from what Swiftsong had said. Where might he find an ocean in these barren hills that framed the Desert?

Could the vision have meant the Desert? It was an ocean of sorts, one of sand and rock instead of water. No. How could the Desert help them, when it was killing them? And how could the rope help? Boats had ropes. No, that made even less sense. He was too thirsty to think, his mind muddled because of it. The answer was there, right before him, and he was too sun addled and dehydrated to see it. They might all die because he couldn't.

"Rion, you must go to Athanark! You gave Andra your remaining water, and she and Ara and Ron and Rarnak yet have what's left of theirs. We'll all live, but none of us will, if you don't go for help," Gar said desperately, dismounting beside him.

Rion put his fingers to his lips, indicating Gar should be silent. It was hard enough to try to think without Gar speaking, and Rion knew he was lying. Rion slid his pack off his shoulders, set it on the ground, and stretched his aching muscles, reaching behind his back to rub his shoulder.

Seafoam whickered and bumped his other shoulder.

Not now, Seafoam, he thought, appreciating her effort to rub it for him but wishing he could tell her aloud not to.

She pawed at his pack with her hoof, and he glared at her in surprise. He tried to whistle *Stop,* harshly, his frustration and aggravation getting the best of him, and was almost relieved when he failed to make a sound. He felt immediately guilty. Likely she smelled the water beneath the rock, and hoped he might have some more in his pack for her.

She lowered her head and began lipping the flap of his pack, confirming his suspicion. Astonishingly, she somehow managed to open it. He reached down to try to gently pat her face away and was shocked when she lifted her head, the coil of Elven rope held delicately between her teeth. She held it out to him, as if handing him the solution to their problem. He petted her. Now if only Seafoam could find him an ocean... an ocean... the sea!

He smacked himself in the head for his idiocy and took the rope from her, patting her and petting her in his thanks. He had his ocean standing there right before him, the Seafoam he needed to move the mountain of rock, and the rope to do it with, but his thoughts had been too muddled to see it.

The water must still be there, under all that rock. It had to be, or the Enemy would not have needed to bury it so deeply to keep it from them, if it had indeed been Him acting against them. Or perhaps just against anyone who might try to escape from Him this way. Some of the rocks were huge. Could Seafoam truly do it? Could she move such a mountain? Rion began forming the rope into a harness for her.

"Rion, what are you doing?" Gar asked, appearing baffled.

Rion pointed to Seafoam and the rope, then the rock, then put the rope in his hands and mimed pulling.

Gar gaped at him in disbelief. "Rion, you can't be serious! Those rocks weigh hundreds of pounds! Those four toward the bottom must each weigh close to a thousand. There's no way she can do it! You'll kill her if you make her try, especially weak as she is."

Rion hesitated. He swallowed. But then Seafoam nudged him with her head again, as if to reassure him. He pulled out his bedroll and unrolled his blanket and put it over her withers, to pad against the rope. Then he began fitting the impromptu harness about her.

Seafoam snorted but remained motionless. He hugged her and petted her. Then he climbed up part of the rockslide and tied the loose ends of the rope around one of the boulders. He climbed carefully down again. He tried to whistle, *Pull,* but he couldn't do it. His lips were completely dry, even when he tried to wet them with his parched tongue. He signaled drinking to Gar. Even though Seafoam apparently knew what he wanted to do, he needed to be able to command her.

Gar looked at him warily. "You're not giving this to her," he said, holding the skin.

He shook his head, pointing to himself.

Gar stared suspiciously at him and reluctantly handed it to him. Rion squirted out just enough to wet his lips and tongue so he could whistle. It was hot and stale and nothing had ever tasted so good in his life. He fought the urge to drink a stream of it, to gulp down all of it. If this worked, he'd have plenty. If not....

He closed the skin and handed it to Gar and whistled, *Pull.* Seafoam walked forward, pulling the rope taut, then lowered her head and began pulling in earnest, as if she were a draft horse rather than a warhorse and riding horse.

The rope stretched tighter. Rion hoped it didn't break, but it wasn't only made of metal, it was made of pallenteum, and it was Elven besides. Surely it should hold?

The rock shifted ever so slightly. *Pull right,* Rion whistled, indicating the direction with his hands to ensure she truly understood, and she obeyed. *Pull left,* he whistled and she did so. He continued urging her to rock it right, then left, and suddenly the boulder rolled free, sending a shower of others crashing free as well, all of them narrowly missing Seafoam. Rion's heart was hammering. He'd misjudged how the rock might shift. He'd have to be more careful with the next one.

Rion hugged and patted Seafoam until his heart calmed. Then he selected the next boulder more carefully and tied the rope around it. This time, it went much more smoothly.

"Amazing. You just might be able to do it, Rion. How can I help?" Gar asked.

Rion pointed to Thenagar and shrugged.

"No, I don't think he'd be able to. Also, my rope would snap. It's not Elven like yours. But I could help by moving some of the smaller rocks out of the way, by hand. I could even climb up and brace my back and use my feet on some of the bigger ones. Those few there look ready to come down, if I push them just right, now that you've made a dent in it."

Rion nodded eagerly.

Gar tied Thenagar securely to one of the boulders a safe distance away from the main body of the slide so he'd not be injured from falling rock; then he proceeded to aid Rion as he'd described. Rion tied another rock off after carefully studying the slide. He was ready to pull, but Gar was still moving some smaller rocks, after knocking down the first few. He tapped Gar and whistled, careful to make the tone different from any of Seafoam's commands, and mimed walking.

Gar grinned. "I get it. I'll know next time to get out of the way when you signal me with just the whistle. Seafoam's not the only one who can respond to your commands." Rion blushed, but Gar hugged him. "If this works, you'll have saved us," he said, and Rion felt better.

Rock by rock they removed the slide. Seafoam was trembling now from the effort, and Gar was as well. Rion gave him the skin back and mimed drinking.

"No, I'm all right," Gar said weakly.

Rion indicated that he should sit and rest, and Gar didn't argue the point. Then Rion went over to Seafoam and soothed her. He headed for the remaining pile of rock, trying to determine which one to move next. He pulled upon a few, to test their stability, and then felt eagerly. Damp, it was damp! That rock was cooler than the ones before, too.

Rion took the waterskin and walked to Seafoam, then gave her a drink. She drank eagerly, the two small mouthfuls that had been left, then begged him for more. He looked at Gar. Gar was still sitting with his head tilted back. He'd not seen him give her the water. Rion was worried about him. He feared he might be unconscious rather than asleep.

Rion patted Seafoam and tied another rock, and whistled, *Pull.* She pulled. This time, when the rock rolled free, there was no question. There was a tiny puddle of water where it had lain. Rion sucked at it eagerly. It was muddy but cool. He had her remove two more rocks. Then he tied her to one of the large ones and patted her, then whistled, and she began to pull, as instructed. The rope stretched taut, but the rock would not budge. *Pull, pull, pull,* he whistled. Her head was down, muscles bulging with the strain. Her whole body was shaking. She couldn't do it.

He whistled for her to stop, afraid the effort might kill her. But she refused to stop. Instead she pulled right, then left, then right, of her own accord, without Rion telling her to. Rion ran to the rock and pressed his back to one of the other boulders and pushed against the one she was trying to shift with his feet, throwing all of his weight into it. His whole body started to shake, but then there was finally the sound of grinding stone. They both redoubled their efforts, encouraged.

Slowly, tortuously, the boulder moved. Rion was exhausted and dizzy, but he fought to stay conscious. He couldn't fail them all now, when he was so close. He refused to give up when Seafoam would not. Eventually, the boulder shifted free enough to reveal a shallow basin with perhaps an inch of water in it. Rion jumped clear and, whistling musically, pulled Seafoam's mane hard, forcing her to turn toward the basin, so she could see the water, so she could see she'd done it. He hugged her and kissed her proud head.

Rion led Seafoam to the water and she drank eagerly, though she didn't finish it. She stepped back and butted his head with hers, as if indicating it was his turn. He didn't need to be told twice. He sucked up all that was left eagerly. Seeing them, and smelling the water, Thenagar trumpeted his frustration. Rion was relieved Gar had tied him securely to one of the rocks before aiding them, but concerned that Gar didn't rouse at all at the sound. He felt guilty for not trying to bring some of the water to Gar.

Rion and Seafoam pulled another of the boulders away and a trickle of water began running into the empty basin. He pulled away some of the smaller rocks by hand and the flow increased. He eagerly watched the basin slowly fill. When Seafoam bent to drink again, he whistled, *Stop.* She snorted at him, for she was still terribly thirsty, but she obeyed.

Rion filled five of the waterskins, then signaled *Go* and splashed the water to ensure she understood, and she drank, then nuzzled him with her wet, velvety nose. Rion untied Thenagar, who was stomping his foot and snorting angrily, and let him drink as well. Then he retied him and went to Gar, put the waterskin into his mouth, and squirted. Gar awoke with a start, coughing.

He pulled back. "Rion, what are you doing! There won't be any left for your journey to Athanark if this doesn't work," he said, voice hoarse.

Rion grinned, shook his head, and pointed. Seafoam was drinking again.

"She might drink it all," Gar said, worried, but Rion held up the other four waterskins by their straps and grinned.

"You've done it! Rion, by Elmoth, you've done it!" Gar said and then drank greedily from the skin Rion held out to him. Rion drank his fill as well.

Gar stared in amazement at the last two boulders they'd shifted. "I can't believe I passed out and missed seeing that! I still can't believe you two moved them, but you must have."

Rion patted Seafoam again, and hugged her strong neck.

They waited until the basin filled again and then filled more of the skins. He knew better than to drink too much, too fast. Then they drank, followed by the horses. They alternated filling skins, drinking, and letting the horses drink until all the skins they'd brought were full, and they were all sated.

"Without us to drain it, it will soon overflow. It's a shame the rest of the basin is yet buried. It seems wasteful, but there's nothing we can do about it, I suppose. We should start heading back. I know we'll only be able to travel a short distance before the sun sets and we lose the light, but we'll at least get a little closer to the others. They'll already be terribly worried when we don't return before nightfall. They won't guess this might have delayed us. I only hope they have sense enough to make camp and not try to walk all the way to us on foot in the dark, otherwise we might miss each other. We'll make camp ourselves, as soon as the light starts to fail. Help me gather some of these broken branches to bring with us. I'll feel happier and safer if we have a fire tonight."

RON cursed. It was too dark to see their trail even with his unusually keen night vision. Clouds had shrouded the moon. If only they were rainclouds! But they didn't have the look of them. "I begged them not to go," Ron said bitterly, frustrated and fearful that both Rion and Gar might already be dead.

"They must have found this water hole dried up as well, and entered the Pass," Andra said.

"That's what I'm afraid of," Ron said. "There are ogres in the Coroden north of here, and I don't doubt they're probably here as well. And there are obearn in these hills and likely in the Pass as well. And both they and their horses are weak from thirst."

"Have faith, Ron," Andra said. "Elmoth will see them safe."

Ron scowled at her. He'd forgotten how devout she was. He was tired enough of Ara spouting such nonsense. But he didn't dare tell her so. He realized her faith might see her through this. He'd not weaken it when she needed it most. What little glimmer of faith he'd started to have had dried up with their water.

"All right. We make camp here. But we move at dawn, two of us, on foot. We leave the other two with the horses," Ron said.

None of them ate dinner, for fear they'd be unable to swallow and would choke.

The others slept deeply, too deeply. Ron alone stayed awake, marveling at his own endurance. He hadn't drunk a drop in three days, yet he still seemed stronger than them. Not for the first time, he wondered who his true father might have been. Had he inherited yet another odd ability from him, to go without water when others couldn't? He'd long ago learned he could survive blows with merely a bruise that should break bone; that he had an unnaturally high tolerance for pain, when he was injured; that he could lift twice the weight others his size could; that unaccustomed to alcohol as he was, he could drink others under the table, and scarcely feel the effects himself; that he could see easily in what others claimed was total darkness; that he had an unerring sense of direction and could not get lost; that he radiated heat like an oven, causing his brothers to gather around him in bed in the winter and complain bitterly in the summer; and now he found he could live without water for longer than he should be able to, to no apparent ill effect.

He looked toward Andra. He never should have let the others talk him into letting her come. Now she'd die out here with the rest of them. At least Van was safe. Little Van. Only he was not so little anymore. He was going to be a father. Ron had thought he'd get to meet his niece or nephew, or that if he didn't, it would be because he'd died in the War. He never thought he'd die of thirst or that he'd doom Rion, and the brothers and sister he loved, and a good friend to such an early death. He cursed. The second dawn broke, or the clouds moved and he could see their tracks, he'd set out after Rion and Gar. He'd see them safe, somehow. He had to.

GAR and Rion sat by their fire, a pot of stew bubbling over it. Rion was amazed at how good it smelled, although Gar had warned him it might taste awful, as he wasn't the cook Ron was. Rion knew if he'd cooked it that it would likely have been inedible. It had been so hard to eat before, with his mouth so dry. He felt his mouth water at the scent, now that he could salivate again.

Gar was almost ready to dish it up when there was a low, bellowing roar, just beyond the light the fire cast, where Thenagar was tethered to one of the desert rocks. Thenagar screamed and bolted past them, nearly trampling them, veering away to avoid the fire at the last moment, the cut rein flapping unevenly along her side.

An obearn came lunging out of the dark after Thenagar, heading straight for them. Gar cried out and ran from it in terror, and Rion realized that memory of the attack he'd barely survived would have driven all reason from him.

Rion leapt to his feet, no less terrified, drawing his sword, knowing he'd never survive its mad charge but that he could not outrun it. He was nowhere near as skilled as Ara with a blade, and Ara had almost died as well, when he and Gar had fought the other obearn. That one had been relatively small, scarcely over seven feet tall. This one was huge; it would tower well over ten feet, when standing.

The obearn lost all interest in Thenagar when it saw much easier prey waiting for it. It reached outward to swipe at Rion with one massive paw, but plunging from out of the dark, Seafoam attacked. She rammed into the obearn with her shoulder, screaming in rage, and it tumbled past Rion, missing him with its deadly six inch claws.

Then Seafoam was rearing, and her hooves sliced into the obearn's thick fur. Trumpeting furiously, she kicked and trampled the beast. The obearn roared and tried to swat her, but she bit its leg. It screamed and tried to bite her back, its mouth opening wide, displaying rows of razor-sharp yellowed teeth, but her hooves crashed into its muzzle. Howling in pain, the obearn lumbered off, fleeing into the night. Seafoam started to follow.

Rion was terrified she might be killed, that he'd lose her, but also, that he would be left alone here in the dark, when another obearn or something even worse might come for him out of the night. Memory of the horrid monsters from his nightmares and the real ones that had attacked him in the Market and on the road to Salenia all but paralyzed him.

Stop, come, protect! Rion whistled desperately, afraid Seafoam would not obey him, as she'd disobeyed him in Salenia when she'd followed him, and at the spring when she'd insisted upon pulling the boulders. But she instantly halted and trotted to him, standing beside him, nickering softly.

Rion dropped his sword and hugged her. He couldn't stop shaking. She whickered softly again and nibbled at his hair, until he slowly calmed.

Another terrifying thought sent his heart hammering. The obearn was wounded now. It would be angry and still hungry. It could easily scent Gar and come for him, kill him. Rion picked up his sword. He'd never be able to track Gar, even in daylight he probably couldn't, but maybe Seafoam could. He dumped the stew, buried it, and threw more wood on the fire, to make it larger and brighter, so he'd be able to find it again, in the rocky terrain. Hopefully, other predators would stay away too, now that there wasn't the smell of food to tempt them. He took Gar's bedroll and held it to Seafoam's nose. *Find,* he whistled.

Seafoam sniffed the blanket curiously.

Find, he whistled again. *Go, find.* He began pulling her along the direction Gar had fled, pulling her head down to the ground, then back to the blanket. Of her own accord, she bent down and sniffed the ground again, then began smelling along it. Rion hoped she was truly tracking Gar's scent and that she'd not lose it. He prayed they might find Gar alive, that the obearn wouldn't have found him first.

After tripping in the dark for the fifth time, Rion told Seafoam to bow, and he mounted her. Then he had her rise and continue along Gar's trail. They walked even farther into the dark Desert. Could Gar truly have run so far? Perhaps Seafoam didn't have his scent after all.

A moment later, when he heard the sound of sobbing in the dark, he felt ashamed for having doubted her. Seafoam had heard, too, and trotted forward eagerly.

The sobbing stopped. "Thenagar?" a familiar but terrified voice called raggedly. "Is that you?"

Rion whistled to Gar in greeting, though he couldn't see his face. He only saw the most vague impression of a dark shadow crouched in the dirt, until a stray beam of moonlight broke through the clouds.

"Rion? Elmoth! Rion? You're alive!" Gar yelled and ran to him.

Rion dismounted and Gar hugged him frantically, saying, "Are you hurt? I can barely see you. Let me help you. I can't believe you're alive!" Gar stiffened and drew back in sudden fear. "Rion? Is that really you? Are you alive?"

Rion reached out and took Gar's hand. Gar trembled and started to pull away from him, but he placed Gar's hand over his heart, so Gar could feel it beating, and whistled reassuringly.

Gar hugged him again, in obvious relief. Then Gar said, "Rion, nod yes or shake your head no. Are you hurt?"

Rion shook his head, *No.*

"But how—is it dead?" Gar asked.

Again, Rion shook his head, *No.*

"Did you wound it?" Gar asked.

Rion shook his head, *No,* then pointed to Seafoam and nodded, *Yes.*

"You mean Seafoam wounded it? An obearn? She attacked an obearn?" Gar asked in astonishment.

Rion nodded, *Yes,* then realized the enormity of what she had done. Horses were terrified of obearn. Yet although he'd not even commanded her to, she'd attacked it, when she might instead have easily run to safety. She'd done it out of love for him, all on her own. Rion hugged her fiercely.

Gar said, "Rion, I'm so sorry! I left you. I just ran away and left you to die. I couldn't help it. When it came for me... my reason fled. I ran and ran, and then when I could finally think again, I had no idea which direction our camp was in. I was sure it must have killed you. However did you find me?"

Rion pointed to Seafoam.

"You mean she found me?" Gar asked in surprise.

Rion nodded and handed him his blanket, then pointed to her and his nose and to Gar.

"What, you mean she scented me? Like a dog would?" Gar asked in disbelief.

Rion nodded, *Yes.*

"Can she find her way back to our camp? Thenagar might be miles from here. We shouldn't try to look for him until daylight," Gar said.

Rion whistled for Seafoam to bow. She did and he mounted and pulled on Gar's arm.

"What, you want me to ride double? All right. I fell a number of times while running, so I certainly won't mind the ride, if Seafoam doesn't mind carrying me," Gar said, as he mounted up behind him, impulsively hugging Rion again and then releasing him abruptly. "Forgive me. I needed to prove to myself you're all right. I'd never forgive myself if you'd been hurt. I still can't forgive myself. I wish I could do it over again. How could I have run and left you?"

Rion patted him reassuringly on the leg. He forgave him for it. After what Gar had lived through on their earlier journey, how could he not? He was only glad he was safe. Rion whistled, *Find backward,* wishing Seafoam knew the word "camp."

Seafoam snorted. He tried again. She did the same.

"What's wrong? She doesn't understand? I'd started to believe she could do anything, that she'd even fly if you told her to. Let me try. Seafoam, find the fire. *Famsala, thelesa faer,*" he said, in Elvish. "I hope that's right. I think it is. I'm pretty sure that's 'find' and 'fire,'" Gar said.

Rion knew Gar should have said, "*Famsala, faer thelesa,*" but he hoped Seafoam would understand Gar's poor grammar. *Find,* Rion whistled again, in encouragement.

Seafoam whickered her understanding and turned and began trotting.

"Amazing. I think that did it. I think she understood us," Gar said. Then a moment later, he asked fearfully, "Rion? Is Thenagar all right?"

Rion shrugged and patted his leg.

"You don't know, but I should try not to worry?" Gar asked.

Rion nodded, *Yes.*

"I left him and you both to die," Gar said mournfully, his voice filled with recrimination.

Rion shook his head, *No.*

"All right. I'll try to forgive myself for it," Gar said.

They reached the fire more quickly than it had taken for them to find Gar.

"How'd the fire get so big?" Gar asked in surprise.

Rion pointed to himself.

"You built it up before you left to look for me? That was smart. But you should have stayed by it. It would have served me right if the obearn came after me in the dark and…."

Rion punched him in the leg.

"Ow! All right, you win. I'll forgive myself. Eventually," Gar said.

Rion asked Seafoam to bow so they could dismount easily. Once they were on the ground, Gar picked up the stewpot and dumped the dirt from it. "I guess I should be glad it ate our dinner instead of either of us, but I'm still hungry."

Rion shook his head and mimed burying it, as he had mimed burying Lerdon's body outside Salenia. The memory sent a shiver down his spine. He'd ridden off into the night. What if he'd found something other than Gar?

"Rion, it's all right. I'm safe and so are you. We just have to hope the others are, too," Gar said, apparently seeing the look on his face by the fire's light. "It was smart of you to bury the stew. That might be what attracted the obearn, if it wasn't only the scent of the horses, or even the water. I bet that spring is going to be pretty busy tonight. It's a good thing we decided to ride partway back. I'd not even thought of that, before. I hope that obearn doesn't go too far hunting for food. If it's wounded, it'll be more dangerous than ever. I hope the others are nowhere near here. In any case, I don't think any of us will be getting much sleep tonight."

RON woke the others at dawn, or tried to. Ara and Andra awoke sluggishly, but Rarnak only moaned and wouldn't rise. Ron cursed. "Andra, I thought you said you'd gotten him to drink," Ron accused.

"I did," she said defensively. "I watched him. I even touched his tongue to be sure, when I realized he was trying to trick me. It startled him, you can well imagine, but his mouth was wet." She hefted his skin and cursed. "It's as full as it was when you gave it to him. He must have put two drops onto his tongue each time, just enough so his lips would look wet, to fool me. Ragnar's fire! You pigheaded, noble…." She thrust the skin through his parched lips and squirted water carefully into his mouth, so none might be lost. He coughed and then began struggling feebly.

There was a whinny from behind them, and Ron turned in surprise. Had one of the horses gotten loose in the night, looking for water? Then he paled. It was Thenagar and he was riderless. Ron went to him, talking soothingly, careful not to frighten him. He grabbed his dangling rein, fingering the uneven cut leather in growing dread and began checking him for injury. He walked around him and paled further. There were four deep parallel grooves in his right flank, filled with dried blood. "No. No, not Gar, not again," Ron whispered horrified, shaking.

"Ron, what is it, what…?" Ara stared in horror at the bloody gashes, recognizing them instantly as obearn claw marks, as Ron had. "Gar! Gar! Rion!" Ara yelled and then bent to the ground and began following Thenagar's hoofprints, back the way he had come.

Ron called after him. "Ara, wait! Bring your bow! Wait for me! Andra, you stay here. Ready your bow, guard Rarnak. We'll come back for you, as soon as we can," Ron said, grabbing his own bow and Ara's, running to catch up to his brother.

"RON, Gar can't be dead. Thenagar survived. Maybe…," Ara began desperately.

"Thenagar survived last time, too, by running off and leaving Gar. It's my fault! How could I have done it again? I sent them off to die," Ron said bitterly, his voice filled with anguish and self-recrimination.

"Stop it, Ron! Rion ran off, remember? You tried to stop him. Gar should have brought him back to us, not gone off with him. He—at least it will have been quick. Not like with Thorn and the ogres. They might not even have seen it, in the dark. It would have killed them both quickly. Elmoth, please hear me, I beg you. If there's any way you might have spared them...." Ara trailed off. It was too late to ask the God to intervene.

Ara tracked the prints quietly, dreading what he would find. He kept picturing the terror on Gar's face as the beast came for him, knowing what it would feel like when it slashed him. And Rion, poor gentle little Rion. He vividly remembered the feel of the obearn raking its claws across his own back.

They walked for what seemed like forever, staring intently at the ground. Ara forced himself to look up every now and then so they'd not be surprised by an obearn themselves, but he was focused on the ground when Ron suddenly grabbed his arm.

"Do you hear that?" Ron demanded. At almost the same instant, Ara heard a whinny. He looked up, startled. Had Thenagar somehow gotten away from Andra and followed them? Then he yelled in amazement, "Rion? Gar? You're alive!" and ran to them, Ron at his side.

"I GUESS she's not so smart after all, Rion. We told her to find Thenagar, not these two," Gar joked lamely.

Ron yanked him off Seafoam.

Gar was amazed he didn't fall in a tangled heap on top of him. Ron was so strong! "I'm not the one you should be happy to see," Gar said, face flushing hotly. "An obearn attacked us last night. I ran and left Rion to die. He would have, if Seafoam hadn't saved him. And I lost Thenagar. We thought we were following his trail."

Ron was hugging him, grinning like a fool, eyes lit with brotherly love.

"Didn't you hear me? Why are you hugging me? Yell at me! I left Rion to die! I ran. Yell at me, hit me, for Elmoth's sake, do something! Stop hugging me and scream at me!" Gar snapped, tugging away from him.

"Gar, stop it. Of course you ran! You're a Man, not a God. Am I to expect you to do any less, after one of those vile things tore your face to ribbons, after you lay dying for days, until the Elves healed you? Are you supposed to have stood there calmly and fired arrows at it? Did it give you time to? Or did it leap at you out of the black of the night and scare you witless? We found Thenagar, or he found us. We saw his wound and guessed what had happened. It's a wonder any of you lived. It must have been a monster, from how far apart the claw marks on his flank were."

Ara was hugging Rion but then he turned and hugged Gar as well.

"It's plain enough Rion doesn't blame you, either. So be a man, admit you were terrified and aren't as perfect as you'd hoped to be and do better next time," Ron admonished.

"I had something far more brutal and biting in mind, but at least you scolded me a little," Gar said, forcing a smile. "Will Thenagar live? Was he badly injured?"

"He wasn't badly hurt. He'll live. It's a wonder he looked so well. You'd never guess he's not had water for so long. The spring was dry, wasn't it? You'd not have been gone so long, otherwise."

Gar said, "It was buried under tons of rock. There was a rockslide. I've no idea if it was an ogre or the Enemy, or it might have just been poor luck."

At Ron's expression of dismay he grinned and dug into his pack and held up two handfuls of full waterskins by the straps. "Fortunately, Rion refused to listen to my plan of having him take my water and riding to Athanark. He must have realized he'd never make it back in time to save us. Instead, he made a harness for Seafoam and had her pull away all the rock. Drink deeply. There's plenty more for the others and the horses," Gar said, grinning.

Ron snatched at one skin and Ara at another, and they started to drink eagerly.

"Let's get these back to camp," Ron said once his thirst appeared to be quenched. "Rarnak's not doing well. I'm hoping he'll recover, once he's had a chance to drink his fill, though we need to make sure he drinks more slowly, lest he vomit it all back up again."

ANDRA was stroking Rarnak's forehead gently. "Please, Rarnak, drink it. I've no need of it. Areth wants you to drink, she wants you to live. I want you to." Andra wasn't sure he could understand her. But he wouldn't swallow, when she tried forcing him to.

"Please, Elmoth, keep Rarnak alive. And Gar. You couldn't have let him die so terribly. Ron told me Gar still wakes up screaming some nights and clutching his face or calling for Ara. Please, when you take him to your side, don't let it be an obearn.

"Take me, instead, if you must take one of us. Ron and Ara and Van and Father all love Gar so. The whole town loves him. Everyone does. The world needs people like that. I never used to see it before, for being so jealous of Gar. He's so pretty. He's the prettiest of all of them, prettier even than Van, and they're all pretty. But he's not vain about it as he might be. He never was. I know he used to tease me about how ugly I am, but I've forgiven him for it. He's changed. He's someone I might love now, if you only give me time enough to learn to. Please, Elmoth! I've ever asked for so little. Save Gar and Rion and Rarnak, and I swear, I'll be content to live and die alone. Exchange my happiness for theirs.

"Oh, what's the use? I've nothing to offer, no happiness to barter. Take my life, Elmoth. One life for three, for the children I'll never bear." That sound... hoofbeats? Andra looked up in surprise and then amazed joy. "Gar? Rion? You found them! They're alive!" Rion was on Seafoam, and the other three were walking beside them.

Andra ran to them, whooping, and she grabbed Gar and hugged him tightly, until he pulled away and looked at her in astonishment and with a slight wince of pain. She flushed, embarrassed that she'd half crushed him in her enthusiasm.

She turned and hugged Rion, who'd dismounted, and then Ron and even Ara, for good measure.

"We found them and they found water," Ron said, holding up a full skin.

"Water!" She snatched it and ran to Rarnak, the four of them momentarily forgotten. "Praise Elmoth, blessed be He. Thank you, mighty and merciful Elmoth, protector of the innocent," she intoned. "Rarnak, please drink. It's water, they found it. Gar's alive, and Rion, too. Drink it, all of it, and live. Elmoth wants you to. Areth does too. You said she'd provide for you, for your sacrifice to her, and she has." She squirted a thin stream of water into his mouth at first. She saw his tongue brush against his lips and gave him a little more. His jaw moved. She put the mouth of the skin between his lips and he began sucking on the waterskin thirstily, as if a baby nursing from its mother.

Andra felt a sharp pain at the thought. She'd made her bargain with Elmoth. She'd die soon, alone and childless. But Gar and Rion and Rarnak would live. She wondered how it would happen and when. Elmoth was just and merciful. He'd try to make it painless and quick.

She pulled the skin away from Rarnak's lips, talking soothingly to him, explaining that he shouldn't drink too much too quickly.

Everyone drank more, watered the horses, and rested and ate, as Gar told them what had happened. They all marveled at Seafoam and showered her with affection.

When they were ready to leave, Rarnak was able to mount his horse, but Andra was worried for him. He still did not seem well to her.

"I'll be fine, Andra, now that I've had the water," he assured her.

They broke camp and headed toward the Pass, moving at a slow but steady pace, careful not to overexert themselves and keeping a watchful eye out for obearn and other predators.

When they reached the spring, they found a jumbled mass of tracks in the mud surrounding it. More than one obearn had apparently discovered the spring. They filled all their waterskins again, in shifts, guarding against obearn and possible ogres, though there were no tracks of the latter. They gathered as much firewood as they could carry, too, broken branches from the formerly buried trees, uncertain what they'd find later, and then headed into the Pass.

IT WAS terrible in the Pass. It was so narrow, they had to ride single file, half the time dismounting and leading their horses over small slides that partly choked the way. More than once the first day, they found themselves traveling along a constricted ledge, over a steep drop. Ron was afraid they might come to a larger slide, find their way blocked altogether and realize they had to turn around and go back to the Gelthor Pass, after all they'd been through to come here.

They finally found an area to stop for a late lunch that was wide enough to accommodate their party, and defensible. To Ron's relief, Rarnak ate well and was looking stronger, in spite of the harrowing ride, but Ron was concerned for Andra. She seemed especially somber and quiet. Worse, when Ara or Gar teased her, trying to get a rise out of her, she only smiled at them sadly.

"Ron, what's wrong with her? Why did she just hug me, when she should have punched me?" Gar asked Ron softly, unnerved.

"I'm not sure," Ron replied. "I thought it was worry for Rarnak, but he's getting better and she's getting worse. I think perhaps this trip's been too much for her, more than she bargained for. I'm hoping once we get to Athanark, she might recover."

They packed their gear and pressed on. The way became increasingly perilous, forcing them to slow their pace to a crawl.

Just before sunset they found a shallow, unoccupied cavern, barely deep enough to accommodate all of them, including the horses, and made camp, relieved for the meager shelter. It was fortunate they yet had food as well as feed for the horses, and that they'd brought the firewood from the spring. They hadn't seen a single tree all day, only scraggly bushes and anemic grasses clinging to the cracks and crevices along the inhospitable trail. After eating dinner, they posted watch and slept in shifts.

THE next morning, they left the cave at first light after a hurried breakfast, eager to move on. To Rion's dismay, they found the going was even worse than before, the footing treacherous and the route nearly impassable. They all expressed regret over not having a heartier breakfast, after traveling well past midday without finding a suitable place to stop for lunch. They finally ate handfuls of nuts and dried fruit while they walked.

Rion was relieved when the Pass opened up a little, in the early evening. Now they were once again on the floor of the ravine, rather than traveling along one of the narrow ledges above it. Gar was leading, followed by Ron, Ara, and Rion himself, and then Rarnak and Andra. Ron had wanted their two best bowmen at front and back, in case of trouble. But when the attack came, it came so swiftly and unexpectedly, they had no time to nock their arrows.

The ogre was apparently starving and half-mad with thirst, or it would have crushed them all with boulders from a safe distance and then feasted upon them. But the sight of all that meat and the smell of water must have been too much for it. It let the first three riders pass and then slid onto the other three, taking a large portion of the mountainside with it.

Seafoam was ambushed as effectively as the others. She screamed in pain as she was felled, her hindquarters crushed by hundreds of pounds of stone, even as she tried desperately to twist away, so Rion might be spared. Behind them, Rarnak and Andra and their horses were buried by the rock.

Rion half fell and half rolled free of Seafoam and stared up in terror from the ground at the tremendous ogre that towered a full ten feet or more above him. But it was not interested in him. Instead, it attacked the three who were still a potential danger to it: Gar, Ron, and Ara.

It slammed its meaty hand into Ara, and he went flying from the saddle, crashing into the sheer rock face of the side of the ravine. Ara fell limply to the ground and lay still. Then it strode toward Ron and Gar.

Gar wheeled Thenagar about and nocked and fired an arrow, which flew true and imbedded in the ogre's left eye. Ron tried to do the same, but Blaze was less well trained and bolted, heading up the ravine, taking Ron with him, as Ron dropped his bow and desperately tried to stay astride him, scrabbling for the reins that had slipped from his grasp.

The creature reached for Gar, appearing intent upon grabbing him so it could crush the life from the one who had harmed it. Gar nocked another arrow, but Rion saw Gar would not have time to fire it, that he was as good as dead.

Fighting off the momentary shock of his fall, Rion scrabbled to his feet and lunged for the ogre. As much as this creature still terrified him, as its cousins in the Gelthor Pass had, Rion had faced wizards, bandits, chimaera, Revenants, and obearn since then. Knowing that more of his friends now lay dead, he was no longer paralyzed by his fear.

He drew his sword and slashed viciously with all his strength at the ogre's right ankle, hamstringing it, as they'd told him Rarnak had done to the one in the Gelthor Pass. The ogre stumbled, howling, its grasping fingertips all that hit Gar, but its frustrated attack was disastrous enough. Gar was knocked from Thenagar, and his bow fell from his hands.

The ogre turned around and bellowed in rage at Rion, lifting its great fist over Rion's head to smash him. But Rion dove toward its left ankle and slashed again. The beast toppled to its knees, and Rion barely rolled clear.

Rion heard running steps coming from up the ravine. It must be Ron, on foot. He must have abandoned Blaze or been thrown from him. But Rion knew Ron would be too late to save him. The ogre was glaring at him in hate with its good eye, and both its fists came for him.

But then Seafoam was there. She'd dragged herself by her forelegs and threw herself over Rion to protect him, shielding him, taking the full force of the ogre's crushing blow, her proud head and back shattered by it. Rion desperately tried to roll free as she fell, but he could not get clear in time. He fought to free the leg that was pinned under her.

Then someone leapt from a boulder behind the ogre onto its broad back, clinging to its hair with one hand and slashing its throat with the sword held in the other hand. Blood flowed freely but did not spurt, and the ogre reached for its tormentor. But the sword sliced again, and this time, blood spewed outward in a great fountain.

The creature clutched desperately at its throat and the erupting gush of blood splattered against its hands, spraying everywhere. Then it fell with a loud thud and lay twitching as the life drained from it into the dry rock and parched soil of the ravine. Rion saw to his shock and relief that it was Andra who had killed it. She was still alive!

Andra stood staring at the dead monster, trembling visibly with unspent energy from the fight. Then she turned to Gar. He was climbing shakily to his feet. She went to Ara, who lay in a crumpled heap from the ogre's blow, and felt his throat. "He's still alive," she called, to Rion's relief. Finally, she ran to where Rarnak lay so still, half buried by rock, as she had been. She collapsed to her knees, an expression of utter devastation on her face.

Rion pulled his leg free from Seafoam and started stroking her, his hand shaking violently, as the tears began to flow. Then he wrapped his arms around her neck and began sobbing. He couldn't bear that she was dead, after all she had done, after all she had been to him, knowing she'd died saving him.

He forced himself away from her. She was dead. Ara needed him now, and Rarnak, if he still lived. He'd thought Andra and Rarnak both dead. If she'd lived, Rarnak might also.

Rion dug through his pack, pulled out his healer's kit, and headed for Rarnak. Andra was desperately digging him out from the rock. Gar had joined her, but he was limping badly, apparently unable to put much weight on his right foot.

Rion could do nothing for Rarnak until they freed him and perhaps nothing even then. He stumbled toward Ara. Ron reached him at the same time. Rion began bandaging the wounds he could see, more afraid of those he couldn't.

"I TRIED," Ron said, his voice shaking in anguish. "I hauled on the reins, but Blaze wouldn't turn. I leapt from him, but he'd already carried me so far. Elmoth, please, you can't let Ara die! Not him, of all of us. He's the only one who honors you as he should, save for Andra." He looked toward where she'd fallen and cried in shock, "Andra's alive?" He ran to her.

Andra was shaking and crying, covered in blood from head to toe, frantically moving stones from Rarnak.

"Andra! Where are you hurt? Let us free him," Ron begged.

"I'm not hurt, not so it matters. My horse took the brunt of the rock. I dug myself out. I couldn't let that thing kill them, but I wasn't fast enough. It hit Ara so hard, and then it came for Rion. It's the ogre's blood, not mine.

"There! Gar, Ron, pull, while I hold it," she said, grunting with effort as she held a rock bigger than her waist up just enough for them to slide Rarnak out from under it. Then the rock slipped, tearing the skin from her fingertips as it crashed down where Rarnak had been. Like her own, his horse had protected him from much of the weight of the rock by the way it had fallen.

Ron cursed. "We need a wagon for them, but even if we had one, we couldn't get it along the trail. We've only the two horses, three if Blaze hasn't run the rest of the way to Athanark by now. Maybe we can find that thing's lair. It might have something we can use to make stretchers for them. There are no trees here to make poles from, but we've got our blankets. Rion, you tend to them as best you can. I'm going to go see what I can find."

"Not alone you're not," Andra said. "What if there are more of these things?"

"That's why I need you and Gar here, with your bows, to protect the others. It's not only Rion we're guarding now, it's Ara and Rarnak, too. And Gar's hurt. He needs your help to guard them," Ron argued.

She clenched her jaw and nodded. "Help me dig my bow out before you go," she said, and he did so. Andra eyed the Elven bow critically, but it was undamaged.

"Be quick as you can, Ron, and be careful," Andra said.

Ron nodded.

The climb up the side of the ravine was treacherous. Ron was exhausted by the time he made it to the ledge the ogre had spied upon them and ambushed them from. "I'm too old for this," he muttered, drawing his sword and eyeing the ground carefully. The ogre's tracks were barely visible in the dry dirt and loose rock. He saw mostly shifted stone from where its feet had pushed aside crumbled bits of rock.

Fortunately its lair was close by. The creature had lived in a cave. It reeked of rotted meat and worse. It hadn't even had the sense to dig a latrine outside its den, but instead had fouled it with its own waste. Ron took off his shirt and tied it about his face to minimize the smell, keeping a cautious eye out, though he was relatively certain this ogre had been one of the rogue males Jargas had spoken about, and had been alone.

He entered the cave cautiously. There were bones everywhere: obearn, horse, Man's, a child's. No, that was a Dwarf's. What had a Dwarf been doing in these Mountains?

Then he felt ill. Those bones there, though, those were definitely a child's, a young one. Its skull had been crushed, just like the others. All the bones were old. The creature apparently hadn't eaten in some time.

There were smashed and torn goods as well. The old leather had been chewed on recently: the thing had been hungry. Amongst a collection of broken, rusted weapons, were two intact stout wooden staves. They'd do. Ron headed out with his find.

It was dark outside. He was surprised he'd not noticed the light fade in the cave. He'd had no trouble seeing while he was inside. But it shouldn't be so dark. He'd not taken that long. Then he heard a crack of thunder and he swore. Areth had picked a fine time to answer Rarnak's earlier prayers for water!

There was no shelter they could get the wounded to. It had been treacherous even for him to climb here. They'd never be able to bring the injured up here, and he'd not leave the horses, either. At least they'd be able to wash the blood off, without wasting the water in their skins. It was dangerous to be smelling of blood with obearn and ogres about.

The rain began pelting him, the clouds dark and roiling. It looked like the storm would be a violent one. He hoped the ravine wouldn't suddenly swell with a flash flood. The ground was too dry to soak up the rain easily, and much of it seemed to be made of clay. It would be more treacherous to climb the wetter it got. He'd best climb down now, lest he break something on the way down.

He quickened his pace and slipped, landing hard on the jagged rock. He cursed. He'd have to be fast but more careful. A slip like that on the nearly vertical sides of the ravine might have killed him.

Ron climbed down carefully, eyes on his feet. He was shocked to see Andra smiling when he finally reached the bottom and looked up. "Ron! They're awake! They're both awake! The rain woke them!" He hurried to Rarnak and Ara, setting down the staves. Rarnak was sitting up. His arm was splinted and bandaged, held in a sling tied about his neck. Ara was lying down, but his eyes were open.

"Thank Elmoth you're awake! What hurts?" Ron asked Ara.

"Everything. But if you mean what's broken, I don't think anything is, though I wrenched my knee, and my leg's splinted and bandaged because of it. I likely shouldn't put any weight on it, but I was lucky. My insides feel all right," Ara assured him.

"We'll put out our pans to catch the rain, while we can, and refill all our skins," Ron said. "I don't think we're in danger of flooding right away at least. It's almost night, and the clay around these rocks is terribly slippery. We can't risk one of us, or worse yet one of the horses, falling. I'll use these poles and some of our blankets to make what shelter I can. We'll use that rock face there for one wall of it, like the City Guard in Thenalon showed us."

Ron went over to Rion. Rion was at Seafoam's side again, sobbing, his tears mixing with the rain.

RION saw Ron coming but didn't care. Seafoam was dead. After all she'd done, saving them by freeing the water for them and then fighting the obearn to save him. She'd protected him to the last, shielding him with her own body. Rion understood better now Ron attacking the already dead obearn that had nearly killed Gar and Ara. He wanted to hack the ogre to pieces for what it had done. Instead, he stroked Seafoam's velvety nose. She was getting cold already. He hugged her more tightly and cried harder. He'd never ride another horse. He couldn't.

"Rion? Rion, I know how you feel, but you have to let her go," Ron said, setting his hand on his shoulder. "We're going to build a shelter, to try to get out of this rain. We have to keep Ara and Rarnak warm, in particular. They're injured the worst and more apt to take ill from it."

Rion looked up at Ron. He pointed to Seafoam and mimed burying her.

"Rion, we can't. She's so large, and we've nothing to dig with," Ron reasoned.

Rion shook his head. He pointed to the pile of rock and mimed laying rocks over her.

"A cairn? You want us to build a cairn?" Ron asked incredulously, and Rion nodded.

"Rion, I know how you loved her. But...," Ron began, but Rion was no longer listening. He went to the jumble of rock around Rarnak's dead horse and lifted one and walked back over to Seafoam's body and laid it beside her. He'd not let some obearn or another ogre eat her. At least, he'd not make it easy for them to.

"All right, you win," Ron said. "As soon as I get the shelter built, I'll help you, so please, don't strain yourself. We can't risk you getting hurt. You're the only one of us that knows anything at all of healing."

Ron built the impromptu shelter and saw Ara, Rarnak, and Gar inside it; then he and Andra helped Rion bury Seafoam in the cairn of stone. As Rion laid the last rock, Ron said softly, "Rion will miss you, Seafoam, *Famsala*, we all will. You saved him. You saved all of us. May the Elves call your spirit home to the River to rest."

Rarnak came slowly over to them and looked up into the sky and turned to Rion. "Areth's crying for her, Rion. It's her tears we're feeling. Areth will bring her spirit home to the Elves."

Rion nodded and then started sobbing so hard he could scarcely stand.

Andra put her hand on his shoulder. "Come, Rion. Seafoam wouldn't want you to take ill for her. She was ever trying to protect you. It's up to us now, to see you safe, since she no longer can. There's room under the shelter for all of us if we're friendly enough."

Rion let her lead him. The six of them sat huddled under the poor roof of blankets. Ron lay between Ara and Rarnak. Rion was glad Ron was sharing the extra heat of his body with them. They were the ones who needed it most. But he desperately missed Ron's warmth, as well as the reassuring beat of his heart. Rion spent a miserable night; he couldn't sleep, and it appeared no one else could either. Despite the meager shelter, they were all quickly soaked to the skin.

THE clouds lifted and the sun shone brightly the following morning, but it was cold. Rarnak and Ara seemed to feel it the worst. Ara was shivering so hard his teeth were chattering. Rion was afraid they might develop a fever, but he had nothing to treat one. It was the one medicine he hadn't been able to find before setting out on their journey, or in the two cities they'd stayed in since.

Ron said, "We have to get to Athanark as quickly as we can. Both of you need to see a healer, and a hot meal and a dry bed wouldn't do any of us any harm. We'll ride double. Ara, you ride with Gar on Thenagar. Use the staves, that rock over there, and Gar's help to mount. We'll bring the staves with us. Rion, you ride with Rarnak on Ara's horse. Andra and I will walk for now. We'll take turns riding, so at least one of our able-bodied bowmen is always on the ground. I'll not risk a repeat of what happened before."

Rion shook his head. He'd not ride. He couldn't. He pointed to Ron and then to Ara's horse and indicated he would walk.

"No, Rion. We'll alternate riders, as I said. You can't walk all the way to Athanark. I couldn't either. I know you loved her, but riding is the only way we can see you safely there. I'm hoping we'll yet find Blaze, so all six of us can ride double. Please, Rion. She'd understand."

Rion gazed mournfully at the cold cairn of stone, turning quickly away. He would not cry again. He was a man. He had to start acting like one. What would Talon and Aras say if they saw him crying over a horse?

The thought of Aras almost brought the tears he was trying to fight. He so desperately needed to see an Elf again, especially Aras or Eladar. He swallowed. No. He forced himself to be honest. It was not them he was desperate to see: it was Elanara. If only she were safe. Eladar had been in Erenia, but if he no longer was, perhaps his sister wasn't either. Was she with him? Would she be waiting for him, at the Watchtower? Thoughts of her made him strong enough to mount the horse, feeling the unfamiliar stiffness of the saddle under him, instead of a warm, broad back. He held the reins clumsily, then turned and looked at Rarnak.

"Here, let me guide him, Rion. I can do so, even one-handed," he said, and Rion handed the reins to him in relief. They began the slow walk to Athanark.

ONLY a short while later they found Blaze, alive and well, looking rather sheepish and incredibly relieved to see them. Ron had no trouble catching him. "Rion, why don't you ride behind me? Andra, you guide Ara's horse, and let Rarnak ride behind you," he said, and she nodded.

Andra was more than happy to have Rarnak's strong arm wrapped around her waist, as she began guiding their horse after Ron. She'd never had a man other than her brothers or father hold her, and seldom had even they done so. Surely Elmoth wasn't taunting her with his nearness? Perhaps Elmoth had a different plan for her than what she had thought.

"IF WE ride straight through, and the terrain stays like this so we can keep up a decent pace, we might reach Athanark by the end of the day," Ron said. "Remember, we need to keep an eye out for obearn, but there may also be wolven-riders, like Rion warned us about, or other dark things. We all need to be extra cautious."

He looked at the two staves they'd brought with them, for Ara and Gar to use, to help them walk. He was worried about Ara. He feared Ara might be hurt far worse than he'd let on. He was looking gray, though he no longer seemed to be in such severe pain. Rion had given him something to ease it. Ron was anxious to have a healer examine his brother.

Rion mounted up behind him, and they continued on.

A RA fought to stay conscious, clinging to Gar's broad back. He'd not have been able to ride further were it not for the medicine Rion had given him for the pain. Whatever it was, it was strong. The agony of his injuries had dulled to a steady throb, but he knew though the pain was now masked, his injuries were grave.

He'd lied to Ron when he'd asked before how badly Ara was hurt. They'd needed to leave and he knew he'd still be able to ride, because he had to. He wouldn't endanger his siblings and Rarnak and Rion, even if it meant worsening his injuries. Even Rion hadn't suspected he had broken bones. Rion knew how to bandage a wound, but he'd not had a healer's training.

Fortunately, the terrain grew even easier to navigate and the day passed uneventfully. It was just dusk when they finally reached Athanark. As the last time Ara and his brothers had come, the gate was closed. But this time the City Guard ordered them to throw all their weapons down and dismount before they would come out to check them over.

Ara slid from the saddle with difficulty. He fought to stay standing, clutching the staff, swaying, his weight all on his good leg, but he lost the battle.

He was unconscious before he hit the ground.

G AR cursed and leaned over Ara awkwardly, hissing in pain as he bent his leg. "He's burning with fever, Ron. I was afraid he was hurt worse than he let on, but I think it's worse even than I feared."

"Stand away from him," an imperious voice commanded.

"But he's injured. He's ill," Gar said hotly.

"The sooner you obey us, the sooner you can bring him inside," the Guard called out stonily.

Gar cursed again, but stood. Twenty City Guard came out, with drawn bows and nocked arrows. They appraised them from a distance, and questioned them, and then approached more closely to examine them. Gar could see they did not believe Ron when he told them they'd come through the Thinabar Pass.

"No one's come through that way in over a year," the Captain of the Guard said, for the third time.

R ON lost his temper. "Well we did! We lost three horses, and all of us were injured, some of us badly. Please, we swear we won't cause any harm. Look at us, for Elmoth's sake! How can we, the shape we're in?"

"All right. I don't suppose you'll cause too much trouble at that. We've far worse inside already," the Captain said cryptically.

"Thank you, Captain. Please, if you could tell us where we might find the nearest healer? My brother appears to be hurt worse than we'd feared," Gar said.

"You'll have a hard time finding a healer at all, inside. They've no shortage of patients. And you'll not find a room at an inn, either. You can pitch a tent on the Commons, if you can find a spot. I hope you brought food or lots of coin, too, or you'll not soon eat. Prices have gone through the roof with the flood of refugees we've had and the dearth of caravans. There's war to the south of us. Ardock's been burnt. The refugees are from there and further south, the ones that had fled to Ardock for safety."

Ron winced as Rion stared in dismay at the Guard. They had all known Ardock had been in danger, but for Rion to hear his home had fallen to the Enemy! Ron was not surprised to see Rion begin to cry again.

The Guard scowled at Rion. "What's wrong with the boy?"

"He's not a boy, he's a man!" Ron snapped, speaking more hotly than he'd meant to. At the Guard's expression, he tried to get a rein on his temper, but he couldn't. "He's from Ardock. We'd not known she had fallen. He's lost more than a few friends this past month, and he's been injured. He can't speak. And you've just told him his City's gone. I'd be crying too, were it my home," Ron said in Rion's defense.

"Don't get testy with me! And you'd better watch your tongue in the City, unless you want to lose it. People will kill you for less offense than that, nowadays," the Guard threatened.

"Please, he didn't mean to anger you. You can see we've had a hard journey. He's worried for our brother and our friends. You'll still let us in, won't you?" Gar pleaded.

"That's better. Of course we'll let you in, now that you asked nicely enough. But see you keep that one in check. You've been warned," the Captain said, pointing to Ron. Then he signaled and the gate was raised.

Ron told Gar to mount. He lifted Ara's limp form, and Gar grabbed hold of him and pulled him onto the saddle in front of him, so he could hold him as he rode. Then Ron mounted, and the others as well. They made their way into the City. It was slow going. The streets were packed with people, and it was hard to keep the horses together.

They tried the first inn they came to, but it was full: rooms, floor, stables, everything. They tried the next, and the next. Fifteen inns later Ron was becoming desperate. They'd tried the Brightwater, hoping Lonas might take pity on them, for Rion's sake, but Lonas no longer owned it. They were told he'd sold it a month ago.

"We have to find something," Gar said anxiously. "Ara's still unconscious and he's shaking so badly I can barely hold him."

Rion tapped Ron and wrote on his hand, *BLOODHAND,* apparently hoping that Vargas might be at his shop, that he might take them in. "It's worth a try," Ron agreed.

They were barely able to make their way to it. Ron saw to his dismay the sign was gone from above the door. Rion climbed clumsily down from Ara's horse and began banging on the door. Ron joined him, pounding relentlessly. Finally, a voice from within called, "If you want to keep your arm, you'll leave. We're closed."

"Vargas, is that you?" Ron yelled in relief, his mouth pressed to the door. "It's Ronamark, with my brothers and Master Rion. We need help."

The door opened a crack. Four heavy chains kept it from opening further.

"Step into the light so I can see your faces, both of you," Vargas said, suspiciously, holding up a lantern to the crack.

They did as he asked.

"It's you all right. Just a moment," he said and closed the door.

They heard the sound of the chains releasing, and then the door opened fully. Vargas was standing there, looking much like he had the last time they'd seen him. There was no sign of Argo. "Come in, quickly, and bring your horses as well, or you'll not see them again."

They led the nervous animals inside the former weapons shop. There wasn't a blade left in the shop. It was empty, save for the display cabinets that once held the stock.

"I can see you're needing help," Vargas said. "You can put the horses in the backyard. No one can take them from there. The houses go right up to the fence. No, wait, they're so hungry now, I'd not be surprised if they'd go through their back doors or even come in over the roofs from the street to butcher them, if they heard them in the yard. Leave them in here, as long as you clean up their mess. All the stock's been sold, and I've sold the shop as well. I'm leaving town tomorrow morning. I've organized a caravan. It'll be just like old times, me and Lonas and Harnel, on the road again. But I'm rambling, I must be getting old. Come into the back. You need to lay Aramark and Rarnak down at least. I can see that much. You can tell me what's happened on the way. Didn't you make it through to Gosa, Master Rion?"

Rion nodded, *Yes.*

Ron said, "I'm sorry, Vargas. Rion can't talk. We made it safely to Gosa, without losing a man, but a lot's happened since. You've no idea how grateful we are to you for letting us in. We came here by way of the Thinabar Pass and had to fight an ogre to get here. Aramark's been badly hurt, and Garamark and Rarnak are hurt as well," he said, using his brothers' full names, the ones Vargas knew them by. "Do you know a healer that can see them? We'll pay whatever he asks," Ron said desperately.

"Aye, there's one leaving with us tomorrow," Vargas said. "He's an old friend, though not quite so old as the other two. Here, lay Aramark down on my bed. Garamark and Rarnak can take Argo's. Lucky for you I sold the beds with the shop, or they'd not still be here. I'll send Argo out for the healer, as soon as he returns. I'm worried about him. He should have been back by now. The City is dangerous now, even for him. People are scared and hungry, and there's far too many of them."

"I'd wondered before, but not asked. Is Argo your son?" Ron asked.

Vargas smiled. "No, he's my sister's son. But I've cared for him since he turned thirteen. He was without a father and heading for trouble, but I turned him around. Swordsmanship's all about discipline. He's a natural at it. He'll surpass me someday, and that day won't be long in coming. But he should have been back by now. I'd thought you were him, at first, until you didn't give the right knock. Then you gave me a fright. It sounded like you might cave the door in with your pounding. It was smart of you to come here. I'll do anything I can to help Oberas's apprentice," he said, gazing at Rion with fond sadness.

"I'm sorry, I'm not thinking clearly and rambling again. I'm tired. It's been bad here. I should go out for the healer myself, if one of you will accompany me. Some folks might think me an easy target, due to my age and my lost arm. I've no interest in injuring myself before a long journey while proving otherwise. Some of my personal belongings are still here, but I trust the rest of you to watch the shop. You all had excellent references, and I'm a good judge of character besides. You've not introduced me to the Lady."

"Forgive me. This is my sister, Lisandra, but everyone calls her Andra. Andra, this is Vargas. We told you about him, when we told you and Father the details of our journey," Ron said.

Andra nodded in greeting to him, but most of her attention seemed focused upon Rarnak. He looked as gray as Ara, Ron saw to his concern, and he was shivering as well.

"I wish I'd taken Talon's advice earlier. I should have left the City weeks ago. But it's not easy leaving twenty-five years of home behind to start fresh again, especially not at my age. I've few good years left to me. Ronamark, you come with me. The others should stay here," Vargas instructed, and headed for the former display room of his shop.

"Please, can you spare some water?" Andra asked. Vargas nodded and left the room, then returned and handed Andra a pitcher. Andra wet a cloth and began patting Ara's face with it. Just then there was a knock on the door, in an odd pattern.

"That'll be Argo," Vargas said in relief. "Argo?" he called at the door, to be sure.

"It's me. Open up, Uncle!" a voice replied.

Vargas opened the door and stared, then ushered Argo inside. Argo wasn't alone. There was a beautiful girl with him, in a ragged and torn dress. Argo had his arm around her protectively. She was perhaps sixteen, with long, red hair and bright green eyes. She was petite but appeared strong. She clutched Argo in fear when she saw the others in the room.

"Audra, I swear I didn't lie to you. You're safe. I don't know who these people are, but they'll not hurt you," Argo assured her, glaring defiantly at them.

"All right," she said, but her voice was trembling.

RION was puzzled by the girl's reaction, and his eyes followed her gaze, trying to discover why she seemed so afraid of them. He belatedly understood. Ron was ragged and filthy. His clothes were stained by dried clay and blood, and he had over a week's growth of beard. They'd not had the water to waste for shaving, nor the time since they'd gotten some. Ron looked like a brigand. Rion realized he must look nearly as bad, save for the beard. He'd yet the ability to grow one. It was a wonder Vargas had let them in, looking as they did.

"Argo, I sent you out to get another horse, not a girl," Vargas scolded gently.

"I got the horse, and brought him to Denahar. But on my way back, I heard someone scream from an alley off Losiris. Some men had seen Audra was alone and followed her and attacked her. They'd dragged her into the alley. I needn't tell you why. She bit the one's hand and he loosened his grip just enough that she was able to scream. I was barely in time to save her. I couldn't just leave her alone after that. Someone else would have attacked her," Argo reasoned.

"No, of course you couldn't. You can see I've picked up strays of my own, although mine at least can fight. You remember Master Rion and his guards?" Vargas asked.

"Of course! I'd not recognized you at first. But I'd not soon forget you, nor the men who tested you. I'd never thought I'd meet an Elf, although Aras was nothing like what you'd told me of them, Vargas," Argo said.

"Aras! You know Aras? Please, is he here in the City? Father said he was coming here with Talon. Can you take me to him?" Audra pleaded, trembling with apparent excitement now, instead of fear.

Rion had been watching Audra with quiet interest. He'd never seen hair like hers before: it was the color of flame. And she was so young and so lovely. She had the fine-boned features almost of an Elf. But she knew Talon and Aras! And she was in love with Aras. He could see it in her eyes and hear it in her voice when she spoke of him.

"Argo, I need you to get Aradon for me. We've three injured men in the back, as well as these two and a woman. We'll take care of Audra for you," Vargas said.

Argo nodded and headed for the door without hesitation. Vargas turned to Audra. "Talon and Aras left months ago, after testing Master Rion's guards. I've not seen them since, nor do I expect to. Elves do not usually walk amongst Men, Audra. It's too painful for them. An Elf might live to be one thousand and a man or woman only to sixty. It is easy for a man or woman to love an Elf. With a single smile, many can be lost to one. When you are blessed enough to know one, you must hold those memories close to your heart, always, but you must not let them steal your heart."

"But Aras didn't just smile at me!" Audra protested. "He was warm and sweet and wonderful. And he gave me... a gift," she said, watching Ron suspiciously, obviously afraid he might yet prove to be a brigand.

Vargas eyed her thoughtfully, then reached to his neck and from under his shirt, pulled out a heavy chain. It was black with tarnish, but there was a thick, large, shiny silver locket at the end of it. He opened it, peered reverently inside, and pulled something from it. "A gift like this?" Vargas asked kindly. He held out his palm. In it was a brilliant emerald-green Elfstone.

Audra gasped and took out a similar gem, though hers was larger and of a slightly darker hue. "Yes, an Elfstone. He wouldn't give me such a gift if he didn't love me," she said fiercely.

Rion's eyes welled with tears, and his heart ached. He'd lost his own Elfstone. How could he have lost it? Only Elanara hadn't given it to him for his love of her, nor certainly for hers of him. She'd meant it for Jargas, to pay him for the horse he'd traded to the ogres for the life of her brother Eladar.

"Aye, he loved you, in his way," Vargas said. "The Elves give us these so we might have some small comfort, some little bit of light left in our lives to remind us that the sun still shines, that it's not really so cold and dark as it seems once they're gone.

"I was given this twenty-five years ago. I was twenty-five at the time, old enough to know she loved me, but would never love me as a woman loves a man. I cherish my memory of her, I always will, but I learned to find happiness without her. I hope you can do the same, Audra. You must find the strength to. Aras was special, I saw as much, even from the short time I knew him. I'll treasure my memories of him always. But he lives in such light and joy. It would break his heart if he were ever to find out he'd broken yours," Vargas said.

Audra started crying and Vargas hugged her as a father would have. They were each clutching their Elfstones as tightly as they held one another.

Rion left the room. He went through the beaded curtain to the kitchen. He didn't want the others to see his tears. He'd already cried far too often in front of them. He had a flash of memory when he saw the familiar room, of Talon and Vargas and him and Tarrell, all seated at the table, with Aras behind them, teasing and laughing and joking. He'd been such a boy then! So much had happened since.

It hurt to be a man. He'd been so desperate to be one, but he hadn't known how much it would hurt. He'd lost his heart and his voice, and he'd tried not to lose his smile, but it was hard, so very hard. He'd lost Lerdon and Jathran. They'd died protecting him, as Elkrum and the others had. Even Seafoam had died for him. She'd been taken from him just as suddenly and violently. What was the loss of an Elfstone compared to the loss of her? But it had come from Elanara. Now he had nothing to fill the dark emptiness where Elanara belonged.

He cursed himself for a fool. He was as bad as Audra. She looked his age, sixteen, as well, but he'd never been so naïve. Well, perhaps in Ardock, but not since that first caravan. He wondered why Audra was here, why she was alone. Had her parents been killed? If so, how had she survived?

If he had his voice, he'd ask her. He'd comfort her. Argo had a strong but gentle voice. Maybe Argo might fall in love with her. She was so beautiful and so vulnerable. It would be easy for Argo to lose his heart to her. He'd rescued her, so she had cause to love him as well. Perhaps they might find happiness together. He liked to think they might. It seemed as if so few of those he'd met, especially those he particularly cared for, might ever be happy. Or if they might be, he'd yet to see how.

Rion went into the bedroom. Andra was pressing a wet cloth to Ara's forehead. She looked up eagerly when she heard Rion, then scowled. "I thought you were the healer," she said and turned away.

Tears welled in Rion's eyes again. No, he wasn't the one who healed, the one who helped. He was the one everyone was hurt for, everyone died for.

Andra turned back to him, the scowl still on her face, and he quickly spun away from her. He hadn't wanted her to see his tears. He was surprised to feel a hand on his shoulder a moment later. He turned. Her face had softened. Her expression was gentle, now. "I'm sorry, Rion. I hadn't meant to sound so harsh. I know you're worried about them too."

She hugged him. She was so tall and strong. She felt nothing like Elanara; she was all bone and muscle. But she was warm, and he'd been feeling cold again, cold and alone. Rion hugged her back, then let go and smiled at her sheepishly. He'd needed a hug and he couldn't even say, "Thank you," for it. He hoped his smile was thanks enough.

Andra went back to Ara, and Rion headed toward the front room again, until he heard Vargas in the kitchen. "If I'd known I'd have an army to feed, I'd have left more supplies here," he muttered.

Rion went to the horses and pulled the last of their food from their packs. He'd brought one hundred gold with him and spent little of it so far, in Westhaven and Falnor. He could buy supplies tomorrow. He brought the food they had to the kitchen and his artist's lead and paper. He handed the food to Vargas, and Vargas accepted it gratefully.

Rion wrote, *Where is your caravan heading?*

"I had planned to take Talon's advice and go all the way to Gosa, but Ronamark's told me I'd better plan on going elsewhere. I've been thinking Maraden, to the north of there. Most of the refugees from Gosa will likely go to Ocanton in the south. It's closer and Ronamark's told me Gosa's Princess is there, with her new husband. Or perhaps I'll go to Ogaten. That town will turn into a City fast enough, now," Vargas said.

Rion swallowed. Vargas knew more about Gosa than he did, and from what he'd said, it sounded like Gosa might have been completely destroyed. He'd feared as much, but to hear Vargas speaking of refugees made him feel ill. He wrote quickly, *Can we travel with you as far as the intersection of the Southern Road with the Western, until just before the Gelthor Pass? Ara and Rarnak will need a wagon and a healer. That way your healer friend could continue to tend them. I've gold and we can work as guards. We'll do whatever you ask. Please take us with you.*

"You needn't beg, lad. Ronamark's already spoken to me about it. We've already worked it out between us. He just hasn't had a chance to tell you all. I'd certainly not leave you here. This City won't last for much longer. Even if it's not attacked, it's ready to boil over. It's a hair's breadth from chaos now. That's why I was so worried before for Argo," Vargas said.

Is there time to shop tomorrow, before we leave? We need food and clothes and some other things, Rion wrote.

"Save your coin, as far as the food goes. It'll be much cheaper in Logareth and we've enough to get us there. You'll barter guard services for the wagon ride and food. The clothes prices here shouldn't be too bad, though, maybe double what they should be, not quadruple or more, like the food. Can you be done and dressed by midmorning? The Market opens at sunrise," Vargas said.

Rion nodded. Then he bit his lip and wrote, *You should know I might be a danger to you all. I think it's safe enough, or I'd not risk going with you. But a wizard is searching for me.*

Vargas looked at him intently. "Ronamark says you know more about that than you've told them."

Rion looked at him guiltily. *And they know more about Gosa than they've told me. You know more than I do. Was the whole City destroyed? How many died? It wasn't truly all because of me, was it?*

"I can't answer that," Vargas said. "I know some of the answers, but I can't say. You should be honest with Ronamark, Rion. He's been risking his life and his brothers' lives for you, and now even his sister's."

Rion nodded. He still felt guilty that they were. Just then there was a familiar knock. Argo was back. Vargas let his nephew and the man with him in. "Aradon! Thank you for coming. Sorry to call you out before tomorrow, but we've had a bit of an emergency," Vargas apologized.

"So Argo's told me. You've wounded already. Starting a little early, aren't you, Vargas? We've not even left the City yet," he said, speaking with the easy familiarity of an old friend.

Audra seemed greatly relieved to see Argo. She'd been sitting off to one side, as if trying to make herself invisible. But now she went to Vargas's nephew and he seemed not to mind her attentions at all.

"Come, your patients are in the back," Vargas said. He led Aradon, and the others followed.

Aradon ran a quick but critical eye over the three on the beds. "Tell me their names and then what happened, so I know what to look for," he said, leaning over Ara.

Ron said, "This is my brother, Aramark. An ogre hit him, hard. It knocked him from his horse into rock. He was unconscious. The rain woke him. He said he hurt all over but nothing seemed broken, though he said he wrenched his knee, which is why we splinted and bandaged it. We camped in the rain, then rode for a day to get here. He'd been shivering, but we didn't realize it was a fever until we got to the City gates and he collapsed. I'd feared he was hurt worse than he was admitting to."

Aradon nodded and stripped the blanket from him. Ara moaned and shivered, reaching deliriously for the blanket.

"I took off his wet things and cloth-bathed him," Andra volunteered. "I've been doing what I can to cool him."

The healer nodded distractedly as he examined his patient's bruises intently. He was bruised everywhere, but the healer studied certain ones with more interest than others. He carefully and gently removed the splint and bandages from his leg, revealing dark bruising there as well, though little upon the knee. Aradon shook his head. "You're from Thenalon, aren't you?"

Ron seemed surprised by the question. "Our grandfather was. You know that from his name?"

"A little from that and a little from your lack of accent, to my ear, at any rate," Aradon said. "But mostly because only a fellow countryman would be mad enough to ride a horse in the rain for a full day saying he wasn't badly hurt after an ogre broke his shoulder, his arm, his leg, and cracked at least four of his ribs. I'll give him something for his fever and the pain and then I'll see to the other two, before I begin setting Aramark's bones and wrapping them. It will take a while."

Rion shook his head and grasped the healer's arm as he reached for two flasks.

"What's the matter, son?" the Healer asked.

Rion wrote, *We already gave him soforath earlier, for the pain. I've been taught he shouldn't take any more or anything else for it until morning.*

Aradon's eyes widened. "*Soforath*! No wonder he could ride! I hope you know what you're doing, son. You can kill a man with that, easily, if you don't."

Rion nodded and went to his healer's kit, which was already in the room, and took out an oilskin pouch of powder and a strip of paper with directions. The healer read them and said, "There's nothing warning you here about severity of injury. I'd not have given a man this wounded *soforath*. Not that you knew how badly hurt he was."

Rion was devastated.

"It's all right, lad. You meant well. You're fortunate he was strong enough, and it's not harmed him. You were right to warn me not to give him something else, though. *Soforath* is the Elven name for it. Men usually call it Elmoth's Blessing, or sometimes just The Blessing. They often use it after battle to ease the passing of someone too injured to recover, so they need not suffer. It's called 'administering The Blessing,' when they use it for that. The Dwarves call it Ragnar's Blood. Dwarven assassins use it as a poison, but their warriors sometimes use it as well, in the same manner as Men do. Since it's treasured as a gift from Ragnar, a mortally injured Dwarf who is removed from the field and given it to ease his passing is still considered to have died honorably, in battle.

"Don't look so grim. If Aramark dies it won't be your doing, and I'll do all I can to see that he survives. I don't mean to alarm you. He should recover—his injuries aren't mortal—but fevers can be tricky things."

Rion was still shaken.

The healer gave Ara the medicine for the fever. Then he went to Rarnak. "And this one?"

Andra spoke, since Rarnak was as delirious as Ara. "His name's Rarnak. He and his horse were buried in a rockslide. He also was awakened by the rain. He at least had the sense to tell us his arm felt like it might be broken. But he also camped in the rain, and rode for a day," she said, brushing a lock of hair from his forehead. The healer removed his splint and bandages and checked him over thoroughly.

"His broken arm seems to be the extent of his injuries, save for the bruises. He was extremely lucky, from what you've said. He also has a fever. Did you give him something for his pain as well?" he asked, turning toward Rion.

Rion shook his head.

"Rarnak wouldn't take anything for it," Andra supplied.

The healer gave him something for his pain and the fever.

"How about you, son?" he asked Gar.

"I'm Garamark. The ogre knocked me from my horse as well, but he barely struck me. My leg's hurt, it's hard to stand and worse to walk, but I don't think it's broken."

The healer told him to take off his pants and he did so, leaving on his undergarment. Then he felt along Gar's leg and had him walk.

"All right, don't try any further. You're to stay off of it as much as you can, to give it a chance to heal." He felt his skin. "At least you don't seem to have gotten a fever. Do you want something for the pain?"

"For tonight, so I can sleep, sure. But after that, I'd rather not have my wits dulled. I'll be needing them for the trip," Gar said.

Aradon had him drink from a flask.

Ron said, "Once you've bandaged Ara and Rarnak, can they journey safely by wagon?"

Aradon said, "Normally I'd say, 'Of course not. They need to recover here, first.' But if you don't leave with our caravan tomorrow, you'll probably not leave, and they'd be more likely to die here in the City in a few weeks' time than they will in the next few days on the Road." The healer proceeded to set Ara's and Rarnak's bones, and bandage them, while the others watched.

"Will you stay for dinner, Aradon? They brought their own food, fortunately. We've enough for one more," Vargas said.

"Certainly. It'll save me having to make something, and it's getting late. In fact, if you don't mind, I'll sleep here tonight on the floor. I don't relish going out into the City so late, even with Argo by my side. I think we're leaving not a day too soon. I wish we'd done so weeks ago. I keep having nightmares that the enemy will come to take the City just before we can escape," Aradon said.

They went into the kitchen. "I'm not used to cooking for so many," Vargas grumbled.

Ron said, "Then please, allow me to, if that would be all right. You've done more than we had any right to expect already. You've saved Ara's life with your hospitality. We had nowhere else to turn."

"Then I'm glad for your sake we'd not already left. And I'd certainly not mind not being the one to cook for tonight. I'm about done in. I'm getting too old for this," Vargas said.

Aradon laughed. "You said the same thing to me fifteen years ago, the night we first met. It's as true now as it was then, meaning not at all."

Argo smiled affectionately at his uncle.

They ate heartily and kept the talk light during dinner. Rion could scarcely keep his eyes open, after a while.

Vargas said, "We should all try to get some sleep. I'm sorry, but I've no extra blankets for you. You can use your packs for pillows, if they're dry enough. Andra and Audra can sleep here in the kitchen. It's warmer in here, with the stove. The rest of us, save for the injured, will be in the display room, with the horses."

Everyone began settling for the night. They laid their blankets and spare clothes out to dry and then lay down. Rion lay down too, but now he was wide awake. The horses were there, shifting their feet and snorting, but Seafoam wasn't. There would be no fog of warm breath on his face tonight, no gentle pulls on his hair. Seafoam was lying dead and broken under a mountain of cold, wet stone.

Rion hugged his pack tightly and began to cry, desperately trying to keep quiet enough so no one would hear him. Seafoam's death had been devastating enough. But after first thinking Rarnak, Andra, and Ara dead in the attack, he'd then thought none of them seriously hurt. But now Ara lay so wrapped in bandages he almost had no need for clothes. And he'd been right: something terrible had happened to Gosa. It was far more than the bakery. It was the whole City. And it was because of him. Why else keep it secret from him? And Elanara didn't love him, not even enough to pity him by gifting him with an Elfstone.

If Tarrell were here, he might help. But Tarrell was hundreds of miles away. Rion felt as lonely as if he were chained by himself in the cell again. The thought brought shivers, and he didn't even have a dry blanket to huddle under.

"Rion, why didn't you say you were cold? I'll not have you falling to fever as well." Ron reached over and drew him in, hugging him. "I've warmth enough for both of us. My brothers are always complaining I make the bed too hot for them, though they sing a different tune in the winter."

Rion's shivering subsided as he felt Ron's warmth around him, and not just the heat from his body, though it was certainly welcome. The warmth of his presence was incredibly reassuring. He thought he might even be able to sleep. What would he do if something ever happened to Ron? The thought brought new terror and his heart started hammering.

"It's all right, Rion. You're safe, I'm here. And Gar's doing well and Ara and Rarnak will be all right now, you'll see. Please try to sleep, Rion," Ron soothed.

Rion nodded and calmed. Ron's heartbeat was so strong, so steady, so comforting. Rion finally drifted off to sleep listening to it.

THE next morning, Ron and Rion awoke together, early. Rion wrote to Ron that he needed him to come shopping with him, and Ron agreed to. They got dressed in their spare clothes.

Before they left, Ron checked on Ara. He was surprised to see Andra asleep in the chair beside Rarnak's bed. He felt Ara's brow and then Rarnak's gently, so as not to waken them, and was relieved that both of them felt cooler to the touch than they had the night before. He crept quietly from the room.

"Their fevers seem to have broken," Ron said softly to Rion, who appeared anxious.

Rion seemed relieved.

"I don't want to leave the door unlocked, but I don't relish waking anyone else," Ron whispered.

"I'll lock it," Argo said from behind them.

Ron spun about in surprise. "I hadn't realized you were awake. Not many men manage to sneak up on me."

Argo smiled. "It's my job to guard Uncle Vargas."

He let them out and they heard the locks sliding into place. The City was not so crowded this morning. Many people were apparently still in bed, those who were lucky enough to have them. More than a few people were sleeping in the alleyways they passed. They walked quickly to the Market.

RION was proud of himself. He found his way unerringly, without Ron having to ask directions for them, though the City had changed much in the few months they'd been gone.

He priced food out of curiosity, but decided against buying any, since Vargas had said the caravan could provide what they needed. Instead, he focused first on finding them new blankets. The old ones were worn, torn, and dirty, and they stank. The prices were steeper than he expected, even forewarned, but Ron was able to negotiate them down somewhat.

Rion felt a pang of guilt. Ron was good at trading; it was what he should be doing. Ron would be doing it still, if it weren't for him. Only Ron might have died in Gosa, then, with the rest of the City.

The Market here reminded him of Gosa, except it was already far busier, though it was yet early. It was a beautiful day. The rain had left the sky a sparkling blue. Rion's heart started hammering, and he gazed up at the perfect, cloudless sky fearfully, half expecting to see more monsters coming for him. He felt a hand upon his shoulder and he jumped, startled, and started to draw his sword as he turned to face the danger.

"Easy, Rion! It's only me," Ron soothed, and Rion stopped his draw, face flushing.

"I saw how frightened you were, and I'd only meant to reassure you. It's safe, for the moment at least," Ron promised.

Rion nodded, feeling foolish.

"There's no need to be embarrassed, Rion, after all you've been through. You have a right to be uneasy. I'm on edge as well," Ron said, looking him in the eye.

Rion nodded, and some of the tension left him. He began viewing the wares at the different stalls selling ready-made clothing. He bought new shirts and pants for all of them, carefully selecting styles and colors and sizes to fit both their bodies and tastes, including Andra. Rion bought two sets for himself. He was through playing the part of Master Trader. He planned to work his way to the Pass as a guard, along with the rest of them, and wanted to dress accordingly.

Then he went to the three different herbalist shops he found, looking for Ghostlips, the medicine for fever Aras had taught him about, to add to his healer's kit. He'd felt helpless, not being able to aid Ara and Rarnak. But it was hard to find what he was searching for. Most people thought of Ghostlips as a deadly poison. Reputable herbalists wouldn't carry it. Finally at the last place he tried, he was able to purchase four flowers, all the man had. He'd hoped to get more, but it was better than nothing. Of course, they'd be traveling with at least one healer now, but he wanted to be prepared, in case something happened to Aradon. Rion had traveled enough now to know he had to be ready for any contingency.

As Rion passed by a stall selling roasted meat-on-a-stick, the delicious aroma was tempting, but the price they were asking was nearly five times what it should be. How could anyone afford to eat in this City?

He noticed Ron was keeping a wary eye out for thieves. Rion had been watching as well, when he wasn't too engrossed with the merchandise he was viewing. They could ill afford to lose their purses or sustain injury. Fortunately, they made it back to the shop without incident.

The others had apparently just finished cleaning up after the horses. "I'm not sorry I missed that," Ron muttered.

Rion fought tears at the thought of Seafoam again. He forced those thoughts aside. He handed Ron his new clothes and blanket and Ron thanked him. Then he passed out the clothes and blankets for the others, placing Ara's and Rarnak's near their beds.

Andra was still sitting by Rarnak, though she was awake now. Rion thought he'd heard her talking to Rarnak when he entered the room, but Rarnak wasn't awake.

"What's this?" she asked, when Rion handed her clothes and blanket to her.

Ron said, "Rion's bought us all new clothes and a blanket."

Andra scowled. "But I've got a blanket, and I like my uniform. I'll not wear a dress, not now," she argued, pushing it back toward him without even unfolding and looking at what he'd given her.

Ron sighed. "The proper thing to say is, 'Thank you, Rion, I appreciate your gift.' Our blankets need replacing and our clothes. And Rion bought you a man's clothes as well. Rion has always treated his friends well, and his guards, although for the most part he doesn't make any distinction between the two."

Andra appeared embarrassed. "Oh. Well, that's different, then. Thank you, Rion," she said, accepting the bundle and setting it on the bed.

Rion smiled at her and then looked questioningly at Ara and Rarnak and pointed to them.

"They're doing better," Andra said, her voice betraying her relief. "Their fevers have broken at least. They're asleep now, rather than unconscious, Aradon told me. He left for his wagon with Argo a little while ago, though Argo's coming back. We're supposed to try to wake them in a little while. We should try to carry Ara to where their wagons are, rather than allow him to walk or ride, if he'll let us. A cart would be better, but from what Vargas said, it would be folly to even try to find one. The refugees have been buying up every cart, wagon and horse in the City, those that can afford them. They fear they'll need to flee Athanark, too."

Ron shook his head, disagreeing with her suggestion. "Ara will be jostled less on horseback, with one of us on either side of him to protect him and someone riding with him, than if we try to carry him. It's astonishing, how crowded the streets are. You can scarcely walk without bumping into or brushing against someone. It's a cutpurse's dream."

"Horseback it is, then," she said, accepting his recommendation without question.

Everyone washed, dressed, and ate breakfast, except for Ara and Rarnak. Ron looked at Rion appraisingly, after he'd changed into his new clothes. Rion knew he looked like one of them, now—a swordsman, not a merchant. "I never thought I'd see you in such clothes," Ron commented neutrally, but his expression betrayed his thoughts. Ron was suspicious Rion planned to be a guard, now, as they were. Few guardsmen were as young as sixteen; they'd not the height nor muscle to go up against a fully grown man. Most started at eighteen and finished before they were twenty-five. A man could do well for himself doing seven years of such work, if he worked hard, saved his coin, was careful, and had both the skill and luck enough to survive.

Rion felt better in the clothes he now wore. He felt part of the group, not set apart from them, as he had been. He understood now why Tarrell had chafed at the finery he had forced him to wear. Oberas had always told him that clothes make the man, that they garner respect, but Rion had since met Lords and Princes who dressed like swordsmen and foresters, beggars and even ogres, to suit whatever need arose. Besides, it would be safer for the caravan. A chimaera flying overhead might not give him a second glance, dressed as he was. *SAFER,* he wrote on Ron's hand with his finger, giving him the response he knew would disturb Ron the least.

"As long as it's for safety's sake, that's fine," Ron conceded. "I know you won't listen if I tell you not to help us fight. But I don't want you drawing your sword at the first sign of trouble and riding full tilt into it. Use caution and your head. You did well against the ogre when you could have gotten killed otherwise."

Rion realized he'd not deceived Ron at all. But the praise made him feel warm again, for a little while, at least. He nodded solemnly, showing he took Ron's words seriously.

Now that they were almost ready to go, they went into the bedroom and roused Ara and Rarnak.

ARA realized he was naked under the blanket and extensively bandaged, and knew a healer must have tended to him and told them how injured he was. When he saw the others were dressed to travel, a lead weight settled in his stomach. "You can't leave me here! You can't go on without me!" Ara argued desperately, struggling to sit, grimacing silently in pain. "I can still ride. I did so before. I have to come with you!"

"Easy, Ara!" Ron scolded, gently pushing him back. "No one's leaving you, although the only riding you'll be doing is just enough to get you to the wagon. We would leave you in Athanark, so you could recover, but it's safer with us than it is here. We're at the Bloodhand. Vargas has sold it. We've signed onto a caravan Vargas is leading, as guards. There's a healer traveling with them, Aradon, the man who tended you. He's a fellow countryman from Thenalon. Come, we'll help you dress. Rion's bought us all new clothes and blankets."

Ara nodded, weak with relief. He looked pointedly at Andra, when he realized that she showed no signs of leaving. She was still dressed in a man's clothes, though new ones, not her guard's livery, now. It suited her. She looked far more at home in pants and a shirt than she ever had in a dress. "Andra, do you plan to stand there while I dress?" he challenged.

She scowled at him. "Who do you think undressed you and cloth-bathed you while you slept, idiot? I'll not stare. You've nothing under that blanket I've any interest in seeing again," she snapped.

Ara flushed, embarrassed.

"Well, even so, now that I'm aware enough, I'd prefer the privacy," Rarnak said.

To everyone's surprise, Andra was the one to blush, then, and she promptly left the room.

Gar muttered to Ara, but loudly enough for the others to hear, "Perhaps what Rarnak's got under his blanket is more to Andra's liking."

Rarnak looked at Gar levelly. "I mind your sister's attentions not at all, Gar, but I'll ask you to watch your tongue when speaking about her."

RON was pleasantly surprised by Rarnak's defense of Andra. He'd been about to swat Gar for what he'd said.

Gar, for his part, appeared sheepish. "Forgive me. I'd started to think of her as one of us, and as such a fair target. I hadn't meant to sound cruel. I've been trying to make amends for my past mistakes."

"If that was your intent, that's different, then," Rarnak conceded. "I'm happy to hear you say so. It's past time the two of you learned to appreciate her as Ron and Van do."

Ron looked appraisingly at Rarnak, as if seeing him again for the first time, and nodded, liking what he saw.

Rarnak began dressing himself awkwardly. Rion went over to him, obviously eager to help, while Gar assisted Ara. Rarnak smiled at Rion. "You remember what it's like, having a broken arm?" he asked, and Rion nodded. "So, we're to join a caravan again. Where will we leave it?"

Ron answered, "At the intersection of the Southern Road with the Western. They'll be heading west from there, through the Gelthor Pass. We'll be heading east. It's a big caravan. Vargas told me last night they have twenty wagons. He said he has room for both of you in his wagon. He sold all his stock and is taking his coin with him to reopen his shop elsewhere. Weapons are in demand here, and he made a substantial profit. He said there are many families with children in the caravan, and there's a full forty guards, most of them family men: the fathers, husbands, uncles, cousins, nephews, and older brothers of those in the wagons. Many have worked as guards before, too. With so many guards, the ogres at least might leave us alone for easier prey, and hopefully the brigands will think twice about attacking such a well-protected caravan, though their lust for goods might outweigh their common sense.

"Still, with luck we'll go unnoticed amongst so many, now that the Enemy's apparently lost track of Rion. We'll pick up replacement horses in Logareth for those we lost and be sure we're amply stocked with food and other supplies. Then it's only a few hundred miles from there to Thorn and the help he's promised."

Ron could see the others weren't fooled for a moment. They knew it would not be nearly as easy as he made it sound.

VARGAS left with Argo and Audra on foot for the rendezvous, with the others riding double on horseback. Rion saw Vargas take a long look at the shop as he locked it for the last time. He told Rion the new owner already had a key as he slipped his own under the door. Then Vargas gazed up at the empty hooks that had held the sign for his shop, which he'd told them was now packed in his wagon.

Rion felt bad for Vargas. He knew how Vargas felt. Rion had been forced from his home twice now, once in Ardock and once in Gosa. It had hurt both times. And he'd liked Athanark, which was supposed to have been his new home, far better than he had liked Gosa, for people like Lonas and Vargas. He'd never felt as welcome in Gosa. He wondered for the hundredth time how differently he might have viewed Gosa had he not been attacked and almost killed his second night there. He'd never felt safe there after that. It had not truly been home to him and never could be, now. But Athanark was too changed, now, to ever be either. He was glad to be leaving.

Rion saw Audra was clinging to Argo. She'd lost her home and it appeared her family as well. He should not be feeling sorry for himself, or Vargas. They were survivors. Only time would tell whether Audra might be, or whether she'd join the ranks of the haunted-eyed refugees he'd seen huddled in the mouths of the alleys here and in Ardock. He'd do what little he could for her, without his voice.

They tried to stick close to Ara so he didn't get too jostled, but it wasn't easy riding three abreast in such crowded streets. They ignored the grumbles of those around them. Ara was looking peaked after even the short ride to the wagon yard. With a painful flash, Rion remembered how Tarrell had looked, months ago, after the walk to the Bloodhand, with his injured arm weakening him.

The wagon yard was abuzz in the controlled chaos of all good caravans. Rion could tell it was a good one, an organized one, because the guards didn't just let them through without challenging them.

All but Ara and Rarnak dismounted. Ron said to the two guards who'd spoken to them, "We're looking for Jonas. We hired on last night with Vargas as guards. Vargas knows us from months ago. He's on his way on foot with Argo, he'll be here soon. He'll vouch for us when he comes."

One of them glanced skeptically at Ara and Rarnak, and Ron grimaced. "The four of us, the ones that can still hold a sword and a bow, will be guarding."

Rion was pleased Ron had included him. He had thought he might still need a little convincing.

One of the guards left to get Jonas. He returned with a large, imposing man. Jonas was at least six and a half feet tall, broad of shoulder, and well muscled. He eyed the four of them who were standing critically. "Vargas is getting feeble in his old age, recommending the four of you," he said, looking them over from head to toe disdainfully. "You're too old to be a guard," he said to Ron. He turned to Andra. "And we've no need for a cook who thinks she can be." Then he dismissed Rion with a glance. "Nor a boy with delusions of manhood." He sneered at Gar. "Nor someone who might run from danger, sooner than mar his pretty looks."

Rion was glad he had no voice, for they needed the protection of the caravan, but it would not have been easy for him to keep silent. His estimation of the man plummeted.

Ron was the one who always spoke for his brothers, and he did so now, for all of them.

RON kept his temper with an effort, for Rion's sake, and Ara's, and Rarnak's. "I'm Ronamark of Ogaten. I've not been too old to see my brothers safely across from Gosa to Thenalon to Athanark to Gosa and back again. You can test my sword hand. I'd be surprised if you can find one better amongst your men, yourself included, or you can ask Vargas when he comes, and he'll tell you as much. And the same goes for my bow work. And I can cook as well as my sister Lisandra can."

He turned to Andra, who was staring coldly at Jonas. "Lisandra is a master at the bow. She was taught by the River Elves of Salenia, as we all were, but they honored her alone by gifting her with one of their bows. As for her bravery and her swordwork, she jumped onto the back of a rogue ogre and slit its throat, in the Thinabar Pass, when we came here, after she'd first fought her way clear of the rock it had buried her under."

Ron turned to Rion. "Rion's a man by age, he's sixteen, but he's more a man by deeds. He was Caravan Master on our previous journey. He led our caravan, two merchants, two wagons, and fourteen guards safely from here to Gosa without losing a single man, and it was not an easy crossing. He'd tell you about it himself, had he not lost his voice fighting a chimaera and a werewolven. But he didn't need a voice to hamstring the ogre we fought in the Pass on the way here. I'll not have him belittled by any man on this journey, when he hasn't the voice to defend himself. You send any with such issues to me, and I'll show them the error of their thoughts."

Then he turned to Gar. "And this is my brother Garamark. His bow work is second only to Lisandra's of any I've ever seen. He's taken down a chimaera and a werewolven single-handed and driven an arrow into the eye of more than one ogre. His swordwork is better than most men's. And he knows more than any man alive what it means to lose his pretty looks, yet still keep them, but we don't know you well enough to tell you that story."

He turned to Ara and Rarnak. "And my brother Aramark and our friend Rarnak fight as well as the rest of us. They are injured as they are through poorer luck not poorer skill."

Jonas scowled at them. "I'm Captain of the Guard of this caravan. Will you follow my orders alone, without hesitation, whether you think them folly or not?"

Ron looked at him intently. "I don't like what I've seen of you so far, but if Vargas chose you as Captain, he must have had good reason. I trust his judgment with my life and the lives of my friends and family. I'll follow your orders," Ron said.

"As will I," said Andra.

Rion nodded that he would.

Gar said, "I will as well," and Ara and Rarnak echoed his words.

Jonas's face burst into a grin. "Then welcome, Ronamark, Lisandra, Rion, Garamark, Aramark, and Rarnak! I'm pleased to see Vargas didn't warn you about me ahead of time. I'll not have men under me who will fold or fight when faced with hard words: they tend to crumble all too easily under harsh conditions, or before strong foes. I welcome your experience, also. We've few amongst us who have ever traveled by caravan, and since you've taken a similar route, we'd welcome any advice you might give." The two men beside Jonas warmed instantly to them at Jonas's words.

Ron nodded. "In that case, my brothers and I go by Ara, Gar, and Ron, to our comrades and friends, and our sister is Andra. We'd be pleased to aid you. You should know, though, we've only signed on with you as far as the Western Road. We'll not be heading west with you through the Coroden Mountains, but we'd be happy to tell you all we know of what you might face on the rest of your journey as well."

"So noted. Have you only the three horses?" Jonas asked.

Ron nodded. "The ogre killed the other three. Vargas is letting Ara and Rarnak ride in his wagon. Rion's an experienced wagon driver, as is Gar. They can work as such as needed, or guard from a wagon, plus night duty around the camp will be on foot in any case, so we'll not hamper you for lack of horses."

Jonas nodded. "I'd lead you to Vargas's wagon, but I still need him to vouch for you. I hope you understand."

Ron said, "Of course."

Vargas entered the yard a few moments later, with Argo and Audra. He smiled as he saw them. "How'd they fare, Jonas?" he asked.

"They passed. You vouch for all six of them, then?" Jonas asked.

"Aye," Vargas said.

"Then I'll put the four to work, and you can lead the other two to your wagon," Jonas said.

"Excellent. This is Audra," Vargas said, introducing her. Audra smiled timidly at Jonas, holding tightly to Argo. "She's another late addition. She'll be riding with me as well. Have you found me a relief driver, yet?"

"Rion and Gar both qualify, according to Ron. Take your pick. They've only three horses between them," Jonas said.

"Then I'll take Rion, since Garamark's a bowman," Vargas said.

Ron was pleased. He'd prefer Rion not work as a guard at all. Vargas had found a way to see him safer, without hurting his feelings.

ARGO, Ron, Andra, and even Gar were quickly put to work. Rion was relieved to see Gar was given a task where he'd be seated, so he wouldn't strain his injured leg. Rion accompanied Vargas and Audra along with Ara and Rarnak to the wagons. Audra looked nervously back at Argo as Vargas led her away, but soon seemed to relax. Vargas was very solicitous of her.

Rion saw that Ara looked like he was in pain again as he settled himself into the wagon, trying to get as comfortable as possible. Rion unrolled their new blankets and laid them out for him to lie on. He bunched them here and there to support Ara's arm and leg better. Ara thanked him gratefully. Then Rion offered him some *soforath*, and Ara took it without protest. He offered some to Rarnak as well, but he declined. Rarnak was watching the bustle around them, appearing frustrated. Rion knew how he felt, but Vargas told him his job for now was to aid Ara and Rarnak, as they'd all discussed earlier, to ensure they rested comfortably and did not worsen.

A short while later, Aradon, the healer, stopped by their wagon. He spoke with Vargas for a moment and then turned his attentions to Ara and Rarnak. When he saw Rion watching anxiously as he examined and treated the two injured men, he said, "Don't worry. Ara will be fine with the medicine you gave him. I suspect he'll sleep for much of the day. They show no sign of the fever returning, though I've given them each one more dose to be on the safe side. They'll recover fully," he assured him. Rion smiled in relief.

"Master Alarion? Is that truly you?" Rion heard a familiar voice ask. He turned in surprise at hearing his given name. He no longer spoke it to anyone. He smiled warmly and nodded in greeting when he saw Lonas, the innkeeper from the Brightwater, who had been so solicitous after Oberas had died.

"Whatever are you doing back here?" Lonas asked.

Rion pointed to his mouth and shook his head.

Vargas said, "He's lost his voice, Lonas. It's a long tale, and I've only heard a portion of it, but you need not worry. He's with good friends, and he's well provided for. He's still young yet. His adventures just aren't over is all. Though it looks like ours aren't either. I should be riding the perimeter, not driving a wagon," he said gruffly.

"Me, I can't believe I'm wearing a sword again! Neither can Harnel. I'm glad we've used your yard to keep in practice here and there over the years, though I've done so out of pride. I'd never thought I'd need such skills again. It'll not be the same, traveling like this without Oberas, Terhannon, and Loessen, though," Lonas said wistfully.

Rion's eyes widened in surprise. Vargas saw his expression and guessed his thoughts. "Oberas traveled and fought beside us long, long ago, when we were young. Do you mean he never told you?" Vargas asked, surprised.

Rion shook his head, eager to hear more.

"You've done it now, lad," Lonas said, smiling. "Vargas will talk your ear off the whole trip, about our adventures."

Rion grinned and nodded, *Yes,* eagerly. Oberas had never said anything to him about such things. No wonder when the wolven-riders had attacked them outside of Athanark he had stood his ground and fought them! Rion had known Oberas had been to the Dwarven Lands, that he'd been rumored to have found his fortune there, but still, he'd never suspected Oberas might have ever been anything other than a merchant, with others to guard him. He felt his loss again more keenly.

A short while later, as the caravan pulled out onto the street, Rion was on the wagon bench next to Vargas, listening with rapt attention to the stories of Oberas as a young man.

Ron had cautioned Jonas and the others about the woods around Athanark. They'd seen no sign of the wolven-riders that had attacked Rarnak's and Rion's caravans when they entered the City, but they'd come from the Coroden Mountains to the west, not the Lost Road to the east. He'd made sure everyone understood about the danger from the poisoned blades both Rion and Rarnak had warned him of.

They all hoped most potential dangers might avoid the caravan. Forty-four guards were a formidable number. But twenty wagons were a tempting target for bandits and ogres and others. These people were carrying all they owned, and many had sold most of their possessions and carried substantial coin. There were women the bandits might desire and children the ogres would find a delicacy. Each of them feared it was only a matter of time before trouble would find them.

Chapter 7
The Road to Logareth

THE first day of their journey passed without incident. Rion drove Vargas's team for half the day. The entire time Vargas told him tales of Oberas and his adventures in the Dwarven Lands, and their time in Riviera with the Elves. Rion was fascinated. He'd heard little of the Dwarven Lands or of the Elven Kingdoms, other than what scant information his mother had known and told him. Elanara was from Riviera, the River Elf Kingdom neighboring Ardock. Hearing about her home made him feel closer to her, somehow.

He wondered whether the Elves of Riviera were yet safe, now that he knew Ardock had been burnt. Had the Elves been forced to flee as well? He couldn't imagine any enemy being so powerful that it might endanger the Elves, though one that used fire as a weapon might prove formidable, even to them.

Here and there he would ask questions, using his lead and paper. It was fortunate for him Vargas knew how to read. Few Men ever had the need to learn. Rarnak and Audra seemed to be as entertained as he was by Vargas's tales. Ara had fallen asleep even before their wagon had made it down the crowded streets and left through the gate.

That evening, after the caravan stopped and made camp for the night, before dinner, Rion took the flowers he'd obtained in Athanark and ground the petals, carefully discarding the poisonous leaves and stems without touching them as Aras had instructed him.

After dinner, Rion had night watch. He could not speak, but he could still make the earsplitting whistle Hardred had taught him so very long ago. He'd demonstrated it for Jonas and the others, indicating that he would use it to signal danger.

He patrolled his section of the perimeter for his shift and then fell asleep, exhausted, almost as soon as he lay down. It was the first night he'd slept without Meander or Seafoam or Ron to watch over him.

RION awoke with the rising sun, feeling calm and well rested. He was relieved he'd not had any nightmares. He had instead dreamt of Elanara again, as he had almost every night for some time now, but this time she was in Riviera as Vargas had described it to him, in one of the beautiful gardens between the marble buildings, beside the crystal waters of one of the many fountains.

That day in the wagon, Vargas suggested Rarnak and Audra tell their stories. Rarnak told of his life as a farmer, and how he'd left at eighteen to work as a guard. He spoke of the caravans he'd been on and the time in between, and of their journey to and from Gosa. Audra listened wide-eyed. Rion thought she looked at him with new respect after hearing Rarnak speak so well of him.

When it was Audra's turn, she said, "I was born and raised in Gower, a village to the north and east of here. My father owned an inn there. I helped him and my mother run it." She described her life in Gower in detail with a sad smile on her face, and then grew grim. "A number of months ago, the wolven came. Those first ones were wild and did not bear riders. They killed all the deer and rabbits and other game in the forest. Then they came to the village to hunt. At first, they took our livestock. Some of the men tried to hunt them, but the wolven were too smart. None of the men who'd gone out after them returned. But one night a man named Talon came.

"It was the night little Billy was taken by the wolven, right out of his bed." She shuddered. "Talon went into the woods after them. He returned with Billy's remains and then went back out, to hunt them. He was gone for days, and we assumed he'd been killed too. But he came back, with an Elf named Aras, whom he'd met in the woods. Aras had slain all of the wolven, all seven, by himself, and nearly died doing it," she said, her eyes alight with hero worship.

"Then they left Gower, and for a while everything was all right again. But a few weeks ago, I was out picking mushrooms with my mother. We'd taken a picnic lunch. We were gone for hours. We'd collected two whole buckets full. We were almost back to the village before we realized something was wrong." Her voice was haunted now, so very soft.

"There was so much smoke in the air. Even the nights we'd rimmed the village with bonfires to keep the wolven out it hadn't smelled like that. My mother told me to hide. She said she'd see what was wrong. She'd call for me if it was safe. She said...." Audra swallowed, hard. "She said she'd be careful. I was so scared! I begged her not to go, all in whispers. I...." She ended the last sentence with a sob and tears started streaming down her face.

"Please, I can't! Don't make me say it!" she sobbed.

Rion was distressed and frustrated. He was driving the wagon; he could not help her. Vargas was on the bench beside him. He climbed down and hugged Audra with his single arm. "Of course you need not say more, child. I should have realized and stopped you earlier. We hadn't meant to stir up such terrible memories. Forgive us."

Audra was sobbing against him. After a long while, she was able to calm down. By early evening she seemed all right again.

It was shortly before dusk, when the caravan was almost ready to make camp for the evening, that the wolven-riders attacked. One moment the woods around them were still and peaceful, and the next the wolven came lunging from the trees on all sides, snarling and growling. To Rion, it was more horrible than the last time. This time there were the screams of women and children, mixed with the screams of the horses and the shouts of the men. This time he knew the slightest touch by one of their poisoned blades would mean death.

He drew his sword, heart hammering. One of them was coming for their wagon, the lead wagon. Audra was screaming hysterically. "Don't let them take me! Not like Mother! Don't let them take me!"

Rion's sword met the wolven-rider's with a loud clang. The force of the blow knocked him from the wagon. The rider was so strong! Rion was on his back on the ground and desperately brought his sword up as teeth and blade came for him, but both wolven and rider turned from him to meet a second attack from the wagon. Vargas and Rarnak, only two arms between them, gave Rion the precious moments he needed to spring back to his feet. He plunged his sword into the heart of the wolven even as Rarnak's sword found the rider's throat, as Vargas parried the swing of his poisonous blade, preventing it from striking either of them. The rider and the wolven fell, twitching.

Rion looked for the nearest foe. The caravan had erupted into chaos, but it was well defended. He saw Andra and Gar, their hands a blur, nocking arrows to their bows on the right. He ran toward the left flank, which was not faring as well. Ron was on the left flank, but he was using his sword instead of his bow, for some reason, and there was only a single bowman at work there. Rion feared their other archers had all been killed, that these wolven-riders had targeted their bowmen first, just as the ones who had attacked Oberas's caravan had. There was a snarl from Rion's left, and his attention was drawn to his own immediate danger. He ducked the wolven-rider's blow, thrusting his sword under the man's guard and skewering him. The rider fell from his mount, and then the wolven was upon him.

Rion fell backward hard again beneath the weight of the beast, the air forced from his lungs. The wolven's teeth were coming for his throat! He drew both arms up, his left to defend his throat and his right to attack with his sword, knowing neither would suffice. Unexpectedly, the creature fell to the right, tumbling from him.

Rion scrambled to his feet, astonished. It was dead. An arrow had been driven through its throat. From the fletching, he knew it was one of Andra's. He looked around and spotted her. She was still on the right side of the caravan. How could she have made such a shot, past people and loaded wagons, to save him?

In that instant, she disappeared from view. Her horse had been felled from under her! Rion scrambled over the wagon blocking her from his sight, terrified of what he would find. These riders' blades dripped with the same sickly green poison as the ones that had felled their guards months ago, outside Athanark.

But Andra was alive. She stood over a rider, her sword red with his blood. She spun toward Rion, sword raised, and then smiled grimly when she saw it was him and not a foe. Then her eyes widened and her blade came toward him, and he ducked instinctively to the left. A wolven sailed past him. It must have been on the wagon behind him, coming for his back. Andra's sword plunged through its ribs, and the blade was wrenched from her hand.

There was a loud whistle; it was impossible to tell where it came from. At that same moment, a wolven galloped up from the front of the caravan toward Andra. She spun to face it, weaponless. Rion ran to defend her, knowing he wouldn't be fast enough. But the rider held no sword, and his beast did not bite her. Instead, the man's arm snaked about her waist and he lifted her, flinging her onto her stomach in front of him, across the creature's broad back, moments before plunging into the woods with his prize.

Rion let out a desperate, piercing whistle of his own, his danger whistle, and ran into the woods after them without waiting to see if anyone had heard his cry for help. The beast was fast. He would lose it amongst the trees if he waited for assistance.

It disappeared quickly enough, but it left deep tracks that were easy to follow, from the speed and the double burden it carried. He went deeper into the woods. He had to save Andra!

R ON retrieved his fallen bow from where he had dropped it after the string had been cut while parrying one of the rider's blades. The wood was hacked nearly in half; it was useless now. He dropped it again in disgust. He saw Jonas and went to him. "How bad?" he asked.

"Seven dead so far, six of them guards: two fathers, a son, and three hired men. And a child," Jonas said, his voice raw with pain. "At least a dozen injured. But we've also two missing, a mother and her daughter. We're trying to do a count now, to see if others are missing as well. Some of the riders got away. That whistle seems to have signaled their withdrawal."

Ron nodded. "I heard Rion whistle just after that. Have you seen him?"

"No, I haven't, but I'll ask after him," Jonas assured him.

Ron went to the front of the caravan, to Vargas's wagon. Ara, Rarnak, and Vargas were there with Audra, who was sobbing hysterically in Argo's arms, but there was no sign of Rion. "Where's Rion?" Ron asked, voicing his concern.

Rarnak said, "We haven't seen him since the start of the attack. He felled a wolven that attacked us, and I got the rider, while Vargas protected us both. Then Rion headed to the left of the caravan."

"He's not there. I'll check the right. And Vargas, Jonas says so far seven dead, six guards, three of them family, plus a child. Over a dozen injured, and a mother and daughter missing. He's doing a full count."

Vargas nodded grimly.

Rarnak climbed from the wagon. "I'll help you look. Knowing Rion, he's helping someone in need, probably bandaging them."

They passed by the bodies of fallen riders and wolven. They were halfway down the length of the caravan when Ron saw something in the dirt that set his heart hammering. It was an Elven bow; the graceful line of it was unmistakable. Ron picked it up, his hand shaking, and called out loudly, "Andra! Andra, where are you?" He turned to Rarnak, whose face had grown pale. "She'd not have dropped this, ever, and left it lying in the dirt."

They searched for her but didn't find her. Nor Rion. And Ron realized Gar was missing as well. They went to Jonas. He was grim.

"They're not the only ones. We've three women missing and two girls, plus your sister and brother and Rion, that's eight. Seven dead, thirteen injured, and two of those may yet die. If you hadn't warned us of the poisoned blades, or if we'd had fewer guards, or ones of poorer skill, our losses would have been at least triple that. We could well have been completely overrun: nearly a full score of riders and wolven each were slain.

"We can't leave the caravan poorly defended to search for the missing, but we've at least one tracker amongst us. Show us where you found the bow. It sounds like there are at least eight of the wolven-riders still alive, if they each took one of those who are missing. You can have ten men, the tracker included. I can't give you more: this might be a trick to weaken our defenses for a second attack."

"I'm coming too," Rarnak said. "I helped in the battle and I can help now, and I'll not cost you a guard."

"All right. May Elmoth protect you both and aid you in your quest," Jonas intoned.

Volunteers were easily found: the four husbands and fathers of the missing, five others, and the tracker. The latter was quick to find the tracks of a heavily burdened wolven and the tracks of two men on foot, following it. Ron felt hope then. "I thought they'd carried Rion and Gar off as well. But it looks like they went after Andra of their own will."

"Which means the riders only took women and girls," Rarnak said grimly, clutching his sword hilt tightly, the bones of his knuckles standing out whitely against his weathered hand.

The fear and anger of those around them grew. They all knew what that meant.

RION was a little hopeful at first. It was easy to see that Andra was not a helpless captive from the erratic prints the wolven had left. But then he swallowed, hard. There was a bloodied knife lying amidst the disturbed leaves of the trail of paw prints he was following. He knew it must be Andra's knife; the rider wouldn't have left it. Worse, now the tracks were steady, which meant Andra was either too hurt to fight, bound and helpless, or unconscious. His only solace was the knowledge that she wasn't dead; he'd have found her body as well.

Rion looked anxiously behind him but neither heard nor saw anyone following. He picked up the knife. He'd need every weapon he could find. He alone could save her.

ANDRA awoke to the sound of crying. Her arms hurt, and she discovered they were bound tightly behind her. She tried to sit, forcing herself up with her elbow, then fell back, breath hissing at the pain in her head.

She struggled to rise again, muscles straining, and she sat up more slowly. She was in a camp. Andra saw ten wolven-riders, their mounts roaming freely amongst them. The crying came from a woman and girl. They were leaning against one another. Their arms were bound, like her own.

Andra whispered to them, "You can cry later. One of you, put your back to mine and help me with these ropes." But the two weren't listening. She cursed at them and even begged, but they would not help. They were hysterical, completely oblivious to her, regardless of what she said to them.

She gave up in disgust and felt around for a sharp rock, even a stick, anything that might aid her in loosening her bonds. Her knife was gone, along with her bow and sword. Still, if she could free herself, the riders would have a fight on their hands.

Three more riders came into camp over the next short while, each with a woman or girl slung on his mount. They dumped their burdens next to the trees where Andra and the other two already sat and bound them. All together there were four women, including herself, and two girls. There were thirteen riders and at least close to that number of wolven. The beasts were far harder to count. They all looked too similar, and they moved quickly and unpredictably amongst the men.

The riders were talking in a guttural language Andra had never heard before, gesturing and leering at their trophies. They were also scanning the trees, as if expecting more riders to join them, but no others came. The men were grim, then, and their voices grew angry. Andra took some small comfort in knowing she had done much to reduce their numbers, to keep those who weren't coming from returning.

She'd fired her entire quiver. She'd felled seven riders and five wolven with her arrows, and she'd slain one other rider with her sword, as well as three wolven. She suspected they'd been attacked by close to three dozen men and beasts each, from what she'd seen. She'd made them pay dearly for their prize. She'd hurt them.

She shuddered. Now they would hurt her, and in the end, she'd pay just as dearly, with her own life. She'd never have expected Elmoth to make her pay such a price. She'd thought she'd die quickly, in battle, with her honor intact. She had even started to think Elmoth had planned for her to live, perhaps that she might be blessed with a husband, and even children.

The men raked their eyes over their captives, talking and gesturing. She couldn't understand their words, but they appeared to be arguing. Then they seemed to reach an agreement. Their hands went to their pants and they started to unlace them. One of the men came toward them. The other prisoners shrank from him. He walked up to the girl Andra had seen first: she couldn't have been more than thirteen.

The girl screamed, she begged, she sobbed as he reached for her. She was screaming for her mother, who was helpless beside her, sobbing and trying vainly to shield her daughter with her body, but she was pushed roughly aside. The other riders kept their distance; they were working themselves into a frenzy.

Andra had known they were to be raped and killed, but it looked like they were going to take them one at a time, that all thirteen men were going to take turns on each of them, and they were taking the littlest first, in front of her mother.

Anger burned over her fear. Andra knew they'd take her last: she was the ugliest. She'd have to sit and watch and listen for hours, perhaps days. No man had ever wanted to touch her, and now thirteen men such as these were going to pleasure themselves upon her.

No! She'd make them kill her now, without raping her. Perhaps that was what Elmoth wanted. She might yet have a quick, merciful death. At the very least, she'd make them rape and kill her first, so she'd not have to watch the others suffer.

She twisted, and with a cry of rage, she leapt to her feet, her arms still bound tightly behind her, and charged the man, her head slamming into his stomach. He fell back, hard, and the girl shrank from him, then crawled on her knees back to her mother. She collapsed against her, sobbing.

Andra had fallen over from the impact with the guard. Now she rolled to her feet and kicked the man on the ground hard between the legs. That was one less that would take her. He'd not be using his for a long time, if ever again.

The other men had been amused before, but now they surged forward, enraged. She was able to kick one other, felling him. He was clutching his manhood in agony, but then the rest were upon her. A fist slammed into her already throbbing head and she reeled, dizzy. Another smashed into her stomach. She would have doubled over, but rough hands had grabbed her arms. Then their hands and arms were about her waist, her legs. She felt her clothes tearing off of her as she was pushed to the ground, kicking and struggling vainly. Their hands were everywhere. Her clothes were in tatters as she felt her legs being forced apart.

Then there was a man's yelp of surprise and another and a gurgle, and the men began pulling back from her. She looked, dazed, from where she lay and saw three of the riders had fallen to the ground. The one nearest her had an arrow through his eye. Someone was firing from the trees! It must be Gar or Ron. She doubted anyone else in the caravan could shoot so well. With the two men she'd felled, that meant eight were left standing, but at least a dozen wolven and those men were heading into the trees. Her brother would be killed!

Then someone ran toward her from the opposite direction, from the forest to her right. It was Rion!

He scooped up one of the fallen riders' swords and laid it by her as he knelt and then cut her bonds with a knife, looking at her pleadingly. He handed her the rider's poisoned blade and pointed desperately at the trees. Then he was running to the women and girls, who were bound and helpless and cowering.

Andra lurched to her feet and began to run into the woods, stumbling. Elmoth, from the fear in Rion's face, it must be only the two of them come to save them, him and one of her brothers. She ran past two more of the riders' bodies at the edge of the woods, each with an arrow in him.

RION cut all the prisoners free, and they sat, trembling and crying. He gestured desperately to the woods, but they just huddled in terror. "R... r... run!" he forced out, stamping his foot. It was the first word he'd spoken in weeks. He no longer even tried to speak anymore. Then he took off into the woods after Andra. He'd given the others their chance; he couldn't waste any more time on them.

He passed two dead riders, both killed with arrows, then two dead wolven and another rider, all sword kills, likely Andra's. The poisoned blades were working to their advantage this time. He sheathed his own blade and took the fallen rider's. The poison would more than compensate for the unfamiliar feel of the blade.

He had hoped Andra would still be able to fight. When they'd swarmed over her like that, he'd been afraid she might be too injured, but he'd kept to Gar's plan anyway and hoped for the best. They hadn't expected Andra to attack the man going for the girl, not with her hands bound.

Rion hoped Gar was still alive. Then he came across the first of Gar's pursuers Andra had missed and no longer had time to worry. He stabbed the man from behind before he knew Rion was there. Rion took off running, confident the poison would do its work. He heard the clash of swords to the left and headed that way.

It was Andra! She was fighting two of them at once, her back to a tree. Rion attacked the man on her right, stabbing him in the back, but he twisted to the side just as Rion struck, and it wasn't the fatal blow he'd planned. The man turned and raised his sword, then shuddered and fell as the poison did its work.

Andra skewered the other one. "Thanks," she said. At that moment, they heard the snarl of a wolven and turned. It was leaping for them. Both their blades struck home, and it fell, twitching. They heard more snarling to the right and headed for it.

Then there was a scream, from the way they had come. Rion looked at Andra, agonized, and headed back toward the camp. He'd cut the prisoners free and told them to run! Gar or Andra might die while he helped them again, but he couldn't leave them so helpless, in danger.

When he reached the camp, he found two wolven-riders, on foot, and their wolven surrounding their cowering and whimpering prey. They'd apparently decided to cut their losses and leave with some of the spoils. They had the second young girl and one of the women. There was no sign of the other three. At least some of them had done as Rion had urged and run.

Rion charged the rider who had hold of the girl, slicing at the back of his legs with the sword; he dared not risk hitting the girl with the poisoned blade. The rider fell, and she fell with him. The rider's wolven lunged at Rion, and he thrust his sword into its open mouth. The sword was yanked from his hand. He barely dodged the blade of the other rider, who was now on his mount. They wheeled about and attacked again.

Rion dove for the fallen rider's sword, barely bringing it up in time to parry the blow that was coming for him. But the jaw of the beast the man rode closed about his thigh, and Rion felt agony as its teeth ripped his flesh as it surged past him, nearly yanking him off his feet. Then it wheeled about.

This time instead of parrying the rider's blow, Rion dodged and slashed with his own blade, slicing the rider's leg to the bone. The beast wheeled, and the rider toppled from him. The wolven leapt onto Rion, knocking him to the ground, its teeth biting deeply into his arm. His sword fell, as the strength left his hand.

He was dead. The wolven would mangle his arm and tear out his throat. His luck had finally run out. Rion knew it was hopeless, but still he struggled.

Then, miraculously, the creature shuddered and fell limply upon him, its jaws releasing his arm. To his amazement he saw the girl he had saved. She was standing there, a wild look in her eyes, one of the rider's blades in her hands, the green of the poison mingling with the red of the blood on the blade. She was trembling.

Rion got shakily to his feet. The borrowed sword he'd wielded was pinned beneath the fallen beast. The girl might yet need the one she wielded. He drew his own blade as he looked from her to the woods and took off, limping badly, unable to run. Gar and Andra still needed him.

He'd barely gotten back into the trees when a wolven slammed into him from the left. He'd neither heard nor seen it. Its teeth sank into his thigh, but it had wrapped its mouth about his scabbard as well as his leg. Rion reversed the grip on his blade and stabbed backward into the creature, confident he'd dealt it a mortal wound when he felt it start convulsing, even as it bit harder. Rion fell as he felt the scabbard break under the force of its jaws and the teeth sink deeper into his leg. Then it lay twitching and finally stilled.

Rion tried to pull the beast's jaws from him, but he wasn't strong enough. They were locked tightly about him. He lay there, breathing raggedly. If he whistled for help, more enemies might come, and he was helpless to defend himself.

The woods were ominously quiet now. He listened desperately for signs that his friends yet lived.

"Rion? Andra?" he heard Gar's voice call out. He was alive! But he sounded like he was in pain.

There was silence for a moment. Then Rion heard Andra call out, "Gar? I knew it was either you or Ron. Is that all of them?"

Rion whistled, now that it sounded like the danger might be past.

Gar called out, "Thank Elmoth! Rion's still alive, too. I can't walk. Andra, can you find me?"

"Keep talking, I'll find you. Rion, try to meet us," Andra said.

Rion whistled. He tried to make it sound like talking, starting and stopping and changing pitch and tone.

"Something's wrong. Rion's trying to call us to him instead," Gar said, his voice thick with worry.

"He might be hurt worse than you. I might need you to help me with him. Gar!" she cried. Then it was quiet. Rion knew they must be together, talking more softly. He kept whistling, knowing his whistles would be harder to follow than even a calling voice.

They found him a short while later. Gar had a long, dead branch in one hand that he was using as a walking stick and an arm about Andra's waist. Gar's right leg was crudely bandaged and bloody. He'd taken off his shirt. Andra was wearing it. Fortunately it was long enough that it fell past her bare hips, as well as covering her torso. Her shredded pants were completely gone now.

"Rion!" Andra cried in concern, seeing him pinned.

Rion forced a smile through the pain, trying to reassure them.

"No wonder he couldn't come! It's a wonder he's still alive," Gar said.

Andra cursed and let go of Gar. She tried to pry the jaws from about Rion's leg with her hands, but couldn't. "Gar, give me your sword," she ordered. She took it and carefully severed the wolven's jaw muscles, then used the sword to pry the jaws apart.

"It's not as bad as we feared. The beast had the scabbard in his mouth as well. Rion's leg's not even as bad as yours, Gar," she said. She made to tear the hem off the shirt she was wearing, but Rion shook his head, pointed to his own, and mimed tearing. He suspected she was naked under the shirt, and it was barely long enough as it was.

She tore the hem from his instead. "As soon as I'm done here, I'll get you both to their camp. I think it's just past these trees. Then we'll try to round up the women and girls, if we can find them."

RON cursed. The trail was clearly visible. After finding where the wolven had entered the woods, he could have followed it himself. Instead, he'd wasted time while the men had assembled and the tracker had come. He should have gone after Andra without them.

The tracks changed after a while. The tracker studied the jumble of Men's and wolven's tracks and told them Andra must have stopped fighting, and that something had dropped and the littler of the two following her had picked it up. Ron wondered what Rion had found.

They continued on. They still hadn't reached her when they heard something crashing through the brush up ahead. The men clutched their sword hilts tighter; they'd already drawn their blades before even entering the woods.

A girl burst through the trees and brush ahead of them as if running for her life. She saw them and screamed and fell back, tripping over her own feet, crashing to the ground. One of the men ran to her. "Sasha? Praise Laneth! Where's your mother?"

"Papa!" she cried, hugging him fiercely, sobbing. "I don't know! We got separated. They grabbed me. They took all of us and tied us until all the rest came back. When they came, they picked me. He came and he was dragging me to the others. And then that guard, she was truly mad! She attacked them, even with her hands tied behind her. She knocked down the one who was holding me and kicked him and I ran back to Mama."

"What happened to Andra, to the guard, to my sister?" Ron asked intently, trying not to frighten her into silence.

She looked at him in horror. "They were so angry. They ran to her, all of them. They were tearing her clothes and grabbing her and hitting her and they pushed her to the ground and… and…." She began sobbing.

Ron took off down the path the wolven had left, not caring if the others followed. He was too late to save her. Even if she lived, Andra would never be the same after such a terrible thing, and he knew her: she'd take a knife to herself. The world had been too cruel to her. He never should have let her come! They all might have died in the Pass without her, but now he wished they had. How could he live with himself, knowing he'd failed her, knowing Andra had been hurt like that?"

"WE'VE no other choice," Andra argued. She was wearing the remains of Rion's shirt about her waist now, after bandaging both his legs and his arm with strips from it. "Neither of you can walk, and someone has to go for help. It could be hours before someone finds us here, if then. It will be dark, soon. And that mother and daughter are still out there, somewhere. We need help to find them." They'd found the others, but those two had managed to truly disappear into the woods.

Rion shook his head adamantly and Gar was vocal enough for both of them. "We don't know whether we got all of them. There could still be wolven or riders or both out there," he argued.

They heard someone then, charging through the trees. Andra's sword came up as she headed for the edge of the clearing toward the sound, and Gar cursed and struggled to his feet. But it wasn't a wolven or a rider—it was Ron!

Andra lowered her blade. "Elmoth, Ron! You sounded like a wolven and rider together, you were so loud," she scolded him. Then seeing his expression she asked, "Why are you looking at me like that? I'm fine. Gar and Rion are the ones with their legs torn open." She looked past him and saw Rarnak, his expression mirroring her brother's. "Rarnak! What's gotten into the two of you?"

Rarnak was looking at her in pain and compassion and something more. He approached her slowly, as if she were a fawn who might be frightened by him. "Sasha told us what happened," he said softly, keeping his eyes focused carefully on her face.

Andra flushed darkly then, realizing how she must look, wearing nothing but Gar's and Rion's torn and bloody shirts, and understood now what they thought. "I wasn't hurt, Rarnak, Ron. Rion and Gar saved me. They're the two needing help now, not me."

Ron looked intently at her, obviously afraid she was lying to protect him.

Gar spoke up. "Honestly, Ron, she's all right. We were barely in time, but we saved her."

Ron exhaled and his features relaxed in relief. He sheathed his sword and hugged her. Andra stiffened and pulled away from him. He let her go, appearing devastated, and she glared at him angrily. "Stop looking at me like that! I'm fine! It's just—they were all over me. I don't want anyone touching me."

RION looked at her compassionately. He remembered how he'd felt when Tarrell tried to hug him after that horrible nightmare where his dead friends had almost violated him when he was bound and helpless. He'd tell her tonight. Perhaps it would help her to know someone understood.

They heard voices and footfalls. More men from the caravan entered the clearing, and Rion saw to his relief the missing girl was with them. Her clothes were intact and she appeared to be unharmed.

The men gave a glad cry, embracing their missing wives and daughter. The man holding the missing girl looked about anxiously. "Where's Sara? Where's my wife?"

Andra said. "We cut them all free and had them run while we fought the enemy. We've not found her yet."

The tracker asked the girl, whom he called Sasha, to show him where she'd last seen her mother. Then he and some of the others disappeared into the woods, following the trail, while the rest stood guard.

They came back with the missing woman a short while later, and she had a joyful, tearful reunion with her husband and daughter. The men that were with them explained she'd tripped and twisted her ankle, and they'd found her huddled under a tree. Sara had thought her daughter Sasha was dead and wouldn't believe it when they tried to tell her otherwise. Now she couldn't stop crying.

RON helped Gar back to the caravan, and Andra helped Rion. Ron was surprised to see Rion's arm about her didn't seem to upset her as his own had. Perhaps Rion reminded her enough of Van to be safe? Maybe she yet thought of him as a boy. The other men in the party kept their eyes averted from Andra, believing what Sasha had told them.

Aradon, Jonas, and Vargas were together when they emerged from the woods. They were overjoyed to see everyone had survived but were concerned for Rion, Gar, and Andra.

"Stop fussing over me!" Andra snapped. "Gar and Rion are the ones who are hurt. I only got my clothes torn. But that didn't stop me from adding to the body count. I felled eight men here and four more there, and a dozen wolven all told. I helped save your daughters and wives, so I want no pity from any of you. All I want is a bath and some clothes and a shot of oushka." She stormed over to Vargas's wagon to get her clothes. They heard her yelling at poor Ara there.

"Tell me what happened," Ron demanded, as Aradon treated Gar's leg.

"I heard Rion whistle," Gar recounted. "I barely saw him run into the woods. I'd no idea why, but I couldn't let him go alone. He was fast, and I lost sight of him, but I saw the wolven tracks and his. I finally caught up to him just outside their camp. He was hiding in the trees, watching them. There were women and girls from the caravan in their camp. They all had their hands tied behind their backs, and Andra was with them.

"I told Rion I'd fire the arrows I had left, but I only had six, and there were thirteen men and at least as many wolven. I told Rion to get to the women and girls and cut them free and have them run. Andra looked like she could fight if she were freed.

"Rion went off to do as I'd told him to. But the men were ready to start on one of the prisoners. The men were all in a group, unlacing their pants, and one of them grabbed hold of the little one, Sasha, and he started dragging her to them.

"Andra was so brave! She wouldn't let him take her, even with her hands tied behind her back. She attacked him. She drove her head into him and then kicked him in his manhood. But then the other men all attacked her. It was terrible, Ron! It happened so fast! They were all over her, hitting her, grabbing her, tearing her clothes. She felled another one, but the rest pulled her to the ground. I couldn't wait for Rion's whistle. I started firing arrows as fast as I could. I had to get them off of her before... before they really hurt her. You know how I mean. And it worked. They all came after me instead. I thought she was all right, Ron. I didn't understand she's not. I wish I knew what to say to her, but I'm afraid to even try, she's so angry."

Ron said, agonized, "Can you blame her? No man's wanted her for her whole life, and then this happens."

"I want her," Rarnak said softly. "I should have told her so before now. Now she'll think I'm only pitying her." He walked away.

Ron cursed. "She'll calm down. It might take a while, but she's strong. She'll be all right." At least he hoped she'd be.

Rion's injuries were treated next. "A fine job we're doing, guarding you," Ron said bitterly. "You're guarding us, instead. Thank you for saving Andra, Rion. And I thought you were brave in the mountains. After what you went through months ago, it's a wonder you've done all you have today. You're more of a man than most I've ever met. I only wish I could help you, as you've helped us."

Rion smiled reassuringly at him.

THE caravan was making camp for the night where it had stopped. There were dead to bury. They could hear the sounds of mourning.

Dinner was cooking. They'd have extra fires tonight. Some of the wolven might have lived, perhaps even one or two of the riders.

Rion sat in the wagon writing intently in his journal in the fading light. Audra was asleep in the wagon. The healer had given her something. They'd had to force it down her throat. She couldn't stop screaming and crying. From all they'd seen and heard and how distraught she was, they figured it must have been the wolven-riders that had attacked her village and killed her parents, that she might even have witnessed them raping and killing her mother. There was nothing Rion could do for Audra, at least not yet, but he hoped he might be able to help Andra.

Rion joined Andra by the fire. She'd bathed off in the trees using waterskins, as there was no stream nearby. They had barrels of water with them in the wagons to replenish the skins with when they weren't traveling near a stream or river. Andra smelled soapy clean; not perfumed, like most women, just clean. She had her legs pulled up to her chin with her arms wrapped around them and she was staring into the fire, huddled into a ball. There was a flask of oushka beside her, but it didn't look like she was drinking from it.

Rion held his journal out to her, the page saying simply, *Can I talk to you?*

She shook her head. "I'm not much in the mood for company, Rion."

He could see she was surprised and intrigued when he flipped to another page and showed it to her. He'd expected what her answer would be. *Please, let me help you. I know you don't think I can understand, but I'm probably the only one here who can. I've been through what you have. I was attacked like that too, when I was bound and helpless. I know what it's like. I've been too ashamed to tell anyone. It's so hard not being able to speak, and I hadn't wanted to put it on paper. Writing it makes it more real, somehow, and it was real enough before. But I wrote it all out now, for you. Please read it. Then you'll understand.*

ANDRA studied his face intently then. She could see how upset he was, and it wasn't only over her. She saw shame and fear and anger in his eyes. It was the anger that swayed her. "I'll read it," she said, although she didn't know how a man might ever know how she felt now.

Rion appeared both relieved and afraid. He turned the page.

He'd written all about a terrible dream that haunted him, but one that was somehow real, not a dream at all: it was memory for him. It had been forced upon him by the evil wizard who hunted him, who'd killed his friends Lerdon and Jathran. Rion wrote that he still didn't understand why the wizard was after him.

He'd written that Incuban had taken his voice, then taunted him, how He'd laughed at Rion as he tried to speak to stop them. He'd written every horrible, sick, twisted thing that had been done to him and almost done. There were dried tearstains on the page.

Andra looked up at Rion and saw that there were tears in his eyes now. He looked so small and vulnerable. He looked ill. Then she read the last lines.

And I've felt terrified and sick and ashamed. And angry, so angry, for being so helpless. I've lashed out at my friends, when I knew they were only trying to help me. But I've learned to get past it. I had to. Someone once told me when I was hurt to never let anyone, least of all the dead, make me feel less than I am. He told me how special I am. And you're special too, Andra. I wish you could see how much Ron and Ara and Gar and Van and Rarnak and I all love you. Please try to love yourself as much as we do.

RION blushed darkly when he saw she was reading that last part. He hoped she understood. He forced himself to look her in the eye.

She had tears in her eyes. He hadn't meant to make her cry. He felt panic building; he couldn't speak, he couldn't help. He'd wanted to help, and he'd hurt her instead.

But then she surprised him. She leaned over and hugged him, like she'd done twice before, all muscle and bone. He was stiff at first, but then he returned her hug. "You are very special, Rion. It took great courage to tell me all this. Thank you. And I love you, too. You're like another brother to me."

He relaxed then, relieved. She'd understood all of it, all he'd meant.

"I don't know if I'll ever love myself as you want me to. But maybe I can at least learn to accept myself. And I'll learn to put this behind me, too, as you have. I realize I was lucky now. We both were. It could have been so much worse, for both of us. I'll never let Him get you, Rion, I swear it," she promised and kissed him on the forehead before letting him go.

He smiled at her and headed for the wagon. He laid his bedroll out on the ground beside it. He wouldn't feel right lying in the wagon with Audra there.

It was hard for him to fall asleep. Writing it all had made the memories that much more vivid. He was afraid Incuban might come to him again. What if He'd sent the wolven-riders to find him and they'd not recognized him, because he was dressed as a guard? Or they had, and they would attack him in his dreams?

Andra came over and laid down on her bedroll beside the wagon. She fell asleep quickly. The day had taken its toll upon her. In sleep her face looked softer; the scowl she so often wore was gone.

Rion got up again. It was useless to try to sleep. He sat up drinking kakla until he couldn't keep his eyes open. He desperately hoped that if he dreamt, his dreams would be of Elanara. He wrapped his blanket tightly about himself and finally succumbed to sleep.

RION awoke before dawn, his heart hammering. He'd been dreaming. He couldn't remember it, but it had frightened him. Andra was still asleep. The whole camp was still asleep. But at least he was no more frightened than normal nightmares had ever made him. It hadn't been Incuban trying to drive him mad again. He knew he'd remember the dream if it had been that, and he'd be terrified, not just upset. But he'd wanted to dream of Elanara, and he hadn't. Then he felt suddenly uneasy as memory stirred. He had dreamt of her, but it had not been a good dream. He didn't want to remember it then. He fought not to, and won.

Rion started breakfast for his friends. It gave him something to do. He couldn't walk easily. They'd told him he would be off wagon-driver duty for a while, as would Gar. Andra had refused to be taken off the guard rotation. Ron had hoped she might rest first.

Rion reached for the pot of kakla and cursed silently, yanking his hand away. He'd forgotten the handle would be hot and hadn't used a cloth.

"Rion, you've no need to cook for us," Andra said, scolding him gently. He hadn't seen her approach. "But the kakla smells good. Thank you."

Rion looked her over carefully, trying to be discreet. She looked well rested, relaxed. She had apparently slept peacefully, at least.

She studied him just as intently, and the concern was naked on her face. "You didn't sleep well?"

He shook his head.

"Nightmares?" she asked. He nodded both *yes* and *no*.

"You mean nightmares, but normal ones, not like before?" she asked, and he nodded *yes* once more.

"If ever you have the other kind again, I want you to tell them to me. I'll not have you face that alone again," she said.

"FACE what alone?" Ron asked, walking up and sitting down by the fire.

"Never mind. Good morning, Ron. Would you like some kakla? Rion made it," Andra said.

Ron nodded and looked at her appraisingly.

She blushed. "I'm sorry I was so difficult yesterday. I'd not meant to yell. I feel better now. Rion had a talk with me last night. He helped me a lot."

Ron looked at Rion, intrigued. He must have written to her. He wouldn't be sitting here so quietly if his voice had suddenly returned. So he'd found a way to help her, even without his voice. Andra certainly looked and sounded better. Ron was relieved and even more grateful to Rion.

ANDRA brought Ara and Rarnak cups of kakla, and they thanked her. "I've something for you, also," Ara said, and he handed her a bundle of nine of her Elven arrows. "I asked Vargas to see they salvaged what they could for you. The other three were broken."

"Thank you, Ara. I'd not soon be able to replace these, and I've only the one other dozen," she said. She had the second dozen in the quiver on her back and had strung her bow. "I'm off to the perimeter, as soon as I put these safely away. We'll be moving again soon."

"I'd like to walk with you, Andra, if I may," Rarnak said.

She looked at him curiously. "All right," she said.

Rarnak headed toward the horses with her. "I want to tell you how I feel, Andra. I should have told you before. I meant to, but I didn't think I could until Rion was safe. I was afraid it might make things awkward, if you felt the same as I did, or worse, if you didn't."

Andra eyed him suspiciously.

He continued on, "And then I almost lost you, without you knowing how I felt, and that was worse."

"How do you feel about me, Rarnak?" she asked softly.

"I love you. And I hope that you might love me, too. I think you might, or might learn to. I want to marry you," Rarnak said.

"Why?" she asked bluntly.

His lip curled up in a ghost of a smile, but his voice was serious when he spoke. "Because any other woman would have said 'yes' or 'no' or asked to have time to think about it, in spite of what she truly thought or felt, but not you. You speak your mind. Mostly, I love you because you're kind and sweet, for all you try to appear otherwise. You're brave and you're smart. I admire you and respect you. You're tender and gentle. You'd make a good mother. And you're tough and strong. You can work hard. And you'd not die bearing children. You'd not turn joy to heartbreak. I want children. I want a family. Family is what truly matters. I've saved more than a little from the guard work I've done. I could work in the mill or on a farm or find something to do in Ogaten, or a City, if that's where you wanted to live. The type of work's not important to me, only that I provide for you."

Andra looked at him carefully. "I'm old for a wife. I'm twenty-four, and I'm no joy to look at. I've a fierce temper and a shrill tongue. And I've no idea how to pleasure a man in bed. I've never tried. I might be terrible at it. You've a good face, a strong body, and skills and coin and rich friends. Are you sure you'd be happy with me? That you'd not regret it later and leave me? I'd rather stay alone than that."

Rarnak touched her cheek tenderly. "You're who I want. I've never felt this way about anyone before. Twenty-four is not so old that you can't still bear children. And I like your face. It's plain, but honest. I don't cower at harsh words, but I think you'd find less call to use them with me for company. And a woman should know only her husband's touch. It's his job to teach her how to pleasure him and no other man's, and his responsibility to pleasure her as well. You need never worry that I'd not be faithful. I would never leave you. I'm not that type of man, even without knowing I'd lose Areth's grace for it."

"There's that, too," Andra said. "I've never had any use for Areth, as She's never had any for me. I follow Elmoth, as grandfather did and Ara does. Would you want me to do otherwise?"

"I hope once we're wed you might see Areth in a better light," Rarnak said sincerely. "She can be hard, even to those who follow Her faithfully, but She can also reward faith generously. I owe Her much. But Elmoth has been good to me also. He's forgiven me for not following Him, as perhaps I should for being a guard. If you were to follow only Elmoth, I'd have no cause for complaint. And our children would be raised with both and decide when they were old enough whom they would follow. There are other Gods and Goddesses besides. I've never understood intolerance in such things."

Andra looked intently at him. "I've never had a man want me or even look twice at me. I never thought one might love me. I thought my heart had grown too hard over the years for love. But I've liked you since I first met you, Rarnak. You were nice to me and wanted to help me. You talked to me. You even brought gifts to me and came to Ogaten just to see me. I was afraid to let you into my heart, afraid I'd only see myself get hurt. But my heart opened to you anyway. You need not wait for me to love you, Rarnak. I already love you." She said it as if it were a challenge, as if he might suddenly turn and flee from her.

"Will you be my wife, Andra?"

"If you're willing to have me as one, I'd be a fool to say no."

Rarnak looked reproachfully at her and her face flushed. "Yes, Rarnak. I'll marry you and gladly. Do you think in all these wagons there might be a Temple priest?"

"We'll leave the caravan earlier than we'd planned," Rarnak said. "We'll wed in Logareth, and spend a couple of nights there, in an inn. We can all use the rest. It will give Ara and me a chance to heal more before we have to ride on horseback again. I'll tell Ron."

Andra nodded, pleased he hadn't first sought Ron's permission to wed her. She was certainly of age and capable of making her own decisions. "I'll go with you."

They approached Ron. He was still at the fire, with Rion and Ara, and Gar had joined them. Ara was sitting carefully, braced against Gar's back.

"Ron, Rion? Andra and I want to stop in Logareth for a few days," Rarnak said. "We know it will mean leaving the caravan a day or so early, but we don't think you'll mind. We need to go to the Temple there and spend a few days at an inn. I've asked Andra to be my wife, and she's said yes."

Ara and Gar looked at Rarnak in surprise. But Ron's face broke into the biggest grin Andra had ever seen him wear. "In that case, of course we can!" Ron said, and then belatedly looked over at Rion for his approval.

Rion was grinning as well and nodding enthusiastically. Then Gar and Ara started smiling and congratulating them, and Andra began to smile, too.

Vargas came to the fire, appearing serious, and seemed surprised at all the smiling faces. Ron turned to him and said, "We'll be leaving the caravan at Logareth, Vargas. Rarnak and Andra are getting married there."

"Married?" He looked from one to the other and smiled. "Congratulations! That's news I needed to hear this morning."

As Andra left with Ron for guard duty, she heard Rarnak sigh behind her as he watched her go, obviously frustrated he couldn't yet stand guard beside her.

RION, who had been thinking intently since Rarnak announced his happy news and watched the couple part, wrote in his book and showed it to Rarnak. *I think you and Andra should get married quickly in Logareth and catch up with the caravan. You can ride fast enough to, and go west with them. Ron and Ara and Gar can accompany me from there.* He could not bear the thought of one of them losing the other after only having just found one another. It was bad enough the brothers risked their lives guarding him.

Rarnak shook his head. "I'll not leave you when you still need me."

Rion wrote, *I have the right to discharge you when I wish.*

Rarnak read it. "Fine. You can do so now, then. It doesn't matter. You're not paying the others. You shouldn't be paying me, either. But you can't stop me from riding my horse next to yours. I'm your friend, Rion. I won't see you hurt when I might help you."

Frustrated, Rion wrote quickly. *But you and Andra are the ones who have been hurt. I won't have her lose her chance at happiness.*

"Do you think Andra would go, either? I'll not have that battle with her. You can if you wish, once she's off duty."

Rion frowned, dismayed.

"Rion, you need us," Rarnak reasoned. "You were hurt this time, too. How would we feel if none of you returned? How happy could Andra be then? People die, Rion. You can't keep them alive when the Gods call them to their sides. You're only a Man. You've no power over life and death, much as you might wish to. None of us have. But we can do our best to help you. The Gods will see we try and might lend their aid, as well."

Rion sighed and closed his book.

"We'll be fine, Rion. Have faith. Faith in us, if you must. But try talking to Areth. She's helped you before, though you might not have realized it," Rarnak urged.

Rion couldn't pray to Areth. He didn't believe in her. He didn't believe in any of the Gods. He wished he did. He wished a lot of things: that the evil had never come; that he'd never had to leave Ardock; that Oberas and Elkrum and their other lost guards were still alive; that Talon and Aras had stayed with him; that he'd never been attacked; that there were no such things as wizards; that he could speak; that Elanara loved him and that he were an Elf, too, so that he could spend hundreds of years with her. But if his first wishes had come true, he never would have known Elanara and the other Elves, the brothers and Andra and Rarnak, Talon and Aras, or so many others. He sighed.

He asked for too much, he knew, when he'd been so fortunate already, to be alive and mostly well, to have found such friends, and for most of his friends to have lived. It was bad enough to have the wizards angered at him. He couldn't risk angering the Gods as well.

His arm hurt, and his legs, and his head was starting to throb as well. But, much as he hated being injured again and feeling so helpless, he was truly thankful he hadn't been hurt worse.

"Rion, you need to rest. You're looking ill," a fatherly voice said. It was Vargas. "Let others do the work for a change. You've more than earned a break, after what you did. We'd not have found any of the women if you hadn't followed Andra. There were too many wolven tracks. We could have spent days until we found some of the right ones, and it would have been too late for all of them. Rarnak would be in mourning now, instead of planning his wedding."

Rion sighed and nodded. He stretched out his blanket and lay down wearily, wishing he had someone to lie beside. Vargas left and Rion gathered his blanket around him, shivering. When had it gotten so cold? It felt as if his very bones were turning to ice. He pulled the blanket up around his chin. His hand was shaking from the cold. He wished Ron was lying beside him.

RION jerked awake. He was thirsty. His waterskin was in his pack beside him. But it was too great an effort to get to it, and it was so cold, as if winter had suddenly come. He shouldn't be sleeping, despite what Vargas had said. He could still do useful work, even injured. He should sit beside one of the wagon drivers. Surely there was someone he could aid, to help the caravan get under way? Except the wagon was already moving; he felt it now. He must have fallen asleep. He was so tired. Maybe he'd sleep just a little more.

RION flung the blanket off. It was so hot! It must be noon already, for the sun to be so hot. He looked at the sky, puzzled. Where was the sun? It was so cloudy he couldn't even see it. No wonder he had been so cold before! But why was he so hot now?

Was he asleep and dreaming? He didn't feel quite awake. His legs and arm and head hurt terribly.

He shivered. It was so cold without the sun. Where was his blanket?

ARADON thought it was early for the caravan to be stopping for lunch. He went to the lead wagons, to check on the wounded and talk to Vargas. Gar was sitting and shivering. He had a blanket wrapped around him. Rion was asleep, but he was shivering as well. Audra was still asleep.

Vargas greeted Aradon in relief. "I'm glad you came. I was going to come get you. Rion and Gar seem feverish to me and Audra's still asleep. Ara's gone to stretch his legs. I thought it a good idea that he not be here when you check on them. I don't think he's aware anything's wrong."

"Audra will wake soon," Aradon assured his friend. "I had to give her something strong because she was so hysterical." He put his hand to Gar's face and Rion's. "But you're right about the other two." He unwrapped Gar's bandages. "The wound looks clean, but I'll clean it again, to be sure, and I've something for the fever."

He treated Rion similarly, and spoke out of Gar's earshot, as he was still conscious and seemed at least somewhat lucid. "Gar's wound is deeper, but I'm more worried for Rion. Rion's been wounded in three places, and he's littler. He's not got Gar's strength, and he's much hotter. I'm going to ride with these two. Go tell Jonas I'll need a driver for my own wagon."

ARA hobbled up to the wagon. He'd been eager to stretch his legs, but he was concerned now, seeing Aradon's grim face, when he saw it was Gar and Rion he'd been tending. He'd gone to sleep as soon as they'd started out in the morning, with the wagon's motion, and gotten up as soon as they stopped. He'd not paid any attention to Gar and Rion. He'd thought they were sleeping too.

Aradon turned to Ara. "At least you seem to be doing well. Watch them for me. I want to check the others who were bitten and see if there are any more with fevers."

"All right," Ara said, looking worriedly from the healer to Rion and Gar. He waited anxiously for the healer's return.

A short while later Aradon came back and reported to Vargas. "We've thirteen with bites, but only six have the fever, including Rion and Gar. Rion, Larson, and Vellis seem to be the most ill, so far."

"You can help them, can't you?" Ara asked, concerned. "You cured my fever, and Rarnak's."

"I did," Aradon said gravely. "But some fevers are easier to cool than others. These are wolven bites. I know from past experience they can be particularly nasty. I'd thought they might only get the fever if the wounds were left untreated. I thought that by cleaning theirs right away, they'd be all right. There's no sign of the wounds festering, but they're ill anyway. They're running very hot, all of them. It's come upon them quickly, and their injuries have already weakened them. I'll do my best. But it wouldn't hurt for you to ask Elmoth for his aid. Jarnath won't mind."

RARNAK came back to the wagon and got a sudden chill. Ara was sitting awkwardly with Rion's hand in his lap, and Gar's, and his hand over both of theirs. He was praying. Rarnak went over to Vargas and whispered, "What's wrong. What's happened?"

Vargas seemed troubled. "It's a fever. They've both taken ill from their bites, them and four others of the thirteen who were bitten. You'd best tell Ron and Andra. Gar's not in any immediate danger, but he may yet be."

"And Rion?" Rarnak prompted when Vargas didn't mention him.

Vargas appeared grim. "Perhaps you could speak a few words to Areth for him. I was told you're a follower of Hers, and he can use the extra words on his behalf. I'd pray for him myself, but I had a falling out with Elmoth decades ago and I've not spoken to Him since. I'd do so now, for Rion, but I wouldn't want to risk bringing His anger down on Rion instead of His help." Vargas stared at the two ill men intently. "In fact, why don't you stay here and pray? I'll tell Ron and Andra."

VARGAS headed for the perimeter. Rion was so young, and Gar not that much older. Memory flooded him, of them setting Terhannon in that cold hole in the ground, the hole Vargas couldn't even help them dig, for the loss of his arm. They'd had to behead the body, to ensure Terhannon wasn't turned into a monster, but they'd buried his head with him. Vargas remembered the first of the dirt upon his young face, before he and the others had to look away. They'd shoveled the dirt blindly then.

That had been the end of their band. Oberas couldn't forgive himself, and he couldn't face the rest of them after that. And Vargas had lost his sword arm. But they no longer needed to fight. They had all the coin they'd ever wanted, more than they'd ever dreamt of. He'd opened the weapons shop with his, and Lonas and Harnel had opened inns in Athanark. Loessen had opened a stable in Thenalon. Oberas had become a trader in Ardock. It was years before any of them saw Oberas again, and they never saw Loessen again, not alive. He hadn't wanted them to. He was the one who'd had to behead Terhannon's body. He'd never forgiven them for it. The next time they saw Loessen, it was only his grave. They'd each gotten a letter, from his nephew, and gone to pay their respects. That was when they first saw Oberas again.

Vargas sighed. He'd have given every gold piece away if it could have brought Terhannon back. Losing him was worse than losing his arm. Losing him was like losing his heart. He'd been as a brother to all of them, save for Oberas, of course. He'd been as a wife to Oberas, though they'd never really understood it.

None of them had ever married. They couldn't bear the thought of having a wife or a child, someone they might love that much, who might die. They couldn't have survived that kind of pain again. Now Rarnak and Andra had just promised themselves to each other, so Elmoth found it necessary to take their friend and maybe Andra's brother from them, the insatiable, voracious bastard. As if He'd not taken enough.

Vargas hadn't told Ara all of it. He not only didn't follow Elmoth, he hated Him. He'd hated Him ever since Terhannon died. Elmoth didn't care, though. He thrived on hate as He thrived on death. He might play at being the God of Innocents, or of Warriors, but He was really the God of War, of Death, no matter that most thought Ragnar was. And to think, he'd once worshipped that treacherous, vicious, vindictive bastard. He'd once loved Him as much as Oberas had. He'd once loved Him as much as he'd loved Terhannon.

"Vargas, what's wrong? You look angry," Ron said in concern.

Vargas got control of his expression with effort. "Don't worry about me. I'm not worth the trouble. I've come to tell you about Rion and Gar. They've taken ill with fever, from their wounds. Aradon's doing all he can for them."

Ron paled at his words, and Vargas belatedly realized he'd said it the way someone does when they know "all he can" means it won't be enough. "Find Andra and tell her for me, if you would," Vargas said with a heavy sigh. "I've got to get back to my wagon. We'll be pulling out now that Aradon's tended them and the others. Four more have the fever as well."

The caravan set out, grimly this time, the weight of the dead and the dying heavily upon them.

RON came by to check on Gar and Rion again as soon as they stopped for dinner. "How are they?" he asked Aradon.

"Worse than before," the healer said, appearing visibly shaken.

Rarnak was laying a wet cloth over Rion's forehead, and Ara was taking one from Gar's face. Gar appeared to be unconscious too, now, and Ara looked frightened.

Aradon said, "I'm trying something else. I'm hoping it might make the fever break."

At that moment, a boy of perhaps ten ran up to Aradon. "Aradon, please, come quick! Papa can't breathe!"

Aradon leapt up and followed the boy. A short while later he was back again, looking grim. "Lanis is dead," he said to Vargas.

"The fever?" Ron asked, his voice haunted.

"No. He was one of the two who were badly injured but not killed outright, the ones we feared might not make it. A wolven tore his arm off and his chest took great injury as well."

Vargas sighed. "I knew we would lose people this journey, but I'd hoped there would not be so many at once or so soon. But we were just as doomed if we'd stayed in Athanark. No, we'd have been worse off. That City won't last much longer. At least we've a chance on the road. I was a fool for not leaving earlier. I'd let myself get soft. I let my instincts dull. Years ago I'd never have let it get so far."

They buried Lanis and settled in for a watchful night.

LATER that night, Ara overheard Aradon speaking softly to Vargas. "It's hopeless, Vargas. I've tried both medicines and neither has done any of them any good. A fever this hot is dangerous even in healthy men. Sometimes fevers burn themselves out on their own. But they'll not survive it, none of them will. It's only a matter of time now, waiting to see who goes first."

Ara couldn't believe Elmoth would have spared Gar from the obearn and the ogre and the poisoned blades and the claws and teeth only to let him die slowly and horribly of fever. And Rion, after all he'd been through, when they'd come so far to help him. Ara had always been pious, but now he prayed as he'd never prayed before. "Elmoth, please spare them. Tell me how I can help them. I can't just sit by and watch them die. I swear to you, if you help them, I'll... I'll... I'll build you a Temple," he said in a sudden flash of inspiration. "In Ogaten. Ogaten will become a City, now, with Gosa destroyed.

"You were right to take that City. It was an evil place. But you spared the people, most of them, the ones who deserved to live. It was the buildings that burned. You were merciful. Most people don't see that aspect of you. They don't understand you as I do.

"That's it! I'll build you a Temple, but I'll do more. I'll give every coin I ever earn to you. I'll become a priest. I'll help others understand. You could have taken my life many times, but you didn't. Now I offer it to you freely, as your servant. Only please, find some way for me to help Gar and Rion." He didn't expect an answer immediately. He knew miracles take time.

Rion moaned and Ara went to him. The cool, wet cloths were next to useless, but at least they made him feel like he was helping. Ara tripped and cursed, nearly falling. He couldn't even kick what he'd nearly fallen over; he had only the one good leg to stand on.

He scowled down at it. It was Rion's pack. No wonder it had hurt. His journal was in it. That book was massive. He placed a wet cloth over Rion's forehead. Rion was shivering violently, but his skin was burning to the touch.

Ara looked thoughtfully at the pack. In all the many days of the long months he'd seen Rion write in his journal, he'd never once gotten to see what he'd written. It would be comforting to read it now. Rion would be talking to Ara if someone else were sick, if he had his voice. He'd be trying to make Ara feel better, if he could. Perhaps if he read some of what Rion had written, he might feel better anyway.

He glanced at Rion guiltily. Perhaps he shouldn't; it was private. But he found his hands were opening the pack anyway. He'd go mad just watching them die, tending them as they did. Rion would understand.

Ara removed the protective oilskin covering from the journal. The book did not look as if the rains and the rough journey it had been subjected to had damaged it at all.

Ara began reading. The journal began when Rion was leaving Ardock. Rion wrote that Oberas had suggested he keep one, to record the trip, but Rion thought that it was so he wouldn't have time to worry. If he wrote every night and then slept and kept busy with their travels during the day, before he knew it, he'd be safely in Athanark.

That first month of entries had been so innocent. He'd been such a boy, still. Then there was a completely different passage. This page was tearstained, and the ink had smeared in more than one place.

Oberas and Elkrum are dead. Everyone is dead. Almost everyone: only Tarrell and I survived. We were attacked outside of Athanark, only half a day's journey from the safety of the City's walls. A month's journey, and only half a day away! It was horrible.

There were nearly two dozen wolven-riding bandits. They came at us out of the trees, without warning. It had been such a beautiful day. The sky had been so blue and we were all in such good spirits. The men were all talking about how they would be spending their wages. Elkrum was talking about a brothel he knew of in Athanark. He was boasting of the women there and.... He can't be dead! They can't all be! I don't want to remember. It hurts too much!

I feel a little better now. I've had a cry. I feel like such a child, crying, but I keep looking at Tarrell, and he's so pale. I fear he might be taken from me as well. It's my fault he might die. It's all my fault!

Oberas sent Tarrell into the woods with me for safety, after I was stunned in the first few moments of the attack. When I realized Tarrell was carrying me away from the danger, I tried to make him go back. I still had the sword I'd picked up and I wanted to help fight, but then I saw a wolven had followed us, that it was coming for Tarrell's back, and I yelled a warning.

Tarrell dropped me, and spun around and faced it, yelling for me to climb a tree, to get to safety. He was so brave! But it was so big and strong and fast. It slammed right into him; it just knocked him to the ground, and it bit him. It tore his sword arm to shreds. There was so much blood and it was going for his throat. I remember screaming and hacking at the beast with the sword I'd taken. I hadn't realized it then, but the blade was poisoned. The wolven shuddered and convulsed a few times and then it fell on Tarrell and finally died.

I dragged it off of Tarrell. It was so heavy! I was covered in blood, but the wolven's blood, not my own. Not like Tarrell. Then I heard voices coming near. I hadn't thought Tarrell was even conscious, but he was. He ordered me to climb the tree behind him, but I wouldn't. I wanted to help him fight them. But then he begged me. He looked as if he might cry. I couldn't bear to see that, after he'd been so brave. So I climbed. He brushed away my tracks, though he could hardly move and he raised his sword in his other hand, though he couldn't even stand. He'd have been flat on his back, if he weren't leaning against the trunk.

Two men came, and one knocked the sword out of Tarrell's hand, and knelt in front of him, and the other started looking around, as if he were looking for me. I jumped down out of the tree onto him. I meant to stab him, but he was so fast, and so strong! The blade just fell from my hand. I still don't know how he disarmed me. Then the other one grabbed me, and I saw he was injured. He'd been bitten on the arm, only I didn't realize then that it was a bite. I only saw that he was wounded, bleeding, that he had a weakness I could exploit, like Tarrell had taught me to. I hit him on his wound, as hard as I could. I could tell I hurt him. But then he hit me in the face. He knocked me out with a single blow.

When I woke up, Tarrell was lying so still and pale, I thought he was dead. And I got a better look at the man I'd attacked and realized he wasn't a Man at all: he was an Elf! A real live Elf, just like in the stories Mother used to tell me. I could have killed him! The other one, the man who hit me, he'd looked so fierce, so dangerous, but he actually apologized to me. He told me he was Talon and that the Elf was Aras, and that Tarrell was still alive and that they were there to help us."

Ara read about the rest of that day and the others in Athanark. He was fascinated. He had assumed Rion and Tarrell had known Talon and Aras for a long time, but they had not. Yet here Rion was, crossing mountain ranges to reach him, all on faith that Talon would help him! Even more surprising, Aras had scarcely known Talon for much longer than Rion had. There was a passage relating to how Aras had met Talon. Rion had written the story Aras had told him about what had happened.

Ara was surprised by the next page. There were notes in a different hand, a smooth, flowing script, and pictures as well. Such pictures! There was a portrait of Talon, done in ink, in loving detail, and one of Aras also, and underneath it read: *There. Now you need never worry that you might forget us. Even once we leave, you can still see us whenever you wish, and know that we will ever aid you when you are in need of us.*

On the next page it said:

Aras drew that for me, as if it were nothing. I've never seen such beautiful art! He is not yet gone and already I miss him terribly. But we've gotten gifts for him and Talon; wait until they see! Oops, I won't say any more. I've asked Aras to write a few more things, and I don't want to spoil the surprise. He might read this. He's as curious as I am.

Ara's heart tore anew. Rion was so joyous, so giving. Why would Elmoth take him from them so soon? He turned the page and was again surprised. Those pages were also in Aras's hand, and there were more sketches, but these were of plants. Flowers and trees and close-up views of bark, all so realistically drawn that he thought he might be able to smell the flowers and feel the rough texture of the wood. He read the paragraphs under each.

They were all plants that could be used as medicines, with the names in Common for some of them and apparently then the names in Elvish and again in phonetic Elvish.

A small note at the bottom in Rion's hand said:

These first three are the medicines Aras used to save Talon's life, when he lay dying of fever and cough. The others are plants Aras has gathered that he thought they might need.

Aras told me he couldn't have had a better teacher for healing if Jarnath himself had taught him, and he'd laughed, as if he'd said something very witty. I don't always understand his jokes, but he says Men aren't supposed to understand Elves as well as Talon and I already do, that he's bound to get into trouble for it, once his father hears about it.

I plan to learn all I can of medicines and healing, and never travel without medicine again. We did not even have bandages with us when we were attacked! I've even made sure at least one of our guards knows something about it: Lerdon. He may yet save our lives someday.

We leave tomorrow, and I've had Aras and Talon prepare a healer's kit for me, complete with instructions, just in case we might need it.

Ara stared at the page, stunned. Rion's healer's kit! He'd brought one on this journey as well! Ara put the book down and began digging through Rion's pack, his hand closing upon the kit and drawing it forth triumphantly.

His hands were shaking as he opened the kit. There were at least a dozen little oilskin pouches with drawstrings, and little scraps of paper tied to each. But the paper looked as if it had been drenched and then dried, and the ink had dyed the paper a black smear.

He cursed. The rain! The rain had done this, in the Pass. Dismayed, he carefully opened the first bag and his breath caught. There was a second scrap of paper, one that had stayed dry: the oilskin had protected it and the powder it contained. *Soforath, for pain,* it read, with instructions for use.

He found what he was looking for in the eleventh pouch he tried. *Thasheera, for fever; men call it Ghostlips. Reputable herbalists won't carry it, as the leaves and stems are deadly poison. Pale pink to pure white flowers.* <u>*Don't touch without gloves.*</u> *Dry and grind* the <u>*petals only,*</u> *one teaspoon per cup of boiling water. Drink one cup evenly spaced, four times in a single day and night. Found in rotting logs. See Aras's picture in my journal.*

Ara sealed the bag carefully, terrified he might spill it. It only looked like there were four teaspoons in it, not enough even for the six who were ill, but enough for at least one dose for the three who were most ill and for Gar. Or two doses each for Rion and Gar. Or four for Gar. Or for Rion. It had sounded from the story of Talon and Aras and the instructions that one dose would not be enough.

Blessed Elmoth! Elmoth had made him trip on the pack so he'd open it and find the healer's kit, or read the book and find it. What did Elmoth want him to do? Elmoth was merciful. He'd not provide a cure to save only one, or even two.

VARGAS approached his wagon, where Rion and Gar lay dying, wearily.

"Vargas! I need you to fetch Aradon. And we need to organize search parties. We've got to comb the woods. I'm sure there's more near here. Elmoth wouldn't give me the answer and let them die."

Vargas studied Ara in concern. He was trembling and his eyes were unnaturally bright. "Of course, Ara. Let me fetch Aradon," Vargas said. Ara had apparently caught the fever somehow as well. If even the uninjured were becoming ill, they were all doomed. Or perhaps the strain of tending to his brother and friend as they lay dying was bringing him to madness. He hurried off to find Aradon.

Vargas found Aradon, and on his way back to the wagon with him saw Ron and called him over. "Your brother's ill, Ron." He'd begun calling the brothers by their nicknames, once he realized the others did so.

"You mean Gar's worse?" Ron asked in concern.

"No, I mean Ara," Vargas said, and Ron paled. "He's either caught the fever too, or he's going mad watching Gar and Rion dying from it. Either way, we may need your help to restrain him."

THEY approached the wagon. Ron was surprised to see Rion's book open on the bed of the wagon and the contents of his pack partly dumped out as well. Just as Vargas had said, Ara was trembling, and his eyes were too bright.

"Ron! Elmoth's saved them! Rion and Aras have told me what to do! I knew Elmoth wouldn't let them die!" Ara cried excitedly.

Vargas was right. Ara sounded mad or delirious, to be speaking of Rion and Aras like that. Rion couldn't have spoken, and they'd not seen Aras in months, since Athanark.

"It's all right, Ara. You need to calm down. We're here to help you," Ron said soothingly.

"We'll need lots of men. It might not be easy to find, and they'll have to be warned about the poison," Ara said.

"Ron, what's wrong? Why are you looking at Ara like that?" Andra asked, coming from the back of the caravan.

"How's he looking at me?" Ara asked in puzzlement.

"Andra, don't get so close. Let us handle it," Ron said. He had to keep Ara talking. Vargas was circling behind him. He'd be in place in a moment.

Andra hurried forward instead of staying back. "Ara, sit down, now, and don't say another word, before they hurt you," she commanded.

Ara gaped at her openmouthed but then sat, wordlessly.

Vargas stopped his approach in surprise.

"Now, Ara, try telling us what you mean without looking like you've gone mad. I can tell it's important," Andra said.

Ara took two deep breaths and his trembling eased. "Rion's healer's kit. He has medicine for fever in it, the same kind Aras used to save Talon's life when they first met. Only there's not enough of it. But in Rion's book I've found out how to gather more. It's from a flower." He held out his hand with the little bag in it.

Ron smacked himself in the head with the palm of his hand. "Rion's kit! It's the first thing he would have done if one of us had a fever."

"What's it called, do you know?" Aradon asked, holding out his hand.

"*Thasheera*, though that's the Elven name for it. He didn't write a Common name, but the flower it's from is called Ghostlips," Ara said.

"Ghostlips! That's no cure, son. That plant's poisonous," the healer said, disappointment in his voice.

"Not the petals. Read the paper inside," Ara urged. "Aras saved Talon's life with it when he was dying of fever. I know it will work. And I've a picture here, and there's a note on where to find it. Try it on Rion and Gar first, if you doubt it."

Aradon read the note and the page in the journal. "All right. It's a chance, perhaps. I just pray it's not a false hope. Even so, we've nothing to lose by trying. Vargas, I'll need some boiling water and two cups. Then see if you can get some men to start the search. We've yet some time before sunset."

"You'll find it near here. Elmoth's done his part," Ara said confidently.

Ron looked suspiciously at Ara. "What did you mean by that, Ara?"

"That's between me and Elmoth, Ron," Ara said.

"Ara, what have you promised Him?" Ron asked fearfully. "I'll not have you take your own life in exchange for theirs."

"I've promised Elmoth my life, Ron, but not as a sacrifice. Those who do such things are misguided. I'm giving Him my life, but as His servant. I'm going to build a Temple to Him, give Him all my coin, and become a Priest. He's called to me before, but I hadn't listened. It's why He spared me from the obearn last trip and from the ogre in the Pass and the fever. I should have done so before now, Ron. Then Rion and Gar need not have suffered."

Ron kept silent. The important thing was Rion and Gar had a chance, now, and Ara wasn't throwing away his life for theirs. He might be happy as a Priest. He wouldn't back down on such a vow. He'd think Gar and Rion would die if he did.

He and Ara had spent a single month as traders, and they'd loved it, too, but now he was a guard again and Ara would be a Priest. Life never went the way you planned.

Vargas brought the men over, and Ara showed them the picture in the book and told them where to look. He warned them not to touch the stem or leaves with their bare hands. Ron and Andra and even Rarnak set out with them.

ARADON watched Rion and Gar carefully, hoping for a change, that the Ghostlips he'd given them might cause the fever to break. A change came, but not the one he'd hoped for. Rion began convulsing, his body racked with spasms.

Vargas asked fearfully, "Is it the medicine? Was it poison after all?"

Ara looked on, horrified, but Aradon shook his head. "No, it's the fever. I warned you he'd be one of the first. He's so little compared to the others, and so hot. His body can't take the strain anymore. If this keeps up much longer, his heart will stop. Ara, in my kit there's a metal flask, the one with the blue stopper. Get it. Hurry."

Ara dug in Aradon's pack and found the flask. He uncorked it and handed it to Aradon, his hand shaking.

"Vargas, force his mouth open carefully. The way he's convulsing he could bite your finger off without meaning to, or you could break his jaw," Aradon said.

Vargas forced Rion's mouth open, and Aradon poured some of the flask's contents into his open mouth. Rion choked and spit up but also swallowed.

"Keep him pinned," Aradon said urgently. The two of them battled grimly with Rion. Ara was praying, softly and rapidly, pleading, begging. With a small cry Rion went suddenly limp.

"Rion! Rion!" Ara cried out in panic.

Aradon put his ear to Rion's chest and sighed and smiled weakly. "It's all right, Ara. The convulsions have stopped, but they've not killed him, and neither have I, praise Jarnath."

Ara eyed him warily. "What was in the flask?"

"Amongst other things, Deathshead venom," Aradon said.

Ara stared at him as if he were mad. "And you were worried I would poison him!"

"I had no choice," Aradon explained. "Little and weak as he is, it might have killed him. But he was dying anyway. I needed something that would act fast. When you dilute it and drink it, it works differently than when it goes directly into your blood. It's a muscle relaxant. The snakebite kills you because your heart is a muscle, too, or so Jarnath teaches us. But this wasn't strong enough to stop his heart, just sufficient to calm the convulsions, praise Jarnath. We've bought him a little more time. Time for the other medicine to work, I hope."

ANDRA was the one to find it. There was a fallen tree, the trunk completely hollowed with rot, and inside were six large clusters of Ghostlips, like bouquets, almost. She called out to the others that she'd found it, that there were six bunches, one for each of the ill. She picked them carefully, mindful not to touch the stem or leaves with her bare hand. They made it back just before sundown, as she'd said they would. She'd been a fool for thinking Elmoth wanted her life. She served Him far better alive than with her death.

MOMENTS before the sun set below the horizon, there was a commotion at the edge of camp. Aradon wondered what new disaster was striking. But it was the search party. They told him they'd been ready to give up and turn back, but Andra insisted they could search for a few more moments and still make it back before dark, and she'd found the flowers.

Aradon started carefully preparing the petals. They gave the last two doses from Rion's kit to the other two who were most ill, now that they'd seen no ill effect upon Gar and Rion. Aradon gave the last two men doses of the fresh medicine, then some to the others, when it was time to. Then in the morning, each got another dose.

Gar's fever was the first to break. He woke up a little before lunch and complained he was famished. He couldn't understand why they were all standing around grinning from ear to ear as if he were Rarnak announcing his wedding. They gave him some broth and told him what had happened.

Aradon was concerned about Rion, though. He was still flushed, still burning, barely tossing and turning, he was so weak. Aradon hoped his fever might break next. But Sanis was next, then Fenlon. There was still no change in Rion or Larson or Vellis, the three who had it the worst, but at least the other two hadn't gone into convulsions. He hoped Rion wouldn't again. He was so weak, the convulsions would surely kill him, but the medicine that had proven effective before and might prevent them would kill him just as certainly. He feared the cure for the fever might have come too late for Rion, and perhaps for the other two, as well, though he kept his fears to himself as he gave them a fourth dose. He'd not take faith nor hope from the others.

Unfortunately, his fears were well founded. Vellis died less than an hour after they'd started the caravan back up again, after lunch. He just stopped breathing. Aradon rushed to his side, but there was nothing he could do. They buried him by the side of the road, and hope turned to despair, as the caravan resumed a deathwatch on Rion and Larson.

Larson awoke shortly after the caravan stopped for the evening, his fever gone. But joy turned quickly to horror. Aradon explained it to the brothers and Andra and Rarnak, so they'd be prepared in case Rion awoke.

"Larson was too hot for too long, though we tried to cool him down the best we could, as with the others. His memory's gone. The fever's taken it. Not his old memories. He remembers everything that happened before the fever. But he can't remember new things. Somehow the ability to make memory is gone.

"You can talk to him at length, but then if he turns his head for a moment and turns back, he'll act like he hasn't set eyes on you since before the fever. He asks the same questions, over and over again. I don't know what we'll do with him. Perhaps we'll leave him with the Temple Priests of Jarnath in Logareth. They sometimes care for the afflicted."

RON felt ill. "It would have been better for Larson had he died instead. If Rion...." He choked on his words. He couldn't even say them. The thought of Rion's curious, eager mind, always asking questions, but doomed to forever ask the same ones over and over, without even a voice to ask them with, was too terrible to even speak of.

Ara looked shaken, but said firmly, "Elmoth must have had a reason for taking Vellis and for harming Larson."

Ron lost his already frayed temper. "I've heard enough about Elmoth! Some men live, others die, and there's no point to any of it, no pattern! Praying doesn't help, sacrifices don't help! The Gods don't care about us, Ara! If there even are any Gods, if Men didn't just make Them up in desperation that there be someone bigger and stronger than they were, that might help them."

Ara launched himself at Ron, grabbing him by the neck of his shirt with his good hand and shaking him. "Don't you dare shout such blasphemy at me! It's your fault Rion's still ill! Elmoth knows the doubt in your heart! He won't heal Rion until you repent. Get on your knees and pray to Him, now!" he demanded, trying to force Ron to his knees.

Ron broke away from him, and all reason fled Ara. He fell upon Ron literally, unable to keep his balance because of his bound leg. Ara balled his good hand into a tight fist and began striking Ron in the head with it.

Vargas, Gar, and Rarnak all fought to restrain Ara, but they were afraid they'd hurt him, that they'd rebreak one of his healing bones.

It was Andra who struck him hard across the face and stunned him. Then she held his face in her hands and spoke intently to him. "Ara, this isn't what Elmoth wants. He's testing your faith, but you'll fail if you let your anger rule you, instead of your head. All the love for Him in the world won't matter to Him then. Elmoth's a soldier, and anger's the enemy of a soldier."

Ara nodded, listening, still shaking from the fight.

"You've said before Elmoth is merciful. Would he truly let Rion die to punish Ron for his lack of faith? Is that mercy?" Andra asked.

"No. No, of course not. Elmoth is merciful. He wouldn't do that," Ara said.

"And should Elmoth even care whether Ron worships him or not? He's a God, Ara. Gods don't need people. It's people who need Gods. Men are children, Ara. The Elves are right in that. We need the Gods. We need their love, their aid, their protection, the same way children need their parents. Parents love their children. Though it hurts them when they are sick or injured or no longer love them, they can still survive without them. Children can sometimes survive without their parents, though their lives are often needlessly filled with pain and emptiness and despair, instead of health and joy and love."

Ara nodded, clearly hanging onto Andra's every word.

"Ron's never been very religious, Ara. He's had reason not to find faith, as he's had reason to lose what little faith he once had. But Elmoth understands Ron, better than you could ever hope to. Elmoth still loves Ron, as a parent loves a child who hurts him, who thinks he doesn't need him. Ron needs Elmoth's love all the more for it, just as that child would. And Elmoth will still love him, even if Ron no longer thinks he wants that love."

Ara nodded again.

"So please, Ara, don't blame Ron for Rion being ill. Ron blames himself enough already. It's eating away at his heart. Ron needs your love now more than ever, Ara. Don't give him your anger instead. Don't try to hurt him when he's already hurt. You should do what Elmoth would, if Ron would only let Him. Comfort him. Show him you love him."

Ara nodded, amazed. "You should become a Temple Priest, Andra. You'd make a better one than me."

She smiled sadly. "I can't, Ara. They don't let women become Priests to Elmoth. I'm not even supposed to be worshipping him. If I ever even tried to enter one of his Temples, they'd flog me for it."

Ara looked shocked.

"But those are the Priests' rules, not the God's. I worship Elmoth anyway. It's Areth's mistake I was born a woman instead of a man, not Elmoth's," Andra said.

RARNAK held his tongue. He didn't think Areth had made a mistake, giving him Andra for a wife. He'd never loved her more than hearing her talk about Elmoth with such understanding.

RON had been listening to Andra and Ara, rubbing his jaw and testing his teeth. Two were a little loose, but he'd not lost any.

Ara approached Ron awkwardly. "I'm sorry, Ron. Please forgive me. I'd no right to say what I did, and less right to hit you," Ara apologized.

"Your words hurt more than your fist, Ara, and you hit hard," Ron accused.

Ara winced and hugged him with his good arm. "No matter what happens, it's not your fault, Ron."

Andra said, "I'm trying to accept it's not mine, for needing to be rescued."

"Nor mine, for not staying by his side," Gar said.

Ron nodded, comforted. If only Rion would wake up. If only he'd be all right. He glanced at Rion and his breath caught. Rion's eyes were open. They closed again as he watched.

Ron was at his side in an instant, gently shaking him. "Rion, open your eyes again, if you can hear me! Open your eyes."

Rion opened his eyes again slowly, as if his eyelids were almost too heavy for him to lift.

Ron felt Rion's face. It was still hot, but it didn't seem to be burning as hotly as before. He put his hand under Rion's. "Rion, I want you to tap my hand with your finger, twice, if you can understand me."

He felt two gentle taps and he hugged him.

"Do you know what happened? Do you remember the wolven? Tap twice for yes, once for no."

Rion tapped twice.

"You've been sick, Rion. Do you understand? Tap again, just like before." Ron held his breath.

There were two taps.

Rion had remembered two meant yes! "I think he's all right. Rarnak, get Aradon," Ron ordered, and Rarnak left quickly.

Aradon came and Ron explained all he'd done. Aradon sat, and began asking Rion questions. When the healer asked Rion who had first spoken to him when he awoke, and gave him choices, Rion gave the three correct taps for Ron.

"You need to try to drink something. We'll get you some meat broth. You need to build your strength again. Don't worry that you're so weak. You've been ill with a serious fever and unconscious, but you'll recover fully from it. All you need is food and rest and care, and you've plenty of friends here for all three."

Rion nodded his head, barely moving.

"Ron, you make the broth. I'll help him to eat it," Andra said, and Ron agreed.

Rion would live, and his mind was intact, his reason, his memory. Ron started the meat boiling to make the broth and then self-consciously sank to his knees and closed his eyes. The old, familiar litany ran through his head: *Mighty and merciful Elmoth, I come to You, Your humble servant Ronamark, son of Markara...* but he went no further. He felt no need to curry favor through flattery, nor introduce himself to the God. If Elmoth didn't know who he was, the prayer was pointless. He was far from humble. And he'd not said the part about being Markara's son since he was twelve and found out he wasn't. Instead, he spoke from his heart. If he were a God, that's what he would want his worshippers to do.

"Thank You, Elmoth, for saving Rion and Gar. Forgive me for my words before. And thank You for Your protection of my brothers and my sister and Rarnak, whom she loves. Ara will make a fine Priest. It's a shame Your other Priests won't let Andra become one as well. But You've found a husband for her, and happiness, when I'd never thought she might have either. Please continue to watch over my family and friends, and I'll try my best to appreciate You for it. Hameen."

Then he opened his eyes and rose and looked around. Good, no one had seen. He'd not wanted them to. Prayer was a private thing, between a man and his God. But he'd wanted to kneel, to show his respect, if not humility.

ANDRA smiled fondly at Ron from the wagon. Ara had seen too; she could tell from the joy in his eyes. She was glad Ara had had the sense not to go to Ron after he'd been praying.

Ron came by a short while later with the broth. "I let it cool a bit and put it in a bowl instead of a mug. I thought he wouldn't be up to holding it himself yet, and it would spill less if you had a spoon to feed him. It's hard to judge when to stop tilting a cup."

Rion appeared embarrassed and struggled to sit.

"Easy, Rion. You've no shortage of friends wanting to help you," Ron said, and Rion relaxed and let them lift him upright.

Andra said, "Rion was curious as to why his journal was out, and his pack unpacked, so I explained how Ara had read some of his journal and discovered the cure. He's asked that none of us read it again without his permission. He wrote to me that there are things written in it now that he should never have put to paper, that he has much to tell us when he's got his voice back, and he swears he will. It took him a long time to write those few sentences. He could scarcely hold the lead." She looked at him, concern naked on her face.

Rion pointed weakly to the bowl and Andra.

Ron laughed. "That was plain enough. He says if you'd stop scowling and start feeding him, he'll get strong again soon enough."

Rion looked like he wanted to protest Ron's interpretation of his simple gestures, but Andra smiled and reached for the spoon, and he relaxed.

Andra began feeding him. She moved the spoon too quickly on the third bite and spilled some of the broth on Rion. She cursed. "I haven't fed anyone since Van was sick when he was eight," she grumbled, embarrassed.

Rarnak had come up on them quietly and was watching. "Then you can use the practice for mothering, wife-to-be," he said, his eyes twinkling.

Andra saw that Rion appeared equally embarrassed to her, as Rarnak smiled at the expression on each of their faces.

Rion finished the broth, and Andra helped him lie down again.

RION wondered what it would be like to have a woman look at him the way Andra looked at Rarnak. He wished Elanara were the one tending to him now, that she was the one looking at him that way.

"Rion, you're going to be fine," Andra said, misreading his expression. She stroked the hair back from his eyes. "You just rest and get strong again. We'll tend to you as long as you need us to."

Rion took a deep breath, trying to relax, and closed his eyes, then let the breath out slowly. He hated being so helpless. It was bad enough that he couldn't speak. Now he could scarcely move, worse than poor Ara, trapped in his bandages. Rion listened quietly to the sounds of the camp around him.

"How's he doing, Andra?" Rion heard Ron ask in a concerned voice.

"He's fine, Ron. He's only sleeping. His body's been through much," Andra assured him.

"Andra, what you said before, about Elmoth, really made me think. I apologized to Him. I wanted to thank you. I don't think I've told you nearly enough how special you are. I'm so glad you're my sister. I'm so happy for you, that you might find happiness with Rarnak," Ron said sincerely.

"Oh, Ron! You can be so sweet. I hope someday you'll find happiness, too," Andra said.

Rion drifted off to sleep, pleased to hear Ron echo what he'd said to Andra before.

THE days passed slowly for Rion as he healed from the fever and the wolven bites. Yet it seemed they were in Logareth all too soon, saying good-bye to their friends in the caravan. Rion was ashamed to feel tears in his eyes as he watched the wagons pull away, as he caught his last glimpse of Vargas, until he saw Gar's face and Andra's. Their eyes held tears as well.

But Rion couldn't stay sad for long. He had fond memories of Logareth, and he was pleased to see that the City was much as he remembered it. The taint of war had touched it: it was more crowded than it had been, and there was a certain tension in the air, but the flood of refugees that had overwhelmed Athanark had yet to reach here, or perhaps they had already come and continued onward.

They went to the same inn they'd stayed at the last time, the Weary Traveler, and Gar greeted the stable master, Paran, by name. Paran remembered him, and the two were soon deep in a discussion of horses.

Ron said, smiling, "We'll get the rooms, Gar. We'll be back in a while for you," and Gar absently nodded.

Rarnak asked for a room for him and Andra to share, and Ron asked for one for the rest of them.

"Next to each other?" the innkeeper asked.

Andra and Ron both cried, "No!" with equal vehemence. Andra had experience now with how thin inn walls could be, and Ron equally had no desire to hear Rarnak deflowering his sister.

They collected Gar and headed out. "Paran told me who to get the three horses we need from," Gar said. "He has a friend on Remis Road with a stable. Paran says he's got the best horseflesh in the City, and if we use his name, we'll get a fair price without having to haggle half the day for it."

Ron said, "Good. We'll go tomorrow, then. Today's the wedding," and Gar nodded.

ANDRA had thought they'd be going straight to the Temple and was surprised when Rarnak instead led them to the Market. "What are we doing here?" she asked.

"We've not the time to have a dress made for you, but we can find one ready-made here. Then we'll get the shoes and the ribbons for your hair, and I'll buy my clothes, and we'll go back to the inn and bathe and change. Or did you think to get married dressed in the same dirty and sweat-stained man's clothes you've been wearing?"

Andra looked sheepish, and he knew then that she had.

A long time later, they were no closer to buying a dress for her than they had been before, and Andra's face had taken on the panicked look of a deer who's seen the hunter and knows it can't leap away fast enough before the arrow strikes. Gar and Ara and Ron were trying to help, Rarnak knew, but Andra looked like she was either going to start screaming at them or, worse, burst into tears. Rarnak convinced them they'd be a better help if they went to the stables Paran had told them of and bought their horses instead, that they'd meet back at the inn after they were done. Rion had not given Andra any suggestions, though he had searched meticulously though the stock at each stall they entered.

"They're all so hideously bright and frilly and pretty! How can I wear something like that? I'd look like a toad stuck in a crystal vase," she moaned.

At that moment a grin of delight lit Rion's face, as he pulled a dress off the rack and showed it to Andra. It was of a simple cut, the color of fresh milk before the cream settles out, with long sleeves with only a hint of lace at the cuffs, and a high neckline. The skirt hung straight down to the ankles, without pleats or petticoats.

Andra studied it critically. "I like it," she finally admitted, to Rarnak's incredible relief.

Rarnak asked the price.

"Fifteen gold," the proprietor said, reading the expression on Rarnak's face and knowing he'd pay any price for it.

Rion was busy writing and handed his book to the proprietor when he finished. The shopkeeper read it and looked at Rion, surprised. "How does a mute swordsman come to know so much about cloth and dressmaking?" he asked.

Rion wrote more, and he read and nodded.

"All right, then. Eight gold it is. I shudder to think what you might have talked me down to had you the voice for it," he said, smiling, and Rion grinned. The merchant gave them a matching ribbon for her hair. Rion paid the merchant, over Rarnak's and Andra's objections.

Rion wrote, *Consider it a wedding gift, for until we are back in Ogaten, it would not be practical to get you another.*

They thanked him.

The shoes proved to be less of a struggle, as did Rarnak's clothes.

They returned to the inn and Rarnak took his bath in Rion and the brothers' room and Andra took hers in the room they'd later share.

There was a tentative knock on their door, and Rarnak opened it. He stood staring at Andra. Rion stared too and then grinned. Andra looked radiant—not beautiful, but wonderful, softer than she ever had.

"You look beautiful," Andra said to Rarnak. "Handsome's not a pretty enough word for you in those clothes. Don't even tell me how I look. I don't want you to have to start our marriage off with lies."

"You look wonderful, Andra, and I have every right to tell you so," Rarnak said.

She blushed then and smiled. Her brothers came back from the stable and were suitably impressed.

"Rion found the dress. He bought it for me," Andra said.

"Well, then, as you both appear to be ready, if you'll give us a few moments, you'll have a four swordsman escort," Ron said. Ara had acquired a crutch for the walk to the Temple.

"We were lucky as well," Ara said. "We found three solid mounts. Gar's friend saved us coin and time. They only cost us seventy-five gold for all three, when I'd expected to pay at least ninety."

They left a short while later, Ron and Gar in front of Rarnak, with Andra, and Rion and Ara behind, as if they were protecting a Lord and his Lady. It was a long walk to the Temple of Areth, and a slow one, at Ara's hobbling pace.

RION looked up at the Temple of Areth curiously. It was a lot different than the one in Gosa. He wondered how different it would be inside.

The six of them entered. An Acolyte came toward them, and Rarnak reminded them to surrender their swords to him. Rion could see the brothers felt odd doing so. No one ever disarmed in the Temple of Elmoth; even the Acolytes and the Priest bore conspicuous arms.

Rarnak told the Acolyte that they were there to be married. The Acolyte nodded, as if he'd guessed as much by the way they were dressed and their guards. Rarnak handed him forty gold, which he accepted with thanks.

Rarnak had explained to the others that a wedding was one of the rare times Areth's Temple expected an offering of coin, rather than goods. The amount could be as small as a single copper, for those who could not pay more; however, it was a commonly held belief that the higher the amount given, the more blessed the marriage would be. Rarnak had given half the coin he had, to do all he could to ensure his marriage would be a joyous and fruitful one. He'd been concerned he might not have been able to give so much, because he had needed to buy a new horse, but Rion had made it clear before they arrived that he was paying for all three horses, since they'd lost theirs in service to him, and they'd not been able to dissuade him.

The Acolyte led them before the Priest. Rarnak and Andra held hands as he began the simple ceremony.

Rion thought it was beautiful. He could see why even those who worshipped Gods with Temples that had Priests who would consent to perform such ceremonies might come here instead. It was one of the few instances where there was no question of the propriety of doing so. People had been wed on the altar to Areth for thousands of years.

When the Priest spoke the final blessing, Rarnak and Andra kissed. Rion turned his face from them, blushing hotly. Kisses such as that one should only be made in private. He was surprised at the two of them.

As they were leaving, Rarnak looked embarrassed at the looks they gave him. "I forgot to mention the part about the kiss. You're supposed to put as much passion into it as you can muster, to please the Goddess and to inspire others who are watching as well."

"You might at least have warned me, Rarnak!" Andra complained breathlessly. "Whose brilliant idea was it to get a room at an inn so far from the Temple, anyway?" she asked, gazing at Rarnak with such passion that Rion blushed even more darkly.

Ara said, "Just remember, we said three days, so don't be surprised when you hear us knock on the morning of the fourth day. We'll make sure the innkeeper knows to bring your meals to your room, so you don't starve."

It was Andra's turn to blush then.

"I've never seen you look so lovely, Andra," Gar said spontaneously. Andra looked like she was about to snap at him when she realized he wasn't teasing her as well. He truly meant it.

"Thank you, Gar. It's nice to know that three of the four of you can be sweet to me," Andra said.

Ara started to protest until he realized she was merely teasing him back.

They saw the happy couple safely back to the inn, as Rarnak had not worn his sword to the ceremony. Then Ron said, "Well, we've three days with no duties. The usual rules apply: no one goes anywhere without a partner." He turned to Rion. "Doing so has seen us safely through a number of tight spots, so don't feel it's for your sake."

Rion nodded.

Ara said, "Well, I've business at the Temple to Elmoth, if anyone would care to accompany me."

Rion nodded eagerly. He'd never been to a Temple to Elmoth before. He felt he ought to go, now that he was a swordsman.

Ara smiled at Rion.

Ron appeared pensive and turned to Gar. "Would you mind going as well?" he asked Gar.

Rion's face fell at the realization that Ron didn't trust him to watch Ara's back, with Ara too hurt to fight himself. But to Rion's chagrin, Ron continued, "I'd like to go too. I want to make an offering, and I don't want you wandering about the City alone." Rion felt bad for doubting Ron's trust in him.

Gar said, "Of course. I feel I should, after surviving the bites and the fever. Elmoth had a hand it that, I'm sure of it."

Rion indicated he wanted Ron's hand and wrote with his finger upon it, *JARNATH TOO.*

Ron nodded. "You're right. We should all offer to Jarnath as well, for the healing. Let's go to a weapons shop first and get the offering for Elmoth, though. We can all chip in for it."

Rion got to see Ron's and Ara's haggling skills for weapons firsthand this time and was as impressed as Tarrell had been by them. He realized with a sudden pang he'd not even thought of Tarrell since the wolven attack, not even when checking into the inn they'd stayed at together the last time he was here. Thinking about him now, he missed him fiercely. He hoped Tarrell was happy and safe. Talia might even be pregnant by now. He wondered if he'd ever get a chance to see the baby, or even to see Tarrell again.

"Rion, are you all right?" Ron asked, gently, and Rion nodded and tried to smile.

Ron put his hand on Rion's shoulder. "That's the problem with idleness. It gives you too much time to think, doesn't it?"

Rion had been idle ever since the fever. He had thought he might never feel well and strong again. But at least he'd had his journal. He'd recorded all of their journey in it, everything he hadn't had time to write about before. He had been relieved when he'd asked

Ara what parts he'd read, and Ara told him. He'd not read anything about the wizards or the terrible dream, the things he needed to have his voice back for, to try to explain.

Then they were at the Temple of Elmoth, and he pushed his dark thoughts aside. The building was solid stone. It looked strong as a fortress, yet it was as beautifully detailed as a Palace. They climbed the long flight of stone stairs and entered. There were weapons everywhere, on the walls, on the worshippers, and on the Acolytes. There were oil lamps instead of candles lighting the inside, save for the candles upon the altar. Elmoth's Temple was far more rich than Areth's, to be able to afford the oil for so many lamps.

Ron laid their offering at the foot of the altar. It was a beautifully crafted blade, and the sheath was of well-tooled leather. Then Ron and Gar knelt. Ara bowed his head, as he could not yet kneel. Rion saw that the other worshippers were looking at Ara in approval and some in admiration. Rion realized it was for Ara being so bandaged, yet still being on his feet, with a sword by his side. Rion knelt too. They all prayed silently, and Rion joined them.

Ara finished first. Rion guessed that Ron and Gar had much more to say to the God this time. Ara seemed more interested in speaking with one of the Acolytes. He hobbled over to one and began talking to him in hushed tones. Their discussion became quite animated. Ara was apparently being very persistent about something. Finally the Acolyte signaled him to follow, and he escorted him to the Temple Priest. Rion wondered what was going on.

PRIEST Mertan listened to Acolyte Petros and then dismissed him and turned to Ara. "Acolyte Petros has explained to you that, in order to become a Priest, you must enter the God's service first as an Initiate, and that Initiates must be between the ages of ten and twelve. There have been few exceptions to this requirement in the history of the Temple, and never for one as old as you. You could not hope to ever reach Priest. You must first be an Initiate, then a Novice, then an Acolyte. Each step takes years of devotion. Even so, few Acolytes ever rise to the priesthood."

"But I must at least try," Ara argued. "I swore to Elmoth that if he would help me to heal my brother and my friend, I would build a Temple for Him, that I would give Him all my coin, and that I would become a Priest. I cannot go back on such a promise."

"Such a pledge is certainly not something to be forgotten," Priest Mertan conceded. "Come. We will speak at length in the Sanctum. I must learn all I can of you, to determine how best to advise you."

Ara followed him eagerly.

A WHILE later, Ron and Gar looked up from their devotions at almost the same time. "Where's Ara gone off to?" Ron asked, glancing about.

Rion tapped him on the arm to get his attention and then mimed him walking and pointed to the altar. Ron looked at him puzzled. "But Rion, he's not there."

Rion nodded, *Yes,* and mimed a door opening with his hand, and then Ara going inside.

Ron appeared perplexed. "Inside? But he can't have. Only the Temple brothers are allowed to enter the inner areas of the Temple."

Rion asked for his hand and wrote, *PRIEST,* on it, wishing he'd had the sense to bring his journal and lead. He'd not thought he'd have a need of it in the Temple.

"He went with the Priest? But wh—ah, of course. He'd need to talk to the Priest. He's finding out what he needs to do to fulfill his pledge to Elmoth, to become a Priest himself."

Gar asked in astonishment, "To what?"

"Not so loud, Gar. You're still in Elmoth's House," Ron scolded. Then he told them in hushed tones about Ara's pledge. Seeing Rion's expression of shock and dismay, Ron said, "Rion, don't look like that. Ara's always loved Elmoth, more than any of us. You needn't feel guilty about this. He'd make a fine priest. He'd be happy as one."

Rion pointed at him and then at his purse.

"Yes, I know we'd planned to do otherwise. We'd thought to be traders now. But Elmoth had other plans for us. Perhaps someday I'll get to be a trader again, perhaps not. For now, I'm a guard. I've trained almost my whole life to be one, even though I thought at one time I'd never leave the River, that I'd never go further than Ogaten. Who's to say what the next months or years might bring? Anyway, Ara might be a while. We'd best make ourselves comfortable."

Quite a while later Ara emerged, looking elated. Then he saw them and his expression became sheepish. "I'm sorry. I hadn't realized that would take as long as it did. I'd not realized quite what I was promising when I made my pledge. It's not an easy thing to get the Temple to bend its rules. I hadn't realized how strict they were about ages. But Priest Mertan told me what I need to do. After the War, I need to go to Thenalon and obtain special dispensation from the High-Priest. I have a letter of recommendation from Priest Mertan that I'm to show to him. Then, once we return to Ogaten, I'll be off to Maraden. They've a Temple there where I can begin my service."

"Ron told us what you did for us, Ara. We'd no idea. Are you sure this is what you want?" Gar asked.

Ara smiled at him, his eyes shining with joy. "I should have done it long ago, Gar. I'm only sorry I was so deaf to Elmoth that He had to resort to such extreme measures to get me to listen. I'd never meant to have you or Rion suffer for me like that."

Gar said, "I'll not have you believing that, Ara. Elmoth must have had reasons of His own for what happened. I can more believe we'd not had true hardship in our family since Mother died, other than our scare in the Gelthor Pass, that something bad had to happen. It's the nature of things. Perhaps it's that Andra was fated to suffer and die, but Rion and I saved her. Yet still, someone had to suffer, so the God chose us to suffer in her place. Since there was two of us, we were hurt less than she would have been. We healed, we lived. I'd much rather have had the fever than had her so hurt, than to have lost her. I'd have been willing to lose much more to see her safe. I'm thankful the God was satisfied with so little."

Ron said. "It does my heart good to hear you speak of her so fondly now, Gar. Come. Elmoth's not the only one we've to be thankful to, for Their healing. We've thanks to give to Jarnath as well."

They exited the Temple to Elmoth and walked a single block to the Temple to Jarnath. Ron again gave their joint offering. This time it was twenty gold. The Acolyte who accepted it was surprised. It was extremely generous. "We don't often see swordsmen in here. If you're seeking healing…." he began, looking at Ara.

Ron said, "No. We're not asking the God for anything. We're thanking Him for what He's already done. He helped Elmoth heal my brother Gar and our friend Rion from fever. In fact, He's helped heal each of us many times on this trip. We owe Him much. Ara has already been seen to by a healer. His bones are knitting well."

The Acolyte smiled at them. "Thank you for your generous offering. May Jarnath continue to watch over you, but may you have less need of His services in the future," he said and blessed them all. The four of them offered Jarnath a prayer of thanks. Then they headed back into the street.

"What next?" Gar asked.

"I know what I'd like to be doing next, were I not so injured," Ara said wistfully.

Ron eyed him appraisingly. "I didn't know that Aradon had bandaged that as well. Were it intact, I know you'd not let a few broken bones stop you."

Ara looked at Ron in surprise. "I thought you didn't approve."

"Just because I don't indulge doesn't mean you and Gar shouldn't. You're grown men. You know the potential consequences. I trust you'll be as careful as you can be. Rion, you can go with them, if you've a mind to. You can drop me off at the inn. I'll not leave before you return to it."

Rion shook his head, blushing. He wouldn't feel right going to a whorehouse, not after all that had happened with Van and Liana, and Rarnak and Talia.

Ara stared intently at Ron. "You're sure it's all right?"

"Go," Ron said. "But for pity's sake, don't fall in love while you're there."

Gar grinned and they headed off, Ara moving surprisingly swiftly with his crutch.

"All right, Rion, where to?" Ron asked.

Rion mimed eating, and Ron agreed.

They chose an inn near the Temple, instead of heading all the way back to their own. Rion paid for his meal and eyed his purse woefully. Normally, were his purse so lean, he'd replenish it from his true purse. But he'd only brought the hundred gold, and between what little he'd spent in the towns to the west and in Athanark, and the coin for the dress and the horses here, he'd spent almost all of it. He realized with a sinking feeling that he'd not yet paid Ron for his share of the offerings, that he'd already spent more than he had. Nor had he paid coin toward the room they shared. He stared at his plate. He felt terrible. He'd completely lost his appetite.

Ron guessed the problem. "Rion, we told you before, you've no need to pay for Andra's and Rarnak's horses. None of us are poor. You must let us share the expenses."

Rion shook his head emphatically.

"And people tell me I'm thickheaded," Ron grumbled, and Rion smiled affectionately at him.

"That's better. Now, I want you to eat. If you insist, once we're back in Ogaten, after your voice has been healed, you can pay me back for anything you might feel you owe me. But I'll not have you worry about it. I'll not add to the burdens you're already carrying. You're family, Rion. You're like a brother to all of us. Family does for each other. That's what family is all about. There's nothing more important than family."

Rion's eyes lit with joy at hearing Ron say so, and he found his appetite had returned. He began eating enthusiastically. Once they were done, they took some time to explore the City a bit, before heading back.

When they returned to their inn, they found Gar and Ara there, appearing very relaxed and happy.

Gar said, "I could get used to this: lounging about, eating, wenching. We've been working entirely too hard these past years."

Ara agreed, yawning and stretching lazily.

"Don't get any such ideas," Ron said. "We've only three days of this, so enjoy them while you can."

Gar finished his oushka with a contented sigh.

"Come, Rion, I'll show you your new horse," Gar said.

Rion swallowed and nodded without enthusiasm. He followed Gar to the stables, with the others trailing along behind. "You'll need to practice riding him, not only to get used to him, but to get used to using a saddle and bridle."

Rion eyed his new mount critically. He was a handsome animal. He petted him. He felt like a horse, not a rabbit, as Seafoam had.

"Why don't you mount him?" Gar suggested.

Rion put his foot in the stirrup and swung his leg over. The saddle felt huge and awkward between his legs. He couldn't even tell he was on a horse; it felt more like he was sitting in a chair. He held the reins uncertainly. When he'd ridden double before, Rarnak and then Ron had held the reins for him.

"Here, Rion, like this," Gar said. "There, that's better. Now, to get him to go, you move the reins like this and squeeze with your legs." Rion tried it. The horse moved forward.

"To stop him, you pull on the reins. No, not like that, together. The other way is to turn left. And if you pull like this, he'll go right. That's about all there is to it, the basics at least. We'll take this one step at a time. Why don't you ride him around the stable yard? Oh, and his name is Nutmeg, for his color."

Rion practiced riding. He felt terribly clumsy, as if he'd not spent the past weeks on horseback. He was incredibly frustrated and feared he might burst into tears at any moment.

"How about that's it for riding lessons today, Gar?" Ron suggested, apparently sensing his mood. "Remember, we've got three days here. They'll have plenty of time to get used to each other. What say you and I go to the Market, Rion? Neither of us are traders, now, yet still I find I am curious as to what is selling well here." Rion nodded his agreement in relief. "Also, I need to replace my bow. I'll not see us leave here poorly armed."

Rion was cheered by the trip, as he was sure Ron had intended. Ron found a new bow, which he bargained skillfully for, and they spent much of the rest of the day in the Market.

THE three days passed with surprising speed. True to Ara's prediction, they didn't see a sign of Andra or Rarnak for the entire time.

Ron, Ara, Gar, and Rion stood outside their door the morning of the fourth day. Gar said, "I say we draw lots."

Ron shook his head. "Let Ara do it. He's wounded already. She'll not hurt him."

Ara shook his head. "It's the youngest who should."

Rion walked to the door and knocked.

"I meant Gar, Rion. Careful. Her bark's not less painful than her bite."

The door opened, and Andra smiled at Rion. "Good morning, Rion. All set? Rarnak, they're ready," she said, calling over her shoulder.

She was back in her man's clothes. Somehow they didn't seem to fit her as well as they had before. She had a softer edge to her now. They'd never seen her so happy.

They left the City, Rion, Andra, and Rarnak getting used to their new mounts as they went. Andra and Rarnak smiled at each other often as they rode. The days passed quickly as they headed north and then east. They were so near their goal now.

Chapter 8
The Watchtower

RION knew that, now that they were alone on the Western Road and heading due east, they might be in greater danger again. They were making far better time traveling on horseback. Before, their speed had been restricted to that of the slowest wagon. Still, neither Ara nor Rarnak would be able to ride as quickly or for as long as the rest of them. Or fight as well. At least he and Gar were healed well enough both to ride and fight, though riding was still an awkward process for Rion.

Rion found himself looking upward often, both for signs of their friendly eagle and for the Enemy's chimaera, but he saw neither. They were drawing ever nearer to the mountains in the east, the Fromer Mountains, with each day's journey.

RION was feeling increasingly anxious, though there was no rational reason for it. They had finally reached the Fromer Mountains and had discovered a welcoming stream running through the woods at the foot of the mountain, near the Pass they sought. They had begun setting up camp for the night, though they had yet to light their campfire. Andra and Rarnak were out gathering firewood. Rion was eager for the warm glow of the fire. Though the sun had not yet fully set, it seemed especially dark tonight and eerily quiet. Fortunately, they'd seen no sign of either obearn or ogres yet, but a pall of danger, of nameless dread, began settling over Rion's heart.

He tried to convince himself he was safe. Their long journey was nearly over. They would find the Watchtower on the morrow. Soon he would see Talon again; soon he might have his voice restored. But despite Eladar's letter, knowing that he would be seeing Hunter again frightened him. He could not forget the malevolent look upon his face in the dream that was not a dream. Memory of it still burned as brightly as if it had happened the past night, instead of many weeks ago.

He also did not trust Jargas, nor Hunter's wife, Jarina. He still could not believe that Hunter might have married—especially so quickly—of his own free will. And they'd been planning to attack Talon, he was sure of it. Was Talon alive or dead, free or prisoner? Eladar's note had said Talon would help him, so he must be all right, but still, Rion had doubts.

Darker thoughts began to intrude upon his reflections, and he felt a sudden chill. What if the letter wasn't from Eladar at all? He didn't know what Eladar's writing looked like. What if the letter itself had been a trick of the Enemy? What if the fight with the chimaera was to make him trust the eagle? What if that was why they had not been attacked since then? Surely an Enemy so powerful and dangerous would not be frustrated so easily! Had they really eluded Him? Or had He been patiently watching their progress toward Him, enjoying each struggle, each battle? Why had the dreams stopped?

Rion felt a terrible sense of foreboding. The letter had sounded like Eladar, but Rion realized he had not questioned it as he should have because he had wanted it to be from him: the alternative was too horrifying.

At the sound of approaching footsteps from beyond the circle of their camp, Rion's heart almost stopped, and he began fumbling for the hilt of his sword, until he realized to his relief that it was merely Andra and Rarnak returning with the firewood they had gathered. They piled it beside the ring of stones Gar had laid for the fire and began arranging pieces of wood and kindling and tinder within the circle, their hands brushing often as they worked in quiet camaraderie.

"From what Swiftsong told us, we should find the trail marker sometime later tomorrow afternoon or early evening, on the right, within the Pass," Ron said, echoing Rion's earlier thoughts. "We might run into their sentries at any point, especially as we draw nearer, but we all know what to say."

The others appeared eager to be so close to their goal, but Rion could not share their enthusiasm, as the night grew darker with every passing moment. He dug into his pack for his journal and lead, and was shocked upon opening his book to discover he could yet see the pages easily, in the fading light of the setting sun, even without the light of a fire. It had seemed as dark as midnight to him.

Rion began writing quickly. He had to share his fears with the others. The thought that they'd all followed him so blindly into such potential danger was too chilling to bear. The thought that those things from the dream might be lying in wait for them close by was terrifying. Lerdon was safely dead and buried, but there would be Jathran and others. Thousands of others: every person the Enemy killed could be turned into one of His servants.

Why hadn't he thought it might be a trick before? Had the Enemy kept him from questioning it? Or was the Enemy attacking him now, somehow? Was He invading Rion's mind even while he was awake? Were they truly close to friends, to help? Was Incuban trying to make them turn back because of it? Which way did the danger lie?

RON was glad the journey was almost done. He was proud of Gar and Ara. After years of strife with their sister, they seemed to have grown as close to Andra as he was. He was especially proud of Andra. She'd truly proven herself on this journey. He was pleased that her marriage to Rarnak hadn't affected her work. He'd assigned them both to guard duty together more than once and then watched them surreptitiously to ensure they'd done their duty properly. Each time they'd remained alert and focused, and not distracted each other from the job at hand.

He wished his sister was safely back at the mill, or better still, in Ogaten with her new husband. She deserved her chance at happiness. But even Ogaten wasn't safe. Nowhere would be safe until the Enemy had been defeated.

Rion caught his eye; their young friend was scribbling furiously in his book. Something was upsetting him. Ron circled around and approached quietly from behind and began reading over his shoulder in concern, while Rion was still writing, not wanting to interrupt him but eager to find out what was the matter, so he could help him.

He swore silently and began peering into the woods around them, though Ara and Gar were both already on guard. He saw Andra was about to light the fire and realized that, if Rion's fears were founded, the last thing they wanted to do was announce their presence with a fire. "Andra, wait. We might not want a fire tonight."

Rion jumped. He'd been so intent writing, he must not have realized Ron had come up behind him. "Easy, Rion, it's only me. Finish your thought, and then we'll alert the others. We need to talk this through."

Rion nodded, swallowed, and wrote two more sentences, then handed the book to Ron.

Ron got everyone's attention, but ensured Gar and Ara kept an eye out for trouble as he read Rion's fears to them all in a muted voice, loud enough for his two brothers on watch to hear, but not his usual carrying tone.

Andra swore, and Rion's eyes widened at some of the words she used.

Ron was grim. "If it is the Enemy, He's done His job. We're here. We've almost walked right into it."

"What now?" Andra asked. "We turn back, after all we've gone through to come here? Like Rion says, the Enemy might be wanting us to do just that."

Rarnak said, "No, we don't turn back. But we don't go forward, either, at least not all of us. Three of us go, and two others stay here with Rion. Ara and Andra are the ones who should stay with him. Ara shouldn't be put into danger yet. He's not up to a battle, with the severity of the injuries he had. Andra can defend herself well enough for all three of them. With her bow, nothing could get close enough to harm them."

Andra scoffed at his plan with a snort. "What, and let you ride into battle with a broken arm only newly healed? No. I'll not hear of it."

"Gar and I will go," Ron said in a tone that settled the matter. "If we don't return or if we do, but you see there's something wrong about us, flee through the trees on horseback, avoiding the Road until you're far from here, and keep careful watch on the sky for chimaera and that eagle, both. We'll head out tomorrow morning. But before we go, I've an idea as to how you might be safer once we've gone. With men like Hunter working with them, I want to be sure you're as hard to find as possible."

JARINA looked at Farad in concern. He was staring down at his plate but not looking at the food upon it. It was late for lunch, only just before the first shift would begin eating their dinner. She'd been relieved when she'd finally been able to drag her husband to the Dining Hall for it; she should have realized that didn't mean he was going to eat. "Starving yourself will not make them come any faster, Faradan," Jarina said, letting her frustration show. "You are already far too thin. You will soon lose your strength, your very health, if you continue this way."

Farad looked up at her, agitated, almost distraught. "They should have reached us by now, if they were going to make it at all. I've flown in Quickwing over every City and farm and Road and trail between here and Gosa. I searched the marshes and back and forth over the Gelthor Pass. They're not there, they're not anywhere! I know that Incuban would taunt me if He'd captured them, but there are other things that might have happened to them: bandits, snakes, illness, obearn, ogres, wolven. Have I brought Rion and his friends to their deaths, when I sought to protect him?"

The alarm sounded and Farad was on his feet and running to the War Room before the second bell began to clang, Jarina only steps behind him. "What is it, what's happened?" Farad asked Lunahr.

"A party of two horsemen has just started up the trail toward the Watchtower," Lunahr said, but there was worry in his eyes, not excitement.

"Horsemen? An Elf and a boy? Or a Man in guardsman's livery? Is there a boy?" Farad asked in a rush.

Lunahr shook his head. "I'm sorry, Farad. They are only Men: no uniformed guards, no Elves, and no boy. We're hoping it's only hunters or trappers or travelers and that they don't come too far up the trail. We don't want to hurt them, but we can't let them come too near us. They're armed: they've got swords and bows. Renard told Aramis they smell alive, but he's keeping watch over them and hasn't revealed himself to them. We're going to try to scare them off. It would be easier if it was dark.

"If they don't scare easily, we might have to try the King's Voice on them, to make them ride in the other direction for a day or two. Maybe if they suspect something, they'll believe it was Elves who got them turned around."

Lunahr winced and Jarina shared his pain. Farad had been so hopeful. She knew Lunahr hated to be the one to tell him it wasn't Rion. He was as worried about Farad as she was. She knew his young cousin had hoped that by being linked to Farad, he could help him sometimes too, but Farad didn't want to be helped.

"WE'RE being followed," Gar said softly to Ron in Thenalonese, bending over the shoulder of his horse, pretending to adjust one of the straps on the bridle.

"The fox? I've seen it. A fox shouldn't stalk horses. It might be one of theirs, like the eagle," Ron muttered back in the same tongue, aware someone might well be in hiding, listening, though they'd neither seen nor heard anyone.

"I could wound it with an arrow. We could take it prisoner, force their hand," Gar suggested.

"We're far enough from the others, and I'm tired of waiting. Let's pretend to hunt and then do it," Ron agreed. Then louder, in Common, he said, "If we plan to have lunch, we'd best get to work now. This part of the woods certainly looks promising enough, and there's no telling what kind of game there will be further up ahead."

Ron unslung his bow, which was already strung. He held an arrow but didn't nock it as he scanned the treetops. "There must be squirrels in trees like these."

Gar mirrored his older brother's actions, his head tilted up even as he sighted the fox out of the corner of his eye. It had stopped and was watching them intently. "I see one," he said, pointing his bow up and to the right at an imaginary squirrel as he nocked an arrow. Then, in one smooth motion, he lowered it, spun, and fired. The fox had been caught completely off guard. It yipped and thrashed, its right foreleg pinned neatly to the tree beside it.

Ron was already out of his saddle and running to it, bedroll in hand. He quickly unrolled his blanket and tossed it over the fox, confining it.

Gar ran over as Ron adjusted the blanket to only cover its head. "You tie its other three legs and then we'll tie its muzzle shut," he suggested.

The fox was still yipping, though it was muffled by the blanket. Once Gar tied the legs, Ron pulled the blanket aside and cursed as sharp teeth raked his hand. "Feisty little beast. You're not afraid of us at all, are you?"

Ron turned to Gar. "All right. I'll remove the arrow while you hold it and then you staunch the flow of blood and bandage it, so we can tie that leg with the rest."

It struggled more fiercely.

Gar said, "Ron, it's not giving up. It's going to hurt itself worse. Maybe if we keep it in the dark it'll calm down."

Ron agreed and wrapped it up as gently as he could in his blanket, but it kept thrashing.

"Now what?" Gar said. "Do we wait here and see who comes to rescue it?"

Ron smiled grimly. "Why wait? Now we follow its spoor back to its masters."

The fox suddenly went still.

Gar glanced nervously at it and said in Thenalonese, "Do you think it's been listening to us?"

Ron answered in the same language, "It might well be. The eagle understood us well enough. Perhaps we'd best keep speaking Grandfather's tongue. Are you sure you can follow its tracks?"

Gar grinned. "Of course. Ara's not the only one who benefited from Grandfather's teachings. This way," he said, leading Thenagar.

Ron followed, leading his own horse. He shook his head in admiration. "I wish I had your talent for tracking."

"You've other talents that outshine mine," Gar assured his older brother. "For a while we'll just be backtracking our own trail, but it won't be long before we're past that point, and then we should see something interesting."

A short while later, they indeed saw something interesting. "We're being watched, Gar. You'd best look up," Ron warned.

Gar looked up from the tracks he'd been intently following and stared in disbelief. They were surrounded. Neither of their horses had reacted to what he saw: a wolven, a pumar, at least six foxes, a small herd of horses, two snakes, and an eagle, ringed where they stood. The eagle called out loudly to them, and Gar clutched the blanket containing the bound fox tightly.

Ron licked his lips. "We've not hurt the fox more than was necessary," Ron said in Common. "We need Thorn, Prince Eladar, to show himself, to know it's truly him who sent the eagle to us. We've no desire to march like sheep into the Enemy's hands after the journey we've taken."

The wolven stepped forward cautiously. Ron fought the urge to raise his bow toward it. It didn't look like it was preparing to attack them. He looked, puzzled, at Blaze. How could his horse stand so calmly with the wolven approaching? Then he saw the glazed look over Blaze's eyes. No wonder the horses hadn't warned them!

The wolven stopped not five paces before them. It began scratching on a fallen log with its claws and then stepped back. The eagle cried out.

Ron said to Gar in Thenalonese. "See if Thenagar is as frozen as my own mount." Then he walked slowly toward the log, hand at his side, ready to draw his sword, if necessary. He risked a quick glance toward the log.

RION? was scratched into the crumbling bark.

Ron backed up slowly toward Gar. "You'll not learn Rion's fate until we see Eladar."

The wolven appeared agitated at his words. Ron had deliberately phrased it so they might think Rion dead. His plan to have Rion, Andra, and Rarnak walk upstream a distance within the stream's waters to hide their trail might not work well enough against such a menagerie of animal senses. He'd thought it would only be Men looking for them, or things that had once been Men.

The eagle cried out again and then took wing and disappeared over the trees in the direction they had been heading. The rest of the animals stood eerily still.

"Now what?" Gar asked Ron nervously in Thenalonese.

"Now we hope a friend comes, and not the Enemy," Ron said.

"And if it is the Enemy?" Gar asked.

"I don't think it will be. They could have just as easily frozen our horses and had that cat jump out of a tree on top of us, or rush us now. The Enemy wouldn't care about the life of a fox. But if I'm wrong and this is some elaborate trick, and we see it's the Enemy's forces who've come, then we fight. We try to bring as many of them down with us as we can. There's no way we'll escape from this, if it is a trap. It wouldn't hurt to have Elmoth thinking of us though, right now in any case," he said and began softly praying under his breath.

THE sound of Ron praying frightened Gar worse than anything that they'd seen, or that his older brother had said.

Gar touched his shoulder, and Ron quieted for a moment. "If it does come to that, if it looks hopeless, I wouldn't want to come back, like Lerdon. I wouldn't want to hurt anyone. If we both swung at the same moment, I think we could... we could take each other's heads, or near enough, at least, so the Enemy couldn't use us that way."

Ron said, agonized, "I don't think I could. I've spent my life protecting you." Then there was a complex play of emotions over Ron's face, and his eyes hardened in resolve. "No, I'll do it. I can, now that I've thought it through."

Gar could guess what his brother had been thinking. He'd been thinking it too: the two of them coming back as undead monsters and Rion and Andra waiting too long to see if it was truly them. Of what the Enemy would make him do to his sister, to Rion.

He glanced nervously at the various animals around them. They were unnaturally still and quiet, except for the wolven. It was pacing. To Gar's astonishment, the pumar walked over to it and licked its face. It nuzzled the pumar, as if it were another wolven, and stilled its pacing. The fox in the blanket was also motionless. "I hope the fox is all right."

"Don't check on it. That may be what they're waiting for," Ron said. "With it free, the others might attack."

"Don't worry. I've no wish to be clawed again," Gar assured him, thankful that there were only foxes and a single pumar and wolven. He'd not be able to stand here feigning calm were there an obearn as well.

Finally, the eagle returned. Moments later, a familiar voice came through the trees. "I'm here. Now what's happened to Rion?" Eladar asked, emerging from the dense cover of the surrounding woods.

RON eyed him carefully. It sounded like Eladar's voice, save for the hard tone and bluntness of his speech, but he looked far different than he had when they'd met him. He was uninjured now, but his eyes were cold, though his gaze was intense, and the lines of his face taut. He appeared far older: there was no hint of the free-spirited Elf who had traveled with them.

"You've changed. I'm not sure I can trust you. You're different," Ron said carefully.

"Different? Of course I'm different!" Eladar snapped, the chill of his eyes replaced by cold fury. "Did you expect me to come to you smiling? Riviera is destroyed, my people gone, my parents dead, my River dry. Loatia, which we were entrusted to protect, is burnt to the ground. The city, the forest, burnt, the people...." He stopped, and there was agony in his voice, his face.

Ron realized, horrified, that the Elves must have burnt with their Wood. They'd feared the worst, but they'd not truly believed that Riviera and Loatia had fallen. No wonder the Elves of Salenia had looked ill! The mere thought of burns affected them so strongly. For them to know that thousands, perhaps tens of thousands, of their people had burnt to death... and not only to death, he realized in sudden understanding. Meander was a healer. She and the others must have been heading to Erenia to tend whatever survivors had made it there. The thought of hundreds or perhaps thousands of burnt Elven refugees—men, women, and children—made him feel ill.

Eladar continued. "Have they managed to kill Rion now as well? And the Elves who traveled with you? And your brother and your sister and your friend?" He glared at the animals around him. "Tell me, mighty Lords and Ladies of Amontir, are they all dead? How many more pyres shall we light? How many cairns shall we build? Was there anything left of any of them to burn or bury this time?"

Eladar glared at the wolven. "You had me lure Rion here to you, Hunter, because you knew he was afraid of you and wouldn't have come if he knew it was you who wanted him here. You gave him false hope that he'd get his voice back, that Talon would heal him. But you've really no idea whether the Ring can heal him. You're only guessing that it can. What if only a wizard can, what then? Why didn't you come to them as a Man? Are you afraid to face them in a form where you might have to answer their questions?"

The wolven lay down and started to whine deep in its throat. The pumar stood beside it protectively, facing Eladar, and roared.

At the chilling cry of the hunting cat, Ron fought not to run while they were distracted. Instead, he eyed the circle carefully. Rion had been right to be afraid of them.

He and Gar had to get away from them. They might not be minions of the Enemy, but neither were they the friends they remembered and had been hoping to find. They were dissolving into chaos before his eyes. If only the horses weren't entranced! They stood no chance of fleeing fast enough without them.

"Eladar, be silent," a harsh female voice snapped from amidst the trees. "Ronamark, please do not leave, not when you swore yourself to my service. I hold you to that pledge. I will not release you when I have such need of you," the same voice said, but in a completely different tone, and he recognized it now. It was Elanara. She emerged from the cover of the trees and glided along the ground, looking, sounding, moving just as Ron remembered her. Her eyes met his, entreating him. "Please do not judge us by my brother's words. He is overwrought."

She turned to Gar. "Garamark, you pledged your sword and bow to my aid as well. You told me I need only call you and command you. I do not command you, I implore you. Please, tell us what has happened to Rion," she said, and her voice broke upon his name.

Ron studied her carefully. The tension and sadness they'd seen in her in Erenia, when first they met her, were nothing as compared to what he now saw.

Her eyes met his once more. "We never thought to see any of you again. We had given up hope. We expected you long ago. Hunter and Quickwing searched everywhere for you, when you did not come. Please, I must know what has happened to Rion," she begged, and Ron saw to his astonishment that her face was wet with tears.

Ron steeled himself against her tears, her words, fighting the urge to tell her everything she wished to hear. "Was what Eladar said true? That Hunter used him to lure Rion here? That the promise of healing was a false one?"

"Hunter asked Eladar to write to Rion because in the dream the Enemy sent to Rion, He made Hunter appear a villain. Hunter knew Rion would be terrified of him because of it. We truly believe the Ring can heal Rion. It is so strong! It must be able to, with all that it's already been able to do. Are you saying Rion is still alive?" she asked, hope suddenly flaring brightly in her voice, her eyes.

Ron took a deep breath and nodded. "He's under guard, deeper within the Pass," he admitted. Ron saw hope war with fear in her face.

"Is he well? Or terribly injured?" Her voice sank to a whisper. "Has he fallen to madness?"

Ron shook his head again. "He is neither injured nor mad. He escaped from much unharmed, even an ogre, though others nearly died from it. He was injured saving Andra from wolven-riders, and he became very ill from it, but he survived the fever and the bites have healed."

Ron turned to Eladar. "You need not add us to the burden of your grief, Eladar. We sent Swiftsong and the other Elves home when we saw they were in danger. And Ara, Andra, and Rarnak all live as well. Rion saw us safely through again. We lost no one," Ron said. He thought Rion might argue that, were he here, and had he the voice to. Seafoam had been far more than a mount to him. She'd been his friend.

Eladar looked at Ron searchingly, as if he could not believe him. Then he nodded.

Elanara said, "Then we must ride to him and bring him to further safety. I will come with you." She walked over to one of the horses. "Fennel, if I may?" she asked, and the horse tossed its head, as if nodding, *yes.* She mounted his bare back sidesaddle, the skirt of her long dress draped over him, and took his mane in her hands.

"We must let the fox we caught go," Gar said. "Eladar, can you bear it safely to your sanctuary, for healing?"

"Of course," Eladar said.

Gar let it carefully out of the blanket, into Eladar's arms, fearing it might seek to bite and scratch, but it was docile. Eladar held it tenderly and unbound it, speaking softly to it in Common, stroking its face. "It's all right, Renard. You did well. I'm sure Pierce has told you how proud he is of you. You'll soon be back in Pierce's arms. I know mine are a poor substitute. He will see you well."

IT TORE Elanara's heart to hear Eladar. For a moment he sounded like the brother she yet loved, the one that she remembered, that she missed so terribly. Then Eladar walked into the woods with his burden, ignoring both her and the rest of the animals, the latter of whom disappeared silently into the woods, singly and in pairs.

RON eyed Elanara as she watched Eladar go. He had never seen an Elf look distraught before. Then she turned her horse and began heading back down the path they had taken, indicating that they should follow her. Ron studied his own mount. Its eyes were free of whatever influence had controlled it before. He rode to her left, as Gar took up the rear. The trail was not wide enough for three to ride abreast.

"Tell me before I see him: is Rion changed?" Elanara asked, with the voice of someone asking a question she knows she will not like the answer to.

"Changed?" Ron asked, not sure what she meant by it.

"By all that's happened to him," she said sadly.

"Of course he's changed, Elanara," Ron said.

"I know he'd be changed somewhat. Men age so quickly. He is certainly no longer the boy he was when I met him, although even then there was much of the man he would become in him. It sounds like he has been through much in so short a time, yet still I hope, I fear.... Has he forgotten how to smile? Has he become bitter? Does he hate us for what has happened to him?" There was pain and longing in her voice. It hurt Ron's heart to hear it, as it had hurt him to see her tears. Elves should never be sad, nor in pain.

"He still smiles, Elanara. He even laughs. There's been fear and pain and weariness on this trip, but also courage and triumph and even joy. And he does not hate you, any of you. Although he is frightened of Jargas and especially of Jarina and Hunter," Ron admitted. He looked at her carefully and said gently, "Eladar has changed. Is he always like this now, Elanara? Is that what you were afraid you'd hear, that Rion might be the same?"

She nodded silently and he saw her swallow as a single tear fell.

Ron said, "Perhaps Rion might help Eladar find himself again. Rion almost lost himself after the chimaera attacked him and the nightmare came. But he overcame another of those monsters and the others that tormented him. More, he saved my sister, twice: he saved her body, but he also saved her spirit. I still don't know how, or what he told her. He couldn't speak, so he wrote to her, but none of us have been allowed to see." Then Ron smiled; he could not help it. "Andra's even found love and joy. She and Rarnak married in Logareth."

"You're smiling." Elanara gazed at him in wonder. "Ronamark, be careful. None of us smile, anymore. We've forgotten how, all of us. Jarina and Beryl still try, it is so part of their natures, but... don't let us take that from you, when even the Enemy has not," she said intently.

"I'm glad you have all come. We need you: you've begun to see how much." Her voice changed, it lost the note of desperation that had entered it. "Now, tell me all about your journey, everything since I saw you. Then once his voice is back, Rion can tell me again. You won't be spoiling his tale. Each always sees every event differently."

Ron told her all that had happened, all that he knew of it. There was much they still did not understand.

ELANARA was distressed by what she heard, but also by what she did not. "We've been desperate to hear how Rion escaped from Incuban, why that monster could no longer find him, even in his dreams. We suspected He could not, when He did not torture Hunter with more of them. We must learn how He could find Rion in the first place, when his core should not have been strong enough for Him to. Yet you have given me no clue as to why. Incuban never sends a single dream: He sends them night after night, until you are driven to madness or death. And Rion has been keeping secrets from you. You said nothing about him meeting the other two wizards, Arcanus and Magus, when you told me of Circe, yet he told Elavar to tell Talon of them. Surely Rion must have known Elavar would tell me as well."

"Other two wizards? Do you mean to tell me Circe is a wizard? And that Rion has met two others? And that he met your older brother Elavar? When? Where? You told us his name—you whispered it to us—but I didn't think Rion knew it. I certainly didn't know Rion had ever met Elavar. You'll not be seeing my smile again, anytime soon, nor Rion's," Ron said, the shock in his voice giving way to anger.

"Wizards! No wonder a chimaera came for him, if he's been trafficking with wizards! He swore to us he had no idea why! I never thought Rion might lie, ever, especially not about something so important. He endangered all of us with his lie, with his secrets, not only my brothers and sister, but the mill, even Ogaten. Blessed Elmoth, the Enemy burned Gosa looking for Rion! He'd think nothing of burning a town, after that! We'd not the heart to tell him Gosa had burnt because of him, and here he knew all along."

"Ron, he must have had good reason," Gar piped up from behind them. "Please don't be too harsh with him. You were able to forgive me and Ara and Van for keeping things from you, when we thought it was for your own good that you not know. Rion would never have kept something like that secret from us to harm us. He must have been protecting us, somehow, by not telling us. Let him at least get his voice back, so he can talk to you man to man about it."

Ron nodded, but he was still glaring and scowling.

Elanara was despondent. "I warned you about your smile. I wanted so desperately to help you keep it, and instead I've taken it from you myself."

"Elanara, please don't be so upset by it," Gar soothed. "Ron's always been like this. He goes for weeks, even months, without smiling. You've not changed him. It's who he already is. You'll see."

She looked back at Gar intently, then nodded, accepting his words as the truth.

They rode on in silence until they came to the head of the trail, and the stream, and then Ron spoke. "They're to have ridden at a walk up the streambed for as close to five miles as they could gauge and then exit to the left on the first rock or hard ground they came to thereafter, so they don't leave tracks. We'll see how well they've hidden."

They traveled along the path the others were to have taken. There was no firm ground, but no hoofprints in the soft ground they did see. They continued upstream, but still did not see any firm ground, to the right or left. They went miles past where they should have exited.

"LET'S go back. Maybe they left the stream but erased their tracks somehow," Gar suggested. They went back and exited the stream at where they thought they should have left it. Gar dismounted, crouched low, and began studying the ground intently. "Ron, you wait here with Elanara and the horses. I'll come back if I spot anything."

He could tell Ron was reluctant to let him go off on his own, but he agreed to it.

Gar searched, starting at the water's edge, in a fan pattern, from side to side, the arc of it widening the farther he got from the stream. He was almost ready to give up and begin yelling for Rion and Andra and Rarnak when he noticed a small patch of yellow leaves amidst a carpet of yellow-orange ones. He moved them carefully aside and found the mark of a hoof on crushed yellow-orange leaves. He looked past the mark in either direction and saw where the yellow ones had come from. Just beyond them, there were some beech leaves amidst maples, all the same greenish-brown hue, though.

He grinned and headed back along the concealed tracks. He emerged from the woods at the stream and looked up- and downstream. There was no sign of Ron and Elanara. He walked downstream for about half a mile, then gave up, realizing they must have been upstream, and walked back in that direction, past the tracks. About a quarter mile beyond, he saw Ron and Elanara. "I found the tracks," he called.

He led Elanara and Ron back and proudly showed them what he had found. Ron stared at the leaves blankly. "If there are tracks here, they're invisible to me," Ron admitted.

Gar grinned. "The ones closest to the stream are hardest to see," he said and lifted a small pile of leaves, exposing a hoofprint.

"That must be Ara's doing. Grandfather taught him things he never taught the rest of us," Ron said. There was a hint of bitterness and jealousy amidst the admiration in his voice.

"Only because he'd sit for endless hours listening to Grandfather retell the same old stories of Thenalon, not because we've different fathers," Gar said firmly. He never wanted Ron to view him as a half brother again.

"You're right," Ron admitted. "Forgive me, Gar."

They followed the tracks for a considerable distance past where Gar had first seen them, leading their horses to ensure they didn't lose the trail.

"Stop!" a voice commanded from a tree above them, and an arrow dug into the ground at their feet for emphasis.

They stopped, and Gar and Ron peered into the branches, not drawing, for they both recognized their sister's voice.

"You'd no need to loose an arrow," Ron scolded.

"It's them!" Andra called out loudly.

Elanara dismounted. "I thought you said our people left you?" she said, looking puzzled as she reached down and pulled the Elven shaft from the ground.

Gar grinned in pride. "They did. That arrow is my sister Andra's."

There was a rustle of branches, and Andra leapt nimbly to the ground. "You're back sooner than we expected." Then there was a sudden expression of fear on her face as she cried, "Rion, look out!"

The others spun at the sound of a loud creak and crash. Ara and Rion were both on the ground and a tree limb was waving over their heads. There was a row of sharpened branches all along the edge of it.

"Idiot! What's the matter with you? If Ara hadn't tackled you when he did.... Have you gone blind as well as dumb?" Andra snapped, then within the same breath said, "I'm sorry, I didn't mean that, but you scared me. I thought you'd be killed."

Rion smiled sheepishly at her to let her know he had not been hurt by her words, or by Ara or the tree.

Rarnak came out of the woods. "Well, at least we know it works," he said pragmatically.

Ara looked proud as he got to his feet. "You and I had better disarm the rest before we skewer some poor hunter out for his dinner."

"So, you set traps as well as hiding your trail," Ron said, sounding impressed.

RION had climbed to his feet too and had eyes only for Elanara. It was seeing her when he had expected to see Eladar that had distracted him almost to tragedy. She looked as beautiful as the last time he'd seen her, as lovely as she did nightly in his dreams.

ELANARA looked critically at Rion. He had changed. He was no taller, but he was more muscled, his build more a man's now than a boy's. But it was his bearing that was the most different. There was strength and confidence, caution and pride. His clothes were those of a swordsman, and she suspected he might now hold a blade with the same easy familiarity as Talon. Then she saw his face as he watched her. His expression was Talon's: he was looking at her as a man looks at a woman he desires. There was need and longing and passion in his eyes. Then he grinned at her, and she saw he was also still the boy she had fallen in love with.

She smiled back at Rion. His grin was infectious. It felt so good to smile! She could not remember the last time she had.

To her astonishment, she realized the sight of him was not enough. She needed to touch him. She went to him and embraced him. For a moment he hugged her in return, the way a man hugs a woman, not the way a little brother hugs a big sister at all. She felt his heart beating rapidly against her. But then he pulled away, awkwardly but firmly, and when she looked into his beautiful blue eyes she saw loss and regret and pain, and she almost cried out, his look cut her so.

Gar was speaking to Ara. "Ara, you did a masterful job. Grandfather would have been proud of you. It was no easy task to find you."

Ara grinned. "The leaves were my doing. But it was Andra's idea to cover our trail with her bow from the tree, and Rion suggested the traps, though I was the one who figured out what kind to make. Rion and Rarnak helped me construct and set them, after I explained my ideas." He turned to Rion. "Then Rion forgot all about them when Andra called to us and he saw you both safe and that Elanara was with you. I'm surprised Eladar didn't come as well."

Rion looked at Elanara in sudden concern.

"He's fine, Rion. We just thought one was best," she said, and he seemed reassured.

Ron said, "Why don't you reset the one trap, Ara, instead of disarming the others? We may as well make camp here. The sun's already begun to set. I'd hoped we'd be able to start toward the Watchtower tonight, even knowing we wouldn't make it there until tomorrow. But having to work so hard to find you has delayed us enough that it doesn't make sense to start for it tonight."

"That's a good idea, Ron," Andra agreed. "We've already a little camp of sorts, where we tethered the horses. I'll stay on guard duty up here. We should post at least two guards. I'll need another bowman to replace me later so I can get some sleep as well."

Rarnak said, "I'll stand watch with you, Andra. That way we can both be together on our off shift."

She smiled at him, her face softening with it.

Ara started resetting the trap.

GAR said, "I'm surprised they let you leave with us without anyone to guard you, Elanara, though I'd not thought of it before. I hope they realize we won't make it back tonight."

"They are well aware. And I am not so alone as you might think," she said mysteriously.

Just then they heard the cry of an eagle and they looked up. The bird was perched in one of the trees overhead. To Gar it appeared to be the same one from near Ogaten, and from the trail to the Watchtower.

Rion's gaze jerked upward at the cry and his blue eyes were bright with excitement. He pulled out a thick strip of cloth from his pack and tossed it over his forearm, then held up his arm expectantly and whistled at the eagle.

It tilted its head and looked at him. Then it looked around carefully and dove from the tree, flapping its wings at the last moment to slow its descent, to land gracefully and softly upon his arm. Rion grinned in joy, his eyes lit with love, as he stroked the eagle gently along the feathers near its beak.

ELANARA laughed. "It seems you have made a friend, Quickwing. You've missed him too, I suspect." She wondered whether it was Lunahr or Farad who was controlling Quickwing at the moment. She suspected it was Farad. Rion would be horrified to learn it was Farad he was showing such affection toward. She was glad he did not know.

She still could not believe Rion looked so well. She had prepared herself for anything, or had tried to, but she had been so afraid of what she might find. To hear, though, that he had been bitten and ill with fever, that she'd not even known he was in such immediate danger and would have been unable to help him even if she had, tore her heart. As had the hug he had given her. It had felt so good to be in his arms. She had melted in his embrace as she had never melted in Talon's, even as she realized she was betraying them both. She did not care. But then Rion had let her go so soon, too soon! She could have held him forever.

The eagle let out a call again and flapped his wings, taking flight, rising from his perch on Rion's arm, but he did not go far. He settled upon one of the higher branches above them.

Ron watched the bird, a puzzled look on his face. "What's the story behind the eagle, Elanara? And the fox and horses and especially the wolven and pumar, all the animals we saw in the woods? Eladar called them the Lords and Ladies of Amontir, as if they were people. They certainly act enough like them. Are they? Has one of the wizards put a curse on them and turned them all into beasts?"

Rion looked at Ron wide-eyed. He'd not heard the story of what they'd seen, yet.

Elanara smiled and shook her head. "No, they are not people, though they are loved as much as if they were. The eagle, Quickwing, is loved by two. They are truly animals, but ones that the Lords and Ladies have bonded with. They can share their bodies, see what they see, hear what they hear, know what they know."

"Including the fox we injured?" Gar asked.

"Yes. That was Renard. He was on guard duty on the trail when he spotted you and reported your approach to Pierce. You caused quite a stir when Pierce told us what Renard saw. We weren't expecting only two men. We thought there would be more. We thought there would be River Elves and uniformed guards, and the descriptions of you and Ronamark did not match Rion."

"I hope I've not made an enemy, then, for harming Renard," Gar said in concern.

"I think Pierce will forgive you for it. After all, you did not kill him, as you might have, and you tended to his injury. I could not believe it when Pierce told us how you had captured Renard. He told us the bowman might look a Man, but that he must have had either Elven or Aralonese blood in him, to have shot so true."

Gar grinned. "May he never get on Andra's bad side. I pale beside her as an archer. I pale when I get on her bad side, too, and that's an easy enough thing to do," he teased.

Andra looked at him in mild annoyance.

"You've spoiled our fun, Rarnak," Gar complained. "You've taken all the fight out of her. If we'd known a husband would do that, we'd have bought one for her long ago."

Andra glared at him, and he grinned wider. "You always were such an easy target, Andra," he said and smiled at her fondly.

She appeared nonplussed, then grunted. "Your teasing I learned to endure years ago. It's your smiling at me now, after, to take the sting out of it I can't get used to." She looked about at the others with a half-hearted scowl. "Why don't the rest of you leave for camp, already, so I can have some peace and quiet?" She headed for her tree.

Andra called up to the eagle. "And you, why don't you make yourself really useful and circle about and take a look around. A fine lot of good you'll do warning us about chimaera from there. By the time you see them, we would too, and they'd have seen us as well," she scolded.

The eagle cried once then went aloft.

Ron shook his head. "Congratulations, Andra, you've just ordered a Lord or Lady as if she were your scullery maid."

She glared at Ron. "You should know by now, Ron, I've got no use for fancy titles or fancy people, especially not when I've a job to do. And I don't see you heading for camp yet either, Brother. Don't make me climb back down to encourage you," she said as she settled on a limb.

Ron smiled fondly at her. "I wouldn't dream of it. Lead the way, Ara, Rion. It appears we've worn out our welcome."

Elanara could not believe how readily they all smiled, even Ron, whom she'd been so concerned for. The Amontir had lost their resiliency long ago, if ever they'd had it. How could she ever learn to be their Queen?

RION was watching Elanara as surreptitiously as he could. She seemed so sad, so upset. He ached to talk to her, to hold her, to reassure her. He reminded himself again that she was betrothed. Hugging her before had been a mistake: a wonderful, glorious, heartbreaking mistake.

At least Quickwing was here, and now he even knew the eagle's name. Rion felt safer with him here. He'd been overjoyed to see the eagle, especially once he saw the bird remembered him and seemed just as glad to see him. But was it the Lord or the bird?

He wondered what it must be like, to be able to soar the skies as an eagle, or slip through the woods as a fox. He wondered which animal Hunter was bonded to.

Surely he could not truly be as evil as he had seemed in Rion's dream? Talon would not associate with someone cruel. Unless he needed someone like that. Kings did need terrible people, sometimes, to do their evil for them. Only Talon had not seemed like such a King. He wished he was at the Watchtower already, afraid as he was. He wanted this nightmare to end.

FULL darkness fell quickly, and Elanara advised them against lighting a fire. It soon became apparent that it would be impossible to change the watch. Clouds obscured the moon completely. They'd never find their way back to where Andra and Rarnak were in such pitch blackness.

Ron whispered, "We won't even be able to see if an animal is hunting us."

Elanara spoke softly also. The woods seemed to demand it tonight. "We are safe. Slash, Whisper, and Bruin roam far, to keep other predators from our wood. The three of them, and some of the others, will have followed us." She knew that Bruin specifically had kept out of sight before. Once Jargas had seen through his bond obearn's eyes that the two Men were Ronamark and Garamark, he'd purposefully remained hidden, knowing how they felt about obearn after Aramark and Garamark had nearly been slain by one.

She whistled into the night, a haunting, beautiful tone. There was a cry overhead, and Quickwing descended.

"Quickwing, I have told them not to light a fire, but they understand the dangers of the wood. Am I right that Slash and Whisper and Bruin protect us, and perhaps some of the others?"

Quickwing bobbed his head.

"Quickwing says we are safe," she said, suspecting the others could not see him at all in such darkness, other than perhaps a vague image, when his form blocked out some of the stars. She could scarcely see him, and she knew her eyesight was keener than theirs.

"Come, I will lead you to your blankets. I think I can find them, and we will sleep. We can rise with the first rays of dawn, eat, and be on our way. The journey to the Watchtower will not be such a long one. You will feel much better once you have had a chance to bathe and change your clothes, to eat a hot meal and sleep in a real bed."

THEY settled down quickly for the night. Rion listened to everyone's breathing. He was able to tell when Ara fell asleep, and Gar. Ron was yet awake. Elanara... he could not tell. He could not hear her at all.

He imagined her coming to him in the darkness, the wispy feel of her dress, her silken hair as it cascaded about him, the sweet scent of her like a spring rain. He bit back a moan and hugged his pack tightly, feeling the reassuring solidity of his journal within. He wished he could read. Or sleep. He was so tired.

He remembered the last time he had been so exhausted, outside Gosa, when he had gone so long without sleep. He had started to see things and hear things that were not there. He had panicked when Gar had come, thinking him a monster. But there might be real monsters here, in the night. It was so dark. What if some horrible creature slipped by their strange sentries? What if something other than Elanara came for him in the dark, touched him? Something horrific?

Memory seized him, again, of the terrible room, the candles, the voice. No! He had to stop it now, before he saw them. He had become adept at doing so, but tonight he could not. He tried to force himself to calm, snatching other images from memory and focusing on them. Tarrell, warm and smiling. Eladar laughing. Lerdon... no, not him! His compassionate smiling face turned into the dead, monstrous one, his hands reaching for him. But then, unexpectedly, it was as if Lerdon was made of smoke, wispy and gray, and then he vanished altogether. He dissipated on the wind.

Instead, there was an image of green grass and trees and dappled sunlight in Rion's mind. He could even hear the sound of running water, though they were not near enough to the stream that he should be able to. But there was another sound as well. It had started out so softly, rising so naturally from the air beside him, that at first he didn't realize it was a voice, a song.

It was so beautiful! He had not known there could be sunlight in music, or warmth. He breathed slowly, deeply. He could almost scent the water on the air: such a beautiful river, so soothing, the sound of it rushing past the riverbank. There was no danger by such a river. Evil could not come here. The river would not allow it. He breathed more deeply, feeling the peace of the river flow over him. He was part of the river. It flowed around him, through him....

ELANARA ended her song slowly, carefully. It had worked, as she had hoped it might. She could tell by his breathing Rion was asleep. Ron was sleeping as well, and the others had fallen asleep long ago. She could rest now also, knowing Rion was at peace, that she had aided him.

The Enemy was searching for them, all of them. Even she could feel it, though her Power had never been near that of her father or mother. It should not be so dark. The clouds had come so suddenly. She'd felt the evil in the air. That is why she had not let them light a fire, but she had not wanted to frighten them with that knowledge. Though Rion had sensed the danger too, somehow, and Ron, she suspected. But they were safe here. The Enemy was not near, not focusing His search upon this spot or any other. She was confident the Lords and Ladies in the wood would keep them safe. She fell asleep within a few moments of that thought.

THE first rays of the sun burnt away the last shreds of darkness that had shrouded the wood. Rion awoke with a smile on his face, but then his brow crinkled in puzzlement. Why couldn't he hear the river? He looked about, confused. He saw his friends curled up under their blankets on the bed of leaves beneath the tall trees, but there was no river here. A dream. It had only been a dream. No, it had been something more.

He sought Elanara. She was sleeping so peacefully. The worry he had seen on her face yesterday had vanished. The song, the river: it had been her, somehow, he realized in wonder. He reached his hand toward her face and drew it back regretfully. Instead, he sat up carefully, quietly. He wanted to check on Andra and Rarnak. He felt bad that they'd been left on guard all night.

But they were already coming into camp. "I'm glad none of you were fool enough to try to come relieve us last night," Andra said softly to Rion, so as not to wake the others. "I've never seen such darkness. It wasn't natural. I'd not have been able to sleep a wink, in any case. I don't know how the rest of you did."

Rion pointed to Elanara, then himself, and mimed sleep. She looked at the sleeping Elven Princess and then Rion in surprise and eyed him appraisingly. Rion blushed darkly, realizing Andra must be thinking he had lain with Elanara, from her expression, and he shook his head vigorously in denial.

"I didn't think you might, but I know it's not from lack of wanting to. Don't let anything stand in the way of your heart, Rion. Nothing's more important."

He felt a wave of frustration thunder over him at his inability to speak.

"It's all right," she soothed. "You needn't explain nor defend yourself to me. I know you must have an excellent reason for doing otherwise. Come. Let's make breakfast for the others, such as we can without a fire. I'm eager to reach that Watchtower of theirs."

Rion nodded, and the three of them began preparing breakfast. Rion had almost forgotten Rarnak was there, he'd been so silent.

Despite their quietness, the others awoke in short order. They were all eager to be on their way.

Ara yawned and stretched. "What a restful night. I can't remember the last time I slept so well."

Gar said, "Me either."

Ron looked at Elanara intently. "Thank you, Your Highness. We appreciate your aid."

Elanara smiled. "You need not be so formal, Ronamark. You may call me Elanara, as you and your brothers did before. Or Brook, actually, once we are at the Tower. Few there know my given name."

Ron said, "Then please: we are Ron, Ara, Gar, and Andra."

"Of course. And you are most welcome. I am pleased I could be of aid."

They ate sparingly, though they'd not had dinner the night before. Everyone was too anxious to be on their way.

They packed up quickly and were ready to mount when Ara said. "Wait, give me and Rion a few moments to disarm those traps we set. We wouldn't want some innocent hunter to be harmed by them."

WHEN Rion and Ara came back a short while later, they were peaked and agitated.

Ara spoke for both of them. "You should have seen the size of the obearn prints out there, mixed in with those of the wolven and pumar! From what you'd told me, I hadn't known they had an obearn, too. Even knowing they're on our side, it makes my skin crawl, how close to camp they were, while we slept!"

Rion knew Ara was remembering the feel of the obearn clawing his back, even as Rion was remembering the wolven's teeth tearing into his limbs. He was glad for the bright sun. There was a shrill cry from above, and Rion looked at Quickwing in relief. Rion was eager to be on his way to the Watchtower, but also afraid. What if whatever they meant to try didn't work? What if he was never able to speak again?

Rion tried the whistle Elanara had used to call Quickwing before. The tone and pitch sounded identical to his ear. He was glad again for his ear for music and his perfect pitch, which he'd inherited from his mother. Thinking of her stirred a wave of loneliness and longing.

Quickwing called again, and swooped down toward him. Rion extended his arm in surprise. He had not expected the bird to come to him, though he welcomed his attention. He winced as the needle sharp talons dug through the thin material of his sleeve. The bird cocked its head, eyeing him in concern, but somehow he thought it was more concerned about him being upset than for whatever minor injury it might have dealt him.

Rion smiled reassuringly at it, stroking its feathers. He wished he could tell it he felt better now. He waved his hand, indicating the bird should take to the air, and it did so. He felt a thrill that such a proud animal would obey his commands, even though he had no voice to speak them.

ELANARA was grateful to Farad. She was certain now that he was the one within Quickwing. It was evident that Rion had withstood much to make it so far. From what Ron had told her, it sounded as if he had kept his spirits up through the entire grueling journey, but she could see he feared what might lie ahead. He was so brave, so strong of character, of spirit. She must not think about him. It had been hard enough when he had been so far away. Now that he was here, she was not sure what she would do.

THEY broke camp and rode quickly, escorted by the animals that surreptitiously guarded them, and by Elanara, who rode with them. Ron and Gar had told the others everything that had happened the previous day, so when they got to the area where the animals had surrounded them, Rion could imagine what it must have felt like. He noticed that his name had been scratched from the log. Perhaps the wolven had felt uneasy leaving it there.

They reached the Watchtower sooner than they thought they might. It was much more than a tower, they saw, to their surprise. It was a ruined castle. Though the body appeared relatively intact, as did a single tall tower, the remains of a second tower lay as a heap of rubble upon the ground.

"This can't be it. It's deserted, it's in ruins," Ron said, looking at Elanara warily.

She smiled reassuringly at him. "Well, if we cleaned up the outside and posted an army about it, the Enemy might know we're here. We've even a special way of cooking so the smoke from the fires doesn't betray us." They continued on, keeping to the trees; the eagle dove swiftly past, with a single call.

"It is safe. No one is watching," Elanara said, apparently interpreting Quickwing's cry. They headed for the massive steel wrapped doors to the castle. The doors opened as they approached.

Rion relaxed. He could see inside, now. There was a wide stone hallway, well lit, with many guards. To his surprised, he realized they were all Dwarves. Elanara led them right up to the doors.

One of the Dwarves said to her in Common, "We'll take your horses, Highness."

"Thank you," she said and dismounted.

The others dismounted as well, removing their packs from their horses. Rion pulled his book and writing lead from his pack, so he'd be able to communicate more easily and clearly than with hand gestures.

"I'll take you all to see Talon now," Elanara said. Then her face flushed, in apparent embarrassment. "Oh, and I should have said something before: he's the Lord of the Watch, he's the King of the Amontir and deserves such courtesy."

RON said, "Rion and Tarrell told us so months ago, in Gosa. But we didn't expect to see Dwarves here. I guess Rion was wrong to worry. He'd thought Jargas and Hunter were leading the Dwarven army against King Talon."

Elanara shook her head. "No, Rion wasn't wrong. Hunter was marching against King Talon. It's very complicated, and I'm not sure they wish it to be discussed. In any case, it is no longer an issue. They are all friends again and sworn to King Talon now."

Ron was intrigued, but did not press her for more. They approached a door with two Men and six Dwarves on guard before it.

"We've come to see the King," Elanara said. "We are expected."

"None may enter armed," one of the Dwarves said. "Please leave your weapons with us. They will be returned once your audience is concluded."

Ron, Ara, Gar, Andra, Rarnak, and Rion all looked a little nervously at one another.

"I surrender my bow to no one," Andra said. "I'll wait here. I've no need to see the King, nor him to see me."

"I will wait with you," Rarnak said.

"But Andra, he's the Lord of the Watch. Grandfather would want you to appear before him," Ron reasoned.

She answered him in Thenalonese. "Grandfather would want me to keep my kin safe. I'll not leave us defenseless, even here. There's too much we still don't know about these people. If I'm armed, I can come to your aid if you call."

"Very well," Ron said in Common.

Elanara was looking at Andra curiously, obviously wondering what she had said to him. Andra met her gaze levelly.

THE rest of the party surrendered their weapons and were gently but thoroughly searched. The guards asked to see Rion's book. Rion was reluctant to part with it and handed it over with misgivings. But the guard merely flipped through it, fanning the pages quickly to ascertain that nothing was concealed in it, and returned it to him. Meanwhile, Andra and Rarnak were escorted partway down the hall. Then the door was opened for the others. Rion and the three brothers entered with Elanara.

The room was sparsely furnished, with a large, heavy, two-level table and fourteen chairs, plus one oversized chair at the high end of the table. There were maps spread across the table. But Rion only gave the furnishings the most cursory glance. He was mesmerized by the great tapestries that hung upon the walls all around the room. There were four of them, one on each wall. They were enormous, brightly colored, and vividly detailed. Rion could tell even from here the weaving was exquisite. Then he saw movement out of the corner of his eye, and he realized the room was not empty. He saw Talon standing in the corner, and temporarily lost interest in the fantastic tapestries.

Talon appeared even thinner than before. He was better dressed, although not in the clothes of a King, his hair clean and combed, his face still beardless. His eyes were the intense blue Rion remembered, but they looked haunted; there was such sadness in them. Rion realized Talon was studying him as well, assessing him as if he were sizing up an opponent, rather than seeing a friend. Rion smiled uncertainly at him, but Talon did not return his smile as he approached.

Elanara broke the awkward silence. "I have brought them before you, Majesty, as commanded. If I may be excused?" she asked stiffly, formally.

Talon answered just as stiffly. "You may go."

Rion looked from one to the other in concern. They were not acting as a man and woman who were betrothed to one another should. How could they sound so cold? Elanara left, gliding silently from the room, and Talon let out a great sigh once she had gone, as if he was relieved she had left. "It is good to see you again, Rion, especially looking as well as you do," he said, but the warmth of his words was not reflected in his tone at all.

Rion nodded slightly in acknowledgement of his words.

Talon turned his attention to the others. "It is good to see all of you again. But where is your sister Andra and her husband, Rarnak? Surely no ill has befallen them? I would have heard of it."

"They are fine. They decided to wait for us in the hallway," Ron explained.

"But you are all well? None of you are injured, in need of healing?" Talon asked.

"Ara and Rarnak just got their bandages off," Ron said, speaking for the brothers as he usually did, and for Rion too, now that he could not. "The rest of us have healed from our most recent injuries as well. But of course, there is still Rion's voice. Thorn told us that he does not think you can help him. He said Hunter made him say so in the letter he had him write so that Rion would come. But Brook is hopeful you can heal him."

Rion stared at Ron wide-eyed. They had not told him that.

"I didn't want to upset you, Rion," Ron said apologetically. "We'd already come so far, we had to see this through. But I promise you, if they cannot help you, we will find someone who can."

"Of course we can help him," Talon said, a touch of indignation in his voice. "Thorn should not have led you to believe otherwise. Either Hunter or Jargas or Jarina will be able to. I… cannot."

Rion looked at Talon fearfully and opened his book and wrote. *But I betrayed their intent to you. I warned you of their attack, through Thorn's and Brook's older brother. Surely Hunter, Jargas, and Jarina must hate me for it?*

"It is true that you guessed their intent," Talon acknowledged. "They were shocked you saw their intentions so clearly, you who have not the tiniest scrap of Power in you. And they were further amazed that you deceived them so well that they had no inkling of what you had understood, or what you were planning. Hunter in particular cannot believe it. Yet he loves you all the more for it, for you sought to protect me from his betrayal, when he could not protect me himself, much as he wished to.

"But they have all been pardoned for their actions against me, for they were acting in adherence to our most sacred Law. I did not know it previous to that time, but Jargas is the true Heir to the Throne, not I. Jargas is a direct descendent of our murdered King. I am a poor second, a direct descendent of the King's brother, the one who committed fratricide and regicide in a single stroke. But Jargas abdicated his claim in favor of mine, though he has been named my Heir. There is no ill will between any of us over it."

Rion wrote eagerly, *I must hear all of that in detail! I am glad to hear you are friends now. But why can you not help me? I do not trust them, any of them, even if you now do. I cannot, after what I have seen, what I have felt.*

Talon studied him intently. "Do you trust me, Rion?"

Rion looked at him just as critically. Talon had changed. There was such weariness, such sadness about him. But his eyes were still his own. He wrote, *Of course! I only needed to see you and speak to you, in order to be sure you were still the man I knew.*

"So then, as you trust me, won't you trust me when I tell you that any of the three I have named can help you?" Talon said. "Though Hunter would be best."

Rion wrote agitatedly, *No! I don't want to see him. I don't want him anywhere near me! I never would have come had I known he was here.*

"Rion, he saved your life in Gosa, when you were taken by those vicious men. I heard the story of all you endured. I still blame myself for sending you to that cursed city. I had no idea it was such a place of evil, or that it was fated to be destroyed so terribly. But also, it was Hunter who guided Quickwing's attack when you were held prisoner by the chimaera. He fought it and freed you, endangering not only Quickwing's life, but his own. It was he who guided Quickwing in the woods just now as well, who watched over you all night to ensure that you were safe. You greeted the bird so warmly. Can you not show similar courtesy to the Man?"

Rion's eyes were wide with horror that he'd been so deceived, tricked into loving Quickwing when the bird was Hunter, in disguise. *He led the Enemy to me, to torture me in my dreams. He enjoyed watching me suffer. He is punishing me for warning you about him,* Rion wrote, his hand shaking so badly his writing was almost illegible.

Talon shook his head. "No, Rion, he did not. He would never do such an evil thing. He has reason to hate Incuban more than any other man alive. He would never aid Him in harming anyone. The Enemy has tricked you, deceived you. He seeks to keep you from our help. What can I say to convince you?"

"I think I'm the one who needs to convince him," a terrifyingly familiar deep voice said from the doorway.

Rion's hand went immediately to his side, fingers closing on empty air where the hilt of his sword should have been. The brothers closed instantly around him, facing outward, shielding him with their bodies, though there were only three of them and they were unarmed. Rion peered between Ron's and Ara's shoulders. It truly was Hunter. He looked stronger than when Rion had last seen him. His eyes were still warm and bright, when they should not be. There was an eagle perched upon his shoulder. Rion recognized Quickwing and a dagger of betrayal pierced his heart.

"I am not here to harm Rion. I am here to help him," Hunter said, addressing the men who now guarded him. Hunter approached slowly and then sat at the table. Quickwing jumped from his shoulder onto the table and stood looking up at Rion. Rion noticed Hunter did not ask Talon's permission to sit. *He hadn't thought you were supposed to sit before a King without his permission.*

"Will you sit at the table with me?" Hunter asked.

Talon sat in one of the three chairs at the high end of the table, in the chair next to the large one. "Please, sit," he urged, his tone making it a suggestion, rather than the command it could have been.

Rion tapped Ron's shoulder and indicated that he would sit. Rion sat opposite Hunter and Quickwing, with the wide table between them. Ara and Gar sat to either side of Hunter. Ron moved aside the chair next to Rion's left and stood protectively behind him and to the left. Ron turned to Talon. "May I have your permission to stand, Majesty?" He did not treat Talon's presence as casually as Hunter had.

Talon said, "Yes, you may."

Hunter stared at Rion intently. "I did not betray you to the Enemy, Rion. I would never send anyone to Him, live or dead. We still do not understand how He found you, or perhaps, more importantly, how He lost you, for He has never before lost any of His other victims, in all the many decades, the centuries, He has tormented us. Fortunately, He has little Power to act against us in our sleep anymore, through our dreams, now that we hold the Ring, save for that one night when He tormented you, when He focused all His Power against you and me both. But though we do not know how He found you, we do know why He attacked you, when I doubt you do. For if you had figured out that part of it, you would know I am not a minion of the Enemy."

Rion's gaze was riveted upon Hunter.

"He tortured you to harm me. It is not the first time another has suffered for me. I only hope it might be the last. He was taking His revenge upon someone He knew I cared for, the only one He could yet reach. I was as trapped in your dream as you were, Rion, but not as He made it appear to your eyes. He forced me to watch His servants harm you." Hunter's voice was grim, almost emotionless.

"You do not know what that means to me, so I will tell you. We Amontir have special Powers other Men do not possess. You have learned something of this in relation to our bonds with animals. Yet that is a new aspect of our Power we have only recently discovered. We can also bond to other people. We can feel each other's pain, or terror, if we are bonded to them, linked to them. Incuban tortured my father, my mother, and each of my three brothers to death, solely to harm me, remotely, through them. They endured such terrible agonies, unspeakable torments, only so that I might share what they felt. You remind me so much of my youngest brother, Alarad: your eyes, especially your eyes, but also your innocence, so much about you...." Hunter's voice was no longer emotionless, it was choked with emotion, and so low it was nearly inaudible. "He was the last to die. He suffered the most. He suffered terribly for me," Hunter said, his voice raw with anguish.

Talon rose quickly from his chair and went to Hunter, clasping him on the shoulder and speaking to him in a language Rion had never heard another speak aloud before, but one he knew, one he had read and practiced speaking to himself.

"FARAD, you tell him too much. You harm yourself by it," Dewalaren said.

"My pain is nothing compared to what He has done to Rion because of me! You do not know of the dream. I refused to speak of it to anyone. But also, the Enemy killed those he loved and used them against him. Rion's own guards were the tools He chose to harm him. Rion had to battle a chimaera alone with nothing but a sword! The Enemy has taken his voice from him. Rion once told me the most horrible thing anyone could do to him was to take his voice...." Farad was shaking.

Quickwing screeched and jumped upon Farad's shoulder again, peering at him in concern.

"You are shielding yourself from Jarina again, aren't you? You must let her help you," Dewalaren said. He cursed his weakness. He had not bonded to Farad, now that he was no longer crippled by Aras's shield, because his core was crippled far worse, by all he had lost. Aras! Despair crashed over him again in a wave. He fell into the chair beside Farad and fought to breathe.

RION was looking at the two of them agitatedly, his fear warring with his need to help them. He'd understood almost every word. Then to his astonishment, he saw an Elf appear magically from behind one of the tapestries, and for a joyous moment he thought it was Aras. Rion had wondered where he might be, why he was not here, beside Talon. Surely Aras would be able to help him!

Then he realized to his surprise it was not Aras, nor was this stranger even an Elf, although he had the grace and bearing and features of one, save for his ears. The blond-haired, green-eyed Man glared accusingly at Rion and his guards, as he headed for them.

"BERYL! You should not be here," Farad scolded in Common, exasperation and warm concern in his voice rather than anger.

Dewalaren stared at Lunahr agape and chastised his young cousin in Amontirin. "Lunahr! You must be mad, coming in here like this! You betray our secret entrance, and you wear your sword before me! If the Guard were to discover you here... give me Loruthanar, now!"

Lunahr unbuckled his sword belt, saying sheepishly, "I forgot. I'm sorry, Laren. I still can't believe only you and Farad trust me now, but Farad was hurt, and shielding it from me."

Farad looked at him in surprise. "You were in Quickwing? You were spying on us?"

Lunahr appeared crestfallen. "I only thought to see them. It's all you've talked about for weeks and... have I made a mess of things?" he asked, dismayed.

Farad lifted his shield and sent a surge of warmth and love through his bond to Lunahr. He could see the despair vanish from Lunahr's face, to be replaced by joy. And Lunahr's joy reverberated down the link, warming Farad in turn.

Farad turned to Rion to try to explain to him what had been happening. Rion must think them all mad. He would never trust them after all of this. But Rion was writing intently in his book. He slid it over to Farad, and he read, *I understand now. I believe you. I trust you now. I will let you help me. Tell me what I must do.*

Farad said in surprise in Common, "Talon, he says he'll let me help him, that he trusts me, now."

Dewalaren looked at Rion, intrigued. Then he slid the Ring from his finger and handed it to Farad.

AFTER all he'd just seen and heard, Rion was convinced now that these men were truly still his friends, good men, rather than the evil he had feared at least Hunter to be. And he could not bear the thought of being trapped in silence for a single moment longer, when they might return his voice to him. He was reeling from all he had heard, his head swimming with questions he was eager to ask.

Beryl was alive! Aras had told him Talon's kinsman was slain, that Talon had been devastated by his death and had recovered his sword Loruthanar only to bury it, as Beryl was last of House of Eagles, yet here he stood before them, having borne that same blade! Talon had called him Lunahr; that must be his given name. He had heard Talon's and Hunter's given names, Dewalaren and Farad, as they spoke to one another, but he had already known them. Circe had told him Talon's and Incuban had told him Hunter's, which Eladar's letter had later confirmed. He would not otherwise have trusted anything that monster might say.

He forced his thoughts away from the horrible dream, focusing instead upon the ring, which also puzzled him. Talon had not worn jewelry of any type when Rion had met him in Athanark, but he wore the ring as if he had always done so, as if he had been born to. From the glimpse he had seen of it, it was a man's ring, the band only of copper rather than silver or gold, but a large ruby cabochon was set into the metal. It looked like something a King might wear, for the valuable stone, but might it be more? Circe had told him of a ring, one that Talon must never let the wizard Arcanus wear. Could this perhaps be that ring? Could it be magic? Is that why Arcanus coveted it, why Talon was giving it to Hunter now?

To Rion's further consternation, Talon handed Hunter a knife, an odd one. The hilt was black, but the blade made of copper, like the ring. Who would want a copper knife? Copper was too soft a metal to make a good knife from. It bent and dulled far too easily. Yet this knife appeared keen and sharp, for all that it had a look of age about it, and beauty, even for the eeriness of the color. Rion realized it was not truly copper in color at all, but more the hue of copper that had already been dipped in blood.

FARAD saw Rion studying the King's Knife and said reassuringly, "Don't worry. I will not be letting your blood or mine with this. It is not a blade for harming, but for healing." He did not say that it had once been used to harm. His memory of Dewalaren with the Knife in his back was still vivid, of him then desperately trying to save his cousin, his King, with the same blade. But he was careful to shield the thought and the emotions it brought from Lunahr. Lunahr suffered guilt enough from what the Enemy had forced him to do to Eladar, for turning him into an assassin. Even though Dewalaren had been healed by the same blade that slew him and then miraculously brought back to life by Aras's wizardry, Lunahr had not recovered from it, nor had Eladar. None of them had been able to help Eladar. He would not let them.

"Do not," Dewalaren said in Amontirin. "You have both already suffered enough for that day. Please do not torture yourselves any more over it."

Farad looked up in surprise at Dewalaren and at Lunahr. He saw the ghost of despair on Lunahr's face, and realized he had been thinking the same thoughts, yet shielding Farad from them even as Farad had tried to shield his own from Lunahr. He sent another surge of love and reassurance to Lunahr and was almost overwhelmed by one that reached him at the same moment. He basked in the warmth of it and then focused outward again, upon Rion, who was waiting patiently and studying the three of them intently.

"Forgive me," Farad said.

RION wondered if Hunter was speaking to him, for the strange delay, or to Talon, for what he had been speaking of, or to both of them. He felt guilty that he knew Amontirin so well, when they did not even suspect that he knew it. He should warn them he could speak Amontirin. He had no right to be privy to all their secrets.

He watched as Hunter slipped on the ring. It began to glow and pulse with a soft light, stronger and then weaker again, the rhythm oddly like that of a heartbeat, and his suspicion that it might be magic was confirmed.

"Rion, I'll need you to lie upon the floor," Hunter said, and Rion complied. The others gathered around him.

Hunter warned those present, "The Ring flares brightly. You must all shield your eyes, or you will be temporarily blinded. I will tell you when it is safe to look. Beryl, be sure you cover Quickwing's eyes as well."

Rion saw the others shield their eyes, and then he both closed and shielded his own. There was a gentle touch upon his forehead and Rion saw a bright red light flare, even through his eyelids and the fingers of his hands. It was like staring at the sun with his eyes closed.

"You may all open your eyes now, including you, Rion, but do not yet move." Hunter touched the dagger to Rion's head and to his heart and his throat, the flat of the blade only, while Rion held his breath. Then Hunter leaned back. "You can sit up now. How do you feel, Rion?"

Rion was puzzled. He felt no different. He shrugged.

Hunter smiled tiredly at him. "Try to speak, Rion."

Rion was suddenly afraid to try. He felt no different. What if nothing had changed? What if he still couldn't speak? Then this would all have been for nothing and he'd need a wizard's aid and....

"Please, Rion. Have faith in me," Hunter urged calmly, cutting into Rion's growing panic.

Rion took a deep breath and spoke. "Thank you for.... Elmoth, it worked! Ron, Ara, Gar, it worked!" Rion said, grinning.

The brothers started hugging him and pounding him on the back as Hunter quickly handed the Ring and Knife back to Talon.

THEIR joy was infectious. Lunahr grinned as well, and found himself hugging Rion and being hugged in return. Even Dewalaren smiled and hugged Rion. Farad smiled also, though he kept his distance. Lunahr's heart flooded with joy to see both the cousins he loved happy, even if for only a fleeting moment, for neither had smiled in a very long time. Lunahr went to Farad and hugged him tightly.

"Talon, I mean, your Majesty, I have so many questions to ask you! And so much to tell you! I mean… that is, I know you are the King, and you must be terribly busy, but…." Rion's face flushed. "I sound like a boy again."

"You are not yet seventeen, Rion. You are entitled to sound like a boy, every now and then," Dewalaren said, with an affectionate smile.

Lunahr laughed. "I'm twenty-four and I still do. Of course, I am still a boy by our custom."

"I couldn't believe it when I heard your name and your sword's and realized who you were," Rion said. "Aras told me the Enemy had killed you. I'm glad to see he was wrong." He turned from Lunahr toward Dewalaren, and missed the look of terror and despair that flashed across Lunahr's face at his words.

"Where is Aras, Talon? I can't believe he's not…. Talon? Talon, what's wrong?" Rion asked in concern.

Dewalaren's face was twisted in pain. He turned away from Rion without a word, stumbling for the tapestry Lunahr had appeared from behind and the hidden door it concealed.

Rion turned to Farad and Lunahr in concern and confusion. Farad was hugging Lunahr tightly, trying to calm his wild trembling. "It's all right, Lunahr. You are safe. He'll not take you again, I swear it," Farad soothed in Amontirin.

"You swore before, you all did! You told me I was safe and… oh Farad, I am so afraid! But Laren…. Please, Farad! You must leave me and go to him. He has no one. He is in such pain, but he will not let me help him. I could not believe it when he hugged Rion. He has not let any of us even touch him," Lunahr sobbed.

"Hunter, forgive me! I didn't mean to upset them. I had no idea I would! I wish now I'd never gotten my voice back at all. Please, what did I say wrong? How can I help?" Rion asked, agonized.

Ron said, "Perhaps we should go? They need their privacy."

"NO!" Farad said sharply. "Please, you cannot leave the room without me. I…." He turned his attention back to Lunahr and said in Amontirin, "Lunahr, please, I need your help. Dewalaren needs you and I cannot let them leave here without me. It would be chaos. Please, go to him and do what you can to comfort him. I will have my hands full with our guests, for a while, but I will go to you both when I can."

Lunahr stopped crying. He took great shuddering breaths and nodded. Then he turned and headed for the tapestry Dewalaren had disappeared behind.

Farad turned to them. "Please, Rion, do not blame yourself for this. You could not have known. But there are things you must not speak of. You cannot mention the Enemy to Beryl. He was not killed, that is true, though it was such a close thing… but he was hurt horribly, tortured and worse. He has been through many terrible trials."

"Please, forgive me for it! You're right, I had no idea. He looked so well. I should have guessed. And I upset Talon, by upsetting him, I—no, there's something more," Rion said, paling and his eyes widened in sudden understanding. "No! No it couldn't be that. Not because.... Aras? Please, tell me it's not because something has happened to Aras?" Rion asked.

Farad sighed. "I could not keep it from you, I see, even were I to wish to. Please, you cannot mention Aras's name in front of Talon. You have seen you cannot. I wish I were not the one to have to tell you this. I have some small inkling of how close you became to him in Athanark. Aras is dead."

Rion stared at him, stunned. "Dead? Aras?" he asked softly, his voice that of a lost little boy. "No! No, he cannot be! How can he? He's an Elf! Elves can't die! I mean... he is so young. He has only just come of age. He is forty-nine. He will live almost another thousand years. And he is so bright, so full of life, surely...."

"I am sorry, Rion, truly I am. He was killed," Farad said reluctantly.

"How? How did he die?" Rion asked.

Farad shook his head. "No, I will not tell you that. It is too terrible to hear, too terrible to speak of."

"Please, you must tell me!" Rion begged. "I need to hear. I will imagine such horrific things. You've some idea what I might imagine, from what I've seen of what the Enemy has done."

Farad could see Rion was already torturing himself with images of Aras's death. "Fire," he said. "He burnt to death. We know no more, other than he died in agony, by fire. Talon was linked to him. He felt it. He would have died from what he felt, he did die, but the Ring and the Knife brought him back, even as he died. They saved his life, his mind, but his heart... his heart still screams, still burns. We fear he will never recover from it.

"I have said too much. I always say too much to you, Rion. I would not have only... I hope that you might help Talon, somehow, as you helped me, as you have always helped everyone you have ever met. It is not fair to you that I should place such a burden upon you, when none of us, with all our Power, even with the Ring and the Knife at our disposal, can aid him. But you are special, Rion. I have sensed how special you are. I have told you before. Perhaps there is something you can do."

RION was horrified. Fire! No, not by fire, not Aras! And for Talon to have felt it! He could imagine what it would have been like for him. He could imagine all too clearly: his imagination was as often a curse as a gift. How could he possibly help Talon? What could he say? What could he do? How could Talon ever heal from something so awful?

"You must come with me, all of you," Hunter said. "I will show you to your rooms, get you settled here. You may see the rest of the Tower later. You are in need of your privacy now. I will take you on a tour of it whenever you wish to see it. There is to be a banquet tonight, in your honor. I know you must no longer feel like celebrating, but we are all in such desperate need of something to celebrate, and we must all eat dinner, in any case, so I hope that you will come."

Hunter sighed. "And I fear you will have even greater cause to be upset, by what you are about to see. But your friend and your sister have not been harmed, I swear it, despite how it will appear. I would release them before you see them, but I do not think I would survive it, or worse, the guards would be forced to harm them."

RON said, "What have you…." But Hunter was striding to the door, and he flung it open and slipped quickly into the hall.

Ron followed and stared, appalled. He had begun to suspect Rarnak and Andra had been bound when Hunter said, "released," but he had not expected this. The two of them were lying on the floor, not unconscious, but rigid, as if frozen in the act of fighting invisible demons.

"What have you done to them?" Ron demanded angrily, fighting the fear that threatened to paralyze him as well.

"They are not harmed. I would never harm them. They will recover, I swear it," Hunter asserted. "I bound them by my Voice. I had no choice. When Rarnak saw me, he recognized me from Athanark. He spoke my name. Your sister went mad upon hearing it and attacked me. She lunged for me as if I were the Enemy himself. The Guard tackled her and then they both went completely wild. They would have been hurt, perhaps even killed, for the Dwarves are not used to fighting Men. They forget sometimes how fragile we are. I will release them now."

He turned to the Guard. "They are not to be harmed, no matter what they try to do to me, even if they succeed, is that understood?"

"Yes, Lord," the Dwarves said.

RION saw the Guard were eyeing Hunter as if they were afraid of him, as well they might be if he had been able to do this. Rion had seen Jargas's eyes; he'd seen he was a wizard. Jargas had told him Hunter's eyes had burned with the same fire. He had said more. He had spoken as if Hunter had been there with them at the time, though he had not been. A sudden realization seized him. They were bonded! The way Elanara had told them. Rion had suspected the Amontir Lords might all be wizards, but to see this!

Hunter crouched beside Rarnak. Rion expected to see fire in his eyes, but there was none. He merely touched Rarnak's forehead gently then sprang back from him. It was good that he did so. Rarnak lunged for him the moment he could move again.

"Rarnak, stop! Don't hurt him! He's not your enemy!" Rion commanded.

Rarnak actually stopped, spinning about in astonishment at the sound of Rion's voice. "You spoke!" he said. Then he saw Andra, and a look of murder flashed across his face again, but Ron had grabbed him from behind and was effectively pinning him.

"Don't hurt him. He's going to waken her," Ron said urgently. "He might be the only one who can."

Rarnak stopped struggling and glared at Hunter.

Hunter ignored him, instead touching Andra lightly and springing back again. He was wise to do so. Andra was on her feet in a single powerful roll, her hands going for Hunter's throat, even as Gar and Ara grabbed her from behind and to the side and restrained her.

"Let me go! You don't know who he is, what he did to Rion! I'm going to kill him!" she yelled, fuming.

Rion stepped between her and Hunter and looked at her entreatingly. "Andra, please! I was tricked. It wasn't truly Hunter in the dream. He hasn't hurt me, he's healed me. Listen to me. I've got my voice back. Please don't hurt him," Rion pleaded.

She stopped struggling. "You can speak?" she asked in disbelief. She glared at Hunter, "Then tell this coward to give me my sword back so I can fight him man to man," Andra said.

"I don't wield a sword, only a bow, and sometimes a knife, when I must," Hunter said.

"Then you have your choice. I drive an arrow into your heart at two hundred paces or we knife fight and I kill you that way," she growled.

"Two hundred paces? I don't think even Gar could make such a shot as that, and I have seen how well he shoots," Hunter said.

"I can't make such a shot, but Andra can," Gar said.

"Then please, accept my most humble apologies for binding you, but if I'd let you kill me, who would have healed Rion?" Hunter asked.

Andra glared at him.

"I have grave misgivings about turning my back on you, but I have told the others I will show them to their quarters, and they are in need of rest. They are in need of more. Perhaps I should find you another guide," Hunter said.

"And you insult my honor, as if I've not cause enough to kill you. I'll not kill you in such a dishonorable way. I was raised better than that," Andra said.

Hunter gazed at her somberly. "I hope that I might give you cause to not want to kill me at all. I've enough enemies here and few enough friends anywhere." He turned to the Guard and commanded, "Give them back their weapons, all of them."

The Guard reluctantly obeyed.

Hunter looked at Andra levelly. "Follow, if you wish to." He pivoted and began walking down the stone corridor.

The others followed him after retrieving their weapons.

After a short while, Rion could not stand the silence, for his mind being in such turmoil. His natural curiosity took over. "Who built this castle and who destroyed it, or at least damaged it?"

FARAD was glad for the distraction. "We don't know. It's many hundreds of years old. When we came across it over a hundred years ago, it had already been abandoned for centuries and looked it. Except for the shattered tower, it seemed sound enough. So we cleared out the pumar den and shoveled out the dirt and leaves and cleaned it up inside, careful to leave the outside unchanged. It became one of our refuges. It is our last such refuge now, with Caramore fallen once more. The Dwarves have helped us tremendously. We can cook without the smoke betraying us. In fact, there is the Dining Hall and the Kitchen is just past it," Farad said, opening one of the large double doors. "Originally, we thought to take you on a tour of the Tower. I had thought otherwise, with all that has happened, but we could do so now, if you wish."

Rion peered into the Dining Hall past him and his eyes widened. Farad realized he must have seen the two tapestries that hung on the far wall, from the direction of his gaze and his expression.

"I'd like to see inside, if that's all right with the rest of you," Rion said eagerly.

"Of course, Rion," Ron said.

Farad was relieved the others allowed it. He was glad to see Rion's mind occupied with something other than Aras. Rion's joy at getting his voice back had been so short-lived. It was good to see the sadness leave his face.

THEY entered the Dining Hall. There were hundreds of Dwarves eating. Rion weaved his way past dozens of tables and headed to the nearest of the two tapestries and stared at it reverently. It was a history. He'd heard of these, tapestries that depicted battles or floods or the building of a castle, some major event for a people. This one seemed to be a coronation. He stared in surprise. The features were Talon's, only the hair was silver, so pale it was almost white, though the face was young, not old, and the eyes were nearly the same shade as the hair, not blue like Talon's.

Hunter eyed it reverently. "This is the coronation of King Albinar. This tapestry, all of them, are of the Amontir that once was. Our people made them long ago, back when we had a homeland. This one is the most recent of all those that survive. It is barely over three hundred years old. The art of making such weavings is lost to us," he added sadly.

"Perhaps your people will rediscover it, once the War is over and your Enemy is defeated," Rion said.

"Out of the mouths of innocents. Ah, Rion, we have such desperate need of you here! I am glad you came," Hunter said. "Come, let me show you the Kitchen. I know you have not eaten well these past two days. Quickwing was watching you. We normally eat in shifts. Those in the Kitchen are constantly at work preparing and cleaning up from meals. But they are preparing for the special banquet tonight."

They passed a number of additional rows of long wooden tables with benches and chairs in the Dining Hall. There was not much room to walk. It was obvious the room had never been meant for so many tables.

"Food has not been a problem yet, fortunately," Hunter explained. "We came here well supplied and have not had to forage. We'd soon exhaust the hunting near the Tower, with so many to feed."

Rion saw that one of the tables was set on a platform so it was higher than the rest. That table was odd in another way. It had been cut, and a middle portion added that rose higher than the rest, with three chairs, one large, to the right, and two normal sized ones, an expanded version of the table from the first room they had been in.

"That is the King's table," Hunter explained, apparently seeing where Rion's attention was focused. "King Talon sits in the middle, with the Heir to the Throne and the Heir's wife to his right and the Dwarven High-King to his left. The Lords and Ladies sit to the right of the Heir and the Dwarven Kings to the left of their High-King. You will also be seated at the King's table tonight, as Talon's guests. It will be quite crowded, I fear! After that, you'll eat at one of the other tables."

They continued on to the Kitchen after allowing a few moments for Rion to gaze at the second tapestry. He would have to come back here before dinner and look at them more carefully. It wouldn't be right to delay his friends longer now.

The Kitchen was swarming with Dwarves; it was a bustle of activity. Hunter spoke to some of the cooks, and Rion recognized he was speaking Dwarvish, though he didn't know any of the words Hunter used. One of the Dwarves smiled and nodded at Hunter.

He turned back to them. "I have arranged to have food brought to your rooms, since, as you can see, they are quite busy preparing the feast for tonight. Why don't we get out of their way? I'll show you the Library next. The room you first met us in is called the War Room. You'll be allowed free access to every other room in the Tower except that one. Few are, so don't be insulted by it."

The tour continued through the Library, which apparently contained mostly Dwarven but also a few Amontiri books. Then they proceeded to the Armory.

FARAD eyed the many hundreds of weapons in the room morosely, trying to keep his voice from sounding too grim. "The main Armory is elsewhere. All the war axes are there. This one holds only swords, knives, and bows. If you see a weapon that you prefer to your own, you are welcome to take it. None of these weapons has an owner, save for the few on the far wall, which are tagged." None here had a live owner, at any rate, but Farad would not tell them that.

The main Armory was in the caves. It held almost four thousand war axes. They'd stopped burying their dead with their weapons long ago, after the first thousand men had fallen. They'd stopped burying them altogether. They were forced now to merely behead them and reclaim their fallen weapons so the Enemy might not use their bodies or their weapons against them.

The last thousand men had died beyond their ability to retrieve their weapons. They'd had orders to behead as many of their fallen comrades as they could before they themselves were felled, so that they hopefully might not have to face any of them later, but nothing could be done about their weapons.

RION could not imagine trading the sword Tarrell had given him for his coming-of-age for another blade, no matter how finely made, until he saw the blades in the Armory.

"Most of them are Dwarven," Hunter said. Rion knew some few Dwarves carried both axe and sword. "I have to agree with the Dwarves, that not even the Elves make as fine a blade as they do."

Hunter pulled a sheathed blade off the far wall and held it out to Rion on the palms of both hands, as if he were a man about to be knighted, handing his blade to his King. Rion looked at him in surprise and lifted the blade. The hilt was exquisitely detailed. The tooled leather depicted a wolven running across a field. Instead of vicious and terrifying, it looked lonely and noble and free.

Rion went to draw the blade from the scabbard that held it, stopping for a moment to admire the tooled leatherwork of the scabbard first. The scene upon it matched that on the hilt, only it was larger and more detailed. There was an entire pack of wolven, running past a stand of trees.

He slowly drew the blade. He had never seen his reflection so clearly before as he did in the mirrored smoothness of the blade, save for in the silvered glass mirror in Oberas's shop in Ardock. The blade was beautiful. He had not thought that might be a word he would ever use to describe a sword, but the workmanship was exquisite. It must surely have been crafted by a master of unparalleled skill. He held it carefully, turning it to the right and then the left, then held it as if he might use it, pretending for a single moment that it was his to use. Then, reverently, he slipped it back into the sheath and held it out to Hunter.

Hunter shook his head. "Read the tag upon it."

Puzzled, Rion glanced at the tag. It read *RION* in a clear bold hand. "But... I don't understand. This sword isn't mine. I've never seen it before, and I could certainly never hope to own one like it. This is a King's blade. It must be."

"NOT unless you have undergone a coronation without my knowledge," Farad said, in wry amusement, though he did not think anything Rion might accomplish would surprise him any longer. "The sword is yours, Rion. I selected it for you weeks ago, when first I knew you were coming to us."

Jarina had only just convinced him to put it in the Armory, for when Rion might come. It had been in their room, where he had looked at it often. His wife had finally realized that the more he saw of it, the less he ate, the less he slept. It had become too much a symbol of his missing young friend.

"BUT... but, Hunter! I can't accept such a gift! It is... it is too much...," Rion said. Then, seeing Hunter's expression, he acquiesced. "All right, I... thank you, Hunter, it's wonderful, it.... I'll protect it always."

Hunter smiled at him and Rion was shocked both by the smile and the rueful humor in it. "May your sword protect you at least as well as you protect it, then."

Rion grinned back at Hunter, in joy to see him so happy, when he had ever only been forlorn before, in the short time he'd known him.

None of the brothers selected new weapons, except for Ara. "If you truly meant it, I will select this blade, then, though not for myself, but as an offering to Elmoth, if that would be all right?"

"Certainly. Once you choose the blade it is up to you what you might do with it," Hunter said. "Come, let me show you the Stables."

Rion was puzzled. "I understood there were thousands of Dwarves here, but surely from what we have seen so far the castle is not big enough to hold so many. Where do they all sleep? Where do they all live?"

"There are a series of caves near here, small ones, nothing like the elaborate caverns the Dwarves are used to. They've been turned into dormitories for them. The main Armory I mentioned is there as well. When on the march, the Dwarves use tarps against rock walls, or tents, to house them, the few times they leave their Mountain. But secrecy is crucial, here, so here they live inside the mountain. Our kinsmen all live within the castle, save for Jargas. He is no stranger to life underground. And the Elves live here as well, of course."

"Elves? There are Elves here, other than Brook and Thorn?" Rion asked, both eagerly and in pain, for the one Elf he would not see.

"AH, FORGIVE me," Farad said. "It is habit. We all say it. It is easier than listing the three of them individually. I was referring to Elanara, Eladar, and Elavar. Elanara has told me it is permitted to use their given names when speaking with you. For tonight, though, please remember to call Elanara 'Brook,' Eladar 'Thorn,' and Elavar 'Sylvan.' Those are the only names most of us know them by."

"We actually had an entire Elven army of five thousand with us before, as well as three hundred of our six hundred newly discovered kin, but we've sent them to cover other key strategic points, along with half our Dwarven forces. Just the three Elves remain here." He did not say that it was because they had nowhere else to go, now that their Kingdom had been destroyed. He had once made the mistake of telling Rion the world would end after the seven Elven Kingdoms had been destroyed. He did not know whether Rion knew two of them had fallen, but he did not want him to learn if he did not have to. He did not want Rion to be afraid the world was ending, even though it was. There was yet hope that it might not, now that they had the Sword, the Ring, and the Knife, but victory had not come as easily as they had hoped, and with each passing day, they feared it never might.

"Please, tell me what it is I shouldn't have said, this time. I waited so long to speak again, it was so hard for me to utter even a single word, before, and now that I can, I seem to always be saying the wrong things," Rion said sadly.

"Forgive me, Rion," Farad said sincerely. "I had not meant for you to see me so melancholy. I had thought I was concealing it. I forgot for a moment how remarkably perceptive you are. I doubt most people might have realized my mood. You have said nothing wrong, truly."

Rion looked at him intently and then nodded in relief. "Do you think you might be able to show me which room is Elavar's? I am eager to see him again."

Farad sighed. "Rion, I know you would like to speak with him, that you'd no doubt like to speak with Elanara and Eladar as well, but you cannot. They are all changed from those you once knew. Elanara is the least changed, I think, but Elavar has become so distant from us, I think half the time he does not even see us anymore, or hear us, even when we stand before him. And Eladar is so very bitter, so angry."

Rion swallowed. "Why? What would have changed them so much?"

"Riviera and Loatia have fallen, Rion. Their Kingdom has been destroyed, their parents and their people killed," Ron said.

Farad cursed softly. He had forgotten Eladar's words to Ron and Gar, in the woods, though he remembered hearing them now. He had been too distraught over Rion to process much at the time. The two of them had apparently not shared the knowledge with the others until now. He wished Ron had not decided to do so.

Rion paled. "No. No, you can't mean it. Not only Aras, but two entire Kingdoms? Thousands of Elves?" His eyes brimmed with tears and then widened in fear, and he turned to Farad. "You mean it's already happening? But you said two years. You told me... but the chimaera came and... it's happening already. The world, it's ending."

Farad grasped him by the shoulders and looked him in the eye. "Rion, no! Please, you mustn't lose hope. You of all people must not! And there is hope. I had none when I spoke to you in Gosa, but I do now. That was before the Ring, before the Knife. We have the means to slay the Enemy now. We will slay Him, but first we must reach Him. He has ringed himself with thousands of His servants so that we cannot use them upon Him. But I have already done much damage to Him. If only I'd had the Ring and the Sword with me when I attacked Him, He would already be dead, though I had not even the hands to hold them, then. Please, Rion! I swear to you we will stop Him," Farad said, the ring of conviction in his voice. For a moment, because Rion needed him to be telling the truth, to believe him, it was the truth; he truly felt they would win, that they must win.

"All right. When I heard that two Kingdoms had been destroyed I thought... I didn't understand, Hunter. I am glad you explained it to me," Rion said. Farad could hear the relief in his voice.

"Come, I will show you to your rooms now." Farad led them up the winding stairs of the tower to the second level. He pointed to a door. "Andra and Rarnak will be sharing this room. The four of you will share the one across the hall from them," he said, pointing to another door. "There is a bath at the end of the corridor. Hot water is delivered every half hour until midnight, then beginning again just before dawn. There is a toilet behind the door next to it. The chamber pot is emptied every half hour or so. If you need me, my room is six doors down, to the left of your room, Rion. Please knock first, of course, as Jarina and I share it.

"Dinner usually begins well before dusk and proceeds in four shifts well into the night. Bells mark the hour each day, one to twelve, with the sequence beginning over again after the noon bell for the second half of the day. Tonight dinner will be different. Many will be eating in the caves and the rest of us will begin the feast in the Dining Hall at sixth bell.

"Tomorrow the schedule will return to normal, with four two-hour shifts for each meal. Dwarves do not like to be rushed at the table, but with so many to feed, two hour shifts were the best we could do. Breakfast will be at second, fourth, sixth, and eighth bell. Lunch is tenth, twelfth, second, and fourth bell. Dinner is sixth, eighth, tenth and twelfth bell. You may eat during whichever shift appeals to you.

"I will leave you to your rest now. Please, do not worry about what you have to wear being inappropriate for tonight. We are a poor Kingdom at best and do not stand on formality. Whatever you have with you, even what you are wearing now, will be fine. You may set it out to be washed, if you wish, in front of your door, and your clothes will be returned to you clean and dry as soon as it is possible for them to be. It is quite remarkable to travel with an army of Dwarves. Having now done so, I would not want to ever run a campaign without them." He smiled at them tiredly and left them to get settled.

RION and the brothers entered their room. It was small. Rion thought the single bed would be quite cozy for the four of them, but it would be a welcome change from their bedrolls on the cold ground. He was surprised and pleased to see their saddlebags were already in the room. The promised food was as well. On the table opposite the bed, beside a stack of metal plates and four steins, was an enormous tray containing loaves of bread and an assortment of dried meats, cheeses, and dried fruit, all artfully arranged. There was a cask of mead or wine on the floor as well.

Rion set his book and lead and the smaller pack he had been carrying down beside his saddlebags, stretching his fingers. He pulled out his set of spare clothes. "I'm not hungry right now, but a bath sounds good. I've never sat at a King's table before. I'll feel awfully underdressed in this. It's a far cry from what I used to wear, but at least these are clean," he said, laughing, eyeing the worn swordsman's clothes he'd produced.

Ron hugged him spontaneously. "You can speak again! We've missed your voice, Rion."

Rion grinned. "I've missed it too." Then he became serious and sad. "Now that you've seen me safely here, you'll be heading for home, won't you, for the mill?" he asked wistfully. "No, I didn't mean it to sound that way. You should go. I want you to go, to be safe. I'd be a danger to you and the mill and Ogaten if I went back. After the Enemy is defeated, after the War, then I can return. Tarrell and I can live in Ogaten, where we can still see you and—no. It will be different. He has Talia. They'll want a home of their own, of course. By the time I return, it's likely he'll already have a child. So… I suppose it will just be me on my own. I…." He swallowed, feeling tears threatening to come.

Ron smiled at him fondly. "Can you believe I'd not planned so far in advance? I was afraid to jinx us, I suppose, afraid Elmoth might think me too confident. I've started to truly follow Him now, as Ara does, or at least, more than I did before. I doubt I'll ever show quite as much fervor as he does. But with all that's happened on this trip, and the last one, it seems right to do so."

Ara said. "You need not look so sad, Rion. You'll not be alone. I'm staying right here. Grandfather told us to aid the Watch, whenever we recognized someone as one of them. I swore to Hunter back in Gosa I would aid him, and I mean to keep that promise. This war is ours as much as it is anyone's, with all the Enemy has done and tried to do to us and what happened to Gosa. In fact, I've a pretty strong feeling that this is the same Enemy who burned Thenalon a hundred years ago and killed Grandfather's family and all the others. I mean to see he doesn't hurt anyone else."

Gar nodded. "I'll not leave when I'm needed. It's the Lands of Men the Enemy has his sights on now. I'll not let him take any more Cities without a fight."

Ron nodded, looking thoughtful. "I'd thought myself too old to fight, but there are those here older than I am by far, who show no signs of slowing down. I've still got a strong sword arm. I'll do my part."

Rion said, "I don't like the thought that you will all still be in danger, but I guess none of us are truly safe anywhere now. And I would have missed you terribly if you had gone. At least you'll no longer be fighting to protect me. I'll be fighting by your side, helping you protect them."

Ron eyed Rion carefully. "Rion, after all their concern to see you safe, I don't think Talon or Hunter or Elanara will let you guard or soldier for them."

"We'll see about that," Rion said, determined. "I'm going for that bath now, if the room is free." He left with his clean clothes. He hoped there might be a clean towel inside, as he'd not thought to ask, and his own small washrag was ragged and threadbare.

He walked to the door Hunter had indicated, at the end of the hall. There was a slate hanging from a rope on the door, colored red, with the word "OCCUPIED," written on it in Common, and a word below in an odd hand Rion thought must be Dwarvish, and a third word Rion read in Amontirin, smiling that he could.

He turned to head back, but hesitated. Someone was singing from inside the room. At first, he thought it must be Elanara, as the voice was high-pitched, like a woman's, and sweet, and the song was Elvish. He stood listening, entranced. But then the song ended and another began, and this one was in what he recognized to be Amontirin, though the words flowed so smoothly he almost didn't recognize it. The voice was deeper, singing in a man's range now.

Rion listened, enraptured. It was a love song, haunting and beautiful, as the Elvish song had been, and so sad, Rion fought tears hearing it. But then there was a third song, in Common, another love song, only this one was a happy one. Rion had his ear pressed to the door now, his eyes closed to hear without distraction.

The fourth song was bawdy. Rion recognized it as a drinking song he'd heard Ara and Gar singing once when they'd come back to the shop from a night on the town together.

The fifth song was deep toned and guttural, and he realized it was in Dwarvish. This one had the same tone as the other, and he suspected it might also be a drinking song. He'd have sworn a Dwarf had been singing it, had he not known it was a Man from all he'd heard before.

He was waiting eagerly for the next song to begin when the door opened unexpectedly, and he pitched forward through the doorway. There was a startled exclamation and then warm and somewhat damp strong arms wrapped around him, catching him.

Rion flushed darkly and found his footing, apologizing. "Forgive me! I'm not usually so clumsy," he said, looking up to see whom he'd fallen against. It was Lunahr! He could not think of him as Beryl, after knowing for so long Beryl was dead, though he knew he wasn't supposed to even know Lunahr's given name. Lunahr was gazing at him with a mixture of surprise and amusement, like an Elf might. But there was a hint of something else as well. He was looking at him, just a little, the way Elsa used to look at Tarrell, with wistful longing bordering on lust.

Hunter had told him that the Enemy had captured Lunahr, tortured him and worse. He could guess the form at least some of the torture had taken. Was Lunahr still under the Enemy's influence? Had he been twisted, changed? His embarrassment turned to fear, and he pulled away from Lunahr's arms.

"You're afraid of me?" Lunahr asked perceptively. "Please don't be, Rion. I'd never harm you."

Rion wanted to be able to believe him. He didn't look evil, or feel cold and dead like those horrible things from his dream. He felt warm and strong and alive. Rion remembered the feeling of his arms around him with sudden wistfulness of his own. And those songs! Meloneth himself could not sound so sweet. At the thought of the songs, Rion's fear left him. "I'm sorry! It's just the way you were looking at me made me feel nervous. I know you had been captured and…."

Lunahr paled at his words, his eyes growing wide. He looked almost like Hunter had in Gosa, when he'd grabbed him and shaken him, then fled toward the lamp in their room. He began trembling wildly. Rion put his hand on Lunahr's shoulder in compassion. "I'm sorry! Please forgive me! I shouldn't have said that. Hunter warned me to be cautious. What's wrong with me? First I can't speak and now I've forgotten when not to. I didn't mean to make you remember. I know a little of what you must have gone through, I… please. I was listening to your songs. You were singing so beautifully. I'd never heard anything like it before."

At the mention of the songs, Lunahr's trembling eased. He took five deep breaths, holding them and releasing them slowly, and calmed further. "I couldn't sing anymore, before. I'd forgotten how, until…. Aras reminded me." His eyes filled with sudden tears. "Talon says it's how I can know I'm healed, that I'm free of Him, that I can sing again even… even with Aras… gone," he sobbed.

Rion's eyes welled with tears also, hearing Aras's name, seeing Lunahr cry for him. Instinctively, he hugged Lunahr. "You loved him too," Rion said, and it wasn't a question. "He can't be gone, he just can't! I thought… all this time, on the way here, half of what made me able to make the journey was the thought I'd get to see him again. I knew he couldn't have strayed from Talon's side. I have so much to tell him, so much I wanted to share with him. I… he always wanted to know so much, about everything. Tarrell used to tease me that I'd finally found someone as curious as I was. Aras was like a brother to me. He was more. He was…." Rion began crying against Lunahr, and now Lunahr was the one who was trying to comfort him.

"Rion, please don't! You mustn't. You have been so brave, to have escaped, to have come here, only the six of you against all His might. Aras would not want to see you weep for him. He only ever wanted all of us to be happy. I try, in memory of him. Idare, I try so hard! But no one here laughs, or even smiles. No one sings. I… sometimes I think the Enemy has won already. I look around me, at all of them, and they are like the walking dead. There is no joy, no light, no laughter, no song, only terror and weariness and fear and…. Jarina, even Jarina. She is like me. She was born to smile, but even she cannot.

"Please, Rion! I saw you. I watched you, in the woods. I watched through Quickwing, through my bond to him, even when Hunter was the one inside of him. You are all so alive! We are in such desperate need of you. Please don't let us take such a gift from you, when we instead need you to share it, to spread it amongst us."

"But I am just a Man! You all want so much of me! Hunter hopes I can help Talon and Elanara hopes I can teach you all to smile again, and you seem to want me to as well but… I am not a wizard. I am not even one of you. I have no magic. There is no fire in my eyes," Rion said desperately, still in Lunahr's arms, but now peering intently into his eyes.

"You do not need magic or our Power, Rion. You have power enough of your own, power of heart. Hunter has told me about you, when we were searching for you in Gosa, and later, when we searched for you everywhere. Elanara and Eladar shared so much with me also, when they would still speak with me before... before I lost their love. I.... You are so special, Rion. I think perhaps you might understand. No one does, except perhaps Hunter, and he has Jarina and... I am so lonely, Rion. You have no idea how desperately I need to feel loved again. I...." He gazed down into Rion's eyes and kissed him on the mouth, softly, gently, yet desperately.

Rion let out a "Mphf" of surprise and stiffened in his arms.

Lunahr pulled back, blushing. "Forgive me! I didn't mean to do that, I... I'm keeping you from your bath. I forgot that is why you are here. Thank you for taking the time to speak to me. I... I'd better go now." He stepped farther away, and his tone changed to that of an instructor.

"The towels are in this cabinet. It's customary to dump the tub once you are done. And don't stay longer than it takes the water to cool. The room is busy all day. A Dwarf comes by with more hot water every half hour or so. If he comes by while you are bathing, pay him no mind. Their tastes do not run as exotically as those of the Amontir or the Elves do. He'll not stare nor try to touch you. I... I forgot for a moment you're not one of us. Forgive me if I've offended you." Lunahr turned abruptly and headed down the hall.

Rion watched Lunahr go, his thoughts in turmoil, and then he closed the door to the hall. When he'd hugged Lunahr, it had felt so nice, so comforting and reassuring and warm. But then Lunahr had kissed him, and he'd been shocked but... he'd enjoyed it, too. He'd been so surprised, he'd frozen, and then Lunahr had pulled away, just when he was ready to kiss him back. He couldn't believe he'd thought to do so! Lunahr had kissed him as a man kisses a woman, but it had felt right, somehow. And he'd implied it wasn't unusual for his people or even for the Elves and....

He'd reacted to it. He'd been as excited by it as he was by his dreams of Elanara. He was reacting to thoughts of it now, far more strongly than he had at the time, when he had still been a little afraid. He blushed darkly at how strongly he was reacting, feeling his manhood stiffen painfully, and he groaned. He'd be sharing a bed with the brothers tonight. They'd be warm and pressed up against him, and he'd be in agony by the end of the night. What was he to do now? He certainly couldn't go out into the halls so obviously aroused. Maybe the water might help him?

Rion stripped off his clothes quickly and filled the tub with the buckets set against one wall. The water was warm. He wished it wasn't. If it were cold.... He glanced guiltily at the door, wishing desperately that it had a lock. He stood with his back to it, praying that a Dwarf wouldn't come by with hot water and interrupt him. Surely he'd knock first, seeing the OCCUPIED sign?

His hand went quickly to his manhood and he closed his eyes and pictured Elanara, or tried to. To his mortification, thoughts of Lunahr kept intruding, and then to his surprise and embarrassment, thoughts of Eladar. Groaning, he forced his thoughts back to Elanara and cried out in relief and release. Then, his face darkening in shame, he ducked into the tub and began soaping himself clean.

Slowly, he began to relax, the feel of the water and smell of the soap calming him. He began humming to himself. It seemed to help. He began to sing, softly. He used to sing in Ardock sometimes with his mother, and later when living with Oberas, when he was sure no one could hear him. Oberas had no such modesty. He'd sung while bathing, loudly and enthusiastically, but with little talent.

On the road to Athanark, their guards had sung around the fire at night. At first, Rion had hung back. He was afraid Oberas wouldn't approve of him singing with the men. But Tarrell had gently teased him enough that he finally did, and he was surprised at how the rest of the men seemed to warm up to him for it. He was even more surprised when he saw Oberas watching them. A look had flashed across his face, of memory and pain, of loss too terrible to bear. Rion had not sung with them again. He couldn't after seeing Oberas's face; no amount of teasing by Tarrell and the others could make him.

Tarrell, Hardred, Alnas, and Elkrum had been their original guards in the City. They'd hired extra men for the journey to Athanark, and Tarrell had quickly become friends with all of them. Rion missed all their lost guards fiercely, but especially their original guards, and of them, he missed Hardred most of all. He'd been almost like a father to him, for all Tarrell had been like a brother. Ron reminded him so much of Hardred. But Hardred had been called by Seneth, and he and Alnas had left them, two weeks before Athanark. And then, the day before they'd reached Athanark, everyone had been killed, save for him and Tarrell.

Were Hardred and Alnas yet alive, or were they dead too? Had they reached Meria? Would he ever see either of them again? He began to sing a song he'd learned by listening to Hardred sing it. It seemed so very long ago, back in Ardock, when the world had been such a simple and safe place, before the refugees, before the journey to Athanark, before the wolven-riders and all the terror since. It was a haunting tale that he called the "Lost Mariner of Meria." He didn't know what others might have called it. He'd never asked Hardred. It had seemed too personal somehow. It was a song about a girl who loses her one true love to the sea.

He finished the last strains and sighed. It had felt good, at first, to stretch his voice, but that song always left him almost in tears. He wished he'd picked something else. Today the tears had come. They'd streamed down his face as he sang. He couldn't help it. His mind had filled with images of all those he'd lost, all those now dead, and he feared Hardred was now one of them.

There was a knock on the door. It startled him. He quickly washed the tears from his face. "Yes?" he called.

"May I come in? I've come with the water," a gruff voice said.

"Oh, of course. Sure. I'm sorry. Lu.... Beryl told me," Rion said awkwardly, drawing his legs up to his chin self-consciously.

A Dwarf came in. He had two huge buckets on a yoke. They were steaming. "I'm sorry I'm so late with them. The water you've got must be cold by now, but every fire in the kitchen's been busy with cooking for the feast tonight. I finally reminded them that some Men like to be clean for such things as well: some of you groom yourselves almost as thoroughly as we do, and we've never a shortage of hot water in the caves. I got them to keep a fire free long enough to heat some water."

"It's all right. I'm about done anyway. Thank you, but I'll save it for the next person," Rion said. He realized the Dwarf was looking at him. Lunahr had told him he wouldn't. Rion blushed darkly, wondering what he might be thinking. He felt very naked and very self-conscious.

The Dwarf surprised him with what he said next. "You've a beautiful voice, lad. I thought Beryl was the only one who sang in here. I was angry at them for making me miss him. He usually is in here before this. The Amontir are a fastidious bunch, when given half a chance. It's a miracle they survive as well as they do in the wild. You should have seen how their King appeared the first time I saw him! And I saw Beryl heading down the hall earlier, with his hair wet, and I knew I'd missed him."

He said sheepishly, "I confess, I sometimes stand by the door and listen to him sing. It does my heart good to hear it. For the most part, we dread when we have to leave the caves, when it's our turn for watch in the Tower. This place will drive you quickly mad if you let it. They're all so grim all the time. Pretty soon you find yourself walking about the same way, too. Anyway, when I heard your singing, I stopped to listen. That song, I'd never heard it before. What's it called?"

Rion blushed darker. He'd never meant for anyone to actually hear him sing. "I'm not sure, actually. I learned if from someone by hearing him sing it. I never asked him. I call it the 'Lost Mariner of Meria.' Hardred, the Man who used to sing it, was from the port city of Meria, originally. I've never been to the sea. I asked him how he could leave it. I told him I'd heard the sea gets into your blood. He laughed and said he'd left and never looked back, that the smell of rotting fish is easy enough to part with." Rion's voice grew soft. "But I knew that wasn't the real reason. I knew he'd lost someone to the sea. Alnas told me as much, thought he wouldn't say more about it.

"I know what that's like, to lose someone you love. When I was a child, only ten, my mother died. I didn't think anything else could ever hurt so much. But she'd been sick for so long and could no longer sing. She could barely move or talk or even breathe toward the end. It was almost a mercy, when she left us. She was finally free of her struggle, her fear and sorrow. Not that she was bitter. She wasn't at all. She kept her smile to the very end. She mourned, not for herself, but the thought of how we'd miss her, my father and me. She drew comfort, though, knowing we'd yet have each other.

"But then, my father and uncle, they were both so young, so strong when… they died too, together. They were City Guards, killed in a riot. After that, I never thought I could lose anyone again. There was no one left to lose. I was all alone. Only I wasn't. I still had Hardred and Alnas, and Tarrell. Hardred was almost like a second father to me, and Alnas an uncle, and Tarrell an older brother. And there was Oberas, of course. I think I loved him too, though I wasn't certain how he felt about me, until….

"We'd all fled Ardock together, before it was destroyed. I thought we'd stay together. But on the road to Athanark, only a fortnight from the city, Hardred surprised me. He told me he and Alnas were leaving, that they were heading back to Meria. He said Seneth, the Goddess of the Sea, was calling him home.

"He'd been with us for over five years. He'd come the week before I began my apprenticeship with Oberas, though I first met him when he saved my life before I even knew him, and suddenly, he was leaving! I couldn't believe he was abandoning me when I needed him most. I asked him how he could and he said, 'I have to go, Rion. I've been thinking about Her, dreaming about Her. The creak of the wagons sounds so like a ship at sea. I miss the sound of the waves on the shore, lulling me to sleep at night. She's calling me to Her, Rion. She's calling me home.'"

Tears started spilling from his eyes and he brushed them angrily away. "I'm sorry. It's just… I don't have a home anymore. And Hardred… I don't even know if he's still alive. All the others… everyone was killed outside of Athanark, save for me and Tarrell. We would have died too, but Talon and Aras saved us. Aras was so wonderful: warm and kind, gentle and compassionate. Nothing like what Elves were supposed to be. I... he was my friend. He was...." A sob escaped, and Rion rubbed angrily at the tears streaming down his face.

"Oh Elmoth! Here I don't even know you, and I've been carrying on like.... You must think me such a child!" Rion said fiercely, angry with himself and humiliated for embarrassing himself like that before this Dwarven warrior, when he'd be living amongst them for weeks or months or even years now, until the War was over.

"Nay lad, nothing of the kind," the Dwarf said gently, his voice even more gruff than it had been before. "It's a sad song and a sad tale. I've many a friend now buried far from the mountains of home too. And many a friend we've not been able to bury at all. We all hope to go home again someday, lad. Ragnar be willing, most of us who are left might yet get the chance. I'm sorry for making you sadder than you'd already been. I'll not trouble you again," he said and turned to go.

"No, please. It's all right. I'm not usually like this. I took my mother's words to heart and I've kept my smile. It's just, I only learned today of Aras and... I'm tired, that's all; it's been quite a journey. My name is Rion, son of Anorion of Ardock," he said, not quite speaking his true name, but speaking it in the Dwarven fashion of naming his father and Kingdom, or in his case, City. "Although I suppose you might know part of that already. Hunter's been making quite a fuss about me," he added, embarrassed. "I'm glad you spoke to me. I like to make new friends." Then he took a deep breath and said as loudly and gutturally as he could manage one of the few phrases he'd gotten Jargas to teach him in Dwarvish. Jargas had told him it translated as, "Will you honor me with your name?"

The Dwarf seemed surprised and impressed. "I am Hernon, son of Dernon, of Malar in Holoren. It's a pleasure to meet you, Rion. Few of your kind bother to learn our tongue, and fewer still can speak it so it sounds right. I'd not have thought you might have the lungs and voice for it, but you seem to have Beryl's talent for languages, as well as singing. I hope to see more of you hereabouts. You've given me another reason not to mind coming here. Now, I'll leave you to your privacy. I'll see you at dinner tonight."

Rion smiled at him, his cheeks still sticky with his unfamiliar tears. Hernon smiled back—a big, warm smile—and then he left. Feeling considerably lighter of heart, Rion washed his face again and then got out of the tub, carefully dumped it, and watched the water spiral down the hole in the floor. He wondered where the hole led to. Then he toweled off, dressed in his clean clothes, and exited the room. He saw Ron heading down the hall toward him, a bundle in his hands.

"There you are," Ron said. "We'd thought to send out a search party for you, if you didn't come back soon."

Rion smiled at him. "I had to wait for the tub. I figured I might as well, that there's probably always a wait. You're in luck, though. They just brought in some hot water." He explained the tub customs and then headed for the room he shared with the brothers.

Gar was in the room, but Ara wasn't. Rion unpacked the rest of his small pack and then pulled out his journal and wrote in it for a while. Then he looked at Gar, trying to work up the nerve to ask him the question he wanted to. Gar was finishing waxing his bowstring, when his eye caught Rion's watching him. "Is there something on your mind, Rion?"

Rion couldn't have asked if Ara was there too, but with just Gar.... He took a deep breath and took the plunge. "Someone told me something about Elves I'd not heard before. I was wondering if it was really true or not."

"I'll answer your question if I can, Rion," Gar said.

Rion felt embarrassed to ask it. He couldn't believe he was going to, but he'd committed himself already. "Is it true that their customs are different, that Elves, maybe not all Elves, but some Elves, well, when they're in love, or maybe just in bed, that…. Do male Elves ever make love to other male Elves?" he asked in a rush, blushing.

Gar stared at him wide-eyed. "Who told you that? You're not telling me someone told you that Eladar and Elavar have been…."

"No! No, not them. Just Elves, any Elves. Besides, they're brothers, they couldn't, I mean, brothers shouldn't. Well, at least brothers and sisters shouldn't," Rion said, feeling extremely foolish.

Gar was eyeing him oddly. "Rion, have you been talking to Eladar? I know you like him, Rion, but I don't think he…."

Rion flushed darkly. "No! I didn't and this isn't about him, anyway, it's about…. Never mind. I wish I'd kept my mouth shut. It's been getting me into all sorts of trouble today."

Gar was still eyeing him strangely.

"Gar, stop looking at me like that! This isn't the first time we've slept in the same bed. I don't plan on jumping you in the middle of the night," Rion snapped, aggravated.

"Well, this is an interesting conversation," Ara said from the doorway, and both Rion and Gar blushed. "What brought this on?" Ara asked.

Rion wished he could spiral down into the floor like the water in the bathing room had.

"Rion wanted to know if male Elves have sex with each other," Gar said bluntly.

Rion blushed darker. But to his surprise, Ara didn't laugh at him. He instead appeared interested. "They do, and not only with each other. Sometimes with Men, also. They've a special word for it: they call it *lythenia*, for when they bond to one another for life. It truly means 'heart's mate' but has come to mean lifemate. It's the same commitment to one another as a marriage. But they also take lovers for shorter times, sometimes even just pleasure-loves, for a night or two. Swiftsong and Grandfather were lovers for a while, after Grandmother died, while Grandfather needed him to ease the pain of losing her. They weren't *lythenia*. It was only for two months or so."

"What?" Gar asked. He sounded scandalized. "But he never…. Grandfather? Our Grandfather?"

"I hadn't thought he'd have told the rest of you. He seldom spoke of such private things. But he wasn't ashamed of it, although Father was repulsed by it. I've heard rumor that the Temple Brothers of Elmoth practice a similar custom, with their fellow Brothers. I've always wondered whether or not they truly do. I suppose I'll be finding out soon enough. Why did you ask, Rion?" Ara asked, sounding intrigued.

"Never mind. Gar's speculating wildly enough for all of you already. I'll not add fuel to the fire," Rion said, wishing he'd never spoken.

"You've got a comely face, Rion, for a Man. Even the Elves would think so. And the right build. I could see how Eladar might…," Ara began.

"Enough! It's not Eladar who was batting his eyes at me and trying to kiss me!" Rion snapped, his temper fraying.

"I see I picked the wrong time for my bath," Ron said from the doorway.

Rion hadn't thought Ron might be so quick, but he should have realized he was used to sharing tubs with at least his three brothers, if not an entire inn. "Don't you start on me!" Rion snarled.

"Don't take your sexual frustrations out on me, Rion. I had enough of that with Van...." Ron began.

"That's it! Out of my way!" Rion said, heading for the door.

"Where are you going?" Ron asked.

Rion opened the door. "To have sex with Eladar and Elavar and half a troop of Dwarves, if I can find any who are willing," Rion yelled and slammed the door behind him. Rion turned from the door and almost ran into Elanara. She was standing in the hall staring at him in stunned surprise. She'd heard him!

Rion's face burned with embarrassment and, mortified, he put his hand over his face and shook his head. "Elanara, I swear I didn't mean what I just said," he mumbled. He could hear the brothers' laughter through the door. "They were teasing me! They knew all along.... I'm going to kill them!"

"You are lucky it was I who heard you, Rion, and not my brothers. Or a Dwarf," Elanara said, smiling mischievously.

"Well, at least that's something. I've gotten you to smile again. From what you and Hunter and Beryl and Hernon have said, I feel I've accomplished much," Rion said.

ELANARA gazed at him sadly. "I've been so worried about Eladar; it's hard to smile, thinking about him. He is so young to have lost both Mother and Father so suddenly and violently. And his home, the Kingdom, the River, everything and almost everyone he ever loved is gone. It is too much for even an Elf to endure. And there has been more, but I won't speak of it," she said sorrowfully.

Lunahr's betrayal, warping him into a tool of the Enemy, was what had harmed Eladar the most. He had loved Lunahr as a brother. She strongly suspected he had loved him as more than one, though she knew Eladar had never acted upon his love. They had both still been children when they were parted from one another. But Eladar could not forgive Lunahr for what he had done, even knowing Lunahr had been a helpless pawn of the Enemy at the time. She knew how Eladar felt. She was trying so hard to forgive Lunahr, but she also found herself hating him for what he had done to her.

"That's the real reason he didn't come with you to see us, isn't it?" Rion asked forlornly.

She nodded. "I hadn't wanted you to see Eladar yet. You were frightened enough to come here already. You might have thought ill of us and fled without seeing us. I'm so glad Hunter was able to help you, Rion, to heal you," she said, peering at him intently.

HER eyes. Rion could lose himself forever in them. "What does it mean, now, with your Kingdom gone? Are you still betrothed to Talon?" Rion asked, daring to hope she might not be.

"Not exactly," Elanara said evasively.

"You're not already married to him, are you?" Rion asked, feeling panic at the thought, like an ogre had thrust his hand into his chest, grabbed his heart, and was squeezing it.

She studied his face. "Why do you ask, Rion?"

Hunter had said those same words to him on the Road, when he'd spoken about Talon, for a different reason. He'd lied to Hunter, but he could never lie to Elanara.

"Because I love you, Elanara. It's just taken me a while to know it. I've dreamt of you since leaving you. It's been worse since seeing Elavar in Salenia. I dream of you every night now. I try not to, but I can't help my dreams. But I shouldn't have told you. You're married to Talon, or soon will be. It doesn't truly matter which. I knew I could never have you. Talon is my friend. I owe him my life. I should be glad for his happiness. Only he doesn't look happy, Elanara, and neither do you.

"Forgive me. I've said too much again. Hunter's magic has worked too well upon me. I think it's best if you not speak to me again," Rion said, and he walked past her down the hallway.

ELANARA turned to call after him, but stayed silent. High-King Laedrin still commanded her. She was still a Princess, although one without a Kingdom. She had suspected that Rion might share her love for him, but she had not expected him to speak of it.

Why did life have to be so complicated? Aras, Dewalaren, Rion… if only she could have chosen her own love. But she had already chosen, little good that it did her. She had warned Rion before that he would only ever give his heart once, and her heart was bound by the same rules. At least before she had been able to speak to Eladar. He had been able to console her, to counsel her. But now she had no one she could turn to. She would not speak to Elavar of this, and she'd not further add to the burden of Eladar's heart.

She suspected dinner tonight would be interminable.

HOW can I possibly show my face at dinner after what I've done? Lunahr thought in despair. Rion was Laren's friend and Farad's. He'd been so frightened to come here already, and he'd all but attacked him. He'd held him and kissed him and… the memory of that kiss still set his heart hammering. Rion was so warm and sweet, so young and innocent and tender of heart, so alive, that Lunahr couldn't help but want him. Rion hadn't seemed offended. Shocked, certainly.

Perhaps he wouldn't say anything to Laren or to Farad? He'd apologize to Rion again after dinner, if he could. But he'd have to be careful that he not be fully alone with Rion, lest Rion get nervous of his intent, yet ensure that there not be anyone too nearby who might overhear. He had better dress for dinner, before he lost his nerve entirely.

Lunahr found himself considering each item of clothing carefully, posing in front of the mirror as he had not done since the days he used to preen for Incuban. Incuban! At the thought of Him, a wave of intense longing and pain arced through him. No! He must not think of Him. Certainly not that way!

He snatched up his lyre and began to play and sing, with a vehemence that did not match the delicate nature of the instrument at all. He dropped the lyre and looked wildly about the room. The bells! He had a set of Dwarven bells, as well as a set of their drums. The drums! He began playing the drums and singing as loudly as he could, drowning out the sound of Incuban's tender whispers, pounding away the feeling of His gentle caresses on the taut drumskins.

He did not hear a knock upon the door, so when it opened, it startled him. He yelped and knocked the drums over, in sudden terror that Incuban had heard his longing and was coming for him.

"Lunahr, it's all right, it's me," Farad said, crossing quickly to him. "What's wrong? What's happened? I tried to check on you, and you were shielded from me. I tried to touch you anyway, but you did not hear me."

"It's nothing, Farad. It's foolish of me. It's just I… please, Farad, can you hold me? Only for a moment? I just… I need to feel someone hold me and…." He was begging. He fought the urge to fawn at Farad's feet. He was a man; he should not want to grovel, to feel subservient to someone he loved.

FARAD saw the war his young cousin was fighting within himself. "Oh, Lunahr! Please, you must try to be strong, but you must seek me out, you must allow me to help you, when you feel like this," Farad said and embraced Lunahr, who let out a single sob and clung to him tightly. "Come, we will sit and we will talk. It will help," Farad encouraged.

"No, I can't. You'll be ashamed of me. You'll… you'll be angry with me and… you might not love me anymore, and Farad, you must! I have no one to love me. I need to be loved. I need…. Please don't hate me! Please don't be angry with me! I didn't mean to. I didn't hurt him by it. I don't think I did. He seemed all right. I…," Lunahr stammered.

Farad felt a sudden chill. He held Lunahr by his upper arms and looked him in the eye, his eyes kindling. "Tell me what you've done, Lunahr," he commanded, dreading Lunahr might somehow have fallen to the Enemy again without them realizing. He was a fool for trying this without the Ring! He'd not thought it through. But fortunately, he did not find what he feared to. Lunahr was still himself, as much himself as he could be after all that had happened to him. Rion, it was Rion he was talking about. He saw the memory of what had happened. It hadn't truly been Lunahr's fault; the circumstances had certainly influenced his actions. From Lunahr's memory of it, Rion seemed more confused than traumatized. He breathed a sigh of relief.

"It's all right, Lunahr. You didn't hurt Rion, but you well might have. I've told you enough of what's happened to Rion for you to know you must take care around him, as he must take care around you, for similar reasons. We are all of us walking on moss-covered river stones, even with the Ring to sustain us. We'd be truly lost by now without it.

"You must not seal yourself off from me when you are feeling alone. That is when you most need to know you are not. Jarina will certainly not be jealous of you for needing a hug from me every now and then, and I'm more than willing to give you one. I know what it is like to need to feel loved. Of all of you, I have ever been the least-loved amongst you," Farad said, unable to keep the bitterness, the memory of loneliness from his voice.

"Oh, Farad! They have been so unfair to you," Lunahr said, hugging him tightly. "I am so glad you found Jarina and that she loves you as she does, that you've found a chance at happiness. I only wish... perhaps, someday, that I might find someone to love," Lunahr said wistfully.

"Lunahr, you are still so young, yet! I do not say still a child, for with all that has happened, you cannot be. Love will find you, but it takes time." Farad laughed. "Hopefully not so much time for you as it did for me! Nearly a century-and-a-half is too long a wait for any man!"

Lunahr smiled and Farad could feel that he was amazed Farad could joke about it, that he could now laugh about something that should make him weep. Farad was incredibly relieved to see it. "There! That is much better! I have missed you terribly, Lunahr, before when you were gone, but also now, when you forget how to smile. I am glad to hear you sing and play again as well, though those of our kin in the rooms beside you probably do not share my enthusiasm!" Farad teased.

Lunahr laughed—he could not help himself—as Farad sent across his link an image of Denric and Tanris, both House of Foxes, two of his most dour and insular kin, who were less than fond of their Dwarven allies, scowling harshly with pillows pressed tightly over their ears.

"Come, I would have you walk with me to my room. I have yet to get changed for dinner, but it will take me little time, and Jarina is already dressed and her hair braided. We will walk with you to the hall," Farad encouraged.

Lunahr nodded, at ease again, and Farad could feel him basking in the warmth of his love.

DINNER was endless. Rion had been excited at first: he'd never eaten at a King's table before. He'd been thrilled to see first Eladar and then Elanara and Elavar, but the Elves had arrived later than the others and were seated far down at the opposite end of the table, and he'd not had a chance to speak with them.

He'd been surprised at some of the people at their table. Hunter had said the three middle seats were for the Heir to the Throne, the King, and the Dwarven High-King. Talon had told him Jargas was his Heir, so he'd not been surprised when he'd sat down in the large chair by Talon's side, but he had certainly not expected that the Dwarven High-King might be a Man, not a Dwarf at all, though he certainly groomed himself as one.

Rion was also surprised to see two Dwarven ladies, not one. He recognized Jarina from her eyes above her veil. He'd seen her on the road to Salenia and would not soon forget her. But upon introductions, he learned that the other was both daughter to High-King Archer and Jargas's wife. Also, he learned that Archer was Lord of House Serpents, which explained at least a little how he might be High-King; he was an Amontir Lord, so he must have Power like the rest of them. There were other Lords and their cousins, mostly male. There were few ladies at the table, and none at all in the rest of the room.

He'd been surprised to see that many of the Men at the table wore conspicuous jewelry, even Talon and Hunter. They each had an armband, most of them of a blazingly pure silver that they wore around their biceps, on the outside of their long sleeves. Could they truly all be pallenteum? He could see that there was some kind of etching on most of the bands, but he'd not gotten close enough to any of them yet to see them in detail.

Talon's was different, though. His was of that same odd reddish copper metal as the knife Hunter had used to help heal him, and he suspected the ring, though he'd not gotten a good enough look at the latter to be sure. And instead of an etched design, Talon's armband was graced with a ruby cabochon, the same size and shape as the one on the ring.

Then Jargas raised his stein, and Rion saw to his surprise he was wearing an armband on his wrist, as if it were a bracelet, of the same bright silver as the others, yet decorated with a cabochon like Talon's. Perhaps Talon wore the King's armband, and Jargas wore the Heir's?

Were the other armbands symbols to show who amongst them might be Captains of the Watch, Lords of their Houses? If Lunahr's bore the image of an eagle, that would probably mean they did. Rion wished he were sitting next to him and not the two Men he'd been seated between.

Rion squirmed uncomfortably in his chair. He could see everyone was straining to appear happy and interested in them being there, when it was so obviously apparent they didn't understand at all what the big fuss had been about with their arrival. Rion sighed. He should have realized he'd not get to speak to Talon or Elanara at dinner, but he'd at least thought he'd speak to his friends. Instead, he was seated between two Amontir Knights, both House of Foxes, Todd and Rekel. After an initial stiff smile at him, following introductions, they'd proceeded to ignore him completely and talk over his head with each other in Amontirin, as if he weren't there. They were all so tall!

He thought it was rude, them speaking Amontirin, thinking he didn't know it. He took secret delight in the fact that he actually understood many of the words they used, and was able to piece together much of their conversation, enough to know he liked them as little as they liked him and his friends. Apparently, their disdain included the Dwarves as well. They'd even said some things in whispered tones to each other about Jargas and Jarina, who were kin to them.

They didn't seem to tolerate anyone other than full-blooded Amontir. He thought that was a pretty lonely attitude to have, considering how few of their kind were left, although Hunter had mentioned they'd had three hundred new kin fighting with them, of six hundred. He was burning with curiosity to hear what that had all been about.

The man to his left, whom Talon had introduced as Todd, said in Amontirin, "Must we stay the entire length of the meal, Denric? Can't you complain you're ill or something? Idare only knows these Dwarves cook like they mean to poison us! I don't know how the others can stand eating such things. And I still cannot believe those barbarians actually eat with their hands! You'd think after months of eating with us, at least their Kings might have learned what a fork is for."

"Courage, Tanris! We must wait until the third course, at least, or the King is liable to send that poor excuse for a healer of theirs to us and make us eat some more of those vile fungi of theirs," the one on his right Talon had called Rekel replied contemptuously.

Rion gritted his teeth, fighting the urge to teach them some respect for their allies. He couldn't believe men such as these might be kin to Talon and Hunter and Lunahr!

Lunahr. He couldn't help glancing in his direction, now that he'd been thinking of him again. Lunahr turned at the same moment as he did so, and their eyes locked. Lunahr smiled timidly at Rion, and Rion blushed and looked down at his plate. Lunahr's smile was like an Elf's; it had the same effect on him as Aras's had on some of the women, and even the men they'd seen in Athanark, while they were with him.

He'd felt his own heart quicken more than once when Aras had smiled at him. He'd not thought twice about why it might have before; he had attributed it to Aras being an Elf. He'd thought it was an effect they might have upon Men. Now he wondered more about what it might signify, after what he'd learned. Although he couldn't imagine that Aras had ever intentionally been trying to entice, let alone seduce, him, with his smile. The pain was new and raw and agonizing, and he fought not to gasp. He'd been thinking about Aras as if he might see him again, forgetting for a moment that he was gone forever, and why.

DEWALAREN looked about in dismay. The seating arrangements had been a mistake. He'd expected his people to be courteous and curious and talkative, rather than insular. He'd hoped there might be at least a hint of festivity tonight. "Lunahr? Why don't you fetch an instrument or two? It's been a while since you've sung for us," he said softly, encouraging his young cousin in Amontirin.

Lunahr's face broke into a relieved smile and he hurried from the Dining Hall.

RION saw Lunahr leave the room after Talon spoke to him and wondered where he was going, in such an excited rush.

He was intrigued to see Lunahr return a few minutes later with a lute and realized he was going to play for them. As the son of a minstrel, Rion knew the instrument would lend itself well to whatever type of music he might be called upon to play. When the others noticed the instrument, the sparse conversation at their table and the loud conversation amongst the Dwarven tables quieted.

"First, I'll take a request from our honored guests," Lunahr announced, looking around at them expectantly.

"Do you know 'The Ballad of Lord Halon'?" Ara piped up.

Lunahr grinned. "In Common or Thenalonese?"

Ara appeared surprised. "Thenalonese. May we sing it with you?"

"Of course," Lunahr said. "Hunter, Fennel, maybe you'll join us?" Then he began, in a clear alto. The brothers joined in, after a moment's hesitation, and Rion was surprised to see that Hunter had indeed decided to sing as well as a Man he'd not met; if Talon had introduced him to the others, he'd not been able to hear. He sat back and enjoyed the song. The men's voices mixed harmoniously and when they were done, there was enthusiastic applause from the Dwarven tables.

"Rion, Rarnak, Andra, is there a song any of you might like?" Lunahr asked, turning his attentions to the other end of the table.

When the others didn't seem like they might suggest one, Rion asked eagerly, "Do you know 'A Summer's Faire'?" He hadn't heard it since leaving Ardock and it had been his favorite.

"I'm sorry, Rion. I don't know that one. Is there another?" Lunahr asked, sounding reluctant to disappoint him.

Rion shook his head, his face flushing as, unexpectedly and inappropriately, a half dozen other love songs came to mind.

"Maybe Rion will teach it to you, Beryl. He was singing earlier today, and his voice was quite pleasing to the ear," Hernon said with a mischievous twinkle in his eye.

"Now you've done it, Hernon! The poor lad won't have a moment's rest, now that Beryl knows there's new songs to learn," another laughed.

Others laughed too, and Lunahr looked embarrassed, but then laughed along with them.

Rarnak asked, "How about 'The Flower Most Fair'?"

Lunahr grinned and began the sweet melody, in Common, about the most beautiful woman in the world always being the one beside you. Rarnak gazed into Andra's eyes as if there were no one else in the room, and she did the same to him. Rion saw that Jargas and his wife, and Farad and Jarina, were doing the same. He glanced at Talon and Elanara. Talon was staring at his plate, his expression hidden. Rion's breath caught. Elanara was looking not at Talon, but at him. She blushed and looked away when she saw Rion's eyes upon her. He wondered what it might mean.

Lunahr finished the song and then turned to the Elves, "Thorn, Brook, Sylvan? Have you a song you'd like to hear?"

They shook their heads, and Lunahr sighed.

He turned to the center of the table. "High-King? Is there a Dwarven tune you'd relish?"

"'The Axe and the Stein,'" Archer called out loudly, and there were shouts of approval from the tables of Dwarven warriors who had been listening impatiently to the songs after the first ballad.

Lunahr began a quick-paced, guttural tune, and from the reaction around him, Rion realized it must be a Dwarven drinking song. Lusty voices joined in enthusiastically and steins were swung back and forth, mead spilling freely from many of them.

After the song was done, another title was shouted out from one of the Dwarves at the other tables, in Dwarvish, and there was a rousing cheer. Lunahr began a second drinking song.

After the sixth such song, Talon got up and said, "Please, continue, but I am making an early night of it, I think." He passed by Rion's chair on the way out as the next song began. Talon bent down and yelled to be heard. "Do you and the others want to stay? We can talk in the morning, if you'd like."

"No, I'd love to come," Rion yelled over the din and stood. This last part had been fun, at least, but he still felt out of place here. He waved the others over, and the brothers rose, as well as Andra and Rarnak. Many of the Amontir took advantage of the King's departure to do the same. The Elves had already quietly slipped away.

Talon asked them all if they'd mind speaking with him, and they were all as eager as Rion. They followed Talon to the War Room, and Hunter came up behind them. "I'd like to hear too, if I may?" he asked in Amontirin.

"I'd welcome your company, if you're sure Jarina won't mind," Talon said in the same language.

"Certainly you must know better by now," Hunter said, his tone gently scolding.

"I only wish to ensure you have the long, happy marriage you so richly deserve, cousin. No matter my need, or the Kingdom's, I'll never do anything to jeopardize your happiness," Talon said. "You're welcome to join us, of course," he added in Common, for the benefit of the rest of them.

Rion again felt guilty for not telling them he knew Amontirin.

They entered the War Room and all settled into chairs around the table. Talon went to a cabinet and retrieved a glass bottle of wine and a number of metal goblets.

Rion recognized it was wine from Thenalon. Talon poured for all of them, except for him and Ron, who politely declined. Rion took advantage of his proximity to Talon and Hunter to eye their bands more closely. He could see the detailed metalwork of the exquisitely crafted ruby armband Talon wore now. Hunter's pallenteum band bore a magnificently detailed etching of a wolven that reminded him of the sword Hunter had gifted him with. It appeared he was right, if Hunter—Farad—was Lord of House of Wolven.

"It's time we heard your story," Talon said. "Why not begin where I left you in Athanark, for much happened even before you reached Gosa that is of interest to us, and Jargas has told us little of it, and Elanara and Eladar even less."

Rion nodded and began the story of their travels. When Rion came to the part about buying supplies in Logareth to trade with the ogres, Hunter was incensed. "Trade with ogres? Jargas must have been sun mad! Ogres only understand the bow and the sword."

Rarnak, who had once loudly voiced much the same objection to Jargas in front of his fellow guards and questioned Jargas's honesty regarding his battles with ogres, spoke up in their absent friend's defense. "I thought so too, and told him as much. I challenged him in front of everyone. But he was right. We'd never have made it through those mountains alive, and Thorn would have been dead as well, had we not done as he told us."

Hunter quieted but did not appear appeased.

"We learned all sorts of things about ogres I'd never heard of. I even speak Ogrish now, such as it is. Jargas taught me. I learned more about how they live, as well, that I'd never even suspected." Rion continued the story of the crossing, of Thorn's rescue, and of the attack by the rogue ogre, where Thorn was terribly injured.

Talon said, "They didn't tell us any of that. We'd no idea Thorn had almost been killed. Please, go on."

Rion glanced at Gar and Ara nervously.

"It's all right, Rion. We've put it past us," Gar said softly.

Then Rion told of the obearn attack and Gar and Ara's injuries, and their desperate journey to the Elves, and about Thorn's message for them. Rion hesitated when mentioning Thorn's message. "It was very secret. It mentions things that are long past.

Can I tell you in Elvish, Talon, I mean Majesty, the way he taught it to me, so the others cannot understand?"

"Rion, please call me Talon in intimate gatherings such as this. As for your message, we are all friends here. You may speak it in Common, if you know it."

"Even the part about Beryl trying to assassinate the Elven High-King Laedrin?" Rion asked in Elvish.

Talon looked at him sharply. "You speak Elvish, now?" he asked in that language.

"I do," Rion replied.

"Eladar said that? No, it's best that not be spoken of here. It was not Beryl's fault, Rion. He never would have done such a thing of his own free will. Laedrin fortunately survived and has pardoned him for it, and he is not a forgiving Elf."

"I understand. And I would not want you to think badly of Eladar. In his message, he denied most vehemently that Beryl might be guilty," Rion replied in Elvish.

Ron frowned at Rion and scolded him. "Rion, are you keeping more secrets from us? I'd hoped you'd reveal more tonight, rather than conceal more."

"I will, I swear," Rion promised sincerely. "I don't ever want to keep secrets again. The last ones might have gotten you all killed. But this wasn't about me, and it would hurt someone who is innocent."

"All right," Ron said, though he did not sound pleased.

Rion told them the message, the part of it that it was safe for them to hear. He spoke of meeting the Elven soldiers in the woods and their capture. Then he told of Elanara questioning him and about the book.

"Father's book? It's safe? I thought it had burned with Riviera," Talon said, sounding both astonished and pleased.

"No, it is safe. I still have it, or rather, Tarrell's keeping it for me now. It's at the mill, or perhaps in Ogaten, with him. Elavar told me I should keep it. You'll hear about that, later. I met him in Salenia." Then he told them about being dragged before the Elven Council and drugged and interrogated.

"We didn't know about that," Ron said, looking and sounding pained by it. Rion knew they'd known he'd been hurt somehow while there, but none of the details.

Then Rion told them about finding the brothers healed and returning to find the others awake, and the soldiers attacking them, drugging them again, and returning them to their wagons on the other side of the forest.

"And you still went to Salenia for aid, after all that? You amaze me, Rion," Talon said sincerely.

Rion said, "I still love the Elves. They're wonderful. The soldiers are different. It's like they're not really Elves at all."

"I remember feeling the same, when I first saw them in Nalea," Talon said. "But we've fought beside them now, worked with them. They're still Elves, Rion. It's their training and how they live that makes them seem so different. I wish you could have met some of the soldiers we got to know here. I think you'd have liked them."

Then Rion told them about meeting Circe. And he took a deep breath, looked at the others, and told the rest, about meeting the wizards Arcanus and Magus. He didn't betray the secrets he had learned about them, the ones Talon already knew, from what he had told Elavar, nor did he reveal their given names, those that he had learned. But he told them that Arcanus had wanted to kill him for knowing too much, but that Circe wouldn't let him. And he told them about Circe charming his Elfstone to use it to waken Jargas.

"Where did you get an Elfstone?" Talon asked in surprise. "The Elfstones are rare and valuable, powerful. The Elves do not part with them lightly."

"Oh, I forgot to mention that. Elanara gave it to me to give to Jargas, to pay him for the horse he traded for Eladar's life, but Jargas didn't want it. He was angry with Elanara for tricking him and drugging us all. He said I could keep it."

"Do you still have it? We might be able to find a use for it," Talon said.

"No," Rion said, still despondent over losing it. "I left it behind in Gosa, by mistake, when we left."

Talon looked like he wanted to ask more, but he only nodded and indicated he should continue.

"Then we went to Gosa," Rion said. He told about being captured and held for ransom and about Hunter saving him, and that he left soon after to find Jargas. He left out the part about Hunter going mad. He obviously wasn't now, and he felt it wouldn't be right to mention it.

"We left a while later to go to Ogaten. Van had fallen in love and was going to get married and build an inn with his new bride. And we had to pick up river pearls for the Princess's dress, for her wedding. Tarrell's sweetheart, Talia, Rarnak's sister, was making it. It was on that trip that we met the Dwarven army." Rion glanced sheepishly at Hunter.

Hunter looked at Rion ruefully. "And you somehow guessed Jargas and I were riding against Talon, managed to keep me from realizing what you knew, and sent a warning to Talon to boot. I still have a hard time believing that part of it, that we simply let you ride away, never suspecting the trouble you would cause us. But I know it to be true, from what happened when we did come. How did you know, Rion?"

"I'll tell you if you tell me what happened," Rion said.

Hunter sighed. "Then I guess my curiosity must go unfulfilled. I won't speak of any of it. I'm still dealing with the repercussions from it."

Rion squirmed in his chair, feeling guilty and uncomfortable that his minor attempt at blackmail had failed so spectacularly. "All right. I'll tell you anyway," he said, and did so.

Hunter shook his head. "Not a scrap of Power, yet you read all that from me. You are a dangerous Man, Rion. Arcanus is right to fear you, and Incuban is a fool for trying to catch you. It has already cost Him much."

"It's cost the people of Gosa more," Rion said. "But that part's been kept from me, so far. It'll be up to Gar to tell it, once I tell you about the chimaera and Revenant in the Market."

He told them of it, and of losing his voice, and being jailed and questioned and exiled from the City. And he told them of the dream, although he said no more about it than that Incuban was using Lerdon and Jathran, come back from the dead, to torture him. Then he told them they had left Gosa, and headed for Salenia, hoping the River Elves might help him regain his voice and keep him from suffering any more terrible nightmares. He told them that a day out from Gosa, he realized he'd left the Elfstone behind, that it was still in his bedroom, where he had dropped it during the nightmare.

He'd gone to sleep holding it. He told them he had sent Gar back for it, almost at the cost of his life. He was gone days longer than he should have been, and when he finally caught up to them just outside Salenia, he had Van's wife's two sisters with him. Rion turned to Gar. "Now Gar, it's your turn. Tell us what happened in Gosa."

Gar shook his head. "No, I won't. None of us will. The bakery burned, Rion. That's all you need to know."

"If it was only the bakery, you'd not have brought the two of them in their nightdresses all the way to the mill and hunted for food on the way. You'd have bought them clothes and food and blankets. The whole city was destroyed, wasn't it? Thousands upon thousands of people dead, and it was all because of me, somehow, wasn't it?" Rion asked in a haunted whisper.

Ron sighed. "Thousands didn't die. Perhaps hundreds. And a third of the City was left standing."

"And it was because of me, wasn't it," Rion pressed.

"I've said all I'm going to," Ron said.

Gar said, "He's already figured it out, Ron." He turned to Rion. "The fire started on Amster Way, the street your house was on. We figure the Enemy was looking for you and got angry when He couldn't find you, when He saw you'd gone for good. We think He set the fire to try to flush you out, that He thought you were still in the City somewhere. Three chimaera searched the crowd in the Commons for you. They gathered up all the boys near your age they could find, one by one, looking for you."

Rion was devastated, but the expression on Talon's face was far different.

"The Elfstone! It was in the house! That's how Incuban found Rion, and that's how He lost him! Rion's core isn't strong enough, but Circe charmed the Elfstone and Incuban tracked him through it, through the traces of magic in it, and used it as a focus to channel His dreams through. Rion, the luckiest thing that ever happened to you in your life was losing that stone! The Enemy never sends a single dream. He couldn't even find you in your sleep to torment you. Even one more nightmare would have driven you to madness. If Gar had found it and brought it back to you, you'd be Incuban's prisoner, and they'd all be dead."

Rion stared at Talon wide-eyed. "And if I never told you all about the wizards and Circe and Gar hadn't told us about Gosa, you'd never have figured it out! I was right. Secrets are terrible. Even when you think they're for the best, they're not. People have always thought of me as honest before. I've been miserable trying to be otherwise, but I've learned my lesson. I won't ever keep secrets again.

"I don't just speak Ogrish, as I've told you, and Elvish passably well, as you've seen. I also know a handful of Dwarvish. But mostly, you should know I speak Amontirin. It's not right that you think I don't. I know you still like your secrets. I already listened to a conversation taking place around me at dinner, although they didn't say anything particularly interesting, and I thought it served them right for being so rude."

Talon looked at him astonished. "You cannot possibly speak Amontirin."

"But I do. Forgive me my accent. I understand it better than I speak it," Rion said in Amontirin.

Talon turned to Hunter, his shock apparent. "Did you teach it to him?"

Hunter appeared equally surprised. "Of course. I just casually betrayed our language to him, in the day I spent with him in Gosa. Or perhaps while I was in Quickwing, I screeched it to him," Hunter said dryly.

Rion laughed. "Actually, Talon, it was your father who taught it to me, as he taught me Elvish. I learned both languages from reading his book. The dictionary in the back was in Common and Elvish and Amontirin, though I had no idea what the latter language was at first, until I read far enough. I thought it a good idea to learn it anyway, as I was learning Elvish."

Dewalaren shook his head. "You never cease to amaze me, Rion. Come, finish your story. Hunter is dying to find out how you slipped past him, when he was watching for you so carefully."

Rion told them that they had left with two parties of Elves, but explained why they had to send the four who were guarding them back to Salenia. He stopped and asked Talon, "How can the Elves live here, without a river?"

Talon said, "There's an underground river beneath the castle, that runs through the caves. It's where our water comes from and is why there are woods around us. Farther up the Pass is very harsh, desolate, and inhospitable, almost entirely rock."

"So that's it," Rion said. Then he told them of their trip to Athanark, of the search for water and unearthing the spring, and their disastrous fight with the rogue ogre in the Pass.

Dewalaren looked upset. "You mean you came through by way of the Thinabar Pass? But that pass was completely sealed by a rockslide decades ago. I saw it myself."

"It's open now. Perhaps the rogue ogres reopen it when it seals," Rion suggested.

"But this is terrible! That means the Enemy need only go through the Velmar Mountains and take Athanark and then go through the Coroden there, bypassing both us here and our people and the Dwarves guarding the Gelthor Pass. He's not as contained as we thought. We'll have to plan around that, now. Go on, Rion. We'll worry about that later."

Rion told them about Vargas, and Talon was pleased to hear they'd found safe haven with him.

"And we met a friend of yours there too," Rion said, almost mentioning Aras, barely stopping himself in time. He continued quickly. "A refugee named Audra, a young girl with red hair and green eyes." He didn't mention the Elfstone, since Aras was the one who had given it to her.

"Audra? So far south? A refugee? Were her parents with her? Goras and Millicent?" Dewalaren asked, remembering the sweet young innkeeper's daughter they had met in Gower. He forced the memories of Aras those thoughts brought aside, successfully suppressing them before they crippled him.

Idare help him, he might actually learn to survive without Aras. He had no desire to lead such a bleak existence. As soon as the Enemy was destroyed, he would finally be free to join Aras in the release of oblivion.

He had been planning exactly how and when he would take his own life in minute detail, mentally wording the letter he would leave for his kin, not foolish enough to put pen to paper. He kept even those thoughts carefully shielded from Farad, lest he inadvertently hear them.

He was so distracted by his musings, he almost missed Rion's answer.

"I'm afraid not," Rion said. Rion told him about how Argo had rescued Audra and how they joined Vargas's caravan, and of the trip. He told about the attack by the wolven-riders and Andra's capture and rescue, and the illness that resulted from it. "Audra had been completely hysterical during the attack, and for days afterward. The healer had to keep her drugged, at first. We were afraid she was going mad. But finally she was able to calm down enough to talk about it, and I think doing so helped her.

"The wolven-riders had come to her village. They'd burned it and killed all the men and boys. They killed the women and girls too, only first… they raped them. Audra had been out with her mother in the woods, gathering mushrooms. When they came back, the wolven-riders were there, only they didn't know. Her mother went to see where all the smoke was coming from, while Audra stayed hidden in the woods. Audra heard them capture her mother. She… she heard her screaming as they savaged her, and after a while… she heard her stop. She climbed one of the trees. She knew they'd leave soon, and she was terrified they'd find her, too.

"It got so quiet, she knew they must be gone, but she stayed in the tree for two whole days. Then she climbed down and snuck into the village. She… she found them, all of them, including her parents. The whole village. The wolven-riders had eaten or taken everything they hadn't burned. She was able to find a single waterskin and took the mushrooms they'd gathered and some of the few vegetables left in her parents' garden and left.

"She walked, all alone, through the woods for weeks. She had no idea where she was going. It was a miracle she found Athanark. She'd managed to miss Fenemal and Logareth. She crossed the river too early. Anyway, after the attack, Argo, Vargas's nephew, became even more protective of her. We all hope the two of them, the whole caravan, makes it to Ogaten, that they might find some happiness there.

"We left the caravan in Logareth. Andra and Rarnak needed to get married there. We'd have had to have left it right after there, anyway. Then we came here. Only I started to worry that maybe the letter and the eagle were a trick by the Enemy, that He was luring me to Him all along. I thought I'd better be cautious." He told them of all they'd done to ensure they survived.

"Remarkable," Talon said. He'd grown very solemn hearing about Audra. "I'd not want you as my enemy, Rion. You are deceptively formidable."

Rion smiled in pride, hearing him say so.

"Now, it's well past midnight, I think, and probably halfway to dawn. You should all get some rest," Talon suggested.

Rion was terribly disappointed. "But I wanted to hear your story."

"Tomorrow, Rion. There will be time enough then. Right now you are tired, and I yet have work to do tonight," Talon said. "Sleep well, Rion, everyone. May you have only pleasant dreams. If you can find your way back to your rooms, I'll see you all tomorrow."

Rion reluctantly said good night, as did the others. As they left, Talon and Hunter began speaking intently to one another in Amontirin.

Rion retired to the room he shared with the brothers, but tired as he was, Rion found it impossible to sleep. So much had happened, in only a single day! He had gotten his voice back and had learned Aras was dead and had told Elanara he loved her and Lunahr…. Lunahr had kissed him.

He groaned and turned over, away from Gar, whom he was lying against. Gar was warm and lean and… he tossed his blanket on the floor in frustration and lay upon it, hugging it around him. He kept seeing different images, wonderful ones and terrible ones. He was still lying awake on the floor when the sixth bell signaling the third breakfast shift sounded. He sprang to his feet, eager to speak with Talon and Hunter. He realized he'd lain down in his clothes again. He changed, hoping to get the other set laundered today. Then he washed up quickly in the bathing room and headed downstairs.

The Dining Hall was crowded, abuzz with activity, except for the King's table. It was empty. He stood at a loss for a moment and then remembered Hunter had said he'd be sitting with the others after last night in any case. He began looking for a free spot, a bit intimidated by the rowdiness of the Dwarven troops so early in the morning. Although it was relatively late for them, he realized, since this was already the third shift.

"Rion, lad, come sit with us, if you've a mind to," a friendly voice called. He recognized Hernon, in relief, and went to join him. There was still a second empty chair to his right when he sat.

Hernon introduced him to those immediately surround him at the long table. A huge tray of sausages was set down before them. The Dwarves eagerly dug into them, skewering them on their knives and slapping them down onto the metal chargers in front of them. Rion followed suit. Then a wheel of cheese, a giant bowl of fruit, and half a dozen loaves of bread appeared, and Rion helped himself to some of each, mimicking the mannerisms of those around him.

He hoped to see a pot of kakla as well, but instead, a keg of mead began making its way around the table. Rion had resigned himself to it with a sigh when a steaming mug of kakla was set down in front of him, by someone who sat down next to him. He glanced over in surprise.

It was Lunahr, with a second mug in his other hand. "When will you loutish brutes learn to drink a civilized beverage with your breakfast," Lunahr sniped in a haughty voice not his own, which Rion immediately recognized as Tanris, the one they'd called Todd. The Dwarves around the table roared with laughter, and Rion couldn't help but join them. He laughed until tears came to his eyes.

"Can you believe the King sat Rion between Todd and Rekel last night?" Hernon said, his voice full of sympathy. "It's a wonder the poor lad could eat a mouthful. Except I'm sure they didn't speak a word of Common the whole night, the arrogant whoresons."

"Nay, Hernon, not whoresons. Whoresons are for commoners. It's bastards you're meaning to say. When a Lord begets a child off a she-goat, it's called a bastard," another Dwarf said, coming to join them, laughing. That set off another round of laughter, which Lunahr joined in wholeheartedly.

"Well spoken, Donovar! It's no wonder the King sent all his new kin back to Nalea. After the warm reception they received from those two, he was too embarrassed to keep them here!" Lornan said.

From the introductions at the banquet, Rion knew Donovar was the Advisor to the Dwarven High-King, Archer. He felt a little awkward. Their teasing had been funny until now, but he was afraid they might say other things that he'd not find so amusing.

"Don't worry, lad. We know when to stop," Donovar assured him. "None of us ever insults King Talon. We'd not dream of it. We've got nothing but respect for him. He's a fine man and a great King, both. But it's important he hears about things regarding his people that might otherwise be kept from him. So, I make my rounds of the tables and hear what I can, then casually mention what's important to High-King Archer, who lets what he feels should slip in front of King Talon, or Hunter, or Beryl here, so they can tell him about it. King Talon well knows his people are far from being as perfect as he'd like them to be, though he loves them fiercely and would die to protect every last one of them. It's not an easy thing, being a King," Donovar said, his voice suddenly soft and serious.

Something in his tone made Rion look at him sharply. He supposed if the High-King listened to Donovar so readily, he might have some empathy for the man in that position, but Rion sensed this was something more than that.

Lunahr said, "Rion, before I forget, Talon asked me to tell you he'd see you at lunch. He and Hunter have been up all night, strategizing. Whatever you and the others told them has shaken them up more than a little. It sounds like troop movements are being affected considerably. They spent the night trying to work it out. They're finally getting some sleep now," he said. His eyes unfocussed for a moment, and his face suddenly darkened in a blush. "Or at least, Hunter soon will be," Lunahr said and then grinned, as if at a private joke.

Rion tried to not look disappointed. "What about Brook and Thorn and Sylvan? Do they usually come to breakfast at this time?" he asked hopefully.

Lunahr sighed. "Last night was the first time the three of them have taken a meal with us in many, many days. Of course, there's always me," he said, apparently trying to sound flippant about it, but his eagerness showed through. "I'm not really such terrible company, once you get to know me."

Donovar laughed. "I warned Hernon last night he'd sealed your fate, Rion. I've seen that look before. Beryl's learned you've songs to teach him, and he'll not let you rest until you do. He even had Archer trapped for two solid days after we joined them, only a week after we'd come to unseat the King, and he's grilled many others of us mercilessly since then as well. He knows more Dwarven songs now than I do, and I've three-hundred-twelve years to his twenty-four."

Lunahr blushed, but then grinned. "I wish I had as much sway over the High-King as you, Donovar. I'd have him cornered in my room still. He knows some Amontiri songs the others have never heard of, let alone the Dwarven ones, and I'm still not sure he's taught me all of even those yet." He turned to Rion. "I don't think you've formally met, Rion. This is Donovar, Healer of Cavernas and Confidant and Advisor to High-King Archer. Donovar, you already know who Rion is."

"I just missed seeing you on the march here. I almost rode forward with Prince Jargas. It's a pleasure, Rion," Donovar said.

"Likewise," Rion said. If he hadn't already known better, he wouldn't have realized he was speaking to someone in so lofty a position. He had sounded like any other of the Dwarves around him. But then, he had no idea what their status or standing might be either, he realized belatedly. They might all be Princes, for all he knew. Though Hernon had been carrying water to the bathing room.

"So, Rion, now that I know you sing, I'd love to hear you," Lunahr said eagerly.

Rion blushed. "I've only ever sung amongst family or to myself, and not much for a while now. I couldn't sing for you, not after hearing you twice, now. Even Meloneth couldn't sound as sweet as you."

Lunahr smiled, his eyes taking on a distant cast, as if at a fond memory. "No, I can't claim to have a voice as fair as his, now that I've heard him. But he said with a thousand or so years' practice I might sound as sweet. And the songs he taught me!"

Rion stared at Lunahr in open-mouthed astonishment. Lunahr made it sound as if he knew the God personally!

Donovar said mildly enough, but with a firm voice, "Lunahr, you forget yourself," in Amontirin. Rion was surprised Donovar knew the language, after what Talon had said last night. Apparently few did. But he was more surprised to hear what he said.

Lunahr broke out of his reverie in dawning dismay. "I didn't mean that, of course! How could I? I just had a dream that I did." He looked like he wished he could run away.

Donovar said in Amontirin, "Calm yourself, Lunahr. No harm done. I doubt he follows Meloneth, for all he sings. But most Men follow one or another of the Gods. It wouldn't do at all to have you mention Jarnath or Areth or any of the others to him. It wouldn't be right to shake their faith. They need it in war more than ever."

Rion understood every word Donovar had said to him. Hunter and Talon apparently hadn't had the chance to warn the others yet that he spoke Amontirin. He had to learn more from Lunahr. It should be easy enough. He'd been reluctant to give Lunahr a chance to get him alone again, before, but now he thought he was all right with it. "I can teach you 'A Summer's Faire,' 'The Lost Mariner of Meria,' and a number of other songs I heard in Ardock, if you'd like," Rion offered. "Ardock's gone now. It's been burnt, from what they said in Athanark. The songs shouldn't die, even if the people have. Songs should be forever."

Lunahr was gazing intently at him, a look of eagerness and wonder on his face, and perhaps something more. "Have you finished eating?" Lunahr asked.

Donovar said, "Beryl, the lad's not even had a chance to start. You've not given him a moment to take a bite."

"I can take my plate with me so it doesn't go to waste, though I'm not really very hungry," Rion offered.

"Then come with me to my room," Lunahr said. He turned to Donovar, and the intensity left his face for a moment. "If I don't have him back by dinnertime a week from tonight, send out a search party for him," he said, laughing.

"You can bet I will, Beryl," Donovar said, smiling.

Rion followed Lunahr to his room, which was not very far from the one he shared with the brothers. Lunahr's room was larger and less sparsely furnished than their own. It had a bed, a bureau, a mirror, and a writing desk and chair, but also a large cabinet and a rack of shelves. There were sheets of music scattered about the desk and at least fifteen different instruments on the shelves, the floor, and some even hanging from hooks on the walls.

Lunahr scooped up the papers from the desk and opened the cabinet. He put them into one of several bins there. There were also dozens of bound volumes in the cabinet and on the shelves, and many loose sheets everywhere.

"It's a good thing I'm so paranoid about losing music forever. I'd copied all the songs I brought to Riviera with me. I had Talon keep the originals for me. I lost hundreds of new ones when Riviera burned, but I still had them in my memory. I was able to write them again, once Aras unlocked them for me." He looked suddenly in pain.

Rion put his hand on Lunahr's arm in concern.

Lunahr shook his head and forced a smile. "I'm sorry. I think about it too much sometimes, about Aras and Riviera being gone. And King Laranela and Queen Naraena. They were like foster parents to me, for all Elanara is my guardian. I... but you've promised me songs. I won't be able to stay melancholy once I hear them."

He picked up his lute and sat on the bed, breathed deeply, and began strumming it gently, his fingers playing across the strings. After a moment's hesitation, Rion sat beside him. He'd thought about sitting in the chair, but he thought Lunahr might feel calmer with him nearer. Of course, getting so close to Lunahr, Rion felt anything but calm.

Lunahr said, "I can't tell you how thrilled I am to know I'll be learning more songs of Ardock. I was devastated to hear she'd fallen. Ardock was the first City of Man I ever visited. It was six years ago, on my way to live with the Elves in Riviera. Talon and Eladar and I spent a few days there, just before Feast Day. With all that happened, though, I only got to hear a few handfuls of songs."

Rion was intrigued. "Really? Were you at the Games? Were you in the Arena when the chimaera attacked?"

"No. We left before then," Lunahr said, looking upset.

"I missed it too. It was the first year we didn't attend the Games. I can't believe that at the time I was foolish enough to wish I'd been there. I was such a child then! But it seemed like everyone in the City saw it, except for me, and it's all everyone talked about for months. Well, that and the wizard, of course.

"My Uncle Farion was there, though. He was a City Guard, one of the ones helping people afterward. There wasn't much he and the other City Guard could do when it attacked, though they tried. They were lucky the wizard was there to save everyone. Uncle Farion actually even spoke to the wizard. My friends were so envious when they heard. Though Uncle Farion didn't say much to us at all about it. I think the wizard really frightened him, though he tried to hide it. I realize why, now that I've actually met wizards. He was in more danger from the wizard than the chimaera, I think. He's fortunate to have survived."

Lunahr was studying his face, his eyes widening in surprise. "Farion was your uncle? I see the resemblance now, to both of them. You have your uncle's eyes, and your mother's smile. You're Alissa's son, aren't you? The one she told us of?"

"You knew my mother? And Uncle Farion?" Rion asked, stunned.

Lunahr nodded, setting the lute down. "I met them right after we entered the City. I was so excited to be there, so happy, and then I heard the most beautiful voice. I followed the singing to a window. I couldn't help myself. I didn't even realize I'd wandered off. Talon snuck up behind me and tried to take my purse, to teach me a lesson, and Farion and another of the City Guard almost arrested both of us, until your mother convinced them not to."

"That was you? And Talon? I can't believe it! I could have met you years ago. And Eladar too, you said he was with…. Oh Elmoth! Don't tell me…. Lunahr, was Eladar going by the name Fisher back then?" Rion asked, his breath held, thinking of the Elf who had so inexplicably come to his mother, fulfilling her fondest wish, that she might see one before she died.

"Yes. I was the one who chose that name for him, because he fished a man named Hardred from the River. He saved his life. He breathed for him after he'd drowned, until he could breathe again on his own," Lunahr said, appearing just as amazed.

"But that's incredible! Eladar's the one who saved Hardred, who taught him how to do that? Hardred saved my life after I was dragged into the shark tank and drowned. And Eladar's the one who sang to Mother, who helped her die in peace?" Rion was reeling from all he was learning.

Lunahr looked suddenly bereft, and his eyes welled with tears. "Then… she's dead? I knew she must be, if even Talon couldn't save her, but still I'd hoped that maybe somehow…. But she's not truly gone, nor her music, if she taught it to you. No wonder Hernon said you sing sweetly, if you've her voice! I'd never heard a voice as sweet, until I went to Riviera and heard the Elves sing. Do you play as well? The mandolin, as she did?" Lunahr asked, hope and despair warring in his voice.

"No, I… I never learned. We… we buried it with her. But also, I didn't really have an aptitude for it. She tried teaching it to me, when she taught me to read and write, and then later once more. She told me I might need to wait until I was nearer a man, that I might just not be coordinated enough to learn yet. I think I might be able to learn now. Tarrell taught me the sword when I was fifteen, and I learned quickly and well, but earlier, when I used to spar with my friends, their fathers were City Guard too, like mine, I was never much good at it. But now even Ron has complimented me on my swordwork, and he's as much of a Sword Master as Talon is," Rion finished proudly.

"Would you like me to teach you to play? It could be an exchange: I teach you to play and you teach me the songs you know," Lunahr proposed eagerly.

"That's a pretty ingenious way to get to hear all I know without me feeling you've cornered me, like you tried to snare the High-King," Rion teased. "I'll be locked away in your bedroom a lot longer than the week you threatened if I'm not careful," he added, grinning. He gazed into Lunahr's eyes and his own widened at the desire he saw. His heart began beating wildly and he felt his face flush darkly.

LUNAHR tore his eyes away from Rion and picked up the lute from beside him on the bed, lest he instead embrace Rion, or stroke his face, or do any one of the number of inappropriate things he suddenly wanted to do with his hands. "If you can sing the song for me once, I'll try to play it, and once I've got the music right I'll write it down, and the lyrics. You can correct me on any I forget," he said, forcing such thoughts aside. He looked expectantly at Rion, once he was certain he had subsumed his desire.

Rion blushed and squirmed. "I've only ever sung to myself or with family, and your voice is so beautiful," he said self-consciously.

Lunahr's head swam with dozens of other ways he might make Rion blush and squirm like that. "Please, Rion, it doesn't matter how you sound. I'll know how you meant it to sound," Lunahr said, desperately trying to think of the music instead. "Last night, after you left with Talon, Hernon told me more about hearing you sing. He even remembered some of the words and a tiny bit of the melody. Why don't you start with the 'Lost Mariner of Meria'?" Surely such a heart-wrenching piece would curb his desire?

"ALL right. Although that song isn't from Ardock, though I learned it there." Rion took a deep breath, then another, and closed his eyes and began to sing. He opened his eyes once he'd started. His voice warbled at first—he was nervous—but then the song flowed easily from him, as if it had a life of his own. When he was done he looked at Lunahr. He was surprised and alarmed to see tears in Lunahr's eyes. This hadn't been a good idea after all, he thought, panicking.

"Hernon was right. It is a sad song," Lunahr said. "But beautiful." He breathed deeply and then began to play and sing it back to Rion. The tears were streaming from Rion's eyes by the time he was done. It was so haunting the way Lunahr sang it.

"You already knew it," he said. "What's it really called? I've always wondered," he asked, wiping the tears away. He'd have felt more self-conscious about it, except Lunahr had cried as well, even as he sang it.

"I've no idea. I'd never heard it before you sang it," Lunahr said.

"But… but you must have! You knew the melody and the lyrics," Rion said.

"Of course. You just sang it for me," Lunahr said.

Rion looked at him astonished. "You mean you figured out the music from one hearing and memorized the words as well?" he asked in disbelief.

Lunahr nodded. "I've an ear for music, a talent for it, like others have for painting or the bow or cooking."

"A talent? You're a genius!" Rion argued. "My mother would have given anything for such a gift. I've an ear for languages and a talent for knowing people's hearts, but you…." Rion blushed darkly. "About that—languages—I already warned Talon and Hunter last night, but I guess they didn't get a chance to warn the rest of you yet. I speak Amontirin. I know what you and Donovar were saying before, and I've figured out a lot by it," he admitted.

Lunahr put down the lute. "What do you think you know?" he asked carefully.

"That you've met Meloneth, you've heard Him sing, you know Him. And He's not the only one. You've met Jarnath and Areth and the rest, all those we call Gods. They're not really Gods at all, are They? They're Elves, elder Elves, or maybe Elven Lords, with Power the way the Lords of your people have Power. Don't look so grim. Donovar gave away much more than you. I was surprised to hear him speak Amontirin. I didn't think anyone outside your people and me might know it, from what Talon said. How did he learn it?"

"He learned it while Archer was teaching it to his daughter, Shanti," Lunahr said, eyeing Rion strangely. "Rion, may I touch your face?"

Rion felt nervous again. "My face? Why?"

"Please, just humor me for a moment?" Lunahr asked.

"Um... sure. All right," Rion said uncertainly.

LUNAHR gently touched his face, and his eyes focused inward. Tentatively, carefully, he felt outward with his mind. But Rion's core was only that of a normal Man's, small and brittle and dark, somewhat brighter than most Men's, but definitely lacking in any Power.

"You are remarkable, Rion," Lunahr said, eyes focusing on his face. He gently caressed Rion's cheek with his hand, then blushed and removed his hand as Rion's face flushed darkly.

"How... how about I sing another song?" Rion asked, his voice squeaking a bit as it filled the awkward silence.

Lunahr smiled, relieved. "I'd like that. But give me a chance to write the other one down, first, or I might forget some of it or get the two mixed up." He began quickly penning the music and the lyrics at the same time, writing the music with his left hand and the lyrics with his right.

Rion stared, astonished. "How can you do that? Write both at once like that? And you called me remarkable! I've never met anyone like you, Lunahr," he said, his voice warm with admiration, but then his expression became sheepish. "I'm sorry! Forgive me! I didn't mean to speak your given name. I know I'm not even supposed to know it, but I can't help it. I think of you by that name.

"It's easier with Talon and Hunter. Those were the names they went by when I first met them. Although I have almost called Hunter Farad once or twice, after hearing Talon say it. He knows that I know it, though, after being in my dream and telling Eladar to put it in the letter and... oh, Lunahr! Please sing something, anything. I'm talking too much again, too fast. I've had so much I wanted to say so desperately for so long that now I can't seem to help myself. Please help me stop. Sing something in Amontirin. I'll have to really concentrate to understand the words. It will help, I know it will," he begged.

"Of course," Lunahr said, and began a different Amontirin song than the one he'd sung in the bath. This one was just as beautiful but cheerful, rather than haunting. "It's a ballroom song. In the days of long ago, we used to hold dances. Heather was born to dance. Every movement she makes is executed with such grace. It is a hope of mine that someday she might learn how to dance. There has been no one to teach her and no chance for her to learn.

"I wish our dances had not been lost. So much was: our music, our art. Only the tapestries remain, and... I'm sorry, I am making you sad again. I had not meant to. Please, I must write down the song you sang before, while I can still hear it. Then I will have you sing more of them, on the condition you only pick cheerful ones. It tears my heart to see the smile leave your face, Rion. You were as born to smile as I was, as Jarina was."

"It's all right, Beryl. Please write it. I'll be fine," Rion said.

"Rion... could you perhaps still call me Lunahr? I like the way you say it and I hear my real name so seldom," he asked, wistfully.

"Of course. But I'll be sure to remember to only use Beryl before the others. I understand about given names and true names. Elanara told me. I know you know her name already. You must, as she is your guardian."

Lunahr was unable to suppress a flash of pain at his innocent words. Rion's face fell. "I've done it again, haven't I?"

"Rion, it is not your fault, it is just…. Elanara said she is my guardian still, after Caramore, but… she no longer loves me as she once did. I was like a brother to her, to Elavar as well, but now… they hate me, both of them. And Eladar…. Oh Idare! He was so much more than a brother and now… I cannot blame them for it. I deserve their hate, for what I did to them only… I would never have done such a thing had I a choice! I… I'm sorry Rion, I'm frightening you. This is not working, is it? I wanted so desperately to hear new songs, only the music helps, but… it's all right. You can go, Rion," Lunahr said, knowing his voice betrayed how miserable he felt.

"Don't be silly, Lunahr. I won't leave you so sad. What kind of friend would I be?" Rion said.

"Friend? Do you truly mean that, Rion? You consider yourself my friend?" Lunahr asked in wonder.

RION'S heart tore at Lunahr's words, at the loneliness in his voice. "Of course! How could I be otherwise? You're wonderful, Lunahr. I wish you could still see how wonderful you are. Come. Write down the 'Lost Mariner of Meria.' I'll sing it for you one more time. Then I've some happier songs to sing," Rion said.

Lunahr smiled shyly at Rion as Rion began to sing, and he listened enraptured. Lunahr penned both the music and lyrics.

"I'll try 'A Summer's Faire,' next. I know it well. It was always my favorite." Rion sang the sweet song he remembered, the story of a young man finding his true love at the faire.

"You've a beautiful voice, Rion. Hernon was right. All you need is a little practice and training and I'll have to watch myself. I can't wait to teach you, both new songs to sing and how to play," he said, looking at Rion eagerly, in joy and something more. "There is so much I might teach you," Lunahr promised, eyes locked upon Rion's own through long blond lashes.

Rion's heart was racing as Lunahr leaned toward him, as he remembered the silky feeling of Lunahr's lips upon his own.

A loud knock on the door shattered the moment, and both of them jumped, jerking guiltily back from one another, blushing furiously.

LUNAHR licked suddenly dry lips. "Come in," Lunahr said reluctantly, stealing one last look at Rion, his eyes widening when he saw Rion's eyes riveted to his mouth, just as he turned to face the unwelcome intrusion. "Hunter," Lunahr said in surprise. He had not felt his cousin so near.

"Ah, so that's why! No wonder you didn't hear me calling to you. I heard the music, but I did not realize you had company as well. I'm sorry, Beryl, Rion, but Talon has need of you, Beryl. I'm afraid the music will have to wait," Farad said.

"But... but we only just got started! I...." He looked at Rion in dismay and disappointment, then back at Farad. "Forgive me. Of course Laren wouldn't call me if he didn't need me," Lunahr said.

"YOU and Talon will still be joining me for lunch, won't you?" Rion asked Hunter, concerned. "And Beryl?" he asked hopefully, his question directed at both of them, no longer knowing who he was most eager to see.

"I'm sorry, Rion, but I doubt we will. There's much strategy we need to rethink, with the intelligence you gave us. You look tired. Perhaps you should rest? Have you been having trouble sleeping?" he asked concern in his voice.

"Yes, but it's nothing. I mean, nothing you should worry about," Rion said. "Please, I know you've great responsibilities. I don't mean to keep you from them. Perhaps I will rest. Will I see you all at dinner?" he asked hopefully.

"Perhaps. If we can come, we'll send word which shift. But if you do not hear from us, you should eat without us," Hunter cautioned.

"Oh. Of course," Rion said, his hope failing.

He left Lunahr's room and headed to his own. No one was there. He decided to familiarize himself with the castle more. He hoped to spot the brothers or Andra and Rarnak, but he didn't see anyone he knew.

Discouraged, he finally went back to his room and lay down, not intending to actually sleep. He didn't think he'd be able to. How could he want Lunahr the way he did, when it was Elanara he loved?

He sighed in dismay. Because Lunahr had the same grace and beauty of body and spirit as she did, but Lunahr also wanted him, when Elanara never could. He forced his thoughts from her. It hurt too much, thinking of her.

He began singing "A Summer's Faire," remembering singing it in Ardock with his mother and father, remembering the last time she'd sung it to him, her voice scarcely a whisper. He turned his face into his pillow and began to cry, for all those he loved who he would never see again, for his mother and father, Uncle Farion, Matt and Ric and Drew, even Cedric and Justin, Oberas and Elkrum, Lerdon and Jathran, and Seafoam, all those who were dead, gone forever. He cried for Hardred and Alnas too, terrified they might have joined everyone else he loved in death. And he cried for himself, for all he'd lost, and all he'd never have.

Chapter 9
Alone in the Night

RION awoke in the windowless room to the ringing echo of a bell, humiliated when he realized he'd cried himself to sleep like a child. He wondered which bell it might have been. He yawned and stretched and rose. The room was thankfully empty, save for him. He combed his hair and splashed some water onto his face from the basin on the bureau. Then he headed to the Dining Hall. He didn't want to be alone, and there were always people there. Hopefully, he'd see a familiar face. He was dismayed when he passed a window to see that it was dark outside. He'd slept the entire day away! He felt slothful for having done so. Worse, he'd not be able to sleep at all again tonight, he feared.

"Oh, Idare, there's another one of them," he heard in Amontirin. Denric and Tanris were walking up the hallway.

"Just smile and nod and maybe he'll go away," Tanris said.

"The way Dewalaren's been acting, you'd think they were visiting nobility or something. But this one's got the mind of an animal, like all the others. In fact Dasher has more to say than he did last night at dinner! I touched his hand for a moment, to be sure. And only because I could tell he'd just bathed. It was bad enough that Dewalaren filled Caramore with Dwarves and Elves and those half-barbarian cousins of ours. Now he's bringing Lesser Men here as well," Denric said.

"He might at least have brought some women here, if he were going to do that. The one he did bring hardly qualifies," Tanris sniped, laughing rudely.

Rion's face flushed as he realized they were talking about Andra. He bit back what he wanted to say and headed quickly down the hall, toward the stairs. He'd completely lost his appetite, but he was anxious to see some friendly faces. He especially wanted to see Lunahr or the brothers, or Andra, or even Rarnak. Any of them might be able to lift the burden of his heart.

When he got to the Dining Hall, he scanned the crowded room in vain. He didn't see anyone he knew at first. Then finally he spied the brothers, at a far table, and rushed over in relief.

"Rion! If we'd known you'd waken so soon, we'd have woken you for dinner. We've just finished ours. I'm sorry, we'd stay, but we're off to a meeting with King Talon. We'll see you later," Ron said, getting up.

"I'm not really hungry. I'll go with you," Rion said, eager to see Talon again.

"I'm sorry, Rion, but there's been a series of reconnaissance and strategy meetings today. They're only for those of us being reassigned to other strategic locations. Gar, Ara, Andra, Rarnak, and I are all going to be heading out to Thenalon in three days' time, with King Velnar's forces. Jargas's father King Rongas is going to be heading to Athanark with him. King Talon's spreading us out more evenly. There's no telling where the Enemy will strike next, now that He has another Pass He can go through. He might decide to attack the west first, then come back to finish us off here."

"But what about me? Where am I to go?" Rion asked, panicking at the thought of being left behind.

"You'll stay here of course, where it's safest," Ron said. "After all it took to get you here, King Talon's not about to risk you in the field."

Rion protested, "But I can fight too! I've proven that to you, haven't I?"

Ron sighed. "Rion, no one's doubting your ability. But I warned you before that this might happen. We'll all feel better knowing you're here. The Enemy has yet to discover this stronghold. You're safer here than you'd be anywhere else, even in the Elven Kingdoms. Riviera and Loatia fell far more easily than their worst fears of how they might."

"But I don't want to be safe! I want to help," Rion protested, frustrated.

"By staying safe here, you are helping," Ron assured him. "Rion, it's about to get pretty terrible everywhere else. King Talon's people have gotten word that the Reservists from the five surviving Kingdoms have all been called to active duty. It's full-scale war now. Quickwing's been delivering messages without rest. They're wishing they had a couple of dozen more like him. Come, Gar, Ara. The King will be wondering what's keeping us," Ron said.

Rion watched them go, not believing what was happening. He'd spent a short while with Lunahr and slept for less than a day, and now the world was swirling past him. He'd been completely overlooked, forgotten. He had to find someone to listen to him! He tried Rarnak and Andra's room, but fortunately heard enough through the closed door that he didn't knock. He wished he knew which rooms the Elves were in. He desperately missed Eladar, but even Elavar might help him. Not Elanara, though. He couldn't speak to her.

They couldn't leave him with nothing to do! He'd spend all his time thinking about her, and worrying about the brothers and Rarnak and Andra. How could they even think to leave him here all by himself? Would Lunahr be leaving too? The weight of his despair was crushing him. He'd never felt like this before. He felt so lost, so alone.

Maybe some fresh air would make him feel better. He'd not even seen the sun today, but at least he could see the stars.

He went to the tower, climbing up the stone steps, past the floor their rooms were on, all the way up the winding spiral staircase. He finally reached the top. He walked out into the night. It was freezing, and he shivered. He wasn't dressed for it. He'd forgotten how frigid it was at night. The castle was surprisingly warm. That must be the Dwarves' doing, he realized. Castles were notorious for being cold and drafty.

He looked up and sighed. It was cloudy. There were only a couple of stars visible. He peered out at the wooded land surrounding the castle. He could barely see the outline of the Pass into the Mountains. Did the Dwarven Kingdom of Malar in Fromer really lie at the end of it? He'd like to go there, to be in a real Dwarven Kingdom, but that was the last place they'd let him go.

He heard a noise behind him and turned. He was surprised to see it was Jargas. He'd been so quiet. Rion had forgotten how quickly and quietly Jargas moved. Rion swallowed. He hadn't expected to see Jargas. He didn't know what to say, how Jargas felt about his warning Talon. He slipped past him without a word, hurrying inside, all but running down the stairs.

With nowhere else to go, he headed for his room. He tried to write in his journal, but his thoughts were in such chaos he couldn't focus them enough to write. He threw himself upon the bed with a sigh. It was soft but far too big, without the brothers. It had sounded like they might be busy for hours. Maybe he could at least take advantage of the privacy. Perhaps if he tired himself out in such a fashion, he might be able to fall asleep again.

He took off his boots, and after a moment's hesitation, stripped off his clothes as well. The brothers usually slept naked, when indoors at least. If he fell asleep afterward they might be surprised to see him undressed, but they hopefully wouldn't think too much of it.

Rion lay down and tried to think of something to get his heart racing. He pictured Elsa and some of the other girls he'd seen in Gosa, without any result. He couldn't think of Elanara. He shouldn't have before, in the bathing room, but that was before he'd told her he loved her and knew for sure she could never reciprocate his feelings for her. Certainly he could not think of Audra. She was beautiful enough, but he couldn't, not after what had happened to her.

Oh Elmoth, he'd never get to sleep tonight! What's worse, now he'd worked himself up into wanting something. In desperation he pictured Heather, but he kept imagining Denric and Tanris scoffing at him. Then finally he pictured Elanara. He had no choice. He really needed some release tonight, and he wasn't nearly excited enough. But he felt too guilty, thinking of her like that. She was Talon's wife, not his.

His thoughts drifted to Lunahr. His heart quickened at the thought of Lunahr, and he felt his face flush. He'd sat with Lunahr alone in his room, on his bed. And the way Lunahr had looked at him, right before Hunter had knocked. He'd looked like he might have kissed him again, like before, and Rion had been shockingly eager for him to.

The thought of that single kiss they'd shared made his manhood stiffen. He remembered watching Lunahr's hands as he played the lute. He had such wonderful hands: long, slender fingers, like an Elf. And his lips. No wonder he sang so sweetly, with lips such as those. Without quite realizing what he was doing he touched himself, and suddenly his body was spasming, as he released upon the sheets. The intensity of his release left him gasping, and he felt his face flush from the shame of it.

He leapt out of the bed and yanked on his clothes and then he lay back down, pulling the covers over his head, carefully avoiding the wet spot. His heart was pounding. How could he possibly sleep now, with what he'd just done? He didn't love Lunahr, not that way. He was a man. How could he? He already loved him like he loved Aras. It was as if Lunahr were an Elf also. He couldn't help but love the Elves. He tried to justify it. He'd loved Meander, too.

He loved Elanara, but in a different way, of course. He sighed. He loved her, but he could never be with her. She belonged to Talon. He pictured Talon touching her and her touching him, the way he'd just touched himself, and groaned. It hurt to think of them together. He needed fresh air. He'd soon drive himself mad.

He got out of bed and belatedly toweled off the sheet. Then he went back up the winding stairs to the very top of the tower. Thankfully, it was deserted now. But he'd forgotten how cold it was. He shivered. But he'd not go back inside. He sat with his back against the wall, arms about his legs, huddled and miserable.

He didn't hear footsteps at all this time. The first he realized someone else had come outside was when he heard them speak.

"But Elavar, you can't leave! Not now, when Eladar needs you so desperately," Elanara said in Elvish.

Rion groaned soundlessly. No, not her! Why did it have to be her?

"King Talon needs me also, and so does High-King Laedrin. How am I supposed to deny such a need? How could we ever hope to revive Riviera? Certainly not by angering the High-King, and you know as well as I he is quick to anger. I only wish it was he who had died and Aras who had lived," Elavar replied bitterly.

"Elavar!" Elanara hissed, shocked. "Are you mad, saying such a thing? That's treason! You're lucky the Army's not still here. They had spies everywhere. You might easily have been overheard."

Rion sat perfectly still, afraid to breathe, lest he betray himself. Could this day possibly get any worse?

"You're in love with him, aren't you, Elanara?" Elavar asked softly.

"Who, Talon? You already know the answer to that, Elavar," Elanara said.

"No, not Talon. Rion. You love him. And he loves you. I've seen it. Everyone's seen it," Elavar said.

In love? Elanara? With him? Rion couldn't believe Elavar might think such a thing.

"Rion? Don't be absurd, Elavar! He was just a boy, a Man-child, when I met him in Erenia. I offered to help him. How could I do otherwise? I'd have done the same had it been a wounded deer in need of my aid. You mistake pity and compassion for love. Rion is no one. He has no station. Talon is a King. I am a Princess. The High-King has approved our betrothal. He has commanded it. Talon and I spent three weeks last summer consummating it. We'd already be married had Riviera not fallen," Elanara said.

"You're shivering, Sister," Elavar said softly.

"I'm cold," Elanara said.

"Then perhaps we should go inside," Elavar said. Rion heard the faintest whisper of silk on stone. The Elves were gone.

Rion sat alone in the cold and dark, trembling, devastated by what he had heard. He was nothing but a child to her. Worse, she'd compared him to a wounded animal. She'd said she pitied him and… that she and Talon had… they'd spent three weeks…. He wanted to scream, or perhaps cry again. For a single wild moment, he thought of simply running across the cold stone and leaping over the edge of the parapet, to plunge down to the rocks below. The thought frightened him. Whatever was he to do now?

ELAVAR entered his sister's room. Elanara still had her arms about herself; she was still shivering. Elavar put his arms around her, hugging her. "You need not pretend any longer, Sister, at least not with me. Talon told me what you said, and what he told you. He released you from your pledge to him, Elanara. Rion is yours now, if you wish him to be. I am your brother, but once I am recognized as such, I will be your King. I would never command you to do something so against your heart as marrying Talon. He is my friend, and I have sworn to him as my King, but I will not stand by and see you destroy your one chance at happiness for him.

"Rion is a fine Man. He is remarkable. He should have been born a King. It was an accident of his birth that he was not. But he is a King amongst Men in every other sense of the word. I am not the only one who has recognized it: Hunter, Jargas, even Talon, sees it in him. And I know you do as well," Elavar challenged.

"Oh Elavar! What am I to do? If only my heart were as free as you make it sound! You don't understand. You cannot! I do what I must. Please, go! I cannot speak of it any more. I am not strong enough. I cannot break my promise, nor betray this trust, though it is all I can do to keep myself from running to Rion even now, and I must not," Elanara said despondently.

"Elanara, please! I am your brother. We are family. Can you not...." Elavar said in frustration.

"Oh Elavar! You are my brother, and I love you dearly. But you are not my only family, and I am a Princess. I do what I must. Please, as you love me, go," she begged, opening the door.

Elavar left Elanara reluctantly, awash in frustration. Never before had he felt so helpless to aid one he loved. She was in such pain, and he could do nothing to aid her. She would not confide in him. He knew there must be a reason for her to sacrifice her happiness, but he could not fathom what it might be. It was then he saw Eladar coming down the hall, at the same moment Eladar looked up and saw him. Eladar turned quickly, changing his direction to head for the tower, for the stairs.

"Eladar, I would speak with you," Elavar commanded, his tone that of King, not brother.

"Yes, Majesty?" Eladar said, his voice dripping sarcasm at the title.

Elavar's control, tenuous at best in recent weeks, stretched beyond its limits, snapped. Eyes narrowed, he commanded in his coldest, most imperious voice, "Kneel to me."

"What?" Eladar asked, in shock.

"I am Heir to the Throne. Father is dead. I am the rightful King of Riviera. You will kneel before your King," Elavar demanded glacially.

"You can't be serious! You swore oath to Talon, remember? Have you forgotten there is no Riviera anymore? I'll not grovel before you so you can pretend everything is as it should be," Eladar scoffed in disdain.

Eladar never saw the attack coming. One moment they were steps apart and the next, Elavar was beside his younger brother. His leg lashed out and Eladar crashed to his knees onto the cold stone floor, Elavar's hand around his throat, restraining rather than crushing, though it shook with the effort of his control. "Do not mock me, ever again. I will not stand by and watch the two of you destroy yourselves, after all I've done to save you."

"Elavar, release him!" Talon commanded.

Elavar looked up angrily and saw to his surprise that Talon had half drawn his sword, and the look he was giving him boded ill.

Elavar released his brother and bowed to Talon. "Forgive me, Majesty, for concerning you. I was merely attempting to instruct my brother in protocol."

Eladar sprang to his feet, enraged.

"Eladar, leave us," Talon commanded.

"I'm not some pet dog you can order away, Talon! I'll not...." Eladar said, but Talon did not let him finish.

"I said leave us! I can see now why Elavar felt it necessary to instruct you so forcefully. You are treading upon dangerous ground with such insubordination, Eladar. We are at war, in case you had not noticed. Even in times of peace, orders from your King should be obeyed without question. In times of war they must be. Now either leave voluntarily, or I'll have the Dwarves lock you in one of the storerooms until you learn some discipline, as this castle is woefully lacking a proper dungeon."

Eladar's face darkened in rage. He spun on his heel and left, heading for the tower stairs.

When he was gone, Talon sighed. "Elavar, this has to stop. The three of you have become a disruptive influence I cannot ignore. Unless you can all show some restraint, I'm going to have to send you to the caves. I'd have done it already, but the Dwarves haven't done anything wrong, and I'd be punishing them as much as you by doing so."

Elavar felt ill from shame at his words. He had failed his people and Loatia's, his parents and siblings, and now he failed his friend and King. He drew himself up and carefully removed all expression from his face. "It will not happen again, Majesty."

"No! No, I will not have you do that, either! Elavar, please! Can't you see how much we need you? I find I cannot trust your advice anymore, when I am in such desperate need of it, because half the time now when you speak it's out of pride or tradition, rather than common sense. I…. What's the use? You've done it again. You've donned your mask. You've erected a wall between us. You cannot understand a word of what I am trying to tell you.

"You have one day, Elavar. One day, or it's to the caves with the three of you. Dismissed," Talon snapped coldly, as Laedrin might have said it. The tone was bad enough, but just before he spun on his heel, Elavar saw the bottomless pain in his friend's eyes, the despair, the hopelessness that so mirrored his own, and he nearly crumpled to the ground.

He reached out a hand, but Talon was walking rapidly away. Wordlessly, he turned in the other direction, reinforcing the mask of cold aloofness that concealed his pain, and headed in the opposite direction.

RION emerged from the tower stairwell, when he saw it was safe to. He'd overheard more that he shouldn't have. He hadn't meant to spy on Elavar a second time. At least Eladar hadn't seen him. Rion had guessed correctly that Eladar would go down, not up, when he reached the stairs. Rion had only come in to get out of the cold, and because of his dark thoughts. He'd hoped the light and warmth inside might help. But there was no light, no warmth. None of the Elves here shed either.

He wished he'd never come. He'd rather have been mute his entire life than see the friends he loved brought to this. He had to leave this place before it drove him mad. He'd find some way to convince Talon to let him go with one of the armies, with any of them. He didn't care which. Except, he did care. He wanted to go to Thenalon, to stay with Ron and the others. Even if they didn't want him. No one wanted him. He fought despair.

He headed for his room. Not to sleep, he could not sleep. He got his journal and the writing lead and headed for the Library. He'd either write in his journal or perhaps read. A few of the books had been in Amontirin.

The Library was mostly bare stone walls with only a few small racks of books, along with bins of maps, a few tables, and some chairs set in front of a large stone fireplace. Though there was a welcoming fire in the hearth, the Library was deserted, he saw to his relief. He put his journal down, began scanning the titles of the books on the shelves, and sighed in dismay. The few Amontiri ones were gone. The only ones in here now were Dwarven. He should have known. He opened one of the maps. It was Dwarven also, apparently, though all the notations were written in Common as well. Still, it must not be important, or be something they had another copy of, to be in here and not the War Room.

There was a curse from the doorway. Rion looked up in surprise. The curse had been Elvish, one he recognized. There had been five whole pages of expletives in the *Understanding Elves* book. Talon's father had written a note at the bottom of the fifth page that he could devote an entire book to Elvish curses, but he'd stop there, with the ones he'd already written. "Eladar!" Rion said in surprise, his excitement freezing on his face at the glare Eladar was giving him.

"The one night I seek refuge, and you have to be here," Eladar snapped.

"I... I'm sorry... I didn't know...." Rion swallowed hard against tears and headed for the door, slipping past Eladar without a word. He headed back for his room, miserable. He'd just made it to his room when he remembered his journal. He'd left it in the Library.

He couldn't believe he'd been so careless! He dreaded facing Eladar again, but he had to go back. He made his way slowly. Perhaps he could sneak in, grab it, and sneak back out? But when he stood in the doorway, trying to see where Eladar was in the large room, he saw that his book was no longer where he'd left it.

Rion ran into the room, looking at the floor in concern. He couldn't have knocked it down, when he went past, could he have? He looked up and to his surprise saw Eladar was in front of the fire, sitting upon the rug, instead of in one of the chairs, a book in his lap, so absorbed in reading that he didn't seem to notice Rion at all. He hadn't realized Eladar could read Dwarvish. He peeked, curious, and his cheeks colored. "Eladar, please. You can't read that. It's my journal. I wrote it. No one else should read it, only me."

Eladar looked up, a spark of something else in his eyes, before they flashed with annoyance. "Then why did you leave it in here, if you didn't want anyone to read it?" he challenged.

"I'd not meant to. I was upset. I left it here without realizing. Please, Eladar, give it back," Rion urged.

A look of longing and loneliness so intense it cut Rion like a knife flashed across Eladar's face. "Please, Rion, can't I read it? I've had nothing to read for weeks and weeks now. I can speak Dwarvish well enough, but their written language is appalling. I'm going mad here. What harm could there be in my reading it? It's innocuous enough so far. It's... it's you, Rion. You're here, on these pages, the way you were in the Pass. So much must have happened between the start of the journal and then, yet you'd not changed. You still haven't, or at least you hadn't until you came here. They've all been talking about it, how you still smile and laugh. You cannot imagine how envious we all are of you for that. Please, Rion, I need to read it. I need to see how you still can smile after all you've been through. Can you understand how I need to?"

Rion thought of Eladar as he'd been in the Gelthor Pass, compared to what he had heard and seen of him here. Eladar had granted Rion's mother's fondest wish. Could he deny Eladar his? If this book might somehow help him find himself again... but so much of what he had written could not be shared. "But it's not innocent. I… there are secrets in it, Eladar. Terrible secrets. I can't let you read it. I'm sorry. Truly I am."

"You don't trust me with your book? There was a time you trusted me with your life. You followed blindly where I led, spoke what I told you to, though you'd no idea what you said. I'm still the man I was, Rion, I swear I am, only… no one sees me, anymore. They look at me as if I were a Resemblant, when I'm not. I'm still me. Only even I have a hard time seeing it, lately. What if I swore to you I'd not tell anyone about anything I read? I can tell it's precious to you. If I swore I'd not damage it? That I'd return it tomorrow and never ask to borrow it again? One night, Rion? Please. One night of peace. Even one night might help," Eladar pleaded.

Rion swallowed. Perhaps if Eladar read it, it might help him. If he saw how much reason Rion had had to lose his smile, yet he hadn't, at least not until today. If he saw Rion knew pain, too, maybe he'd share his own with him. Maybe he'd want to talk to him again. Maybe he could help Eladar. And maybe, in turn, Eladar might help him. He'd not be so terribly alone if he had Eladar and Lunahr for friends, if when one was busy, the other might not be.

He took a deep breath. "All right. If you swear not to tell anyone what you read, and to return it tomorrow, and that you'll be careful with it, then I suppose you can read it," Rion said, putting aside his misgivings. Elavar had told Elanara that it was no secret he loved her, that everyone already knew it. And he'd told Talon and the brothers about the wizards, and Andra about the dream, and Hunter already knew too. He hadn't told them everything. But he trusted Eladar not to betray his secrets.

"I swear. Thank you, Rion. May you have pleasant dreams, or at least not remember the others," Eladar said and then bent down to the pages before Rion could reply.

Rion left reluctantly. It felt wrong, leaving his book. The climb upstairs seemed interminable. He entered his room and lay upon the bed, taking off only his boots. He'd not lay naked in this bed again. It was hard to lie down at all. Sleep still had not come, hours later, when the brothers crept in. He'd heard the bells announcing each subsequent hour in dismay.

"You needn't tiptoe. I'm awake," Rion said, unable to keep the wistfulness from his voice.

"You shouldn't be. It's only a few hours till dawn," Ron scolded gently. "You haven't been having nightmares, have you?"

"No. I'd need to be able to sleep in order to dream," Rion said sullenly.

"You slept too much during the day. You'll be able to sleep tomorrow night, if you don't. Gar, Ara, and I certainly are tired enough, and we've an early morning of it again tomorrow. Good night, Rion," he said, and his brothers echoed him.

"Good night," he said, fighting to keep the loneliness from his voice. They might get injured in Thenalon, if they were distracted worrying about him at the wrong moment. He'd put on a brave face until they left. He wouldn't risk them getting hurt because of him.

He tried to sleep, but he couldn't. He lay in bed listening to their steady breathing, cherishing the sound. Soon they would be gone, and he would be alone. Tears began to fall silently one by one, dripping down his cheeks onto the pillow.

ELADAR was frustrated. It seemed he'd been reading Rion's book for such a short time, but he couldn't keep his eyes open any longer. He stretched, and from the stiffness of his muscles realized it must have been longer than he thought. In the journal, they'd just arrived in Erenia. He had been amused by Rion's initial impression of him, and touched to see how highly Rion thought of him thereafter. With his words, he remembered who he had been, for a few moments, what it had been like as a captive of the ogres, but how quickly despair had fled with his rescue. If such a thing had happened to him now, he knew he'd not survive it. The thought frightened him. How could he be so changed? How could he have so lost sight of who he was?

He yawned. Perhaps he might even be able to sleep tonight. It had been many, many nights since he'd slept more than a handful of hours. He kept having dreams, terrible dreams, not only of Riviera burning, of his parents and his people dying, but of Elanara and Elavar screaming at him, hating him. He'd sleep a little at least, perhaps, and then begin reading again in the morning. He'd sworn he'd return the journal tomorrow, but Rion hadn't said when. Perhaps he could read it all day, or even convince Rion to let him read it a second day? No, he'd promised he wouldn't.

Although Rion hadn't acknowledged that part. Besides, if he didn't return it, he'd not be borrowing it a second time, just extending the loan by a day. He grinned at his ingenuity. It was reasoning like that that drove Men mad when dealing with his kind. Men were so easy to trick, to confuse. Except for Rion. But that only meant that Rion was a challenge. He enjoyed a challenge.

How odd. He was feeling like himself again. He clung to the tenuous feeling, knowing it could flee at any instant. It was so good to have something to do again. He had little else to do. Talon and Elavar had seen to that. They'd not let him into any of the strategy meetings.

He began fuming again at the thought of being excluded, of not being allowed to help, when he had the knowledge and ability to. He cursed. His brief moment of self had vanished.

He went back to the fire and opened the book again. He'd read the part about Erenia, and perhaps a little beyond, and then quickly head off to bed without thinking about Talon and Elavar. The two of them were driving him mad.

DEWALAREN stretched out on his bed, futilely trying to relax enough that he might sleep. He had to sleep: Farad had threatened to have Donovar give him something that might force him to, even knowing they could not risk it. The Enemy might attack at any time, and he could not be drugged when the chance finally came to slay Incuban. But every time he closed his eyes, he saw Aras's face, or when he was fortunate, maps, or he rethought the positioning of some crucial element of their forces.

He made a quick note on the paper by his bed as another such thought occurred. He had meant to ask Rion for one of his writing leads for that purpose, but he'd not had the chance. He was still using pen and ink.

He thought fondly of Rion for a moment. Thank Idare he was safely here! Ron had told him in tonight's meeting how much Rion wanted to go with them to Thenalon, or at least to be included in the planning, but he'd not hear of it. Rion was still a boy. War was no place for boys.

It was bad enough Lunahr had to be included, but he couldn't exclude him. To do so would damage his fragile ego terribly. Lunahr would think Dewalaren didn't trust him again.

Lunahr had sung again, to all of them, the night of the banquet, and Farad said he had been singing with Rion as well. Dewalaren smiled at the image that brought. He wished he'd been able to hear it. Still, it relieved him greatly to know Lunahr had. The Enemy could not touch Lunahr while he still held his music. Aras had crafted music into a shield for him.

Aras! The agony of his death tore across his heart again. The room darkened as if the oil lamp illuminating it had suddenly been extinguished. Aras was gone, lost to him forever, and it was his fault. How could he survive long enough to kill the Enemy, knowing what he had done to Aras? But he could not abandon his people while they so desperately needed him. He had to live long enough to see Incuban dead. Then he could finally join Aras in oblivion. The eternal darkness of it held no fear for him. It was already so dark all around him. He would link to no one, lest they see what lay in his wounded heart. Lest he lose them as well. He was so achingly alone, even here, surrounded by his people and his few friends.

He stiffened on the bed. He was not alone. Someone was in the room! He sprang to his feet, grabbing his sheathed Sword from the table by the bed and drawing it, all in a single smooth motion. There was a muted yelp of surprise. "Laren! It's all right! It's only me," Lunahr cried softly, drawn back in a defensive stance against the wall.

This was not the first time his young cousin had visited him in the middle of the night, using the secret door to the room to bypass the Guard at his door. Only he, Lunahr, Farad, Desmond, and the Elves knew of the passages that honeycombed the castle. Farad had been the one to discover them, a century ago. They'd not told any of the others for fear the Enemy might learn of the tunnels and use them against them in an attack, if ever they discovered the castle.

But the other nights Lunahr had come, there had been fear upon his face, often bordering on hysteria. Though his memories of his captivity and torment were safely sealed away in a chest within his core, Lunahr still sometimes suffered from nightmares from his ordeal, although ordinary ones. Not frequently, but when they did come, they were intense and terrifying, and he could not face them alone. But tonight was different.

When first he saw Lunahr, his cousin's face was flushed. There had been a look on his face of longing, even of lust; it was chilling to see it. He would not sheathe his Sword, nor would he yet call his Guard. "Why are you here, Lunahr?" Dewalaren asked, wariness in his voice.

Lunahr blushed and stammered and looked shyly at him for a moment, but then the embarrassment turned to dismay. "You're afraid of me! You think…. I'm not, Laren! I swear I'm not. Test me and see."

The Ring pulsed as Dewalaren extended his core out and touched Lunahr. He saw to his relief Lunahr had spoken the truth. His mind was his own. The Enemy was not there, not this time. Then why…? He hadn't meant to see it; he'd meant to ask. He was startled by the desire he saw, the seductive images in Lunahr's mind, and he drew back from Lunahr's core.

"YOU… you saw. I didn't think you would…." Lunahr headed for the passageway, panic rising. The look on Laren's face! He couldn't bear it. He'd been so afraid Laren might reject him, but even more so that he might be indignant or insulted by the thought of touching him intimately, even repulsed by it, knowing what Incuban had done to him. He had so feared that Laren might lose what little respect he yet had for him, what tattered fragments of love might remain, even after all his cousin's declarations to the contrary.

Lunahr was trembling, fighting the urge to sob. He could not cry in front of Laren! Not again. Idare, why had he ever come?

Then he felt strong arms around him. It was Laren. He was hugging him, holding him. Laren turned Lunahr around to face him, and Lunahr looked into his eyes, fearing what he might see. But there was only love there. Whatever might happen or might not, Laren yet loved him.

"Ah, Lunahr. You were so very brave to come to me tonight, as you have. Forgive me for the poor welcome I gave you," Laren said softly.

"I tried not to. I've wanted to before, but… I'm so lonely, Laren! I need so desperately to be held, to know I am loved," Lunahr said.

"You are loved, Lunahr. Very much so," Laren said, holding him, gazing into his eyes. "And you are not the only one who is lonely, who needs to be held," he added softly. Then very gently, he placed his hand under Lunahr's chin, tilted his face upward and kissed him tenderly upon his lips.

Lunahr shuddered and then melted against him.

LUNAHR kissed him back, responding with such desperate passion it stole Dewalaren's breath away.

"Stay here. Do not move. This will only take a moment," Dewalaren said, reluctantly pulling free of Lunahr's embrace. He breathed deeply, forcing his desire down for the moment.

Dewalaren went to the door to his room and opened it. His door Guard looked at him curiously. He knew they had not expected to see him again tonight. He was grateful the walls were thick stone and the door solid oak, and that Lunahr had kept his voice low, even in his alarm. He did not want his Guard to know Lunahr was within. Fortunately, they had never overheard any of his cousin's previous visits.

"I will be working for a while yet. I must meditate, and I must run through my Sword exercises. I must practice with the Ring. I am not to be disturbed, no matter what you might hear. It might be dangerous for you to enter. Do you understand?" he lied, hoping to explain any sounds they might hear, though he and Lunahr would do their best to be quiet in their passion.

FENLON nodded. "Aye, Majesty. We'll not disturb you, now that you've alerted us. We know better than to meddle in such things. But please, you must try to get some rest as well."

King Talon smiled reassuringly at him. "You need not worry on that account. I suspect tonight I will sleep well indeed."

Fenlon was greatly relieved to see the smile that warmed the King's face. They had all been extremely worried about him. He had not looked well to them since the night he had fallen. Those who were there swore he had died and risen again, as Hunter had. The two of them were blessed by Ragnar and Aralyn as no others, for having done so. Every Dwarf in the caves would be honored to die in service of the two who had been God-touched.

DEWALAREN closed the door and turned toward his bed. He was dismayed to see the room empty. Lunahr had gone. He headed anxiously for the passageway, but the door opened before he reached it, and Lunahr emerged. "Don't look so distressed, Laren. I haven't gone. I was merely being discreet, in case the Guards had been suspicious and decided to search your room." He smiled coyly. "Although I must admit, it did my heart good to see your disappointment, to know you truly want me."

"I want you, Lunahr, and I need you," Dewalaren said and embraced him and kissed him again.

RION was at the second shift of breakfast before the bell rang. The brothers were, of course, still asleep. Rion was surprised by how many in the Dining Hall seemed wide awake and how many others seemed so tired. Had everyone been having trouble sleeping? Then he realized the tired ones might well be the night shift of the Guard, that they were eating after coming off shift, before going to bed. He looked for Hernon and Donovar, for Andra and Rarnak, and for Lunahr, but he didn't see anyone he knew. They must all still be asleep. He envied them that. He envied them much.

Then, unexpectedly, he saw a face he recognized, and she saw him at the same instant and began heading toward his table. It was Jarina, Jargas's sister, Hunter's wife. He recognized her petite size and the eyes above the veil. It was disturbing how much she looked like Circe. Rion could not face her. He was afraid of her. He still didn't understand how Hunter could have married her only a few days after leaving them. Rion still thought she must have cast some sort of spell upon him, as well as Hunter appeared to be now, but he did not have the nerve to ask anyone about it.

Rion got up quickly, darted around two other tables, and headed for the door. He saw Jarina watching him in surprise, but to his relief, she did not follow him. He breathed easier in the hallway, but still, he didn't want to be easy to find if she changed her mind and came looking for him.

He went to the Library. It seemed seldom used. Perhaps someone had returned one of the Amontiri books, and he could find something to read. If not, he could look at that map. That would at least give him something to do for a little while. He could eat later, in one of the other shifts. In spite of not having eaten the day before, he was surprisingly not hungry.

LUNAHR nuzzled Dewalaren gently in his sleep. Dewalaren smiled at him and lightly traced his finger along Lunahr's shoulder, remembering the shiver of delight he'd felt when Lunahr had done the same to him last night. Lunahr looked so peaceful, so relaxed, so content. He was smiling, even in his sleep.

Dewalaren stroked his hand down his bare arm, to his fingers. Lunahr had such wonderful hands, as talented in bed as they were playing one of his many instruments.

Dewalaren stole a final admiring glance at Lunahr's smooth, lean body. Then he reached over him and pulled the blanket over his bare torso. It was chilly this morning. The Dwarves had respected his commands and not come in during the night, even to light the fire, as they normally did, before he wakened, though truthfully, he had yet to ever sleep through the intrusion. His survival instincts were too keenly honed to allow it. But he did not miss the fire. Lunahr was warmth enough.

It had been a long time since he had felt such warmth pressed against him. He fought the memory of Elanara aside. He did not want to spoil the feeling of contentment he still enjoyed. Elanara had been a reluctant lover, skilled but reserved. She had been afraid of him, he had finally realized. He sighed. He was thinking of her, and he should not be.

He focused on Lunahr's face. Lunahr had been eager. His enthusiasm had been almost overwhelming. And he had been so very skilled, when he should not have been. Lunahr had not known such arts before he had left for Riviera, and the Elves had certainly not taught him. They thought of him as a child. He truly was yet a child. Dewalaren would normally never think to bed one so young. Lunahr was still a few months shy of coming-of-age. He was still only twenty-four. But the Enemy had no such moral restrictions. He delighted in destroying innocence.

Lunahr had never known the touch of love, though he had been touched many times. Child he may be, but by age alone. He was unquestionably a man by his experience. They'd healed him, as well as he could be healed. Dewalaren had wanted to take all memory of the Enemy from him, even the knowledge that he had ever been captured. The Ring was strong enough to do so. It frightened him, what the Ring might be capable of, what he might be capable of, wielding it. But Lunahr and Farad would not allow him to. They argued Lunahr was stronger for the memories. He was no longer the innocent he had been when first he was captured. If his memories were gone, and Incuban found him again, he could steal his innocence a second time, instead of Lunahr being strong enough that he might resist him, perhaps even successfully fight against him.

Lunahr moaned softly and shifted in his sleep, his former tranquility gone. Dewalaren realized his thoughts might be what was disturbing his young cousin. Though they were not linked, the Ring might be sharing his consciousness with Lunahr again, as it had unexpectedly last night, in the heat of their passion.

He'd not had such a joining of the minds with Elanara, though he loved her. He'd spent three glorious weeks with her last year, so very long ago. But she'd stayed distant from him even during their lovemaking. She feared his Power, and the Madness she knew might grip him at any moment. And she did not have a core strong enough to bond to. That special ecstasy of the twining of minds along with bodies had been missing. Yet he had loved her. He still loved her, though she was lost to him. And she was not the only one.

He had not had another lover since Elanara, though he had loved another. Aras had tempted him, almost beyond rational thought. But Aras was still such an innocent, a man by age alone. Dewalaren had not wanted to rob him of his innocence when his own future was so uncertain. Also, he'd loved Aras too much to bed him. He'd never have been able to return to Elanara if ever he had shared himself so intimately with Aras. He'd been promised to Elanara, and it was his duty to wed her, for the sake of the alliance with the Elves, but also to provide an Heir to his House, to the Throne. But Elanara loved Rion, not him, and Aras was lost to him.

He felt the terrible darkness and emptiness rising again, but this time, with Lunahr beside him, it did not overwhelm him. He forced thoughts of the two he had lost aside and filled his mind with thoughts of Lunahr. He had lost Lunahr as well. He had thought it was forever.

Dewalaren put his arm protectively around his young cousin. He'd not lose him again, ever. Lunahr smiled in his sleep again, as if he'd heard and felt the fierce protectiveness, the love that drove the need.

He should let Lunahr sleep. He had great need of it. But he had needs of another kind also. Perhaps it was early enough that both needs might yet be fulfilled? He shifted his weight upon the bed and woke Lunahr with a kiss. Then he froze. There were raised voices at the door, disturbingly loud, for him to hear them at all. Quickly he tossed the blanket over Lunahr, leaping from the bed naked, Sword in hand. But the voices quieted and the door did not open. He glared at it and put the Sword down, climbing back into bed.

Lunahr was shivering, under the covers. "It's all right, Lunahr. It must have been someone particularly insistent about wanting to see me, but Fenlon is still following my orders about not disturbing me."

Dewalaren pulled the blanket off of Lunahr and ran his eyes down his long, leanly muscled frame, drinking in the smooth perfection of his satiny skin, his young yet virile form.

He saw Lunahr's fear vanish, to be replaced by playful lust at the admiring look he had received. "I did not know it was possible to undress someone with your eyes when they are already naked," Lunahr said, laughing.

Dewalaren looked lecherously at him and rolled on top of him again.

"What are you doing!" an indignant voice cried from near the far wall. Dewalaren and Lunahr both jumped at the unexpected interruption.

"What does it look like!" Dewalaren snarled angrily, covering Lunahr with the blanket and rolling from the bed to face Farad, ignoring his own nakedness.

Farad was just as incensed. "I thought for a moment it was Elanara. I was going to leave quietly. But Lunahr! Have you gone mad, Dewalaren? He's a child! Did you think he could replace Aras? After what's happened to him, how could you even think to…."

Dewalaren paled and crumpled to his knees. Aras! Idare, had he made love to Lunahr only to ease the pain of his loss of Aras, for a moment's respite? Had he done something so selfish, so potentially damaging to one he loved as a brother, almost as a son? He had thought he would be helping Lunahr, not harming him. What had he done? "Out. Both of you. Get out," he said hoarsely.

The anger fled Farad's face, to be replaced by concern. "Dewalaren, no! Please, wait. Let me stay. Let me…."

"Out!" Dewalaren commanded, shaking. He could not stand; he could scarcely breathe.

Lunahr leapt from the bed, grabbing his clothes off the floor and running past Farad into the passageway, in tears.

Farad looked from Dewalaren to the tunnel Lunahr had disappeared into and followed him, closing the passageway door behind him.

Dewalaren fell forward, collapsing fully onto the cold stone floor, and began sobbing.

ELADAR had slept well, for the first time in many weeks. He awoke refreshed. He almost felt himself again, and this time the feeling was not tenuous, like before. It was early yet. He bathed and dressed, then curled up on his bed to read more of Rion's book. Last night he had finished their encounter in Erenia and their travels thereafter, until they were only a week from Gosa. He'd forced himself not to peek at the next page, lest he be drawn into reading more. He found Rion's journal irresistible. Rion's heart and spirit and voice were all contained within these pages.

He opened the book, removing the ribbon he'd used to hold his place, and turned the page. His eyes widened as he stared in horror at the title across the top of the page: "The War of the Wind: The Story of the Destruction of the Elven Homeland." No, it could not be! Not here, written in Common, as if it were just another tale to tell.

I never knew that each Wood Elf Kingdom, save for Erenia, is built beside a River Elf Kingdom, for protection, of all things. That it is the duty of the River Elves to aid the Wood Elves in case of fire. The tradition is apparently an old one, a remnant of a time when the Elves lived in war, rather than tranquility, in horror, rather than joy.

I was told that it has been three thousand years since the Elves have had armies or needed them. If they had armies now, it might mean they were ready to destroy the world again, only this time, there would be nowhere left for them to flee to. I was told by someone who did not know of the soldiers in Erenia. It frightens me, what their presence might mean, after what I have learned.

Prince Thorn of Riviera had told me that the Elves once had a war, that their history might make me weep. Now that I know the details of what happened to them, I will be able to tell him he is right. As you can see by the stains upon this page, I am crying as I write this. The thought of what I have heard is too heart-wrenching to bear.

Once, long ago, the Elves had a catastrophic war, The War of the Wind. The Seven Kingdoms, four Wood Elf Kingdoms and three River Elf Kingdoms we know here, are but a pale reflection, a dying shadow of the glory the Elves once knew. How could they be more, when only two of the four races of Elves yet live? In the Elven Homeland, there had been four races: Aerta, Oceana, Faeren, and Aerie.

The Aerta or Elves of the Earth, held a love for all life, for growing things, plant and animal, but especially for the forests of the Elven Homeland. The lost trees of those woods were not like the poor specimens in these lands. The trees of the Homeland could walk and move and speak. The Wood Elves of these lands are the shadowy remnants of the Aerta.

The Oceana or Elves of the Water dwelt in every river and lake, even in the great ocean surrounding the Homeland. They drew their Power from the crystal waters. The River Elves are all that remains of them.

The Faeren or Elves of Fire dwelt in the faeraelen, the mountains of fire of the Homeland. There are none here in these lands. We have no word for them. There were few of the Faeren, for there were few mountains of fire, even in the Homeland, but they were hardy and strong. The story of the destruction of the Faeren would make the strongest heart weep.

The fourth race, the Aerie or Elves of the Air, those most hated, most reviled, once dwelt on the highest mountaintops of the Homeland. They began the War that destroyed the Elves' world. The mountains were not high enough for them. They were so aloof that they sought to remove themselves from the world below completely. They sought true flight, more than flight; they sought a way to put their great strongholds into the very air.

They began chopping down the forests, to create the charcoal they needed to melt the ores they dug from the earth. They rent the land with fantastic tools, great machines, like waterwheels or windmills, but made of metal and powered not by water and wind but by wood and charcoal and then oil and coal and things for which I know no name. They mined more of the earth, digging for the materials they needed. They poisoned the waters with their mining, with their building. They dammed many of the rivers, to drive their great waterwheels, leaving huge tracts of land to shrivel up and die. They poisoned the very air all the Elves breathed with smoke from their fantastic machines. They even harnessed the power of the few fire-mountains of the Homeland, using the heat for energy. They built wings of metal, which they thrust into the sky. They finally achieved their dream, but it had come at a terrible price.

The Aerta, the Oceana, and especially the Faeren had begun dying by the thousands, by the tens of thousands, without the trees and waters and fire-mountains they each needed to sustain them. The Aerie had turned a deaf ear to all their pleas; they were cold and aloof and cared not that their cousins perished. It was the Faeren who finally found the strength of spirit to challenge them. If they would not listen to words, to reason, they must be made to listen, by force of arms.

That was the beginning of the War of the Wind. The Faeren begged the Aerta and Oceana to aid them. But their will was weak. They had instead decided to flee the Homeland. Centuries earlier, the Oceana had begun crossing the great oceans with ships of deadwood they had built. They already had formed small colonies on those lands. They decided to all leave, and the Aerta were determined to go with them. The Faeren realized that such an exodus would take time. They told the Oceana and Aerta they would protect them from the Aerie, so they might build enough ships to reach the safety of the New Land. And so they fought, all alone, against a great Army of the Air. They fought bravely, valiantly, but they finally realized they were losing.

Then they feared for their cousins, for the Aerie had so despoiled the Homeland, even they now sought a new land, with clean, clear air they might breathe and water they might drink. And new forests to chop down and new rivers to dam, new lands to lay to waste. Then, the remnants of the Faeren Army knew what they must do. They had been working upon a great weapon of flame, to be used only if all was lost. A weapon that would obliterate the Homeland and themselves with it, but a weapon of such great power it would reach into the very sky and smite the Aerie. And that is what they did. For the sake of the Aerta and the Oceana, the Faeren died as a race: they died proudly, knowing that their Enemy, the Aerie, died with them.

I was told that it is the fate of the good, the valiant, the noble, to die for their cause when faced with such an enemy. I was told that the enemy is not dead, that the enemy can never be dead. There is always some new terror to replace the old. I pray that is not the case. I hope to never see such a war in my lifetime. But I am afraid. There is war coming, from the south and the east. We fled Ardock to escape from it. But can you truly flee such a war? Surely there comes a time when you must fight. If only the Aerta and Oceana had stayed. If only they had helped the Faeren instead of fleeing, the Faeren might have lived! Thousands upon thousands of Aerta and Oceana might have lived as well. How can they not have fought?

How could they not have fought? At the thought of the hundreds of thousands of his people who had perished on the battlefields desperately trying to stem the mad advance of the Faeren, Eladar screamed in rage and tore the offending pages from the book, crumpling them in his tightly clenched fist. How could Rion write such lies? He painted the Faeren as heroes, as martyrs, when it was they who had begun the War of Flame, when it was they who had ended it by annihilating the world!

Eladar knew the history of the War; every Oceana Prince did. They were all taught, lest the lessons they had learned be forgotten, lest they ease their vigilance, lest they ever forget why every Elf, male and female both, spent five years training in Nalea, what the coming-of-age ceremony meant, how the Reservists might be called to arms at any moment to defend the fragile remnants of their civilization.

The Faeren had not been content to live amongst the natural *faeraelen* of their land. They had sought to expand their territory, by consuming the Great Forests with fire and drilling down into the ground to where the rock was so hot it flowed like water. They had created entire new ranges of fire-mountains, where once forests and rivers and lakes had stood.

The Faeren hated all their cousins, the Aerta, for the soil that quenches fire, and the Oceana for the water that drowns it, but most of all, the lofty Aerie, whom they could not reach. The Aerta and Oceana had sent army after army against the Faeren, only to see them perish horribly, to see them all burnt to death. They had begged the aloof Aerie to aid them, but the Aerie had turned a deaf ear. The problems of the land below were not their concern. They cared only for their cold machines, until the smoke came. Once the forests began to burn and the mountains began spewing rock and ash into their perfect, pristine world, the Aerie were finally awakened to battle. They flew down out of the skies to smite the Faeren. They fought like two ogres battling, caring not for what they destroyed.

The Oceana and Aerta had seen that all hope was lost. They had fled in their twenty-five Great Ships and two thousand or more lesser craft, desperately seeking the safety of their colonies. But horrifically, when still in sight of the coast of their Homeland, a great pillar of fire roared up from the east, and a wave of roaring flame raced across the sea. Much of the fleet was consumed in the fire that claimed their Homeland. Many more ships were lost to storms upon the enraged seas. Their records showed that of the Evacuation Fleet that had set sail for the colonies, twenty-one Great Ships and only one-hundred-ninety-six others arrived. Some tens of thousands of their peoples survived, when hundreds of thousands had fled, when once they had numbered in the millions.

But their kind had not thrived on these new lands. The soil here was different from the soil of home. The trees here could not walk or speak or even think. The water that flowed over the land was weak as well. His people could no longer live for ten thousand years or more, but for a scant thousand. And they bore so few children. How could they bear children into such despair? Their numbers dwindled.

They had sworn an oath of peace. They did everything they could to aid Man, lest they be drawn into conflict with him. But now Talon's people had brought their Enemy across the mountains to their doorstep. They had lost Riviera and Loatia both, two of the Seven Kingdoms. They had lost thousands of people. And Rion, whom he thought was his friend, whom he had thought understood so much about them, Rion had written this heresy!

Shaking, Eladar ran from the room, Rion's book clutched tightly under one arm, and the crumpled pages of lies in his other hand.

RION was comparing three of the maps in the Library, studying them intently, when an angry voice from near the doorway made him jump. "How could you write this?" Eladar roared. He was enraged, trembling, his hand clenched in a tight fist. He held a crumpled piece of paper, and he was shaking his fist at Rion for emphasis. Rion's book was under his other arm.

"Write what? How could you tear a page from my book, after you swore you would be careful with it?" Rion asked, incensed.

"It never should have been written! It's forbidden to speak of it, ever, to anyone other than the King's family, or to write it, and you write it in Common, so the whole world may read it and believe such lies!"

Rion's anger evaporated in the heat of Eladar's own. "Eladar, please! I'm sorry, whatever it is I wrote that I didn't know I shouldn't have. You can't believe I'd ever mean to hurt Talon. I owe my life to him, more than once."

"What's Talon got to do with this?" Thorn asked, in a tone that implied Rion was a backward child.

Rion was hurt. Eladar had never used such a tone against him before. "He's the King. You said…," Rion began.

NEITHER Rion nor Eladar noticed Dewalaren in the doorway, they were so focused upon each other. Dewalaren hadn't believed the voices he'd heard coming from down the hall could be Eladar and Rion, that Rion might be becoming just as fractious as the Elves, or that even Eladar might speak his name with such rancor.

"HE'S not my King!" Eladar yelled. "Just because you don't have a King, don't think the rest of us don't! My King is dead because of him! But I've still a brother and the High-King, if I feel the need to grovel at someone's feet. I'm sick to death of kowtowing to Talon as if he were Laedrin!

"Do you think after the War Talon is going to go back and reclaim his Kingdom, free his people? There's no one to free! The Amontir are all dead! They should be dead, after what they unleashed on the world!

"Do you have any idea what they've done? So few of us survived the War of Flame, and now two of the Seven Kingdoms are dead, Riviera is dead, my Kingdom, dead, all my people. My father, my mother, they are dead and burned. Burned," he said, and the pages from his hand fell to the floor, as did the book. His voice was hollow now. All the anger had burned away. He turned from Rion. He had no more to say.

He saw Talon then, staring at him, his face an unreadable mask. Talon backed from the doorway, wordlessly, his eyes never leaving Eladar. Eladar left, turning his head as he passed, eyes upon Talon's.

RION watched Eladar go and realized to his horror that Talon had heard Eladar's treasonous words. Only Rion thought he was right to feel as he did. Talon was not his King. And he'd spoken the truth about Talon's people, if viciously. Many a King would still have him executed or exiled for it. He did not think Talon would, but he had a temper, he'd seen it, and Eladar had said terrible things.

Talon's eyes had followed Eladar from the room. Rion took a deep breath and approached him. "Majesty?" he asked tentatively.

Talon turned toward him. His eyes were a deep, bottomless blue, like the evening sky, but a ghost of flame crackled around them, as if lightning in an azure sky, and Talon quickly averted his eyes from Rion's. "Why do you call me that, Rion?" he asked, picking up the book and the pages. He straightened and looked at him, and his eyes were only eyes again. "I am not your King. I would not have you feign respect for me as Eladar has."

It was hard for Rion to answer, and he was about to tread upon very dangerous ground, but he would never again remain silent when he felt the need to speak. He could not, after having regained his voice, after it being so long lost to him. But he did not kneel. He did not think Talon might want him to.

"I call you Majesty because you are my King. I have never had a King, before you, and I would wish to have no other after you, when you are gone, should I outlive you. I hope I do not, for you should enjoy the fruits of your labors, your sacrifices, and live a long life of peace after the War is done. And though I am younger, I am only a Lesser Man. I will not live nearly as long as one of your people."

"You are not a Lesser Man. How do you even know the term? None of us uses it anymore. We've learned the folly of our arrogance. It's been beaten into us these two hundred and fifty years past," Talon said bitterly, still scowling.

"Perhaps you are not as perfect as you need to be," Rion said, but then winced, for it was something Aras had said to him once.

Pain flashed across Talon's face, as if he too heard Aras's voice speak the same words, but he stayed silent.

"I need to explain to you what was said before you came, for I'll not have you think it was you that Eladar was truly angry with, in spite of how it sounded. He was angry with me," Rion said.

"Yet he spoke treason, for despite his denial of it, he knelt to me and swore oath to me as his King, and I do not take such acts lightly," Talon said.

"Might I see what upset him so, Majesty?" Rion asked.

Talon handed him the crumpled pages. Rion flattened them out and looked at them. It was the account of the Elven War that Selene had told him. He had not thought she had lied to him, but either she had, or the truth was other than she had known it to be, or perhaps, other than Eladar knew it to be.

"To understand why Eladar is so upset by this, first I must find out what part of this is true. What do you know about the Elven War?"

"What war?" Talon asked. "The Elves never had a war."

Rion shook his head. "But they did, Talon. Even Eladar told me that much, when first we rescued him, and he admitted as much again tonight. And how could they have such an Army and Navy, without knowing of war?"

Talon looked thoughtful.

"I cannot understand how you people can live without going mad!" Rion cried, all his frustrations boiling over. "You keep such secrets from each other: the Amontir, the Elves, everyone. Secrets breed mistrust, mistrust breeds fear and deceit, and deceit breeds treachery and treason and war. You saw what we gained when I shed my own secrets, yet you keep so many! You hoard knowledge as if its value decreases the more people who possess it, when knowledge is at its most powerful when everyone shares it."

Talon looked at him intently. "Our secrets keep us safe. I would have been dead decades ago had Incuban known my identity. Hunter has been tortured for over a century out of Incuban's frustration in not being able to learn my identity, and my father's before me. Secrets are necessary."

Rion sighed and said, "There are better ways. You all value me so highly because I see through your secrets. I make connections where you see none."

DEWALAREN was surprised by his words. He had not thought of Rion in such terms. He had first valued him for his youth, his innocence. Later, he had been impressed by his resiliency, his enthusiasm, his love for everyone, his understanding, his caring. But also, his honesty and his integrity. His core was still so pure, even after darkness had not only touched him, but been directed at him, after it had battered him relentlessly. He was a survivor, but unlike the rest of them, he did not merely survive, he truly lived. He could still smile and laugh and love. And he had not yet become a man when his trials had begun.

Incuban must never take him from them. The thought blazed across his core anew. "I am learning much, but little of Eladar. May I see what you have written, so I can at least know what he saw? Then you may tell me the words he spoke to you, that I did not hear," Dewalaren said.

Rion nodded and handed him the pages. Dewalaren read the Elven history in wide-eyed horror. "*Aerie*," he whispered. "No wonder he was so terrified of her. She was *Aerie*, he told me, but I did not understand. She destroyed their world with fire and I sent him to her. And she burned him."

RION paled, taking the Elven history back, looking at it in horror. "You can't mean... not Aras? No, it's not possible. They are dead, the *Aerie* and the *Faeren* both. Only the *Aerta* and *Oceana*, the Wood Elves and the River Elves, survived the War of the Wind... only Eladar called it the War of Flame. And the world was burned, and the *Aerie* were the Air Elves. It was the *Faeren* who were the Fire Elves, who fed off fire the way the others feed off the trees and the rivers.

"Elmoth! What if it truly was the *Faeren* who destroyed their world, not the *Aerie* at all! And Circe made them out to be heroes! No wonder Eladar was incensed. But who would have taught the story to her, and why? She's a Dwarf. Why would a Dwarf even know of their War?" He looked up at Talon and was frightened by what he saw. There was a nimbus of red light about his hand, but worse, all the light had gone from his eyes. They were dead, empty, like Hunter's had once been.

"Rion, please go. Talon is ill," Hunter said from behind him.

Rion jumped. Hunter had come from the back of the Library, yet it had been empty before. Rion had been the only one there, and they were standing in the doorway. How could Hunter have entered?

Rion looked at him, then back at Talon, and nodded. He could not help, or if he could, they would not let him. He left, with his journal tucked under one arm and the pages in his hand.

"DEWALAREN, the Ring has called me to your aid. You must let me help you," Farad said, the concern naked upon his face.

"You cannot. No one can. He is dead. She has killed him. I have killed him," Dewalaren said and turned and stumbled from the room.

"YOU'RE looking lost, lad," Donovar said kindly.

"I am not lost," Eladar said indignantly. "I've navigated caverns far bigger and more complex than this, in Dorolingas and Ironhand, without ever once getting lost. Why is it you Dwarves can't accept the fact that some of us can manage just as well as you underground?" Eladar snapped. "Where do you think River Elves live, in the River? We've our own tunnels in the riverbanks, not as big as yours perhaps, but no less a labyrinth—more so. They're low and narrow. You can't see what lies up ahead."

"You may know where you are, lad, but you don't know where you are going. And none of us can see what lies ahead. It's easy enough to get lost under those circumstances, isn't it?" Donovar asked.

Eladar glared at him, then thought about what he had said and felt suddenly sheepish. "I'd not expected such philosophy from a Dwarf. Forgive me, Advisor Donovar. It was foolish of me to say so, and I'd not recognized you. And no, it's not that I think you all look alike, I... ah, forgive me. I seem to be doing it again. I would have asked your forgiveness, regardless. It shouldn't matter you're the High-King's Advisor. It doesn't matter, other than I'm more likely to have my older brother scold me again for insulting someone of higher rank, than lower. I hate it when he's so pompous like that, when he plays into the reputation we already have, just for being Elves.

"I'm ranting again. Forgive me. I'm sure you're busy and have little time or patience for the ramblings of an Elf. I have little enough patience for my own moods. Everyone's busy it seems, except for me. I'm looking for someone."

"You've found someone," Donovar said. "If you can't locate who you're searching for perhaps I could help you. But first, who is it who is expecting you?"

Eladar smiled grimly. "He'll not be expecting me. I'd just hoped to speak with him. I'm looking for Sarnon, King Rongas's Steward."

"Ah, Sarnon. I know many a King who wishes he had a Steward like him. I'm sure he could help you with whatever it is you need, except for your timing. He's preparing King Rongas's meal. If you came back...."

Eladar scowled. "But it's well past breakfast and hours until lunch, for those of you who eat within the caves! I came now because I knew he'd not be preparing food. I know he has other duties. It's amazing all he does, but... so why is Jargas always complaining his father's not eating? Or is it that it takes hours to prepare? I can't believe that it does, with the feast he produced for me in a scant few minutes. I'd never have thought.... It's pointless, I'll have gone completely mad by then. If you think I'm ranting now you should hear what I might sound like by then," Eladar said, frustrated.

"The King's not had his breakfast yet. It's breakfast Sarnon's making. He was delighted, actually: the King ate dinner last night, and here it is less than a day later and he's eating again, or has said he might. At least two thirds of the meals Sarnon prepares for him go uneaten, or at least, not eaten by him. We don't waste food here. The King often neglects to eat when he has important things on his mind. He says he cannot waste the time to.

"We all keep trying to see that he eats. Jargas and Jarina have enough to worry about without trying to make sure he does. Sarnon doesn't let them worry but... well, we worry about Sarnon sometimes, too. It's a stressful job, being Steward to a King, especially a King such as Rongas, and Sarnon is old to be going to war, though we'd not think of saying so in front of him. I used to know a King like Rongas, once, long ago. So very long ago," Donovar said, and he looked deeply lost in memory.

"Forgive me lad, now I'm the one rambling. It's just... well, it's nice to talk to somebody for a change, I mean other than, 'Where should the troops be heading?' and 'How many have we lost today?' and hearing how many wounded are coming. This is one of the first times since marching to the Fromer that I've actually had the chance to chat. But you've other important things to do, I'm sure, and no time to listen. No one has the time to listen anymore. I'll let Sarnon know you need to speak with him. I'm sure he'll come as soon as he's free," Donovar said, turning to go.

"No, wait! Please, don't go," Eladar beseeched.

DONOVAR turned back, concerned by the desperation in the young Prince's voice.

"I... I need someone to talk to. I've been thinking too much. Though as an Elf, I suppose I'm doomed to, aren't I?" Eladar said with the ghost of a smile, which quickly fled his face.

"That's why I was looking for Sarnon. When I was being held prisoner in Jargas's camp, he was so solicitous of me. And I've not gotten the chance to really speak with any others of you. He's really the only one I feel like I know at all, and... I'd not met you yet and.... But I forget, High-King Archer must need you. You're trying to be polite and not say so. You're afraid I'll be offended: 'The only thing worse than an Elf is an Elven Prince,' isn't that how the saying goes?

"Never mind. I should never have come here. I knew I shouldn't. I should have just lain in the River again listening to you all, as I've been doing. It's just... I miss it. I never really liked Dorolingas nor Ironhand while I was there, but after I left... when I was being held prisoner, I... it's silly, but I felt alive again, more alive than I've been since.... No, I'm doing it again. Excuse me. I'll leave you to your duties," Eladar said and turned to go.

"Prince Eladar, you need not go. I'd be honored if you'd come speak with me. I've no other duties right now that might preclude it," Donovar said.

"YOU know my given name?" Eladar asked, stunned.

"Aye, and I did not speak it lightly. I am, after all, Confidant and Advisor to the High-King. I know all your names, even those of the Amontir," Donovar said.

"Since you know it anyway, might you call me Eladar, Advisor? Not Prince, just Eladar. I've never stood on ceremony, though I'm young yet. I suppose I'll eventually learn to be as haughty as the rest of us, though I would hope not. But not Prince. How can you be a Prince without a Kingdom?" Eladar said sadly.

"Of course, Eladar, but only if you'll call me Donovar. Everyone only calls me that. It's been many decades since I've gone by a title. And you're Prince enough, lad, from all I've seen and heard, Kingdom or no. It's not the rock that makes the King, it's the man inside."

Eladar looked at him in surprise. "I think it was fortunate for me you saw how lost I am. Perhaps by the time we are done speaking, I might have found myself again, at least for a little while. I can't seem to keep myself in sight anymore. It frightens me, how far away I am from where I should be."

"You're just in need of a friend, lad. I've stood in the spot you are standing in myself. I still stand there, oftener than I would like. I think Archer might be relieved to see me speaking with you. He's been worried about me lately. He's good reason to be, but I hate to be such a burden to him, when I've ever always only wanted to lighten his own. It's not easy being a King. It's far less easy being a High-King, effortless as he makes it appear," Donovar said. "Come, Eladar. I'll show you to my quarters. There's no wounded there at the moment, thankfully. We'll be able to speak without interruption, I hope."

Chapter 10
Little Brother

RION spent another morning being studiously ignored by everyone around him, with thoughts of another miserable night ahead of him. He had hoped to speak to Eladar again, and Talon, but it was as if both had vanished. He did spot Lunahr in the hall, once. He looked like he'd been crying. Rion had called out after him, but he'd not stopped, though Rion was certain Lunahr must have seen and heard him. He'd followed Lunahr to the Library—he was sure he'd seen him go inside—but when he got there, the room was empty. Frustrated and concerned for his new friend, he'd left. When he saw the brothers a while later, they were all on their way to another meeting, with no time to talk. He didn't even see Andra or Rarnak.

He checked the Dining Hall every shift of lunch, hoping to find someone, anyone, he knew, to sit with, to talk with. Each time he was discouraged and left without eating, until finally at the fourth lunch shift he admitted defeat, sat down for a quick moment, put a few mouthfuls of food onto his plate, and then left with apologies for his rudeness, pretending to see someone he knew across the room.

He took the plate up to his room and choked down a few bites, more to pass a few more moments of time with something to do than because he was hungry. The thought of dinner by himself was discouraging, and the thought of the many empty hours in between disheartening. Perhaps a walk might help. He missed the fresh air and sun.

He fetched his sword, the one Hunter had gifted to him. After a moment's hesitation, he filled and brought his waterskin. He did not think he'd have need of it on such a brief journey, but he would feel odd without it. He'd certainly not bring his journal, nor his healer's kit. It would feel good to travel so unencumbered. On the way out, he ducked back into the Dining Hall and deposited his plate, after giving the room a long, slow scan, still hoping to miraculously see a familiar face.

It was easier leaving the castle than he had thought it would be. The sentry merely told him to stick to the trees and other cover when he could, so he'd not be too visible from the air in case of enemy flyovers. Rion almost went back inside then. He hadn't realized chimaera flew over the castle, but when he said so, the Guard told him they didn't, that it was just their standard precaution. Reassured, Rion entered the woods, heading back down toward the Pass. He'd looked down the Pass from the Tower, and it had seemed safe enough. He only wanted to explore it a bit. It was still early. He'd have plenty of time to make it back to the Tower by sundown.

Rion had seen from the Tower how quickly the vegetation thinned toward the east, within the Pass. The underground river that kept the rest so green must not extend out that far. Rion glanced up frequently as he walked, but the sky remained clear of chimaera. Perhaps Gar could teach him the bow. He should know how to shoot. Only he should have had him do so before. The brothers were leaving for Thenalon soon. It was all so terribly anticlimactic: now that he had his voice back, there was no one to talk to.

Rion continued to walk until he reached bare, loose rock, for as far as he could see. It looked lonely, desolate. It suited his mood. Perhaps he could explore just a little bit further? Not far, but enough to justify the long walk. There was still plenty of time until dusk.

He was getting hungry, from walking so far. Perhaps he'd actually be able to sit and eat dinner when he returned, even if he were alone again, as he feared he would be. The brothers would be gone the day after tomorrow. He might never see them again, yet he'd not said more than a handful of words to them the past couple of days.

Rion took a long drink from his waterskin and pressed on cautiously. The footing was treacherous. Loose rock shifted at every step. He remembered Eladar's story of his falling amongst the ogres when the ledge he was on gave way, and how he'd broken his leg and lost all his weapons. But this was the floor of the Pass. He'd not fall here.

It felt good to be away from everyone and on his own, instead of alone in a crowd. He kept walking, penetrating much further into the Pass than he had originally planned. He looked over his shoulder, back the way he had come and then toward the sun. It had sunk a lot lower than he had expected. He'd not thought it through, that the walls of the Pass would block the sun. Perhaps it was time for him to be heading back? In fact, he'd probably walked too far already. The sun would be setting as he returned.

His heart fluttered as he realized he would likely be returning after dark. He'd come too far and been careless. He should have paid more attention to the position of the sun. Still, if he walked quickly, he might make it. Rion turned to start the long journey back. A wisp of wind tickled his neck as he did so, and he heard a faint noise from along the direction he had been traveling, a sound that did not fit this barren place. It sounded like crying.

Rion felt a sudden chill of fear. Who could be crying out here, so far from the Tower? Surely not Lunahr? When he'd seen him in the hall earlier, his eyes had been red-rimmed from crying. Rion had wanted to help him, but Lunahr had managed to elude him. What if he had come out here for privacy, as Rion had? Perhaps he had even been hurt somehow.

He had to check and see. He couldn't risk not doing so, and then returning and finding out it had been Lunahr out here after all. He swallowed. Of course, it might always be some sort of trap by the Enemy. But if it were, that would mean the Enemy knew they were here. Either way, he had to look.

Rion crept cautiously along the floor of the Pass, trying not to make a sound, picking his way carefully through the loose rock for the firmest footing. He tensed. There, up ahead, by that pile of rock: something had moved. He approached the wall of the Pass as cautiously as he could, glad now for the fading light that might conceal him from whomever was there. He stared, stunned. Elmoth! It was a child, but not a Dwarven child, nor a child of Man, nor an Elf. It was an ogre. He hadn't realized ogres could cry.

It was shorter than he was. By its height and features, it appeared to be perhaps eight years old. But it was much broader than he was. He was sure it could still crush him easily. Only it was the one crushed. There had been a rockslide. The ogre may or may not have been intentionally part of it, but a boulder had fallen against two others and pinned its leg.

Rion watched it carefully. It wasn't aware of him yet. It was facing the other direction. The memories of the ogres in the Gelthor and Thinabar Passes were still vivid. It was a monster, like the one that had killed Seafoam. He should leave it to die.

He swallowed. The crying was clearer from here. It was the thin, hopeless, pitiable wail of a child whose cries have long been ignored. It sounded like it might have been crying for many hours. It sounded weak. It looked far from threatening.

It must be terribly thirsty, Rion thought in sudden compassion. "I must be sun mad," he muttered softly. Rion carefully unslung his waterskin. "Gata lata brata. Wa wata?" Rion said in the Ogrish Jargas had taught him, in as deep and gravelly a voice as he could muster, from the safety of the rock outcrop that was sheltering him from view. There was no way he could make himself appear ogre-like, as Jargas had, but he hoped he might sound enough like one, and that its own dialect was similar enough to that of the Rakakala that it might understand him. He had said, "Good little brother. Want water?"

The ogre stopped crying. "Wata? Wata! Wata!" it cried enthusiastically, looking around for the owner of the voice.

Rion stepped carefully from the rocks. The ogre's eyes widened, and it started trembling and cowering. "Bata Man! Na haat Mak!"

Rion stared at it in surprise. The ogre was scared of him! In fact, it looked terrified. He'd understood it, too. It had said, "Bad Man! No hurt Mak!" Mak must be its name. He belatedly realized the ogre was a boy; he'd been thinking of him as an "it" before.

"Na haat Mak," Rion assured soothingly. "Rion," he said, approaching slowly, thumping his chest for emphasis. "Mak taka wata," he said, and opened his mouth and pointed to it, holding up the waterskin. Mak seemed puzzled. Rion demonstrated by squirting a stream of water into his own mouth. Then Mak opened his mouth eagerly, and Rion repeated the process, this time for the little ogre.

"Mar wata, Ran!" the ogre demanded when he stopped. The ogre had spoken his name! He reminded Rion of a large, ugly, overeager mastiff puppy he'd once played with. Rion grinned at him and gave him some more water and studied Mak in growing surprise. He didn't look the same as the other ogres he'd seen. They'd all been filthy, covered in dirt and flies and rotting animal skins. Their stench had been almost unbearable. But Mak was relatively clean; dirty, certainly, but perhaps with days or weeks of dirt, not months or years. And he was wearing some sort of rough homespun fabric, held together somehow: not quite clothes, really, but a far cry from what the others wore.

"Rion gata. Help Mak," Rion said, frustrated with the limited vocabulary of Ogrish. They had no word for "help." It probably was a foreign concept to them. He hoped Mak understood.

He risked getting a little closer to Mak to inspect the rocks trapping his leg. He couldn't tell if Mak's leg was only pinned, or crushed. Rion searched for something he could use as a lever to pry the rock off of him. He could tell by looking at it that he'd not be able to lift it otherwise. He wished he had Jargas's strength, or at least his staff. Perhaps he could use his sword? In the scabbard. It was Dwarven. He hoped it might not bend or break from the strain. He didn't want to damage it, but he couldn't weigh a sword against the life of a child.

"Ran ga raka," he told Mak. "Mak na faat Ran." (Rion move rock. Mak no fight Rion.) He hoped Mak would realize he meant to pull his leg free when he pried the rock off him and not attack. The little guy was probably hungry, and Rion knew he might look pretty tasty to him. He wished he'd brought some food with him. But he was fairly confident he could outrun Mak, if need be, plus he'd have his sword, and Mak was unarmed. Except for rocks he could throw, of course. Rion hesitated.

"Ran haap Mak? Ran ga raka?" Mak encouraged.

"Elmoth, please don't let this be a mistake," Rion prayed softly. Then he wedged the scabbard underneath the boulder and pushed down with all his might. The rock moved a slight bit. Rion grunted and forced all his weight down onto the sheathed blade, throwing every bit of strength he had into it. He could do this. He had to.

Memory of moving the rocks with Seafoam outside the Thinabar Pass flooded him, followed immediately by the horrible images of her being crushed by the rockslide the ogre had unleashed, of her dragging herself to stand protectively over him as the ogre smashed her head and back with rock. Why was he trying to free this monster?

At that moment the rock unexpectedly shifted and the scabbard slipped. Off balance, Rion fell upon it, and suddenly the boulder rolled free. Rion crashed face first into the rocks of the slide. He lay there, dazed and gasping. He'd bashed his sword arm, but at least it didn't feel broken. He had no idea where his sword was. It had escaped his grasp.

A shadow fell over him. Mak was free and he was standing over him. Rion felt sudden terror. He'd never be able to get to his sword in time. He wasn't even sure he could sit up. He must have been mad, setting this thing free! It would crush his head with a rock and eat him.

He tried to sit up and fell back dizzily. Then he felt something wet upon his face and panicked. His eyes found focus. Mak was standing over him with the waterskin. Rion had set it down, when he went to pry him free. Mak had figured out how to make it squirt water. He was giving him water!

"Wata, Ran," Mak said, grinning a big, toothy smile, showing a mouthful of large, terrible teeth.

"Gata Mak," Rion said, weak with relief. This ogre, at least, understood gratitude. Mak squirted more water and Rion swallowed some. Then Mak stopped and studied Rion in concern. "Ran haat?"

"I hope not. If I'm lucky I'll be able to sit, maybe even stand," Rion said, though he knew Mak would not be able to understand any of that. Rion tried to sit up again. He closed his eyes for a moment as the world spun around him. Then he reopened them. Thankfully, the wave of dizziness passed. There, that was better.

Cautiously, he tried to stand and, to his relief, found he could. He could see his sword now as well. Trying not to appear too eager, Rion stepped cautiously toward it and grinned in relief. He could still walk! He bent down to retrieve his sword and saw stars, and almost fell over. He sat down abruptly on the hard rock.

"Ran haat," Mak said in concern.

"No, it's all right Mak, I'm only dizzy. I'll be fine. Ran gata, na haat," he said. He examined Mak's leg. It didn't look as bad as it could have, but it was bloody. He'd been a fool not to bring his healer's kit! He'd never traveled anywhere without one since that first trip to Athanark. "Mak haat. Ran mak gata," he said, hoping "make good" might suffice for bandage or make it better. Rion took out his knife and cut a notch in his shirt, then tore a strip off the bottom edge. Then he repeated the process, improvising bandages.

He carefully washed the ogre's wound with water from his skin and blotted it with one of the strips from his shirt that hadn't torn well and would be useless as a bandage. The skin had been scraped off completely along Mak's shin. Rion discarded the bloody fabric, impressed further by Mak. He'd not squirmed at all, and Rion was certain it must have hurt. Once Rion finished bandaging him, Mak shook his leg, his face crinkled in a scowl. The bandage must have felt odd, but he didn't try to peel it off with his fingers.

"You're a smart fellow, aren't you, Mak?" Rion said, impressed.

Mak stared at him intently. "Mak smat."

Rion's eyes widened. Had Mak truly understood him when he'd spoken true Common, a whole sentence of it? Smart wasn't an Ogrish word. No, he couldn't possibly have. He was simply mimicking him, that's all. But he could test him to be sure. "Mak, do you know the way home? Where is your home?" Rion asked, curious to see whether Mak might understand him.

"Na hama," Mak said, pointing down the Pass in the direction Rion had been traveling, before he'd decided to turn back. "Hama haat. Bata Man da. Na ga hama."

Mak knew the way home, but he didn't want to go back. He'd said, "Home hurt. Bad men there. No go home." Had he been running away from some kind of danger, from his home, when he'd gotten trapped and hurt?

"Ran gata. Mak hapa. Mak ga Ran," the little ogre said and grinned.

Rion was nervous. Mak had said, "Rion good. Mak happy. Mak go Rion." It sounded like Mak wanted to stay with him, that he wanted to go home with him.

"But what about Baga Mama?" Rion asked. Surely he wouldn't leave the Ogress so willingly at such a young age?

Mak's expression turned grim. "Bata Man wa kala Baga Mama. Wa maka Mak, Mak kasan, Mak fran faga, tra fara, tak ada Man, Tawa Man Ancaban." He stared intently at Rion. "Wa mak Mak tak Ran Ancaban."

Rion repeated what Mak said, in his words first, then, in dawning comprehension and horror, translated them into true Common. "You mean bad Men threatened to kill the Ogress, the Baga Mama, so that you and your cousins and your friends would fight, would… throw fire? At… tawa… what is…. Oh Elmoth! At the Tower Men? You said take other Men, Tower Men to… Incuban? That… they want you to take me to Him? Because I'm from the Tower too, you know that? You couldn't possibly know more than that. Mak, did you know my name before I told it to you? Had you heard it before?" Rion asked fearfully.

Mak appeared to be thinking hard about that. "Na," he finally said, but it was small comfort. Incuban knew about the Tower! He'd been planning an attack against it all this time! Rion pictured an army of ogres descending upon the Tower bearing fire, as they'd done a century ago in Thenalon. He'd had Ara tell him all the stories his grandfather had told him. The ogres had laid the greatest city of Man, the Jewel of the East, to waste in a scant few days. The Tower would fall far faster. The ogres would carry them all off to the

Enemy, to be tortured and consumed by Incuban. And they'd no idea such danger was near! They'd thought the Tower still secret, still safe. But the Enemy knew of it, even what they called it. He had to warn them!

Mak hadn't wanted to go back to help them attack. He'd instead warned Rion. That meant he wasn't evil, not yet. But if they recaptured him, he'd grow up being taught by them to do terrible things, evil things. "Mak, can you walk?" Rion asked.

Mak had been standing. He seemed to be doing so easily enough.

"Mak wak," he said. But when he tried, he almost fell. He scowled at his leg. "Mak na wak," he said sadly.

Rion wished again for Jargas's staff. Mak could have used it as a walking stick. He looked at Mak nervously. "I will help you walk," he said, fighting the terror of memory of the ogres from the Passes, as he slowly put his arm around Mak's waist to support him. His skin crawled when he did so. But Mak held him with surprising gentleness.

They proceeded awkwardly, a little like two people in a three-legged race. Rion was carefully tracing his steps back to the Tower. He had no idea what he would do with Mak once he got there. The others would think him mad, except perhaps for Jargas. No, even he would. But Mak had warned them of the coming attack. They owed it to Mak to help him.

Rion heard a loud screeching call coming down the valley. It sounded like an eagle. Quickwing! Lunahr must be searching for him, or perhaps Hunter. He sighed in relief.

"Had, Ran! Had! Hap Mak had! Hapgraf!" Mak was frantic, terrified.

Rion swallowed. The call had been loud, too loud, and it had come from the wrong direction, from deeper within the Pass, from the east. Not a chimaera, not a cat's cry, but.... Rion moved as quickly as he could to the side of the valley. There was an overhanging ledge with a shadow underneath it. They could hide there. They barely made it. A huge shadow passed over the floor of the valley and the screeching cry it made now was earsplitting. Then Rion saw it.

It was as large as a horse. In fact, the hindquarters were that of a horse, but the forelegs and head and wings were those of an eagle. Mak had called it a hapgraf. There was a rider on it; he could see that much as it flew over the length of the Pass, disappearing from sight toward the end that led to the Tower. Rion hoped furiously that it might be gone but stayed hidden in case it decided to return. It was well that he did so. They heard the cry again before they saw it.

At first he thought it was less well trained; the chimaera were so silent, they could attack by surprise. But then he realized that bone-chilling cry had made him want to run, even knowing he could not escape from it. An army faced with one or more such shrieking beasts might easily break ranks and crumble.

Rion hoped it would fly back the way it had come, but it didn't. It flew over to a ledge on the opposite side of the Pass and landed, perching upon it. They were trapped. Until it left, they could not move.

Rion studied it. Why was it here? It was as if it were waiting for something. The rider was cloaked, his face hidden. Was it a scout? Was the Enemy already sneaking up on the Watchtower? Was it a guard? Was the enemy moving something of value down the Pass? Or was it searching for something or someone, perhaps for Mak?

"Mak na ga bak, Mak na ga bak!" Mak started chanting softly. To his surprise Rion realized Mak was trembling. A whine was starting deep in his throat. He was starting to whimper as a dog would. Rion shivered. Mak sounded like Rion had, that terrible night after the horrible nightmare. Mak was terrified. "Shh. You must be quiet, Mak. You won't go back. We'll stay hidden. I'll protect you," Rion swore.

He tried to think of how to say it in Ogrish, but Mak said, "Ran kap Mak saf," in obvious relief.

Exactly how many words did this ogre know? He'd already spoken ones he shouldn't and apparently knew the meanings of many others.

Time crept past. The hapgraf was quiet now, and it camouflaged well with the rock. It was the same brownish gray. Rion realized how lucky he was that it hadn't come earlier. He'd never have known it was there.

He hoped it would fly off soon. He'd not realized it was planning to stay so long. He'd not thought that they might lose their shadow, if it stayed too long on its perch. But it looked like the shadow might actually be lengthening slightly. He hadn't paid attention to where the sun was in relation to the ledge when he'd chosen it. He'd not had the time for such details, crucial though they now were. It was blind luck that sunset was working in his favor.

There was no way he'd ever make it back to the Tower before dark now. He should have told someone he was going out. But he'd been afraid they wouldn't have let him go, then. They'd worked so hard to get him here to them, to safety, but they'd done it out of pity, as Elanara had. They didn't need him, or really even want him. He'd worked his way from Athanark as a guard, but they wouldn't let him fight for them. He'd begun to feel so useless here.

Rion missed Talon, as he had been in Athanark. He was so changed. And he missed Aras fiercely. He still couldn't believe Aras was dead. Such a bright light shouldn't be able to be extinguished. And Elanara and Eladar no longer cared about him. Elanara never had; she'd only pitied him. And Eladar hated him now, for what he'd written. Hunter was too busy for him and still frightened him a little. Hunter had given him the sword, a Dwarven blade, but there had been a room full of such blades. He hadn't meant anything by it, as Rion had thought he had at first. It was like giving a child a piece of candy so he'd be quiet and do what he was told. Lunahr…. Lunahr had spoken with him, he'd been eager to… because he wanted to learn the songs he knew. Or maybe because Lunahr had wanted to pleasure himself on him, because he was younger than Lunahr was, smaller, and inexperienced. Lunahr certainly hadn't thought of him as a true friend, or he'd not have run from him earlier.

Ron, Gar, Ara, Andra, and Rarnak were glad to be rid of him, or else why wouldn't they have tried to get Talon to let him come with them? He'd been a burden to them. They'd helped him out of pity, or loyalty for when he'd been their employer. Their sense of duty had made them help him. No, that last wasn't fair. He knew it wasn't. They were his friends, truly, but they still didn't have time for him here. They had important work to do. War was no place for a boy, and they all still thought of him as one, as someone to be protected.

He might as well still be without a voice. No one ever listened to him here. Rion was dismayed to feel tears welling up in his eyes. He'd thought himself older than that, stronger than that. No wonder they thought of him as a boy. He still acted like one.

"Ran na cra," Mak whispered, patting him on the back.

That did it. He started to sob. He was so pathetic even an ogre felt sorry for him. He forced himself to cry quietly, lest the hapgraf hear.

Mak was very concerned. "Ran hat haat," Mak whispered.

Rion stopped crying, trying to puzzle out what Mak said. "What is hat?" he asked.

The little ogre tapped his chest, then at Rion's puzzled expression, gently held his hand and placed it where his had been. Rion felt the strong beat of Mak's heart.

Rion's eyes widened, in sudden understanding, and he nodded. "Yes, my heart hurts," he said. How could Mak be so smart?

"Mak Ran fran," Mak said. "Hat na haat."

"You're my friend? So my heart shouldn't hurt?" Rion asked.

"Ya," Mak said, nodding yes with a big toothy grin.

Elmoth, he was ugly! He'd forgotten, hearing his words, until he saw those teeth again. He felt sorry for the ogre. Mak would be even more miserable than he was, at the Tower.

Rion's breath caught. A figure was coming down the Pass. It was a Dwarf. Rion's heart began hammering. The hapgraf and rider would see him! He'd be killed, or worse, captured. What could he do? He only had his sword. If he tried to help, he'd die too.

The figure drew nearer. Oh no! Rion recognized him. It was Donovar, the High-King's Advisor. He took a deep breath. He had to try to help. Donovar had seemed nice, the little he'd seen of him, but he also knew all their plans. If he were captured, tortured and interrogated, they'd not only lose the Tower, but the entire War.

Rion started to rise from his hiding place, but then the hapgraf let out a shrill cry and leapt off the ledge, diving for Donovar. Rion saw Donovar jump at the sound, but he didn't run. He was either frozen with fear or brave beyond measure. Either way, Rion realized he was too late to save him. Donovar was as good as dead.

The creature soared over the Dwarf's head and landed a few feet behind him. Rion finally got a decent look at the rider's face as she pushed back the hood of her cloak and his heart froze. The rider was small and her face clearly visible: she wore no veil this time. It was Circe! For her to be riding a creature like that, to be here, she must be here because the Enemy sent her. She'd apparently lost her battle. She'd turned fully to darkness, just as he'd seen her in his dream. Donovar was doomed.

Circe jumped down from the creature and ran to Donovar and embraced him. Donovar hugged her back. It made Rion's stomach turn to see it. She was using her magic on him. He was under her spell, exactly as Jargas had been. She'd fornicate with him and drain his life away. But she didn't climb on top of him. Instead, she seated herself once again upon the hapgraf, and Donovar mounted it behind her. Then, with a great beating of wings, they took to the air. Rion watched them fly down the Pass, the way the creature had originally come from. She was taking him to Incuban, so they could both feed upon him. They'd share him. And he'd betray all their secrets to Incuban.

Rion paled. Unless he already had! She'd been waiting for him, expecting him. No wonder the Enemy knew of the Tower! Donovar was one of their pawns. Either he'd been all along, or he'd been turned, captured in one of the battles they'd fought and then released before he was missed so no one knew. Or they'd come to him in the middle of the night, in his tent, before he reached the relative safety of the Tower. And now the ogres would come and everyone would die: his friends, the Amontir, the Dwarven army, everyone.

"Mak, when were your friends and cousins supposed to attack the Tower, do you know?"

"Tamawa nat," Mak said confidently.

"Tomorrow night? You're sure?" Rion asked.

Mak nodded.

Of course! The troops were already starting to move out, to reposition. There would be less than two thousand Dwarves left. One thousand had already left, and another thousand were to leave tomorrow morning, and then the final thousand who were being repositioned. Talon was leaving himself practically defenseless! "Then there's still time. How far is it to your home, Mak? How long to walk?" Rion asked.

"Na ga hama. Bata man da," Mak said adamantly.

"I know there are bad men there. But if I go back to the Tower and warn my friends yours are coming, they'll be ready for them. They'll fight them, and your friends will all die. But many of mine will die too. That isn't right, Mak, that your friends and mine should die. The Enemy is the one who should die, Incuban should. Maybe if you take me near your home, not all the way there, or I'd be captured, but near enough, maybe I can figure out how to help, what to do."

Mak had been studying him intently, probably trying to puzzle out what he'd been saying. He should have spoken more slowly. "Ran Mak fran. Mak tak Ran hama," Mak said. "Hap Mak wak, hap Mak fran, Mak kasan, na kala."

"That's right. I'm your friend. You take me home. I'll help you walk there and help your friends and cousin so they don't try to kill us or get killed," Rion said, relieved. Mak had understood! He was going to do it! "Come on, let's go. I think it's safe now, and it will be dark soon. We need to hurry."

Part of him thought what he was doing was foolhardy. He had to warn everyone about Donovar, about the attack. But if he went back to the Tower, his friends wouldn't be safe, not from an attack by ogres. The ogres could tear the Tower apart with their bare hands, or at least smash it to bits with rocks. And Mak's friends would die in the carnage too.

Hunter hated ogres; Rion had seen it. All of them hated or feared them. Only Jargas or Jarina might care a little about their survival. Denric and Tanris had scorned even the Elves. He could imagine what they might think about Mak. They'd not think twice about killing Mak and all his friends.

It was hard for Mak to walk. He was leaning heavily on Rion.

"Can we reach there by dark?" Rion asked anxiously.

Mak nodded. "Mak wak fas," he said and picked up the pace a little, but Rion could tell it hurt him. Rion remembered Ara in the Pass, saying he was all right and riding his horse with so many broken bones. Mak's face looked drawn like that. Could Mak be walking on his leg if it were broken? From what Rion had seen of the ogre fight in the mountains, they didn't seem to get injured as easily as men, or feel pain as keenly. Besides, even were Mak's leg broken, he could do nothing to aid him here. But they could heal him with the Ring and the Knife, at the Tower. Only Hunter would sooner kill him. Hunter had reacted so angrily to their talk of ogres! Rion wondered what terrible experience he'd had with them that he hated them so. He'd probably never hear. It might be another one of their secrets.

Mak had such faith in him, a child's faith, that even injured as he was, he would go back to the home he feared. Was his faith misplaced? Was Rion causing Mak unnecessary pain? Should he have taken Mak back to the Tower and gotten their help? Was he only doing otherwise to force the others to see he was a man? No. They might not help Mak. Rion sighed. His thoughts were running in circles, but at least his feet were heading in a single direction.

The walk seemed endless, but it was almost dark. They must be close.

"Da canyan! Amast da," Mak said, confirming his suspicion.

Canyon? Rion eyed the crack in the wall of the pass dubiously. "That's a canyon?"

"Ya. Cafa. Gads. Na lad nas, Ran," Mak said softly.

Careful? Guards. No loud noise? "All right," he whispered. There were fresh-looking rockslides to either end of the crack, the stone all sharp and jagged. Was it really the mouth of a canyon? If so, was it a box canyon, or an open-ended one? The thought of being trapped by the hapgraf terrified him. "Mak, is there any other way out of the canyon? Another exit, like this?"

"Ya. Mach baga. Al cam dat wa. Ancaban dat wa," Mak said, shuddering.

There was a much bigger opening at the other end? Everyone came that way? Incuban was that way?

Without hesitation, Mak stepped into the crack. Rion followed, his heart pounding in trepidation. He followed where Mak led, stopping when he did, clinging to the rock. Finally, Mak let out a soft sigh. "Har," he whispered.

Here? Rion didn't see anything that looked like a village, even an ogre one. He'd expected crude houses of stone, as there were no trees here for ogres to uproot, for them to snap off the branches and use the logs to build with, as they otherwise might.

"Had!" Mak cried, pulling Rion to an outcropping.

It was the hapgraf, or perhaps another one. It was coming from the opposite end of the canyon, from where that wider entrance must be, but it could easily have flown over it and circled around. Rion saw only a single rider. Was it the same one? If so, where was Donovar? Rion waited for the hapgraf to turn aside, but it didn't. It flew straight at the rock face of the canyon wall, then vanished into a shadow. Elmoth! It was the entrance to a cave. Rion studied the cliffside carefully. There were many such shadows.

"Mak," Rion whispered. "How many ogres, how many of your people, are here? Which caves do they use? How many live in each?

Mak scrunched his brow.

Rion realized he had asked too much, that his words must have been too confusing for the limited intelligence of even this amazing ogre prodigy. He'd find out first how many ogres lived there altogether and worry about how many in which caves later.

He held up his closed hands, two fists. "Pretend each finger is an ogre," he whispered, and counted to ten slowly, extending each finger as he counted aloud. "Show me how many ogres live here." Even as he said so, he belatedly realized how futile it would be, to expect an ogre to be able to count.

Mak shook his head. "Ma," he said and held out his own thick fingers, all ten of them.

Rion was convinced Mak was merely mimicking him, playing some kind of game, when to his shock, Mak said, "Alavan, twalv, thartan, fartan, faftan, saxtan, savantan, aatan, nantan, twanta," and then grinned proudly.

No! Mak could not possibly have just counted to twenty! "Twenty?" he asked dubiously, to confirm the number.

Mak grinned and nodded. "Ya. Twanta an cav."

"Twenty? So many? But Jargas told me ogres only live in tribes of fifteen or less, that more is too hard to feed. Which cave do they live in?"

"All," Mak said. "Twanta an cav."

"All? What? You can't mean there are ogres in every cave here? Twenty ogres in each?" Rion asked, his heart thudding at the thought of so many ogres so near.

Mak grinned again, showing those enormous teeth. "Ya."

Rion swallowed. "But… but that can't be right! There must be at least thirty caves here! Twenty in each cave would mean over six hundred ogres!" he hissed.

Mak nodded, grinning. "Ran smat," he said, apparently impressed that he'd come up with the figure so quickly.

What had he gotten himself into? Six hundred ogres? They'd smash the Tower to powder! And he'd been worried Mak's friends were the ones who would die, when it was his friends who would! "How many Ogresses have been captured. Baga Mama. How many Baga Mama?" Rion asked.

"Wan," Mak said. "Wan Baga Mama, all cav."

"One? But that can't be right. Ogres live in tribes of fifteen. More is too many to feed. Even twenty per cave is too much. Are you trying to tell me this is an ogre village, a city, that you all live here with only one Ogress? It's so desolate here. How could you possibly feed so many?"

"Fam. Fam anma, fam plan. Bata man tak wata, kala anma, kala plan. Na fata," Mak said sadly.

"Fam… you mean farm? But ogres can't farm!" Rion said indignantly.

"Wha na?" Mak asked, sounding puzzled.

"Why not? Well because… because…." Rion couldn't say it. *Because they're not smart enough to.* Only Mak spoke almost like a Man. He could reason and count. Elmoth, he'd even been able to add or multiply: he'd had some way of coming to six hundred, unless he somehow knew the number. But how could an ogre even conceive of a number so high? And they farmed. He saw no fields here, even ruined ones, as Mak had described. There was no soil, only rock. Wherever their fields were, the enemy had taken their water and killed their plants and animals so they'd starve and weaken and had taken their Ogress hostage. The ogres must hate the Enemy, for what He had done. Rion wondered if the Enemy underestimated the ogres' intelligence the way he had. Mak had gotten away. Others might have as well. He wondered how well the Ogress was guarded.

"How many hapgraf are there, Mak?" Rion asked.

"Wan, ta, tra," Mak counted quickly on his fingers, holding three fingers out, beaming in pride.

Rion swallowed. He'd hoped there might have only been the one.

"Do they guard Baga Mama? She is still here, isn't she?" he asked in sudden fear. What if she wasn't? What if they'd taken her elsewhere? How would they ever find her?

"Ya. Baga Mama da," Mak said, pointing to one of the shadows that indicated the mouth of a cave.

"Is she heavily guarded? Did you ever try to rescue her?" Rion asked.

Mak looked scared. "Ya. Bata man angra, kala ada. Tra cav. Twanta, twanta, twanta kala," Mak said, and Rion saw there were tears in his eyes. "Lata, baga, all."

"The bad men punished you for trying to free her? They killed all the ogres in three caves? Twenty plus twenty plus twenty? Sixty ogres? Little ogres and big ones? Oh Elmoth, you mean children! Not... not even babies?" he asked in sudden dread, knowing the answer, as he mimed holding an infant.

The tears started to stream down Mak's face. "Ya," he said hoarsely.

Ron was appalled. "But that's horrible!" he cried softly, fighting the urge to shout. "How am I supposed to rescue her? I had no idea how dangerous all this would be! I thought there'd be fifteen of you, hopefully poorly guarded, not six hundred, and three hapgrafs, and they'll kill babies if I fail!"

"Ran, ta fas, ta fas. Mak sla. Na andasta." Mak said, agitated, tapping his head in frustration.

"I'm sorry, Mak, I didn't mean to talk so fast and say so much, faster than you could understand," he said more slowly and clearly. "I know Common must sound very strange to you, the way I speak it, almost like another language sometimes. You're not slow, Mak. You're so smart, I forgot you're an ogre. I forgot you're still a child. An eight-year-old Man couldn't do better than you've done. Please don't feel bad."

Mak calmed at Rion's words. "Ran hap," he said confidently.

He'd said "Rion help" with the confidence of a child. *Oh Elmoth, I wish I was as confident of myself as he is of me,* Rion thought. And here he was, swearing to Elmoth a dozen times, asking Him for aid, when he knew now that Elmoth wasn't even a God; He was only an Elf. He wished Donovar hadn't said so, that Lunahr hadn't. He needed to believe. This was too big for him to face alone. Except he wasn't totally alone. "Mak, how did you get away? How did you escape?"

Mak said proudly, "Mak fan hal an cav."

Rion was puzzled. Something about a cave. His head was starting to hurt, Mak's Common was so bad. But at least he was speaking it. Imagine if he were a normal ogre, if he only knew twenty words!

"What was that about a cave? Say it again, Mak, and show me with your hands if you can," Rion said.

Mak bent down and dug a little ditch in the dry soil of the rocky ground. "Mak... fan... hal... an... cav," Mak said, pointing to the hole he'd dug.

"Hole? You found a hole in the cave? You mean a tunnel?" Rion asked, and made an arch with one hand and used two fingers of his other hand to walk through.

"Tana? Ya, tana, tana!" Mak said enthusiastically. He'd learned a new word and was overjoyed.

"So there's a secret way out of one cave, at least. Can you point to your cave, Mak?"

Mak pointed.

"Can we get back in that way? How many guards are inside the cave?"

Mak started trembling. "Na ga bak. All kala. Mak papa, Mak mama, Mak brada, Mak sasta." He said the last miming holding a baby.

Rion swallowed. "You mean you're from one of the three caves? The ones where they killed everybody? The Enemy killed your whole family?"

Mak started sobbing and Rion put his arms around him and hugged him. "Shh, Mak, it's all right. I know your heart hurts. The Enemy's minions killed all my friends but one, too. They killed more. They killed my whole City, two cities, Ardock and Gosa. And more friends there. Everywhere I go, He kills those I love. I know what it's like to lose those you love, to live when everyone else dies."

Mak quieted at his words. "Ran Mak fran. Ran na kala."

Rion was surprised. Mak knew the word "die," apparently, yet he still said the Ogrish word for it, which meant both kill and die. "Yes, Mak, I'm your friend and I'll try not to die. But if I'm to live, I need to know how you got away safely. Why didn't they follow you through the tunnel?"

"Bata man ta baga. Mak small," he said. He eyed Rion appraisingly. "Ran small. Ran can ga hal... tana," he said, correcting himself with the new word he'd learned.

"The Men were too big to follow you? But I'm small enough, you think I'd fit?" Rion asked, to be sure he understood him correctly.

"Ya. Mak tak Ran da?" Mak asked, and began trembling more violently.

"I don't know, Mak. I might need you to show me how to go in, but that doesn't mean you'd have to go with me. I couldn't ask you to do that," Rion said.

Mak shook his head fiercely. "Ran na ga alan. Mak ga ta."

"But you don't have to come, Mak. If it's some sort of crevice tunnel, it should be easy enough to follow. Unless it's too dark inside, or it branches and there is more than one tunnel," he said in dismay at the thought.

He could barely see Mak now, the sun was so low in the sky. The last rays were fading. But Mak's eyes were almost glowing, two bright yellow spots in the dark of their hiding place, like wolven eyes. He wondered if Mak was able to see in the dark, the way some animals and even the Dwarves could, or perhaps even better. Could all ogres? Jargas hadn't mentioned that about ogres, but Jargas would never believe him about Mak, unless he met him.

Rion swallowed hard, forcing tears back. He might never see Jargas or any of them again. Jargas didn't seem so frightening now. Rion wished Jargas were here to guard him. Jargas might be able to survive such a rescue attempt. He couldn't. It was hopeless.

Mak's eyes were focused on him, but in the fading light, Rion couldn't read the expression on his face, though he must have been able to see his from the despondency in his voice when he said, "Ran na hap. Ran ga Tawa, ga saf?"

"I never said that, Mak. I never even thought it. Of course I'll help. I can't go back to the Tower with you and leave your friends here in danger," Rion said.

"Ran ga Mak?" There was joy in his voice and Rion realized Mak hadn't only started to fear he'd leave, but that he'd leave without him!

"I told you, Mak, I'm your friend. Friends take care of each other. Friends help each other. Even if I discover I can't help you here and now, I'll take you with me to my other friends. I'll have them all come aid you."

Mak lunged at him and Rion was terrified that Mak had misunderstood him somehow. Then he realized the strong arms around him weren't crushing him, and Mak let him go. He'd hugged him, spontaneously, enthusiastically, with all the adoration of any eight-year-old boy hugging his big brother.

He had no idea how he was going to do it, but there must be some way to save the ogres and his own friends as well. He just had to plan, to think this through. There must be a way.

FARAD watched as Ron yawned, touching off a series of other people's yawns and a few stretches at the table.

Dewalaren said, "Ron, why don't you and the others get some sleep? I've given you scarcely a moment's peace since Rion told us about your trip and I realized how vulnerable we are. You've told me all you can about Thenalon and Logareth and Athanark. At this rate you'll make yourselves ill or be too tired to sit in the saddle when it's time for you to leave us."

Ron poured more kakla. Sarnon had put a fresh pot on the table. Ron took a sip of the scalding liquid. "No, let's finish tonight, if we can. We can still catch a few hours' sleep and then have some time tomorrow to spend with Rion. I've barely seen him in days, and who knows when we'll see each other again after this?"

"All right, if you're sure," Dewalaren reluctantly agreed.

Farad knew better than to suggest Dewalaren get some sleep. One look at him and Farad could tell he'd not sleep again anytime soon. Farad cursed himself for the hundredth time for barging in upon him and Lunahr like that, for saying what he had. He'd give anything to undo the harm he'd caused both of them by it. He'd tried, but he'd shattered their tenuous happiness.

Dewalaren looked like the walking dead. It was unnerving seeing him like this after the many decades he'd stayed strong for them. And Lunahr was shielding himself from Farad completely so he wouldn't feel his pain and hear his thoughts. Farad only took solace in the fact that Lunahr had not broken the bond, wounded as he'd been by him. Lunahr had at least recognized how dangerous it would have been for him to have done so. He forced his worries about his friends down and concentrated on the discussion at hand.

It was well after second bell when they finished. Farad walked upstairs with the brothers and Lunahr. He bid the brothers good night as they entered their room, and headed for his own. Jarina would already be there. She'd left the meeting hours earlier, once her part was done.

Lunahr passed him silently, without saying good night to him, heading for his own room. Farad winced at the slight and was about to enter his own room when he saw Ron and his brothers head back out of their room. He was surprised. He'd not have thought to see them again until morning, and they appeared troubled. "Have you thought of something you forgot to tell us? Or is something wrong?"

"I'm not sure. Rion's not in our room, and the bed's not been slept in," Ron said, his concern evident. "Rion folds the bedding around the pillows differently than we do when he makes the bed. I'd have thought he might be up writing in the Library or somewhere, only his journal is still on the desk. He might be at first shift of breakfast. We thought we'd go look for him. We've scarcely seen him at all these past couple of days, and he's seemed troubled the times we have, unlike his usual self. I'm sure he's fine, but I'd not be able to get to sleep, knowing he's sitting up awake somewhere."

"I'll help you search. With the four of us, we should find him quickly enough," Farad said.

"Hunter, please, get some sleep. There's no need for you to come, too. I'm sure we'll find him easily," Ron assured him.

"I'll be better able to sleep once I've said good night to him," Farad argued.

BY THE sound of fourth bell, Farad was starting to get worried: they'd checked the Dining Hall, Kitchen, Stable, Library, even the Armory and War Room, to no avail. They'd looked everywhere on the first level of the building. "He must be here somewhere. Let's try your room again, in case he got past us, and then check the rest of upstairs and in the Tower," Farad suggested.

Rion wasn't in their room or the Tower or any of the hallways or the bathing room or privy. Reluctantly, Farad knocked on Lunahr's door, wanting neither to waken him nor interrupt him. He suspected Rion might be there, that perhaps he'd been waiting in Lunahr's room for him, and if he had been, he had a fair notion of why he might be, from what he'd seen and heard earlier. But Lunahr was alone in his room, still wide-awake and dressed. When he heard they were looking for Rion, he said he wasn't tired and he'd help them search.

Farad thought Rion might perhaps be in Elanara's room, but he wasn't about to knock on her door. It had been hard enough to knock on Lunahr's. Farad wondered if perhaps Rion had discovered the secret tunnels, if he'd decided to find out how Farad had appeared in the Library when he'd known it to be empty. He sent the brothers to the Dwarven caves to look for him; then he and Lunahr began searching both of the series of passageways. Lunahr searched the downstairs tunnels connecting the Library to the War Room and the underground river grotto, the passages Farad had discovered and explored over a century ago. Farad searched the upper passages, which connected the bedrooms, tunnels he hadn't even discovered until they had come here after Caramore fell.

RON was surprised to see Eladar on his way out of the caves as he entered. He'd not expected to see one of the Elves here. Eladar was scowling. "Eladar, forgive me for troubling you when you're already troubled, but have you seen Rion?"

Eladar appeared uncomfortable. "Not since yesterday morning. I looked for him yesterday evening. I'd wanted to speak with him, after talking to Donovar. I'd hoped to apologize, but I wasn't able to find him. You haven't seen Donovar by any chance, have you? He doesn't seem to be anywhere in the caves. I suppose he's eating breakfast, though I checked the Dining Hall for him before coming here. I must have missed him somehow. I was about to look for him in the Dining Hall again."

"No, we've not seen him anywhere in the Tower, and we've searched everywhere but the bedrooms there for Rion. But we split up to search. Hunter and Beryl might have seen Donovar. We thought Rion might be here, but it doesn't sound as if you've seen him. Do you think maybe the two of them are together? That perhaps they've gone for a walk or something?" Ron asked, running out of ideas.

"I doubt it. The Perimeter Guard doesn't let anyone out after dark, and the sun has not yet risen, but we can check," Eladar said, the look of annoyance on his face having changed to concern, as they spoke. They asked the Perimeter Guard, but no one had seen either of them leave, although they said they were the night shift and had only begun their duty at sundown.

Ron, Ara, Gar, and Eladar went back to the Tower. Hunter and Beryl met them. "He wasn't in the caves?" Hunter asked tensely.

"No, and Donovar seems to have gone missing as well," Ron said worriedly. "We were going to try the Dining Hall again. The Perimeter Guard said they didn't leave while they were on shift, but they might have on the previous one."

"We just came from the Dining Hall. Rion wasn't there, and I didn't see Donovar, either. We'll speak to those of the Perimeter Guard who were on duty earlier. We checked with Elanara and Elavar as well, and neither has seen Rion," Hunter said in frustration.

THEY went back to the caves and Farad spoke to the Captain of the Perimeter Guard, who sent for the previous shift. They assembled, and were asked about Rion and Donovar.

"Aye, I saw the lad," Galen said. "It was about midway between fourth and fifth bell in the afternoon. He said he was going for a walk. I warned him to be careful of flyovers and to stay under cover where he could. He didn't come back my way, but people often don't come the same way they leave."

"Was Donovar with him?" Farad asked.

"Nay. I didn't see the Advisor all day," Galen said apologetically.

"I saw Donovar," Venron volunteered. "He left a while after fifth bell, in the afternoon. He said he was going for a walk. He's done so often enough. I didn't think anything of it. He didn't come back past me, but he doesn't usually."

Farad cursed. "Did any of the rest of you see either of them return?"

There was a chorus of "Nays."

Ron paled. "That was twelve hours ago! You mean he's still out there, alone in the dark, in the Pass, with ogres and obearn and pumar?"

Farad said grimly, "There won't be ogres or obearn. The ogres in these Mountains were all exterminated a century ago, in retaliation for Thenalon, and fortunately obearn are extremely rare here. Jargas's bond obearn is the only one we've encountered, and Bruin's not seen another of his kind since his mother died protecting him from a pumar, years ago, and he's roamed far. But there are snakes and pumar and other hazards. Also, the rock is dangerously unstable along portions of the wall. There are frequent rockslides."

Gar said anxiously, "Rion would never have stayed out so long, especially not past dark. He'd know it's not safe. Something's happened to him."

"We have to find them both," Farad said. He turned to the Captain. "I want you to mobilize two search parties, one hundred men each. And I want you to quadruple the Guard around the Tower. This may be the Enemy's work. We need to be ready for an attack."

"Aye, sir. Since Donovar is one of the ones missing, should we wake the High-King?" he asked.

"He'd not soon forgive you if you didn't. I'll go wake Talon as well, and my wife," Farad said. "We'll use Slash and Whisper to track them by scent, and we'll need to use torches too. It's too dark to see otherwise tonight."

"That'll provide a tempting target, if it is the Enemy, and lead them right to us," the Captain said, his voice thick with worry.

Farad didn't answer. He was well aware of the risks. Twelve hours! And a little over eleven for Donovar. Anything might have happened to them. Farad felt panic and despair rising and fought it down.

Shortly after fifth bell, they were off. The two groups expected to diverge from each other relatively quickly. They were surprised when Slash and Whisper strayed little from each other. It soon became apparent why. "The Pass! They've both gone into the Pass! Whatever possessed them to do something so foolish?" Jarina asked, dismayed.

Farad was glad Dewalaren had ordered Lunahr to stay in the Tower, though the rest of their kin had joined the search. Dewalaren had ordered Eladar and Elanara to stay behind as well, although they had begged to help. Dewalaren had only let Elavar come with them. He was afraid what they would find. The woods around the Tower were dangerous enough: pumar roamed them freely. It was there Jarina had met and bonded to Whisper. But the Pass was far more dangerous.

Was the Enemy here as well, now? Had He gotten past the Dwarves of Malar somehow, by using chimaera or hippogryphs? His forces had certainly infiltrated the Fromer Mountains deeply enough to attack Caramore. They still didn't know what portion of their defenses had been overlooked for that to happen. There might be dozens of other, smaller passes like the Thinabar Pass that they knew nothing of that the Enemy had discovered and was utilizing. The Enemy had also managed to launch a major offensive against the Lands of Men south of the Velmar Mountains, coming upriver from the Sea, from what they'd learned, when they'd never suspected He might. He'd destroyed Riviera and Loatia because they'd failed to anticipate His strategy. Farad forced those thoughts aside. For now, he had to concentrate on finding Rion and Donovar.

They followed the trail for quite some time when it unexpectedly diverged. Rion's trail, which Slash was following, headed toward one wall of the Pass, while Donovar's trail, which Whisper followed, went down the center of the valley.

Farad and his men followed Slash. A feeling of dread washed over Farad as he realized Slash was heading for a rockslide. No, not that! It couldn't be they'd find him buried under the rock. Slash began sniffing along the jagged, broken rock and then started growling and gnashing his teeth. "Stay here," Farad commanded the others as he approached Slash alone. "Easy, boy, what is it? What have you found?"

He bent down to look, holding the torch close to the ground. Someone had been here, buried in the rock, but he was gone now. But… blood, there was blood on the rock. He bent and retrieved something. It was a dark, raggedly torn scrap of fabric. He smelled it. Blood. Slash was still growling. He searched further and found a small patch of dirt amidst the loose rock, with a clear footprint, a bare foot, too wide to be a Man's and misshapen in an all-too-familiar way. Idare, no! It couldn't be; not here! He'd never have thought that the rockslide might have been more than a tragic accident, but it had been. An ogre!

Farad followed the tracks, but quickly lost them on the bare rock, but he'd seen enough. It was definitely an ogre. It had unleashed a shower of rock upon Rion, buried him in it, and now it was dragging him along with it. It was a small one from the tracks, not big enough to carry him, but big enough that it could have crushed him, easily, and was bringing him back to its lair to eat. He clutched the scrap of fabric in his clenched fist and fell to his knees as memory flooded him.

He was in Thenalon again, a century ago, amidst the carnage, the horror, the terror, the pain and the blood and the fire. There had been a boy there, too. There had been many, but this one he remembered vividly, as if it had only been yesterday. An ogre had torn his arm off and eaten it in front of him, then left him bleeding, to die. Only he'd lived. Farad had found him, saved him. But the boy had seen and heard his father burn alive in the fire. He'd seen his mother and sister both savaged by the ogres. Farad still got ill remembering their bloodied, ravaged bodies as he'd found them, hearing the sobbing boy tell him what had happened.

A wave of warmth and strength flooded him. It was Jarina. He forced himself to his feet, following Slash, who still had the scent, his men trailing at a distance. Then he heard a roar. Whisper! He told Slash to stay put and went to the search party Jarina was with.

"What is it? What have you found?" Farad asked.

"Not found, lost. Whisper has lost the trail, and she is furious. There is something else here that has her enraged. I have never seen her like this. Hold me while I extend myself into the link. I must smell what she smells. I must know what she knows."

Farad held her as she went limp in his arms. A few moments later, Jarina recovered, her face creasing in puzzlement. "I do not know what it is. It is infuriating for me as well. I smelled both horse and eagle, but more than that, somehow. It was so strong, as if a flock of eagles had landed here, in this spot, beside a horse. But eagles do not flock."

Dewalaren said in horror, "A hippogryph. It is a creature, like a chimaera, only part eagle, part horse. The Enemy created them, uses them. It must have seen Donovar, landed here, and flown off with him." He turned to Desmond. "I am sorry, Archer. If we are lucky, it will have been one of theirs out hunting. He might only be dead. If not, he will have been taken to the Enemy. Rion must also have been taken."

Jarina said, "No, not by such a creature. I saw what my husband has, through our link. There was blood, a rockslide, footprints. An ogre has injured Rion, taken him," Jarina said to the others.

"BUT you told us there are no ogres here!" Ron cried in denial, heart pounding. An ogre had Rion! The chance that he might yet live was small, diminishing with each moment it took to find him. He pictured Rion, alone and terrified and helpless, desperately trying to be brave, as the ogre carried him off, knowing he would die, that his friends would never even find a body.

"He might still be alive," Gar said. "The ogres kept Thorn alive, as their prisoner, so… they like having fresh…."

Ron silently finished the thought his brother could not voice: *They like having fresh meat to eat.*

"I will not abandon Rion to them. I will save him or avenge him," Hunter said, turning toward Slash.

DEWALAREN addressed his men. "Fenlon, I want you and three others to report back what we've found. We're already braced for an attack, but they need to know about the hippogryph and how close to the Tower it was." He'd not have Farad send such a message over his link to Lunahr. He knew Farad must be shielding his thoughts carefully from their young cousin.

"Aye, Majesty. We'll warn them," Fenlon swore.

The combined search party set out grimly now, not hoping to find either of the lost men alive but hoping they might at least recover their bodies.

A short while later, Whisper suddenly thrust her head into the air, her face into the wind. She began bounding up the Pass, and then veered to the left wall. Everyone followed, not knowing what to expect.

"Whisper! Stop. Stay," Jarina commanded as a figure emerged warily from the shadow of the rock into the light of their torches.

"Donovar!" Desmond cried in relief and joy. "We thought you dead! How did you escape?"

"Archer! You gave me a fright! I saw the torches and hid. I'd not realized it was you, at first. I'd thought the Enemy had found me! I'm sorry if I panicked all of you so much that you'd send a search party out to look for me, that you'd fear I might have been captured. I'd not meant to be gone so long. But it's dangerous to be using torches at night here. You'll be seen. We must get back to the Tower as quickly as we can," Donovar urged.

Desmond stiffened. "You're saying you weren't captured, old friend?"

"Would I be standing here if I had been?" Donovar challenged.

Jargas grabbed him from behind, pinning his arms, as Jarina took his axe from him.

"What are you doing?" Donovar demanded indignantly.

Dewalaren tensed as Farad touched his hand to Donovar's face, knowing his cousin was reading Donovar's core, willing him to be safe.

"The shield is still there. I can sense nothing from him," Farad reported, his voice thick with frustration.

"What shield?" Dewalaren said. "He can't have a shield. He's not one of us. Or are you saying he's a wizard?"

"He has a pyrenteum shield around his core. It's been there since I first met him. If it's still there, yet we know he's been consorting with the Enemy, then that means the

Enemy's been controlling him from the beginning. No wonder we've been losing this War, even with the Ring!" Farad accused, glaring at Donovar.

"I can't believe that," Desmond denied. "I've known him for over thirty years. In all that time, he's never once caused anyone any harm, but he's helped many."

"We must remove the shield and test him," Dewalaren declared, and the Ring on his hand began to glow.

Donovar's eyes widened in fear. "No! You can't! You mustn't! You'll put her in terrible danger if you destroy the shield!"

Dewalaren stayed his hand for the moment. "Who would it put in danger?"

Donovar swallowed; he looked trapped. He exhaled strongly. "Circe. You can't endanger her. Please! He'd hurt her, worse than He has already. He'd kill her."

"Circe is the one who took you. She was riding the hippogryph," Dewalaren said in a flash of insight.

Donovar said, stunned, "How could you know about that?"

Dewalaren cursed in Amontirin. "That can mean only one thing. She's no longer Arcanus's pawn. She's Incuban's."

"No! No, she's not! You have to believe me! You have to understand," Donovar argued desperately.

"Talon, he's lost to us, but we still might save Rion. Let me take my men and continue the search, while you find out what you can from his core," Farad urged.

"Rion? You mean it wasn't me you were searching for, it was Rion? What's happened to him?" Donovar asked, sounding genuinely distressed.

"We were looking for you both. Rion was in the Pass too. He was taken too. An ogre has him," Desmond explained.

"No! Ragnar, not the ogres! If the ogres have him, you're too late. The Enemy's got him. Unless Circe saw him first and was able to save him."

Jargas said in disgust, "She's not only lain with him and fed off of him, she's twisted him. She's made him love her. He thinks her a hero, not a villain."

"Talon, we can't believe a word, you know we can't," Farad said. "Donovar's trying to get us to stop searching, to give the Enemy time to find Rion."

Dewalaren said apologetically but firmly, "Hunter, we can't risk it. I'm going to remove the shield. I'll find out whatever I can. You'll have to stay here until I do."

Donovar beseeched Desmond, "Please, Archer, don't let him do this! I've been your friend for three decades. Surely you trust me to still be?"

Desmond said, agonized, "I am sorry, Donovar, but I cannot."

Donovar turned to Desenia in desperation. "Shanti, please! You're like a daughter to me. Don't let him destroy it! Anything but that. I'd rather he just killed me outright. I'll not live through that again. No one could live through that again. I should be dead already."

Shanti's eyes welled with tears. "It's the only way to save you, if you can be saved."

Donovar turned back to Dewalaren. "If you destroy the shield, he'll feel it. You'll harm him, but worse, he'll think the Enemy's taken me. He'll think Incuban knows about Circe, that He knows too much about his plans. You'll make him act too soon. You'll kill him."

"Who? If not the Enemy, then who has shielded you like this? Who are you trying to protect?" Dewalaren demanded.

Donovar slumped in Jargas's grasp. "Arcanus."

"Arcanus!" Dewalaren said his name as if it was a curse. "He is as bad as Incuban! He is worse!"

Donovar stiffened and stared at Dewalaren in challenge. "If you truly believe so, if you would fight against Arcanus as if he were the Enemy, then we are already lost. But he is not the villain you fear him to be, nor is Circe whom you think her to be. I love Circe, that much is true, but not for the reason you fear. Circe is my granddaughter."

Desenia looked at him in shock, and Desmond said in surprise, "Donovar, old friend, you never told me you had a granddaughter."

"There is much I never told you, Archer. I was trying to protect you. I'll still not have you hear it. I'd not so harm one I love. I'll tell only King Talon and Lord Hunter. I'll let them judge me. King Talon has the Ring to protect him from me, were I a tool of the Enemy, which I am not. Hunter has the ability to judge whether or not I am telling the truth even with the shield. I've seen him use it. If they still feel I am a tool of the Enemy, when they are done, then I ask them to kill me rather than remove the shield. If I'm dead, Arcanus will think me only a lost friend. If the shield is destroyed, he will think me lost to the Enemy. He will act too soon.

"Arcanus, Magus, and Circe have put themselves in such terrible danger. They seek to ally themselves with the Elves and all the other forces of good in this world against Incuban. They are the one chance we have, the only chance left to us, now that Aras is gone. I'll not see you doom the world to destruction, King Talon, when you have suffered and sacrificed so much to save it. If it means my death to ensure that you don't make that mistake, then it is a small price to pay, one I gladly will. Please, I beg you. Talk to me, where no one else can hear."

Dewalaren studied Donovar. Donovar had said he would make Arcanus act too soon, that he would kill him, as he had killed Aras. And Donovar had offered to die, rather than have the shield destroyed. "I cannot risk that he might be telling the truth. I cannot pay another such price. Come Donovar, Hunter. We will talk where the others cannot hear. Ron, Gar, Ara, Andra, you're to target him with your bows. If he makes a single act against either me or Hunter, or does anything else remotely threatening or suspicious, if he endangers anyone, you are to slay him."

The four of them readied their bows. When Dewalaren saw they were aimed, he commanded Jargas to release Donovar.

Jargas did so with obvious reluctance.

They walked toward the wall of the Pass, Dewalaren bearing a torch and Farad's hands unencumbered, in case it was a trick of some sort. But Donovar sat upon a large, flat rock. He held out his wrist to Farad. "Go ahead. Test me as you have tested others without Power, Farad, though we risk much in doing this here. The Enemy is far nearer than you had suspected, than any of us had. But you'll not believe any of what I have to say until you hear my story, so we'll have to risk it. First, I must tell you my true name, for it's not right for a Dwarf to be known by another, and it is part of the story I must tell. I was not always Donovar of Cavernas, Westhold, nor was I always a healer. I was once and am still, in my heart, King Donovar of Armsguard, though not even Desmond knows it. He must never know it."

Dewalaren started. Armsguard was not one of the thirty Kingdoms of the West. It was truly a Lost Kingdom. And he claimed to be a King!

Donovar nodded. "Aye, I'm the King of a Lost Kingdom. Now you know how a healer can be Confidant and Advisor to the High-King. It was thirty-four years ago that Armsguard fell. Desmond was no longer saving the life's-blood of the Kingdoms when my own was under siege, when my own fell.

"We withstood the Enemy's attacks for six long years. We lived upon the great stockpile of food we had, the mushrooms we grew. Our underground river sustained us, but it was the river that was ultimately our undoing. Somehow the Enemy finally found the source of it. He poisoned it. Thousands upon thousands of us died quickly, thousands more by disease the rotting dead brought. The rest of us held out until we had all but died of thirst. That's when Incuban forced the doors, when we were too weak to fight.

"I was locked in the Treasure Vault, my two greatest treasures beside me: my wife, Irene"—his voice caught—"and our daughter...." His voice broke and a sob escaped him. "Our daughter, Ilene," he forced out. "The few Guard who could still stand were outside. We'd kept hoping that Desmond might come, that someone might. We'd heard rumor of him. It's when we heard the Vault door being forced that I knew it was truly hopeless.

"We'd talked about what we would do. Calm as you please, my wife...." He sobbed and continued through his tears. Dewalaren could scarcely understand him. "Irene, she kissed me, then knelt before me, head bowed, and I raised my war axe...." He fell upon the stone, sobbing. He could no longer speak.

Dewalaren's heart went out to him, but he remembered Lunahr tricking him in the cell in precisely such a fashion. He dared not console him. "Donovar, you don't have to tell us this to show us how you've suffered at the Enemy's hands. I understand that part. I can see you have. We all have."

Donovar shook his head. "No, you don't understand. How can you, unless I tell you? I beheaded her," he said, speaking quickly to get the words out. "I had to. Then I held the axe over Ilene, my daughter. She was so brave! She just waited for me to kill her. And I hesitated. She looked up, and I saw terror in her eyes as we heard the door crash in. She saw them coming for us, and I swung, but I was too late.

"They drove three arrows into me. As I fell, I saw her scrambling for my knife, but they were so fast! I saw them dash the knife from her hand. I heard her scream, and then there was only darkness. But I was not dead. They'd not allowed me such a mercy. When I awoke I was healed, but I was in chains. My daughter was chained too. Only I was on the wall and she... she was on His bed. He'd waited days for me to waken, so He could make me watch."

The tears were flowing freely, but his voice was a steady low monotone now, lifeless. "And help. He made me hold her down while He took her, over and over again. He made me whip her. He made me brand her. I can still hear her begging and screaming as He violated her and I tortured her, endless days and nights, for weeks, until she fell quiet. She was still alive, her body at least, but her mind was gone. He'd raped it away.

"It was no fun for Him anymore, with His plaything broken. I thought He'd kill us then, but He had His servants bring us to His herd. That's what He called it. There were thousands of us, in these great fenced pens. He called us bulls and heifers and calves. His servants would come and thin the herd, that's when they'd drag some of us off for Him to feed upon. I thought the children were the worst part—there were so many, so terrified— until I saw the breeding pens. The Kingdoms were falling too fast. He'd soon have none to feed upon, so He'd started making more livestock.

"I thought I'd go mad, like poor Ilene with her blank-eyed stare. I swore I'd see her out of there. I studied all of it. I knew tactics, strategy. It took months to plan. I found men I could trust. I knew how to rouse them, how to lead them. Over six hundred of us escaped, all at once. We killed hundreds of his servants, arming ourselves as we went. We died by the dozens at first. They hunted us down mercilessly. Only seven of us made it to the Fromer Mountains, where they finally lost track of us. All but Ilene and I died crossing them.

"It was outside of Thenalon that Arcanus found us, lying upon the ground, within sight of the City wall, yet too weak to reach it. He tended us and forced me to tell him what had happened. He hoped to see us well again. He tried so desperately to help Ilene. He had to at least keep her alive for as long as he could, not for her sake, but for the baby's. She lasted almost the full term. It was an easy birth, but her body had finally found an excuse for her to die. It was a mercy when she finally stopped breathing. We named the baby after her, as is our custom. We used the last part of Ilene's name. She'd borne a little girl, tiny and perfect: Selene." He looked Dewalaren in the eye. "You know her as Circe. Circe's my granddaughter, as I've told you, but Arcanus isn't truly her father, for all he's raised her as his own. Incuban is."

Dewalaren stared at him, astonished, as so much clicked into place.

But Donovar was not finished. "But she's not who you think she is. She's not evil, for who her true father is, nor for having started down the wrong path since, when she did those terrible things you've heard of. It was the only way she could save her brother Magus. She'd do anything for him. She truly loves him. I told you Arcanus made the shield. He knew Incuban must never learn about Selene. He could have killed me to keep the secret, but instead, he shielded me. Then he took me to live in exile, as far from Incuban as possible. He took me to Gosa. Arcanus had no idea how evil that City is. It deceives many."

Dewalaren winced, remembering Rion's trials there. Rion! "We've heard enough, Donovar. We have to find Rion. We…."

"No, I've not finished. You have to let me finish," Donovar insisted. "The rest has been eating away at my spirit for decades. I can't live with my dirty secret anymore. You still need to judge me, but in order to do so, first you must hear the truth about me.

"It wasn't easy being a Dwarf amongst Men in that wretched City. I was set upon, time and time again. I'd have died many times, were it not for the strength of body my kind possesses. I remember dragging myself from an alleyway, the last time I was beaten and left for dead. There was the sound of hoofbeats, then a loud thud and a curse. The rider had been thrown, when I'd startled his horse by moving in the dirt in front of it. I was so dazed that I didn't even realize the curse was in Dwarvish, at first. I heard many men, all calling "Majesty," and for a moment I thought I was somehow being rescued, until I saw them cluster about the man on the ground.

"But he shoved them aside and came over to me. His hands were gentle, and he lifted me onto his horse and told his men they'd stay at an inn that night, instead of heading home. He sent one of his men to fetch a healer for me. They were Dwarves, all of them, except for the one who'd carried me. He was a Man, for all he'd groomed himself as one of us. They called him Archer. Later I learned that their home was in the Saravan Mountains.

"Archer tended to me and spoke to me. And when he found I had no home of my own, he invited me to his. I'd learned by then who he was, the Savior of the Lost Kingdoms, and I went with him willingly. I met his wife and his daughter. They were beautiful. It was then I decided it. He'd liked me. He'd trusted me from the start. I learned to be a healer, so they'd all value me, so they'd all trust me, and they did. If only they'd known. I wasn't there to serve him, as they all did, to honor him as High-King. I was there to kill him."

Dewalaren looked at him sharply, astonished that he might have thought to do so, and that he would admit to such a thing, knowing he would likely die for it. Farad still held his wrist. He was still staring intently into his eyes.

Donovar continued. "I hated him. He had a wife, a daughter. He'd saved twenty-nine Kingdoms, thousands of sons and daughters, but he'd left Armsguard to die, slowly, terribly. He'd left my daughter too. So I planned and I plotted and I waited. He was never alone. There were always people watching him, aiding him. They all loved him. They had reason to. He'd saved them.

"My skill as a healer grew. Arcanus had taught me something of the art, and I'd learned much more as I waited. I was there nearly a year when finally I got my chance at revenge. He came to see me one night, but he left his Guard outside. He wanted a sleeping draught. I began mixing something for him to see that he'd not awaken, something that would burn his guts out as it killed him.

"I talked to him, to keep him distracted, lest he sense what I was planning, even with Arcanus's shield about my thoughts. He was so perceptive, and I was afraid my body language might give me away. I asked him what troubled his sleep. He said it happened every year, when the first flowers bloomed in the spring, the first sunny, perfect day after the rains. That's the day his wife and sons were taken from him. Then he grew silent.

"I stopped stirring, and I told him to tell me. He said he couldn't. It had been forty-five years, and he'd never spoken of it to anyone. He told me he'd already said too much.

"I told him he needed to tell me. He'd already started to, and I could see it was eating away at him. I told him I'd never once seen him smile at his little daughter, that Shanti deserved a father who could love her. But still he wouldn't speak.

"I grew angry. I told him he should be grateful he had a wife and daughter, that he'd not been forced to kill his own wife to save her, that he'd not been forced to watch his daughter raped and tortured to death, that he'd not seen his Kingdom turn to rubble around him. By the end I was screaming at him.

"His Guard ran in and Desmond ordered them back out. He started screaming back at me. He told me he'd seen his wife and two young sons killed before his eyes, while he was helpless to save them. That it was their screams that kept him awake on the anniversary of their death every year. That he'd only been able to save so few survivors of twenty-nine Kingdoms, only tens of thousands of lives, when over one hundred other entire Kingdoms had perished. Millions had died. He blamed himself for not being strong enough. He said that they'd dragged him from the rubble of the last three Kingdoms and forced him to stop trying because they loved him. He told me he hated them for it, but he hated himself most of all, because it was his fault he'd not been able to save more, that so many had died. That he wished someone would kill him and end it, because he couldn't. He'd tried to, but his wife's eyes and his daughter's kept stopping him. And he fell to his knees sobbing at my feet.

"It was then that Shanti came running in. She started screaming at me for hurting him. She was so fierce! And suddenly her eyes lashed fire at me. I felt her anger trying to burn me. I felt the fierce love of a girl for her father behind it, even through the shield, as I fell, as the poison I'd held poured out onto the ground. Desmond was horrified. He thought she'd killed me. And she was terrified at what she'd done. I heard him screaming at the Guard again to leave us. He was hugging Shanti, telling her he loved her, that it was his fault, not hers, that he'd watch over her, he'd teach her to control her Power. He'd not known she'd had it. He swore he'd help her.

"And I remembered. I remembered what it was like, to hold the child you loved and keep the world from harming her, to feel her love for you, her faith in you. There'd been so much horror and pain and anger, I thought the love in me had all burned way. But it was still there, deep inside me. I loved Shanti too, for showing it to me again. And I sat up, and they were shocked to see me alive, when I should be dead. Then Shanti hugged me too, and I held her. I felt her strong little arms about my neck, her tears on my face. I thought of Selene, how some day she might need me to hold her like that. She deserved for me to be there for her.

"The two of them, Desmond and Shanti, have loved me ever since, never dreaming how close I'd come to killing him. And I've loved them. We've taught each other how to smile, to laugh, to get beyond the pain and truly live again. And then one day, Selene did come to me. She found out about me from Arcanus's mind when he was too weakened to shield his thoughts from her. She searched for me, for the shield surrounding me. She knew she'd be able to sense it. And she found me.

"She's not the pawn you think she is. She's playing a dangerous role in that nasty Game of theirs, and she may well die playing it. But I'll not have our people be the ones to kill her, nor yours, when she's fighting on our side, against Him, from within. She's shown me all she's plotting, and I believe her, I trust her. She called to me today, drew me to her, to warn me so I could warn you all of an attack the Enemy has planned. He's sending an army of ogres to storm the Tower tomorrow night, and poisonous water snakes into the underground river, and an army of Revenants into the caves. She's hoping now that we know, we might survive it, that we can flee the Tower before the attack comes."

Dewalaren was stunned by all he had heard. He turned to Farad. "Well?"

Farad sighed. "He's told the truth. Every word of it, or at least what he believes to be the truth."

Dewalaren studied Donovar's face intently. "Tell us again about the shield and why it can't be removed," he commanded, and Donovar did so.

Farad said, "That was true also."

Dewalaren took a deep breath. "All right. We'll trust you. We've no other choice. I can't risk destroying the shield, from what you've told me of it."

Donovar breathed deeply. "So I'm to live after all? I almost wish... nay, I cannot. I'd hurt Shanti and Selene by it. I'd hurt Desmond as well. I'll live for their sakes, if not for my own. Please, Dewalaren, promise me you'll not tell Desmond. Not about me trying to kill him, though I hope you won't. I fear he'd never trust me so fully again, and a King has so few he can truly trust. But promise me you'll not tell him I was a King. He'd not treat me any different—he's always made me feel King enough—but he'd blame himself all over again for losing Armsguard. I'll not see him hurt, ever, when I can spare him further pain. He's suffered enough for us."

Dewalaren nodded. "I promise."

They walked slowly back to the others, to a sea of anxious faces. "Donovar has not been compromised by Circe or the Enemy. He's still to be trusted. He's told us of an attack the Enemy has planned to make on the Tower and caves tomorrow night, using ogres and poisonous water snakes and Revenants. We need to go back, to strategize and implement a withdrawal, before the Enemy suspects we know his plans. There could be a flyover of this Pass at any time. If he sees an army of us here bearing torches, he might strike immediately."

"But what about Rion?" Farad argued. "We can't just leave him to the ogres, to the Enemy."

Dewalaren was flooded by remorse and pity. "Rion is gone, Hunter. He is lost to us. Either the ogres have killed him already, or they've taken him to the Enemy. Either way, he is beyond saving."

"No. We can't believe that. We won't, not after everything he's lived through," Ron argued. "He speaks Ogrish. He might have been able to talk them into keeping him alive, the way he talked those Men in Gosa into doing so. We're going after him."

"I'll not let you endanger us all, nor will I let you sacrifice yourselves to save him, when there is no hope," Dewalaren insisted.

"Ron's right, Talon. There's still a chance we can save him. Please, you must let me try!" Farad pleaded. "Let me go alone. I won't use a torch. I'll use Slash. I'll let him guide me, or I'll bond with him, like before, when I saved Jarina."

"I'll go with him. My eyes can see in the dark as well as any of our people," Jargas said, stepping to his side.

"As can mine. The three of us will go, with Slash and Whisper to aid us," Jarina added.

"I'm sorry, Hunter, Jargas, Jarina. I can't let you. I won't risk you like that. It's suicide. Rion's dead, or soon will be. There's nothing you nor I nor anyone can do about it," Dewalaren said forlornly but firmly.

"Dead? I'm not dead! But we all soon may be. You must be mad, hundreds of you with torches, when any of the Enemy's hapgraf might fly over you at any moment! Whatever are you doing out here?" a young voice asked loudly from the shadows around an outcropping of rock.

Dozens of heads turned in astonishment in the direction of the voice.

"Rion?" Ron shouted in joy, echoed by his brothers and sister and Rarnak, as well as Farad, Dewalaren, and many others.

"IDARE, we thought we'd lost you!" Farad cried, his voice choked with emotion. He ran to Rion and embraced him.

"You mean you're all out here looking for me?" Rion asked, sounding astonished. "I'm sorry, Hunter. I didn't think you might worry about me when I didn't come back. I didn't think anyone would even notice I'd gone."

Farad doubted that in the poor light Rion could see how his friends winced at his words. He'd hit the mark squarely, all unknowing.

"But I'm so glad to see you here! We thought we'd have to walk all the way back to the Tower. We might still be able to rescue her before dawn now, before the Enemy suspects we even know about His plan to storm the Tower tomorrow night... well tonight, I guess. It's nearly dawn."

Farad stiffened and reached out with his core to test Rion. Idare, no! How could he have escaped from the ogres, and even so, how could he have learned the Enemy's plans? But his mind was his own. Still he was wary. "Rescue who? Circe? And who is with you? You said, 'we.'"

"Circe! Are you mad? I want nothing to do with her! How did you even know she's here? She.... Donovar! Talon, Hunter, Jargas, quick, grab him! You're in terrible danger from him! Circe's taken him. You mustn't trust him!" Rion said, his hand going to his sword hilt, but Farad prevented him from drawing his sword.

"It's all right, Rion. We know all about Circe and the hippogryph. It's not how it appeared. It's you we are worried about now. Who's with you? Where are they?" Farad asked.

"There's someone hiding in the rocks, forty paces behind the boy," Fenris said softly, and the Ogaten siblings targeted the spot with their bows.

"No! Don't hurt him! That's Mak. He's my friend. He's only a child!" Rion cried out, pulling away from Farad. "Mak, stay down!" he commanded desperately.

"How could a child be here, Rion?" Farad asked suspiciously.

"He escaped from the Enemy, but he got trapped in a rockslide and.... Mak, look out!" Rion yelled. Farad saw Slash's shadowy shape heading for the rocks where Mak was hiding. There was a crack of rock on rock and then a sharp yelp of pain. Farad winced at Slash's pain, as he was hit by a second, better-aimed rock.

A dozen Men and Dwarves surged toward the child's hiding place, as Farad grabbed Rion from behind and held him fast, trying not to hurt him. But Rion was under no such limitations. He cracked his head into Farad's jaw and twisted and bit, kneeing Farad in the groin, apparently using every dirty trick he knew trying to free himself. But Farad wouldn't let go. Even as he fell gasping from the pain, he took Rion down with him.

"Na haat Ran!" a panicked voice bleated from the shadows.

"Please, don't hurt him! He's only a child and his leg's broken. He can't hurt you. Please, Jargas, Jarina, protect him from them. You at least will understand. You have to!" Rion pleaded.

"That's no child, it's an ogre!" someone cried, and the advancing men drew back.

Jargas moved quickly forward. "Stay back, all of you. Leave this to me," he said. From where he lay on the ground, his legs wrapped around Rion, who was still struggling fiercely, Farad saw Jargas wave away a torch. "Nay, I won't need a torch. I can see him even in the shadows. He's just a little fellow. Rion's right in that, at least: he's only a child, sure enough. It's all right, Little One. I'll not hurt you. Jarg na haat Mak."

"Ran!" Mak cried out piteously, his voice quavering with fear. "Bata Man cam!"

"No, Mak, it's all right! They're not bad, they're my friends. They're only trying to protect me. They don't understand. They thought I'd been caught by Incuban. Come out slowly, Mak, into the torchlight, so they can see you don't mean them any harm," Rion called out.

Then softer, more intently, he pleaded, "Hunter, please, let me go to him. I'm sorry I hurt you, but I couldn't let you harm him. He's hurt and he's terrified. He's been through enough already. The Enemy killed his entire family, even his baby sister. Incuban's taken their Ogress hostage, to force the ogres to attack the Tower. You've no idea what's happening. I know you hate ogres. I can guess why. Ara told me about Thenalon. But Mak's not like that. His people aren't. They're farmers. They don't hunt and eat people like other ogres do. Hunter please, let me up," Rion begged.

Farad let Rion stand, but didn't let go of him.

Slowly and fearfully, Mak came out into the torchlight, crawling.

"See, it's exactly like I told you. He can't even walk without me to lean against. Please, let me go to him," Rion said.

"We go together," Farad compromised, and Rion agreed.

"It's all right Mak. I'm here. Come, let me help you stand. These men are my friends. They're the ones from the Tower, the ones you're helping me save," Rion said. He turned to the others. "I found Mak pinned by a rockslide. I felt sorry for him and helped him, and in turn, he's told me of an attack the Enemy's planning against us. There's a City of six hundred ogres in a canyon further down the Pass. They used to be farmers, but the Enemy killed their livestock and destroyed their crops and captured their Ogress, to force them to work for Him, and brought them here. They're going to attack the Tower with fire tomorrow night, so the Enemy's minions can carry us all off to Incuban, so He can feed on us.

"Mak led me back to the City. There's thirty caves with twenty ogres in each: men, women, and children, whole families. He's shown me the one the Ogress is being held in, and I know a secret way into one of the caves not far from her. There's a tunnel. It's too small for full-grown Men to go through, but I was able to make it and the more slender Dwarves should be able to make it too, I'm sure of it. We've planned the whole rescue out, only we couldn't do it with only the two of us, especially with Mak not being able to walk, so we went to get help. Now that you're here, you can maybe even attack while it's still dark, if you can reach it in time. The wall of the canyon will help keep it shadowed even once the sun has risen. It will work much better than I'd feared it might, for you already being here.

"The ogres hate the Enemy for all he's done. He didn't just destroy their crops and livestock. When they tried to free the Ogress themselves, they failed, and Incuban killed three whole caves of them to punish them: sixty ogres, even children, even babies. Please, Talon, Hunter, you have to listen to me! I'm not a boy, I'm a man. I can help you. I know you don't want me to, but I have to. I promise I'll be careful."

DEWALAREN took a deep breath. He still couldn't believe Rion was alive, when he'd given him up for dead. "All right, Rion, I'll listen. Tell me what you know and your plan."

"Thank you, Majesty! But first, please, can you or Hunter or Jargas use the Ring and the Knife to heal Mak, if they are able to? He's in excruciating pain, though he's been very brave about it, but he can only walk holding me. You can't let him suffer like that. He's an innocent, a child. You all have told me you'd never let an innocent suffer," Rion urged.

Dewalaren looked from Rion's pleading face to the ogre and back again. "Idare, I must be mad to even consider it." He could not use them; his core was too chaotic. He could not imagine Farad would do it. He held them both out to Jargas. "Jargas, please help him."

Jargas took the Ring and Knife and approached Mak cautiously.

Farad finally let Rion go, and Rion went to Mak and hugged him. "Mak, this is Jargas, as he told you. He's the son of a Dwarven King. A King is like a Baga Mama, only a man. He's going to help you. The knife he's holding is special, it's magic. It's not for cutting, for hurting, but for healing. He healed me with it too, when Incuban took my voice from me. He only needs to touch you with it, but you have to close your eyes. There's also a bright light, but I'll be holding you, Mak. Don't be afraid."

"Ran kap Mak saf. Mak na afrad," Mak said.

"That's a good boy, Mak. All right, Jargas, please help him. We're ready," Rion said.

The Ring glowed in Jargas's hand and he touched the Knife to Mak's leg. It took longer than it had to return Rion's voice.

"Talon, I don't want to distract Jargas, but why is it taking so long? It healed me so quickly. Is everything all right?"

"It depends upon the injury, from what we've been able to discover. His bone is broken, and bone takes so long to heal naturally, to knit back together, that even using the Ring, it takes time. But it shouldn't be much longer," Talon assured him.

Finally, the light dimmed, and Rion opened his eyes. "All right, Mak, you can open your eyes. How do you feel?"

Mak grinned. "Lag na haat." He tested it. "Mak wak!" he said excitedly and hugged Rion. Then he bowed to Jargas. "Tanka Kang san Jargas."

Dewalaren said in astonishment, "Rion, did he just say 'thank you'?"

Rion grinned. "I told you his people are not like other ogres. They know gratitude and understand Common almost as well as we do. He speaks it well, too. He knows hundreds, maybe thousands of words, not only twenty, and he can count and maybe even add or multiply in his head. Let me tell you all I've learned, all we've planned about saving Ogress Tana," Rion said.

Rion told them all he knew and drew a map of the ogre City in the dirt, indicating the locations of the different caves. He seemed surprised by the amount of detail Dewalaren asked.

"It sounds like Rion's plan will work," Dewalaren said. "If we free the Ogress, not only will we prevent the ogres from attacking us, but we may well gain a powerful ally. We'll discuss the details of the attack again. We have to plan carefully. But first, Rion, it's time for you and Mak to go back to the Tower. I'll send six Dwarves off with you. You should be safe enough. You can't see well in the dark, but they can, and from what you've told me, Mak can as well. They'll guide you both. It would be too dangerous to bring a torch. We'll be extinguishing our own shortly, once we're done mapping out the attack. The Dwarves with us will guide us."

"MAJESTY, please! You can't mean that! Mak and I are supposed to be the ones to lead the forces to the tunnel," Rion protested, devastated. They couldn't mean to keep him from even joining them!

"King Rongas will lead that arm of the assault. I'll not have a child on the battlefield," Talon said.

In frustration, Rion realized he meant that he wouldn't have two. No matter what he did, Talon would never think of him as more than a child, someone who needed protecting.

"Rion, I'm charging you with keeping Mak safe. I'm giving you an important mission, the safety of an innocent. There is no role more vital than that here," Talon assured him, obviously trying to lessen the blow. "You may well face hippogryphs on the way back to the Tower, and they see well in the dark. That's why I'm sending six Dwarves with you, but Mak's safety is your responsibility."

"Yes, Majesty. I'll see him safe," Rion said, but he could not keep the disappointment and rejection from his voice. "Come, Mak. We've still got a ways to walk. But at least now it won't hurt you."

"Mak ga Tawa!" Mak said happily. "Mak fran sav Baga Mama Tana, Mak kasan, Mak fran."

"That's right, Mak. And King Talon will let her know you're safe. He'll tell Ogress Tana how brave you've been, how it's thanks to you they were able to rescue her, rescue everyone. You're a hero, Mak," Rion said over the lump in his throat, trying desperately not to cry.

Mak grinned and Rion forced a smile. After all of this, they still didn't want him, didn't need him. He breathed deeply, trying to calm himself. Mak needed him, at least. He'd not let him down.

The men Talon assigned formed up around him, and they began the long march back to the Tower. Rion couldn't believe that they'd let Donovar stay, that they still trusted him, after what he'd told them. Circe had hugged Donovar; he'd seen it. How had Donovar been able to convince them he hadn't been twisted by her? All his instincts screamed at him to go back, to lead the attack, to help see his friends safe, but Talon had commanded him to do otherwise. He'd told Talon he acknowledged him as his King. He couldn't disobey him now.

He realized bitterly that the Dwarves surrounding them were more likely to ensure that he didn't double back to join in the attack, rather than to lead and protect him and Mak. He doubted they'd be in any danger. Talon obviously didn't trust him. He wished Hernon had at least been one of the ones assigned to Guard him, or the brothers, or anyone he knew.

The march to the Tower seemed endless, but finally they approached. The Dwarven Guard eyed Mak warily, but Lunahr was at the door as well, and though he kept a cautious eye on Mak, he greeted Rion warmly, hugging him tightly. "We'd thought we'd lost you, until Hunter contacted me across our link and told me what happened and let me know you were safe, that you were coming."

Rion returned the hug, feeling his face flush. But it felt good to hold Lunahr. He didn't care how confused it also made him feel. "I'm sorry if I frightened you, Beryl," Rion said sincerely, careful not to use his given name in front of the others.

Then Lunahr turned to Mak and looked sheepish. "Forgive me. I'm forgetting my manners. My name is Beryl. Welcome to the Tower, Mak," he enunciated, slowly and clearly.

"Bar Ran fran. Bar Mak fran," Mak said, grinning.

"That's right, Mak," Rion said, interpreting for Lunahr, who appeared politely confused. "Beryl's my friend, and my friends will now be your friends too." Rion looked about wistfully. "I thought Brook and Thorn might greet me as well."

Lunahr looked uncomfortable. "I'm afraid that now that they know you are safe, they've gone to ground again, though they were both quite upset before. I tried to get them to come out to see you. Come. I'm sure you're both hungry and thirsty. I can at least offer you my company while you eat.

"I know how you feel, Rion, being sent back here. They wouldn't let me help search for you. I begged Talon," Lunahr said and then blushed darkly. "I even cried, but he wouldn't let me." He hugged Rion again, spontaneously. "I was so afraid you were gone forever. You've no idea how happy I am to see you safe." Then he looked embarrassed and let him go. "But about that food I promised you," he said and began leading them to the Dining Hall.

Rion was about to say he wasn't really hungry, but Mak turned to him and grinned. "Fata!" he said eagerly. Rion realized it had probably been some time since he'd eaten. He'd been trapped a while. But also, the Enemy might not have fed His prisoners very well.

"We'll be reporting to our Captain," the Dwarves said. Rion wondered if it might be they had no wish to eat beside an ogre. He was a little concerned about that himself. They entered the Dining Hall. Rion was shocked to see it was empty. "Where is everyone?" The Dining Hall was never empty, with four two-hour shifts for breakfast, lunch, and dinner.

"Another thousand Dwarves are heading out this morning. And there's the two hundred men that went to find you and Donovar. But there is plenty of food in the Kitchen."

As they approached the Kitchen, Rion asked, "Um... Mak... what do you eat? I mean, you're not like the other ogres I know of. Do you... do you prefer animals live or dead? Cooked? I mean, do you use fire or...."

As they entered the Kitchen, they saw a number of Dwarves inside, cooking. Mak's eyes widened in delight at the sight of food laid out all around them. "Brat, cas, frat, anma!" he said excitedly, and headed for the table containing bread, cheese, fruit and cooked meat. He stopped, uncertainly, as one of the kitchen Dwarves glared at him. He was holding a large knife and looking at Mak suspiciously.

"Let me get you a plate, Mak," Rion said. He and Lunahr filled a platter and took three plates and cups. "What would you like to drink, Mak?" Rion asked. "Water?"

"Hapa wata?" Mak asked eagerly.

When Rion asked one of the Dwarves, "Would you mind carrying that keg of wine for us?" Mak grinned so slyly that Rion hesitated, suddenly understanding. "Mak, are you allowed to have hapa wata at home?" Rion asked.

"Na," Mak said sheepishly, looking down.

Rion grinned at him. "Well, then, we'll let you have one cup, as a special treat, and then it's water. But there's honeycake for dessert."

Mak grinned and nodded.

They went into the Dining Hall and sat. Rion wondered if Mak used a fork at home. The Dwarves didn't use them, nor did the Amontir when dining in their company, though the Elves did. But Mak dug in eagerly with his bare hands, not even using a knife as the Dwarves did. Rion followed suit, and after a moment's hesitation, Lunahr did also. Rion was thrilled enough that Mak wasn't eating a live goat or something in front of them.

Lunahr's face took on a distant expression, and he stopped eating.

"Beryl, what is it, what's wrong?" Rion asked, concerned.

LUNAHR shook his head and focused on Rion. "Nothing. The fighting's started, that's all. They're rescuing the Ogress. I was drawn into it by Hunter. I'm worried about him, and Talon too, of course. I'm worried about all of them. I should be there, fighting beside them," he said, frustrated, and pushed his plate away.

Rion looked at him forlornly and did the same.

Mak said with obvious concern, "Ran na hangra?"

"No Mak. We're not hungry anymore. We're worried about our friends," Rion explained.

Lunahr heard an odd sound, coming from behind the closed door to the Dining Hall. It was the clang of metal on metal. For a moment, he thought that it was the sound of battle, but how could it be? He had just convinced himself he must have imagined it, thinking of his kin fighting without him, when a Dwarf suddenly swung the doors to the Dining Hall wide and stumbled inside, bleeding from half a dozen wounds. It was one of the men who had accompanied Rion and Mak to the Tower.

"Quick, the Enemy's forces are inside the Tower! Use the Kitchen exit! Run! We'll try to hold them!" he said desperately, dragging one of the heavy tables toward the door as two other Dwarves sprang through, bloodied axes in hand, and slammed the doors shut.

Lunahr sprang to his feet, shaking in terror. Rion and Mak jumped up too. Lunahr sent a panicked call down his bond to Farad. *Farad! The Enemy's forces are in the Tower!*

He felt a wave of horror course down the bond. *We're coming! We'll get there as soon as we can. Take Rion and hide in the passageways!*

They burst through the doors to the Kitchen, and Lunahr told the Dwarves there what was happening. They immediately began arming themselves with knives, cleavers, and everything they could bring quickly to hand. Mak snatched up a large butcher's knife from one of the work tables, and a heavy metal mallet used for pounding meat.

"Follow me," Lunahr ordered Rion and Mak. They exited out a back door to the hall, after Lunahr ensured there were no foes there.

Lunahr led them to the War Room.

RION saw there were no Guards at the door. There were always Guards there! They must be elsewhere, already engaging the Enemy's troops.

Lunahr ran into the room, straight for one of the tapestries. Sudden understanding flashed across Rion's mind as Lunahr yanked it aside, touched a certain spot, and a concealed panel swung open. There were secret passages here! He'd looked for one in the Library, after Hunter had so miraculously appeared there, but he had not been able to find it. They were reassuringly well hidden.

Lunahr closed the panel behind him. "We have to find Eladar and Elanara and warn them. Elavar's with the others in the valley."

Rion hadn't known that. He hadn't seen him.

"Eladar might still be at the River," Lunahr said and began heading down the corridor, snatching a lit torch from a sconce in the hall and then turning and heading down a flight of stairs. He stopped before reaching the bottom. "Idare, no!" he cried in horror. "Eladar!" His name was a sob.

Rion peered around Lunahr's shoulder. Eladar was there, but he was not alone. The floor was a teaming, writhing mass of snakes. Eladar was lying on the cold stone, one leg in the River, his normally pale skin gray, his lips blue, his face a frozen, twisted mask of agony. Five of the snakes reared up to strike at them. Lunahr's blade flashed out and two heads flew as three others bit futilely upon his blade. "Back up the stairs! Quickly," Lunahr commanded.

"But Eladar…," Rion protested.

"He's dead! Now move!" Lunahr ordered, shoving Rion, his voice rough with emotion. Rion saw the tears welling in Lunahr's eyes as he turned.

Rion urged Mak up the stairs and wiped the tears from his own cheeks. They passed the War Room passageway entrance they'd entered from. Lunahr turned left and headed along the corridor, then turned this way and that, listening at various doors and the intersections of tunnels as they went. Outside each door was the sound of pitched battle.

Rion's heart was hammering. The Enemy had changed his plans, either because they had attacked His forces in the Pass, or because He had found out about Circe and Donovar. Or was the whole thing a trap laid out from the beginning, designed to split their already weakened forces, to catch them out in the open? If he and Donovar hadn't entered the Pass, would some other event have lured their troops there?

It didn't matter. From what they heard, it sounded like the Enemy didn't need the ogres to take the Tower. They'd already weakened their own defenses too badly by sending thousands to other key strategic locations. The Enemy's minions must be in the caves in full force, or else He'd sealed them off. There should have been close to two thousand Dwarves still here. The Enemy would find the tunnels. Rion knew it was inevitable. He'd find them and capture them.

Finally, they found a door with silence beyond it. Lunahr peeked out, sword at the ready, and then waved them frantically onward. They emerged from the tunnels and raced for the tower stairs. They dove into the first bedroom they came to, and Lunahr led them into what was apparently a second series of passages.

It was quieter now, in these passages. They proceeded on, and then Lunahr stopped at a panel and listened. "This is Talon's room. It sounds clear, but I'll go first. You stay here. Be ready for anything. If you hear anything, you're to run. You're not to come in after me. Get as far from here as you can," Lunahr commanded. Then he swung the door out, plunged into the room, and yelped. Rion dove through the door after him. He'd not leave Lunahr to be captured again.

"Lunahr! Rion!" Elanara cried, the fear in her eyes turning to relief. "Lunahr, I could have killed you!" she chastised.

Lunahr was getting shakily to his feet. Elanara had a sword in her hands and had apparently attacked him, before she realized who it was.

"Elanara! Thank Elmoth!" Rion said, hugging her one armed, not caring whether it might be proper or not, his sword still in his other hand.

"We have to reach Eladar. He was at the river. I tried, but…. Lunahr, what's happened?" she asked, the fear returning to her eyes. She'd obviously seen the pain in Lunahr's eyes.

"I'm sorry, Elanara. There was nothing we could do. It was water snakes. There's dozens of them, perhaps hundreds. They must be all over the caves as well. He'd already been bitten," Lunahr said, his voice anguished.

"Dead?" she asked in disbelief, in dawning horror. "Eladar?" Then she fell to her knees, sobbing, the sword clanging loudly onto the stone floor as it fell from her hand.

"There's no time to grieve, Elanara. Please, we have to hide. We have to give the others time to save us," Rion begged, tears streaming from his eyes. No one could watch an Elf weep and not cry as well, but this was Elanara: he would have cried regardless. He mourned Eladar too. He could see Lunahr and even Mak crying along with her.

They heard a shuffling sound from the hall outside Talon's room and Rion saw to his horror that the door wasn't secure. It was open a crack. Elanara had either just entered or been about to leave when Lunahr surprised her. Lunahr slapped his hand over Elanara's mouth, grasped her arm, pulled her to her feet, and began dragging her to the wall. Rion held her as Lunahr opened the panel again, and they went inside and shut the door and headed deeper into the passageways.

"THESE tunnels link Talon's room to the other bedrooms," Lunahr explained. His room was one of them. The master of this castle had at one time enjoyed easy access to the guests' and servants' quarters. Lunahr had tried not to think about why, whether hundreds of years ago the owner of this castle, a lesser monster, had preyed upon those in his care as well as unsuspecting guests in the same manner the Enemy did. Whether perhaps that was why the castle had been half destroyed. Had the family of one of his victims sought revenge? He forced his thoughts back to the corridor, desperately hoping to find a way out of the Watchtower. But now everywhere they went, there was the sound of the Enemy outside the panels, even up here.

Lunahr took a moment to focus over the link to Farad and drew back instantly. Farad was fighting for his life. The three hippogryphs had been reinforced by at least a dozen chimaera and an army of Revenants. He'd not risk distracting Farad and killing him. "I just checked. The battle is not going well. There won't be any help coming for a while. Even if they left immediately, it would take them too long to come. We'll try Talon's room again."

They circled back in the passages and stopped before the panel they had used before. Elanara was still crying quietly in Rion's arms. Rion looked just as anguished, as hopeless. Mak was patting Rion on the back, his face showing his fear. Outside, Lunahr could hear the sounds of fighting, but they quickly diminished and then vanished altogether.

RION thought the silence was more terrifying than the sounds of battle had been. How many of their men lay dead? Had the Watchtower fallen? Then he heard a voice he dreaded. "R-i-o-n. I know you are here. I can feel your fear, your despair. There's no reason to hide, Rion. It is over. Your friends are all dead. They all died for you, Rion," the voice taunted.

Rion bit back a sob and began trembling. He knew that voice, that horrible, wonderful voice. He'd heard it in his dream.

"I've killed thousands, Rion, to find you. I can feel you. You are near. It's time to go, Rion. It's terrible to be so alone, isn't it?" He asked silkily. Then His tone changed. "**COME TO ME,**" He commanded, His voice rumbling as if with thunder.

Rion felt the pull of His Power drawing him, even though Incuban could not see him, and the Power was not focused directly upon him. But it wasn't Incuban's Power that swayed him; it was His words. He could sense Rion, somehow. And He thought Rion was alone. The Enemy had not found the second set of passages, at least, even if He had found the first; otherwise the passageway would already be swarming with His minions. If he went to Incuban, Elanara and Lunahr and Mak would be safe. If he stayed hidden, Incuban would still find him, but He would find his friends, too.

Rion pictured Incuban torturing Elanara or Lunahr or Mak as he'd been tortured in his dream. He pictured the Enemy forcing him to hurt his friends or them to hurt him. He turned to the others. "Stay here. It's me He wants. You'll be safe if I go to Him," he whispered.

LUNAHR fought an irrational surge of jealousy and desire. Incuban no longer wanted him. He wanted Rion. He bit down hard upon his tongue to keep from calling out to Incuban, from betraying them all to Him.

RION reached for the latch to the panel, but Elanara clung to him. "No, Rion, I won't let you."

"Tear the Watchtower apart, stone by stone if you have to," Incuban commanded.

There was the sound of many feet and a raspy voice. "Master, we have brought the prisoners."

Rion's heart raced. He had recognized that voice as well. Jathran, it was Jathran, or what once had been him.

"Excellent. Rion, I know you can hear me. I feel you. Listen to this," Incuban said.

They heard a scream, then many voices in Dwarvish uttering curses.

"I have prisoners here, Rion. I have just killed one of them, because you are hiding from me. There are ten more, Rion. You don't want to hear them all die because of you, do you?" Incuban's voice had become sickly sweet. "Come out, come out, wherever you are," he crooned in a childlike singsong.

Rion tore himself away from Elanara's grip and knocked her to the ground, then attacked Lunahr viciously, hitting him hard in the stomach. Lunahr bent over double, gasping, as Rion sprang to the panel and his fingers danced across the spot he'd seen Lunahr touch. The panel swung open, and he closed it carefully behind him, running for Talon's door. He flung it open, charging into the corridor, sword at the ready. "Stop! Don't hurt them!"

There were four Dwarven bodies in front of the door; they looked like they'd died fighting. There was a cluster of Men at the end of the corridor. They all turned toward him. Not Men, Elves, or what once had been Elves. They were Revenants now. And there were five Dwarven Revenants. And Jathran. There were no live Dwarves, no prisoners, not even a dead one. It had been a trick. But there was someone else there. He was beautiful. His hair was red orange and fell down His back in waves. His eyes were red, His features divine, His body perfection.

"Ah, there you are, Rion," He said and laughed. It was Him. It was Incuban. "Forgive me my little trick. My servants played their part quite convincingly, did they not? I have so desired to meet you, Rion," He said, emphasizing the word "desired" as He approached, His servants walking and shuffling behind Him. "And you have desired me as well, Rion. You desire me now. I saw how you looked at me just now. There was hunger in your gaze."

"Stay back or I'll slit my own throat!" Rion cried desperately, but his hand was steady as he held his blade to his neck.

Incuban held up His hand and His servants stopped. "I know you are frightened, Rion," Incuban soothed, His voice dripping with compassion. "You have every right to be. Your friends have abandoned you. They left you here, all alone, ill defended. The Dwarves have all fled, Rion. So few stayed to fight. Why should they? Why die for a mere Man, a Lesser Man? Have you heard them call you that, Rion? Those high and mighty Lords and Ladies of Amontir? They command the Dwarves, even as they despise them. They've scorned you as well, haven't they?"

Rion remembered Denric and Tanris and what they'd said, how they'd acted around him.

"Ah, I see you have indeed heard their cruel whispers, felt their coldness toward one whom they should have honored. You risked much to come to their aid, didn't you, Rion? But they don't want you. They don't love you. No one loves you, Rion. Farad enticed you here, but he has a wife. He does not want you. Lunahr chose Talon, Dewalaren, over you. Surely you know that they fornicated with one another?"

Incuban was closer now. Rion belatedly realized He'd been steadily approaching as He spoke. Rion backed a few steps farther away, but not too far. His feet were reluctant to obey him.

"You need so desperately to feel loved, don't you, Rion? As you try so hard to be a man. But you are still a boy. You cannot be a man until you lose your innocence. But you need someone to teach you, do you not? Come with me, Rion. I can give you the love you crave. Let me teach you to be a man." Incuban was reaching His hand toward him.

Rion gazed at Him in wonder. He was not terrible at all! He was so gentle. And He understood, He truly did. Rion began to lower his sword as he felt his face flush and his heart quicken, the way it did when he saw Elanara, when he saw Lunahr, when he saw Aras. Elanara! Lunahr! He pictured them as he'd last seen them, in hiding, eyes wide with terror, red from tears, because of Eladar. Eladar! He pictured Eladar's laughing face transformed into the bitter, angry one Rion had seen here. He pictured Eladar as he'd last seen him, cold and dead, his face a twisted mask of agony. This monster had killed him! He'd killed Eladar's entire Kingdom, two Elven Kingdoms, almost all the Dwarven ones, and so many cities of Man. Ardock: He had burnt Ardock! And His minions had killed Oberas and all his guards, all Tarrell's friends. Tarrell! Tarrell still loved him, even with a wife he did. And so did Ron and his brothers, and Andra and Rarnak.

Rion lunged and slashed at Incuban's arm with his sword. "Don't touch me, you monster! I don't love you, I hate you! I'm going to kill you for all you've done!" he cried, lunging forward.

The blade was all but at Incuban's throat when He uttered a single word, "**STOP**," and Rion's body froze.

"Good. Very good!" Incuban said, laughing. He reached out and caressed Rion's face. "So, I will have a fight on my hands after all. I had feared you would succumb too easily. I will enjoy taking you, Rion, making you love me, turning you against your friends. You will do such wonderful things for me. You will be a tool of my victory. You will not disappoint me. You will not fail me as Lunahr did." He kissed Rion upon the mouth, gently forcing his tongue between Rion's lips and then deepening the kiss, holding Rion helpless in his thrall.

LUNAHR was shaking. Farad's presence could not still his body as it had stopped him before. When Incuban had been seducing Rion, he'd felt a terrible wave of longing and jealousy crash over him. He would have run to Incuban, begged Him to take him back, if Farad had not sensed the danger.

Still, he would not listen to Farad. He was about to cry out, to reveal himself, when suddenly Farad used the King's Voice upon him, from within his head, paralyzing him, forcing him to silence. He listened helplessly as Rion did what he could not. Rion resisted Incuban, tried to attack Him. But still, when Incuban told Rion that Lunahr had failed Him, he would have sobbed at Incuban's feet if it weren't for Farad.

ELANARA heard every sick, twisted word the depraved monster spoke. She saw the desire on Lunahr's face, saw that something held him back, something restrained him. She tried to stay still, stay silent, but she could not bear to hear Rion seduced and corrupted, as Lunahr had been. She knew that Rion had been trying to save them, that Rion's sacrifice would be in vain if she revealed herself, that she'd put Lunahr and Mak in danger as well, but her head could no longer control her when her heart was being so torn. She could not let Rion be taken from her as Lunahr had been.

She drew her concealed knife and sprang toward the panel, taking advantage of Lunahr's distraction, and flung it open. She ran for Talon's door. She leapt into the hallway, screamed in rage, and sprang for Incuban as she saw Rion frozen and helpless before Him, being kissed by Him. Only a few more feet and she could end this!

Incuban smiled at her and uttered, "**STOP**," and suddenly she froze, her knife less than a foot from Him. She realized He had let her get so close, to taunt her with the victory just out of reach.

"Ah. Elanara. I did not know you were here. You were an important piece in the Game, once. When Dewalaren loved you, I could have used you. When your Kingdom still stood, I still could have. But now you are nothing. You are no longer of any value: a bride without a groom, a Princess without a Kingdom. Dewalaren's Queen has become the lowliest of pawns, now. But perhaps I can yet find a purpose for you."

RION could hear everything, see everything within range of his vision without turning his head, but he could not move. He was helpless to save Elanara. Why had she done it? Why had she come out of hiding, after what he had sacrificed to save her? His heart froze at the thought of how Incuban would use her now.

Incuban turned to Rion. Smiling sweetly, He said, "**KILL HER FOR ME, RION.** That's a good boy." Rion saw the horror in Elanara's eyes as he turned toward her with his sword. It matched the horror in his heart. He fought desperately to lower the blade, but he could not. But still, he resisted, and his movements seemed to slow.

MAK had crept out of the passage, closing the door carefully behind him, and had been peeking out of the crack between the door and the wall. He was appalled at what Rion was about to do. "Ran na haat Nara!" his desperate young voice bleated, as he sprang from Talon's room, the metal mallet in one hand and the knife in the other.

RION'S attention was forced to Incuban and Mak, as Incuban drew back in apparent surprise and commanded, "**STOP!**"

Mak stumbled but did not stop.

Incuban's Revenants interposed themselves between their master and the enraged ogre. The Revenants fell upon Mak, smashing their fists into him with the strength of Elves and Dwarves.

Incuban watched dispassionately as they beat him into the ground. "Enough," He said, and they drew back.

Mak lay limp, his face and body bloodied. Incuban turned back to Rion and looked at him and an expression of surprise again crossed His face. Rion realized there were tears streaming down his frozen face.

Incuban traced the path of a tear with His finger, and then licked the tear sensually from it. "You actually cared for that creature? A pity. Had I known I might have let you keep it as a pet. Much as I will keep you," He said, wrapping his fingers lightly around Rion's throat. "You will enjoy wearing a collar for me, having your leash tied to my bed. Ah, but first, before we were so rudely interrupted, I had given you a command. When I give you a command, Rion, you are to obey it, without hesitation." His eyes were bright with anger, with madness, as His hand closed relentlessly about Rion's throat.

Rion gasped for breath, as Incuban began choking the life from him.

"But I forget for a moment, you are as yet untrained. I will teach you your first lesson in obedience: it is futile to resist me, Rion. You are only a Man. I am a God!" He laughed and His hand eased from Rion's throat.

"You *will* do as I command. **YOU WILL SLAY HER, NOW!**"

Time suddenly resumed its speed. With terrifying quickness, the sword in Rion's hand was arcing up and out. Rion knew he could not hope to stop it, but he focused all his will upon his hand. He had to turn the blade, divert it just enough so that it did not pierce her heart, so that she might yet live.

Elmoth aid me! he screamed in his mind as he fought to wrench his hand over. He felt sharp metal pierce soft flesh as the keen Dwarven blade Farad had gifted to him thrust deeply into Elanara, then withdrew, stained red with her life's blood. He saw the terror in her eyes turn to pain and then darkness as she fell to the floor.

Incuban laughed. "Very good, Rion."

Rion fought against more tears, terrified his tears would betray him. If Incuban ever suspected that he felt anything more than friendship for Elanara, He would take her with them. And she was not yet dead, not yet. The blood had not spurted as it would have had he pierced her heart. Incuban would torture and rape her if He took her with Him. He would make Rion help Him hurt her. Or He'd finish killing her and then turn her into a Revenant.

"Tell me, Rion, should I take you here, now, perhaps in Dewalaren's bed?" Incuban said, fondling him through his pants.

To Rion's horror his manhood stiffened instantly under the monster's vile touch.

"Are his sheets still stained with Lunahr's love of him? It's a pity Lunahr was not here to see me favor you over him." Incuban laughed. "He is so devoted to me. He still has his uses, even though I have tired of him. He can teach Dewalaren so very much. He weakens the King with his love of him. I have taught him much, but I will teach you more.

"Yet you are still a virgin, are you not? As Lunahr was, when first I took him. A virgin must be taken carefully. **COME, RION.** I have a special room I would use. Not the one from your dream. There are delights in this room that you cannot imagine. I will show them to you, all of them, as I showed them to Lunahr."

He turned to the Revenants. "Search that room. There may be others hiding there, though I doubt it. It does not matter. The others will come to me soon enough, if they yet live, now that I have my prize. Kill anything that moves—animal, Man, Dwarf or Elf— and then return to me. Tell the others. Go."

The Revenants headed for Talon's room as Rion left with Incuban, as helpless to save Lunahr as he had been to save Elanara or Mak or himself.

Chapter 11
Those Who Endure

LUNAHR had listened in helpless horror as Elanara and then Mak had revealed themselves to Incuban, while Farad's Voice held him fast. He felt Farad's rage grow as Incuban tormented Rion, as He twisted him into His tool, while Farad was powerless to save him. Incuban's hold upon Lunahr had disintegrated with what he had heard. Incuban was forcing Rion to kill Elanara, when he loved her. He'd seen how much Rion loved her. And she loved Rion, Eladar had told him—it seemed so very long ago—in Caramore.

Both Farad's control and his hold upon Lunahr had shattered as he heard Rion's torment. Farad was screaming now, inside Lunahr's mind, for Lunahr to stop Rion from killing Elanara, but Lunahr would not. "I cannot reveal myself as they have. If I do, then Rion's sacrifice will have been for nothing. All the tortures that follow will have been for naught."

Even hearing Incuban's taunts, Lunahr was no longer tempted to go to Him. But then He mentioned the room, the terrible, wonderful room, and Lunahr fell to the floor fondling himself, writhing upon the floor in memory of it, his mind flooded with images, his body awash in sensations, of pleasure and pain so intermingled he had not been able to distinguish one from the other, until he had longed for both, for either, until he had fawned at Incuban's feet and begged for the whip, for the brand, for other awful things.

Farad was incoherent now from the images and sensations Lunahr had sent coursing down the link toward him, identical to the ones Farad had felt when his parents and brothers were raped and tortured to death. With a tremendous effort of will, Lunahr shattered their bond, praying he had not truly driven his cousin to madness, when he feared he had.

With Farad gone, it was quiet. He was able to hear the music that had been thrumming with desperate insistence in his core. He concentrated on the melody and fought his memory of the room, forcing it back into the chest Farad had forged, slamming the lid closed, and locking the chest with the melody. He lay panting and gasping, fighting to breathe steadily, to focus.

When he was finally able to shakily stand, it was quiet, too quiet. He waited and he listened. Cautiously, carefully, he opened the panel the tiniest of cracks. Dewalaren's room was empty. The Revenants had gone. They had left the room a shambles, tearing everything that could be torn, smashing everything that could be smashed, but they had not found the panel to the passageway.

Lunahr drew Loruthanar and crept out, stepping carefully around the torn pages of Laren's journals that now littered his bedroom floor, lest the sound of crinkling paper betray him. He headed fearfully for the door, terrified the silence was a trick, that a host of Revenants might be waiting for him on the other side of it. But there was silence there as well.

He peeked through the narrow crack between the door and the doorframe. Nothing moved within his line of sight, but he could see bodies upon the floor. Hand shaking, he opened the door. The hall was empty, save for four Dwarven bodies and the bodies of an Elf and an ogre. He looked in dismay at Elanara and Mak and went to them. He knelt by Elanara's side.

Her diaphanous silver dress was stained a deep red: a misshapen rose had bloomed upon her chest. He touched her face tenderly, and a tear ran down his cheek and splashed upon hers. To his terror, her eyes opened.

He scrambled back from her, horrified. Incuban had transformed her! She was a Revenant! He was astonished Incuban could have performed the ritual here. He must have laid her there as a trap for the others, when they returned. But she did not spring up and attack him. She did not move at all. Then she spoke, and her voice was so weak, it was a scarcely audible whisper. "Lunahr."

Lunahr dove toward her, hands tearing desperately at his shirt, shaking. She was alive! He ripped off his shirt and crumpled it into a ball and pressed it firmly against her wound. Rion was a swordsman, a good one, now. She'd been paralyzed, he knew she'd been. Rion could not have missed her heart, unless he had meant to, unless he'd forced his hand not to obey Incuban's command completely.

Rion had still been fighting Incuban, when Lunahr had thought him already lost. He would not have let Incuban take Rion so easily, had he known. He would have fought Farad to go to him. But then he would have been killed, and Elanara would have bled to death. She might yet die. The wound was grievous, and she had bled much while he had lain helpless in the passageway. But the cloth did not immediately saturate with blood.

There was a soft moan from beside them, and Lunahr jumped but then realized it was coming from Mak. He swallowed. "Mak? Mak, is that you? Please let it be you, really you. I can't leave her. She'll die."

"Ran?" the little voice cried out piteously, full of pain and fear.

"No, Mak, it's Beryl. Rion is…. Rion is gone," he forced himself to say with a sob. "Incuban's taken him. He forced him to hurt Elanara, and then He took him."

"Nara kala?" Mak asked, and Lunahr could hear him crying.

"She's hurt, Mak. I need to carry her to the passageway. The Enemy didn't find it. We can't stay here. We might be found. They might still be here, downstairs, or in any of the rooms. Please, Mak, can you walk? Try to walk, Mak," he urged, as he picked Elanara up. She was deceptively heavy, for her dense Elven bones. He could scarcely hold her.

"Mak wak," the injured ogre said and got shakily to his feet. He swayed and steadied. Lunahr could see he was in pain.

They entered Dewalaren's room and then the passageway, and Lunahr sealed the panel behind them. He laid Elanara against the wall. "Mak, I need you to be brave. I need you to do something important. Elanara has been badly hurt. She will die if I don't help her. I need to get a healer's kit. I need you to stay with her, to press this against her chest like this, so she doesn't bleed so much, like I've been doing. Can you do that, Mak? I'll be back soon, I swear I will. I'll only be gone a short while," Lunahr said intently.

"Mak hap Nara," he said, and moved his hand to press against the cloth.

Lunahr was weak with relief. It had been a desperate hope. He'd not thought Mak would understand him.

He headed down the passageway, torch in one hand, sword in the other, as quietly as he could, knowing that at any moment he might face the Enemy or his minions. But the passage was deserted, and all the panels he passed were closed.

He entered Rion's room. To his relief it appeared undisturbed. He looked about desperately. He found a pack, but it was the wrong one. There, that other one, the oilskin pouch. There were bandages and a dozen smaller oilskin pouches with drawstrings. He took it and turned for the door, his eye falling upon the journal on the desk. Rion's journal, the one he'd had with him when Lunahr had first met him in the War Room, the one Eladar had been reading.

He took it from the desk and clutched it tightly to his chest. It was all they would have left of Rion. He'd not risk it being destroyed. He spied the pitcher of water on the stand by the bed and took that as well. It was mostly full. He had to sheathe his sword to carry everything. He hoped he'd not regret it. He reentered the tunnels, closing the panel tightly behind him. He retraced his steps quickly.

"Bar?" he heard a soft fearful whisper as he approached.

"Yes, Mak, it's me," Lunahr reassured Mak just as quietly.

"Hap Nara, Bar," Mak pleaded.

"I'll try, Mak. I've medicines, now, at least, which I hope I can use. Ara told me about Rion's healer's kit in one of our meetings, about reading his journal and saving Rion's and Gar's lives with it. I'm hoping Rion's kit has what we need to save Elanara as well. There are bandages too." He fought tears at the thought that, even lost to them, Rion was still helping his friends.

He began opening the little pouches, reading all the scraps of paper. Then he said, "All right, Mak, you can let go now. I'm going to cut her dress, to expose the wound. Then I'll sprinkle this powder on like this. Then this one. That should stop the bleeding and keep it from festering. Next she needs to drink this one. I need to put this powder into the water and mix it, but there's too much water in here and I don't have a cup. There aren't any in Talon's room either. I'm going to drink some of this. We shouldn't waste it. Mak, drink some also. Leave about a fist's worth of water in the bottom of the pitcher. Can you do that? Do you understand?" Lunahr asked hopefully.

Mak closed his fist and pointed to it. "Das mach wata," he said, nodding, and held his hands out for the pitcher. He drank, eyeing it carefully a few times, then handed it back. There were tears in his eyes.

"Mak, what is it, what's wrong?" he asked, checking in sudden fear that he'd drunk it all and was crying from guilt, but he hadn't. He'd left exactly the right amount.

"Ran gav Mak hapa wata ta drank. Ran sad hana cak. Tat saf. Na saf. Ancaban cam," he said in despair. "Ran gan! Ran las! Mak famla kala, Ran kala, Nara kala, all kala!" he was sobbing.

Lunahr had understood part of it, at least. He carefully put down the pitcher and held out his arms to Mak, and Mak dove into his embrace. "Shh, Mak. I'm still here. I'm Rion's friend. I'll keep you safe, now, because he can't. I have to help Elanara, Mak.

She'll die if I don't, but I can't risk you crying too loudly. Please, Mak, try to calm down, all right?" he soothed.

Mak took a great shuddering breath and nodded. "Nara na kala? Sawa, Bar. Mak na cra mar."

"That's a good boy, Mak. You're very brave. I'm so proud of you. They hurt you, Mak, but I'm not sure what to do to help. Does it hurt a lot? I can give you something to ease the pain."

"Na. Na haat," Mak said, though Lunahr knew he was. But he was not sure what he could do for him, in any case. They'd beaten him, pummeled him. There was no wound for him to bind and he'd never learned the healing arts as Laren had.

Lunahr mixed the final powder into the remaining water, sloshing it around until it dissolved as well as it could in the cold water, knowing it was better to boil it. He held the pitcher to Elanara's lips and tried to make her drink it. He couldn't be sure she swallowed any, though he tried to see that she did.

"We have to keep her warm, Mak. And we have to talk to her, to let her know we're here, that she's safe, in case she can hear us," he said, and he began speaking softly to her in Elvish.

"Wat Bar sa?" Mak asked, puzzled.

Lunahr turned to him. "I'm sorry, Mak, I'm speaking Elvish to her, so she'll understand it easier. She'll be comforted by it, I hope. I know you can't understand it. I'll talk to you, too, some, all right? But right now she needs to hear me."

Mak nodded. He stroked her arm gently, as Lunahr talked to her.

Lunahr wondered whether the others were winning or losing their battle to free the Ogress. With his link to Farad severed, he didn't know what was happening to them. They might all be dead.

He forced the thought aside, and the despair that it brought. But he kept picturing Farad, screaming incoherently on the battlefield, lost to madness, helpless to defend himself. He pictured Laren falling, trying to defend him. He forced his thoughts away from the battle, but then he pictured Rion with Incuban. They would be flying on a hippogryph or chimaera. They would soon be nearing Ironforge.

He pictured the terrible room that awaited Rion there. He visualized Rion inside it, helpless, at Incuban's mercy, when He had none. The chest in his mind was rattling, trembling; the horrific memories of his own capture, violation, and torment were threatening to burst the chest open. He'd be lost if the memories sprang free with his link to Farad gone.

He stopped speaking to Elanara. "Mak, please, talk to me. Speak of good things. I need to hear the voice of a friend," he said desperately.

Mak said proudly, "Mak Bar fran." He began speaking, and Lunahr had to strain to understand him, but he could, if he tried hard enough, listened carefully enough. It was working. The concentration and effort it required was so great his mind was focusing on Mak's words, on his voice, instead of on memory, on Rion's face, on Incuban's voice.

He had no idea how long it had been when there were sounds from outside the room, and he desperately urged Mak to be quiet. He heard footsteps, purposeful ones, and then a cry of agony, a heart-wrenching cry of loss. "They've taken her body!"

Lunahr let out his held breath in relief. It was Elavar!

"It's my friends, Mak. They've come back. That's Elanara's older brother." His heart stuttered in fear. "Although I'd better check to be sure, after the way Incuban tricked Rion before. You stay here with Elanara. I'm going to peek, to be sure. It might be some sort of trap. I'll not have you taken."

Mak nodded his understanding.

Lunahr opened up the panel and exited quickly, quietly, and closed it again. He crossed the room as silently as an Elf and peeked through the crack between the door and the frame. He could see the bodies of the Dwarves in front of the room as before. But now there were other Dwarves there, standing. He couldn't see Elavar, but he could hear the sound of sobbing. His heart ached for the man who had been like an older brother to him. He opened the door to the hall.

The Dwarves immediately spun about and faced him, axes raised.

"Wait, it's me!" Lunahr called, arms held high in surrender.

They sprang at him and he yelped in terror that they'd kill him now, out of fear, when he had survived the Enemy's attack.

He fell to his knees before them. "Please, don't kill me!" he begged.

Elavar ran to him, grabbed his shirt at the throat, and shook him. "Where is she? What have you done with her?"

"Elavar, it's me, Lunahr! I swear it's me. She's safe, she's not dead, but she's grievously wounded. She needs Laren. She needs the Ring and the Knife. She's so weak," Lunahr babbled, hoping to make him realize he wasn't a Resemblant or in Incuban's thrall.

"Of course. I take you to Talon and you kill him and take the Ring. Elanara is dead. Hunter heard her die before you attacked him, before you drove him mad. Jarina told us what you did to him. Talon should have killed you in Caramore, the last time you betrayed us. I should have killed you, for what you did to Elanara and Eladar there. It's your fault Eladar's dead! He died in Caramore with what you did to him, what you made him do! He couldn't live knowing it. She couldn't. You've killed them both! I'll kill you now for it," Elavar said, and his other hand darted out and wrapped viselike around Lunahr's throat.

Lunahr fought desperately for breath, vainly pulling at the hand around his throat as the world disappeared in a red haze. But then strong Dwarven hands pulled Elavar's away.

"Nay, Prince Sylvan. We can't let you kill him. It's up to the King to decide his fate," Hernon said.

"What's the matter with you? Elanara's still alive, but she'll die unless Laren helps her, and you try to kill me!" Lunahr gasped, between breaths. "I didn't drive Hunter mad, at least not intentionally. I'd never hurt him. I didn't mean to make him see what he saw, feel what he felt. I couldn't help it! For Idare's sake, I was battling Incuban as much as Rion was! Where's Laren? He'll believe me. He has to."

"He's in the grotto, trying to bring Eladar back from the dead," Elavar said, his voice tortured. "It's too late. I told him. Eladar died with Riviera. He died in Caramore. It doesn't matter that what was left has died now." He turned to Hernon. "Take his sword. I'll not risk him finding my back as tempting a target as he found Talon's."

Lunahr looked at Elavar as if he was the one who had been stabbed in the back. He didn't resist or even object as Hernon took Loruthanar from him.

"Bar? Bar fran? Na kala Mak?" Mak asked cautiously, from the door.

The Dwarves eyed Mak suspiciously.

"Mak, I told you to stay with her," Lunahr scolded.

"Nara sad hap Bar. Mak cam ha," Mak said piteously.

"What do you mean Elanara said... you mean she's awake? Elanara's awake?" Lunahr asked, in sudden hope.

"Ya," Mak said, nodding.

Lunahr ran for the door but was stopped by the Dwarves. Hernon said, "You, Mak, away from the door. Lorgas, Denton, take a look but be careful. It could be a trap."

The two Dwarves entered and searched then came out, scowling. "There's no one there. The room's a shambles."

"Mak, you closed the panel? Good boy. That was smart, Mak, but they don't know about the secret passageways. They need to find Elanara. Can you open it too, Mak?" Lunahr asked.

"Ya," Mak said confidently.

"What are you talking about?" Hernon asked, eyes narrowed in suspicion.

"There are secret tunnels that crisscross the castle. There are two sets, the downstairs ones and these. I think the Enemy probably was able to discover the others because of the River, but He didn't send His minions into the ones we were hiding in. I don't think He knew of them. Elanara's in the passageway, near the panel. But please be gentle. I've treated her wound but she's already bled heavily."

Hernon said, "You two follow him, carefully. See if what he says is true or not."

The two Dwarves reentered the room and watched warily as Mak walked confidently to the wall and opened the panel there. They told him not to go in, and they entered the passageway with axes at the ready. "Blessed Aralyn! It's exactly as he said, Prince Sylvan! It's your sister, Princess Brook! She's alive!"

ELAVAR ran into the room, to the doorway to the passageway. His eyes filled with tears again as he saw his sister, bloodied and bandaged, pale as moonlight, but alive, her hand reaching weakly toward him. He spoke to her in Elvish. "Elanara, sweet sister! I thought I had lost you both," he sobbed, stroking her hair with a butterfly soft touch.

Her eyes brimmed with tears. "Rion!" she sobbed, her face anguished.

"Forgive me, Elanara. I came too late to save him for you," Elavar said guiltily.

"Eladar! Elavar, Eladar is... he's...." She sobbed then gasped in pain and clutched weakly at her chest.

Elavar fought panic. "Please, Elanara! You have to stay calm. I must bring you to Talon. He will heal you," he said and lifted her as one would lift a child, holding her against him, then carrying her through the doorway.

"Bring the two of them, but watch them carefully. I still don't trust them," Elavar said, his voice as cold as a stream in spring thaw.

Lunahr looked as if Elavar had just stabbed him through the heart.

"Come, lads," Hernon said gently.

THEY headed down the hall to the tower, then down the stairs and toward the War Room. Lunahr saw that the dead lined the corridors. Incuban hadn't taken them, this time, to replenish his ranks. He had no need. He was winning. He'd lost few, while they had lost many. Rion! They'd lost Rion!

They entered the War Room. Lunahr was horrified. Piles of ash lay everywhere. Their books, their maps—the Enemy had burned them. And the tapestries! Lunahr's eyes filled with tears. The Enemy had sliced them to ribbons. They were gone forever. Books should never be burned, art should never be destroyed. It was like music. Music! His music! It did not matter. Eladar! Rion! He would never sing again if only he could have saved them.

Mak staggered and swayed and unexpectedly fell against him. Lunahr barely kept him from sliding to the ground; Mak was heavy. He felt his heart and to his relief found it still beat strongly. He turned to Hernon. "Please, stay here with him. He's Rion's friend. He was so brave. He tried to save Rion and he helped me save Elanara, but he's been hurt again. The Enemy thought He'd killed him."

Hernon nodded and wrapped his arms about the little ogre with surprising gentleness.

The lower passageways were definitely no longer secret. The doors had been ripped from their hinges. A voice he scarcely recognized as Dewalaren's, for the devastation in it, floated up the stairs from below, as they began to climb down to the cold, damp grotto. "Elves are different than us. They're harder to kill. Poisons don't work the same on them. I know it will work. It has to."

Lunahr entered the grotto. There were dead snakes everywhere. Dewalaren didn't seem to even see them. He was concentrating all his attention on Eladar. He was sitting on the floor, Eladar's head and shoulders in his lap. Eladar's legs were swaying gently in the underground River's current. "Please, Eladar! We need you. Don't leave us now. Elavar can't have lost you both. You're in the River. You can't have died. The River wouldn't have let you, not when it was giving you its strength. Elavar told me of the Power it has."

Jargas appeared frustrated, discouraged. "I've tried, Talon, but I can't do it, I tell you. I've not the skill. His core is dark. If there's a spark there, I can't find it. It would be different if there was yet light. If he were still alive, then I could help him."

"He's not dead!" Dewalaren argued. "I did not give him permission to die for me." He turned to Eladar. "Do you hear me, Eladar? I do not give you leave to die! I am still your King. You swore oath to me. I bind you to that oath. You swore when I forgave you your treason that you would never break my commands again. I command you to live!" he said, shaking him.

Jargas looked at him intently. "Talon, please. Hunter has already gone mad and almost taken my sister with him. I need you to be strong. I need you to be my King. Don't make me unseat you again."

Lunahr spoke up. "Give me the Ring and the Knife. Elanara is still alive. We can still save her, but she's so weak."

Dewalaren looked up in shock. "Alive? No, she can't be. Hunter heard her die. He heard Rion kill her before you attacked Hunter, before you drove him mad."

He glared at Lunahr in loathing and Lunahr cried out in pain from the look. "Please, Laren, have Jargas test me. I've not fallen to darkness again. I won't resist, I swear I won't."

"I'll do it, Talon. I must," Jargas said. Jargas reached for Lunahr, the Ring clutched tightly in his fist. His eyes lost their focus for a few moments. He shuddered and gasped, and Dewalaren tensed, but then Jargas looked outward again.

"Nay, don't hurt him. The poor lad's been hurt enough. I made him show me what drove Hunter mad. It's a wonder Beryl's still alive. I'd have taken my own life long ago. Nay, I'd not even have lived through what he has. He's telling the truth. He didn't mean to harm Hunter. And Elanara is truly still alive, but she won't be for long if we don't aid her."

He handed Lunahr the Ring and the Knife. "I've not the subtlety to use these upon her, weak as she is. I might kill her when I mean to help her. I've seen your core. You've the Power and the skill to save her."

Lunahr slipped on the Ring and took the Knife. He walked to Elavar. He was beside Eladar, by the river. Elanara was still in his arms. He'd removed her slippers and put her feet in the River, so she might draw upon the strength of the waters.

Lunahr gently touched the Knife to Elanara. The Ring flared to life. Lunahr felt a rush of Power crashing over him, like a thundering waterfall, threatening to drown him. But he held fast; he banked it, channeled it, and turned it into a river, focusing it through the Knife and then into Elanara. Her breathing grew stronger, and the pain and paleness left her face, as severed flesh and muscle and skin knitted whole again, and then she opened her eyes. Lunahr stepped back.

Elanara began to cry. "What have I done? Rion sacrificed himself to save me. Now he'll think it's all for nothing. Worse, he'll think he's killed me. Oh, Elavar! What am I to do without him? And Eladar! Not Eladar! We can't have lost Father and Mother and him too!" she said, kneeling beside their younger brother and sobbing.

Lunahr knelt beside Eladar also and touched his cheek, his hand shaking. Eladar was still warm, despite his ashen skin and blue lips. He did not feel dead, though Lunahr could detect neither his breath nor the beat of his heart. He drew Eladar onto his lap, the way Dewalaren had held him, while Elavar was temporarily distracted comforting his sister.

He focused again, with the Power of the Ring, carefully feeling for any sign that Eladar might yet live, searching for his light, no matter how faint. There! Within his core, not a flame, not even a spark, but a glowing ember, darkening as he watched. He focused on the ember.

"Please don't leave me! I love you, Eladar. I have always loved you, since first I met you. Come, Eladar, your sister is calling you. She is frightened. She needs you. Elavar has been weeping. Don't let them be alone. They need you, we all need you. Please come back to us," Lunahr begged in Elvish.

The Ring began to glow, so faintly that at first Lunahr did not realize it. This time, the Ring's Power was like a spring rain, as if the Knife and Ring somehow knew more would snuff out the ember. He fed the energy to Eladar as it came, and it changed. Now it felt like fire, not water, the comforting fire that warms you on a cold winter's night. But it was not enough. The ember was almost dark.

The chest in Lunahr's mind trembled and shook and creaked open, only the tiniest crack. The Ring kept it from springing wide open. From the darkest recesses of Lunahr's mind, awakened by the touch of flame, words came, ones he had overheard, not with his ears, but with his mind, words of Power.

"FEK NA TARO LA FAER." As he uttered the terrible, familiar words, in a voice not his own, he felt his mind bend the Ring to his will, the skill somehow awakened within him.

Elavar and Elanara shrank back from him in horror, and he heard their thoughts as clearly as if he was bonded to them both. They knew that tongue, though they had never heard it spoken. It was forbidden to speak it. None yet lived who did.

"REME FA MELA TOTHA." Lunahr felt the Power build and grow. It pulsed with life, new life, old life. He recognized in revulsion the flame, the words, the bending, the ritual he was using, but the words leapt upon his tongue and sprang from his mouth, and he did not dare stop them. *"NOREZ LE SAFAREN."*

Dewalaren's face reflected his terror at seeing Elavar's and Elanara's. He reached for Lunahr, but then froze, as did the others, save for Lunahr.

Lunahr would let no one interfere. The horror that would result would drive them all mad, beyond even the Ring's Power to save them.

"ME KATA NO SALEZ." He felt a thin thread form. A strand no stronger than spider silk extended from his core and touched Eladar's. He was there, still there! Lunahr felt his spirit and held it fast. He would not let him slip away, not now, not ever. ***"RA NIERMA SOTEN!"***

Lunahr moved the Knife gently from Eladar's head to his heart. The thread of spider silk held. He saw Eladar's chest rise, then fall, then rise again. He placed his hand on Eladar's chest and felt the strong beat of his heart. He bent over him and kissed him, slowly, tenderly, upon the mouth, and Eladar returned the kiss with equal tenderness as his eyes fluttered open.

Eladar laughed. "I thought I heard Elanara. I wondered why she might kiss me like that. That was not a sisterly kiss! And here it is you, Lunahr. You have never turned such attentions upon me before. You have instead been as a brother to me, but that was not a brotherly kiss either!"

He looked thoughtful and made no attempt to sit. He seemed content to gaze into Lunahr's eyes, his head in his lap. "I had the oddest dream. I dreamt that I had died. I had thought before I would welcome death, though why I should have thought so escapes me. In my dream I fought desperately against it, but I feared I had finally lost. I am glad to be awake again. I am awake now, aren't I? Might I kiss you again, Lunahr, to be sure?" He reached up and pulled Lunahr's head toward him.

Lunahr started to respond, instantly submissive to Eladar's desire, his own desire, both within his heart and his body, swelling at the familiar, welcome feeling of submissiveness.

He pulled back from Eladar. This was not right. He had only kissed him to finish the ritual. "The Kiss of Life," Incuban had called it, laughing. He'd given others his "Kiss of Death" so many times, He was amused by the duality of it. Lunahr had reanimated Eladar with the ritual Incuban had used to turn others into Resemblants. Only Eladar wasn't one.

The ember had still glowed. Lunahr had rekindled it, instead of extinguishing it. He'd not replaced Eladar's mind with some dark shadow from his own, had he?

Eladar was looking at him now, in concern and pain and loss and longing. His core was astonishingly bright, far brighter than it should be, as it had always been, as bright as that of one of his kin. His feelings were so strong! They raged across the link like an angry river. Lunahr was afraid they would snap the tenuous link between them.

Lunahr said softly, "I'm sorry, Eladar, I truly am. You can feel my sorrow, can't you? But this is neither the time nor the place to explore the bond we have forged. You don't know what's happened. The others will come soon. Jargas will have called Jarina for aid. I had no choice. I couldn't let them stop me.

"The other Lords, they'll all try to kill me for what I've done, even though Laren commanded me to. They won't let me explain. They won't even hear me for their fear of me. Even your brother and sister are terrified of me now. And of you. You are in deadly peril from all of them."

"But why would they...? What do you mean they will think I am a Resemblant? How could I... dead? But I wasn't... but Incuban didn't... but how could you know how to.... Lunahr, stop! Maybe you Lords are used to talking without speaking, but I certainly am not! You will soon drive me mad if you keep doing so!" Eladar exclaimed.

Lunahr's face flushed as he slowed the torrent of mental words and images that had been overwhelming Eladar. "I'm sorry, but it's so much faster than speaking, and there's little time. They're coming. I can hear them. There is such Power in the Ring! You have no idea how it weakens Incuban to create a Resemblant. He used to kill dozens before, and then after to replenish Himself, for the Power He needed to create a single life of shadow. The others have no idea. They do not even suspect the true potential of the Ring! Laren has only touched upon its Power. Only Arcanus knows its potential. But there is no time to dwell upon it. Rion...." He trailed off, but his thoughts could not quiet as his tongue had.

ELADAR'S eyes widened in horror as he heard in his mind what Lunahr did not speak. "No! Incuban has Rion? He forced him to.... Elanara, where is she?"

He struggled to sit, pushing Lunahr back from him. "She is not fine! What have you done to them? Why have you... shh, it's all right, Lunahr! Forgive me. Calm down. I'm not afraid of you. You are not alone. You can feel me, can't you? You'll never be alone again, and neither will I." Eladar hugged him with his arms as he hugged him with his mind and his voice.

Eladar felt the frantic beating of Lunahr's heart calm as he held him. "If only we knew how Hunter and Jarina kept Talon from killing them when they stole the Ring and the Knife to bring Hunter back from the dead.

"You were there? They... all right, then, we'll try that. If it worked for them, it might for us. You didn't seize the Ring, Jargas gave it to you.

"Really? You mean they can still hear us? You only froze their bodies, not their minds? Then I'm sure it will work.

"What? You are blocking his Power? Jarina and Shanti cannot hear Jargas? No wonder they are coming! Don't be afraid, Lunahr. Talon loves you. I'd no idea how much!" Eladar said, suddenly laughing, the flare of jealousy and rage he would have expected to feel noticeably absent.

"I know you didn't mean to show me. It's so good to be able to laugh again. It wasn't today I died. It was many weeks ago, with Riviera. Elanara was right. I should have let them help me. Only, I didn't want their help. I didn't want to be able to smile and laugh, with Mother and Father and everyone else dead and gone. And then in Caramore, when you betrayed me, in spite of my love for you, I blamed you for it. How could I have? I see I was wrong. I see so much, now. Kiss me again, Lunahr, please? In case it doesn't work, in case I'm fated to die today. Even if Talon hasn't given me his leave to. And people say Elves are arrogant!" He hugged Lunahr and they kissed, slowly and sweetly.

Eladar was the first to draw back. "I'm sorry, but if I hadn't stopped then, I could not have. Give me the Ring and the Knife, Lunahr."

Lunahr handed them to him.

Eladar said, "Now we'll kneel to him, as Hunter and Jarina did. He'll like that. I've only twice before knelt to him. I seem to kneel to him only when he is angry with me, although he's never wanted to kill me before. Was he really so despondent over me before? I hadn't thought he even liked me. People say we Elves are aloof. That's only because few Men have met the Amontir!"

"Eladar, you're stalling," Lunahr said.

"All right, all right. I'll kneel to him if I must, to save us both. I'm sorry, Lunahr, it's all so ridiculous to me, that they have fought so hard to see me live and now might try to kill me for it." Then he grew grim. "Meanwhile, the Enemy has Rion. I'd almost forgotten. Come, let's get this over with, one way or another."

Eladar knelt before Talon and held out the Knife and the Ring. Lunahr knelt beside him. Eladar took a deep breath and let it out slowly. "Release them," he said to Lunahr.

LUNAHR could hear voices now, with his ears as well as his mind, and the sound of many feet at the top of the stairs. "Please don't let them kill us, Laren," he pleaded, as he released the four of them.

DEWALAREN snatched the Ring and the Knife from Eladar's hands. Jargas was looking warily at both Lunahr and Eladar. Elavar's and Elanara's expressions were impossible to read.

Dewalaren turned to them. "Elavar, Elanara, you know him better than anyone. I know what I feel, but I must hear from you also. Is he still your brother? Is he real, or is he a monster in Eladar's form? I must know before the others enter. You've only moments to decide."

"It's him. Save him," Elanara said, turning her back to Eladar, placing herself between him and those who were coming. Elavar protected Lunahr similarly.

"Jargas, are you with us?" Dewalaren asked desperately, eyes boring into his.

"Aye, I'll back you on this. He's the lad I remember again, more than that ghost who's been living with us was. I'll not see anyone harm him."

The six of them faced the oncoming warriors, weapons sheathed, for they'd not harm any of their own, even to save themselves.

A dozen Dwarves spilled into the grotto, axes raised. Hernon was leading them. They hesitated when they saw that none had raised a weapon against them, and that they stood united. Hernon called up the stairs, "They're all here, all alive, even Thorn and Brook, when they're not supposed to be," he added in a suspicious tone. "But they've not attacked us. They've not even drawn their weapons. What do we do?"

Desmond's voice floated down the stairs. "Shanti, can you hear Jargas again?"

"He's all right, Father! He's not harmed, nor frozen, nor controlled. He's not even frightened anymore," his daughter replied.

"Watch them, weapons at the ready. We're coming down," Desmond said.

Moments later, Desmond and a dozen Dwarves appeared. Desmond eyed the six of them coolly. "Talon, give me the Knife and the Ring."

"How am I supposed to respond to such a command, Archer? You are not my King, I am yours. If I don't surrender them, you might fear I covet them, but if I do, you might fault me for not protecting them with my life. Pick a different test, if you must test me," Dewalaren said.

"Tell me how it is that Thorn and Brook appear to live when they were dead," Desmond said.

"Brook was not dead, only badly wounded, despite how it appeared. As for Thorn, I commanded Jargas to bring him back when we all thought him forever lost, and he could not. But Lunahr did, and then I almost slew him for it, out of fear for what he had done."

"If I am to die again, I'd like to have some say in it, this time. The snakes did not show me the courtesy of asking me if I would like to be bitten. I could have used your aid then, Archer," Eladar said whimsically. "You survived the poison of Beryl's arrow because it was from water snakes, and as Lord of House of Serpents, you are immune to their venom. Would that I had your Power, or at least your protection."

"He does not sound himself," Desmond said, eyeing Eladar suspiciously.

Elanara said, "On the contrary, he is exactly who he should be again. Please, Rion is slipping further from us as we stand here debating."

Desmond said to Dewalaren, "Command us, Majesty," and the Dwarves lowered their axes.

"Come," Dewalaren said, heading for the stairs.

THEY climbed the stairs and Lunahr knelt by Mak, whom Hernon had left with another Dwarf. Lunahr turned to Laren. "Mak's been hurt again, I'm afraid worse than before. Incuban tried to kill him. He thought his servants had. Please, he's only a child, and he's fought so bravely. Use the Knife to heal him, Laren, or let Jargas wield it for you."

Jargas looked at Lunahr in surprise. "You've grown as fond of him as Rion has," he said and then winced at his own words. "Aye, I'll help him, if Talon will allow it. He'll not be beyond my ability."

Lunahr added in Amontirin, "Laren, what of Farad? I would help him if I could."

Laren said, "I hope you can. Jarina has tried, but she almost went mad as well, even though she wore the Ring at the time. We're keeping him unconscious. He's dangerous, even to himself." He put his head in his hands. "How could we have let the Enemy take Rion? We cannot save him. We don't even know where to look for him."

"I know where Incuban has taken Rion," Lunahr said, a shudder passing through him. "I heard Him tell Rion. I know the place He was speaking of. He's taken him to the Queen's Chamber, in Ironforge." Every Dwarven Queen lost her virginity in her Chamber, the night she was married. But there was far more than a soft bed in this one. Lunahr remembered the chains and the whips, the wax and the brands. He fought not to remember so well. The chest Farad had made threatened to burst open and release all his memories again. Farad! He was no longer linked to him! He was not strong enough to keep the memories at bay alone.

Lunahr heard the faintest of whispers in his mind and shrank from them in terror. He felt strong arms around him and he fought them, until he recognized the voice and the arms were Eladar's. Now he heard the words as well. "You are not alone, Lunahr. I am always with you," Eladar said aloud. Lunahr embraced Eladar in relief and felt joy burn away the darkness that had threatened to overwhelm him.

"WE MUST heal those in need and then leave at once. We will strike while Incuban is distracted," Dewalaren said. Incuban did not know they knew where he had gone, this time, that they could follow him to his lair and end it. Rion would be avenged. And Aras. All those who had fallen. Then, finally, he could join them in oblivion.

RION was on a chimaera again, but this time he was astride it. Incuban rode behind him, His arms about Rion's waist, His hands upon his manhood, fondling him. Rion was still frozen, still helpless, or he would have twisted to make himself fall off. He would have taken Incuban with him, to plummet to the rock below.

"Are you thinking sweet thoughts of the pleasures your Master will bring you?" Incuban asked Rion.

Incuban could not hear his thoughts! Of course! He had no Power. Rion remembered how Mak had been able to resist Him enough to attack Him. Maybe his thoughts and Mak's weren't strong enough, loud enough for Him to hear. Maybe Rion could surprise Incuban somehow because of it, attack Him, injure Him, weaken Him, so the others might find victory. He knew he could not escape from Him.

Rion felt Incuban's tongue trace the curve of his ear. "You are so delicate, so tasty, Rion. I will try to remember how fragile you are. I will try not to break you too quickly," He said, laughing. "If only I could have Farad chained beside you, to watch us together. But his dreams will have to do."

The chimaera was descending now, Rion realized. He steeled himself for what would come, wishing he'd not listened to Oberas and Tarrell. They'd urged him not to take a woman to his bed until he was older, afraid he'd lose his heart, that he'd be hurt. But now he was weaker than he should be, because of his inexperience.

A shattered metal door was inset into the side of the mountain. Well above it, hundreds of feet up on a sheer rock face was a second door, sealed, smaller. It swung open as Incuban and all his winged servants approached. Rion's last ray of hope died. His friends could not fly. They would never be able to enter here.

They flew inside the Mountain. The shrill cries of the hippogryphs and the roars of the chimaera were terrifying. Rion felt the weight of the cold stone of the Mountain all around him.

"Come, Rion," Incuban said, and Rion obeyed meekly, as helpless to resist as if he were on an invisible leash.

A figure approached them. She was dark haired and dark eyed, petite and perfect, nearly naked, except for a transparent, filmy bolt of fabric the color of blood, which hung loosely from one shoulder, covering her left breast and part of her thigh. Rion recognized her instantly. Circe!

"Ah, Selene, how good of you to welcome your daddy home," Incuban said, kissing her fully on the mouth and running his finger along the crevice amidst the dark curls between her thighs.

"I've missed you, Father," Circe said, wrapping one leg around him.

Rion stared, appalled. Was Incuban truly her father? Could a father treat a daughter so? He had thought Arcanus was her father.

Incuban turned to Rion, Circe still clinging to him. He pulled his hand away from her soft mound and with a terrible smile said, "I give you a rare treat, Rion, a taste of what is to come." He gently thrust the wet fingers that had fondled Circe into Rion's mouth. Rion found himself sucking hungrily upon them. His body still would not obey him.

Circe smiled seductively at Rion. "Hello, Rion. It is a pleasure to see you again." The way she said "pleasure" sent a wave of terror through him.

"Have you readied the Queen's Chamber for my virgin bride?" Incuban asked Circe.

"Yes, Father. Ninety-nine red candles ring the room. The incense is lit, the wax is melted, and the brands are so hot they are almost white. Oh, and I put white sheets on the bed. I know the red ones disappointed you the last time. These will show the blood much better."

Rion would have fallen to his knees in terror had Incuban's hold not kept him standing. Blood! Brands! He fought the debilitating panic. Incuban might let go of his body in that horrible room. Incuban would enjoy watching him struggle. If he could seize a brand while he was free of His control, he could blind Him with it, or better still, maybe even castrate Him. They'd kill him for it, but maybe it would be quick. Or maybe if he threw himself upon the coals.... He felt his gorge rise and forced it back down. He knew he was fair of face. Maybe Incuban wouldn't want him if he wasn't.

Rion was led down corridor after corridor, past hundreds and hundreds of Revenants, each more hideous than the last: Men and Dwarves and most monstrous of all, Elves. At least Aras wasn't amongst them. He'd died terribly, by fire, but his body would have been destroyed by it. Incuban couldn't have used him. Then he saw something too horrific to imagine, and bound as he was by Incuban, a whimper still rose in his throat.

Incuban turned to him in surprise. "What's this?" He looked about, as if noticing the Revenants around Him for the first time. He backed up a few steps and brought some of them before Rion. "I will give your voice back to you, for a moment, so you may tell me your thoughts."

Rion stared in terror at her. She had been an Elf, once. The half of her face that was not burnt away was still ethereally beautiful, despite the chilling dead eyes. He knew those eyes, that hair, that face: it was Elanara, as she might have looked three hundred years from now. It must be her mother, River, Queen Naraena of Riviera. Lunahr had told him her given name. Rion bit his tongue and forced himself to remain silent.

Incuban scowled at him. He turned to the Revenant he had been staring at. "Perhaps his mouth is parched, his tongue too dry for him to speak. Wet his lips, refresh his tongue for me. Kiss him so that he may find his voice."

Rion's body was still frozen. He could not turn from her, he could not run. In an awful parody of his previous muteness, he could only speak. "No, stop! It's...," he began, but her cold, burnt mouth was upon him, her dead tongue forcing itself into his mouth, and he gagged upon it, his heart pounding. He felt the blackness closing in upon him like it had in the cell when he'd been screaming, after the rat had scurried up his leg, and he embraced the darkness. But Incuban would not let him escape so easily. Suddenly the world snapped back into focus.

The horrible thing that had been Elanara's mother backed away from him, and he began retching, but he could not move his head. He vomited all over himself; a cascade of it fell everywhere. Incuban glared at him in sudden fury, grabbing him by the throat. Rion prayed to Elmoth that He would snap his neck, or strangle him, that it might end now, quickly.

"Oh, Father, surely you won't let such a minor thing spoil your fun? Not when you have worked so hard and waited so long to catch him?" Circe said soothingly, running her finger along Incuban's ear.

Incuban flung Rion down upon the ground. Pain exploded in Rion's temple as he hit the stone floor, landing on his face, helpless to break his fall. "Clean it up. Then I will decide if I should punish it or pleasure it," He snapped and stalked off down the hall.

Rion turned his head and glared at Circe in hate and fear. She had kept Incuban from killing him, all to fulfill her own sick, twisted desires. Then he realized he had turned his head. He could move! He tried to leap to his feet, but a wave of dizziness made him stumble.

"NO, RION. YOU WILL NOT ESCAPE. I have need of you," Circe said, and again his body was not his own, nor his voice, though strangely, her voice had sounded sad rather than seductive. "I'm sorry it had to be you, Rion. I had hoped He might bring back one of the others. Come. I must ready you for Him, or He will be angry with me." She escorted him down corridor after corridor, through a confusing maze of twisting and turning passageways.

Circe finally led him into a stone room. There was a large sunken basin in the floor and what appeared to be solid gold spigots set into one wall. She turned one of them, and to his astonishment, water began flowing from a gold pipe set under it. Steam rose from the water. Was she going to scald him? But then she turned on the other and periodically tested the water carefully. She poured different scented soaps and oils into the water.

She looked longingly at him. "You and I could have much fun here, soaped and oiled. I would slide against you and you would slide inside of me," she said, then bit her lip so hard that it bled. "I know! I'm sorry! I am trying, truly I am! I won't, I promise," she said, so softly he could scarcely hear her. It had sounded as though she were speaking to someone. Rion wondered if she heard Incuban's voice in her head, scolding her, if even now He was taking sick pleasure watching them through her eyes.

Circe stripped Rion of his clothes, her hands gently caressing him as she did so. Then she guided him into the bath and began washing him with the warm water, a soft cloth in her hand. She washed his hair and then soaped him everywhere. His body thrilled to her touch, betraying him. He had stiffened at her first caress. "Please, I can't wait. I know I'm supposed to, but I need him. I'll go mad if I don't take him."

"Selene, where is my bride?" a voice called silkily from the hall, and her eyes widened in terror.

"I am drying him now, Master!" she said, quickly flinging a towel onto him. "He will be dressed and in the room in moments."

Rion fought terror of his own at the voice. If it was not Incuban she had been speaking to, then who was it? And she had called Him "Master" now, not "Father," and she looked terrified of Him.

"Do not make me wait, Daughter," the cold, hard voice threatened, and Circe began trembling wildly.

"No, Master." She touched the wall and a door opened in the solid stone. She took out a long silk tunic of the purest white, and soft white slippers. The tunic fell to the middle of Rion's thighs. There were no pants given to him. She pulled on the slippers and then ran a comb quickly through his hair. She yanked his hand, propelling him toward the door. "He is ready, Master," she said breathlessly.

Incuban narrowed his eyes at her and studied them both intently. "It is well you did not betray me and pleasure yourself upon him, Daughter."

She laughed, but it sounded forced to Rion's ear.

Rion was escorted down more corridors, until he came to a door. The smell coming from behind it made him want to retch, but his body shook with dry heaves. He had nothing left to vomit. Even through the closed door, the room smelled of the same sickly sweet incense as in his dream.

Incuban's scowl metamorphosed into a silky smile. "Ah, you remember this sweet scent, I see," He said, laughing, His good mood apparently restored. The door opened, and Rion beheld a cavernous room. They entered. There was an enormous bed with white sheets. Reddish-copper manacles, the same oddly colored metal as Talon's magic knife and ring and armband, hung from the walls over the bed, and from a number of other spots within the room, including at the edges of a grate over the floor. Were they magic too? Rion saw shimmers of heat coming from the grate, like rock will give off in summertime. He saw glowing white brands and was escorted past a bubbling cauldron filled with boiling red wax. There was a table with many different types of whips, some leather, others barbed metal. Then he saw the chair, the red, bottomless chair from his dream, and he whimpered.

Incuban laughed in delight. He escorted Rion slowly about the room, making sure he saw everything it contained. Then He led Rion to the bed and, with a laugh, pushed against his chest. Rion fell backward onto the bed. He could feel the softness of it against his bare legs and arms. "Shackle him," Incuban said.

"Upon his back?" Circe asked.

"For now," He said.

Circe fastened reddish-copper cuffs about each wrist. "His feet, also?" she asked.

Incuban shook His head. "No, this will be sufficient. We must give him some small glimmer of hope, mustn't we? **I FREE YOU NOW**," He said, then laughed. "In a manner of speaking."

Suddenly Rion could move and speak again. He fought the urge to writhe on the bed, to test the chains. Incuban wanted him to, so he would not. He lay still.

"Ah, I can see you are going to be an enjoyable plaything for me, Rion. You think you will not move? Fetch the wax, Selene. It is time Rion receives his first lesson," Incuban said.

Rion paled but did not move.

Circe said, "Father, I am sure I can get a rise out of him for you. Please, may I taste him?"

Incuban eyed her appraisingly. "No. You will kneel before me, instead," He said, watching her carefully. She knelt eagerly, instead of obediently, and Rion watched, sickened and, to his horror, excited, as she pleasured Him with her mouth. Rion felt himself stiffen with desire and, shamefaced, turned from them, trying to hide his humiliation in the sheets.

Incuban grabbed Circe by the hair and forced her to keep her face against Him as He spasmed in release. Rion saw her throat work as she swallowed hungrily.

"I had begun to wonder at your interest in him, but your enthusiasm for me has not waned," Incuban said. Then he turned toward Rion and laughed. "And it seems your technique has worked upon my toy as well, Daughter."

She batted her eyes, cream dribbling from her mouth. "May I taste him, Father? Please, just a single taste?"

"Ah, I am such an indulgent parent. I fear I spoil you, Daughter, but go ahead, one taste, and then he is mine."

Mouth still dripping, she bent over Rion as he struggled to get away from her. He felt her lips upon him. At her touch there was a voice, a man's voice, in Rion's mind. It whispered softly to him, speaking his true name: "**ALARION, SON OF ANORION OF ARDOCK, I CLAIM THEE.**" Rion heard the roar of blood in his ears and then the world became strangely silent.

THEY were half a day's march from the Watchtower. They'd left it deserted, abandoned. Lunahr had carefully hidden his music and Rion's journal in the caves, in case the Enemy yet decided to destroy the Tower. They had left their bond animals behind as well. None of them expected to see them again. Two-thousand-sixteen Dwarves, two-hundred-fourteen ogres, three River Elves, fifteen Amontir, ninety-four Men, and a woman of Men all marched with a single purpose. They would fight to the last person left standing. They would defeat the Enemy once and for all, or they would all perish in the attempt.

"Laren, Mak should not be with us. I still cannot believe you and Ogress Tana allowed it. He is an eight-year-old boy. You would not let an eight-year-old of our own people march to war because he loves Rion and wants to help him," Lunahr accused.

Dewalaren said tiredly, "I am allowing a twenty-four-year-old boy of my own people march to war because he loves Rion and wants to help him. Despite the special dangers he faces in doing so." Dewalaren seemed to have aged decades in the hours since Rion had been taken.

Lunahr swallowed and nodded. He felt a faint thrum of warmth across his bond with Eladar. He embraced it desperately. Farad was still lost. Lunahr had been unable to help him and had not been allowed to renew his bond with Farad. They could not risk letting Farad waken. They were slowly giving him Theodas's precious vial of *sharesh*, along with a sedative, to keep him in his dreamless slumber. They had brought Farad with them only because they could not risk leaving him poorly guarded at the Watchtower, where the Enemy might strike at them by seizing him.

RON, Ara, Gar, Andra, and Rarnak were all clustered tightly together. Ron's and Andra's eyes were still red from the tears they'd shed earlier. They knew they were marching to avenge Rion, not to save him. They'd known it from the first. It was more than a two-hundred-mile march to Ironforge, and then they would have to lay siege once they arrived. It might be months before they could enter. Perhaps far longer. Some of the Dwarven keeps had withstood years of siege by the Enemy's forces.

DESMOND wished the rest of his army were here beside them, instead of in Nalea and elsewhere. They marched with so few men. But he was glad the rest of his people, the Urwani-Amontir, and the few other kin Dewalaren had assigned elsewhere were not here. He did not think any of them would survive the coming battle. It was good to know the Amontir as a people still would, though they would lose Obearn, Wolven, Pumar, Serpents, and Eagles, five of their smallest yet strongest Houses. And they would lose their King, along with every potential Heir to the Throne. But Shadala and Haran would lead their people, as they had before the coming of the King.

He was disturbed to see his daughter, Desenia, was almost gleeful, knowing that she was finally going to be able to confront the Enemy who had tormented her.

JARGAS was deeply troubled, concerned for his wife, but especially for his sister and her husband. He had argued and lost that Jarina and Farad should stay behind, with some others. He did not want to risk losing his sister to the Enemy, not after He'd come so close to taking her from him forever. Jargas took some small comfort in knowing every one of the surviving ninety Varash and every Dwarf of Malar who marched with them would die to protect her.

ELAVAR and Elanara marched with grim purpose. They shared their thoughts with no one. But Eladar shared every waking thought with Lunahr. Eladar had neither the skill nor the desire to shield any of them from him. Eladar's thoughts gave Lunahr the strength he needed to make the march, to fight the terror of what they would find.

Their army had not stopped for lunch, and the Dwarves had marched through the full heat of the day without complaint. Laren and Desmond both knew that they could not do so thereafter, but there was still a sense of urgency, despite the hopelessness of the situation.

There was a cry from the air, and Quickwing banked away from them, heading west. Lunahr wondered what he'd seen, and extended his thoughts down his link to his bond eagle. His eyes lost their focus for a moment, then focus returned and his eyes were wide and white with fear. "Laren! The Enemy! Chimaera, hundreds of them, coming from the west!"

DEWALAREN cursed, wishing in vain for the Elven bowmen he'd sent back to Nalea. He called out orders that everyone get as close to the walls of the Pass as possible, to make it hardest for them to attack, and Desmond and Jargas relayed the orders in Dwarvish to their men.

They prepared as best as they could, as dozens, then hundreds of tiny black specks became visible on the horizon. They drew nearer quickly, and hundreds upon hundreds of dark shapes began to take form.

So, their march was to end in disaster even before it had truly begun! So be it. Dewalaren was through running. He would fight to the death, here, and end it.

The flap of wings could be heard now, and the harsh, screeching cry of eagles.

So, Quickwing had been mistaken. They would not fall to the fanged mouths of chimaera after all; they would be rent by the chiseled beaks of hippogryphs.

The Dwarves raised their axes bravely, as the four Ogaten siblings and three Elves nocked arrows and raised their bows.

Lunahr called Quickwing back desperately, but his bond eagle defied him and flew instead to meet the onrushing army. Then Lunahr paled. "Laren, it's Arcanus who comes for us!" he yelled. Dewalaren had told Lunahr of Arcanus's attack upon him.

Dewalaren cursed again. So now they would have to face Arcanus's might as well as such an army of flying creatures.

Then Lunahr yelled in astonishment. "But... but it's not an army of chimaera or hippogryphs at all. I can't believe it! I don't understand. How can it be? It's Gryphon! A flight of Gryphon! And there are other riders. Laren, it's the Elves! I see High-King Laedrin! And Dwarves! And our cousins! I see Veran and Shadala!"

Dewalaren stared at him in shock. "Beryl, are you sure? You must be sure!"

"It is, Laren! It's not the Enemy's army at all! It's ours!" Lunahr cried in relief.

"But why would Arcanus ride with them? We must still take care. There is something odd about this," Dewalaren said.

Aramis said dryly, "What, odd to encounter hundreds of Gryphon, when we know them to be extinct?"

"They are not extinct. I have seen a Gryphon before." Dewalaren said. He thought painfully of the memory of that meeting, when Aras had come on the back of a Gryphon to save his life after Arcanus had nearly drained it away.

The screech of the Gryphon was all but deafening, now, as the sound echoed back and forth across the valley. Then they began to land, dozens at a time.

Laedrin and Shadala dismounted and walked toward Dewalaren, while Arcanus hung back with the others, along with a figure in a blue cloak, guarded by two Elves and Veran.

"High-King, Chieftess," Dewalaren called out in greeting. "What brings you to us in such a manner?"

Laedrin boomed, "It is time for the final battle of the Enemy's War. Magus has cast a scry and seen it. It is time for us to pay the Enemy back for the destruction of Riviera, Loatia, and Nalea, as well as the Dwarven Kingdoms and your own, King Talon."

"Nalea? Nalea has fallen?" Dewalaren asked in shock.

"No, she is burnt but not fallen, thanks to the timely arrival of your army. We beat back the Enemy. Now we return the favor. We bring one-thousand-twenty-three Gryphon to your aid. Each now only bears a single rider, but may carry two with ease, or three with some loss of maneuverability. Magus had foreseen that you go to attack a target in the sky. Arcanus told us he had the means to reach such an Enemy and summoned a flight of Gryphon to our aid. We are here to fight beside you, to victory against Incuban."

"I welcome your aid, High-King, but I cannot welcome Arcanus's. He has shown himself to be our enemy, not our ally. You are in great danger from him," Dewalaren said softly, for the High-King's ear alone.

"Nay, he is not whom you fear him to be, King Talon. But you might not be able to believe as readily my own words as those of my son," Laedrin said.

For a moment of desperate hope, Dewalaren looked eagerly toward the Gryphon for a face he longed to see.

"Forgive me, King Talon. I did not mean to bring such hope to your heart, only to see it taken from you. Aras is dead, dead and gone these many weeks ago. But his voice lives on through this letter. It is in his own hand. You will know it is his voice that speaks when you read it." He handed Dewalaren a letter.

Dewalaren's hand shook as he took it and recognized Aras's writing, though the only other time he had seen such a missive, Aras had written it in his own blood. Tears sprang to his eyes as he read the final desperate words of hope and love. There could be no hope, not for him. His love was dead.

He handed the letter wordlessly back to the High-King and then walked to where Arcanus stood, next to a Gryphon. Dewalaren saw then that, as he suspected, the figure in blue was Magus.

"Greetings, King Talon," Arcanus said formally.

"Why are you here?" Dewalaren asked, pointedly.

"To destroy Incuban. Do you fear I seek the Ring?" he asked, and Dewalaren barely kept from stiffening at mention of it. "I do not. I seek vengeance upon Incuban for all the harm He has done to the children of my blood, both the Amontir and my son Magus, as well as for the harm He has done and might yet do to the child of my heart, Circe, whom He holds as His prisoner."

Dewalaren's eyes narrowed. "I have not seen that you hold love in your heart for any of your children. You tried to kill me," he said, and his voice was firm. "You tried to kill Aras," he said, and his voice shook; that he could not forgive.

"I did," Arcanus admitted, and Dewalaren was surprised. "It was wrong of me to do so. I have been shown the error of my ways. Aras forgave me for it, both for the attack upon him and for the attack upon you. You see from his letter that we became allies, though our allegiance was unhappily short-lived."

"You killed him," Dewalaren accused, his voice dark with hatred. "You are the one who burned him."

Arcanus shook his head tiredly. "I was not the one who sought his death. It was his own mother, Ithelia, who thought to slay him, when she saw he was lost to her. Fortunately, she was weakened enough in her battle with him that I was able to overcome her. She is dead. Do you think High-King Laedrin would fight beside the man who killed his son?"

"You are King of Lies," Dewalaren said. "You twist and turn the truth to suit your needs. You care nothing for my people."

"Take care, King Talon. Do not presume to tell me where my affections or my allegiances lie. Ring or not, you do not wish to have me for your enemy. Would you not rather have me as an ally? Or can you forgive the Enemy so easily for what he has done to Hunter's entire family, to Beryl, and so many others? For what he is even now doing to Rion? Do you truly wish to see it? We have already done so. Magus's scry led us to you. Magus can show you Rion as well, but I do not think you will like what he shows you."

"I will not," Magus said. "It is terrible. You must know how Rion is being tortured. I will not weaken you by showing you Rion's torment when you most need strength." He looked as if the very thought of what he'd seen made him ill.

Magus continued, his voice softening, "King Talon, I can see you are in pain. We give you the means to strike at your Enemy, to end this war of annihilation. Would you turn that aid aside for the sake of your pride? Would you have the deaths of all those you have loved and lost be meaningless, be for naught?"

Dewalaren turned to Shadala. "Chieftess, you are one of my people, and I value your counsel. You once showed me the error of what I perceived. Will you so guide me again?"

"Arcanus does not come to you as your enemy, but as your ally," Shadala swore. "He knows you wear the Ring. He admits that he once coveted it, but he has now chosen a different path. He will not tell us more. I can see that he is keeping more than one secret from us, but we know enough. The Trees of the Lords' Grove have told us he is to be trusted. My people are not easily led, yet though we acknowledge you as our King, we now follow him to War. Ride with me, my King. I will not see you fall," Shadala said, with more than one meaning to her words.

Dewalaren exhaled. "Then we ride."

Shadala smiled. "We can take two-thousand forty-six of your people, two more people per Gryphon." She eyed the ogres in surprise. "Or somewhat less, if the ogres join us, for each weighs at least as much as two men."

They began determining who would fly with them. The rest would continue on foot, to reinforce those coming by air.

"While we are readying, do you have any injured who need tending?" Shadala asked.

Dewalaren shook his head. "Only Hunter, and his injury is not something you can tend to."

She asked him what had happened to him, and he told her. She nodded and left.

A short time later, Magus approached. He looked at Dewalaren nervously. "Shadala has told me one of your people is in need of aid. I think my Power is such that I might be able to help him."

"I will not let you near him," Dewalaren said coldly.

Lunahr spoke up then. Dewalaren had not seen him approach. "Laren, please let him try. Think what it would mean to Hunter! He has fought the Enemy his whole life. He should ride amongst us, now. He should be able to fight. Do not leave him feeling he did not do his part. I will link to him again, to be sure Magus does not harm him."

Magus shook his head. "I cannot aid him, then. I am truly sorry."

Jarina approached and spoke to Dewalaren. "King Talon, he is your friend, your cousin, your subject, but he is my husband. He needs to fight. Please do not take that from him, when the Enemy has already taken so much. I trust this wizard to aid him."

Dewalaren looked from one to the other. "I will not stand in the way of your heart, when my own heart is already dead. Do as you must."

Magus watched him go, and Lunahr saw pain in his eyes, and wondered at it. Then Magus turned to Farad and his eyes were clear again. He placed his hand lightly on Farad's forehead, and his eyes lost their focus.

"Lunahr!" Farad said, some moments later, and sat up suddenly.

"It's all right, Faradan. He is well, he is safe," Jarina said, eyeing him carefully.

Farad nodded. "He is safe. It is Rion who was taken," he said, but his voice was calm. "We will save him." His voice was firm, confident.

"Husband, more than half a day has already passed since you fell and he was taken. Rion has already been grievously harmed," Jarina cautioned.

Farad turned to her, and there was the light of conviction in his eyes instead of madness. "We will save him."

Lunahr saw Jarina eye Magus, but he had already returned to the Gryphon.

"Farad?" Lunahr asked cautiously, fear in his face, his voice soft, so no one might overhear. "Can you ever forgive me? I never meant to hurt you. I could not stop the memories. I did not mean to harm you by them. They harmed me as well."

Farad said, "I know, Lunahr. What drove me to madness was seeing you hurt like that, when you never should have suffered so. I never should have left you. You are not the one who should ask for forgiveness. Can you ever forgive me, for failing you so utterly, for abandoning you? How can you not hate me at least as much as I despise myself?"

"I don't hate you, Farad, I love you. I have always loved you. Please, Farad, may I renew my bond to you?" Lunahr pleaded.

Farad smiled fondly at Lunahr and nodded. Lunahr touched his face eagerly. Farad said, surprised, "You are already linked, but such a fragile thread!"

Lunahr said joyfully, "Eladar is with me now, always. He is the one I am bonded to."

Farad looked at him, puzzled. "You cannot be."

Lunahr grinned. "Much has happened while you slept, cousin." Then the grin left his face. "Both for good and for ill."

"Beryl!" an excited voice called, and Lunahr looked up. His face broke into a wide grin again. "Leonas! Gaius!" He ran to them and hugged them both tightly. He felt something odd and tried to figure out what was wrong. Then he saw Eladar was watching him, jealousy plain upon his face, and realized that was what he had felt, across their bond. He sent a gentle wave of warmth through his link to Eladar. He saw the dark expression replaced by one of cautious interest. Lunahr waved him over and Eladar came, eyeing the two Elves before him warily.

"Leonas, Gaius, this is Prince Eladar of Riviera, my *lythenia*," Lunahr said, although the past night had not afforded them the opportunity of truly exploring the bond they now shared. They had yet to lie together. They should not, until he came-of-age, but after all that had transpired, they no longer wanted to wait. The future was too uncertain.

Eladar's coolness vanished at Lunahr acknowledging him publicly to his friends as his lover, his lifemate. "Eladar, these are my friends, Leonas, Lord of the Grove, Protector of the Trees, and Gaius, Captain of the Grove Guard."

Leonas smiled at them both. "Actually, Gaius is now Commander. And we are also *lythenia*."

Lunahr smiled in joy, and they began catching up on all that had happened to each of them.

As soon as the mounts were selected for everyone, they took to the sky. Dewalaren rode with Shadala and no third so they would maintain their maneuverability. Lunahr and Eladar rode with Leonas. Farad and Jarina rode with Veran. Rarnak and Andra rode with Gaius. Now their journey to Ironforge would take hours, rather than days.

SELENE approached the door to the Mountain carefully. Her father had finally dismissed her. He had called some of His other servants to aid Him in His pleasures with Rion. The Revenants at the door stared vapidly at her as she coolly touched the handle that would release the lock. Some of them retained little of their intellect, while others were almost as intelligent as they had been in life, those who had been reanimated most quickly after death.

She did not open the door, not yet. She stared at the hand upon the handle in revulsion, remembering all that hand had done the past many hours. She rubbed at the dried blood. It flaked off easily but still left a red stain upon her hand. But the screams, she could not remove those from her ears, nor the smell of burning flesh from her nose.

Selene shuddered, remembering how she had found Magus quivering in the dirt, how she had thought he had undergone something so terrible, when his body had at least been safely upon the road, affected only by the shadow touches from his dreams. Rion was no longer screaming, nor crying, nor begging. When she had left, he was scarcely whimpering. She had not thought Incuban would be so severe with him, so soon. He had said He knew Rion was fragile, and He could not yet share what He did to Rion with Hunter. But it was as if Incuban had forgotten all about Hunter, as if Rion himself was now the focus of His merciless rage. If only Rion stayed alive! If only he kept Incuban's attention a little while longer!

The hand upon the lock was shaking. She fought to still it. The Revenants were like wild animals. They could sense fear. She must not let them see her fear. It would all be over soon.

Finally, she sensed those she awaited approaching, aloft, as planned. When they were directly outside the Mountain, she released the lever, and the door swung open.

The Revenants nearest her stared stupidly as dozens of Gryphon descended upon the landing area. The attackers were springing from their mounts onto them before they even realized there was something amiss.

She ran to Arcanus. "Come, quickly, before the others raise the alarm! Where is the Sword? Where is the Ring? Oh hurry! He will find us!" she begged him, all but sobbing.

Arcanus hugged her. "You are safe now, daughter-of-my-heart. You have played your part well. Lead. We will follow."

DEWALAREN heard dozens of roars as a wave of chimaera sprang from a bank of tunnels toward the rear of the cave. The flight of Gryphon raced toward the pride of chimaera, and they began tearing at each other viciously, even as the Revenant guards were slaughtered by their army.

More Revenants began to arrive, as Dewalaren headed for Circe and Arcanus, with Magus, Farad, Jargas, Jarina, Desmond, Shanti, Donovar, Lunahr, Shadala, Laedrin, Jarnath, Haran, Veran, Ron, Andra, Rarnak, Ara, Gar, Mak, Elavar, Elanara, and Eladar.

SELENE ran down the corridor, leading them, heart pounding. Finally, they reached the Queen's Chamber. The door to the room was still closed. Selene flung it open and started inside, then began to scream, as she saw the wall of fire heading toward her.

FARAD saw Magus slam Circe aside and thrust both hands forward, palms outward, and a great wind sprang forth, dissolving the fire. Then Magus darted into the room, followed by the rest of them.

A quick check showed the room was empty. There was a sword beside the bed, Dwarven, beautiful, but the blade was stained with dried blood. There was a leather sheath next to it, intricately tooled with images of wolven.

Farad stared at the familiar sword and sheath and the empty bed in horror. The once white sheets were striped in blood, marred by burns, covered in uneven splotches of dried wax, and other drying fluids. "Where is he?" Farad demanded, grabbing Circe by the arms, shaking her. "Where is Rion!"

"He was here, I swear he was still here, still alive...," she said, but then she screamed and her body spasmed.

Arcanus pushed Farad away, hugging Circe tightly, and began incanting. Lunahr's shock resonated across his bond to Farad as his young cousin recognized the language, though not most of the words. Arcanus was speaking in the same forbidden language that had so terrified Elanara and Elavar.

Magus's eyes grew distant for a moment and then he started to run. The others followed. Farad grabbed the sword and sheathed it in the scabbard without cleaning the blade. Clutching it to his chest, he ran after them.

Magus led them back out to the floor of the cavern where the Gryphon were. It was a scene of utter carnage. Bodies of Dwarves, Elves, Men, Ogres, Revenants, chimaera, hippogryphs, and Gryphon were everywhere. Many hundreds of Revenants were pouring into the room from formerly concealed doorways in what had previously appeared to be solid rock, reinforcing the forces already there. The Ogres broke away from the battle and ran for the mouths of the tunnels leading to the cavern, to stem the tide of new combatants.

Farad's blood boiled with hatred as he saw that Incuban was in the cavern now, on a protruding shelf of rock. He was laughing wildly, as if all He beheld had been put there for His amusement. He extended His hands and flames shot from them, aiming for them.

But Magus extended his own hands and silver lightning crackled from his fingertips and smashed into Incuban, even as Farad and the others realized to their confusion that the fire did not burn. It reached them, but there was no heat from it. It was illusion only.

Incuban's body jerked as the lightning hit, then wavered and changed to that of a naked, bruised, bloodied, and burnt boy, barely a man, who toppled from the shelf toward the stone floor below. Farad and Magus simultaneously exclaimed in horror as the masking spell dissolved and revealed it was Rion whom Magus had attacked. Magus shifted his Power, cushioning his fall with wind.

From almost directly behind Magus, Farad heard Incuban's voice thunder, **"THETELA, MARCUS, SENET ETH ESCOLIER, FAEREN ET SCHLIEREN!"** and a thundering wave of liquid flame slammed into Magus, engulfing him completely. Farad cursed in helpless frustration. While they were distracted with Rion, Incuban had positioned himself between Farad and Dewalaren, effectively neutralizing the most critical element of their plans. Farad could not reach his cousin to aid him.

Ron's, Andra's, Ara's, and Gar's bows sang, but their arrows were incinerated in midflight before they could reach Incuban.

Dewalaren screamed and charged toward the Enemy, his Sword blazing. To his horror, Farad saw the cascade of fire arc toward his King. Heart hammering in terror, Farad lunged for his cousin in vain, knowing he had no hope of reaching him in time, cursing their battle strategy of keeping him safely to the side, in reserve for when they most needed him. What would it matter, if Dewalaren fell?

"YOU WILL NOT HARM HIM!" roared a voice from where a pool of fire had been only a moment ago, and bolts of silver lightning slammed into Incuban. **"THETELA, HOUERFASHANG PYRFIER, SERVIERE ETH ESCOLIER, FAEREN ET SCHLIEREN!"**

Incuban stumbled back from the lightning, and His flame arced harmlessly away from Dewalaren, although Dewalaren was knocked from his feet by the proximity of the blast. Seeing he was alive, for the moment miraculously unharmed, Farad angled toward him, as Desmond ran toward Incuban, double-bladed axe raised.

Incuban carelessly waved His hand and a gout of flame slammed into the Dwarven High-King's chest, blasting him backward.

Donovar, who had been running for Incuban, axe held high, checked his charge and instead ran to his fallen friend.

Desenia, seeing her father fall, screamed in grief and rage and ran for Incuban.

Jargas slammed into her, barely knocking her to the floor in time as another burst of flame blazed from Incuban's outstretched fingertips. Jargas writhed for a moment as his back burned, then rolled upon it, and the flames extinguished.

Shadala ran to him as Laedrin ran for Incuban.

"Father, no!" Magus cried, looking at Laedrin in horror as a wave of flame arced unchecked for the Elven High-King. But it never reached him. It instead curled away from him harmlessly, as if sucked toward something else.

"THETELA, HOUERFASHANG PYRFIER, SERVIERE ETH ESCOLIER, FAEREN ET SCHLIEREN!" a terrible Voice roared, as red lightning crackled forth from Arcanus's outstretched hands. "Magus, now, hold him! Talon, quickly, your Sword!"

Finally, at long last, they would slay this monster! Farad ran full tilt for them, then cursed as something unexpectedly slammed into him from behind, knocking him to the ground. No! A Dwarven Revenant! He had been so focused upon Incuban, he had forgotten the cavern was swarming with other enemies, ones the bulk of their forces were battling. His blood froze and he fought back a wave of both bile and tears as he recognized him. It was Devron, one of the Throne Guard of the Lost Kingdom of Axemore. He'd last seen him the day before the Mountain fell.

Fortunately, the monster that was once his friend had apparently been instructed to subdue him, not slay him, or the double-bladed axe it carried would have been imbedded in his back, not held at his throat. Screaming in frustration, loss, and rage, Farad wrenched the axe backward with his Power, jerking the blade into the stunned Revenant's throat, though not forcefully enough to behead him. The Dwarven blade King Valar had gifted him completed that grisly task.

Farad lurched to his feet and saw that silver lightning had joined the red as the two wizards fought side by side. Incuban was beaten back against a wall, pinned helplessly by the combined assault. To his dismay Farad saw Dewalaren run for Incuban, thrusting the King's Sword toward Him, without Farad's crucial aid.

To Farad's horror, Incuban laughed wildly, joyously, at the bold attack. He flicked His finger toward Dewalaren, and Kathalanar spun harmlessly away, clattering to the floor.

His other hand reached out, and moved as if He were swatting a fly, and both Arcanus and Magus were slammed against the stone floor by a similar invisible wave of Power.

"Foolish mortals!" Incuban roared as He grabbed Dewalaren by the throat, reaching for his hand to claw the King's Ring from his finger. His eyes showed confusion when he realized it was not upon Dewalaren's hand, and then narrowed in hatred and rage. **"DEWALAREN, SON OF EVANAREN...,"** He began, but His words ended in a gurgle, as He clawed at His throat with the hand that had been searching for the Ring, struggling to pull out the blade that was now imbedded in His neck. He dropped Dewalaren, and the Ring gleamed from the finger of Farad's outstretched hand, exposed when he had thrown his dagger.

Dewalaren gasped raggedly, fighting to breathe, as he started dragging himself toward Kathalanar.

LUNAHR ran forward, snatching up the Sword Dewalaren had dropped, running toward Incuban. Kathalanar blazed as he used his link to Farad to call upon the Power of the Ring. But he stopped in confusion, only feet from Incuban, as Incuban exerted all His will upon him, battling against the Power of the Ring, commanding him to surrender Kathalanar. The light left the Sword and slowly, reluctantly but obediently, Lunahr extended his hand out to Incuban, to hand Kathalanar to Him, instead of skewering Him with it.

"Lunahr, no! As you love Dewalaren and Farad, as you love me and Leonas and Rion, kill him!" Magus yelled, but the voice was no longer his.

Lunahr turned to him in astonishment. The figure on the ground wavered and flowed. The silver hair changed to gold, the blue eyes to green, and the features shimmered and reformed to ones he loved and had never thought to see again. "Aras?" Lunahr asked in joy and astonished wonder.

"For me, for Aranahr, for Meloneth, hear us sing to you!" Aras cried, and Lunahr's eyes lost their focus as he turned his attention inward for a moment and his face lit with a beatific smile. Then his eyes turned hard and cold and deadly, and the Sword blazed to life again. In a single smooth motion he thrust it forward, into Incuban's heart. Incuban gurgled a final scream, then with a tremendous thunderclap, He vanished, leaving only a pile of ash where He had leaned against the wall.

Lunahr sat upon the ground, where he'd been thrown by the force of the blast, looking, dazed, at the twisted, smoking, blackened mass that was once his right hand. The remains of the Sword's hilt had been welded to his flesh by the blast. The impervious pyrenteum blade was completely gone.

Dewalaren dragged himself over to Lunahr, calling for Farad, for the Ring.

Donovar ran to them, leaving Desmond where he lay.

RON, Andra, Ara, Gar, and Rarnak ran to where Rion had fallen. Rion was completely naked, save for a collar about his neck, the kind a disobedient dog might wear. His small, lean body was splotched everywhere with brutal bruises, crisscrossed by lash marks, blade slashes, brand marks and other burns. He was sprawled across the cold stone floor, eyes wide open but unseeing.

Ron knelt beside him and felt for his heartbeat with shaking hands, but there was none to find. Wordlessly, he took Rion tenderly in his arms.

Andra brushed the hair from Rion's sightless eyes, then stroked her hand against his eyelids, closing them, as tears began streaming down her face. Ara and Gar began to cry as well, and Rarnak, who was holding Andra, both trying to comfort her and desperately seeking comfort from her.

Ron carried Rion toward the others, oblivious of the fighting dying down around them as the now masterless Revenants were slaughtered by Talon's army.

DESENIA checked Jargas frantically for injury and he did his best to calm her. "It's all right, beloved. It was my shirt and hair that caught. The flame only grazed me. Even then the armor bore the worst of it, though it almost melted even from such a glancing blow."

"Then Father…," she sobbed, falling into Jargas's arms, knowing that he could not have survived such a direct blast. Jargas held her and turned to where Desmond lay.

Desmond sat up, a dazed expression upon his face.

Jargas stared at him in astonishment.

Desenia felt it across their bond, rather than seeing it. She looked up in disbelief, ran to him, and sobbed, "Father! I thought you dead! His flame hit you squarely. How can you still live? Don't try to sit! Wait until Jargas can use the Knife upon you."

"I'm fine, Desenia, I have no need of the Knife. Remember, this is Rowanar's armor. Fire cannot harm me, as long as I wear it," he reminded her soothingly.

SELENE ran up to Arcanus and hugged him tightly. "Oh, Father, you did it! It worked! We tricked Him!" she sobbed joyfully, tears flowing down her face.

"Hush, child. It's all right now," Arcanus soothed, holding her gently.

"Magus is all right, isn't he?" she asked, and Arcanus nodded.

"Magus is safe, in the Grove, in Nalea. He is very well guarded. He played his part well, as did you, Daughter, and Aras. Magus channeled Aranas's energy to Aras, through their bond, just as we had planned. Aras would not have had such Power were it not for your brother. It is fortunate Aras was not Magus. Magus would have died from that attack, when his true name was spoken, while the High-Prince was all but unharmed." Arcanus's gaze fell upon Lunahr. "Beryl had the Power of the Ring, through his bond to Hunter, but not its protection, to shield him from the blast. He is fortunate he was not killed."

THE glow of the Knife faded, and Lunahr looked at his uninjured hand and wiggled his fingers in relief. He smiled, but his smile quickly faded as he saw Ron and his burden. "Rion!" he cried in agony, as Ron gently laid him upon the ground.

"Rion is dead," Ron said, his voice wooden, but tears were flowing freely down his face.

Elanara burst into tears and began sobbing against her brothers.

Eladar said in stunned denial, "No, he is not dead. He cannot be. Talon did not give him leave to die."

Lunahr touched Rion gently, eyes unfocused, and then focused again. "I cannot, not this time. There is nothing, not even an ember," he said and began to cry also.

Eladar left Elanara with Elavar and went to comfort him.

"He is not dead," Aras said, limping over to them. "Talon, you must heal his body. His spirit is elsewhere."

DEWALAREN stared at Aras, still reeling from seeing him alive when he knew him to be dead. He wanted to hug him, to hold him, to tell him how he loved him, to never let him go. He wanted to scream at him for deceiving him, for forcing him to endure the agony of the past weeks. Instead, he spoke in a soft voice. "Aras, he is dead. You cannot bring him back. I cannot, not this time. We knew we would be too late to save him. Even had he lived, after what the Enemy did to him, he would no longer have been the Man we loved. He has no Power. We could not have suppressed his memories nor removed them, even with the Ring. We could not have healed his core. It is better this way. But the Enemy has, even in his defeat, claimed his final victory against us."

Aras smiled at Dewalaren wearily. "Things are not always what they seem, Talon, or do you forget you thought me dead, also? You and Aranas both felt me burn. I almost killed you and him and Leonas because of it, when I had not even died myself.

"I had already made my alliance with Arcanus. I saved Magus from Incuban for him, but I weakened myself greatly doing so. It was then that Mother finally discovered my deceptions and attacked. She had overpowered me, but Arcanus fought for control of me. The fire you felt was his fire, in my core, as he wrenched me away from her. He burned her away. She did not survive it. I almost did not survive it. It incinerated my links to you and to Aranas, and so, you thought me dead.

"I realized that, were I to remain dead, much as it would hurt those who loved me, I would be safer to attack Incuban. But I needed to have the Power of the Grove still, somehow, although I could not touch Aranas to restore my link to him. So I wrote the letter to my father, linked to Magus, and then sent him to Nalea, to the Grove. I tried to give you all hope, at the end of my letter, without revealing myself, though I was truly terrified of dying, after having come so very close.

"Magus linked to Aranas for me. Magus has been channeling the Grove's Power to me, so I would be strong enough to fight Incuban. And we put Circe here. We let Incuban think she came out of weakness, rather than strength, so that she could betray Him from within. She sacrificed terribly so that we might be able to defeat Him. She did so to keep Magus safe from Him, for she loves him. I think she is glad to know that he is not truly her brother, now," he said, and astonishingly, Circe blushed.

"But we did not plan everything. We did not expect Rion to be captured, though it worked to our great advantage. Circe had no part in Incuban locating Rion in Gosa, through his Elfstone. It was Magus who had given Incuban that knowledge, when he was taken for the second time, though Incuban found Rion through the traces of Circe's Power yet within the Elfstone. It was, unfortunately, Hunter who betrayed the Watchtower to Incuban, while imprisoned in Malar, when Incuban entered his thoughts there. Hunter never realized how deeply he had been compromised, but Incuban taunted Arcanus with that knowledge.

"When Rion was taken, we sought to keep him safe. We have kept him safe, despite how he appears. His body has been horribly damaged here, and my attack has stopped his heart, but his core has not been harmed. His mind and his spirit are safe. He is with Circe. Through her, I took Rion's spirit from him and replaced it with a Resemblant, so that it might scream and beg and fool Incuban into thinking it was truly Rion in torment. I will start Rion's heart again. I can do so, as it is I who stopped it. He should still have lived, even with all the suffering he endured. Then you will heal his body and Circe will rekindle the flame in his core, and he will be returned to us."

THE others were staring at Aras, horrified at what they had heard, the cold calculation of it, the calm recounting of so much suffering. Aras eyed them all sadly and then looked Dewalaren in the eye, expecting to see horror, revulsion. Instead, he saw love—pure, unbridled love—yet still he dared not hold any hope for what it might mean. Dewalaren had loved him and turned against him before.

Aras told Dewalaren and the others to move back, and then he gently placed his right hand on Rion's head and his left over his heart. There was a flash of silver light, and Rion's back arched in a spasm as lightning shot through Rion's slender form.

They watched in awe as Rion's chest rose and fell, but he was otherwise limp, motionless.

Dewalaren knelt beside him and used the Knife, healing Rion's brutally burnt, whipped, and battered body.

"Come, Circe," Aras said, and Selene walked to Rion, knelt beside him, bent over him and kissed him on the mouth.

RION'S eyes snapped open, his heart hammering in terror. He struggled, terrified, away from Circe, who leaned over him. He had to get away from the two of them! He felt strong arms around him and fought them.

"Rion, hush, it's me. It's Aras. It's all right. You're safe now."

Rion stopped struggling, and looked up into Aras's concerned face in shock. "Aras? No, it cannot be! You're dead. Talon told me.... The whisper, it was you, it was your voice, I recognized it. You spoke my true name and then...." He looked about in confusion and saw he was no longer in that awful room, and all his friends, old and new, were clustered around him, expressions of shock and wonder on their faces. Many of their faces were streaked with tears. He thought they must have been overcome with joy seeing Aras lived, when he should be dead. "But what's been happening? Where are we? Where is He, the Enemy? He was here. He was... where are my clothes?" he asked in shock, as he realized he was naked and saw that Elanara was one of the ones staring at him in wonder. Then he remembered the Tower and what he had done to her, and he turned away from her, agonized.

"The Enemy is dead, Rion. The War is over, or soon will be. It has been less than a day since you were taken. You need only know, for now, that you are safe, you are well, and you are amongst friends. Later you will hear all that's happened," Aras assured him.

Rion noticed Lunahr and was incredibly relieved to see he had miraculously survived the invasion of the Tower. Then he belatedly realized who Lunahr was holding, and his eyes widened in astonishment. "Eladar! But how...?"

To Rion's joy Eladar smiled at him, as if he had never forgotten how. "Surely you cannot believe you are the only one they value enough to bring back from the dead," Eladar teased.

The smile left Rion's face and he swallowed. "Dead?" he said, in a small voice. "You mean I...."

Eladar said, "It is in the past, Rion. Much has happened, there is much you must hear, but Aras is right. You need not hear it now. Suffice it to say, you owe your life to Talon and Aras, as much as I owe mine to Beryl." He gazed lovingly at Lunahr. "I will enjoy repaying my debt to him. He is my *lythenia.*"

Rion looked at him in surprise. "*Lythenia?* Congratulations! I... I envy you, Eladar, having someone you might love." He looked wistfully at Elanara, without meaning to.

ELADAR could not bear to see the look of longing on Rion's face. He resolved he would speak to High-King Laedrin on his sister's behalf, as she would not speak to him upon her own.

MAK approached Rion shyly. "Ran na haat, na kala?" he asked.

"Mak! But I thought...." He trailed off and looked at Lunahr questioningly.

"He wasn't killed, Rion. He's an Ogre. We all forgot how tough they are. Even the Enemy thought he was dead, when he wasn't. They hurt him terribly, but Jargas healed him."

"Mak ga Ran? Mak Ran fran?" he asked shyly.

"Of course you're my friend. But what about your people, Mak? We freed them, I can see that much," he said. There were Ogres all over the cavern, working with the Dwarven warriors to behead the last of the Revenants. Some of the Ogres were using clubs and war axes, but some were merely grabbing them and tearing their heads off. Rion felt ill watching and turned away.

His eyes met Hunter's. Hunter approached him, then, as if summoned by him. There was a sword in his hand, a sheathed blade. To Rion's surprise, he recognized it as his own, the one Hunter had gifted to him. To his astonishment Hunter walked up to him and wrapped his arms around him and hugged him tightly. "We have saved you. Aras promised me we would save you, though I did not realize it was him, at the time. He made me believe it. I had to. I could not have gone on otherwise. I have known you for such a short time, Rion, yet you are like a brother to me, perhaps even as a son to me," he said, his voice gruff with emotion.

Rion was shocked and touched. He had never thought to hear someone like Hunter voice such a thing to him.

"My House sword was lost long ago, but this sword would do the Heir to House of Wolven proud, were there ever to be one. Like my father before me, I cherish the bow and am skilled with the knife. Such a sword was not meant for my hands. Please keep it, Rion. Someday it might save your life, though I hope you need never again lift a blade in your own defense or of that of anyone you love. Do not blame the blade for the use to which it was put."

"Thank you, Hunter, I... I am so glad to have known you. I hope you also might finally live in peace, now that the Enemy who has hounded you for so long is dead," Rion said, hugging him back.

JARNATH, Laedrin, Shadala, and Leonas all clustered about Aras now, touching him fearfully, as if they were afraid he was but a dream. He reassured all of them and then sought out the one he most needed to see, to hear, to feel.

"Dewalaren," Aras said softly, his voice embracing the name lovingly. Aras looked at him shyly. "You do not look at me in fear or hatred anymore," he said cautiously. "Even now, having heard so much, you do not. I have tricked you and used you all. I had to, even knowing you would hate me for it. But I do not see hate or even fear now, in your eyes."

Dewalaren shook his head. "I neither fear nor hate you, Aras," he agreed softly.

Aras continued onward carefully. "Then, do you think that perhaps you and I might still be friends?"

"You and I are much more than mere friends, Aras. I once told you that you were becoming many things to me. You are friend, brother, teacher, student, companion, confidant, lifeline, anchor, and healer, both of my body and my spirit. But most of all, Aras, beloved, I hope you might be *lythenia* to me," Dewalaren said, gazing at Aras with hope in his eyes.

Aras's face lit in wonder and he hugged Dewalaren carefully, eyes wet with tears of joy. "I did not think you might.... I was afraid you would think.... My heart sings with such joy, I've not the words to express it."

"Then perhaps this is not the time for words," Dewalaren said, and he kissed Aras tenderly upon the mouth.

Aras let a little whimper of desire escape and responded eagerly. Then he pulled away and blushed darkly, conscious of those around them.

"The Chieftess is right, Aras. In many ways you are still a child," Dewalaren said fondly.

Aras started to protest, but Dewalaren put his finger to his lips. "You make me feel young again," he explained.

"I'm sorry I caused you such pain before. But there was still a good chance the Enemy might slay me, and I didn't want to torment you with false hope," Aras apologized.

"None of our hopes will be false after this. We are a free people again. We need no longer skulk in the alleyways of cities dressed in rags, hiding in the shadows," Dewalaren said.

"Where will you go?" Aras asked.

Dewalaren said carefully, "Not back over the Deathshand. That place is no longer home to us. I was hoping… there are so few of us… do you think the Chieftess and your father might allow us to stay in Nalea? We have caused terrible trouble for them, I know, but…."

"Of course! You are Shadala's King," Aras assured him.

Haran came over to Dewalaren. "Majesty, we've defeated all the Revenants here and the Ogres sealed the corridors so no more could come. But we must root out the rest, now."

Selene spoke up. "And we must free the prisoners. There are thousands of them, in the pens in the lower levels. I can lead you to them, and to the Armory. There are places we should try to seize first. Not all the Revenants are as mindless as these. The shock of Incuban's death will soon pass, and many of them are quite cunning."

Donovar went to her. "You have done enough, Granddaughter, more than enough. Let the others do their part. You shouldn't have to see any of it."

She hugged him. "I have to, Grandfather. I have to help atone for what I've done. Not only here, but before, when I was aiding Magus. Incuban did such terrible things to me, but also, He… He made me do such horrible things to some of the prisoners. Aras could not protect me as he protected Rion. My core is too bright. Incuban would have seen the change. He would have known. Please, Grandfather, I know you want to protect me, but it is too late for that, far too late. Arcanus thinks he has come in time to save me, but it remains to be seen whether or not I can yet be saved." She kissed him softly upon his brow and then quickly turned away from him.

DEWALAREN began issuing orders.

Rion approached him. He was wearing Ron's shirt, which came nearly to his knees, and was barefoot and barelegged. There was a sheathed sword in his hands. Dewalaren recognized it. It was the Dwarven blade Farad had gifted to him. Dewalaren scowled. "No. Absolutely not. You are to stay here, with Elanara and Eladar and Beryl to guard you. I will risk none of you further."

Rion looked innocently at him and smiled. "You misunderstand, Majesty. I do not come to you as a warrior, merely as a sword-bearer. You seem to be without your own sword and you should not enter such a battle without a reliable blade. I offer you mine. It is Dwarven. It will serve you well."

Dewalaren looked at Rion in surprise, and Rion grinned at him. Dewalaren shook his head in wonder to see it as he accepted the blade. "All you have been through, yet still you can smile! I envy you your indomitable spirit, Rion. I once said the Enemy was a fool for trying to catch you, that you would be His undoing."

RION'S face clouded. "But I did nothing to harm Him. I would have tumbled us both to the rocks below, when we flew on the chimaera, but I could not move. I would have used His own brands upon Him, but I was chained. I did nothing to Him, but He…." His face darkened in shame. Almost a full day had passed that he had no memory of. He shuddered, thinking what might have happened during that time that he had been found naked with a collar about his neck and Elanara and Ron and Andra and the others had been crying. He rubbed his throat where the collar had been self-consciously.

Hunter spoke then, from beside them. Neither of them had noticed him arrive. "Rion, you were invaluable. You kept the Enemy distracted so He was unaware of our approach or of Circe's betrayal, until the last moment. But most importantly, He is dead and you are not. Have you forgotten what I told you?"

"No. I greatly value your advice. I even told it to Andra. I helped her with your words, to never let anyone, especially the dead, make me feel less that I am, and how special I am," Rion said.

Rion turned to Talon. The Elves were closer than he would have liked and their ears were keen. "Majesty," he said, this time in Amontirin. "I'm glad you won't let Elanara and Eladar join you. You shouldn't. But please, you must insist Elavar stays to guard me as well. The Revenants here... many of them are Elves, from Riviera and Loatia. And I saw...." he shuddered at the memory and felt faint. He swayed, and both Talon and Hunter steadied him, in concern. "Their mother, the Queen. She is here. She's burnt and... she's terrible. They shouldn't remember her like that."

DEWALAREN closed his eyes and breathed deeply, then swallowed, thinking of Queen Naraena, such a bright, warm, beautiful light, turned into a hideous monster. He opened his eyes. "Thank you, Rion, for the warning. Do not worry. I will take care of it," he assured him.

Rion looked at him compassionately, thanked him sincerely and somberly, and then rejoined the others.

Dewalaren finished relaying his plans and casually commanded Elavar to stay with those guarding Rion and Lunahr. The rest of them were going to free the prisoners and take the Armory. They hoped that, in addition to keeping the weapons from the Enemy's army, they might also convince at least some of the prisoners to bear arms and aid them in their fight, for they were gravely outnumbered. From what Circe told them, there were yet many thousands of Revenants here, perhaps tens of thousands, to their own meager three thousand.

Aras told Dewalaren he would leave with the surviving Gryphon to pick up the rest of their army, to join in the fighting.

"But surely you cannot leave alone with them," Dewalaren protested. "How would you control them?"

"I will not. Though many of them are loyal to me, for my secret aid of them against my mother, it is Aerlyr who will sway them to assist me, out of his love for me, as he did before," Aras explained.

Dewalaren's voice sank to a whisper. "Aras, I cannot let you leave when you have only just returned to me. We are not linked. But I cannot link to you now, here, and without your father's blessing and permission. Aras, please! I would not know if you were in danger. I cannot ever lose you again. I would not survive it."

"Dewalaren, you must let me go," Aras said, hugging him. "Do not worry. I will be safe. You are the one going into terrible danger. Please, it is not easy for me to go when my heart begs me to stay, to keep you safe, always. But we need reinforcements. You must think with the heart of a King, now, not a *lythenia*. I would never want to see you so changed for your love of me."

Dewalaren hugged him tightly. "Do not be long. Go, quickly," he said, and turned from Aras, marching resolutely toward the others, who were awaiting him.

Aras turned and left, heading for the flight of Gryphon, and Aerlyr cried out in joy, apparently sensing he was soon to fly with Aras again.

THOUGH the Revenants in the chamber they had cleared were all beheaded, to ensure they were destroyed, they left their own fallen intact, laid out properly. Incuban was no longer there to animate them, to use their own dead against them. They would be able to bury them without first mutilating the bodies.

Rion aided Shadala, Jarnath, Donovar, and the other healers tending their wounded. Rion was glad he was being kept so busy. He was trying hard not to think of what had happened to him. He could imagine many appalling things. That room! That horrific room! A flash of memory seized him, of Incuban touring him around the room, the feel of the manacles closing about his wrists, Selene on top of him, before the blackness claimed him.

He felt a hand upon his shoulder and shrank from the touch, spinning about to lash out, and barely stopped himself in time. Eladar had sprung back from him but cautiously approached again. "I was going to ask if you are all right, but I can see you are not," he said in concern.

Rion inhaled deeply and exhaled just as deliberately. "No, I'm all right. Really, I'm fine. I just... I was thinking, when I shouldn't have been. I wish Aras and Selene had acted sooner. I... I know they had to wait, so He wouldn't suspect, but...."

"Why don't you talk to Mak?" Eladar said. "Lunahr told me how Mak not only helped him save Elanara, but Mak saved him as well, in the tunnels, when he was thinking too much. Besides, Mak is lonely and worried for his friends. They let him come to help rescue you, but they won't risk him any further. He's feeling left out."

Rion nodded thoughtfully and went to Mak. Eladar was right. He looked so sad and lost, left behind while all his people sought revenge in the tunnels for what the Enemy had done. Rion began speaking to him, comforting him, and felt better himself in doing so.

Rion was worried for his own friends inside the tunnels. Dwarven passages could be treacherous. Many corridors had hidden traps to discourage those who might try to breach their strongholds to plunder their Treasure Vaults. As if affirming his fears, wounded began to arrive from below, with guards to escort them and, too often, to carry them. Rion was soon hard at work bandaging the new wave of injured warriors, with Mak helping him by handing him bandages and other supplies.

"It's good to see you looking so well, lad. The brothers have been worried about you," a familiar voice said, as a Dwarf sat down. He was next to be bandaged. His arm was cut to the bone.

"Hernon! Let me see that. That's a pretty nasty wound. Mak, hand me the vial of... that's right, very good, Mak. I don't even have to ask you anymore, do I?"

He handed Hernon the vial. "Take a tiny sip only. It's Donovar's. It will dull the pain, without dulling your wits as well."

Hernon did so.

"Please, Hernon, tell me how it's going. We've so many wounded! Are we losing?" Rion asked fearfully.

"Nay, lad, we're not, though there's so many of the enemy, sometimes it's hard to tell. We've been destroying twenty Revenants for every one of our men who takes injury. Most of those injuries have not been serious, and fortunately, few have been fatal," Hernon said.

"The brothers, Andra, and Rarnak, are they still all right?" Rion asked, afraid to hear they might not be.

"Aye, lad. We had a bit of a fright, though, when we lost the King," Hernon said.

"Lost? What do you mean, lost? Which King?" Rion asked fearfully.

"King Talon. But don't worry, lad, we found him again. Alive, thanks to the brothers and Andra. King Talon had pulled ahead of the rest of us, too far ahead. Hunter was just trying to call him back, warning him the corridors themselves are dangerous, when the King passed two of them, one on the right, and one on the left. We heard the grinding of stone, and suddenly an army of Revenants came pouring out of the mouths of both, cutting King Talon off from our aid. There must have been a hidden passage they opened, for he later swore they'd been empty when he passed.

"We fought to reach King Talon in time to help him. The brothers and Andra were the first to reach him. No one could touch them, the way they fight as a team. They just cut a swath right through the Enemy's ranks. They were barely in time. The sheer press of numbers had driven King Talon to his knees. The siblings encircled him, protecting him, and then cut their way back over to the rest of us. King Talon got an earful from both Hunter and Jargas for it, after the fighting eased. He'll not soon be taking such a foolish chance again."

"I should be there. I should be helping," Rion said, tying off Hernon's bandage.

Hernon flexed his fingers and closed his hand into a fist, testing it and then hefted his axe. "You have helped enough already, lad. You're the reason we're here. You've already played a bigger part in what has happened than any one man should have to. And you are helping still. It's thanks to you I can rejoin the fray," Hernon said, smiling at him. Then he stood and headed back for the corridors.

With the new influx of wounded, Rion was kept too busy to feel sorry for himself for a long while. Then a party of Dwarves came from the corridors, at least a dozen of them all clustered together. Rion feared one of the Kings might have fallen. Everyone else came up in two's and threes, the healthy often leading or carrying the injured.

The Dwarves parted, and Rion saw to his surprise it was Jarina who was escorted, but she appeared well. She walked over to Lunahr. "Beryl, King Talon has commanded me to bring these to you. It is too dangerous, now, for him to carry them in the tunnels. We cannot risk them being lost. But also, our casualties are becoming greater, more severe. You can still bandage those who are not seriously injured, but we will not lose any more men when we have the Power to save them. You are to use the Knife to heal those who are otherwise beyond helping."

Fenlon cleared his throat awkwardly and spoke up. "Forgive me, Princess Jarina, but King Talon did not command you to bring them to Beryl. He commanded you to bring them here to be used. I was under the impression he thought you would be using them yourself."

Jarina smiled at him sweetly, though her veil hid much of it. "He only did so because Jargas begged it of him. We cannot afford to lose a warrior merely because my brother fears for my safety."

Rion swallowed. "Is it truly as bad as that, that every person is vital?"

"I am afraid so," she said to Rion, the smile leaving her face. "We are seriously outnumbered. But the King fears the prisoners will be killed if we do not reach them soon. We cannot risk waiting for the reinforcements Aras went for. Although King Talon is already concerned that Aras has not yet returned. He expected him before this. I fear his heart is guiding the battle, rather than his head. He has been making mistakes, when he can ill afford to."

"Then we are going with you," Elavar said, and Eladar stepped to his side. Rion had not noticed them approach. "There is no need for us to remain, now that so many wounded are here. They can fight to protect the healers, and Rion and the other noncombatants, if necessary."

"No! Please, Elavar, Eladar! You can't. Talon's your King. You swore oath to him. He commanded you to stay with me. You can't go," Rion said desperately.

Eladar said gently, "Rion, I know you're afraid, I can understand you are, after what's happened, but...."

"No, please, Eladar, you don't understand. I... you can't go, you can't! The Revenants, there are Elves, hundreds or perhaps thousands of them, from Loatia, from Riviera. They're your people, your friends. You can't see them like that," Rion begged.

"Rion, we know. We are prepared for what we might see, but...," Eladar said, but Rion would not let him finish.

"No! Please, I'm begging you not to! You can't. You'll see her and you can't. Not like that. She was so beautiful once, so regal, but now she's so horrible...," Rion said, shaking. He'd said too much. He'd not been able to stop. She was there before his mind's eye again, hideous and burnt, kissing him.

Elanara had approached as they spoke, and she paled. "Mother?" she asked, looking intently into his eyes. He could not hold her gaze. He turned his head away, looking at her brothers, and nodded yes.

Elavar and Eladar looked ill. Eladar said bravely, "Then we must go. We'll see her laid to rest."

Lunahr stepped to his side. "You're not leaving without me. Your parents cared for me as if I was their own. I must help you. And I will not let you go without me, Eladar."

Rion looked about for something he could use as a weapon. There were the dead from earlier, in the initial assault in that cavern. Fortunately, few had died since, but most of them had been armed with axes.

"No, Rion. They need you here, to care for the wounded. And you cannot face an army of Revenants, not after what you've been through," Lunahr argued.

Eladar hugged Lunahr tightly. "Neither can you, my *lythenia,* my love. I can hear the terror in your thoughts, I can feel it. But also, you must stay to use the Knife to heal those who are in danger of dying. You must let Elavar and me go alone. You must stay and keep Rion and Elanara safe for us. You slew Incuban himself, Beryl. Your fighting is done, yet your role in this battle is still of vital importance. There is no telling how many you've yet to save."

LUNAHR wanted to protest, to argue, but he knew he had an important duty to fulfill. He was also truly terrified. He feared he would endanger Eladar by going. He nodded, his eyes wet with unshed tears. He pulled away from Eladar. "Go, quickly, before I beg for you to stay," he said, kissing Eladar lightly on the cheek.

"I swear I will return to you, Lunahr," Eladar said in Elvish. Then he turned and headed with Elavar and Jarina toward the corridor, along with the dozen Dwarves.

RION felt a terrible sense of loss as they left. He turned from their receding forms, and his eyes accidentally fell upon Elanara. He turned quickly away from her, again.

A short while later they heard the shrill screech of eagles, and the flight of Gryphon appeared at the door to the Mountain and began landing in the cavern. Aras dismounted and came over to Rion, his face lined with concern, seeing all the injured.

"Is Talon safe? How is the battle going?" he asked anxiously.

"Aras! We were worried about you! Talon's still safe. At least, he was last I heard from someone," Rion added.

"I didn't mean to take so long, but we had so few men left for the Gryphon to carry, I thought to go to Malar to get more. I figured our allies would want a hand in the final battle. And then I realized to exclude Dorolingas and Ironhand might cause dissent in the future. The alliance between those three Kingdoms is an uneasy one, and I'll not see a future conflict scar this land, once the current War ends. I brought eight hundred warriors from each of the three Kingdoms, including their Kings, as well as healers from each. I thought we might need them. The rest of the Gryphon are carrying supplies. I feared there might be need of them. The dead, even those who walk, do not eat, and the Enemy might well have poisoned what food was here for the prisoners, and we may be fighting here for some time yet," Aras reported.

"Aras, you are wonderful! I'm afraid we need the healers as much as we need the warriors, and you are right that we'll likely be here long enough to need the supplies as well," Rion said. He told Aras what he knew of the fighting in the caverns below.

Aras had the warriors he brought unload the Gryphon. Then he hugged Aerlyr and spoke to him in Elvish, and the flight of Gryphon took off from the cavern, heading out riderless. Rion realized the terrifyingly beautiful winged creatures would not be able to fight effectively in the confines of the tunnels, even were they willing to aid them further.

Aras sent the healers to Rion, and some of the newly tended wounded led Aras and his troops into the caverns.

Lunahr directed some of the walking wounded to begin sorting the supplies and preparing food and water stations for the warriors who were still battling.

Mak eagerly volunteered to help. He began carrying supplies to different areas as directed. He had the strength of his kind, for all his young age and small size. Rion was relieved. Mak had been looking increasingly dejected, though he'd continued to help Rion tend the wounded. Mak was worried about his friends. He still felt he should be fighting beside them. Rion knew how he felt.

Rion introduced Jarnath and Donovar to the other healers, and they soon got to work caring for the wounded, who continued to arrive.

As the night dragged on, Rion kept glancing toward the corridor mouths, eager to see familiar faces, yet afraid he might, knowing that if they were coming out to him, it would likely be because they were injured. He was bandaging someone and didn't see Jargas until he was fifty feet away. He was running and Rion realized he was carrying someone. His heart froze. "Jarina, we've need of the Ring!" Jargas bellowed.

Lunahr ran over to Jargas, and Rion did as well. He had to see who it was. It was a Dwarf he recognized, Sarnon, King Rongas's Steward. He was drenched in blood. "Close your eyes," Lunahr commanded, and the Ring flared with Power.

A few moments later, Sarnon sat up suddenly, crying "Majesty!"

"It's all right, Sarnon. You saved him," Jargas assured Sarnon. "You're the one who almost died, taking the axe that had been meant for him. He'd have carried you here himself, but he knew he wouldn't make it in time. You're to rest here. That's an order from my father. You've done enough for one day. Hernon and I and the others will keep Father safe."

Jargas turned and scowled at Lunahr. "Where is Jarina? Why are you the one wielding the Ring?"

Lunahr swallowed. "Jarina left again for the tunnels hours ago, after delivering the Ring and the Knife to me. She went with Eladar and Elavar, I mean Thorn and Sylvan. She said things were going badly, that you needed all the warriors you had. You mean you haven't seen her?"

Jargas cursed. "In those corridors? I've not seen many. There are corridors you wade through that are waist deep in heads. We've men spread everywhere, just keeping our retreat secure. No wonder she's been shielding herself from me. She must be shielding herself from Hunter as well. I must go back."

Rion said, "Jargas, wait. Tell the others as you see them there's food and water here for them now, as well as healing. And make sure King Talon knows Aras has returned, that he's safe, or at least, he was hours ago. He's brought two-thousand-four-hundred more men, in addition to the last of our army. He went to Malar and Ironhand and Dorolingas for them."

"Aye, I'll tell them. That's good news indeed. No wonder we've been faring better than we had been," he said, looking around, and then he unexpectedly smiled. "Gervan! Arvan!" he called out, and two of the new healers turned to him and smiled back. The elder looking of the two came to him, but the younger was busy treating someone.

"Jargas! It's good seeing you again! Is your kinsman Hunter here as well, or have you parted company with him since leaving us?" Gervan asked.

"Parted and rejoined, more than once. He's here, in the tunnels below. He's well now, fully healed, mind and body both. You'll not recognize him. He's married to my sister," Jargas said, then scowled. "And she's not where she should be. I'm sorry, Gervan,

I'll have to speak with you later. I must go back. There's still a War to fight, when we'd hoped it over. We'd no idea how many troops the Enemy had here, or that they'd be so formidable even without that monster to lead them."

"Of course. Jargas. Please keep an eye out for King Valar as well. Arvan and I are terribly worried about him. He's young yet. This is his first battle," Gervan said, his voice warm with concern.

"I'll be sure to see he is kept safe," Jargas assured him, and then he headed back to the corridors.

Sarnon rose, and Lunahr said, "Didn't Jargas command you to stay here and rest? The Ring has healed your injury, but you still need to rest."

Sarnon said, "I'll stay, but I'll not rest, at least not yet, not when there's an army to feed. Someone's got to see the King and everyone else gets a hot meal." He headed determinedly for the cooking pots lining one wall of the cavern.

Lunahr exhaled loudly. "I was afraid he'd head for the corridors. I'm relieved I needn't be the one to try to stop him. I'd certainly not be able to keep him from King Rongas's side. But neither would I have wanted to be the one to try to explain to King Rongas why we let him go!"

Rion smiled at Lunahr. He'd felt the same. He was glad Lunahr was here with him. He looked for Elanara. He'd not seen her hovering about in a while. He was concerned she might have slipped off into the corridors, without anyone realizing. But then he spotted her. She was by the cook fires, helping prepare the meals for the men. He watched her; he could not help himself. Then someone called for aid, and he got back to work.

Dawn broke, visible through the door to the Mountain, which had been kept open. No one knew what Aras might have told the Gryphon, and they didn't want to accidentally seal them out. Men had been coming up in groups, for food and for rest. Many of them appeared exhausted. Rion was tired as well, but he couldn't rest when he was needed, and he was afraid he'd miss seeing his friends. Then finally he saw a familiar face, but was instantly afraid. It was Andra, but she was carrying someone, not as Jargas had been, in her arms, but over her shoulder, as if he were a sack of flour. She was staggering.

Rion called for Lunahr and then ran to her with some Dwarves. It was Rarnak she was carrying. They took him from her gently, laid him upon the ground, and carefully unwrapped the blood-soaked bandage about his leg. His leg had been almost completely severed just above the knee. The bone was cut clean through; only a small strip of flesh connected the two pieces of his leg. There was a strange second bandage above the wound. When Arvan moved toward it, Andra looked afraid. "Don't touch it or he'll die. Jarnath," she whispered, and then she toppled over. Rion barely caught her before she hit the floor. He checked her anxiously for injury, as Lunahr began using the Ring and Knife on Rarnak.

"Arvan, please, get Jarnath," Rion urged, and Arvan left to do so.

Jarnath approached. "She called for you, Jarnath. She wouldn't let us touch the second bandage," Rion said anxiously.

Jarnath's eyes widened. "It's well she warned you. It's called a *fethana*. It's a special bandage for when an artery or vein is severed, to keep the person from bleeding to death.

It will be safe to remove it once the Ring and the Knife do their work. This is Aras's handiwork. I'm the only other Elven healer here and I doubt any other would know how to do this. I must speak to her, for news of Aras."

Rion felt Andra's heart. It was beating strongly. She must have collapsed from sheer exhaustion. Who knew how long she'd carried Rarnak, on top of having fought all day as well? "Why did no one help her bring him?" he asked, afraid. It boded ill for their men.

Jarnath gave her something to drink. She coughed and choked, but awoke and seemed fully aware. "Rarnak!" she cried in concern and fought to sit.

Rion put his hands on her shoulder gently and held her down. It wasn't hard to do. She had little strength. "He'll be fine, now, Andra. You brought him to us in time," Rion soothed.

"His leg," she said, her eyes welling with tears.

"It's all right, we've saved it. He'll be able to walk again. He'll even be able to run," Lunahr said reassuringly.

Rion said, "Please, Andra, what of the others? Are your brothers and Aras all right? Why was no one with you to help you carry Rarnak?"

"It's madness down there. We've reached the pens where the prisoners are. There are thousands upon thousands of Revenants, but also thousands of prisoners. They've been using them as shields. Oh, Elmoth! The children! I have to go back. They need me."

"Drink this. It will give you what you need. Careful. Only two small sips," Jarnath cautioned.

She drank eagerly, gratefully. Then she stroked Rarnak's face tenderly. He was still unconscious. "Why isn't he awake?" she asked anxiously.

"Because his body knows it still needs to rest after such an injury, even with the Power of the Knife to aid him," Jarnath said.

"I don't feel any different. I am so tired! Perhaps I should drink more," she said to Jarnath. Then she swayed and fell against him.

"What's wrong? What's happened?" Rion asked, afraid for her.

Jarnath said tiredly. "Do not worry, she is merely asleep. As I told her, I gave her what she needed. She would not have lasted more than a few moments in the battle she described. Come, we must rally every able-bodied man here and join those down in the corridors. I can fight as well as heal, and as we have seen, they need the healers where the battle is, now."

Jarnath went to Sarnon and Donovar, and the three of them quickly organized every man who could yet hold a weapon. Rion took Rarnak's sword and joined them. Lunahr was with them, as was Elanara. No, not her! Rion spoke to her, he had no choice. "Please, Elanara, you cannot go," he said in Elvish to her.

"You treat me as if I do not exist for an entire day, and then presume to tell me what I can and cannot do?" she said with all the imperious aloofness he had always heard Elves were supposed to possess.

"I…. Elanara, please! You could be hurt, killed. I won't let you be hurt, not ever again. You must stay here. It's safe here," Rion pleaded.

"I don't want to be safe. I want to help," she said, unknowingly echoing Rion's words in the Tower. "I'll not stand idly by while you walk calmly to your doom a second time."

Calmly? He was terrified. And she truly thought they marched to their deaths? No wonder she needed to come. Both her brothers, her last remaining family, were down there.

Mak came up to Rion, a Dwarven war axe in his hands.

"Mak, you cannot come with us. You have to stay here," Rion pleaded. He had to know at least Mak would be safe.

Mak looked at Rion levelly. "Na. Mak kap Ran saf."

"Mak, please! I can keep myself safe. I can't risk you being hurt, dying. When I saw you fall at the Tower, it was terrible," Rion argued.

"Ran nad Mak. Mak gad Ran. Kap Ran saf," Mak said firmly. "Hap fran. Hap kasan. Hap Baga Mama. Hap Kang Talan. Hap Ran. Hap all."

Rion knew what it was like, wanting so desperately to help his friends, to fight. If he didn't let Mak come now, he might try to follow them, sneak off alone after them. "All right. But you stay beside me, no matter what, so I can help keep you safe too, understand?"

"Ya. Mak sta ba Ran, Mak kap Ran saf, Ran kap Mak saf," he said solemnly.

They gathered almost two hundred men, those whose wounds were not overly severe, and others, who were uninjured and had eaten and rested and were refreshed enough to battle again. More still joined them, who had come to them exhausted and hungry and not had the chance to either eat or rest, but would not see their comrades go into battle without them.

To Rion's surprise it was Donovar who led them, forming them into groups and barking orders as if he had led troops to battle many times before. The men rallied around him without question, as if he were a great warrior champion, or a King, rather than a healer.

They quickly made their way toward the heart of the Mountain. The beheaded dead lined the corridors everywhere. There were indeed waist-high piles of heads, but no longer staggered troops lining the corridors keeping the retreat clear, as Jargas had described. *All the men must be down below*, Rion thought.

The corridors seemed to go on forever, but they kept sloping downward, always downward. Those who had come up before guided Donovar so he did not lead them down any false passages, and they had marked the traps well, so they could be easily avoided.

Rion marveled that Andra could have carried Rarnak so far, all uphill. No wonder she'd been so exhausted! Rion fought his own fatigue. He could help. He had to help.

They lost about twenty men on the way down. Between their injuries and fatigue, they simply couldn't make it so far, though they tried. They left them in the corridors filled with the dead, and hoped they would be able to return to them, after the battle was done.

They could hear the sounds of fighting up ahead now and quickened their pace. The corridor opened up suddenly. They were standing on a wide ledge above a tremendous chamber. Rion thought it might once have been a Great Hall. It was a huge natural cavern. It must have been beautiful once. But it had been turned into a series of pens, divided and fenced with wire mesh, even over the tops. They held not animals, but people. Everywhere there were prisoners: men, women, and children, though only Men and Dwarves. There was no River or Wood here to sustain Elven prisoners.

There were Revenants, thousands of them, as well as wolven-riders, wolven, and pumar, in a pitched battle with their own warriors. Andra had said it was madness, and it truly was. Their warriors were surrounded on all sides by great heaps of corpses. The enemy were climbing over them and springing at their forces.

Donovar bellowed with a commander's voice, "We'll attack them from behind, drive a wedge into them to reach that pen there." He pointed to the target, his booming voice carrying above the din of battle. "There are at least a thousand men there. You can see them, straining to escape, to help join the fight. They can take up the weapons of the fallen and aid us. To victory!" he yelled, and dozens of Dwarven and Men's voices took up the cry as they began racing down the sloping corridor toward the pen.

They charged into the enemy's rear, axes and swords swinging. Rion remembered what Ron had told him of what Swiftsong had taught them about using the bow. He forced himself not to look at the swarming mass of Revenants in its entirety, but focused instead upon a single weapon arm or neck or head and attacked. It was the only way he could keep from running screaming in terror from them. Mak and Elanara matched him blow for blow as they hacked and slashed their way toward the pen. Neither strayed far from him. He tried to keep Lunahr in sight, too, but lost track of him in the chaos of the battle.

More and more of the Enemy's forces began turning toward them to meet their attack, as they recognized the new danger. Rion saw men to the right and to the left of him fall. He realized in cold dread that they would not make it. There were too many enemy before them.

Suddenly, there was a hysterical, shrill babble of incoherent words and then a scream of pure terror. Rion's heart all but stopped as he recognized the voice. Lunahr, it was Lunahr! But where was he? Frantically, he fought to reach him, trying to judge his location by sound alone. Then he saw a flare of blinding red light, at twenty paces to his left. There was an army of Revenants in between.

He fought his way toward the flare. It was not fading but was instead a constant crimson brilliance. Rion beat his way toward it, eyes tearing from the glare.

Then from above, a figure descended toward the flare, flickering faintly with lightning, and Rion recognized it. Circe! He felt panic. She'd seen the red flare. She knew Lunahr had the Ring, and she was going to take it from him. He'd die without its Power to aid the Knife, which was healing him! Rion fought to reach her even as the red flare died. He heard a triumphant yell, and then she rose into the air again.

Now the lightning was coruscating brilliantly all around her. She thrust out her arms, fingers outstretched and tremendous arcs of lightning crashed down upon the enemy forces below her, as thunder cracked and boomed. She began moving the arc outward, fanning it everywhere. Rion saw it coming straight for him. He knocked Elanara and Mak to the ground, trying desperately to shield them with his own body. But miraculously, the lightning never came. Instead, it arced around him, to devastate the enemy before and behind him. He leapt to his feet and ran for Lunahr.

There were dozens of charred, smoking bodies everywhere. Lying amongst them he saw Lunahr. He was not burnt, but his clothes were slashed in a dozen places and red with blood. Rion knelt to him, trembling, feeling for his heartbeat. He was alive! He checked him for injury and was astonished to find none. He realized then what must have happened. As the Revenants had attacked and overwhelmed him, he'd been wounded over and over, only to have the Knife, powered by the Ring, heal him, apparently of its own accord, as he was not conscious.

"The pen! Rion, we can reach it now! We can set them free," Elanara cried.

"Elanara, stay here. Protect Lunahr. Mak and I will go," Rion ordered. "Mak, hurry! Come with me! I'll need your help!" He ran to the metal fence and saw a chained gate. "Stand back!" he cried to those inside. "Mak, use the war axe. Try to cut the chain!" Rion hoped the Dwarven blade might cut through the chain, but the Dwarves had apparently crafted it as well. Mak dropped the axe and began pulling on it. "Ta wak, ta small," he said in dismay.

A towering shape loomed over them and Rion spun around, prepared to fight. It was an Ogre, huge, at least ten feet tall. Rion fought terror. It was all he could do to keep from running, but he forced himself to remember the Ogres were on their side in this fight. At least he hoped all of them were. He stepped away from the fence slowly.

"Taka!" Mak cried in joy.

"Lata Mak, na pas ta faat," the big Ogre scolded. The imprisoned men shrank back from the gate as the Ogre reached out, grabbed the chain in both hands, and pulled it in opposite directions, muscles straining and bulging.

Rion saw the links beginning to deform, to distend and stretch, and finally one of them gave. The Ogre unwound the length of chain from the gate and swung it open. The men inside were cowering back in terror.

Rion ran to the gate. "It's all right! He's not here to eat you. The Ogres are on our side! They're helping us save you. This is your chance to be free, to avenge your Kingdoms, your families, your people! Incuban is dead, but His army still fights! We need your help to save the women and children!"

"Incuban is dead?" a chorus of voices cried in disbelief.

"Please, you must help us! The Watch and the thirty Dwarven Kingdoms of the West are fighting, and the Eastern Kingdoms of Malar and Dorolingas and Ironhand. We've the wizards and the Elven Army and Navy and the Ogres! Even the pumar and wolven are being turned to our side! We can win, if you help us!" Rion cried.

First one man, then three more, then a dozen, then a hundred, and then the rest all ran for the gate, and Rion stepped back to let them pass, pulling Mak aside so he'd not be trampled. The freed Dwarves and Men swarmed over the bodies of the dead, snatching up weapons and running for the enemy.

Rion ran for Lunahr and Elanara. There were no moving enemies near her. Lunahr was in Elanara's arms, now. She was holding him like a child, her sword yet in hand. He was still unconscious.

"Please, Elanara, take him back up to the corridors, to safety," Rion begged.

"I'll not leave you, not again," she said stubbornly.

"You must! You swore you'd protect Lunahr, that you'd not let him be hurt again," he pleaded.

Pain crossed her face. "It was my fault that he was caught the first time. I never should have left him in Riviera. I can't leave you now," she insisted.

"Why? Because you feel sorry for me, you pity me, like a wounded animal, like you told Elavar in the Tower? Why should you care what happens to me? You're a Princess, I'm nobody. I have no station, isn't that what you said? I don't want your pity, Elanara. And I don't want to risk seeing you hurt again. I can't bear that he made me hurt you, that I almost killed you. I still love you, I can't help it that I do. Please, just go! They need me. Come, Mak," he said and turned and ran for the battle that was still raging two hundred feet from where he stood.

MAK looked from Elanara to Rion. "Kap saf, Nara. Tak Bar, had!" Then he was gone.

Elanara fought tears, looking from Lunahr's sweet face to Rion's receding back. How could he know what she'd said? She'd never meant it. Surely Elavar wouldn't have told him, not after what he said in her room? Rion must have heard her somehow, heard her and believed her when Elavar didn't, when he knew the truth about how she loved Rion. Rion might die here, believing such cruel lies. She would rather die herself than lose him again. But Lunahr was helpless. She couldn't leave him. The tears fell as she ran for the corridors, cradling Lunahr in her arms.

WITH the influx of the freed prisoners and the benefit of Circe's lightning, the tide of battle turned. Now it was the Revenants who were on the defensive. Rion fought them with a vengeance. From time to time, when he had a moment's respite, he'd watch Circe. Now that he saw she still aided them, that she hadn't fled with the Ring, taking it for herself, he was worried about her. She was channeling so much Power. He remembered her caution, about how Arcanus must never again hold the Ring. It must be this one she'd been speaking of. Was it dangerous for her to be using it as she was?

He realized too late that an axe was coming for him. He'd been distracted by Circe; he'd not been paying attention. Mak was far to his left, and his own sword was not where it needed to be to block the blow. He saw it in the split instant before the axe head would strike, shrinking from it, knowing he could never dodge it in time. Only it did not connect. It was countered and diverted just enough to miss him. The Revenant who'd swung at him was beheaded in a single powerful swing by a second blade.

"You're supposed to be safely in the cavern above us, with the healers," Ron said sternly, slashing at a third foe even as he scolded Rion.

Rion saw Ara was the one who had countered the first blow, who had saved him, and Ron had destroyed the Revenant who'd tried to kill him.

"I had to come. Donovar and the others are here. We brought close to two hundred men. We're the ones who freed the prisoners," Rion said, slashing at another. "Mak, that's too far! Come closer," Rion called out, trying desperately to keep sight of him.

"You brought Mak! I suppose you were fool enough to bring Beryl and Elanara, too," Ron accused.

Rion couldn't answer. "Where's Gar? He's not with the two of you. Please tell me he's all right."

"He was when last we saw him," Ron said. Then pain tore across his face. "It's Andra we fear for. Rarnak was injured, he was dying," he said grimly. "She left with a party of ten guards guiding twenty other wounded. We saw them on the ledge above us. A swarm of Revenants came out of the corridor right on top of them, and then we were overwhelmed as well. When we looked again, all we saw were bodies. Rion, when you entered, did you see her?" Ron asked, obviously dreading the answer.

"She's alive, Ron, and well, she and Rarnak both. They're both safely above, in the cavern. Lun... I mean Beryl, healed him. Then Jarnath drugged her so she'd sleep. She'd carried Rarnak all the way up the Mountain on her back. They were the only two who came. The others must all have been killed. We wondered how you could have left her to carry him all by herself so far," Rion said.

"Alive? Ara, Andra's alive! And Rarnak's been healed, Rion's seen them!" Ron shouted in sudden joy.

Ara whooped in relief as he beheaded his latest foe with a single fierce blow.

Rion and Mak fought beside Ron and Ara as arcs of lightning continued to crash down everywhere. Gar joined them a while later and was ecstatic, hearing the news about Andra and Rarnak. Then Talon and Aras saw them, and at the expression that crossed Talon's face, Rion wanted to hide behind the brothers.

"I SHOULD have known! You're the one who brought Beryl into this madness, aren't you?" Dewalaren accused. "And now Circe has the Ring! Rion, do you have any idea what you've done? What she or Arcanus might do with it, now that they have it? I'm surprised they're both still here, fighting beside us. We're lucky their thirst for revenge has overcome their thirst for Power for the moment. And where is Beryl? Why isn't he with you?" he asked, fear flashing across his face as he realized Lunahr was not with them.

Rion swallowed. "He was overwhelmed. The Ring and Knife healed him, but he's unconscious. I made Elanara take him to safety. I had to come, Talon, but it wasn't only me. It was Donovar and Sarnon and everyone who could fight. Nearly two hundred of us came. You needed us. You were losing. Andra told us. We're the ones who freed the prisoners to fight with you. And you're wrong about Circe. She won't keep the Ring. I know she won't. To have put herself in Incuban's Power to help us, the terrible things I saw. She's sacrificed everything to help us. You'll see."

Dewalaren shook his head at Rion's idealism. He was a child. Children had no business being in war.

They continued to fight. It was easier now. The splintered forces began regrouping as dozens of Revenants were felled with each flash of lightning, and the tide of battle continued to turn in their favor.

Dewalaren was amazed that Rion was still on his feet. Many grown men in their first major battle would have collapsed in exhaustion long ago. Dewalaren had been battling for endless hours; he had no idea how long. He was ready to collapse, but he did not have the luxury. A King cannot show such weakness in battle, lest his men lose heart. And Aras was still fighting strongly, destroying two Revenants for each one he felled. He'd not appear weak before him.

RION'S sword arm felt as if it were made of lead. He marveled that he could still move it at all, though he was slower with each thrust, with each parry. But he saw the others still fighting, after having fought for so much longer. He couldn't stop while they kept going. The others seemed tireless. He envied them their stamina, wishing he had the same warrior's build they each did.

The lightning attacks crashing down all around them finally slowed and then gradually stilled altogether. Rion looked for Circe in concern. But she was still hovering above them, out of reach of the many weapons the Revenants had thrown at her in frustration. Then Rion realized there were no large clusters of Revenants left, only small groups too interspersed with their own warriors to attack, or ones using prisoners as shields. Rion was relieved to see Circe did not attack them, that she was not harming innocents. He knew he was right about her; he was sure of it.

Then he saw her swoop down and rise again, Donovar in her arms, and she carried him to the ledge where Elanara had gone with Lunahr. Surely she wasn't leaving them, taking the Ring and fleeing with Donovar?

He started to fight his way toward the ledge, knowing he'd never be able to catch her. To his surprise she reappeared and dove down again, this time rising with a limp Dwarf in her arms. She headed for the ledge again. What was she up to? Was she taking the wounded out of the battle, bringing them to safety, to Donovar, for healing? Then a Revenant lunged at him, and he couldn't afford to be distracted by thoughts of her. He'd learned his lesson earlier.

Finally, as the last of the Revenants were being destroyed, Rion made his way over to Circe. He'd seen she was still alternating between transporting the injured and slaying the Enemy's forces, and he wanted to be there when it came time for her to surrender the Ring.

Once all the monsters were destroyed, the men who had been imprisoned were attacking the chains securing the pens that held the women and children. Then some of the Ogres walked over and made quick work of the chains. They freed at least two thousand women and three thousand children.

DEWALAREN climbed a mountain of Revenant bodies and addressed everyone, his voice laced with Power so that it might echo throughout the cavern.

"The Enemy that has plagued these lands for the past two-hundred-fifty years is destroyed! Incuban is dead and His army no more! We have all suffered terribly, but the time of suffering is over. It is time now for us all to build new lives, new homes, new cities, new Kingdoms!

"We will see that you are all safely returned to your own peoples, to the Dwarven Kingdoms of the West or Cities of Man that yet stand. We have food and water and healing for all of you. None of us could have brought this victory about alone. Men, Dwarves, Elves, and even the Ogres, working together, have snatched victory from the jaws of defeat. You bear witness now to the dawn of a new age, an era of peace, of life, of hope! You have been given a rare gift. Cherish it."

The cavern erupted in a spontaneous roar of cheering, and then Dewalaren climbed wearily down to them.

He walked over to Circe, eyeing her warily. "Circe, the battle is over. I believe you have something that belongs to me."

Circe looked innocently at him. "No, King Talon, I do not."

Dewalaren bristled and the men beside him tensed.

Unexpectedly, Farad stepped between them, smiling tiredly. "She is telling the truth, Talon. If you wish to reclaim the Ring, you must see Beryl about it, not Circe. Although he will not relinquish it soon, I think," he said, pointing to the ledge above them. It was aglow in red light that faded and then flared again.

Dewalaren looked in surprise at Farad, then the ledge, then Circe. "My mistake. I thank you for saving us, Enchantress."

"I played no greater a part than any of you. Come, there are other wounded to find to bring to the healers on the ledge. I would not have been able to fly nearly as many as I have, had Beryl not so generously allowed me to hold the Ring after every few flights. Still, I will not miss having its Power at my beck and call. Only a God should wield such Power, and wizard I might be, but I find I cannot style myself a God as some others of you have," she said, looking pointedly at Arcanus and Aras, and then turned to go.

Aras shifted uncomfortably.

Arcanus spoke, then. "Our children teach us much, when we chose to listen and to learn."

"That they do, indeed," Laedrin rumbled, and to Aras's obvious astonishment and joy, his father embraced him. "I, for one, am ready to listen. There is much I would learn from you, Aras, and much you have already taught me. I would hear more. I have lived in silence for five decades. I have lived in silence for far longer. I have been deaf since leaving our Homeland. But the last of the Aerie and the Faeren are now safely dead, and I find Dwarves, Men, and even the Ogres no longer pose the threat that I have feared them to be for so long. It is time all of us found peace. Not that I will disband our forces, though, for evil always thrives when the good lose their vigilance, when they fail to act against it."

Dewalaren turned to his cousins. "We are a free people again. We need no longer skulk in the alleyways of cities dressed in rags and hiding in shadows." He turned to Shadala and laughed. "You will have to retrain us, Chieftess, to perform some useful function amongst you. I fear we know only how to fight!"

She smiled at him. "It will be our pleasure, King Talon. But first, our job here is far from over. It will take many days to see everyone here safely on their way to their new lives. For now, we must eat and rest."

He nodded.

RION kept silent. He was too tired to talk, and he had nothing of importance to say. He was just glad so many of his friends had survived. He knew he should go up to the ledge and help the others to bandage the wounded, but he only made it ten feet, before he stumbled.

Mak caught him. "Ran tad. Ran rast," Mak chastised gently.

"I can't, Mak. People need me. There will be time for rest later," Rion said sadly, fighting against sudden tears.

Mak looked at him in concern. "Ran sat?"

Rion nodded. Mak's concern over his aching heart was too much. He swallowed hard, twice, and barely kept the tears at bay. "I can't help but be sad. It's all over, Mak. I... I won't be seeing any of them again. Everyone is going to go to their own homes and... I'm being silly. I'm glad it's done." But Elanara, Eladar, Aras, Talon, and Lunahr would all leave. He'd never see any of them again. He'd go back to Ogaten, to trading. But Ogaten was so small, and trading seemed so unimportant after all he'd done. At least the brothers would be there, and there were Elves in Salenia. He even knew some of them a little now. Meander was there. But Elanara would not be.

"Mak na sta Ran? Ran ga hama?" Mak asked softly. Rion could hear the sadness in his voice, too.

Rion nodded. "You belong with your people, Mak. You'll be able to farm again. You'll be able to go back to your real home, wherever the farm they forced you to leave was."

Mak shook his head. "Anma kala, plant kala, sal pasan, wata pasan. Na mar gra. Na fata."

Rion swallowed. "Nothing will grow there now because the Enemy poisoned the water and the soil?"

"Ya," Mak said sadly.

"I'm sure King Talon and Chieftess Shadala can find new land for you to farm," Rion assured him. "Maybe... perhaps even near their own. Most men are frightened of Ogres, but his people and hers and the Elves know you're good. They'd not fear you. I'll speak to them later for you, all right? And Aras. I'm sure he could convince his father. They looked so happy together."

Mak grinned, and his smile warmed Rion's heart. He'd miss Mak. But now he had a job to do. He couldn't waste time feeling sorry for himself, when he had the injured to aid.

They reached the ledge, and he was overjoyed to see Lunahr looking well, although busy. He went to work beside him. He managed to stay awake for a while longer, helping those who needed him, before he finally collapsed, completely exhausted.

RION awoke slowly. It felt so good to be lying down, a warm blanket over him, a warm body against him. He started and looked to see who it was and then smiled affectionately: Mak was curled up at his side.

Rion sat up carefully, trying not to wake him, and looked about curiously. He was in the upper cavern again. He blushed, wondering who had carried him so far. There were many people laid out asleep beside them: mostly alone, under blankets, but some in twos or even threes, like the brothers. He saw Lunahr, also sitting up and looking guilty. Rion saw that Eladar was sleeping beside him. Lunahr's eyes lit upon Rion's, and he grinned and rose, and Rion rose and met him.

"I can't believe I fell asleep so deeply that someone carried me here," Rion said sheepishly.

Lunahr laughed. "You've one of the Ogres to thank for that. I think his name was Taka. Ogress Tana herself carried Mak. Mak told them you were his Baga Brata Ran. I think you've been adopted into their tribe, Rion."

Rion felt warm inside, hearing Lunahr say so. He glanced at where Eladar was still lying asleep. "It looks like the Elves have adopted you, too. Eladar once told me you were like a brother to them, but I guess he was mistaken. Or perhaps just being secretive or mischievous. I'm thrilled for you, that you are *lythenia*. But... what about Talon? I mean...." He looked down, embarrassed. Incuban had said some things in the corridor, and Rion thought they might have been true, from the way he'd said them.

Lunahr looked surprised and then blushed. "He's betrothed to Elanara. We really shouldn't have...." He trailed off and looked guilty, and Rion realized his face must have betrayed his pain. "Forgive me, Rion, I didn't think before I said that. I...."

"No, it's all right, really. Please excuse me, Lunahr, I... I must be needed somewhere. I'm sure there's still a lot of work to do," Rion said, heading off.

"I'VE waited long enough. It's past time I spoke to High-King Laedrin," Eladar said, coming up behind Lunahr. He stared at Lunahr speculatively. "The looks you were giving each other, you and Rion. You didn't ever...?" He trailed off.

Lunahr sighed. "No. Not for lack of wanting to, though." He looked in surprise at Eladar's scowl. "You were jealous? You were watching us? I didn't feel anything across the link."

Eladar sighed, then grinned. "I'm an Elf, Lunahr. Of course I was jealous! We're known for that, you know. Which is rather foolish, I agree, especially considering the lasciviousness of our nature. I am yet young, and young Elves are doubly terrible about that sort of thing. As for the link, I'm a quick study, especially when it comes to secrecy."

He wrapped his arms around Lunahr's waist and kissed him softly upon the mouth. "You and I have yet to consummate our bond. There were certainly too many people about last night for us to do so. And that gives me added reason to be jealous, at the thought that you and Rion might have shared something we have yet to.

"I'd better go, before I get carried away here, now, with you, and before I lose my nerve. I do not relish speaking to the High-King. Why don't you have some breakfast? I'll join you when I can."

ABOUT an hour or so after Rion awoke, he was surprised to see Eladar coming toward him, looking very solemn. "Rion, High-King Laedrin wishes to speak with you, on a matter of no small importance. He asked me to escort you to him."

Rion wondered what he might possibly have done to warrant the High-King calling him before him. He was led to a tent that had been erected against the rock wall of the cavern, one of the Dwarven tents. His nervousness grew as he saw the High-King was not alone: Talon, Aras, Elavar, and Elanara were all there. Rion fidgeted in his borrowed clothes, feeling small and unimportant, when he realized that everyone else in the room was at least a Prince or Princess. Why was he here?

Laedrin said, "Certain matters have been brought to my attention that must be addressed, without delay, now that the fighting is done. It had been previously arranged that Princess Elanara of Riviera be wed to King Talon of the Amontir, to unite our forces for the battle we knew we would face. They are, in fact, betrothed. However, the War has ended, and it is my understanding that this arrangement is not only no longer necessary, but ill-advised. Prior to the current arrangement, Princess Elanara was betrothed to my son, High-Prince Aras."

Rion looked at Aras in surprise. He had not known that.

Laedrin continued. "I have learned that King Laranela, Elanara's father, was pleased with the betrothal to Aras, but not the one to King Talon, for reasons I will not mention here. In order to resolve this issue, there are certain matters that must first be addressed." Laedrin turned to Elavar. "Crown Prince Elavar. Kneel before me."

Elavar knelt without hesitation.

"Crown Prince Elavar, you are the Heir to King Laranela and as such, the rightful King of Riviera. It is true that Riviera has been destroyed and that you have, until now, been a Prince without a Kingdom. I hereby restore that Kingdom to you.

"All the survivors from Riviera and those few from Loatia, should the latter chose to leave Erenia, are welcome to resettle in the Wood surrounding Nalea and along our two Rivers, where a new City of Riviera will be built. There they will find peace and protection and healing. We will forgo the traditional coronation ceremony, until you might appear before your restored people, upon your new lands, but I hereby name you King of Riviera. And as such, I bring news to you that should bring you no small measure of joy.

"In addition to the thousands of survivors you knew of in Erenia, whose numbers continue to slowly climb, I learned shortly before we departed Nalea to come to your aid that every child of Riviera, all one thousand two hundred and nine of them, plus the twenty-seven women who are expecting, escaped Riviera uninjured before she fell. They were led by a visiting healer of Tanieria, along with some hundreds of the children's parents, safely to sanctuary in Tanieria.

"Apparently, when your parents learned from the sorrowfully few refugees to escape Loatia that their sister Kingdom fell so easily, without warning, and that their evacuation plans failed so spectacularly, your parents realized Riviera's defenses and emergency protocols had likely been somehow similarly compromised. There was little they could do to bolster their defenses in so short a time, so instead they concentrated all their efforts upon saving the future generation. I now entrust those subjects to you. Rise, King Elavar of Riviera reborn."

Elavar rose, his expression unreadable.

Laedrin continued. "Now then: as King, you must determine the more immediate matter of what might be best for your sister and your Kingdom. Before you pass judgment, I would ask that any of those in this room who wish to speak upon the matter be given voice."

Aras looked at Talon and at Elanara. It was Talon who spoke, turning to Elavar. "Majesty, I would ask that you release Princess Elanara from her betrothal to me. Although our betrothal was once a great joy to me, and I still love her and will treasure our time together always, I do not wish her to be my wife. She has told me she is in love with another, and that she can never love me in return, because of her love for him. Although she is prepared to do what is commanded of her, at the cost of her own happiness, I would not want such a wife or Queen."

Talon turned to Laedrin. "I, in turn, have also found a new love, for whom I must seek your approval, High-King, once the matter regarding Princess Elanara is settled."

Laedrin appeared surprised but nodded.

Aras turned to Elavar and Laedrin. "Majesty, Father, I am not in love with Elanara, nor is she in love with me. I would not seek to be betrothed to her. I withdraw any suit which might have been previously made upon my behalf."

Rion was looking puzzled at everyone. When he'd heard of Aras's betrothal to her, he thought that it must be him who she was in love with, but Aras had just claimed otherwise.

Laedrin looked thoughtful. "Princess Elanara. You find yourself without a suitor. Yet King Talon has stated you are in love. Will you name the one who holds your heart?"

Elanara took a deep breath and turned to Elavar. "With my King's permission," she said. Then she turned to Laedrin. "And my High-King's," she said. Last she turned to Rion. "I ask that I might wed Alarion, son of Anorion of Ardock, known as Rion."

Rion gaped at her, shocked, breath held.

She smiled at him. "Rion, you have confessed your love for me, although you would not press your suit, for you are a Man of honor and would not wound a friend. But I have been released from both my betrothals. My heart is yours. My heart has been yours since first we spoke in Erenia, though you had not yet come-of-age, and I had not been free to follow my heart. But I have thought of you always since then and dreamed of you often, even as you have thought of and dreamt of me. I offer you my hand, if my King and High-King will permit it."

"I want whatever will bring you happiness, Sister," Elavar said. "And I can think of no finer husband for you than Rion."

Rion stared at Elavar, speechless.

High-King Laedrin said, "I also approve this union. I have heard much about Alarion and am likewise impressed by his qualifications as a husband for you."

Rion was stunned.

"How do you feel about this proposal, Alarion, son of Anorion of Ardock?" Laedrin asked formally.

Rion turned to Elanara. "I love you, Elanara. I have loved you since first I saw you, and my love has only grown with time. Yet I have always known you were beyond me. I am only a merchant, perhaps a swordsman. I am not a Prince or a King or even an Elf. I am not even an Amontir. I am only a normal Man. I won't live to be one thousand as an Elf, or even two-hundred-fifty as an Amontir. I will live only to be sixty, at the most, and then I will be gone. And you have told me your heart can only be given once. I cannot doom you to such a lifetime of loneliness."

Elanara smiled at him. "My heart is already yours, Rion, whether you accept the gift or refuse it. But if you should accept it, then we would have perhaps forty-four perfect, joyous years together, and that will be enough. For you are a love of a lifetime, Rion, even for a lifetime as long as my own."

Rion gazed at her in wonder and joy and knelt before her, taking her hand in his own. "Princess Elanara of Riviera, will you be my wife?"

"I will, and joyfully, Alarion, son of Anorion of Ardock."

He rose and they kissed, briefly and gently.

Laedrin turned from the happy pair to Talon. "Now then, King Talon, why might you seek my approval for your own union, when I am not your King?"

DEWALAREN took a slow, deep breath, and stood by Aras's side and took his hand. "Because, High-King, your son Aras and I wish to become *lythenia*," Dewalaren said bravely.

The High-King and the others looked at the two of them in surprise. "Indeed? I was not aware of this. I brought Aras before me now only because he was supposed to have wed Elanara originally, before the betrothal was changed, and I wanted him to have a voice in the matter regarding her. You are a King and the Lord of your House. Do you also intend to have a wife, to bear your heirs?"

"No," Dewalaren said. "If we are to be *lythenia*, I would honor that. I could have no wife. Prince Jargas is already Heir to me and is, in fact, the rightful King, although he abdicated his claim to the throne. Now that the War is over, I will give him the option of claiming the throne now or upon my death, as my Heir, as he will outlive me, barring illness or injury, for his Dwarven blood. His eldest son would then be Heir after him, though he would be of mixed blood on both sides. Many of our newly discovered cousins are also of mixed blood, so none would dispute his claim, nor his progeny's. And he is House of Obearn, so my House would also continue."

"I see. You are, however, aware that I have no heirs, save for my son?" Laedrin asked.

Dewalaren nodded. "I am. However, I am only a Man, though an Amontir. I will not live as long as an Elf would. In less than one-hundred-seventy years, barring accident or illness, I will be gone. Your son is yet young. At that time, Aras could then marry and sire heirs, so that your line would also continue."

Aras clutched Dewalaren's hand more tightly, obviously distressed by talk of his death. Dewalaren wished he was linked to him, so that he might console him, but he had not wanted to form such a bond without the High-King's permission.

Laedrin appeared thoughtful. "You love this Man, and wish him to be *lythenia* to you, Aras?"

"With all my heart, Father," Aras said, looking first at his father and then at Dewalaren.

Laedrin smiled and Aras's eyes widened to see it. "Then I approve and acknowledge your union," Laedrin said simply.

Aras grinned in stunned delight, and Dewalaren slowly smiled, unable to believe the High-King had said yes.

Laedrin said, "I believe we have said all that needed to be said," with an air of dismissal.

"Forgive me, Majesties, but there is one other suit which needs must be brought before the three of you for approval," Eladar said.

The three looked at him, curious. "Indeed?" Laedrin asked, intrigued. "I had thought you were here only as representative for your sister, Prince Eladar, as it was you who brought these matters to my attention."

Elanara looked at Eladar in sudden understanding, and his face flushed. "At the time, my sister's happiness was my only concern. Yet hearing what has been spoken here, I now realize I have been remiss. Come, Lunahr," he called.

LUNAHR, who was standing in the doorway, came forward. Eladar had called to him through their bond.

"Lunahr and I have pledged ourselves to each other as *lythenia*. As a second son, I did not think to obtain approval for such a joining, but now I see that I must seek it, for we did not think about the issue of his heirs when we made our pledge. I had not thought to consider he is Lord and sole Heir to House of Eagles."

Lunahr's eyes filled with sudden fear. He had indeed not considered it. Although his people often found pleasure-loves amongst their own sex, they did not marry them. They had nothing equivalent to the commitment of *lythenia* amongst the Elves, which was as sacred and binding and exclusive as marriage.

Lunahr turned to Laren. "But, Laren, Majesty, I do not want a wife. I want only Eladar. I have ever only wanted him. We already share a bond, and though we have not yet had the opportunity to truly live as *lythenia*, we wish to and…. Laren, please! Don't I deserve the same happiness you and Aras will now share?"

Laren looked torn. "But, Lunahr, House of Eagles has always been one of our strongest Houses. You know our Laws. I cannot allow a House to die for lack of descendants, when so many have already been lost."

"You would force me to marry and to bed someone I do not love?" Lunahr asked and began shivering.

"No!" Laren said, in sharp denial, obviously realizing Lunahr was remembering Incuban. "No, Lunahr, of course not. But…." He sighed and admitted defeat. "If Eagles must die so you might live in happiness, then so be it. You have the approval of your King," he said formally. Then he stepped forward and hugged him. "And the joy of your cousin," he added, smiling at him.

Lunahr's face lit with love and he hugged Laren and then blushed at the feel of his pounding heart, remembering the last time Laren had held him in his arms.

He felt a wave of jealousy race across the bond from Eladar and realized Eladar had felt it as well. He sent a wave of love and reassurance back to him, and he felt Eladar calm as Laedrin and Elavar also gave their approval to their union.

Aras said, "You made the right decision, Talon. Also, do not mourn House of Eagles yet. You told me Hunter's mother was also of that House, as was your own. Surely there must be others? House of Pumar was revived through Jarina. Could not Eagles be revived as well, through Hunter and Jarina?"

Laren appeared pained. "No, at least not through Hunter," he said solemnly.

Lunahr turned to him and said in Amontirin, "Oh, but Laren, Aras is right! I had not thought of that. It can be! Farad is a private man. I am not surprised he has not spoken of it to you, but he is healed. He and Jarina will indeed bear heirs. I can imagine he and the rest of our kin might do so with renewed enthusiasm, now that they know their children will be safe."

Dewalaren smiled in joy, as did Lunahr, that Farad might now be so blessed to have a family about him again, one he need not fear losing.

"Congratulations, Eladar," Rion said, grinning.

Eladar grinned back at him, his arm around Lunahr. "Congratulations to you also, Rion. Welcome to the family, little brother," he said, then sighed. "It will be a strain, being the older, responsible one for a change, but I shall endure."

Chapter 12
A Time of Peace

DEWALAREN stared first in shock and then rapidly increasing alarm as Farad knelt before him upon the granite floor of the Audience Chamber in Kingshome. Instead of moving with his customary quick grace, his cousin, who rarely made such blatant and unnecessary shows of obeisance, had all but collapsed to his knees.

Dewalaren ran to his side and pulled him to his feet. "You have not knelt to me since you and Jarina begged me to spare your lives, in the darkest days of the War. Please, tell me what is troubling you. You look unwell. I fear for you, cousin." Farad looked terrible, more haggard than he had appeared during the harshest moments of the War, worse than he had looked in his death shroud, newly risen.

"I have heard some disturbing news, Majesty, and I need to speak with you concerning it," Farad said formally.

"Majesty? Farad, please! Tell me plainly what is wrong? Is there trouble in the west, something that threatens your home, Malar in Holoren or the village of the Varash? Some new enemy we must face? Or an old one reappeared? Ahrnad? We never found a body we could identify as his. Or some other evil? Are we to be given only six months of peace? I know it cannot concern Arcanus or his children. I saw him only two days ago."

"I am aware of the visit and the result. That is why I am here, why I flew upon Daenlyr. Do not destroy the Ring, Majesty, I beg of you."

Dewalaren stared at him in astonishment. "How can you know what we spoke of? There were only three of us: me, Arcanus, and Aras. Surely Arcanus has not betrayed our plan to you! He was the one who put it forth. He revealed much to me I had not known before.

"The Ring must be destroyed, Farad. Arcanus told to me the true story of the War of the Wind, or the War of Flame: each side had his own name for it. The Elven Homeland was destroyed, millions of Elves incinerated, when the land burned and the sea boiled. The neighboring Dwarven homeland was obliterated because of it, overwhelmed by the wall of water that ensued, though the Dwarves yet remain ignorant of that fact. I forgot for a moment your ties to them. You must swear you will never reveal what I have said to you. But Farad, the horrific War, the death and suffering, was all for possession of the Ring."

"I know that is what Arcanus told you," Farad said. "And I know Arcanus revealed his true form to you at last, that he dimmed the masking spell that has hidden his features for three millennia, lest we see he also was an Elf. Like Incuban, he also was *Faeren*, when Laedrin had thought with Ithelia and Incuban both dead that the last *Aerie* and the last *Faeren* had perished. I know that Arcanus was once a great scholar, more than a healer, an alchemist of the flesh, and that Incuban was once his servant. I know that the

Ring and the Knife in tandem are the key to immortality for one, yet ever only for one, that the Ring is far more: it is Power beyond imagining. It can make a Man a God. I know that even so, Arcanus swears he never coveted it, though he was left holding it, after all the others were dead.

"He told you he used its Power to create our people and gifted it to us for our strength of spirit, and the Knife to heal us, and the Sword to protect us, that he truly thought of us as his children. He told you how Incuban tricked and overpowered him, all to seize the Ring, that He hounded both us and Arcanus so He might reclaim it, when it once again slipped from His grasp. Arcanus claims that now that Incuban is finally dead, he is content to find his immortality through his children, as we all must, but also through the Tree that he, Marcus, and Selene are now bound to.

"Or so he has told you, because he must, because he does not dare let you to know the truth. I cannot hope to guess all he has kept hidden from you, the truth masked by layers of carefully constructed falsehoods, but I do know this: Arcanus fears the Ring. It is the only thing in this world powerful enough to destroy him or his children, should they ever need destroying. You cannot leave us so defenseless, Dewalaren. Arcanus has his own agenda. You cannot imagine that you might ever know it. You cannot guess how he might be deceiving you, none of us can. Even Aras cannot fathom his true past, his motivations, his intent, though he tries."

"Aras?" Dewalaren asked in sudden understanding, in shock, in horror. "Aras has betrayed me? He has told you so much, things that were to have been for my ears alone?" He groped for the arms of his throne blindly and sat down hard.

"He loves you, Dewalaren. He does not want to see you make such a potentially dangerous mistake. But also, his motives are selfish. He cannot bear the thought that you will die so soon, when you might live forever, when the Knife and the Ring together might see you forever young and alive for him. He hoped that I might convince you to keep them, to use them. But I could not deceive you as he wanted me to."

"There is no question now. I must destroy them, both of them. It is too dangerous to allow them to remain. That Aras, of all people, might betray me," Dewalaren whispered raggedly, devastated by the enormity of it.

Tears sprang into Farad's eyes. "I could not keep the truth of it from you. I understand you will do what you feel in your heart you must. I know that you have forgiven Arcanus, that you cannot believe he ever truly wished to harm you. You have convinced yourself that he was brought to it out of desperation, when.... Dewalaren, I no longer care! I cannot! I cannot think of matters so large, so complex, when I fight even to be able to eat, to breathe!" he said, and he fell to his knees once more at Dewalaren's feet.

"Please, I beg you only this: do not destroy them immediately. Wait a year, only a year. That is all that I ask. I have sacrificed everything for you, Dewalaren, and for your father before you. I have suffered more than any Man might ever be expected to survive. I will take my own life if you allow harm to come to me again, instead of joy. I will not lose another I love, I cannot. Please, lend me the Ring and the Knife. I will do anything you ask for them," Farad pleaded.

Dewalaren was kneeling at his side in an instant. "Farad, please! You are frightening me. Never have I seen you so lost to despair! I would not see you beg at my feet," he said, embracing him. "I am aware of my debt to you, that I can never repay it, that I can never return to you those you lost in service to my father. Now please, tell me plainly, what is wrong?"

Dewalaren could see Farad struggling for control. "Jarina is pregnant," Farad said, in a tone that made it sound as if she were instead dying.

Dewalaren looked at him in consternation. "Why is that news that would bring terror and pain to you, instead of joy?"

"Because both she and the healers have said it is twins," Farad said, his voice ragged with fear. "Because her brother was so large he killed their mother with his birth, though their mother was large and strong and of our blood. Yet Jarina is so petite. And even were it not twins, it has been the curse of her mother's line for four generations that the mother dies bearing her first child, though the child lives. When I wanted to kill myself in shame for not being a proper husband to her, for my impotence, she told me why it instead might be a joy to me. But then I was healed, yet still, somehow, I never believed I might be able to father a child. Five months ago we learned she is with child, children. She is so filled with joy for it, but sorrow also.

"Jargas feels only terror. He cannot even rejoice that Desenia is gravid as well with their first, also with twins. And I…. Dewalaren, I have tried, but I can no longer sleep, nor eat, nor hold my wife without crying, though I know I do her harm by it. Please, I beg you! Let her wear the Ring and the Knife, so she might live. I swear I will never lay hands upon her again. I will have fulfilled the duty to my line, though whether these children will be Wolven, Pumar, or Eagle I cannot say. I do not care. I want only that my wife might live."

"Farad, why did you not share this with me before? To think I almost destroyed them! I was angry with Aras, I still am, yet now I owe him much. He saved me from making a grievous mistake. Of course she may wear them," Dewalaren said, removing both the Ring and the sheathed Knife and handing them to him. "Just do not let it be known that she has them, other than to Jargas, so he might live in joy now also, as he should. I would not want her endangered, when we seek to protect her, nor to risk such terrible Power being seized by those who might do evil."

Farad stared in disbelief at the Knife and Ring in his shaking hands. "I… I did not think you would. You felt so strongly about destroying them. I had not thought…. I love you, cousin," Farad said and hugged him tightly.

"Now then, as Jarina is in no immediate danger, you will, I hope, spare the afternoon, at least, so that I may hear more about our western kin? Even with the pairs of Gryphon we have stationed in Malar and each of the three Strongholds of the West to unite those of you who are so far away with the rest of us, we hear less word of you and Jarina, Desenia and Jargas, and Desmond than I would like. I would hear news of Malar in Holoren, Northhold, Westhold, and Southhold, as well as of the twenty-four remaining Kingdoms of the West, and what you might know of the six that have resettled in the Dwarven Lands. News from Malar in Fromer has been spotty at best, since Dorolingas broke their treaty with Ironhand, and the three of them appear ready to go to war with each other over the Malar Pass. Rion and Eladar both have gone there as emissaries. I understand that Rion has already mastered Dwarvish, as has Lunahr, who accompanies Eladar. I miss Lunahr fiercely."

"Elanara has not gone as well?" Farad asked in surprise.

Dewalaren was chagrined. "Of course. She is as skilled a diplomat as her brother and as Lunahr and Rion. I had not meant to exclude mention of her." He sighed. "Old habits die hard, I suppose. I find my ego is still bruised that she chose Rion over me, when I struggled so long and hard to win her love."

Farad looked at him in concern. "Are you not happy with Aras? Has he given you cause, other than today, not to be?"

"No, of course not! I am so happy with him by my side that it frightens me. I find I would do anything he asks of me, only… I will not keep the Ring. I have no wish to live forever, but he will not accept it. I hope he learns to. He is such a dichotomy: part God, yet still part child, though mostly a man. His passions and convictions are unparalleled."

Farad smiled. "Your face lights up when you speak of him. It is good to see you living in such joy, cousin. Please, do not be too harsh with him over this. He would never have told one you did not trust with your very life. I am Protector and King's Friend still. You have not revoked the title, though we live so far apart. He wants only to see you safe, always. I cannot fault him for it. I too wish you might keep the Ring and Knife forever, for even did you not sit upon a throne, you would always be a King amongst men."

"I hear your heart in your words, cousin. Yet still, the Ring must be destroyed, once you no longer have need of it. Now then, about that news from the west," Dewalaren said, firmly changing the subject.

He and Farad spoke the rest of the day and then ate dinner together. Aras was noticeably absent from the table.

It warmed Dewalaren's heart to see the hope and joy on Farad's face when he bade his cousin good night at the door to one of the guest chambers. Farad would be staying the night and leaving at dawn. Gryphon flew at night only in direst necessity, and Farad had all but exhausted his mount by coming in such haste. Daenlyr needed to roost, before making the return journey.

ARAS crept into the bedroom he shared with Dewalaren long after Dewalaren had retired for the night. He was startled when the oil lamp, which was burning dimly, flared to light. Aras looked guiltily at his lythenia. "I had hoped you would be asleep, so I might lie beside you. Please do not be angry, Dewalaren. I felt so much before through the bond, before you shielded yourself from me. I…." Tears sprang to his eyes. "I still cannot feel you, when before… I have not felt such horror toward me from you since I fled from you to confront my mother. I would rather face her again, knowing I was dying, than to stand in the same room with you as if you were not even here." Aras's wild trembling ceased when Dewalaren unexpectedly removed the shield that had separated them and sent a wave of warmth to him. Tears of relief wet Aras's face as he sprang into his love's arms.

"Ah, Aras, my *lythenia*, my life, my love. Why can you not understand? How is it you can hear my thoughts yet not know them?" Dewalaren asked, his exasperation far outweighed by the cascade of love coursing through their bond, permeating Aras's core.

"Because I may be a man, yet I am still part child and part God, and as all three seek to get my own way in all things," Aras said.

Dewalaren looked at him oddly, and Aras heard an echo of his words being spoken aloud by Dewalaren, in memory, across their bond.

"Really? Just today, to Farad? No, Dewalaren, I did not hear you through your shield, or else I would have also heard the words of love you spoke about me to Farad, as I hear them now in your thoughts, and I would not have spent the day weeping against Aranas."

"Truly?" Dewalaren asked, both in surprise and guilt.

Aras's face flushed. "Yes, I truly did." Then he laughed. "I will have to apologize to him for it tomorrow, though he feels the joy in my heart tonight. He did not need to wait for the rains to water him."

He would not tell Dewalaren what Aranas had told him, not tonight. He was yet reeling from it. Aranas had been perplexed that he might be so concerned about Dewalaren's mortality yet not have asked him for his assistance. He was puzzled why Aras had not thought to have him bond to Dewalaren as well, as both Leonas and Gaius were bonded to Aranonas and Lunahr and Eladar were bonded to Aranahr. Both Lunahr and Shadala of the Amontir had already bonded to Trees. Why should their King not as well?

Aras could not believe he had overlooked something so critical, and he had showered Aranas with his thanks as enthusiastically as he had watered him with his tears.

"Why so silent, my love? Perhaps it is because you have other plans for your mouth tonight?" Dewalaren asked teasingly, lasciviously.

Aras kissed him briefly, playfully and drew back, and then laughed at the flummoxed expression on Dewalaren's face. "You need not look so crestfallen, my *lythenia*, my love. I know what you were thinking. The night is yet young."

"As is my heart, for my love of you," Dewalaren said, and then he kissed him with all the passion and love within his heart.

Aras melted against him, knowing that, for this moment at least, all was right with his world.

EIGHT years. He might only have known Dewalaren's love for so short a time, had he not acted in defiance of his wishes, his command.

"Aras, you told me you had destroyed the Ring. Instead, I realize now you altered the King's Band. You have exchanged the ruby in it for the stone of the Ring," Dewalaren accused.

No, that was not technically true. The stone of the band had never been a mere ruby cabochon. Aras had exchanged the inert, damaged gem-battery of the King's Band for the supercharged gem-battery of the King's Ring.

Knowing that Dewalaren was bonded to Aranas was not enough. He had yet feared that Dewalaren might be taken from him. Nearly half the Lords and Ladies had died in the War: their Trees alone had not been enough to protect them, to save them. He would not allow Dewalaren to be jeopardized. And indeed, something catastrophic had occurred. The gem-battery had activated of its own accord to Power the Knife because

Dewalaren had been dying. As he had before, during the War. As Lunahr had. His deception had saved Dewalaren's life.

Dewalaren continued on, as if they were not once again linked, as if Aras had not felt the horror of his death as their bond shattered from it, before he could even attempt to save him.

"I was bitten this morning. A snake startled Shadowdancer. He reared and threw me. The snake struck me on the neck while I was lying, stunned, upon on the ground. I grabbed it and flung it from me, and Shadowdancer trampled it, even as I collapsed. Then the Band under my shirt flared brightly, as if it were the Ring. I rose and calmed Shadowdancer and then bent to see what kind of snake it had been, suspecting already what had happened. I was right. It was a Deathshead. Its head was still intact and its poison sack was empty. Even Jargas would have fallen dead almost instantly, were he bitten as I was. When I went home and beheld myself in the mirror, the marks from its fangs had vanished. My neck was unmarred."

"Is it so bad to live eternally with those who love you? To be forever young and strong? You would have died today. You might yet die today, or tomorrow, or the day after," Aras said softly, striving for calm amidst terror at the thought of losing him.

"Death is a part of life, Aras. All who live must eventually die. I will die happily, knowing I have done all I set out to do, that our Enemy is destroyed and my people safe and thriving. And I love many: all my people, and others besides. I have no wish to live forever while those I love age and die around me. And what might they think, once they realize? Might they not start to see me as a monster, as no better than Incuban?

"And there would be those who would seek to take the King's Band from me. You know this. We have spoken of it often enough. It is too dangerous, Aras. Please, do as you promised and destroy the gem of the Ring and return the stone of my Band to me. I already have the bond to Aranas to sustain me. I will already outlive my people. I agreed to it, for your sake, in spite of what I told your father when he allowed us to become lythenia. But I will not become a monster masquerading as a God."

Aras sighed, as if in defeat. "I will destroy it, because it is you who ask it of me, and I would do anything for you," he lied. He took the Band from Dewalaren. Dewalaren smiled and headed off toward the rooms they shared, as Aras began walking to his sanctum.

Aras knew he could not sway Dewalaren in this. He felt his lythenia's heart, his core. Although he could make Dewalaren think differently. With a simple single twist of thought, he could make him crave immortality, to covet the stone as much as Incuban had coveted the Ring. The thought chilled him. He would never do such a thing to one he loved. There was a time he had thought he could never do so, even to an enemy. He shivered.

It still haunted him, what he had done to Arcanus. He'd altered his very core, he'd altered more, but he had been forced to. The unnamed Tree had refused Arcanus, at first. Aranas had told him what he must do, for the Tree to accept Arcanus and his children. Arcanus was both Faeren and more that they would not speak of: they would not forgive Arcanus for his crimes here, and in the lost Homeland. They had to be sure his nature was changed enough so that they need never fear he would attempt to use their own Power against them, or that he might be capable of harming them, or Jarnath, or him, or any of the Lords and Ladies they were bonded to.

Aras knew he would not destroy the Faeren stone even if he could. It was a gem-battery like no other he had ever seen, not merely for the charge it now held, but for the apparently limitless capacity of the stone to hold such Power. The lives of millions of their four peoples, as well as every iota of Power that had once dwelt in the very rock and soils and waters of their Homeland, as well as that of every plant and animal, now lay dormant within the single stone, just waiting to be called forth.

The art of creating any type of gem-battery had been lost with their Homeland, let alone of manufacturing one of such fantastic Power. Such knowledge might have been preserved in the alchemical tomes of the Library of Riviera, but they had been burned with the rest of the Library when Riviera fell. The loss of the Library, of the literature and nearly the entire culture of their peoples, had been nearly as staggering as the loss of life. So many of the great works of art and music and architecture lost three millennia ago had at least been preserved to some extent within the pictures and texts of those volumes, but now they were truly, irretrievably lost.

He had only the six books retrieved from his mother's sanctum on the Isle of Gryph, along with the contents of her laboratory, with which to try to recreate the lost art. He had been refining his skills within his own sanctum here in Nalea, hoping to one day rediscover the secret of the creation of the stones. He had so pitifully few of the precious gem-batteries. He ached to have more. He was becoming increasingly frustrated in his alchemical pursuits, but he would not allow the limitations of his materials to sabotage his research. He would succeed, in time.

"Aras!"

The unexpected familiar voice calling to him instantly brought a smile to his face. He had not seen his young friend in far too long. "Rion, my friend! I have never seen such a smile upon your face, and you smile often."

Incredibly, Rion's grin widened. "I've reason for joy today. Elanara is pregnant! I couldn't wait to come tell all of you."

"That is truly wonderful news, Rion!"

"We'd been trying for over seven years now. I'd begun to think it just wouldn't work for us. Van, Tarrell, Hunter, and Jargas already have four each, and Rarnak and Gar each have two. Yet Elanara kept insisting I was doing nothing wrong!" Rion said, laughing, and then he blushed.

"You've no idea how happy I am, Aras. This child is more important than most. I've been worried lately, how lonely Elanara will be without me. I know what she said before we were married, that I was the love of a lifetime and forty-four years would be enough, but I'm twenty-three now, I'm in my prime, and I've been thinking how she'll have hundreds of years of loneliness after I'm gone. Now she'll have our child to keep her company. If we're lucky, he or she will be the first of many, although many Elves have only one, so I don't know. Perhaps I'd better build a bigger house to encourage her! Not that we spend much time in it. But even one child is enough. Where is Talon? I must tell him next. I had meant to tell you together."

Aras laughed. "And Talon says I am still part child! I have missed your enthusiasm! Talon is in our rooms. You know the way. How long do you plan on staying this time, Rion?"

"I'll be here at least a few days," Rion replied.

"Good. Be sure you don't leave without seeing me again. I wish to give a special gift to you, in celebration of the new life you and Elanara are bringing to the world," Aras said.

"Don't worry, Aras, I'll see you many times before I go," Rion assured him.

"Perhaps, but I have a task I must do that Talon has set for me, so you might not see as much of me as either of us would like." Inspiration suddenly flared. He hesitated only for a moment. "Rion, for the gift, I'll need a lock of your hair."

Rion looked at him in surprise. He pulled his knife from his belt and cut some strands of his hair and gave them to him. "You'll be sure to keep that away from the wizards, I trust," he said. Aras could tell he said so only halfway in jest. Aras knew Rion was still a little leery of Arcanus, Circe, and Magus, especially Circe, after what had happened in Ironforge and before, although she seemed to have mastered her darker side. Aras was touched, knowing Rion showed his love and faith in him by giving him such a gift.

"No harm will come to you from your gift to me, Rion. Far from it," Aras swore.

Rion smiled, reassured, and told him he would see him again at dinner.

"Actually, you won't see me until I complete the task Talon has given me to perform. It cannot wait. But I will see you again before you go," Aras promised.

Rion looked disappointed for a moment, then grinned again. "You had better. I shall not leave here until you do."

Aras smiled back but grew serious as soon as Rion left. He had much work to do and little time. He fingered the Band through his shirt. He'd told Dewalaren he would destroy the stone, knowing it was not in his Power to do so. If Dewalaren would not accept it, if he must lose Dewalaren one day to accident or to the ravages of time, he could at least see that Elanara would not have to suffer such a loss, so much more quickly. The stone would be safe with Rion.

Rion had no Power, not even the Power of the Amontir. Rion had no ambition, other than to see everyone he met live in joy. And Aras loved Rion, not as deeply as he loved Dewalaren, but still, he would not be so alone if Rion yet lived. Rion would never allow him to succumb to the Siren's song of the Ring's Power, nor to fall to darkness; he could never become a potential danger to those he loved and sought only to protect, with such a friend always beside him.

Aras followed Rion surreptitiously. He made sure he saw Dewalaren leave their rooms with Rion before he entered. Dewalaren often kept the Knife in their bedroom, now, instead of wearing it, as it would not work without the stone of the Ring to Power it. He had been incredibly fortunate Dewalaren had worn it on his ride. It was easy to obtain the Knife.

Aras brought it to his sanctum. No one would disturb him here. His sanctum was off limits to everyone, including his father and Dewalaren. All the lore and artifacts his mother had once owned were there, taken from his mother's sanctum on the Isle of Gryph.

Aras yet journeyed to the Isle, but only to visit the Gryphon there during mating season. The Isle was now deserted the rest of the year. Gryphon were by nature proud, solitary creatures, living alone on distant peaks, far from others of their kind. Normally they had little tolerance for their fellow Gryphon, save for their littermates and their mates. The Isle had originally been a mating ground. Gryphon came from near and far to the windswept, jagged cliffs, to engage in the spectacular aerial mating display used to entice a mate, and later, the aerial mating dance to seal the mating bond. Once paired, the mates would return to either the male's den, or the female's, upon whatever lands they had come from, to bear and raise their litter.

His mother, Aethelia, had corrupted the Isle to a far darker purpose. She had bound the Gryphon who came seeking mates with her Power, forcing them to remain upon the Isle, in service to her. She fed from them, though never enough to slay: only enough to weaken them and strengthen her, to supplement the Power of the winds. At one time, over twelve-hundred Gryphon had lived upon the travesty of their former mating grounds. Forced to live together in such enforced confinement, they had often grown vicious, attacking one another with unparalleled violence. The few hapless fledglings that were born upon the Isle seldom survived.

ARAS remembered the first time his mother had taken him to the Isle, the terror of flying over the waters, of facing the claws and beaks of the animals that would have torn him to shreds for his trespass, were it not for his mother's protection. She had made sure he knew that he lived solely because she wished him to, that the Gryphon around him would rend him to pieces, were he ever to fail her, to betray her. He had been eight years old. He trembled still at the memory of her coldness, her cruelty. She had made his father seem warm by comparison. He had lived in fear for many years, until Aerlyr had freed him from it.

Over time, the Gryphon upon the island had become accustomed to and tolerant of his presence. He was always cautious, always careful. He offered them gentleness and affection, where Aethelia offered them neither. He even named them, all of those he had contact with.

Tolerance gradually turned to respect and, eventually, even to affection. But always, he had to be cautious, lest his mother realize they were no longer the threat she had wished them to be. Still, he had never realized how great those nascent bonds were until one morning, shortly after he turned sixteen. Were he a Man, he would have been considered an adult at that age, but as an Elf, he was still a child, decades from coming-of-age.

There were only twenty-nine fledglings on the Isle. Each year fewer were born. Aras knew of those few, fewer still would reach maturity, in spite of all he tried to do to aid them. The Isle was already so crowded, competition for food and roosting space so fierce, that fights were inevitable, and the gryphlets were often endangered. His mother did not care. She had enough Gryphon for her purposes. But the Gryphon mothers cared.

It was Laethea who had come to him, her fledgling child clasped gently in her talons. Her cry had been so mournful, when she had laid the warm little body at his feet. The fledgling had been attacked by one of the other adults. The injuries he bore were easy enough to identify: claws had torn his wing and rent his back. The gryphlet tried to bite him as he reached for it.

"Of course, I will help him," he promised Laethea, his heart hammering. Never before had he done something so bold, interfered so blatantly. If his mother found out,

she would be furious. He had trembled with the memory of what his mother had done to him the last time she had been angry with him. But he had taken the fledgling Gryphon to his sanctum, the little hidden cave he had found, which he fled to whenever he could. He had tended him. He had healed him.

He had seen him grow strong and well and named him: Aerlyr. And then he had returned him to Laethea. Laethea was killed by an enraged male two years later. But Aerlyr was old enough and strong enough to survive, and he had never forgotten Aras. Aerlyr loved him as much as he loved Aerlyr.

HE HEARD Aerlyr's concerned call now, not with his ears, but with his mind, and Aras smiled, sending a wave of warmth and reassurance down his link to him. Aerlyr had heard the distress of his thoughts, laced with memories of pain.

With Aerlyr soothed, he forced his thoughts back to the task at hand. This would not be easy. He must concentrate.

Slowly, carefully, he crafted a large locket of pallenteum, the metal bending and flowing at the force of his will. He carefully pried the stone from the setting it had lain in for eight years, removing the four strands of Dewalaren's hair from beneath the gem, where he had placed them. When he had pried the stone from the setting of the Ring, eight years ago, he had found eight twined red hairs beneath the gem. He had determined through his Power that they belonged to Arcanus and Incuban, four each, and had carefully preserved them and locked them away, thinking he might have need of them, some unknown time in the future, for reasons he feared to contemplate. He had yet to use them.

He began the careful work of extricating the healing mechanism from the hilt of the Knife, referring more than once to his mother's tomes. This part was delicate, time-consuming work. A single misstep could easily lead to his death.

Finally he was done. He concealed the stone artfully behind the tiny back frame of the locket and placed four of the hairs Rion had given him gently over it, sealing them away. He carefully placed the remaining hairs in a silk cloth and locked them in a chest in one of his cabinets, against the day he might have need of them.

There were four frames; a thin sheet of pallenteum between the two halves of the locket bore a frame on each side. He left to visit Etheria, to obtain the paint and brushes he needed, surprised to see that it was dawn. He had worked the entire day and night. He sighed. He was far from done. He assured Etheria he would speak with her when he could. They had become quite close, after the War.

Etheria had been devastated by the loss of all her art, millennia of work, when Nalea burned, after having lost all her other works when their Homeland fell and even what pictures of them had remained when the Library was burnt. All feared her despair might yet claim her life, when Ahrnad had not. Aras was the one who had brought the six shredded Amontiri tapestries Lunahr had recovered from the Watchtower to her and commanded she work with Falara to reweave them, to rediscover and teach the lost art to her, and other Urwani-Amontir.

The challenge of recreating such beauty without altering it from its original form had managed to rouse Etheria from her despondency. She and Falara had experimented and built loom after loom until they were satisfied, becoming fast friends in the process, and then worked painstakingly to restore each of the six tapestries, which now graced the Hall of History in Kingshome, the new Urwani-Amontir city, located near the new Ogre city of Tanaham, on the banks of the Sarashen River, near both Riviera and Nalea.

Lunahr had similarly worked with Meloneth to restore the lost music of their people. Meloneth had been going mad, trying to replace so much on his own. But Lunahr joined him and wrote the lyrics and melodies as Meloneth sang and played them. Eladar had at first been jealous of the time his lythenia had been spending with another, until he saw the joy it brought them both, and the hope it brought to their peoples. When both Meloneth and Lunahr realized Eladar's jealousy, they invited him to join them, to aid them, to add his hand and voice to theirs. The three of them had become inseparable, and Meloneth had created many new works, as well as replacing the old, inspired by the two young lovers.

Aras smiled as he thought of them, as he returned to his sanctum and began painting miniature images of Rion and Elanara on the cover frame and on the leaf, so they were next to one another. It had been many years since he'd painted; he much preferred music as an art, but he knew he was still better at it than most Men who called themselves artists. He left the other two frames blank. He would paint the child's picture in one, once he or she was sixteen, and his or her sibling beside it, so Rion might always carry those he loved close to his heart.

When he was done, he worked his will upon the metal and the stone and the hair. None would ever be able to steal the locket from Rion. Few would wish to try. The locket would appear quite different to any who saw it: it would seem poorly crafted and to be made only of base iron, of negligible value to any except for Rion. He emerged from his room and blinked at the brightness of the sun. Three days had passed. He would seek out Rion, now, and gift it to him.

RION was relieved to see Aras. "I knew I couldn't leave without seeing you, but you haven't made it easy. What have you been doing all this time?"

"I have done as Talon commanded of me. And I have been painting. This is for you, Rion. May you always wear it close to your heart in happiness." He handed him a locket.

"It's beautiful," Rion said, awed by the pallenteum and metalwork. He opened the locket and saw images of himself and Elanara, and looked at Aras in surprise. "Do you mean to tell me you painted these? I've never seen work so fine! And I thought your sketches were lovely! We look as if we might speak, we look so real."

Aras smiled. "I'm glad you like it. Once your child is sixteen, bring him or her before me, and I will add his or her picture to the next frame. And then, if you have a second child, I will do the same, so you may always have your family with you, even when you are parted from them."

Rion hugged him, tightly. "I will certainly see you many times before then, Aras. You make me wish I might live forever, for there are not enough days left to me to share with you, and I am yet young."

"Rion, before you go, you have given me news enough of the others. They must be well, to be producing children at such an alarming rate," Aras said.

Rion laughed. "You forget, Aras, they are Men, not Elves. We do not have the luxury of waiting two or three hundred years between each child."

Aras smiled. "I am well aware, Rion. But please, is there news of Ara and Ron? Are they also well?"

"They are thriving!" Rion said. "You know Ogaten's grown to be quite a City now. Markara was concerned for the Elves. There had been some trouble. They haven't had a King in Ogaten, you know, just a series of Governors, one after the other, all of them deplorable, each more corrupt and incompetent than the last. None lasted even a full year, and the City was falling to anarchy.

"It would have been worse than Gosa, were it not for the City Guard Ron led, which kept things from getting too bad. Well, Ron had finally been Commander of the Guard long enough to see what was wrong and to figure out what needed to be done to fix it, and since no one else seemed capable of doing so, he decided he'd give it a try himself. As a trader, he certainly had the silver tongue needed. He ran for Governor and was elected. He's in his second year at it now, and it appears the job will be his for life, if he wants it, though they'd have to change their laws to do that. They certainly might, from what I've seen.

"As for Ara, he went to Maraden and became an Initiate to Elmoth as soon as he returned home after the War. He rose quickly, to Novice, then Acolyte. But he missed his family. He was still in Maraden, because Ogaten didn't have a Temple. They'd not had the size nor coin for one. But Ara had only fulfilled part of his oath to Elmoth. He decided he was ready to fulfill the rest.

"He asked the Priest in Maraden if he could leave to build a Temple in Ogaten, and if he could become the Priest of it, once he gained his fourth emblem. The Priest said he could, if he lived long enough. Their Temples are built like fortresses or Palaces, all stone, but very ornate, with lots of carvings. Such a building usually costs tens or even hundreds of thousands of gold pieces, and takes decades, sometimes even centuries to build.

"Well, Ron's not the only one who found a way to put his trader's talents to good use. First he got the Governor to approve three new Temple sites. It wasn't Ron yet. He had to pay the man a substantial bribe to do it. He convinced the Governor to give him the land for free, as long as he paid to build the new Temples. The Governor figured he'd give up and fall to poverty and despair over it, and he'd get the land back anyway. But he didn't know Ara!

"Ara rode to Malar in Holoren and requested an audience with King Rongas. He'd have spoken to Jargas too, he'd hoped to, but Jargas was already living in Cavernas, with Shanti. Anyway, he told King Rongas that if he would send him an army of stonemasons and builders with the materials he needed to build a Temple for Elmoth, he'd give them the other two sites to build a Temple to Ragnar and one to Aralyn, right beside each other. You know how the Dwarves feel about their God and Goddess. The King agreed, and within a month two thousand Dwarves showed up at the City gates with I don't know how many tons of marble and other supplies. It's a good thing Ron was Commander of the Guard and Ara had told him what he was up to. As it was, half the City was convinced they were being invaded!

"The Dwarves came in and went to work. All three Temples were built in only six months' time. Ara showed the Priest from Maraden the Temple, and he thought Elmoth himself must have sent it to them. It was twice as large and ornate as his own! Then the High-Priest came from Thenalon to view it and bless it. He awarded Ara his last two emblems and ordained him as a Priest on the spot."

Rion's eyes suddenly grew bright with tears. "I still can't believe it's partly because of me that he promised Elmoth he'd become a Priest and build the Temple to him and gift him all his coin, all because Gar and I were dying from fever. I've told you that story. It's you and Ara both who saved me: your knowledge of medicine that you taught to me and your picture of the flower."

Aras smiled at him. "If you're about to thank me again for it, please don't, Rion. I'm grateful I was able to help you, even without being beside you. I'm no less grateful to you for all you did to help save Talon and everyone else. If it had not been for you, Rion, we could never have won the War.

"Had you not rescued Eladar from the ogres, my people would have destroyed the Amontir before Talon's people ever realized we were a danger to them. Had you not rescued Circe from the villagers who hunted her, she would have been killed and unable to aid us. Had you not reminded Circe of who she really was, it would have been worse: she would truly have joined with Incuban against us, instead of only feigning to. Had you not aided Hunter, he might not have stayed sane or lived long enough to reach Jargas, and then we might never have recovered the Ring. Had you not told Elavar in Salenia of Elanara's and Eladar's fates, we would have been without their aid. Had you not warned Talon of the Dwarven army coming to oppose him, our Elven soldiers and Jargas's Dwarves would have annihilated each other.

"Had Incuban not become so obsessed with you, He would not have become distracted enough for us to survive. Had you not succored Mak, we would never have gained the Ogres as allies: they would have killed us all, despite Donovar warning us of the pending attack. Had Incuban not captured you, we might never have found Him and reached Him in time to destroy Him. Then, in Ironforge, you were the one who saw Lunahr and the Ring safe, when he was unconscious and helpless. You were the one to free the prisoners. The Ogres would never have been there to break their chains and fight by our side without you. And it was you who inspired the prisoners so eloquently to aid us, despite their terror. You have done so much, Rion. You are our savior."

Rion appeared astonished by his words, and shook his head in denial. "How can you possibly think that? I'm only a Man. I am glad I was able to play some small part in all that happened, but I cannot claim to be anywhere near as important as you make me sound! You were the one who won the War for us, Aras, and Talon, Hunter, and Lunahr, the wizards and the Dwarves and the Ogres, and the rest of the Elves," Rion argued.

Aras shook his head. "No, not me, Rion. The others certainly played an important part. But I made so many mistakes! I would have died without Talon to save me, and Arcanus after him. And I harmed so many I was trying to help! I nearly killed Aranas and Leonas. Worse, I actually killed you, Rion. I killed Talon," he said, his face and voice revealing the depth of his agony of the knowledge of what had happened.

"Don't be ridiculous, Aras. You are wonderful! You saved us all. You saved me. You are the one who saved Talon when Eladar killed him. I heard about what you did. Praise Elmoth Talon was wearing the Ring and the Knife when he died the second time. But none of that was truly your fault, Aras. It's certainly not your fault the Enemy tricked you into thinking I was Him or that Arcanus saving you from your mother killed Talon," Rion said intently, his hand going to Aras's arm instinctively.

He drew his hand back before he touched Aras. "I know I should fear such powerful magic, but how can anything so wonderful, something that saves people, truly be wrong?"

"You are so special, Rion. I am only thankful you survived everything you endured without being altered by it, that your bright light was not extinguished too soon," Aras said sincerely.

Rion grinned. "You see, you are responsible even once more for saving me. I couldn't die, Aras. I couldn't so hurt the ones I love," he said, blushing darkly as he said it, realizing how much he truly meant by it.

Aras looked at him in surprise and then grinned back at him, eyes bright as Elfstones. "I love you, also, Rion. May you have a long, happy, wonderful, peaceful life, my friend," Aras said, embracing him. Rion was startled for a moment, then returned the hug and backed away, blushing. His heart was hammering in the familiar pattern, as it had in the past, only after everything that had happened with Lunahr, he was aware now that it signified more than he'd once thought it did.

"Take care of yourself, Aras. And take care of Talon, too. You and I both know he needs you to," he said, forcing a laugh, to fend off his tears at the thought of leaving. "I've already said good-bye to him and Eladar and Lunahr. We're off to Tanaham next. I'd better get to the stable, or Elanara might drive away in the wagon without me. She is getting willful, now, with the baby inside of her. It signals trouble for me, I think. This child might be more than I bargained for," he said, laughing more naturally.

"I shall miss you incredibly, but I will try not to be gone so long now, between visits. If only I can convince the Dwarves they should have had enough of war, that peace is preferable by far!" In spite of his best efforts, his eyes welled with tears. "You'd think after living with an Elf for so long I'd be able to leave the presence of one without feeling as if darkness were falling," Rion said, shaking his head at his own folly. Then he turned and walked quickly toward the wagon.

WHEN Aras saw Dewalaren a short while later, on his way to the Lords' Grove, Dewalaren asked if he had had a chance to see Rion before he left.

"Yes, I saw him," Aras said, smiling fondly at the memory.

"You were secluded for a long time," Dewalaren said cautiously.

"It was not an easy thing to do," Aras said, sighing. He handed Dewalaren his Band. "I have replaced the stone with the original gem."

Dewalaren nodded, appearing relieved as he snapped the Band back in place over his arm. "And you destroyed the stone of the Ring?" Dewalaren pressed.

Aras sighed again. "The stone is gone," he said, truthfully.

Dewalaren smiled at him and wrapped his arms around him. "I hope you understand, Aras. If it still existed, it would ever be a temptation, a danger. Few Men alive would not covet such a treasure, would not kill, even go to war, to obtain it."

"I understand," Aras said. Even now Aras worried that the locket might somehow be lost, even though it could not be taken, that its secret might one day be discovered. He thrust such dark thoughts aside. Rion's life was worth the price he might one day be forced to pay. Dewalaren would not forgive him for such a deception, not a second time. He knew he risked losing Dewalaren's love.

He forced himself to be honest. He had not only done this out of love for Rion or out of the need to avert his own loneliness. He had done it out of fear. Fear that, one day, he might again need the Ring, to wield it against Arcanus, or against his children, or some unknown foe. But that was not all he feared.

He had learned much from studying his mother's tomes and the fascinating artifacts of their Homeland. He had thought his thirst for knowledge might finally be quenched with them, but it had not been. Each question answered generated many more. There was so much lost knowledge to relearn! But as much as he coveted such knowledge, he feared it as well. He had already learned so many secrets, such terrible secrets. He feared one day he might learn too much.

No, that was not what he feared. He forced himself to be honest. He feared he would instead lose himself in the search, as his mother had. One day, the Ring might be needed again, to save them, as it had saved them before. Only this time, when Dewalaren or Farad or Lunahr wielded it, he might be the Enemy they despised, that they feared.

"Aras, what is it, what's wrong?" Dewalaren asked, caressing his cheek.

"Do you still fear me, Dewalaren? Even a little, in the dark of night, when you lie beside me, do you pull away?" Aras asked, hating how young and desperate and lost he sounded.

"Of course not. For all your great Power, you would never harm me, Aras, my *lythenia*, my love. You would never harm anyone," Dewalaren said confidently.

I harmed Arcanus. I changed him. I had to, Aras thought, but he could not say it. He dared not ever let Dewalaren know. Dewalaren might understand. He might forgive him. But Arcanus had always been like a second father to him, until the day he had almost killed him. His lythenia still did not think clearly in matters involving Arcanus.

"If ever I became a danger to you, to your people, to mine…," Aras began.

"You would not, ever," Dewalaren said, with absolute conviction. "I know you better than that, Aras. If you doubt me, speak to Jarnath or your father, to Meloneth, to Lunahr. Any of us would tell you the same. You have wielded your Power for decades, ever only for the good of those around you, despite all of those who tried to warp you to do ill. I know what it is like, to have great Power, the responsibility that surrounds it, the fear. I have wielded such Power of mind since I was a child. I have wielded the power of my throne for decades. Besides, if it is of any comfort to you, you must know that, even as much as I love you, as my own life would end, should harm ever come to you, I would not hesitate to act against you, if ever you endangered my people, or your own, or any innocent."

Any innocent. Arcanus had not been an innocent. Arcanus had been far from innocent. He had seen much Arcanus had thought to keep hidden. The experiments he had performed in their Homeland, though much of that had yet been kept from him. The experiments here. Arcanus's creation of the Amontir had been one such experiment.

And there was the deception, the lies, all those innocents slain as he posed as one God or another over the centuries, when fleeing from Incuban, in aid of the Amontir. Arcanus had wielded the Power of a God the way a true God might wield it, with coldness and cruelty, all to his own ends. Arcanus had told himself he had done it for his children, the Amontir, as well as Marcus, the child of his body, and Selene, the child of his heart, but he had not.

Farad had killed King Balgar, he had had to, though it went so against his nature he had almost died from it, though he had thought he would lose Dewalaren's love for it. He would have preferred death to such a loss. Farad would do anything to protect an innocent. He had never harmed one, he could never harm one.

Aras thought of all he had ever done. Had he ever done less than Farad? Would he ever?

No. Dewalaren was right. And it comforted him to know that, were he ever to try, Dewalaren would stop him. Aras knew with certainty that he would. So would Rion. So would his father. His friends and family would never let him sink to such depths as Incuban and Arcanus had. He loved them all the more fiercely for it. Aras inhaled deeply and exhaled just as strongly, the weight of the world lifting from his shoulders. He smiled at Dewalaren, who was looking at him in concern.

"Come, Dewalaren, do not look so grim. You must allow me a moment of self-doubt every now and then. You of all people know that I am, after all, still a child." Then he took Dewalaren in his arms and kissed him with such boundless love and passion that he stole Dewalaren's breath away.

Dewalaren gasped and laughed. "You are many, many things Aras, but trust me when I tell you, you are certainly no longer a child," he said, and then he returned the kiss Aras had gifted to him.

It was Aras's turn to gasp and to blush, when he saw more than one set of eyes upon them. Aras had forgotten they were in full view of the Grove Guard, and he saw that Eladar and Lunahr were approaching as well. "I think we had best retire to our rooms, Dewalaren. I find I am suddenly in desperate need of a bed, and it is not at all because I have not slept in three days."

Dewalaren looked at him so lecherously, he felt faint, as his heart hammered wildly and all the blood rushed from his head to his groin.

"And you tell me I'm shameless," Eladar said laughing, his arm around Lunahr. "Your father is looking for you, Aras. He says if Talon is done with you, he'd like you to join him and High-Queen Shadala for dinner." Eladar grinned. "I think I'd better warn him: he might see you at dinner, but it won't be today! From the look he just gave you, I think that, far from being done with you, Talon has yet to begin! Come, Lunahr, they've given me a wonderful idea as to how we might spend the rest of the day."

Smiling happily, Lunahr waved good-bye to them as he and Eladar left arm in arm, heading toward the River. Grinning just as broadly, Aras left with his lythenia for the privacy of their bedroom, secure again in the knowledge that Dewalaren loved him and that no harm could ever come to him or all those he loved with Dewalaren by his side.

The Descent of Kings series by MARIA ALBERT

http://www.dreamspinnerpress.com

MARIA ALBERT lives in California Bay Area with her two daughters and several dozen friends, most of the latter of whom are still confined in binders on her bookshelves. She looks forward to releasing many more of them in the coming months.

Also by MARIA ALBERT

http://www.dreamspinnerpress.com

www.ingramcontent.com/pod-product-compliance
Lightning Source LLC
Chambersburg PA
CBHW050021030726
47506CB00001B/51